K-PAX

THE TRILOGY

K-PAX

THE TRILOGY

gene brewer

BLOOMSBURY

K-PAX first published in Great Britain 1995
First published in the USA as a Wyatt book for St Martin's Press
Copyright © 1995 by Gene Brewer

K-PAX II: On A Beam of Light first published in Great Britain 2001
First published in the USA by St Martin's Press
Copyright © 2001 by Gene Brewer

K-PAX III: The Worlds of prot first published in Great Britain 2002
Copyright © 2002 by Gene Brewer

Prot's Report first published in Great Britain 2004
Copyright © 2004 by Gene Brewer

This paperback edition first published 2004
Copyright © 2004 by Gene Brewer

The moral right of the author has been asserted

Bloomsbury Publishing plc, 36 Soho Square, London W1D 3QY

A CIP catalogue is available from the British Library

ISBN 978 0 7475 6695 3

All paper used by Bloomsbury Publishing, including that in this book,
is a natural, recyclable product made from wood grown in sustainable,
well-managed forests. The manufacturing processes conform to the
environmental regulations of the country of origin.

10 9 8 7 6 5 4

Printed in Great Britain by Clays Ltd, St Ives plc

www.bloomsbury.com/genebrewer

Contents

K-PAX

Prologue

I n April, 1990, I received a call from Dr. William Siegel at the Long Island Psychiatric Hospital. Bill is an old friend of mine, and a distinguished colleague. On this particular occasion the call was a professional one.

Bill was treating a patient who had been at the hospital for several months. The patient, a white male in his early thirties, had been picked up by the New York City police after being found bending over a mugging victim in the Port Authority Bus Terminal in midtown Manhattan. According to their report his answers to routine questions were "daffy" and, after they booked him, he was taken to Bellevue Hospital for evaluation.

Although he was somewhat emaciated, medical examination revealed no organic abnormality, nor was there evidence of formal thought disorder, aphasia, or auditory hallucination, and he presented a near-normal affect. However, he did harbor a rather bizarre delusion: He believed he came from an-

1

other planet. After a few days' observation he was transferred to Long Island, where he remained for the next four months.

Bill was unable to do much for him. Although he remained alert and cooperative throughout the various courses of treatment, the patient was completely unresponsive to the most powerful antipsychotic drugs. At the end of it all he remained firmly convinced that he was a visitor from "K-PAX." What was worse, he was able to enlist many of his fellow patients to this fantasy. Even some of the staff were beginning to listen to him! Knowing that the phenomenology of delusion has long been an interest of mine, Bill asked me to take a crack at him.

It couldn't have come at a worse time. As acting director of the Manhattan Psychiatric Institute I was already swamped with more work than I could handle and, indeed, had been phasing out patient interaction since January of that year. However, the case sounded both interesting and unusual, and I owed Bill a couple of favors. I asked him to send me a copy of the man's file.

When it arrived I was still bogged down by administrative duties, and a few more days went by before I found it lying on my desk under a pile of personnel and budget folders. With renewed dismay over the prospect of another patient I quickly read through the chart. It summarized a puzzling history indeed. Although our "spaceman" was quite lucid and articulate, and demonstrated a strong awareness of time and place, he was unable to provide any reliable information as to his actual origin and background. In short, he was not only delusional, but a total amnesiac as well! I called Bill and asked him to make arrangements for the transfer of this nameless man, who called himself "prot"—not capitalized—to my own institution.

He arrived the first week in May, and a preliminary session with him was scheduled for the ninth, a Wednesday, at the time I usually set aside to prepare for my regular "Principles of Psychiatry" lecture at Columbia University. We met at weekly intervals for several months thereafter. During that period I developed an extraordinary fondness and regard for this patient, as the following narrative, I trust, will show.

Although the results of these sessions have been reported in the scientific literature, I am writing this personal account not only because I think it might be of interest to the general public but also, to paraphrase Dr. Arieti, because of what he taught me about myself.

Session One

My first impression, when he was brought into my examining room, was that he was an athlete—a football player or wrestler. He was a little below average in height, stocky, dark, perhaps even swarthy. His hair was thick and coal-black. He was wearing sky-blue corduroy pants, a denim shirt, and canvas shoes. I didn't see his eyes for the first few encounters; despite the relatively soft lighting, he always wore dark glasses.

I asked him to be seated. Without a word he proceeded to the black vinyl chair and sat down. His demeanor was calm and his step agile and well coordinated. He seemed relaxed. I dismissed the orderlies.

I opened his folder and jotted the date on a clean yellow pad. He watched me quite intently, evincing a hint of a smile. I asked him whether he was comfortable or needed anything. To my surprise he requested an apple. His voice was soft but clear, with no detectable regional or foreign accent. I buzzed our head nurse, Betty McAllister, and asked her to see if there were any available in the hospital kitchens.

While we waited I reviewed his medical record: Temperature, pulse, blood pressure, EKG, and blood values were all within the normal range, according to our chief clinic physician, Dr. Chakraborty. No dental problems. Neurological exam (muscle strength, coordination, reflexes, tone) normal. Left/right discrimination normal. No problem with visual acuity, hearing, sensing hot or cold or a light touch, handling platonic solids, describing pictures, copying figures. No difficulty in solving complex problems and puzzles. The patient was quick-witted, observant, and logical. Except for his peculiar delusion and total amnesia, he was as healthy as a horse.

Betty came in with two large apples. She glanced at me for approval and, when I nodded, offered them to the patient. He took them from the little tray. "Red Delicious!" he exclaimed. "My favorite!" After offering us a taste, which we declined, he took a large, noisy bite. I dismissed my assistant and watched as "prot" devoured the fruit. I had never seen anyone enjoy anything more. He ate every bit of both apples, including the seeds. When he had finished, he said, "Thanks and thanks," and waited for me to begin, his hands on his knees like a little boy's.

Although psychiatric interviews are not normally recorded, we do so routinely at MPI for research and teaching purposes. What follows is a transcript of that first session, interspersed with occasional observations on my part. As usual during initial interviews I planned simply to chat with the man, get to know him, gain his trust.

"Will you tell me your name, please?"

"Yes." Evidence for a sense of humor?

5

"What is your name?"

"My name is prot." He pronounced it to rhyme with "goat," not "hot."

"Is that your first name or your last?"

"That is all of my name. I am prot."

"Do you know where you are, Mr. prot?"

"Just prot. Yes, of course. I am in the manhattan psychiatric institute."

I discovered in due course that prot tended to capitalize the names of planets, stars, etc., but not those of persons, institutions, even countries. For the sake of consistency, and to better depict the character of my patient, I have adopted that convention throughout this report.

"Good. Do you know who I am?"

"You look like a psychiatrist."

"That's right. I'm Doctor Brewer. What day is it?"

"Ah. You're the acting director. Wednesday."

"Uh-huh. What year?"

"1990."

"How many fingers am I holding up?"

"Three."

"Very good. Now, Mr.—excuse me—prot: Do you know why you are here?"

"Of course. You think I'm crazy."

"I prefer to use the term 'ill.' Do you think you are ill?"

"A little homesick, perhaps."

"And where is 'home'?"

"K-PAX."

"Kaypacks?"

"Kay-hyphen-pee-ay-ex. K-PAX."

"With a capital kay?"

"It is all capitals."

"Oh. K-PAX. Is that an island?"

He smiled at this, apparently realizing I already knew he believed himself to be from another world. But he said, simply, "K-PAX is a PLANET." Then: "But don't worry—I'm not going to leap out of your chest."

I smiled back. "I wasn't worried. Where is K-PAX?"

He sighed, tolerantly it seemed, and shook his head. "About seven thousand light-years from here. It's in what you would call the CONSTELLATION LYRA."

"How did you get to Earth?"

"That's somewhat difficult to explain. . . ."

At this point I noted on my pad the surprising observation that, even though we had only been together a few minutes, and despite all my years of experience, I was becoming a little annoyed by the patient's obvious condescension. I said, "Try me."

"It's simply a matter of harnessing the energy of light. You may find this a little hard to believe, but it's done with mirrors."

I couldn't help feeling he was putting me on, but it was a good joke, and I suppressed a chuckle. "You travel at the speed of light?"

"Oh, no. We can travel many times that speed, various multiples of c. Otherwise, I'd have to be at least seven thousand years old, wouldn't I?"

I forced myself to return his smile. "That is very interesting," I said, "but according to Einstein nothing can travel faster than the speed of light, or one hundred and eighty-six thousand miles per second, if I remember correctly."

"You misunderstand einstein. What he said was that nothing can *accelerate* to the speed of light because its mass would become infinite. Einstein said nothing about entities *already* traveling at the speed of light, or faster."

"But if your mass becomes infinite when you—"

His feet plopped onto my desk. "In the first place, doctor brewer—may I call you gene?—if that were true, then photons themselves would have infinite mass, wouldn't they? And beyond that, at tachyon speeds—"

"Tachyon?"

"Entities traveling faster than the speed of light are called tachyons. You can look it up."

"Thank you. I will." My reply sounds a bit peevish on rehearing the tape. "If I understand you correctly, then, you did not come to Earth in a spaceship. You sort of 'hitched a ride' on a beam of light."

"You could call it that."

"How long did it take you to get to Earth from your planet?"

"No time at all. Tachyons, you see, travel faster than light and, therefore, backward in time. Time passes for the *traveler*, of course, and he becomes older than he was when he left."

"And how long have you been here on Earth?"

"Four years and nine months. *Your* years, that is."

"And that makes you how old now? In Earth terms, of course."

"Three hundred and thirty-seven."

"You are three hundred and thirty-seven years old?"

"Yes."

"All right. Please tell me a little more about yourself." Although I recognized the unreality of the man's story, it is standard psychiatric practice to draw out an amnesiacal patient in hopes of obtaining information about his true background.

"You mean before I came to EARTH? Or—"

"Let's start with this: How did you happen to be chosen to make the journey from your planet to ours?"

Now the patient was actually grinning at me. Though

8

it seemed innocent enough, perhaps even ingenuous, I found myself poring through his file rather than gaze at his Cheshire-cat face in dark glasses. He said, "'Chosen.' That's a peculiarly human concept." I looked up to find him scratching his chin and searching the ceiling in an apparent attempt to locate the appropriate words to explain his lofty thoughts to someone as lowly as myself. What he came up with was: "I wanted to come and I am here."

"Anyone who wants to come to Earth may do so?"

"Anyone on K-PAX. And a number of other PLANETS, of course."

"Did anyone come with you?"

"No."

"Why did you want to come to Earth?"

"Several reasons. For one, EARTH is a particularly lively place as seen and heard from space. And it is a Class III-B PLANET."

"Meaning . . .?"

"Meaning early stage of evolution, future uncertain."

"I see. And is this your first trip to our planet?"

"Oh, no. I've been here many times."

"When was the first time?"

"In 1963, your calendar."

"And has anyone else from K-PAX visited us?"

"No. I am the first."

"I'm relieved to hear that."

"Why?"

"Let's just say it would cause a lot of people a certain amount of consternation."

"Why?"

"If you don't mind, I'd rather we talk about you today. Would that be all right?"

"If you wish."

"Good. Now—where else have you been? Around the universe, I mean."

"I have been to sixty-four PLANETS within our GALAXY."

"And on how many of those have you encountered life?"

"Why, on all of them. The ones that are barren don't interest me. Of course there are those who are fascinated by rocks and weather patterns and—"

"Sixty-four planets with intelligent life?"

"All life is intelligent."

"Well, how many have human beings such as ourselves?"

"EARTH is the only one with the species homo sapiens that I have visited so far. But we know there are a few others here and there."

"With intelligent life?"

"No, with human life. The PLANETS that support life number into the millions, possibly the billions. Of course we haven't visited them all. That is only a rough estimate."

"'We' meaning inhabitants of K-PAX."

"K-PAXians, NOLLians, FLORians . . ."

"Those are other races on your home planet?"

"No. They are inhabitants of other WORLDS." Most delusionals are confused to the point that they stutter or stumble considerably when trying to answer complex questions in a consistent manner. This patient was not only knowledgeable about a variety of arcane topics, but also confident enough of his knowledge to weave a cogent story. I scribbled on my pad the speculation that he might have been a scientist, perhaps a physicist or astronomer, and made a further note to determine how far his knowledge extended into those fields. For now, I wanted to learn something about his early life.

10

"Let's back up just a bit, if you don't mind. I'd like you to tell me something about K-PAX itself."

"Certainly. K-PAX is somewhat bigger than your PLANET, about the size of NEPTUNE. It is a beautiful WORLD, as is EARTH, of course, with its color and variety. But K-PAX is also very lovely, especially when K-MON and K-RIL are in conjunction."

"What are K-MON and K-RIL?"

"Those are our two SUNS. What you call AGAPE and SATORI. One is much larger than yours, the other smaller, but both are farther from our PLANET than your SUN is from yours. K-MON is red and K-RIL blue. But owing to our larger and more complex orbital pattern, we have much longer periods of light and darkness than you do, and not so much variation. That is, most of the time on K-PAX it's something like your twilight. One of the things a visitor to your WORLD first notices is how bright it is here."

"Is that why you are wearing dark glasses?"

"Naturally."

"I'd like to clarify something you said earlier."

"Certainly."

"I believe you stated that you have been on Earth for four years and—uh—some odd months."

"Nine."

"Yes, nine. What I'd like very much to know is: Where were you living for those four or five years?"

"Everywhere."

"Everywhere?"

"I have traveled all over your WORLD."

"I see. And where did you begin your travels?"

"In zaire."

"Why Zaire? That's in Africa, isn't it?"

11

"It happened to be pointing toward K-PAX at the time."

"Ah. And how long were you there?"

"A couple of your weeks altogether. Long enough to become familiar with the land. Meet the beings there. All beautiful, especially the birds."

"Mm. Uh—what languages do they speak in Zaire?"

"You mean the humans, I presume."

"Yes."

"Besides the four official languages and french, there are an amazing number of native dialects."

"Can you say something in Zairese? Any dialect will do."

"Certainly. *Ma-ma kotta rampoon.*"

"What does that mean?"

"It means: Your mother is a gorilla."

"Thank you."

"No problem."

"And then where did you go? After Zaire."

"All over africa. Then to europe, asia, australia, antarctica, and finally to the americas."

"And how many countries have you visited?"

"All of them except eastern canada, greenland, and iceland. Those are my last stops."

"All—what—hundred of them?"

"More like two hundred at present, but it seems to change by the minute."

"And you speak all the languages?"

"Only enough to get by."

"How did you travel? Weren't you stopped at various borders?"

"I told you: It's difficult to explain. . . ."

"You mean you did it with mirrors."

12

"Exactly."

"How long does it take to go from country to country at the speed of light or whatever multiples of it you use?"

"No time at all."

"Does your father like to travel?" I detected a brief hesitation, but no strong reaction to the sudden mention of prot's father.

"I imagine. Most K-PAXians do."

"Well, *does* he travel? What kind of work does he do?"

"He does no work."

"What about your mother?"

"What about her?"

"Does she work?"

"Why should she?"

"They are both retired, then?"

"Retired from what?"

"From whatever they did for a living. How old are they?"

"Probably in their late six hundreds."

"Obviously they no longer work."

"Neither of them has ever worked." Apparently the patient considered his parents to be ne'er-do-wells, and the way he phrased his answer led me to believe that he harbored a deep-seated resentment or even hatred not only of his father (not uncommon) but of his mother (relatively rare for a man) as well. He continued: "No one 'works' on K-PAX. That is a human concept."

"No one does *anything*?"

"Of course not. But when you do something you want to do, it's not work, is it?" His grin widened. "You don't consider what you do to be work, do you?"

I ignored this smug comment. "We'll talk more about your parents later, all right?"

"Why not?"

"Fine. There are a couple of other things I'd like to clear up before we go on."

"Anything you say."

"Good. First, how do you account for the fact that, as a visitor from space, you look so much like an Earth person?"

"Why is a soap bubble round?"

"I don't know—why?"

"For an educated person, you don't know much, do you, gene? A soap bubble is round because that is the most energy-efficient configuration. Similarly, many beings around the UNIVERSE look pretty much like we do."

"I see. Okay, you mentioned earlier that—mm— 'EARTH is a particularly lively place as seen and heard from space.' What did you mean by that?"

"Your television and radio waves go out from EARTH in all directions. The whole GALAXY is watching and listening to everything you say and do."

"But these waves travel only at the speed of light, don't they? They couldn't possibly have reached K-PAX as yet."

He sighed again, more loudly this time. "But some of the energy goes into higher overtones, don'tcha know? It's this principle, in fact, that makes light travel possible. Have you studied physics?"

I suddenly remembered my long-suffering high school physics teacher, who had tried to drum this kind of information into my head. I also felt a need for a cigarette, though I hadn't smoked one in years. "I'll take your word for that, Mist—uh—prot. One more thing: Why do you travel around the universe all by yourself?"

"Wouldn't you, if you could?"

"Maybe. I don't know. But what I meant was: Why do you do it *alone?*"

"Is that why you think I'm crazy?"

"Not at all. But doesn't it get kind of lonely, all those years—four years and eight months, wasn't it?—in space?"

"No. And I wasn't in space that long. I've been *here* for four years and nine months."

"How long were you in space?"

"I aged about seven of your months, if that's what you mean."

"You didn't feel a need to have someone to talk to for all that time?"

"No." I jotted down: Patient dislikes *everyone?*

"What did you do to keep yourself occupied?"

He wagged his head. "You don't understand, gene. Although I became seven EARTH months older during the trip, it really seemed like an instant to me. You see, time is warped at superlight speeds. In other words—"

Unforgivably, I was too annoyed to let him go on. "And speaking of time, ours is up for today. Shall we continue the discussion next week?"

"As you wish."

"Good. I'll call Mr. Kowalski and Mr. Jensen to escort you back to your ward."

"I know the way."

"Well, if you don't mind, I'd rather call them. Just routine hospital procedure. I'm sure you understand."

"Perfectly."

"Good." The orderlies arrived in a moment and the patient left with them, nodding complacently to me as he went out. I was surprised to find that I was dripping with perspiration, and I remember getting up to check the thermostat after switching off the recorder.

While the tape was rewinding I copied my scribbled observations for his permanent file, making mention of my dis taste for what seemed to me his arrogant manner, after which I filed the rough notes into a separate cabinet, already stuffed with similar records. Then I listened to part of the tape, adding a comment about the patient's lack of any trace of dialect or accent. Surprisingly, hearing his soft voice, which was rather pleasant, was not at all annoying to me. It had been his demeanor. . . . Suddenly I realized: That cocky, lopsided, derisive grin reminded me of my father.

DAD was an overworked small-town doctor. The only time he ever relaxed—except for Saturday afternoons, when he lay on the sofa with his eyes closed listening to the Metropolitan Opera broadcasts—was at dinnertime, when he would have exactly one glass of wine and relate to my mother and me, in his offhand way, more than we wanted to know about the ringworms and infarctions of his day. Afterwards he would head back to the hospital or make a few house calls. Unless I could think up a good excuse he would take me with him, assuming, erroneously, that I enjoyed the noxious sounds and smells, the bleeding and vomiting as much as he did. It was that insensitivity and arrogance, which I hated in my father, that had annoyed me so much during my first encounter with this man who called himself "prot."

I resolved, as always when something like this happens, to keep my personal life out of the examining room.

ON the train home that evening I got to thinking, as I often do after beginning a difficult or unusual case, about the human mind and reality. My new patient, for example, and Russell, our resident Christ, and thousands like them live in worlds of their own, realms just as real to them as yours and mine are to us. That seems difficult to understand, but is it really? Surely the reader of this account has become, at one time or another, thoroughly involved in a film or absorbed in a novel, utterly "lost" in the experience. Dreams, even daydreams, often seem very real at the time, as do events recalled during hypnosis. On such occasions, who is to say what reality is?

It is quite remarkable what some of those with severe mental disorders are able to do within the boundaries of their illusory worlds. The "idiot" savants are a case in point. Unable to function in our society, they withdraw into recesses of the mind which most of us can never enter. They are capable of feats—with numbers, for example, or music—that others cannot begin to duplicate. We are still in the Dark Ages as far as understanding the human mind is concerned—how it learns, how it remembers, how it *thinks*. If Einstein's brain were transplanted into Wagner's skull, would this individual still be Einstein? Better: Switch half of Einstein's brain with half of Wagner's—which person would be Einstein and which Wagner? Or would each be someone in between? Similarly, in the case of multiple personality syndrome, which of the distinct "identities" is really the person in question, or is he/she a *different* person at different times? Are we *all* different people at different times? Could this explain our changing "moods"? When we see someone talking to himself—to whom is he speaking? Have you ever heard someone say, "I haven't been myself lately."? Or "You're not the man I married!"? And how do we account for the fundamentalist preacher and his clandestine sex life? Are we all Drs. Jekyll and Messrs. Hyde?

I made a note to dwell for a while on prot's imaginary life on his imaginary planet, hoping of course that this would reveal something about his background on Earth—his geographical origin, perhaps, his occupation, his name!—so that we might be able to track down his family and friends and thus, in addition to allaying their fears about his health and whereabouts, get to the underlying cause for his bizarre confabulation. I was beginning to feel the little tingle I always get at the beginning of a challenging case, when all the possibilities are still open. Who was this man? What sorts of alien thoughts filled his head? Would we be able to bring him down to Earth?

Session Two

I have always tried to give my examining room as pleasant an atmosphere as possible, with cheerful pastel walls, a few sylvan watercolors, and soft, indirect lighting. There is no couch: My patient and I sit facing each other in comfortable chairs. There is a clock placed discreetly on the back wall where the patient cannot see it.

Before my second interview with prot I went over Joyce Trexler's transcript of the first week's session with him. Mrs. Trexler has been here almost forever and it is common knowledge that it is she who really runs the place. "Crazy as a loon" was her uninvited comment as she dropped the typed copy onto my desk.

I had looked up "tachyons" and found that they were, as he had indicated, entities traveling faster than light. They are purely theoretical, however, and there is no evidence suggesting their actual existence. I had also tried to check out the "Zairese," but couldn't find anyone who spoke any of its more than two hundred dialects. However, although his story seemed perfectly consistent, it was no less problematic.

In psychoanalysis, one tries to become the patient's peer. Gain his confidence. Build on what grasp he still has of reality, his residue of normal thoughts. But this man had *no* grasp of reality. His alleged travels around the world offered some sort of earthbound experience to pursue, but even that was suspect—he could have spent time in the library, or watched travelogues, for example. I was still pondering how to gain some kind of toehold on prot's psyche when he was escorted into my examining room.

He was wearing the same blue corduroys, dark glasses, and familiar smile. But this time the latter did not annoy me so much—it had been my problem, not his. He requested a few bananas before we began, and offered one to me. I declined, and waited until he had devoured them, skins and all. "Your produce alone," he said, "has made the trip worthwhile."

We chatted for a few minutes about fruit. He reminded me, for example, that their characteristic odors and flavors are due to the presence of specific chemical compounds known as esters. Then we reviewed briefly our previous interview. He maintained that he had arrived on Earth some four years and nine months ago, traveled on a beam of light, etc. Now I learned that "K-PAX" was circled by seven purple moons. "Your planet must be a very romantic place," I prodded. At this point he did a surprising thing, something that no other patient of mine has ever done in the nearly thirty years I have been practicing psychoanalysis: He pulled a pencil and a little red notebook from his shirt pocket and began taking notes of his own! Rather amused by this, I asked him what he was jotting down. He replied that he had thought of something to include in his report. I inquired as to the nature of this "report." He said it was his custom to compile a description of the various places he visited and beings he encountered throughout the galaxy. It appeared that the patient was examining the doctor! It was my turn to smile.

Not wanting to inhibit his activities in any way, I did not press him to show me what he had written, though I was more than a little curious. Instead, I asked him to tell me something about his boyhood on "K-PAX" (i.e., Earth).

He said, "The region I was born in—incidentally, we are *born* on K-PAX, just like you, and the process is much the same, only—well, we'll get into that later, I suppose. . . ."

"Why don't we go into it now?"

He paused briefly, as if taken aback, but quickly recovered. The little grin, however, was gone. "If you wish. Our anatomy is much like yours, as you know from the physical examination. The physiology is also similar, but, unlike on EARTH, the reproduction process is quite unpleasant."

"What makes it unpleasant?"

"It is a very painful procedure."

Ah, I thought, a breakthrough: Mr. "prot" very possibly suffers some sort of sexual terror or dysfunction. I quickly pursued this lead. "Is this pain associated with intercourse itself, with ejaculation, or merely with obtaining an erection?"

"It is associated with the entire process. Where these activities result in pleasurable sensations for beings such as yourself, for us the effect is quite the opposite. This applies both to the males and females of our species and, incidentally, to most other beings around the GALAXY as well."

"Can you compare the sensation to anything else I might be able to understand or identify with? Is it like a toothache, or—"

"It's more like having your gonads caught in a vise, except that we feel it all over. You see, on K-PAX pain is more general, and to make matters worse it is associated with something like your nausea, accompanied by a very bad smell. The moment of climax is like being kicked in the stomach and falling into a pool of mot shit."

"Did you say *mot* shit? What is a 'mot'?"

"An animal something like your skunk, only far more potent."

"I see." Unforgivably I began to laugh. This image coupled with the dark glasses and suddenly serious demeanor—well, as they say, you had to be there. He grinned broadly then, apparently understanding how it must have sounded to me. I managed to regain my composure and carry on. "And you say it is the same for a woman?"

"Exactly the same. As you can imagine, women on K-PAX do not strive very hard to reach orgasm."

"If the experience is so terrible, how do you reproduce?"

"Like your porcupines: as carefully as possible. Needless to say, overpopulation is not a problem for us."

"What about something like surgical implantation?"

"You are distorting the importance of the phenomenon. You have to bear in mind that since the life span for our species is a thousand of your years, there is little need to produce children."

"I see. All right. I'd like to get back to your own childhood. Can you tell me a little about your upbringing? What were your parents like?"

"That's a little difficult to explain. Life on K-PAX is quite different from that on EARTH. In order for you to understand my background, I will have to tell you something about our evolution." He paused at this point, as if wondering whether I would be interested in hearing what he had to say. I encouraged him to proceed. "Well, I suppose the best place to start is at the beginning. Life on K-PAX is much older than life on EARTH, which began about two-point-five billion years ago. Homo sapiens has existed on your PLANET for only a few tens of thousands of years, give or take a millennium or two. On K-PAX, life began nearly nine billion of your years ago, when your WORLD was still a diffuse ball of gas. Our own species has been around for five billion of those years, considerably longer than your bacteria. Furthermore, evolution took a quite different course. You see, we have very little water on our PLANET, compared to EARTH—no oceans at all, no rivers, no lakes—so life began on land or, more precisely, underground. Your species evolved from the fishes; our forefathers were something like your worms."

"And yet you evolved into something very much like us."

"I thought I explained that in our previous discussion. You could check your notes. . . ."

"This is all very interesting—uh—prot, but what does paleontology have to do with your upbringing?"

"Everything—just as it does on EARTH."

"Why don't we proceed with your childhood, and we can come back to this relationship later if I have any questions about it. Would that be all right?"

He bent over the notebook again. "Certainly."

"Very well. First, let's talk about some of the fundamental items, shall we? For example, how often do you see your parents? Are your grandparents still alive? Do you have any brothers or sisters?"

"Gene, gene, gene. You haven't been listening. Things are not the same on K-PAX as they are on EARTH. We don't have 'families' as you know the term. The whole idea of a 'family' would be a non sequitur on our PLANET, and on most others. Children are not raised by their biological parents, but by everyone. They circulate among us, learning from one, then another."

"Would it be fair to say, then, that as a child you had no home to go to?"

"Exactly. Now you've got it."

"In other words you never knew your parents."

"I had thousands of parents."

I made a note that prot's denying his father and mother confirmed my earlier suspicion of a deep-seated hatred of one or both, possibly due to abuse, or perhaps he had been orphaned, or neglected, or even abandoned by them. "Would you say you had a happy childhood?"

"Very."

"Can you think of any unpleasant experiences you had as a child?"

Prot's eyes closed tightly, as they often did when he tried to concentrate or to recollect something. "Not really. Nothing unusual. I was knocked down by an ap a couple of times, and squirted by a mot once or twice. And I had something like your measles and mumps. Little things like that."

"An 'ap'?"

"Like a small elephant."

"Where was this?"

"On K-PAX."

"Yes, but where on K-PAX? Your own country?"

"We don't have countries on K-PAX."

"Well, do elephants run around loose there?"

"Everything runs around loose there. We don't have zoos."

"Are any of the animals dangerous?"

"Only if you get in their way."

"Do you have a wife waiting for you back on K-PAX?" This was another toss from left field, again to determine the effect of a key word on the patient's state of mind. Except for a barely perceptible shift in his chair, he remained calm.

"We don't *have* marriage on K-PAX—no husbands, no wives, no families—get it? Or, to put it more correctly, the entire population is one big family."

"Do you have any biological children of your own?"

"No."

There are many reasons why a person decides not to have children. One of these has to do with abuse by or hatred of his parents. "Let's get back to your mother and father. Do you see them very often?"

He sighed in apparent frustration. "No."

"Do you like them?"

"Are you still beating your wife?"

"I don't understand."

"Your questions are phrased from the point of view of an EARTH person. On K-PAX they would be nonsense."

"Mr. prot—"

"Just prot."

"Let's establish some sort of ground rules for these sessions, shall we? I'm sure you will forgive me if I phrase my questions from the point of view of an Earth person since, in fact, that is what I am. I could not phrase them in K-PAXian terms even if I wanted to because I am not familiar with your way of life. I am going to ask you to humor me, to bear with me in this. Please try to answer the questions in the best way you can, using Earth expressions, which you seem to be quite familiar with, whenever possible. Would that be a fair request under the circumstances?"

"I am happy you have said that. Perhaps we can learn from each other."

"If you are happy, I am happy too. Now, if you are ready, maybe you could tell me a little about your parents. For example, do you know who your mother and father are? Have you ever met them?"

"I have met my mother. I have not yet run across my father."

It's his father the patient hates! " 'Run across'?"

"K-PAX is a big place."

"But surely—"

"Or if I have met him, no one has pointed out our biological relationship."

"Are there many people on your planet who don't know who their fathers are?"

He grinned at this, quickly picking up on the double meaning. "Most do not. It is not an important thing."

"But you know your mother."

"Purely a coincidence. A mutual acquaintance happened to mention our biological connection."

"That is difficult for an Earth person to understand. Perhaps you could explain why your 'biological connections' are not important to you."

"Why should they be?"

"Because—uh, for now, let me ask the questions, and you give the answers, all right?"

"Sometimes a question is the best answer."

"I suppose you don't know how many brothers and sisters you have."

"On K-PAX we are all siblings."

"I meant biological siblings."

"I would be surprised if there were any. Almost no one has more than one child, for reasons I have already explained."

"Isn't there peer pressure or government incentives to make sure your species doesn't die out?"

"There is no government on K-PAX."

"What do you mean—it's an anarchy?"

"That's as good a word as any."

"But who builds the roads? The hospitals? Who runs the schools?"

"Really, gene, it's not that difficult to understand. On K-PAX, one does what needs to be done."

"What if no one notices that something needs to be done? What if someone knows something needs to be done but refuses to do it? What if a person decides to do nothing?"

"That doesn't happen on K-PAX."

"Never?"

"What would be the point?"

"Well, to express dissatisfaction over the wages being paid, for one thing."

"We don't have 'wages' on K-PAX. Or money of any kind."

I jotted this down. "No money? What do you barter with?"

"We don't 'barter.' You really should learn to listen to your patients, doctor. I told you before—if something needs to be done, you do it. If someone needs something you have, you give it to him. This avoids a multitude of problems and has worked pretty well on our PLANET for several billion years."

"All right. How big is your planet?"

"About the size of your NEPTUNE. You'll find this also on the transcript of last week's conversation."

"Thank you. And what is the population?"

"There are about fifteen million of my species, if that is

what you mean. But there are many other beings besides ourselves."

"What kinds of beings?"

"A variety of creatures, some of whom resemble the animals of EARTH, some not."

"Are these wild or domesticated animals?"

"We don't 'domesticate' any of our beings."

"You don't raise any animals for food?"

"No one 'raises' another being for any purpose on K-PAX, and certainly not for food. We are not cannibals." I detected a sudden and unexpected note of anger in this response—why?

"Let me just fill in one or two blanks in your childhood. As I understand it, you were brought up by a number of surrogate parents, is that right?"

"Not exactly."

"Well, who took care of you? Tucked you into bed at night?"

Utterly exasperated: "No one 'tucks you into bed' on K-PAX. When you are sleepy, you sleep. When you are hungry, you eat."

"Who feeds you?"

"No one. Food is always around."

"At what age did you begin school?"

"There are no schools on K-PAX."

"I'm not surprised. But you are obviously an educated person."

"I am not a 'person.' I am a being. All K-PAXians are educated. But education does not come from schools. Education stems from the desire to learn. With that, you don't need schools. Without it, all the schools in the UNIVERSE are useless."

"But how did you learn? Are there teachers?"

"On K-PAX, everyone is a teacher. If you have a question, you just ask whoever is around. And of course there are the libraries."

"Libraries? Who runs the libraries?"

"Gene, gene, gene. No one does. Everyone does."

"Are these libraries structures we Earth people would recognize?"

"Probably. There are books there. But many other things as well. Things you would not recognize or understand."

"Where are these libraries? Does each city have one?"

"Yes, but our 'cities' are more like what you would call 'villages.' We have no vast metropolises such as the one in which we are presently located."

"Does K-PAX have a capital?"

"No."

"How do you get from one village to another? Are there trains? Cars? Airplanes?"

A deep sigh was followed by some incoherent mumbling in a language I couldn't understand (later identified as "pax-o"). He made another entry in his notebook. "I have explained this before, gino. We get from place to place on the energy of light. Why do you find this concept so hard to understand? Is it too simple for you?"

We had been over this before and, with time running out, I did not intend to be sidetracked again. "One final question. You have said that your childhood was a happy one. Did you have other children to play with?"

"Hardly any. There are very few children anywhere on K-PAX, as I have indicated. Besides that, there is no distinction between 'work' and 'play' on our PLANET. On

EARTH, children are encouraged to play all the time. This is because you believe they should remain innocent of their approaching adulthood for as long as possible, apparently because the latter is so distasteful. On K-PAX, children and adults are all part of the same thing. On our PLANET life is fun, and interesting. There is no need for mindless games, either for children or adults. No need for escape into soap operas, football, alcohol, or other drugs. Did I have a happy childhood on K-PAX? Of course. And a happy adulthood as well."

I didn't know whether to feel gladdened or saddened by this cheerful answer. On the one hand, the man seemed genuinely content with his imaginary lot. On the other, it was obvious he was denying not only his family, but his school experiences, his childhood itself. Even his country. Everything. Every aspect of his entire life, which must have been quite abominable, indeed. I felt a great deal of pity for this young man.

I ended the interview with a question about his "home town," but this also led nowhere. K-PAXians seemed to drift from place to place like nomads.

I dismissed the patient and he returned to his ward. I had been so astonished by his utter denial of everything human that I forgot to call the orderlies to go with him.

After he had gone I returned to my adjacent office and went through his entire file again. I had never experienced a case like this, one for which I couldn't seem to find any kind of handle. Only one other in thirty years was even close, and it also involved an amnesiac. A student of mine was eventually able to trace the man's roots through an analysis of his reawakened interest in sports—but it took a couple of years.

I jotted down what I had on prot so far:

1. P hates his parents—had he been abused?
2. P hates his job, the government, perhaps society as a whole—had there been a legal problem resulting in a perceived injustice?
3. Did something happen 4–5 yrs ago that underlay all these apparent hatreds?
4. On top of everything else, the patient has a severe sex hangup.

As I looked over these notes I remembered something that my colleague Klaus Villers has professed on more than one occasion: Extraordinary cases require extraordinary measures. I was thinking of the rare instances in which a delusional of exceptional intelligence has been convinced that his identity was false. The most famous example of this treatment is the one in which a well-known comedian graciously consented to confront a delusional look-alike, and a miraculous cure was quickly effected (but not before they both put on quite a show, evidently). If I could prove to prot that he was, in fact, an ordinary human being and not some alien from another planet . . .

I decided to do a more thorough physical and mental workup on him. I was particularly interested in learning whether he was, in fact, abnormally sensitive to light, as he claimed to be. I also wanted to have the results of an aptitude test and to determine the extent of his general knowledge, particularly in the areas of physics and astronomy. The more we knew about his background, the easier it would be to find out who he really was.

WHEN I was a senior in high school our career counselor advised me to take the one course in physics our school offered. I quickly learned that I had no aptitude for the subject, though the experience did serve to increase my respect for anyone who could master that esoteric material, among them my wife-to-be.

We were next-door neighbors from the day she was born, Karen and I, and we played together all the time. Every morning I would go outside and find her in the yard, smiling and ready for anything. One of the fondest memories I have is of our first day in school, of sitting behind her where I could smell her hair, of walking home with her and leaves burning. Of course we weren't really sweethearts at that age—not until we were twelve, the year my father died.

It happened in the middle of the night. My mother came and got me up because she hoped, vainly as it turned out, that I might be able to do something. When I ran into their bedroom I found him lying on his back, naked, sweating, his pajamas on the floor beside the bed. He was still breathing, but his face was ashen. I had spent enough time in his office and on hospital rounds to suspect what had happened and to recognize the seriousness of the situation. If he had taught me something about closed-chest massage I might have been able to help him, but this was before CPR was generally known and there was nothing I could do except watch him gasp his last breath and expire. Of course I yelled at my mother to call an ambulance, but it was far too late by the time it got there. In the meantime I studied his body with horrible fascination, his graying hands and feet, his knobby knees, his large, dark genitalia. Mother came running back just as I was covering him with the sheet. There was no need to tell her. She knew. Oh, she knew.

Afterwards, I found myself in a state of profound shock and confusion. Not because I loved him, but because I didn't—had almost wished him dead, in fact, so I wouldn't have to become a doctor like him. Ironically, because of the tremendous sense of guilt I felt, I vowed to go into medicine anyway.

At the funeral, Karen, without anyone saying anything, sat beside me and held my hand. It was as though she understood perfectly what I was going through. I squeezed hers too, hard. It was unbelievably soft and warm. I didn't feel any less guilty, but with her hand in mine it seemed as though I might be able to get through life somehow. And I've been holding it ever since.

O N Friday of that week we received a visitor from the State Board of Health. His job is to check our facilities periodically, see that the patients are clean and properly fed, that the plumbing works, etc. Although he had been here many times before, we gave him the usual grand tour: the kitchen, the dining and laundry and furnace rooms, the shop, the grounds, the recreation/exercise room, the quiet room, the medical facilities, and, finally, the wards.

It was in the rec room that we found prot sitting at a card table with two of my other patients. I thought that a bit odd inasmuch as one of them, whom I shall call Ernie, almost always keeps to himself, or talks quietly with Russell, our unofficial chaplain. The other, Howie, is usually too busy to talk to anyone (the white rabbit syndrome). Both Ernie and Howie have been here for years, sharing the same room, and both are very difficult cases.

Ernie, like most people, is afraid of death. Unlike most of us, however, he is unable to think about anything else. He checks his pulse and temperature regularly. He insists on wearing a surgical mask and rubber gloves at all times. He is never without his stethoscope and thermometer and he showers several times a day, demanding fresh clothing after

33

each one, rejecting anything that shows the slightest spot or stain. We humor him in this because otherwise he would wear nothing.

Eating is a serious problem for Ernie, for several reasons. First, because of his fear of food poisoning he will not consume anything that isn't thoroughly cooked and comes to him piping hot. Second, he will only eat food that is broken or cut into tiny pieces so he won't choke to death on something too large to swallow. Finally, there is the problem of preservatives and additives. He will not eat meat or poultry, and is suspicious even of fresh fruits and vegetables.

None of this is unusual, of course, and every psychiatric hospital has an Ernie or two. What makes Ernie different is that he raises his defenses a notch or two higher than most necrophobes. He cannot be induced to venture outside the building, for example, fearing bombardment by meteorites, cosmic rays and the like, poisoning by chemicals in the air, attack by insects and birds, infection by dust-borne organisms, and so on.

But that's not all. Afraid he will unconsciously strangle himself at night he sleeps with his hands tied to his feet, and bites down on a wooden dowel so he won't swallow his tongue. For similar reasons he will not lie under sheets or blankets—he fears they might wrap themselves around his throat—and he sleeps on the floor so as not to fall out of bed and break his neck. As a sort of compensation, perhaps, he sleeps quite soundly once his ritual is complete, though he awakens early to fitfully check his parameters and accouterments, and by the time he has breakfast is his usual nervous wreck.

How could a person get so screwed up? When Ernie was a boy of nine he watched his mother choke to death on a piece of meat. Unable to help, he was condemned to witness her last agonizing moments while his older sister ran around the kitchen, screaming. Before he could get over that horrible experience, his father dug a bomb shelter in the back yard and practiced using it. Here's how it worked: At any moment of the day or night Ernie's father would suddenly leap at him or emit a blood-curdling screech or douse him with something. That would be the signal to run for the bomb shelter. By the time he was eleven Ernie was unable to speak or to stop shaking. When he was brought to MPI it took months just to get him not to jump and run whenever a door opened or someone sneezed. That was nearly twenty years ago, and he has been here ever since. His father, incidentally, is a patient at another institution; his sister committed suicide in 1980.

Fortunately, debilitating phobias like Ernie's are rare. Those who are afraid of snakes, for example, need only stay away from forest and field. Agoraphobics and claustrophobics can usually avoid crowds and elevators and, in any case, are treatable with drugs or by slow acclimation to the offending situation. But how does one acclimate the necrophobic? How to avoid the Grim Reaper?

Howie is forty-three, though he looks to be sixty. Born into a poor Brooklyn family, his musical abilities became evident early on. His father gave him his unused violin when he was four years old and, in his early teens, he played that instrument with a number of well-respected regional orchestras. As time went on, however, he performed less and less frequently, preferring instead to study scores, other instruments, the history of music. His father, a bookseller, was not particularly concerned with this turn of events and went about his tiny shop bragging that Howie was going to become a famous conductor, another Stokowski. But by the time Howie got to college his interests seemed to cover the entire spectrum of human endeavor. He tried to master everything from algebra

35

to Zen. He studied night and day until he finally broke down and ended up with us.

As soon as his physical health was restored, however, he was off and running again, and no tranquilizing drug has proven powerful enough to slow down his endless quest for perfection.

The strain on Howie is terrible. The circles and bags under his eyes attest to his chronic battle with fatigue, and he suffers constantly from colds and other minor afflictions.

What happened to him? Why does one artist end up at Carnegie Hall and another in a mental hospital? Howie's father was a very demanding man, intolerant of mistakes. When little Howie stood up to play the violin he was terrified of making the slightest false note and offending his father, whom he loved deeply. But the better he became the more he realized how much he did *not* know, and how much more room for error there was than he had imagined. In order to be certain of playing his instrument perfectly he threw himself into music in all its aspects, trying to learn everything about the subject. When he realized that even this would not be sufficient, he took up other fields of study with the impossible goal of learning everything there was to know about everything.

But even that isn't enough for Howie, who spends each summer cataloging the birds and insects and counting the blades of grass on the lawn outside. In the winter he catches snowflakes, systematically recording and comparing their structures. On clear nights he scans the skies looking for anomalies, something that wasn't there before. Yet these are mere avocations for Howie. Most of the time he reads dictionaries and encyclopedias while listening to music or language tapes. Afraid he will forget something important he is constantly taking notes and making lists, then organizing and re-organizing them. Until that day in the recreation room I had never seen him when he was not frantically counting, record-ing, or studying. It was a struggle to get him to take time to eat.

I edged up to the table with my guest, trying to catch a bit of the conversation without scaring anyone off. From what I could gather, they were querying prot about life on K-PAX. They clammed up when they finally noticed us, however, and both Ernie and Howie scuttled away.

I introduced prot to our visitor, and took the opportu-nity to ask him whether he would mind submitting to a few additional tests on Wednesday, our regular meeting day. He not only didn't mind, he said, but he looked forward to it. We left him smiling broadly, apparently in eager anticipation.

ALTHOUGH we would not receive the official report from the State Board of Health for several months, the representa-tive did point out two or three minor deficiencies that needed to be corrected, and I brought these up at the regular Monday morning staff meeting. Among the other items discussed at that meeting was the news that the search committee had nar-rowed down their list of possible candidates for permanent director to four—three from outside the hospital, and myself. The chair of that committee was Dr. Klaus Villers.

Villers is the kind of psychiatrist usually portrayed in films: sixtyish, pale, trim gray goatee, heavy German accent, and a strict Freudian. It was clear that he had selected the other three names personally. I was familiar with their work and each, on paper, was a reasonable facsimile of Villers him-self. But all had outstanding credentials, and I was looking forward to meeting them. My own candidacy was not unexpected, but I had mixed feelings about the directorship—it would have meant permanently giving up most of my patients, among other things.

When that business was taken care of I summarized for my colleagues what I had learned so far about prot. Villers and some of the others agreed that it would be a waste of time to proceed with ordinary psychoanalysis, but thought my attempt to "humanize" him would also prove fruitless, suggesting instead some of the newer experimental drugs. Others argued that this approach was premature and, in any case, without the consent of the patient's family, the legal ramifications could become complicated. Thus, it was generally agreed that a greater effort should be made, by the police as well as myself, to determine his true identity. I thought of Meyerbeer's opera *L'Africaine,* in which Inez awaits the return of her long-departed lover, Vasco da Gama, and I wondered: Was there a family somewhere in this wide world fervently hoping and praying for a missing husband and father, brother or son to reappear?

Session Three

T HE testing took all morning and half the afternoon of May twenty-third. I had other pressing duties much of that time, not the least of which was an emergency facilities committee meeting to approve the purchase of a new linen dryer for the laundry room following the irreversible breakdown of one of the two old ones. Betty McAllister served very well in my place, however.

At the time, Betty had been with us for eleven years, the last two in the capacity of head nurse. She was the only person I had ever met who had read all of Taylor Caldwell's novels and, as long as I had known her, had been trying to get pregnant. Although she had resorted to almost every known scientific and folk remedy, she eschewed the so-called fertility pills because, as she put it, "I only want the one, not a whole menagerie." None of this affected her work, however, and she consistently performed her duties cheerfully and well.

According to Betty's report, prot was extremely cooperative throughout the examination period. Indeed, the eagerness with which he attacked the tests and questionnaires supported my earlier speculation of an academic background. How far he had progressed with his education was still a matter of conjecture, but it seemed quite likely, based on his confident demeanor and general articulateness, that he had at least attended college and possibly even a graduate or professional school.

It took a few days to process the data, and I must confess that my curiosity was such that I let lapse some things I had planned to do at home in order to come in on Saturday to finish what Betty had not completed by Friday afternoon. The final results, though generally unremarkable (as I had expected), were nonetheless interesting. They are summarized as follows:

IQ	154 *(well above average, though not in genius category)*
Psychological tests *(left/right, mazes, mirror tests, etc.—addnl. to std. admission exam)*	normal
Neurological tests	normal
EEG *(performed by Dr. Chakraborty)*	normal
Short-term memory	excellent
Reading skill	very good
Artistic ability/eidetic imagery	variable
Musical ability	below average

General knowledge (*history, geography, languages, the arts*)	broad and impressive
Math and science (*particularly physics and astronomy*)	outstanding
Knowledge of sports	minimal
General physical strength	above average
Hearing, taste, smell, tactile acuities	highly sensitive
"Special senses" (*ability to "feel" colors, sense the presence of other people, etc.*)	questionable
Vision 1. Sensitivity to white light 2. Range	marked! can detect light at 300–400 Å (UV)!
Aptitude	could do almost anything; particular affinity for natural history and physical sciences

As can be seen, the only unusual finding was the patient's ability to see light at wavelengths well into the ultraviolet range. His apparent sensitivity to visible light could have been due to a genetic defect; in any case there was no obvious retinal damage (nevertheless, I made a note to call Dr. Rappaport, our ophthalmologist, first thing on Tuesday, Monday being Memorial Day). Otherwise there was no suggestion of any special alien talents.

The patient's knowledge of languages, incidentally, was

not as broad as he pretended. Although he spoke and read a little of most of the common ones, his understanding was limited to everyday phrases and idioms, the types found in books for travelers. Another thing that caught my eye was some information the patient volunteered about the stars in the constellation Lyra—their distances from Earth, types, etc.—nothing that required space travel to obtain, certainly, but I decided to check this out as well.

Driving home that afternoon to the accompaniment of Gounod's *Faust*, I marveled once again, as I bellowed along, at what the human mind can do. There are well-documented cases of superhuman strength arising from a desperate need or fit of madness, of astounding performances far beyond the normal capabilities of athletes or rescue workers, of people who can go into trancelike states or "hibernation," of extraordinary endurance exhibited by victims of natural or man-made disasters, accounts of paralyzed people who get up and walk, of cancer patients who almost seem to cure themselves or, by force of will alone, manage to hang on until a birthday or favorite holiday. No less striking, perhaps, is the case of the unattractive woman who comes across as beautiful merely because she thinks she is. An individual with little talent who becomes a Broadway star on the basis of self-confidence and energy alone. I have personally encountered many patients who have done amazing things they could not do before they became ill. And here we have a man who believes he comes from a planet where people are a little more light-sensitive than we are, and by God he is. At times like these one wonders what the limits of the human mind really are.

ON Memorial Day my oldest daughter and her husband and their two little boys drove up from Princeton for a cookout. Abigail is the reverse of the unattractive woman I mentioned above—she was always a very pretty girl who never realized it. I don't think she has ever used makeup, doesn't do anything with her hair, pays no attention to what she wears. From the beginning she has had a mind of her own. When I think of Abby I see a kid of eight or nine marching with a bunch of others two or three times her age, all with long hair and flared pants, flashing her peace sign and yelling her slogans, serious as a kiss. Now, as a nonpracticing lawyer, she's active in any number of women's/gay/environmental/civil/animal rights groups. How did she turn out this way? Who knows? All of our children are as different from each other as the colors of the rainbow.

Fred, for instance, is the most sensitive of the four. As a boy he always had his nose in a book, and an ear for music as well. In fact, he still has an enormous collection of recordings of Broadway shows. We always thought he would become an artist of some kind, and were quite amazed when he ended up in aeronautics.

Jennifer is very different still. Slim, beautiful, not as serious as Abigail or as quiet as Fred, she is the only one of the four who has shown any interest in following her old man's footsteps. As a girl she loved biology (and slumber parties and chocolate-chip cookies), and she is now a third-year medical student at Stanford.

Will (Chip) is the youngest, eight years younger than Jenny. Probably the brightest of the bunch, he is a star athlete in school, active, popular. Like Abby before him, and unlike Fred and Jenny, he is hardly ever home, preferring instead to spend his time with his friends rather than with his grizzled parents. He hasn't the foggiest idea what he wants to do with his life.

All of which leads to the question: Is the shape of the individual personality due primarily to genetic or to environmental factors? After a great deal of experimentation and debate on this critical issue, the answer is far from clear. All I know is that, despite similar backgrounds and genetic makeup, my four kids are as different from each other as is night from day, winter from summer.

Abby's husband Steve is a professor of astronomy and, while the steaks were sizzling on the grill, I mentioned to him that there was a patient at the hospital who seemed to know something about his field. I showed him prot's figures on the constellation Lyra and the double star system Agape and Satori, around which traveled a putative planet the patient called "K-PAX." Steve studied the information, scratched his reddish beard, and grunted, as he often does when he is thinking. Suddenly he looked up with a ferocious grin and drawled, "Charlie put you up to this, didn' he?"

I assured him that he hadn't, that I didn't even know who "Charlie" was.

He said, "Terrific joke. Ah love it." My grandson Rain was banging him with a Frisbee now, trying to get him to play, after failing to coax Shasta Daisy, our neurotic Dalmatian, out from under the porch.

I told him it was no joke and asked him why he thought so. I don't recall his exact words, but they went something like: "This is somethin' Charlie Flynn and his students have been workin' on for quite a while. It involves a double star in the constellation Lyra. This double shows certain perturbations in its rotation pattern that indicate the possibility of a large dark body, prob'ly a planet, as part of the system. Like your alleged patient said, this planet appears to travel around them in an unusual pattern—Charlie thinks it's a figure eight. Do you see what Ah'm sayin'? This is unpublished work! Except for one or two colleagues, Charlie hasn't told anybody about this yet; he was plannin' to report it at the Astrophysics meeting next month. Where does this 'patient' of yours come from? How long has he been at the hospital? His name id'n 'Charlie,' is it?" He stuffed his mouth with a handful of potato chips.

We drank beer and chatted about astronomy and psychiatry most of the afternoon, Abby and her mother nagging us not to talk shop and to pay some attention to our sons/grandsons, who kept throwing food at Shasta and each other. One thing I wanted to know was his opinion on the possibility of light travel. "It's not," he stated flatly, still not convinced, I think, that I wasn't pulling his leg. But when I asked if he would be willing to help me prove to my new patient that "K-PAX" was a figment of his imagination, he said, "Shore." Before they left I gave him a list of questions to ask Dr. Flynn about the double star system—the types of stars they were, their actual sizes and brightnesses, their rotation period, the duration of a "year" on the putative planet, even something about what the night sky would look like from such a world. He promised to call me with whatever information he could dig up.

Session Four

THE Manhattan Psychiatric Institute is located on Amsterdam Avenue at 112th Street in New York City. It is a private teaching and research hospital affiliated with the nearby Columbia University College of Physicians and Surgeons. MPI is distinct from the Psychiatric Institute at Columbia, which is a general treatment center that deals with far more patients. We refer to it as "the big institute," and ours, in turn, is known as "the little institute." Our concept is unique: We take in only a limited number of adult patients (one hundred to one hundred twenty in all), either cases of unusual interest or those that have proven unresponsive to standard somatic (drug), electroconvulsive, surgical, or psychotherapies.

MPI was constructed in 1907 at a cost of just over a million dollars. Today the physical facility alone is worth one hundred fifty million. The grounds, though small, are well kept, with a grassy lawn to the side and back, and shrubs and flower gardens along the walls and fences. There is also a fountain, "Adonis in the Garden of Eden," situated in the center of what we call "the back forty." I love to stroll these pastoral grounds, listen to the bubbly fountain, contemplate the old stone walls. Entire adult lives have been lived here, both patient and staff. To some, this is the only world they will ever know.

There are five floors at MPI, numbered essentially in order of increasing severity of patient illness. Ward One (ground floor) is for those who suffer only acute neuroses or mild paranoia, and those who have responded to therapy and are nearly ready to be discharged. The other patients know this and often try very hard to be "promoted" to Ward One. Ward Two is occupied by those more severely afflicted: delusionals such as Russell and prot, manic and deep depressives, obdurate misanthropes, and others unable to function in society. Ward Three is divided into 3A, which houses a variety of seriously psychotic individuals, and 3B, the autistic/catatonic section. Finally, Ward Four is reserved for psychopathic patients who might cause harm to the staff and their fellow inmates. This includes certain autists who regularly erupt into uncontrollable rages, as well as otherwise normal individuals who sometimes become violent without warning. The fourth floor also houses the clinic and laboratory, a small research library, and a surgical theater.

Wards One and Two are not restricted in most cases, and the patients are free to mingle. In practice, this takes place primarily in the exercise/recreation and dining rooms (Wards Three and Four maintain separate facilities). Within each ward, of course, there are segregated sleeping and bathing areas for men and women. The staff, incidentally, maintains offices and examining rooms on the fifth floor; it is a common joke among the patients that we are the craziest inmates of all.

Finally, the kitchens are spread over several floors, the laundry, heating, air-conditioning, and maintenance facilities are located in the basement, and there is an amphitheater on (and between) the first and second floors, for classes and seminars.

Before becoming acting director of the hospital I usually spent an hour or two each week in the wards just talking with my patients, on an informal basis, to get a sense of their rate of progress, if any. Unfortunately, the press of administrative duties put an end to that custom, but I still try to have lunch with them occasionally and hang around until my first interview or committee meeting or afternoon lecture. On the day after the Memorial Day weekend I decided to eat in Ward Three before looking over my notes for my three o'clock class.

Besides the autists and catatonics, this ward is populated by patients with certain disorders which would make it difficult for them to interact with those in Wards One and Two. For example, there are several compulsive eaters, who will devour anything they can get their hands on—rocks, paper, weeds, silverware; a coprophagic whose only desire is to consume his own, and sometimes others', feces; and a number of patients with severe sexual problems.

One of the latter, dubbed "Whacky" by a comedic student some time ago, is a man who diddles with himself almost constantly. Virtually anything sets him off: arms, legs, beds, bathrooms—you name it.

Whacky is the son of a prominent New York attorney and his ex-wife, a well-known television soap opera actress. As far as we know he enjoyed a fairly normal childhood, i.e., he wasn't sexually repressed or abused in any way, he owned a Lionel train and Lincoln logs, played baseball and basketball, liked to read, he had friends. In high school he was shy around girls, but in college he became engaged to a beautiful coed. Although convivial and outgoing, she was nevertheless extremely coquettish, leading him on and on but never quite going "all the way." Crazed with desire, Whacky remained as virginal as Russell for two agonizing years—he was saving himself for the woman he loved.

But on their wedding day she ran off with an old boyfriend, recently released from the state prison, leaving Whacky literally standing at the altar (and bursting at the seams). When he received the news that his fiancée had jilted him, he took down his pants and began to masturbate right there in the church, and he has been at it ever since.

Prostitution therapy was completely ineffective in Whacky's case. However, drug treatments have proven marginally successful, and he can usually come to the table and get back to his room without causing a disturbance.

When he is not caught up in his compulsion, Whacky is a very pleasant guy. Now in his mid-forties, he is still youthfully handsome, with closely cropped brown hair, a strong cleft chin, and a terrible melancholy that shows in his sad blue eyes. He enjoys watching televised sporting events and talks about the baseball or football standings whenever I see him. On this particular occasion, however, he did not discuss the Mets, his favorite team. Instead, he brought up the subject of prot.

Whacky had never seen my new patient as far as I knew, since inhabitants of Ward Three are not permitted to visit the other floors. But somehow he had heard about a visitor in Ward Two who had come from a faraway place where life was very different from ours, and he wanted to meet him. I tried to discourage the idea by downplaying prot's imaginary travels, but his pathetic baby-blue eyes were so insistent that I told him I would give the matter some thought. "But why do you want to meet him?" I inquired.

"Why, to see if he will take me back with him, of course!"

The sudden silence was eerie—the place is usually one of noisy confusion and flying food. I glanced around. No one was wailing or giggling or spitting. Everyone was watching us and listening. I mumbled something about "seeing what I could do." By the time I got up to leave, the whole of Ward Three had made it clear that they wanted a chance to take their cases to my "alien" patient, and it took me nearly half an hour to calm everyone down and make my exit.

TALKING with Whacky always reminds me of the awesome power that sex has over all of us, as Freud perceived in a moment of tremendous inspiration a century ago. Indeed, most of us have sexual problems at some time in, if not throughout, our lives.

It wasn't until my wife and I had been married for several years that it suddenly occurred to me what my father had been doing on the night he died. The realization was so intense that I leaped out of bed and stared at myself in the closet-door mirror. What I saw was my father looking back at me: same tired eyes, same graying temples, same knobby knees. It was then that I understood with crystal clarity that I was a mortal human being.

My wife was wonderfully understanding throughout the ensuing ordeal—she is a psychiatric nurse herself—though she finally insisted I seek professional help for my frustrating impotence. The only thing that came from this was the "revelation" that I harbored tremendous guilt feelings about my father's death. But it wasn't until after I finally passed the age he was when he died that the (midlife) crisis mercifully ended and I was able to resume my conjugal duties. During that miserable six-month period I think I hated my father more than ever. Not only had he chosen my career for me and precipitated a lifelong guilt complex, but, thirty years after his death, he had nearly managed to ruin my sex life as well!

STEVE did even better than he promised. He faxed the astronomical data, including a computerized printout of a star chart of the night sky as seen from the hypothetical planet K-PAX, directly to my office. Mrs. Trexler was quite amused by the latter, referring to it as my "connect-the-dots."

Armed with this information, which prot could not possibly have had in his possession, I met with him again at the usual time on Wednesday. Of course I knew he could not be a space traveler any more than our resident Jesus Christ could have stepped out of the New Testament. But I was nonetheless curious as to just what this man could pull from the recesses of his unpredictable, though certainly human, mind.

He came into my examining room preceded by his standard Cheshire-cat grin. I was ready for him with a whole basket of fruit, which he dug into with relish. As he devoured three bananas, two oranges, and an apple he asked me a few questions about Ernie and Howie. Most patients express some curiosity about their fellow inmates and, without divulging anything confidential, I did not hesitate to answer them. When I thought he was relaxed and ready I turned on the recorder and we began.

To summarize, he knew everything about the newly discovered star system. There was some discrepancy in his description of the way K-PAX revolved around the two stars it was associated with—he claimed it was not a figure eight but something simpler—and the corresponding length of the putative planet's year was not what Steve or, rather, Dr. Flynn had calculated. But the rest of it fit quite well: the size and brightness of Agape and Satori (his K-MON and K-RIL), the periodicity of their rotation about each other, the next closest star, etc. Of course it could have been a series of lucky guesses, or perhaps he was reading my mind, though the tests showed no special aptitude for this ability. It seemed to me more likely, however, that this patient could somehow divine arcane astronomical data much like the savants mentioned earlier can make computer-like calculations and pull huge numbers from their heads. But it would have been an astonishing feat indeed if he could have constructed a picture of the night sky as seen from the planet K-PAX, which, incidentally, Professor Flynn had now chosen to call his previously unnamed planet. In anticipation of this result I think I was already contemplating the book the reader is now holding. So it was with some excitement that I nervously watched as he sketched his chart, insisting all the while that he wasn't very good at freehand drawing. I cautioned him to remember that the night sky as observed from K-PAX would look quite different from the way it does on Earth.

"Tell me about it," he replied.

It took him only a few minutes. While he was sketching I mentioned that an astronomer I knew had informed me that light travel was theoretically impossible. He stopped what he was doing and smiled at me tolerantly. "Have you ever studied your EARTH history?" he asked. "Can you think of a single new idea which all the experts in the field did not label 'impossible'?"

He returned to his diagram. As he drew he seemed to focus on the ceiling, but perhaps his eyes were closed. In any case he paid no attention to the map he was working on. It was as if he were simply copying it from an internal picture or screen. This was the result:

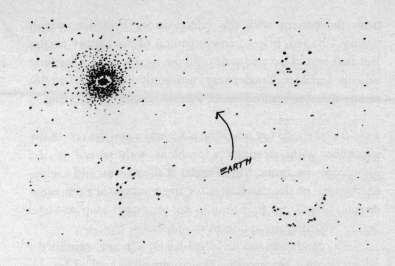

There are several notable features about his sketch: a "constellation" shaped like an *N* (upper right), another like a question mark (lower left), a "smiling mouth" (lower right), and an enormous eye-shaped cluster of stars (upper left). Note that he also indicated the location of the invisible Earth on his chart (center). The reason for the relatively few background stars in the diagram was, according to prot, that it never got completely dark on K-PAX, so there are fewer stars visible in the sky than one can ordinarily see, in rural areas, from the nighttime Earth.

However, it was clear that prot's and Steve's charts were completely different. Although not surprised to find that my "savant" had his limits I was, nonetheless, somewhat disappointed. I am aware that this is not a very scientific attitude, and I can only attribute it to the post-midlife-crisis syndrome first described by E. L. Brown in 1959, something that occurs most often in men who have entered their fifties: a curious desire for something interesting to happen to them.

Be that as it may, at least I would now be able to confront the patient with this contradictory evidence, which would, I hoped, help to convince him of his Earthly origin. But that would have to wait until the next session. Our time was up, and Mrs. Trexler was impatiently flashing me a telephone signal to remind me of a safety committee meeting.

ACCORDING to my notes the place was a zoo the rest of the afternoon with meetings, a problem with several of the photocopy machines, Mrs. Trexler at the dentist, and a seminar by one of the candidates for the position of permanent director. But I did find time to fax prot's star map to Steve before escorting the applicant to dinner.

The candidate, whom I shall call Dr. Choate, exhibited a rather peculiar mannerism: He continually checked his fly, presumably to make sure it was closed. Quite unconsciously, it appeared, since he did it in the conference room, in the dining room, in the wards, with women present or not. And his specialty was human sexuality! It has been said that all psychiatrists are a little crazy. Dr. Choate did nothing to dispel that canard.

I took the candidate to Asti, a lower Manhattan restaurant where the proprietor and his waiters are apt to break into an aria at the drop of a fork and encourage their patrons to do likewise. But Choate had no interest in music and finished his meal in rather glum silence. I had a lovely time, however, catching a flying doughball in my teeth and singing the part of Nadir in the lovely duet from *The Pearl Fishers*, and still made the 9:10 to Connecticut. When I got home, my wife told me Steve had called. I rang him back immediately.

"Pretty amazin' stuff!" he exclaimed.

"Why?" I said. "His drawing didn't look a thing like yours."

"Yes, Ah know. Ah thought your man had just concocted somethin' out of his head, at first. Then Ah saw where he had put in the arrow indicatin' the position of the Earth."

"So?"

"The chart Ah gave you was for the sky as seen *from* Earth, except that it was transposed seven thousand light-years away to the planet he calls K-PAX. Do you see what Ah'm sayin'? Lookin' back *here* from *there,* the sky would appear entirely different. So I went back to my computer, and *voilà!* There was the N constellation, the question mark, the smile, the eyeball cluster—all where he said they'd be. This *is* a joke, idn' it? Ah *know* Charlie put you up to this!"

That night I had a dream. I was floating around in space and utterly lost. No matter which direction I turned, the stars looked exactly the same to me. There was no familiar sun, no moon, not even a recognizable constellation. I wanted to go home but I had no idea which way it was. I was afraid, terrified that I was all alone in the universe. Suddenly I saw prot. He was motioning that I should follow him. Greatly relieved, I did so. As we proceeded he pointed out the eyeball cluster and all the rest, and at last I knew where I was.

Then I woke up and couldn't go back to sleep. I recalled an incident a few days earlier when I was running across the hospital lawn on my way to a consultation with the family of one of my patients. Prot was sitting on the grass clutching, it appeared, a batch of worms. I was late for an appointment and didn't dwell on it then. Later on I realized that I had never seen any of the patients playing with a handful of worms before, and where did he get them? I puzzled over this as I lay in bed awake, until I remembered his saying, in session two, that on K-PAX everything had evolved from wormlike creatures. Was he studying them as we might scrutinize our own cousins, the fishes, whose gills still manifest themselves for a time in the human embryo?

* * *

I hadn't yet found an opportunity to call Dr. Rappaport, our ophthalmologist, about the results of the vision test, but I did so the following morning. It is "highly unlikely," he told me, somewhat testily, I thought, that a human being would be able to detect light at a wavelength of three hundred angstroms. Such a person, he pointed out, would be able to see things only certain insects can see. Though he seemed extremely dubious, as if I were trying to make him the victim of a practical joke, he wouldn't go so far as to deny our examination results.

Once again I reflected on how remarkably complex the human brain really is. How can a sick mind like prot's possibly train itself to see UV light, and figure out how to diagram the sky from seven thousand light-years away? The latter was not completely outside the realm of possibility, but what an astonishing talent! Furthermore, if he *was* a savant, he was an *intelligent, amnesiacal, delusional* one. This was absolutely extraordinary, an entirely new phenomenon. And I suddenly realized: I've got my book!

SAVANT syndrome is one of the most amazing and least understood pathologies in the realm of psychiatry. The affliction takes many forms. Some savants are "calendar calculators," meaning that they can tell you immediately what day of the week July 4, 2990 falls on, though they are often unable to learn to tie their shoes. Others can perform incredible arithmetical feats, such as to add long columns of numbers, mentally calculate large square roots, etc. Still others are wonderfully musically gifted and can sing or play back a song, or even the various parts of a symphony or opera, after a single first hearing.

Most savants are autistic. Some have suffered clinically

detectable brain damage, while others show no such obvious abnormality. But nearly all have IQs well below average, usually in the fifty to seventy-five range. Rarely has a savant been found to exhibit a normal or greater intelligence quotient.

I am privileged to have known one of these remarkable individuals. She was a woman in her sixties who had been diagnosed with a slow-growing brain tumor centered in the left occipital lobe. Because of this malignancy she was almost totally unable to speak, read, or write. She was further plagued by a nearly constant chorea and barely able to feed herself. As if that weren't enough, she was one of the most unattractive women I have ever seen. The staff called her, affectionately, "Catherine Deneuve," after the lovely French film star, who was very popular at that time.

But what an artist! When provided with suitable materials, her head and hands stopped shaking and she began to create, from memory, near-perfect reproductions of works by many of the greatest artists in history. Though they ordinarily took only a few hours to complete, her paintings are virtually indistinguishable from the originals. Amazingly, while she worked she even seemed to become beautiful!

Some of her work now resides in various museums and private collections all over the country. When she died, the family generously donated one of her pictures to the hospital, where it graces the wall of the faculty conference room. It is a perfect copy of van Gogh's "Sunflowers," the original of which hangs in the Metropolitan Museum of Art, and one is just as awestruck by her talent as by the genius of the master himself.

In the past, the emphasis has been on trying to "normalize" such individuals, to mold them into products more suitable to society's needs. Even "Catherine Deneuve" was encouraged to spend less time painting and more time learning to dress and feed herself. If not cultivated, however, these remarkable abilities can be lost, and attempts are now being made, at various institutions, to allow such people to develop their gifts to the fullest.

However, most savants are very difficult to communicate with. Normal discourse with "Catherine," for example, was impossible. But prot was alert, rational, able to function normally. What might we learn from such an individual? What else did he know about the stars, for example? Might there be more ways to arrive at knowledge than we are willing to consider or admit? There is, after all, a fine line between genius and insanity—consider, for example, Blake, Woolf, Schumann, Nijinsky, and, of course, van Gogh. Even Freud was plagued by severe mental problems. The poet John Dryden put it this way:

> Great wits are sure to madness near alli'd
> And thin partitions do their bounds divide.

I brought this up at the Monday morning staff meeting, where I proposed to let prot ramble on about whatever he wanted and try to determine whether there was anything of value he might have to tell us about his (our) world, as well as his own condition and identity. Unfortunately, despite the substantiating presence of "Catherine Deneuve" 's priceless painting, there was little enthusiasm for this idea. Indeed, Klaus Villers, without ever having seen the patient, pronounced him such a hopeless case that more aggressive measures should be instigated "at ze first suitable opportunity," though he's probably more conservative in his approach to his own patients than anyone else on the staff. The consensus, however, was that little was to be lost by giving my patient a few more weeks to have his say before turning him over to the pharmacologists and surgeons.

There was another facet to the case that I did not mention at that meeting: Prot's presence seemed to be having a positive effect on some of the other patients in his ward. For example, Ernie was taking his temperature less frequently, and Howie seemed a bit less frenetic. He even sat down one night and watched a New York Philharmonic concert on television, I was told. Some of the other patients were beginning to take a greater interest in their surroundings as well.

One of these was a twenty-seven-year-old woman whom I shall call Bess. Homeless and emaciated when she was brought to the hospital, she had never—not even once—smiled, as far as I am aware. From the time she was a child, Bess had been treated like a slave by her own family. She did all the cleaning and cooking and laundering. Her Christmas presents, when she got anything at all, consisted of utensils and appliances, a new ironing board. She felt it should have been she who perished in the fire that devastated the family's tenement apartment, rather than her brothers and sisters. It was shortly thereafter that she was brought to us, nearly frozen because she wouldn't go to one of the shelters the city provides for the homeless.

From the beginning it was difficult to get her to eat. Not, like Ernie, because she was afraid to, or like Howie, was too busy, but because she didn't think she deserved to: "Why do *I* get to eat when so many are hungry?" She was certain it was raining on the sunniest days. Everything that happened seemed to remind her of some tragedy, some terrible incident from her past. Neither electroconvulsive therapy nor a variety of neuroleptic drugs had proven effective. She was the saddest person I had ever met.

But on one of my decreasingly frequent travels through the wards I noticed that she was sitting with her knees up and her arms wrapped around them, paying rapt attention to whatever prot might choose to say. Not smiling, but not crying, either.

And seventy-year-old Mrs. Archer, ex-wife of one of America's foremost industrialists, ceased her constant muttering whenever prot was around.

Known in Ward Two as "the Duchess," Mrs. Archer takes her meals on fine china in the privacy of her own room. Trained since birth for a life of luxury, she complains constantly about the service she receives, and about everyone's deportment in general. Amazingly, the Duchess, who once ran naked for a mile down Fifth Avenue when her husband left her for a much younger woman, became a lamb in the presence of my new patient.

The only person who seemed to resent prot's proximity was Russell, who decided that prot was scouting the Earth for the devil. "Get thee behind me, Satan!" he exclaimed periodically, to no one in particular. Although many of the patients continued to flock to him for sympathy and advice, his coterie was shrinking almost daily and gravitating toward prot instead.

But the point I was making was that prot's presence seemed to be beneficial for many of our long-term patients. This raised an interesting dilemma: If we were successful in diagnosing and treating prot's illness, might not his recovery come at the expense of many of his fellow sufferers?

Session Five

B EFORE my next encounter with prot I had a couple of old floor lamps brought in from the storage tunnel and equipped them with fifteen-watt "nightlight" bulbs, hoping the dimmer radiance would induce him to remove his dark glasses so I could see his eyes. That is exactly what happened and, although now it was too dark in my examining room to see the rest of him with clarity, I could discern his obsidian irises shining across the desk like those of some nocturnal animal as he plucked a papaya from the fruit basket and offered me a bite.

While he ate I casually gave him the date of my birth and asked him to tell me what day of the week it fell on. He shrugged and went on chomping. I asked him to give me the square root of 98,596. His reply was: "Mathematics is not my strong suit." Then I asked him to do what I thought he had done earlier, namely to draw the night sky as seen from K-PAX, only in the other direction, away from the Earth.

When he had finished I compared it with the one Steve had faxed me the week before. It contained fewer stars than the computer projection, but I could tell that the general pattern was the same.

I didn't waste time asking him how he knew what the night sky looked like from K-PAX. He would undoubtedly have snorted something about "growing up there." Instead, I turned on the tape recorder and essentially just let him ramble. I wanted to know exactly how well developed his peculiar delusion was and what, if anything, we might be able to learn from it, both about prot's true background and, perhaps, about the universe in general.

"Tell me about K-PAX," I said.

He lit up when I asked him that. Munching a star fruit, the significance of which was not lost on him, he said, "What would you like to know?"

"Everything. Describe a typical day in a typical year."

"Ah," he nodded. "A typical day." Apparently this was not an unpleasant prospect. He finished his snack, and in the dim light I could see his fingertips coming together and his eyes rolling up. It took a few seconds for him to gather his thoughts, or project them onto his internal screen, or whatever he did with them. "Well, to begin with, we don't have 'days' in the sense you mean them. We experience rather dusky light conditions most of the time, you see, much like it is in this room right now." The last phrase was accompanied by a very familiar wry grin. "Also, K-PAXians don't sleep as much as y'all do, nor do we sleep at regular times, but only as the need arises." I had gotten staff reports to this effect on prot's sleeping habits. He stayed up most of the night reading or writing or, apparently, just thinking, and napped at odd times during the day. "And finally, K-PAX doesn't rotate unidirectionally as does EARTH, but reverses itself as it reaches the end of its cycle every twenty-one of your years. Thus, the length of a 'day' varies from about one of your weeks to several months as K-PAX slows and reverses its spin."

At this point I noted down something I had forgotten to mention to Steve: Prot's description of the path of K-PAX around, or between, its suns didn't seem to match Dr. Flynn's "figure eight" pattern.

"Incidentally," he said, and his eyes opened for a moment, "we do have calendars and clocks, though we rarely use them. On the other hand, they never need to be reset or replaced—they are the type you would call 'perpetual.' But to get back to your question, let's say I have just awakened from a little snooze. What would I do? If I were hungry I would eat something. Some soaked grains, perhaps, and some fruit."

I asked him what he meant by a "soaked" grain, and to describe some K-PAXian fruits.

His eyes popped open again and he sat up straighter; he seemed to relish the opportunity to explain the details of his "world." "A soaked grain is just what it sounds like," he said. "You soak a grain long enough and it gets soft, like your rice or oatmeal. On EARTH you prefer to cook them. We just let them soak, usually in fruit juices. There are twenty-one commonly eaten grains on our PLANET, but, like yours, none is a complete food in itself. They have to be mixed to get the proper amino acid balance. My favorite combination is drak and thon and adro. It has a nutty flavor much like your cashew."

"Gesundheit."

Prot had either a well-developed sense of humor or none at all—I was never able to tell. "Thank you," he said, without blinking an eye. "Now the fruits are a different story. We have several wonderful kinds—I especially like the ones we call yorts, or sugar plums—but they can't compare with EARTH's variety, which is due primarily to your great variations in climate. To summarize: If we get hungry we grab some soaked grains, usually in fruit juice, and sit down against a balnok tree and fall to."

"What about vegetables?"

"What about them?"

"Do you have them?"

"Oh, of course. After the next snooze we might munch a bunch of krees or likas."

"Meat? Fish? Seafood?"

"No meat. No fish. No seafood. No *sea.*"

"No animals of any kind?"

He tapped his glasses on the arm of his chair. "Now, gene, I've already told you about the aps and mots—remember?"

"What about pigs and cows and sheep?"

With a deep sigh: "As I pointed out in session two, we don't have any 'domesticated' beings on K-PAX. But we have *wild* pigs, *wild* cows, *wild* sheep—"

"Wild cows??"

"Well, they're called rulis, but they're much like your cows—big, cumbersome, placid. Have you ever noticed how gentle your large beings are? Your elephants and giraffes and whales, even when they are mistreated?"

"So basically you just eat and sleep on your planet?"

"Perhaps I should back up a step. When I told you that we snooze when we feel the need, you probably imagined a bed in a bedroom in a house much like the one you live in. Wroooong! It's different on K-PAX. You see, our weather is very dependable. Every day is about the same as the one before. It is usually quite warm, and it never rains. There are structures scattered around for storage of utensils and the like, for the use of anyone who happens to pass by. Food is kept there, as well as mats and musical instruments—a variety of things—but no beds. For the most part—"

"Who owns these structures?"

"No one 'owns' anything on K-PAX."

"Go on."

"For the most part we sleep out of doors—except there are no doors—usually for an hour or two, your hour, at a time. Where we won't get stepped on by an ap, of course. By the way," he interrupted himself, sitting up again, "since sexual contact is not a desirable thing on our PLANET, or on most others, men and women are free to share everything without fear or the need for guile. You might find yourself lying down for a nap near someone of the opposite gender, but you don't need to worry about what your wife or husband—or whatever—might think if he or she hears about it, or suffer embarrassment or discomfort of any kind, even though we usually wear little or no clothing. Sexual apparati are simply no big deal on K-PAX, especially since there are only two varieties and, as you know, when you've seen both, you've seen them all."

He leaned back and closed his eyes again, obviously enjoying the exposition. "Okay, we've awakened, we've eaten something, we've urinated, picked our teeth, what do we do now? Well, whatever needs to be done. Soak some more grains for next time, wipe out our bowls, fix anything that's broken. Otherwise, anything we want! Some prefer to search the skies, others observe the leafing of the trees or the antics of the aps or the behavior of the korms or homs, or play music or paint or sculpt. When I'm not traveling I usually spend most of my time in one of the libraries, which are usually filled with beings at any given time of cycle."

"Tell me more about the libraries."

"There are some books there, of course, but those are

very old, and there is something much better. Let me see if I can describe it for you." Prot's eyes rolled up again, and his fingers began tapping together, more rapidly this time. "Imagine a computer with a monitor that projects three-dimensional images complete with all-sense capability. Now suppose you are interested in ballooning. Let's say you want to know what it was like to pilot a balloon a hundred million cycles ago, before we learned how to travel with light. You just set up the computer, tap in the instructions, and there you are! You would find yourself in an ancient gondola, floating at whatever location and altitude you specified, at the authentic wind speed and direction on the date you selected. Feel the ropes in your hands and the suns on your face! Smell the trees below! Hear the korms of that time who perch on top of the bladder or join you in the gondola! Taste the fruit and nuts provided for the trip! The surface features you see below you are perfectly accurate. It is exactly like being there!" By now prot was virtually quivering with excitement.

"What happens if you fall off?"

His bright eyes opened once more and his fingers became still. "That's a question only a human being would ask! But the answer is: nothing. You would find yourself back in the library, ready for another adventure."

"What other kinds of adventures might you have?"

"Use your imagination, doc. Anything that has happened on K-PAX in the last few million years is yours to experience, in three dimensions and all senses. You could recreate your own birth, if you wanted to. Or relive any part of your life. Or that of any other being."

"These holograms—do you have any for other planets? Will you be taking something back from Earth?"

"Planetary travel is still somewhat new to us. We've

only been at it for a few hundreds of thousands of your years, mostly just scouting expeditions, and our library is rather incomplete on that subject. As for EARTH—well, I find it to be a very interesting place, and I will so state in my report. But whether anyone will want to set up all the parameters . . ." He shrugged and reached for a mango, bit into it without peeling off the skin. "But that's only the beginning!" he exclaimed, with a noisy slurp. "Suppose you are interested in geology. Tap in the instructions, and samples of any and every rock, ore, gem, slag, or meteorite, complete with name, origin, composition, chemistry, density, from whatever source you specify, will be at your fingertips. You can pick them up, feel them, smell them. Same with flora and fauna or any group or species thereof. Science. Medicine. History. The arts. You like opera, *nicht wahr?* In a matter of seconds you could select anything you wished to see and hear, from a list of everything ever written or performed on K-PAX or certain other PLANETS, organized by title, subject, setting, types of voices, composer, performers, et cetera, et cetera, all cross-referenced. If you had this capability on EARTH you could take part in a performance yourself alongside Ponselle or Caruso! Sound good?" I had to admit that it did. "Or you could sail with Columbus, sign the Magna Carta, drive the Indy Five Hundred, pitch to Babe Ruth—you name it.

"After a time in the library," he continued, a little more placidly now, "I might go for a walk in the woods or just sit or lie down somewhere for a while. That's one of the nicest things of all." He paused for a moment, apparently deep in thought, then said: "A few months ago I sat beside a pond in alabama. There was no wind at all and it was absolutely quiet, wonderfully still except for the occasional jumping of a fish or croaking of a frog or the sound of water bugs making tiny ripples on the surface. Have you ever experienced that? It is beautiful. There are no ponds on K-PAX, but the feeling is the same."

"When was this?"

"Last october." He leaned back with that perpetual smile on his face as if he were, at that moment, actually sitting beside the pond he had just described. Then he sat up and sang, rather loudly and not on key, "And that's a typical daaayyyy" (tap, tap), "in dogpatch (tap), u.s.aaayyyy." A reference, according to my son Fred, to a popular Broadway musical of the fifties called *Li'l Abner*.

And then he said something totally unexpected, something precipitated, apparently, by his "reminiscing" about life on his "world." He said, "No offense intended, gene, but my time is almost up here and I can't wait to get back."

This took me completely by surprise. I said, "What—to K-PAX?"

"Where else?"

Now it was my turn to sit up straighter. "When are you planning to return?"

Without a moment's hesitation: "On august seventeenth."

"August seventeenth. Why August seventeenth?"

He said, "It's 'Beam me up, scotty' time."

"You're 'beaming' back to K-PAX on that date?"

"Yes," he replied. "And I shall miss you. And all the other patients. And," he nodded toward the nearly empty basket, "all your delicious fruits."

I said, "Why does it have to be August seventeenth?"

"Safety reasons."

"Safety reasons?"

"You see, I can go anywhere on EARTH without fear of bumping into anyone traveling at superlight speed. But

68

beings are going to and coming from K-PAX all the time. It has to be coordinated, like your airport control towers."

"August seventeenth."

"At 3:31 A.M. Eastern time."

I was disappointed to find that our own time was up for this session. "I'd like to take this up again next week, if that's all right with you. Oh, and could you draw up a K-PAXian calendar for me some time? Just a typical cycle or so would be fine."

"Anything you say. Until august seventeenth I'm all yours. Except for a little side trip up north, of course. I haven't been to a few places yet, remember?" He was already out the door. *"Ciao,"* he called on his way down the corridor.

AFTER he had gone I returned to my office to recopy my notes. As I was trying to make some sense of them I found myself gazing at Chip's picture sitting on my desk. *"Ciao"* is one of his favorite expressions, along with "Truly," and "You know?" Now on summer vacation, he had gotten a job as a lifeguard at one of the public beaches. A good thing, too, since he had already weaseled two years' advances on his allowance. The last of my children, soon out of the nest.

I should wax philosophical here and report that I pondered long and hard the implications of that inevitable fledging, both for Chip and for myself, but the truth is that it brought me back to prot's "departure date." August seventeenth was only two months away. What did it mean? It would be like Russell's saying that on such-and-such a day he would be returning to heaven. But in all the years he had been with us Russell has never announced a date for that journey and, to my knowledge, neither has any other delusional. It was totally unprecedented in the annals of psychiatry. And since it was patently impossible for prot to travel to K-PAX, or anywhere else, what would happen to him on that day? Would he withdraw completely into his amnesiacal armor? The only possible way I could see to prevent that from happening would be to find out who this man really was and where he had come from before it was too late.

But suddenly it occurred to me that August seventeenth would have been the approximate date that prot claimed he had arrived on Earth nearly five years earlier. With this in mind I asked Mrs. Trexler to put in a call to the precinct where he had been brought in originally, as indicated on his admission records, to request that they check whether anyone answering his description had disappeared on or about that particular date. And to inform them of prot's possible visit to Alabama in October. She came in later with a batch of letters for me to sign, and mentioned that the police had promised to let us know if anything turned up. "But don't hold your breath," she snorted.

W E find out a lot about our patients not only from the nursing staff but also from the other inmates, who love to talk about one another. Thus it was from his roommate Ernie that I first learned that Howie had become an entirely different person—cheerful, even relaxed! I went to see for myself.

Ernie was right. On a cool Thursday afternoon I found him calmly sitting in the wide sill of the second-floor lounge gazing out the window toward the sky. No dictionaries, no encyclopedias, no counting the threads in the big green carpet. His glasses, whose lenses were usually fogged with grime, had been cleaned.

I requested permission to sit down with him, and struck up a casual conversation pertaining to the flowers lining the high wall on the other side of the lawn. He was happy to produce, as he had many times in the past, the common and Latin names of each of them, something of their genetic history, nutritional value, medical and industrial uses. But he never took his eyes from the dark gray sky. He seemed to be looking for something—*scanning* was the word that came to mind. I asked him what it was.

"The bluebird," he said.

"The bluebird?"

"The bluebird of happiness."

That was an odd thing for Howie to say. He might well have known everything about bluebirds, from their eye color to their migratory habits to the total number worldwide. But *the* bluebird? Of *happiness?* And where did he get that gleam in his eye? When I pressed him on this I learned that he had gotten the idea from prot. Indeed, my problem patient had assigned Howie this "task," the first of three. I didn't know at the time what the other two were, and neither did Howie. But the first was assigned and accepted: Find the bluebird of happiness.

Some of the temporaries in Ward One quickly dubbed Howie "the bluenerd of sappiness," and in Ward Four there was talk of a bluebeard stalking the grounds, but Howie was oblivious to all this. Indeed, he was as single-minded as ever toward his illusive goal. Nevertheless, I was struck by the placidity with which he had taken up his stint by the window. Gone were the fitful checking and rechecking, the rushing from book to book, the feverish scratching of pen on reams and reams of paper. In fact, his tablets and ledgers were still spread out all over his desk and the little table he shared with Ernie; apparently he had dropped what he was doing and didn't even care enough about his lifetime of records and notes to file them away. It was such a refreshing sight to see him calmly sitting at the window that I could not help but breathe a sigh of relief myself, as if the weight of the world had been lifted from my own shoulders, as well as Howie's.

Just before I left him the sun came out, illuminating the flowers and bathing the lawn in gold. Howie smiled. "I never noticed how beautiful that is," he said.

Thinking that hell would freeze over before he spotted a bluebird in upper Manhattan I didn't bother to change his semiannual interview, scheduled for September, to an earlier date. But it was only a few days later, on a warm, drizzly morning that the wards were filled with the rare and delightful sound of a happy voice crying, "Bluebird! Bluebird!" Howie was running down the corridors (I didn't witness this personally, but Betty told me about it later), bursting into the exercise room and the quiet room, interrupting card games and meditation, finally grabbing a smiling prot by the hand and tugging him back to the lounge, shouting, "Bluebird! Bluebird!" By this time, of course, all the patients—and staff, too—were rushing to see the bluebird for themselves, and the windows were full of faces peering out at the wet lawn, shouting "Bluebird!" as they spotted it, until everyone was shouting "Bluebird! Bluebird! Bluebird!" Ernie and Russell and even the Duchess were caught up in the excitement. Betty said she could almost hear movie music playing. Only Bess seemed unmoved by the event, recalling all the dead and injured birds she had encountered in her joyless lifetime.

Eventually the bluebird flew away and everything settled back to normal, or almost so. Or was there a subtle change? A gossamer thread of something—hope, maybe?—had been left by the bird, and someone rushed out to retrieve it. It was so fine that, after it had dried out, no one could actually see it, except for prot, perhaps. It remains in Ward Two today, passed invisibly from patient to patient as a sort of talisman to alleviate depression and replace it with hope and good cheer. And, amazingly, it often works.

Session Six

My next session with prot took place the following afternoon. Smiling profusely when he came into my examining room, he handed me what he called a "calendar." It was in the form of a scroll, and so complicated that I could make little sense of it. But I thanked him and motioned to the basket of fruit on the side table by his chair.

I waited to see if he would bring up the subject of Howie and the bluebird, but he never mentioned it. When I finally asked him about it he bit into a cantaloupe and shrugged. "It had been there all the time, but nobody had looked for it." I didn't mention the larger issue of his assigning "tasks" to the patients. As long as the results were positive, I decided to allow it for the time being.

After he had finished the last kiwi, fuzz and all, I turned on the tape recorder. "I'd like to follow up on something you told me earlier."

"Why not?"

"I believe you said there is no government on K-PAX, and no one works. Is that right?"

"Quoit roit, guvnuh."

"I must be dense. I still don't understand how things get done. Who builds the libraries and makes all the equipment for them and installs it and runs it? Who makes all the holographic software, if that's the proper terminology? Who makes your eating utensils and your clothes? Who plants the grains? What about all the other things that you surely need and use on K-PAX?"

Prot smacked his forehead with the palm of his hand and muttered, "*Mama mia.*" Then, "All right. Let me see if I can make it complicated enough for you to understand." He leaned forward in his chair and fixed me with his penetrating black gaze, as he did whenever he wanted to make sure I was paying attention. "In the first place, we hardly ever wear any clothing on K-PAX. Except once each cycle—every twenty-one of your years—when we have some cold weather. And nobody plants the grains. You leave them alone and they plant themselves. As for the libraries, if something needs to be done, someone does it, *capisci*? This goes for everything you would call 'goods and services.' Now do you get it?"

"Surely there are jobs no one wants to do. Hard labor, for example, or cleaning public toilets. That's only human nature."

"There are no humans on K-PAX."

I glared back at him. "Oh yes, I forgot."

"Besides, there is nothing that needs to be done that is really unpleasant. Look. You defecate, don't you?"

"Not as often as I'd like."

"Do you find it unpleasant?"

"Somewhat."

"Do you get someone to do it for you?"

75

"I would if I could."

"But you don't, and you don't think twice about it. You just do it. And it does have its rewards, right?"

The tape indicates that I chuckled here. "Okay. There are no undesirable jobs. But what about the other side of the coin? What about the specialty jobs that take a lot of training? Like medicine. Or law. Who does those?"

"We have no laws, therefore no lawyers. As for the former, everyone practices medicine, so, in general, there is no need for doctors, either. Of course there are some who are more interested in such matters than are others, and they are available whenever anybody needs them. For surgery, primarily."

"Tell me more about medicine on your planet."

"I knew you'd get around to that sooner or later." He settled back into his familiar pose. "As I suggested a moment ago, there isn't much need for it on K-PAX. Since we eat only plants, we have almost no circulatory problems. And since there's no pollution of our air or our food, and no tobacco, there isn't much cancer, either. There's little stress, ergo no GI problems. Also there are few serious accidents, no suicide, no crime—*voilà!* Not much need for doctors! But of course there are occasional outbreaks of disease. Most of these run their course without permanent damage, but there are a few serious afflictions. For these we again have the plants. There is an herb or two for every ailment. You just have to look it up in the library."

"You have an herb for *everything*?"

"So do you. For aids, for all the different kinds of cancer, for parkinson's and alzheimer's, for blocked arteries. Herbs for selective anesthesia. They're all there, in your tropical forests. All you have to do is look for them."

"Selective anesthesia?"

"If you want to do abdominal surgery, there is something to anesthetize that part of the body. You can watch someone take out your appendix. Or do it yourself, if you wish. And so on. Your chinese have the right idea with their acupuncture."

"Are there hospitals?"

"More like small clinics. One for each village."

"What about psychiatry? I suppose you're going to tell me there's no need for it on K-PAX."

"Why should there be? We don't have religious or sexual or financial problems to tear us apart."

"All right. But aren't there those who become mentally ill for organic reasons? What do you do with *them*?"

"Again, these are rare on our PLANET. But such beings are usually not dangerous and are not locked up for the convenience of others. On the contrary, they are well taken care of by everyone else."

"You mean your mental patients aren't treated with any drugs—herbs—to make them well?"

"Mental illness is often in the eye of the beholder. Too often on this PLANET it refers to those who think and act differently from the majority."

"But surely there are those who are obviously unable to cope with reality. . . ."

"Reality is what you make it."

"So no K-PAXians are ever treated for mental problems?"

"Only if they are unhappy, or request it themselves."

"And how do you know whether they are happy or not?"

"If you don't know that, you can't be much of a psychiatrist."

"All right. You said there are no countries and no governments on K-PAX. I deduce from this that there are no armies or military weapons anywhere on your world—is that right?"

"Heaven forbid."

"Tell me—what happens if K-PAX is attacked by inhabitants of another planet?"

"A contradiction in terms. Any beings who would destroy another WORLD always destroy themselves first."

"Then what about your internal affairs? Who keeps order?"

"K-PAX is already orderly."

"But you also said there are no laws on your planet. Correct?"

"Kee-reck."

"Without laws, how does one know what is right and what is wrong?"

"The same way human beings do. Your children don't study law, do they? When they make mistakes, these are pointed out to them."

"Who decides what a 'mistake' is?"

"Everyone knows."

"How? Who created the original behavior codes?"

"No one. They just became obvious over a period of time."

"Would you say there is some moral basis for these codes?"

"Depends on your definition of 'moral.' I presume you are thinking about religion."

"Yes."

"As I said before, we have no religions on K-PAX, thank god."

"God?"

"That was a joke." Prot entered something into his notebook. "Have you no sense of humor on this PLANET?"

"Then you don't believe in God?"

"The idea was kicked around for a few hundred cycles, but it was soon rejected."

"Why?"

"Why kid ourselves?"

"But if it gives comfort . . ."

"A false hope gives only false comfort."

"Do all K-PAXians share this view?"

"I imagine. It's not something that's discussed very much."

"Why not?"

"How often do you discuss dragons and unicorns?"

"What sorts of things *are* discussed on your planet?"

"Information. Ideas."

"What sorts of ideas?"

"Can one travel forward in time? Is there a fourth spatial dimension? Are there other UNIVERSES? Stuff like that."

"One more thing before we move on to something else. What happens—I know this is rare—but what happens when someone breaks one of your behavior codes? Refuses to conform?"

"Nothing."

"Nothing?"

"We reason with him or her."

"That's all?"

"Yes."

"What if he kills someone?"

Somewhat agitated: "Why would any being do a thing like that?"

"But what if someone did?"

79

"We would try to avoid him or her."

"But is there no compassion for the person he has killed? Or for his next victim?"

Prot was staring at me, disgustedly it appeared, or perhaps in disbelief. "You're making a mountain out of a molehill. Beings don't kill other beings on K-PAX. Crime is less popular than sex, even. There's simply no need for it."

I had a hunch I was on to something here. "But if someone did commit a crime, shouldn't such a person—uh, being—be locked up for the good of everyone else?"

Prot was clearly becoming irate. "Let me tell you something, doc," he almost snarled. "Most humans subscribe to the policy of 'an eye for an eye, a life for a life.' Many of your religions are famous for this formula, which is well known throughout the UNIVERSE for its stupidity. Your christ and your buddha had a different vision, but nobody paid any attention to them, not even the christians and buddhists. On K-PAX there is no crime, you dig? And if there were, there would be no punishment. Apparently this is impossible for EARTH beings to understand, but it's the secret of life, believe me!" By now prot's eyes were bugging and his breathing was hard. I sensed it was time to end the day's session, if somewhat prematurely.

"I admit you have a point there. And by the way, I'm afraid I'm going to have to cut our session a little short today. I hope you don't mind. I have an important meeting which couldn't be rescheduled. Would it be all right with you if we continue with this next week?"

Calmer now, but not much: "Perfectly." Without another word he got up and stalked out.

I sat in my examining room for a few minutes after he had gone, thinking. Until that moment I had seen no evidence of anger, and rarely even a frown, in this patient. Now it appeared that just below the surface lay a seething cauldron, a volcano that could erupt at any time. Had it erupted in the past? Hysterical amnesia sometimes results from a violent and irreversible act. Had prot, in fact, killed someone, possibly on August 17, 1985? As a precaution, should I have him transferred to Ward Four?

I decided against the latter move, which might have driven him deeper into his seemingly impenetrable shell. Besides, all this was pure speculation at this point. And even if correct, he was unlikely to become violent unless we made substantial progress toward unraveling his past actions, the precipitants of his amnesia, a development I welcomed. Nevertheless, I would notify the staff and security office of the potential problem, have him watched more closely, and conduct subsequent interviews with greater caution. I decided also to notify the police department about a possible violent altercation some five years earlier, hoping it would help them to track him down, something our previous clues had failed to do.

But August seventeenth was fast approaching. I was frustrated and tired. Perhaps, I thought, I was getting too old for clinical work. Maybe I wasn't good enough any more. Maybe I never was.

I never wanted to be a psychiatrist. I wanted to be a singer.

As a pre-med student in college my only real interest was the annual "Follies Brassière," a talent show for students and faculty, in which I shamelessly belted out Broadway tunes and opera arias, to loud and addictive applause. By the time I graduated, however, I was already married and it made no sense to pursue such a frivolous dream. I was no Don Quixote.

Thus, it wasn't until I got into medical school itself that

I began to have serious doubts about my choice of profession. But just as I was about to confess to my new wife that I might rather try something else, Mother was diagnosed with liver cancer. Although the doctors decided to operate, it turned out to be far too late.

Mother was a courageous woman, though, and she put up a good front until the end. As she was being wheeled into surgery she talked about all the places she wanted to visit and all the things she wanted to take up: watercolors, French, the piano. But she must have known the truth. Her last words to me were, "Be a good doctor, son." She passed away on the operating table, never to see her first grandchild, who was born three months later.

There was only one other moment when I almost decided to chuck the whole thing. It was the afternoon I saw my first cadaver.

He was a forty-six-year-old white male, overweight, balding and unshaven. As we started to work on him his eyes popped open, and they seemed to be appealing to me for help. It wasn't that it made me feel faint or nauseated—I had been on too many hospital rounds as a boy—it was that the body looked exactly like my father the night he died. I had to leave.

When I told Karen what had happened, that I couldn't cut into someone that looked like my own father, she said, "Don't be silly." So I went back and opened that man's arms and legs and chest and abdomen, all the time hearing my father, who considered himself something of a comedian, whispering in my ear, "Ouch, that hurts." But I was more certain than ever that I didn't want to be an internist or surgeon. Instead, I followed the example set by my friend Bill Siegel, and went into psychiatry. Not only because it seemed less sanguinary, but also because it appeared to be a great challenge—so very little seemed to be known about the subject. Unfortunately, that sad state of affairs is as true today as it was nearly thirty years ago.

THE afternoon that prot stalked out of my examining room I got a call from a freelance reporter who was planning to do a story on mental illness for a national magazine. She wanted to know whether she might be able to "set up shop" at MPI for a few weeks to gather background material and "pick our brains," as she put it. That's a phrase I've never liked much, along with "eat your heart out" and "chew someone out"—I think of vultures. However, it was hardly a basis for rejecting her proposal, and I gave her tentative approval to do the article, hoping that the notoriety might get us some additional dollars. I transferred her call to Mrs. Trexler to arrange for an appointment at a time convenient for both of us. I laughed right into the phone when she said that "now" was convenient for her.

A new patient of Dr. Goldfarb's arrived over the weekend. I'll call him "Chuck" because, although that is not his name, that is what he wanted to be called. Chuck was a sixty-three-year-old New York City doorman—or doorperson, as Abby would have it—and a chronic cynic, hopeless pessimist, and classic curmudgeon. He was brought in because he was beginning to inform everyone who walked into his building that he or she "stunk." Everyone within fifty miles of him "stunk." Indeed, his first words, when he entered the hospital, were, "This place stinks." Bald as an eightball and somewhat cross-eyed, he might have made an almost comic figure had not his presence in Ward Two brought terror to the heart of Maria—he reminded her of her father.

Maria had been at MPI for three years and, in all that

time, Russell was the only male who could get near her. At first she had numerous Sunday visitors, as befit her large family, including cousins of all ages. But the visitations soon dwindled to her mother and the odd aunt or uncle every month or two for the simple reason that when they came to see Maria they often found someone else: Maria suffered from multiple personality disorder.

MPD begins to manifest itself in early childhood as an attempt to deal with a terrible physical or mental trauma from which there appears to be no escape. Maria wasn't beaten, Natalie was; Maria wasn't molested, it was Julia; Maria can't bear these attacks but Debra is strong. Many of the victims harbor scores of distinct personalities, depending on the number and severity of the abuses, but the average is about a dozen, each of whom is able to "take over" under certain circumstances. For reasons that are unclear, instances of a single alter ego are relatively rare.

Personality differences among the various alters are often astonishing. Some are much smarter than others, express widely discrepant talents, score uniquely on psychological tests, and even produce disparate EEG patterns! They might also visualize themselves as being very dissimilar in appearance, or even of a different sex, than that of the other identities. Whether these are true individuals is questionable, but, until integration occurs, many of the alters, including the "primary" personality, may be totally unaware of what the others are doing when in control of the body.

Maria was known to harbor more than a hundred separate and distinct personalities, most of whom rarely made an appearance. Otherwise her case is typical for this disorder. She had been raped innumerable times by her father, starting when she was barely three years old. Her devoutly religious mother, who cleaned a dozen large offices at night, never knew about these violations, and her older brothers had been threatened into silence until they were old enough to demand some of the "action" for themselves. Under such circumstances life can become quite unbearable and the desire for escape overwhelming.

A pretty girl with long black hair that shines like the stars, Maria came to us after she, as Carmen, had nearly scratched a boy's eyes out when he tried to make advances. Until that incident she was thought of as "quiet" and "distant." No one has touched her since, with the possible exception of Russell, who, of course, refers to her as "Mother."

But Maria herself is seldom in evidence. Most of the time one of the others is in charge, one of her "defenders" or "protectors." Sometimes, when one of her "persecutors" takes control, we see another facet of Maria, a darker side. One of these, who calls herself Carlotta, has tried to kill Maria, and therefore herself and all the others, on at least two occasions. It is this constant struggle for control among the various identities, often accompanied by anxiety, insomnia, and ceaseless headaches, that makes for the singular horror of the multiple personality sufferer.

Chuck thought *all* of Maria's alters stunk. Also Russell, Mrs. Archer, Ernie and Howie, and even harmless little Bess. The entire staff, including myself, stunk to high heaven. To his credit he admitted that he, himself, smelled worse than all the rest of us put together—"like a gutwagon," as he put it. The only person in the entire hospital who did not stink, in his opinion, was prot.

Session Seven

B E C A U S E of what had happened at the end of our previous encounter I asked Mr. Jensen and Mr. Kowalski to stand by during session seven. However, prot seemed in unusually good spirits as he chomped on a pineapple. "How was your meeting?" he said with his familiar grin.

It took me a moment to figure out what this meant, but I finally remembered the "important meeting" I had dismissed him with at the end of session six. I told him it had gone well. He seemed pleased to hear this. Or was it a smirk? In any case the clock was moving and I turned on the tape recorder. I also switched on my backup machine, this one to play back a Schubert song I had recorded earlier. When it was finished, I asked him to sing it back to me. He couldn't even hum the first phrase. Obviously music was not one of his talents. Nor was sculpture. I asked him to create a human head with a piece of clay—the result looked more like Mr.

Peanut. He couldn't even draw a house or a tree. It all came out looking like the work of a third-grader.

All of this, however, took up half our session. "Okay," I said, somewhat disappointedly, "last time we talked about medicine on K-PAX, or the lack of it. Tell me about your science in general."

"What would you like to know?"

"Who does it and how is it done? Are there, in fact, any scientists?"

"We are all scientists on K-PAX."

"I knew you were going to say that."

"Most human beings I've met have a rather negative opinion of science. They think it is dull and abstruse, possibly even dangerous. But everyone, even on EARTH, is a scientist, really, whether he realizes it or not. Anyone who has ever watched and wondered how a bird flies or a leaf unfurls, or concluded anything on the basis of his own observations, is a scientist. Science is a part of life."

"Well, are there any formal laboratories on K-PAX?"

"They are part of the libraries. Of course the whole UNIVERSE is a laboratory. Anyone can observe."

"What sorts of scientific observations do K-PAXians usually carry out?"

"Every species now living on our PLANET, or that ever lived there, or on several other PLANETS, is catalogued and thoroughly described. The same for the rocks. The same for the STARS and other ASTRONOMICAL OBJECTS. Every medicinal herb and what it can do is indexed. All this from millions and millions of years of observing and recording."

"And what goes on in the laboratories?"

"Oh, identifying the odd new compound that might turn up in a novel plant variant, for example."

"You mean its chemistry?"

"Yes."

"I assume your chemists can produce all these natural products synthetically. Why do you still get them from plants?"

"No one ever 'synthesizes' anything on K-PAX."

"Why not?"

"What's the point?"

"Well, you might find a useful new drug, for example. Or a better floor wax."

"We have a herbal preparation for every known disease. And we don't have floors to wax. Why should we make red grass or blue trees?"

"You're saying that everything is already known."

"Not everything. That's why I'm here."

"Aside from the occasional interstellar trip, though, it sounds pretty dull living on your planet."

He snapped back with: "Is it any duller than on EARTH? Whose inhabitants spend most of their lives trying to get laid, watching sitcoms on television, and grunting for money?"

I noted down this sudden outburst and remarked, casually: "I mean it seems pretty dull with nothing much left to discover."

"Gene, gene, gene." It sounded like a bell tolling. "No single *individual* knows very much. No matter how much one learns, there is always more to know."

"But *someone* already knows it."

"Have you ever listened to a mozart symphony?"

"Once or twice."

"Is it dull the second time, or the third, or the twentieth?"

"No, if anything . . ."

"Exactly."

"What about physics?"

"What about it?"

"Are all the laws of physics known?"

"Have you ever heard of heisenberg?"

"Yes, I've heard of him."

"He was wrong."

"With that in mind, what can you tell us about the fundamental laws of the universe? Light travel, for example."

His customary smile became even broader than usual. "Nothing."

"Nothing?"

"Nothing."

"Why not?"

"If I told you, you'd blow yourselves up. Or worse, someone else."

"Perhaps you could tell me one thing, at least. What do you use for power on K-PAX?"

"That I can tell you because you have it already, or soon will. We use type one and type two solar energies. Except for traveling, and certain other processes, when we use that of light. You'd be surprised how much energy there is in a beam of light."

"What are type one and type two solar energies?"

"Type one is the energy of the stars: nuclear fusion. The other is the type of radiation that warms your planet."

"Isn't there enough of the fusion type? Why do you need the other?"

"Spoken like a true homo sapiens."

"Meaning?"

"You humans just can't seem to learn from your mistakes. You finally discover that burning all that coal and oil and wood destroys your air and your climate. Then what do you do but go hell-bent after solar, wind, geothermal, and tidal energy without any thought whatsoever about the consequences. People!" He sighed and wagged his head.

"You haven't answered my question."

"Isn't it obvious? The use of one produces heat; the other consumes it. The net effect is that we neither warm nor cool our PLANET. And there is no waste or pollution."

"Have you always been able to tap these energy sources?"

"Of course not. Only for the last few billion years."

"What about before that?"

"Well, we fooled around with magnetic fields for a while, and bacterial decay and the like. But we soon realized that no matter what we tried, there was some effect or other on our air, or our temperature, or our climate. Gravitation energy is even worse. So we made do with our muscles until someone figured out how to fuse atoms safely."

"Who figured that out?"

"You mean his name?"

"Yes."

"I have no idea. We don't worship heroes on K-PAX."

"What about nuclear fission?"

"Impossible. Our beings rejected it immediately."

"Why? Because of the danger of an accident?"

"That is a small matter compared to the waste that's produced."

"You never found anything to contain it?"

"Where would we find something that lasts forever?"

"Let's turn to astronomy. Or better yet, cosmology."

"One of my favorite subjects."

"Tell me: What is the fate of the universe?"

"Fate?"

"Is it going to collapse back on itself, or will it go on expanding forever?"

"You'll love this: both."

"Both?"

"It will collapse, then expand again, then repeat and repeat and repeat."

"I don't know whether to take any comfort in that or not."

"Before you decide—there's more."

"More?"

He guffawed, the first time I had ever heard him laugh. "When the UNIVERSE expands again, everything will be as it was before!"

"You mean—"

"Exactly. Whatever mistakes you made this time around you will live through again on the next pass, over and over and over, forever and ever, amen!" His demeanor had suddenly changed. For a second I thought he was going to break into tears. But he quickly became himself again, smiling and confident.

"How do you know that? It's not possible to know that, is it?"

"It's not possible to test that hypothesis, no."

"Then how can you be sure your hypothesis is right? Or any of your other theories?"

"I'm here, ain't I?"

Something suddenly occurred to me. "I'm glad you brought that up. There's one thing you could do for me that would erase any doubts I might have about your story. Do you know what I'm suggesting?"

"I was wondering when that would occur to you." He scribbled something in his notebook.

"When could you give me a little demonstration?"

"How about right now?"

"That would be quite acceptable."

"Shalom," he said. "Aloha." But of course he just sat there grinning at me like a Cheshire cat.

"Well?"

"Well what?"

"When are you going?"

"I'm already back."

I'd been taken in by the old "fastest gun in the West" routine. "I was hoping you would stay away long enough that I might notice your absence."

"You will next week when I leave for canada, iceland, and greenland."

"Next week? I see. And how long will you be gone?"

"A few days." While I was jotting down the suggestion that we increase the surveillance on him, he exclaimed: "Well, I see our time is up, and gunnar and roman are waiting!"

I was still writing, but I vaguely recalled that the clock was positioned in such a way that prot couldn't possibly have seen it. And who told him that Jensen and Kowalski were standing by? I mumbled, "Shouldn't I decide that?" But when I looked up he was already gone.

I rewound the last part of the tape and switched it on. His assertion, in a thick, choked voice, that he was going to have to repeat his mistakes over and over for all time suddenly seemed very moving, and I wondered again: What in God's name had he done? Unless I could find some way to break through his amnesia armor it was going to be very difficult to find out. In the absence of some clue to his background I was literally working in the dark. Given enough time I might have been able to come up with such a lead, and I dearly wished I could increase the number of sessions to twice a week or even more, but I simply had no extra time. There just wasn't enough time.

A couple of days later, after returning from my Friday morning radio talk show where I answer general questions about mental health called in by the listening audience, I discovered that prot had assigned a second task to Howie. The assignment: to cure Ernie of his fear of death.

I could see what he was getting at with his "program" for Howie and perhaps I, as his staff doctor, should have thought of it myself: By encouraging him to focus on a single project, his attention was drawn away from the awesome multiplicity of life's possibilities. I still had mixed feelings about prot's assigning "tasks" to his fellow patients, but as long as no harm came from these endeavors, I continued to allow it.

Howie approached the problem in a typically methodical manner. After scrutinizing his roommate for hours on end, to the point that Ernie finally ran screaming from the room, he asked me for texts on human anatomy and physiology, specifically on the subject of respiration. I assumed he was going to try to prove to him how unusual it is for someone to choke to death, or perhaps construct some sort of breathing apparatus for Ernie's use in case the worst happened. I could see no reason to refuse him on this and I allowed him access to the fourth-floor library. In retrospect I should have realized that these solutions would have been too simplistic for someone as brilliant as Howie. Perhaps my judgment was clouded by the unconscious hope that he might somehow succeed where I had failed, and that both might find a little peace at long last.

Ernie, in the meantime, was doing much the same thing

for some of the other patients; that is, he was beginning to take an interest in their problems as well as his own. For example, he was reading poetry to blind old Mrs. Weathers, who cocked her snowy head with every word like a rapt chicken. He had always spent quite a bit of time with Russell, seeking solace primarily, but now he was chatting with the latter about a variety of secular matters—suggesting he get some exercise, for example.

He was spending a lot of time with prot also, as were most of his fellow patients, asking him about K-PAX and other supposedly inhabited regions of the galaxy. These talks seemed to raise their spirits enormously, or so I was informed by several of the nurses. I finally asked Ernie point-blank what it was about his discussions with prot that seemed to cheer him up so dramatically. His eyebrows lifted a mile high behind his surgical mask and he told me exactly what Whacky had said earlier, "I'm hoping he'll take me with him when he goes back!" I realized then what was drawing the others to our "alien" visitor: the promise of salvation. Not just in the hereafter, but in *this* life, and in the relatively near future. I made a note to talk to prot about this as soon as possible. It was one thing to make a sick person feel better. It was quite another to prop him up temporarily with false hopes, as he himself had asserted. But for the next few days I was unable to ask him anything. He had disappeared!

A search of the building and grounds was initiated immediately upon learning that prot had not shown up for lunch on Sunday, but no trace of him was found. No one had seen him leave the hospital, and none of the security tapes showed him passing through any locked doors or gates.

His room provided no clue as to where he might have gone. As always the bed was made and his desk and dresser were uncluttered. There wasn't even a scrap of paper in his wastebasket.

None of the patients would admit to having any knowledge of prot's whereabouts, yet none was particularly surprised that he was gone. When I asked Chuck about it he replied, "Don't worry—he'll be back."

"How do you know that?"

"Because he took his dark glasses with him."

"What has that got to do with it?"

"When he returns to K-PAX he won't need them."

Some days later a maintenance worker reported that some of the items in the storage tunnel had been shifted around. Whether prot had been hiding there, however, was never determined.

F O R his first twenty-seven years Russell never saw another human being except for his mother and father. His schooling consisted exclusively of Bible reading, four hours every morning and evening. There was no radio, and no one ever came up the long driveway because of the mud and the Doberman pinschers. In the afternoons he was expected to work in the garden or help with the chores. This isolated existence continued until a determined census worker, who also bred Dobermans, stumbled upon him accidentally while his father was at the hardware store and his mother in the back yard hanging out the wash. After he chased the astonished woman down the driveway shouting, "Mary Magdelene, I forgive you!" she reported the matter to the authorities.

Psychotherapy was completely ineffective in Russell's case, and Metrazole shock therapy barely less so. Nevertheless, he was returned to his parents. The young delusional soon escaped from the farm, however, only to be arrested as a "public nuisance." After that he was in and out of jails and

95

hospitals for several years until he was finally brought to MPI, where he has remained to this day.

Neither Howie, who is Jewish, nor Mrs. Archer ("I'm Episcopalian," she would sniff) have ever had much use for Russell. But with his retinue shrinking rapidly—only Maria and a few of her alters seemed to be paying any attention to him—he began to preach the gospel to Howie and to the Duchess, who had begun to emerge from her room on occasion to speak with prot.

Howie simply ignored him, but it was different for Mrs. Archer. It would be a bad joke to state that he was driving her crazy, but that was the net effect. Conversing with Russell requires a certain amount of forbearance under the best of circumstances. He tends to preach right into your face, releasing prodigious amounts of spittle with almost every word. And when she was able to escape his fervent hectoring she found herself being assaulted by Chuck's observations, expressed in no uncertain terms, that she stank.

Mrs Archer, who used nearly a pint of expensive perfumes weekly, was both mortified and irate. "I most certainly do not stink!" she screeched, impatiently lighting a cigarette.

"Those goddamn things reek," Chuck would badger.

She was finally reduced to tears. "Please," she implored, when I happened by. "Let him come back."

"He wouldn't take a stinker like you with him. He's going to take me!" Chuck proclaimed.

But Russell warned, "For there shall arise false Christs, and false prophets, and they shall show great signs and wonders; insomuch that, if it were possible, they shall deceive the very elect!"

"You stink too!" Chuck reminded him.

★ ★ ★

DURING a quick lunch in the doctors' dining room Dr. Goldfarb told me more about Chuck. He had been a middle-level government employee at one time, she said, but blew the whistle on the waste and corruption in his division at the Pentagon. For his efforts he was fired and, for all practical purposes, blackballed, both from government and corporate employment. That alone might be cause enough for disillusionment, but the straw that broke his back was his wife's divorcing him after thirty-five years of marriage. "I couldn't have been happier," he muttered to Dr. Goldfarb. "I had to kiss that malodorous maw every day. P.U.! Stinkeroonie!" But the truth was that he loved his wife passionately and it was more than he could bear. Indeed, he had tried to commit suicide shortly after she left him by blowing his brains out with a shotgun. It must seem incredible to the reader to learn that he missed, but the fact is that many attempted suicides end in "failure" for the simple reason that they are actually desperate attempts to draw attention to the sufferer's terrible, and often silent, unhappiness. Most victims don't actually want to die; they want to communicate.

Of course, not all those who feel rootless or valueless resort to this futile measure. A manic-depressive once assured me that he would never try to kill himself. I asked him how he could be so sure. "Because," he told me, "I still haven't read *Moby Dick*."

As good a reason for living as any, I suppose, and perhaps it explains why so few people have ever finished that book.

IN the midst of all the furor surrounding prot's disappearance, the reporter who had called me the previous week arrived, half an hour early, for her appointment. She was older than she appeared, thirty-three, she said, though she looked more like sixteen. She wore faded jeans, an old checked shirt, and running shoes with no socks. My first impression was that freelance writing must be a poorly paid profession, but I eventually came to realize that she dressed this way for effect—to induce people to feel at ease. To that end she also wore little makeup, and only a hint of perfume that somehow brought to mind our summer place in the Adirondacks. "Pine woods," I would have called it. She was short, about five-two, and her teeth were tiny, like a little girl's. Disarmingly, she curled up into the chair I offered. She asked me to call her Giselle.

She came from a little town in northern Ohio. After graduating with a degree in journalism from the local college she came directly to New York, where she got a job on the now-defunct *Weekly Gazette*. She stayed there nearly eight years before writing an article on drugs and AIDS in Harlem, which won her the Cassady prize. I asked her about the dangers she must have faced researching that story. A friend had accompanied her, she explained, an ex-football player whom everyone in the area knew. "He was huge," she added with a coy smile.

She later quit the *Gazette* to research and write pieces on a variety of subjects—abortion, oil spills, and homelessness—for various periodicals, including several major newspapers and national magazines. She had also written scripts for a number of TV documentaries. She had gotten the idea to do something on mental illness after trying to find background material on Alzheimer's disease and failing to find a good generalized account of the subject "in layperson's language." Her credentials were certainly impressive, and I gave her the go-ahead to "cruise the corridors," as she put it, provided that she was accompanied by a staff member at all times, and that she enter the psychopathic ward for no more than three one-hour visits and only in the presence of a security officer. She cheerfully agreed to abide by these conditions. Nevertheless I asked Betty to keep an eye on her.

Session Eight

I was in a very bad mood when Wednesday afternoon came around, having spent the entire morning waiting to testify in a preliminary hearing, only to have the case resolved out of court. I was glad it was settled, but annoyed that half a day had been wasted, and I had missed lunch as well. Underlying all this, of course, was my concern about prot's well-being.

But he returned exactly in time for our next session. Still wearing his blue corduroys, he sauntered in as if nothing had happened. I shouted at him: "Where the hell have you been?"

"Newfoundland. Labrador. Greenland. Iceland."

"How did you get out of the hospital?"

"I just left."

"Without anyone seeing you?"

"That's right."

"How did you do that?"

"I told you—"

"With mirrors. Yes, I know." I also knew there was no sense in arguing the matter, and the tape at this point in the session is silent except for the distinct sound of my fingers tapping the arm of my chair. I finally said, "Next time tell me when you're going to leave."

"I did," he replied.

"And another thing: I don't think you should be telling the other patients you're going to take them back with you."

"I never said that to any of the patients."

"You didn't?"

"No. In fact I told them I can only take one person back with me."

"I don't think you should be making promises you can't keep."

"I have promised nothing." He bit into a huge strawberry from a bowlful brought in from her garden in Hoboken by Mrs. Trexler.

I was famished. My mouth was watering. This time I joined him. Chewing hungrily, we glared at each other for several minutes like prizefighters sizing up an opponent. "Tell me," I said. "If you can leave here any time you want, why do you stay?"

He swallowed a mouthful of berries, took a deep breath. "Well, it's as good a place as any to write my report, you feed me every day, and the fruit is wonderful. Besides," he added impishly, "I like you."

"Well enough to stay put for a while?"

"Until august seventeenth."

"Good. Now let's get started, shall we?"

"Certainly."

"All right. Can you draw a star map showing the night sky from anywhere in the galaxy? From Sirius, say?"

"No."

101

"Why not?"

"I have never been there."

"But you can do so for all the places you've been?"

"Naturally."

"Will you do a few of those for me before the next session?"

"No problem."

"Good. Now—where have you really been the past few days?"

"I told you: newfoundland, labrador—"

"Uh huh. And how are you feeling after your long journey?"

"Very well, thank you. And how have you been, narr?"

"Narr?"

"Gene, on K-PAX, is narr." It rhymed with "hair."

"I see. Is that from the French, meaning 'to confess'?"

"No, it is from the pax-o, meaning 'one who doubts.' "

"Oh. And what would 'prot' be in English—one who is cocksure?"

"Nope. 'Prot' is derived from an ancient K-PAXian word for 'sojourner.' Believe it or not by ripley."

"If I asked you to translate something from English to pax-o for me, something like *Hamlet,* for example, could you do it?"

"Of course. When would you like to have it?"

"Whenever you can get to it."

"Next week okay?"

"Fine. Now then. We've talked quite a bit about the sciences on K-PAX. Tell me about the arts on your planet."

"You mean painting and music? Stuff like that?"

"Painting, music, sculpture, dance, literature . . ."

The usual smile broke out, and the fingers came together. "It is similar in some ways to the arts on EARTH. But remember that we have had several billion years longer to develop them than you have. Our music is not based on anything as primitive as notes, nor any of our arts on subjective vision."

"Not based on notes? How else—"

"It is continuous."

"Can you give me an example?" With that he tore a sheet of paper from his little notebook and began to draw something on it.

While he did so I asked him why, with all his talents and capabilities, he needed to keep a written record of his observations. "Isn't it obvious?" he replied. "What if something happens to me before I get back to K-PAX?" He then showed me the following:

"This is one of my favorites. I learned it as a boy." As I tried to make sense out of the score, or whatever it was, he added, "You can see why I'm rather partial to your john cage."

"Can you hum a few bars of this thing?"

"You know I can't sing. Besides, it doesn't break down into 'tunes.' "

"May I keep this?"

"Consider it a souvenir of my visit."

"Thank you. Now. You said that your arts are not based on 'subjective vision.' What does that mean?"

"It means we don't have what you call 'fiction.' "

"Why not?"

"What is the point?"

"Well, through fiction, one often gains an understanding of truth."

"Why beat around the bush? Why not go right for the truth in the first place?"

"Truth means different things to different people."

"Truth is truth. What you are talking about is make-believe. Dream worlds. Tell me"—he bent over the notebook—"why do human beings have the peculiar impression that a belief is the same as the truth?"

"Because sometimes the truth hurts. Sometimes we need to believe in a better truth."

"What better truth can there be than truth?"

"There may be more than one kind of truth."

Prot continued to scribble in his notebook. "There is only one truth. Truth is absolute. You can't escape it, no matter how far you run." He said this rather wistfully, it seemed to me.

"There's another factor, too," I countered. "Our beliefs are based on incomplete and conflicting experiences. We need help to sort things out. Maybe you can help us."

He looked up in surprise. "How?"

"Tell me more about your life on K-PAX."

"What else would you like to know?"

"Tell me about your friends and acquaintances there."

"All K-PAXians are my friends. Except there is no word for 'friend' in pax-o. Or 'enemy.' "

"Tell me about some of them. Whoever comes to mind."

"Well, there is brot, and mano, and swon, and fled, and—"

"Who is brot?"

"He lives in the woods RILLward of reldo. Mano is—"

"Reldo?"

"A village near the purple mountains."

"And brot lives there?"

"In the woods."

"Why?"

"Because orfs usually live in the woods."

"What's an orf?"

"Orfs are something between our species and trods. Trods are much like your chimpanzees, only bigger."

"You mean orfs are subhuman?"

"Another of your famous contradictions in terms. But if you mean is he a forebear, the answer is yes. You see, we did not destroy our immediate progenitors as you did on EARTH."

"And you consider the orfs to be your friends?"

"Of course."

"What do you call your own species, by the way?"

"Dremers."

"And how many progenitors are there between trods and dremers?"

"Seven."

"And they are all still in existence on K-PAX?"

"*Mais oui!*"

"What are they like?"

"They are beautiful."

"Do you have to take care of them in some way?"

"Only clean up after them, sometimes. Otherwise they take care of themselves, as all beings do."

"Do they speak? Can you understand them?"

"Certainly. All beings 'speak.' You just have to know their language."

"Okay. Go on."

"Mano is quiet. She spends most of her time studying our insects. Swon is soft and green. Fled is—"

"Green?"

"Of course. Swon is an em. Something like your tree frogs, only they are as big as dogs."

"You call frogs by name?"

"How else would you refer to them?"

"Are you telling me you have names for all the frogs on K-PAX?"

"Of course not. Only the ones I know."

"You know a lot of lower animals?"

"They are not 'lower.' Just different."

"How do these species compare with those we have on Earth?"

"You have more variety, but, on the other hand, we have no carnivores. And," he beamed, "no flies, no mosquitoes, no cockroaches."

"Sounds too good to be true."

"Oh, it's true all right, believe me."

"Let's get back to the people."

"There are no 'people' on K-PAX."

"I meant the beings of your own species. The—uh—dremers."

"As you wish."

"Tell me more about your friend mano."

"I told you: She is fascinated by the behavior of the homs."

"Tell me more about her."

"She has soft brown hair and a smooth forehead and she likes to make things."

"Do you get along well with her?"

"Of course."

"Better than with other K-PAXians?"

"I get along well with everyone."

"Aren't there a few of your fellow dremers that you get along with—that you like—better than others?"

"I like all of them."

"Name a few."

That was a mistake. He named thirty-odd K-PAXians before I could stop him with: "Do you get along well with your father?"

"Really, gene, you've got to do something about that memory of yours. I can give you some tips if—"

"How about your mother?"

"Of course."

"Would you say you love her?"

"Love implies hate."

"You didn't answer my question."

"Love . . . like . . . it's all a matter of semantics."

"All right. Let me turn that around. Is there anyone you *don't* like? Is there anyone you actually *dis*like?"

"Everyone on K-PAX is just like me! Why would I hate anyone? Should I hate myself?"

"On Earth there are those who do hate themselves. Those who haven't lived up to their own standards or expectations. Those who have failed to achieve their goals. Those who have made disastrous mistakes. Those who have caused harm to someone and regretted it later on. . . ."

"I told you before—no one on K-PAX would cause harm to anyone else!"

"Not even unintentionally?"

"No!"

"Never?"

Yelling: "Are you deaf?"

"No. I hear you quite clearly. Please calm down. I'm sorry if I upset you." He nodded brusquely.

I knew I was onto something here, but I wasn't certain as to the best way to proceed. While he was composing himself we talked about some of the patients, including Maria and her protective alter egos—he seemed quite interested in her condition. Who knows where inspiration comes from? Or is it merely a momentary clearing in the fog of stupidity? In any case I realized at that moment that I had been focusing, perhaps for reasons of self-interest, on his delusion. What I should have been attacking was the hysterical amnesia! "Prot?"

His fists slowly unclenched. "What?"

"Something has occurred to me."

"Bully for you, doctor brewer."

"I was wondering whether you'd be willing to undergo hypnosis at our next session?"

"What for?"

"Let's call it an experiment. Sometimes hypnosis can call up recollections and feelings that are too painful to recall otherwise."

"I remember everything I have ever done. There is no need."

"Will you do it as a personal favor to me?" He eyed me suspiciously. "Why do you hesitate—are you afraid to be hypnotized?"

It was a cheap trick, but it worked. "Of course not!"

"Next Wednesday all right?"

"Next wednesday is the fourth of july. Do you work on your american holidays?"

"God, is it July already? All right. We'll test your susceptibility to the procedure next Tuesday, and begin the week after that. Does that suit you?"

Suddenly calm: "Perfectly, my dear sir."

"You're not planning on leaving again, are you?"

108

"I'll say it one more time: not until 3:31 A.M. on the seventeenth of august."

And he returned to Ward Two, where he was welcomed back like the prodigal son.

THE next morning Giselle was waiting at my office door when I arrived at the hospital. She was wearing the same outfit as before, or perhaps one of its clones. She was all tiny-tooth smiles. "Why didn't you tell me about prot?" she demanded.

I had stayed up until two o'clock to finish some editorial work, had come in early to prepare a speech for a Rotary Club luncheon, and was still distraught over prot's temporary disappearance. My office clock began to chime, further jangling my nerves and telling me what I didn't want to know. "What about him?" I snapped.

"I decided to make him the focus of the piece. With your permission, of course."

I dropped my bulging briefcase onto my desk. "Why prot?"

She literally fell into the brown leather chair and curled into the already familiar ball. I wondered whether this was premeditated or whether she was unaware of the charming effect it had on middle-aged men, especially those suffering from Brown's syndrome. I began to understand why she was such a successful reporter. "Because he fascinates me," she said.

"Did you know that he is my patient?"

"Betty told me. That's why I'm here. To see if you would let me look at his records." Her eyelids were fluttering like the wings of some exotic butterfly.

I busied myself with transferring the contents of my case to some logical place on the already overcrowded desk. "Prot is a special patient," I told her. "He requires very delicate treatment."

"I'll be careful. I wouldn't do anything that would jeopardize my own story. Or divulge any confidences," she added in a playful whisper. Then: "I know you're planning to write a book about him."

"Who told you that?" I practically shouted.

"Why, he—prot—told me."

"*Prot?* Who told *him?*"

"I don't know. But I want to assure you that my piece won't affect your book in any way. If anything, it should drum up some business for it. And I'll show it to you before I submit it for publication—how's that?" I stared at her for a moment, trying to think of some way out of this unwanted complication. She must have sensed my doubt. "I'll tell you what," she said. "If I can identify him for you, I get my story. Fair enough?" She had me and she knew it. "Plus any expenses I might incur," she added immediately.

O V E R the weekend I reviewed the transcripts of all eight sessions with prot. Everything pointed to at least one violent episode in his past that precipitated his hysterical "escape" from the real world, which he deeply hated, to a nonexistent, idyllic place where there are no human interactions to cause all the problems, large and small, that the rest of us have to live with every day. Nor the joys that make it all worth-while . . .

I decided to ask prot to spend the Fourth of July at my home in order to see if a more or less normal family environment would bring anything out of him I hadn't seen before. I had done this with a few other patients, sometimes with beneficial results. My wife was in favor of the idea, even though I mentioned to her that prot may have been involved in some sort of violent affair, and there was a possibility that—

"Don't be silly," she interrupted. "Bring him along."

How these things happen I haven't a clue, but by Monday morning everyone in Wards One and Two knew that prot was coming to the house for a barbecue. Almost every patient I ran into that day, including three of Maria's alters, who kept fastening buttons unfastened by other personalities, and vice versa, complained, good-naturedly, "You never invited *me* to your house, Dr. Brewer!" To every one of them I said, "You get well and get out of here, and I'll do exactly that." To which most of them replied, "I won't be here, Dr. Brewer. Prot is taking me with him!"

All but Russell, who had no intention of going to K-PAX: His place was on Earth. Indeed, with everyone in Wards One and Two enjoying a picnic on the hospital lawn, except for Bess, who stayed inside out of an imaginary rainstorm, Russ spent all of the Fourth in the catatonic ward, preaching the gospels. Unfortunately, none of those pathetic creatures jumped up and followed him out.

That same Monday morning Giselle was waiting for me again in her usual outfit, same piney bouquet. I asked her as politely as possible to please call Mrs. Trexler for an appointment whenever she wanted to see me. I started to tell her that I had patients to see, a lot of administrative work, papers to referee, letters to dictate and so on, but I had barely begun when she said, "I think I know how to track down your guy."

I said, "Come in."

Her idea was this: She wanted to have a linguist she knew listen to one of the interview tapes. This was one of those people who can pinpoint the area of the country where one was born and/or grew up, sometimes with uncanny accuracy. It is not based on dialect so much as phrasing—

whether you say "water fountain" or "bubbler," for example. It was a good suggestion, but impossible, of course, owing to patient/client privilege. She was ready for this. "Then can I tape a conversation with him myself?" I saw no compelling reason she should not, and told her I would ask Betty to arrange a time convenient for her and prot. "Never mind." She grinned slyly. "I've already done it." And she literally skipped away like a schoolgirl to get in touch with her expert. Her piney aura, however, stayed with me for the rest of the day.

Session Nine

I т was a beautiful Fourth of July: partly cloudy skies (I wonder why it's always in the plural—how many "skies" are there?), not too hot or humid, the air redolent of charcoal grills and freshly cut grass.

A holiday seems to generate a feeling of timelessness, bringing, as it does, blended memories of all those that came before. Even my father took the Fourth off and we always spent the day around the brick barbecue pit and the evening at the river watching the fireworks. I still live in my father's house, the one I grew up in, but we don't have to go anywhere now; we can see the nearby country club display right from our screened-in terrace. Even so, when the first Roman candle lights up the sky I invariably smell the river and the gunpowder and my father's Independence Day cigar.

I love that house. It's a big white frame with a patio as well as the second-story terrace, and the backyard is loaded with oaks and maples. The roots are deep. Right next door is the house my wife grew up in, and my old basketball coach still lives on the other side. I wondered, as I gathered up the sticks and leaves lying around the yard, whether any of my own children would be living here after we've gone, picking up loose twigs on the Fourth of July, thinking of me as I thought of my father. And I wondered whether similar thoughts might not have been buzzing around Shasta Daisy's head as she sniffed around her predecessor's little wooden marker barely visible in the back corner behind the grill—Daisy the Dog: 1967–1982.

By 2:00 the coals were heating up and the rest of my family began to arrive. First came Abby with Steve and the two boys, then Jennifer, who had brought her roommate, a dental student, from Palo Alto. Not a man, as we had thought, but a tall African-American woman wearing copper earrings the size of salad plates that hung down to and rested on her bare shoulders. And I do mean tall.

As soon as I saw Steve I told him about the variance between Charlie Flynn's description of the figure-eight orbit of K-PAX around its twin suns, and prot's version, which, if I understood it correctly, was more of a retrograde pattern, like that of a pendulum. Later I showed him the calendar and the second star chart prot had concocted—the one describing the sky as seen from K-PAX looking away from Earth. Steve shook his head in disbelief and drawled that Professor Flynn had just left for a vacation in Canada, but said he would mention all this to him when he got back. I asked him whether he knew of any physicists or astronomers who had disappeared in the last five years, particularly on August 17, 1985. To his knowledge there had been no such disappearances, though he joked that there were a few colleagues who he wished might quietly do so.

Freddy arrived from Atlanta, still wearing his airline uniform, alone as usual. Now everyone was here for the first time since Christmas. Chip, however, had better things to do and soon went off somewhere with his friends.

Just after that Betty showed up with her husband, an English professor at NYU, who happens to have a black belt in aikido. They had brought prot and one of our trainees, whom I had invited primarily because he had been an outstanding amateur wrestler and he, too, would be helpful in case prot showed any indication of turbulence. Shasta Daisy, extra nervous when so many people are present, barked at everyone who arrived from the safety of the underside of the back porch, her usual refuge.

Prot came bearing gifts: three more star maps representing the heavens as seen from various places he had "visited," as well as a copy of *Hamlet,* translated into pax-o. He hadn't been out of the car for five seconds, however, before an extraordinary thing happened. Shasta suddenly ran at him from the porch. I yelled, afraid she was going to attack him. But she stopped short, wagged her tail from ear to ear as only a Dalmatian can, and flattened herself against his leg. Prot, for his part, was down on the ground immediately, rolling and feigning with the dog, barking, even, and then they were up running all over the yard, my grandsons chasing along behind, Shakespeare and the charts blowing in the wind. Fortunately, we managed to recover all but the last page of the play.

After a while prot sat down on the grass and Shasta lay down beside him, bathing herself, utterly calm and content. Later, she played with Rain and Star for the very first time. Not once did she retreat to the porch the rest of that afternoon and evening, not even when the nearby country club celebration started off with a tremendous bang. She became a different dog that Fourth of July.

As, so to speak, did we all.

That night, after the fireworks were over and our guests had gone, Fred came into the family room downstairs, where I was shooting some pool and listening to *The Flying Dutchman* on our old hi-fi set.

For years I'd had the feeling that Fred wanted to tell me something. There had been times during pauses in conversations when I was sure he was trying to get something off his chest but couldn't quite bring himself to do it. I never tried to push him, figuring that when he was ready he would tell me or his mother what was bothering him.

That's not entirely true. I didn't press him because I was afraid he was going to tell us he was gay. It is something a father doesn't ordinarily want to hear—most fathers are heterosexual—and I'm sure his mother, who will not be satisfied with less than eight grandchildren, felt the same way.

Apparently motivated by a conversation with prot, Fred decided to come out with it. But it wasn't to tell me about his sexual orientation. The thing he had tried to bring up all those years, and couldn't, was his deep-seated fear of flying!

I have known dentists who quake at the sight of a drill and surgeons who are terrified to go under the knife. Sometimes that's why people get into those fields—it's a form of whistling in the dark. But I had never encountered an airline pilot who was afraid to fly. I asked him why on earth he had decided on that profession, and he told me this: I had mentioned at dinner years before that phobias could be treated by a gradual acclimation to the conditions that triggered them, and had given some examples, such as fear of snakes, of closets, and, yes, of flying. I had taken him with me to a conference near Disneyland when he was a boy, having no idea he was apprehensive about the flight. That was why he went to the airport the day after he graduated from high school and began to take flying lessons—to work out the problem on his own. It didn't help, but he continued the training until he had soloed and flown cross-country and passed his flight test. Even after all that he was still afraid to fly. So he figured the only thing to do was to enroll in an aeronautical school and become a professional pilot. He obtained his commercial license, became an instructor, hauled canceled checks all over the Eastern seaboard, usually in the middle of the night and often in bad weather, and after a couple of years of that he was as horrified as ever at the prospect of leaving terra firma. Then he got his air transport "ticket," as he called it, and went to work for United Airlines. Now, five years later, after a brief conversation with prot, he had finally come to me for help.

We were a long time down in the family room, playing Ping-Pong and throwing darts and shooting pool as we talked. Nine years a pilot and he still had nightmares about plunging to Earth from awesome heights, taking forever to fall through empty space, falling and falling and never reaching the ground.

I have had many patients, over a quarter century of practice, who were afraid of flying. For that matter, it is quite common among the general population, and for a very simple reason: Our ancestors were tree dwellers. As such, a fear of falling was of considerable evolutionary value—those who did not fall survived to reproduce. Most people are able to overcome this fear, at least functionally. On the other hand there are some who never go anywhere they can't get to by car or train or bus, no matter how inconvenient.

I explained all this to Fred and suggested that he very likely fell into the latter category.

He wanted to know what he should do.

I suggested he try some other line of work.

"That's exactly what prot said!" he cried, and for the first time in two decades, he hugged me. "But he thought I should talk to you about it first." I had never seen him so happy.

My sigh of relief turned out to be premature. Right after Freddy had gone, Jennifer came in, pink from a shower. She grabbed his cue stick, took a shot, missed. We talked a while about medical school, shooting all the while, until I noticed that she hadn't pocketed a single ball, which was unusual for her.

I said, "Is there something you wanted to talk to me about?"

"Yes, Daddy, there is." I knew it was something I didn't want to hear. She hadn't called me "Daddy" in years. And she had also been talking to prot.

But it sometimes takes Jenny a while to get to the point. "I saw you hugging Freddy," she said. "That was nice. I never saw you do that before."

"I wanted to lots of times."

"Why didn't you?"

"I don't know."

"Abby thinks you weren't much interested in our problems. She figured it was because you listened to other people's troubles all day long and didn't want to hear any more at home."

"I know. She told me tonight before she left. But it's not true. I care about all of you. I just didn't want you to think I was trying to interfere with your lives."

"Why not? Every other parent I know does."

"It's a long story."

She missed another easy shot. "Try me."

"Well, it's because of my father, mostly. Your grandfather."

"What did he do to you?"

"He wanted me to become a doctor."

"What's wrong with that?"

"I didn't want to be a doctor."

"Dad, how could he have made you go to med school? He died when you were eleven or twelve, didn't he?" Her voice cracked charmingly on "eleven" and "twelve."

"Yes, but he planted the seed and it kept growing. I couldn't seem to stop it. I felt guilty. I guess I wanted to finish the rest of his life for him. And I did it for my mother—your grandmother—too."

"I don't think you can live someone else's life for them, Dad. But if it's any consolation, I think you're a very good doctor."

"Thank you." I missed my next shot. "By the way, you didn't go to medical school because of me, did you?"

"Partly. But not because you wanted me to. If anything, I thought you didn't. You never took me to see your office or the rest of the hospital. Maybe that's why I became interested—it seemed so mysterious."

"I just didn't want to do to you what my father did to me. If I haven't told you before, I'm very happy you decided to become a doctor."

"Thank you, Dad." She studied the table for a long minute, then missed the next ball entirely, sinking the cue ball instead. "What else would you have done? If you hadn't gone into medicine, I mean?"

"I always wanted to be an opera singer."

At that she smiled the warm smile she inherited from her mother—the one that says: "How sweet."

That annoyed me a trifle. "What's the matter?" I said. "Don't you think I could have been a singer?"

"I think anyone should be anything he or she wants to

be," she replied, not smiling anymore. "That's what I wanted to talk to you about." With that she missed the twelveball by a mile.

"Shoot," I said.

"It's your turn."

"I mean, what's the problem?"

She threw herself into my arms and sobbed, "Oh, Daddy, I'm a lesbian!"

That was about midnight. I remember because Chip came in right afterward. He was acting strangely, too, and I braced myself for another revelation. Chip, however, had not talked to prot.

Even my grandsons behaved differently after that momentous Fourth of July. They stopped fighting and throwing things and began to bathe and to comb their hair without arguing about it—an almost miraculous change.

But back to the cookout. Prot wouldn't eat any of the chicken, but he consumed a huge Waldorf salad and a couple of gallons of various fruit juices, shouting something about "going for the gusto." He seemed quite relaxed, and played Frisbee and badminton with Rain and Star and Shasta all afternoon.

Then something happened. When Karen turned on the sprinkler so that the kids could cool off, prot, who appeared to be enjoying himself, suddenly became extremely agitated. He didn't turn violent, thank God, just stared for a moment in utter horror as Jennifer and the two boys splashed into and out of the spray. Suddenly he started screaming and running around the yard. I was thinking, "What the hell have I done?" when he stopped, dropped to his knees, and buried his face in his hands. Shasta was by his side in a second. Betty's husband and our trainee looked at me for instructions, but the only one I had was, "Turn off the goddamn sprinkler!"

I approached him cautiously, but before I could put a hand on his shoulder he raised his head, became as cheerful as ever, and started to frolic with Shasta again.

There were no further incidents that afternoon.

Karen and I had a lot to talk about that night and it was nearly dawn when we finally got to sleep. She wanted to know what Freddy would do after he left the airline, and she cried a little about Jenny—not because of her choice, but because she knew it was going to be difficult for her. Her last words before drifting off, however, were: "I hate opera."

GISELLE was waiting for me the next morning, jumping up and down, nearly beside herself. "He's from the Northwest!" she exclaimed. "Probably western Montana, northern Idaho, or eastern Washington!"

"That what your man said?"

"She's not a man, but that's what she said!"

"Wouldn't the police know if someone, especially a scientist, had disappeared from that part of the country five years ago?"

"They should. I know someone down at the Sixth Precinct. Want me to check for you?"

For the first time in several days I had to laugh. It appeared she knew someone in any line of work one could name. I threw up my arms. "Sure, why not, go ahead." She was out the door like a shot.

That same morning, Betty, wearing an enormous pair of copper earrings in another desperate attempt to get pregnant, I presumed, brought in a stray kitten. She had found it in the subway station, and I assumed she was going to take it home with her that evening. But instead she suggested that we let the patients take care of it.

The presence of small animals in nursing and retirement

homes has proven to be of great benefit to the residents, providing badly needed affection and companionship and generally bolstering their spirits to such a degree that life spans are actually increased significantly. The same may be true for the population at large. To my knowledge, however, such a program had not been introduced in mental institutions.

After due consideration—we are an experimental hospital, after all—I asked Betty to instruct the kitchen staff to see that the kitten was fed regularly, and decided to let it roam Wards One and Two to see what would happen.

It headed straight for prot.

A short time later, after he had nuzzled it for a while and "spoken" to it, it went out to meet the other inhabitants of its new world.

One or two of the patients, notably Ernie and several of Maria's alters, stayed away from it, for reasons of their own. But most of the others were delighted with it. I was especially surprised and gratified to see that Chuck the curmudgeon took to it immediately. "Doesn't stink a bit," he averred. He spent hours tempting it with bits of string and a small rubber ball someone had found on the grounds. Many of the other patients joined in. One of these, to my amazement, was Mrs. Archer, who, I discovered, had owned numerous cats before coming to MPI.

But the most remarkable effect of the kitten was on Bess. Unable to sustain a relationship with another human being, she became totally devoted to "La Belle Chatte." She assumed the responsibility for feeding her and emptying her litter box and taking her for romps on the grounds. If anyone else wanted to play with the kitten, Bess immediately gave her up, of course, with a wise, sad nod, as if to say, "You're right—I don't deserve to have her anyway." But when night came, La Belle invariably sought out Bess, and the staff would find them in the mornings sharing the same pillow.

After a few days of this I began to wonder whether another kitten or two might not have an even greater salutary effect on the patients. I decided to get a tomcat later on and let nature take its course.

Session Ten

THERE are two probes available for penetrating the carapace of hysterical amnesia; each has its proponents, each has its place. The first is sodium pentothal, also called "truth serum." A reasonably safe treatment, it has met with some success in difficult cases, and is favored by many of our own staff, including Dr. Villers. Hypnosis, in experienced hands, offers the same possibilities, but without the potential risk of side effects. With either method events long forgotten are often recalled with amazingly vivid clarity.

When I learned hypnosis as a resident many years ago I was skeptical about its value in psychiatric evaluation and treatment. But it has begun to come into its own in recent years, and is the method of choice in the management of many psychopathologies. Of course, as with other methods, success depends not only on the skill of the practitioner but also, to a great degree, on the disposition of the patient. Thus, the hypnotizability of the subject is routinely determined before treatment is initiated.

The Stanford test is used most often for this assessment. It takes less than an hour and provides a measure of the patient's ability to concentrate, his responsiveness, imagination, and willingness to cooperate. Subjects are rated on a scale of zero to twelve, the higher numbers indicating the greatest hypnotic susceptibility. Psychiatric patients, as well as the general public, average about seven on this test. I have known a few tens. Prot obtained a score of twelve.

My purpose in using hypnosis in prot's case was to uncover the traumatic event which had led to his hysterical amnesia and delusion. When had this incident occurred? My best guess was August 17, 1985, approximately four years and eleven months earlier.

The plan was simple enough: to take prot back to his childhood and carefully bring him up to the time of the putative traumatic event. In this way I hoped not only to determine the circumstances that led to whatever catastrophe had apparently befallen him, but also to get some information on the background and character of my patient.

PROT seemed to be in good spirits when he arrived in my examining room and, while he went to work on a pomegranate, we chatted about Waldorf salads and the infinite number of possible combinations of fruit juices. When he had finished his snack I turned on the tape recorder and asked him to relax.

"I am completely relaxed," he replied.

"Good. All right. I'd like you to focus your attention on that little white spot on the wall behind me." He did this. "Just stay relaxed, breathe deeply, in and out, slowly, in and out, good. Now I'm going to count from one to five. As the numbers increase you will find yourself becoming more and more drowsy, your eyelids becoming heavier and heavier. By the time I get to five you will be in a deep sleep, but you will be able to hear everything I say. Understand?"

"Of course. My beings didn't raise no dummies."

"Okay, let's begin now. One . . ."

Prot was a textbook subject, one of the best I ever had. By the count of three his eyes were tightly closed. On four his breathing had slowed and his facial expression had become completely blank. On five his pulse rate was forty bpm (I was beginning to be concerned—sixty-five was normal for him—though he looked okay) and he made no response when I coughed loudly.

"Can you hear me?"

"Yes."

"Raise your arms over your head." He complied with this request. "Now lower them." His hands dropped into his lap. "Good. Now I'm going to ask you to open your eyes. You will remain in a deep sleep, but you will be able to see me. Now—open your eyes!" Prot's eyes blinked open. "How do you feel?"

"Like nothing."

"Good. That's exactly how you *should* feel. All right. We are going back in time now; it is no longer the present. You are becoming younger. Younger and younger. You are a young man, younger still, now an adolescent, and still you are becoming younger. Now you are a child. I want you to recall the earliest experience you can remember. Think hard. What do you see?"

Without hesitation: "I see a casket. A silver casket with a blue lining."

My own heart began to beat faster. "Whose casket is it?"

"A man's."

"Who is the man?" The patient hesitated for a moment. "Don't be afraid. You can tell me."

"It is the father of someone I know."

"A friend's father?"

"Yes." Prot's words came out rather slowly and sing-songy, as though he were five or six years old.

"Is your friend a boy or girl?"

Prot squirmed around in his chair. "A boy."

"What is his name?"

No response.

"How old is he?"

"Six."

"How old are *you*?"

No response.

"What is *your* name?"

No response.

"Do you live in the same town as the other boy?"

Prot rubbed his nose with the back of his hand. "No."

"You are visiting him?"

"Yes."

"Are you a relative?"

"No."

"Where do you live?"

No response.

"Do you have any brothers or sisters?"

"No."

"Does your friend have any brothers or sisters?"

"Yes."

"How many?"

"Two."

"Brothers or sisters?"

"Sisters."

127

"Older or younger?"

"Older."

"What happened to their father?"

"He died."

"Was he sick?"

"No."

"Did he have an accident?"

"Yes."

"He was killed in an accident?"

"No."

"He was hurt and died later?"

"Yes."

"Was it a car accident?"

"No."

"Was he injured at work?"

"Yes."

"Where did he work?"

"At a place where they make meat."

"A slaughterhouse?"

"Yes."

"Do you know the name of the slaughterhouse?"

"No."

"Do you know the name of the town your friend lives in?"

No response.

"What happened after the funeral?"

"We went home."

"What happened after that?"

"I don't remember."

"Can you remember anything else that happened that day?"

"No, except I got knocked over by a big, shaggy dog."

"What is the next thing you remember?"

Prot sat up a little straighter and stopped squirming. Otherwise there was little change in his demeanor. "It is night. We are in the house. He is playing with his butterfly collection."

"The other boy?"

"Yes."

"And what are you doing?"

"Watching him."

"Do you collect butterflies too?"

"No."

"Why are you watching him?"

"I want him to come outside."

"Why do you want him to come outside?"

"To look at the stars."

"Doesn't he want to go?"

"No."

"Why not?"

"It reminds him of his father. He'd rather mess with his stupid butterflies."

"But you'd rather look at the stars."

"Yes."

"Why do you want to look at the stars?"

"I live there."

"Among the stars?"

"Yes." I remember my initial discouragement at hearing this answer. It seemed to mean that prot's delusion had begun extremely early in life; so early, perhaps, as to preclude a determination of its causative events. But suddenly I understood! Prot was a secondary personality, whose primary was the boy whose father had died when he was six!

"What is your name?"

"Prot."

"Where do you come from?"

"From the planet K-Pax."

"Why are you here?"

"He wanted me to come."

"Why did he want you to come?"

"He calls me when something bad happens."

"Like when his father died."

"Yes."

"Did something bad happen today?"

"Yes."

"What happened?"

"His dog was run over by a truck."

"And that's when he called you."

"Yes."

"How does he do that? How does he call you?"

"I don't know. I just sorta know it."

"How did you get to Earth?"

"I don't know. I just came." Prot hadn't yet "developed" light travel in his mind!

"How old is your friend now?"

"Nine."

"What year is it?"

"Nineteen—uh—sixty-six."

"Can you tell me your friend's name now?"

No response.

"He has a name, doesn't he?"

Prot stared blankly at the spot on the wall behind me. I was about to go on when he said, "It's a secret. He doesn't want me to tell you." But now I knew he was in there somewhere and prot, apparently, could consult with him.

"Why doesn't he want you to tell me?"

"If I tell you, something bad will happen."

"I promise you nothing bad will happen. Tell him I said that."

"All right." Pause. "He still doesn't want me to tell you."

"He doesn't have to tell me right now if he doesn't want to. Let's go back to the stars. Do you know where K-Pax is in the sky?"

"Up there." He pointed. "In the constellation Lyra."

"Do you know the names of all the constellations?"

"Most of them."

"Does your friend know the constellations too?"

"He used to."

"Has he forgotten them?"

"Yes."

"Is he no longer interested in them?"

"No."

"Why not?"

"His father died."

"His father taught him about the stars?"

"Yes."

"He was an amateur astronomer?"

"Yes."

"Was his father always interested in the stars?"

"No."

"When did he become interested in them?"

"After he was hurt at work."

"Because he had nothing to do?"

"No. He couldn't sleep."

"Because of the pain?"

"Yes."

"Did he sleep during the day?"

"Only one or two hours."

"I see. And one of the constellations your friend's father told him about was Lyra?"

"Yes."

"When?"

"Just before he died."

"When he was six?"

"Yes."

"Did he ever tell him there were planets around any of the stars in Lyra?"

"He said there were probably planets around a lot of the stars in the sky."

"One more thing. Why don't you go out and watch the stars by yourself?"

"I can't."

"Why not?"

"He wants me to stay with him." Prot yawned. He was beginning to sound tired. I didn't want to push him too far at this point.

"I think that's enough for one day. You may close your eyes. I'm going to start counting backwards now, from five to one. As I count you will become more and more alert. On the count of one you will be wide awake, refreshed, and feeling fine. Five . . . four . . . three . . . two . . . one." I snapped my fingers.

Prot looked at me and smiled brightly. "When do we begin?" he said.

"It's already over."

"Ah. The old 'fastest gun in the west' routine."

"I know that feeling!"

He had his notebook out; he wanted me to tell him how hypnosis worked. I spent the rest of the hour trying to explain something I didn't fully understand myself. He seemed a little disappointed.

After Jensen and Kowalski had escorted him back to the wards I listened to the tape of the session we had just completed and, with mounting excitement, jotted down my conclusions. It seemed clear to me that prot was a dominant secondary personality who had come into being as a result of the perhaps unexpected death of his alter ego's father, a trauma which was obviously too much for the primary personality to bear. It seemed evident also why he (prot) had chosen an alien existence: His (their) father had instigated in him an interest in the stars and in the possibility of extraterrestrial life occurring among them, and this revelation had come immediately prior to his father's demise.

But this did not account for the extraordinary dominance of prot over the primary personality. It is the secondary identity who ordinarily remains in the background, watching, waiting to take over when the host personality runs into difficulty. My guess was that some far more traumatic event must have drawn the primary—let's call him Pete—into a thick, protective shell, from which he rarely, if ever, ventured. And I was more certain than ever that this terrible incident, whatever it was, occurred on August 17, 1985, the date of prot's most recent "arrival" on Earth. Or perhaps a day or two earlier, if it had taken a while for Pete to "call" prot, or for him to respond.

Why did I not suspect that prot was a secondary personality earlier on? MPD is not an easy diagnosis under the best of circumstances, and prot never showed any of the symptoms usually associated with this disorder: headaches, mood changes, a variety of physical ailments, depression. Except, possibly, for his outbursts of anger in sessions six and eight, and the episode of panic on the Fourth of July, the host personality (Pete) had never made his presence felt. Finally, I was completely thrown off by his other aberrant traits—a dominant secondary personality who is himself delusional, and a savant as well—the odds against such a phenomenon must be astronomical!

But who was Pete, the primary personality? Apparently he was in there somewhere, living the life of a recluse in his own body, refusing to divulge his name or much of his background, except that he was born in 1957, apparently, to a slaughterhouse worker who died in 1963, perhaps somewhere in the northwestern part of the United States, and he had a mother and two older sisters. Not much to go on, but it might help the police trace his origin. Strictly speaking, it was Pete's identity, rather than prot's, that we needed to ascertain. Any information we could get about him, any knowledge of things familiar to him, might facilitate my persuading him to come out.

All this put prot's "departure date" into an entirely new light. It is one thing for a patient to announce an end to a delusion, but quite another for a dominant alter to disappear, leaving behind a hysteric, or maybe worse. If prot were to leave before I could get to Pete, it might well preclude my ever being able to help him at all.

I wondered whether the *un*hypnotized prot knew anything about Pete. If not, the plan would remain as before: to bring prot/Pete slowly and carefully, under hypnosis, up to the time of the traumatic event(s) which precipitated Pete's dramatic withdrawal from conscious existence. Even if he did know about Pete, however, hypnosis might still be necessary, both to facilitate prot's recollection and to make possible direct contact with the host personality.

But there was a dilemma associated with this approach. On the one hand, I needed to talk to Pete as soon as possible. On the other, forcing him to relive that terrible moment prematurely could be devastating, and cause him to withdraw even further into his protective shell.

* * *

GISELLE seemed a little less cheerful than usual the following Monday morning. "My friend down at the Sixth Precinct couldn't find any report of a missing person who disappeared from the upper West in August of 1985," she said, consulting a little red notebook much like the one prot was fond of. "Somebody killed a man and then himself in a little town in Montana on the sixteenth of that month, and in Boise on the eighteenth another guy ran off with his secretary and one hundred fifty thousand dollars of his company's funds. But your guy isn't dead, and the one who ran off with his secretary is still in the Idaho State Penitentiary. My friend is expanding the search to cover January through July of 1985, and then all of the United States and Canada. It will be a while before he gets the results.

"I also know someone in the Research Library at New York Public; during her breaks she's doing some searches for me for the week of August seventeenth. You know—newspaper reports of anything unusual that might have happened during that period in Montana, Idaho, Washington, and Oregon. Nothing there so far, either." She closed the little book. "Of course," she added, "he might have been raised in the Northwest and then moved somewhere else. . . ."

I told her about prot's (Pete's) father and the slaughterhouse. "Ha!" she replied. "I wonder how many of those things there are in the United States?"

"I don't know."

"I'll find out," she said with a wave.

"Wait a minute," I called after her. "He was born in 1957."

"How did you find this stuff out?" she demanded to know.

"Ve haff arrrr vays, mein Mädchen."

135

She ran back and kissed me on the mouth (almost) before dashing out. I felt about thirteen years old again.

KAREN and I were inseparable after my father's funeral. If we could've lived together, we would have. I especially loved her fat, pink cheeks, which became red and shiny, like little apples, in the wintertime. But it took me another year to get up the nerve to kiss her.

I studied the way they did it in the movies, practiced for months on the back of my hand. The problem was, I wasn't sure she wanted me to. Not that she turned away whenever our faces were close together, but she never indicated in any clear way that she was interested. Finally I decided to do it. With all those movies it seemed abnormal not to.

We were sitting on the sofa at her house reading Donald Duck comics, and I had been thinking about it all morning. I knew you were supposed to kiss sort of sideways so your noses wouldn't bang together, and when she turned toward me to show me Donald's nephews carrying picket signs reading: "Unca Donald is stewped," I made my move. I missed, of course, as first kisses often do, as Giselle's did before she ran out.

THAT afternoon I found Giselle in the exercise room talking animatedly with prot. La Belle was asleep in his lap. Both were jotting things down in their respective notebooks, and prot seemed quite comfortable with her. I didn't have time to join them, but she told me later some of the things they had discussed. For instance, they had been comparing the Earth with K-PAX, and one of the questions she had asked him, in a brash attempt to track down my patient's origins, was where he would like to live if he could live anywhere on Earth. She was hoping he would say "Olympia, Washington," or some such town in the upper West. Instead, he answered, "sweden."

"Why Sweden?" she wanted to know.

"Because it's the country most like K-PAX."

The subject then turned to those human beings who seemed most like K-PAXians to him. Here is what he said: Henry Thoreau, Mohandas Gandhi, Albert Schweitzer, John Lennon, and Jane Goodall.

"Can you imagine a world full of Schweitzers?" she hooted.

I said, "John Lennon?"

"Have you ever heard 'Imagine'?"

I told her I would look it up.

Then she said something I had been wondering myself: "You know what else? I think he can talk to animals!"

I said I wasn't surprised.

I had no time for them that afternoon because I was on my way to Ward Four, where Russell was trying to get in. Apparently distraught with the loss of his followers to prot's counsel and advice, and his failure to wake up the catatonic patients, he had decided to convert some of the psychopaths. When I arrived I found the nurses attempting to get him to go back to his own ward. He was up on his toes shouting through the little barred window high in the steel door, "Take heed that no man deceiveth you! For many shall cometh in my name, saying, I am the Christ; and shall deceiveth many!" Apparently his words were not falling on deaf ears, as I could hear laughter coming from inside. But he kept on yelling, even after I pleaded with him to go back to Ward Two. I ordered a shot of Thorazine and had him taken back to his room.

That same day two other things happened that I should have paid more attention to. First, I got a report that Howie had asked one of the residents how to perform a tracheotomy. Dr. Chakraborty finally told him, thinking Howie was going to show Ernie how easily he could be saved even if he were to get choked on something, despite the unfortunate example of his mother's demise.

The other event concerned Maria. One of her alters, a sultry female called Chiquita, somehow got into Ward Three and, before anyone discovered her presence there, offered herself to Whacky. But the results were the same as with the prostitute prescribed earlier. Facing this unexpected rejection, Chiquita quickly exited and Maria appeared. Though finding herself with a naked man engaged in self-manipulation she didn't become hysterical, as you might expect. Rather, she immediately began to pray for Whacky, whose despair she seemed to understand completely!

On the lighter side, Chuck presented prot with a drawing summarizing his assessment of the human race, one of many attempts, I discovered, to impress prot so that he would take Chuck to K-PAX with him. It is reproduced here:

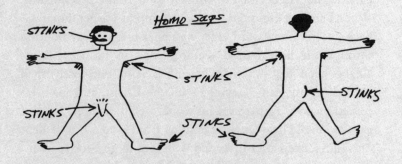

Purely by coincidence this diagram described almost perfectly our second applicant for the position of permanent director. He obviously had not bathed in weeks or even months. A blizzard of dandruff snowed from his head and drifted onto his shoulders. His teeth seemed to be covered with lichen. And, like the previous candidate, Dr. Choate, who checked his fly every few minutes, the man came with excellent references.

Session Eleven

I had been gazing out my office window at a croquet match on the lawn below just before prot came in for his next interview. I nodded toward the fruit basket and asked him what sorts of games he had played as a boy. "We don't have games on K-PAX," he replied. "We don't need them. Nor what you call 'jokes,' " he added, scrutinizing a dried fig. "I've noticed that human beings laugh a lot, even at things that aren't funny. I was puzzled by this at first until I understood how sad your lives really are."

I was sorry I had asked.

"By the way, this fig has a pesticide residue on it."

"How do you know that?"

"I can see it."

"*See* it? Oh." I had forgotten about his ultraviolet vision. With time at a premium, I nonetheless could not resist the opportunity to ask him what our world looked like from his perspective. In response, he spent nearly fifteen minutes trying to describe an incredibly beautiful visage of vibrantly colored flowers, birds, and even ordinary rocks, which lit up like gems for him. The sky itself took on a shimmering, bright, violet aura through his eyes. It appeared that prot's vista was tantamount to being permanently high on one or another psychedelic drug. I wondered whether van Gogh had not enjoyed a similar experience.

He had put down the offensive fig while he expounded on his exceptional faculty, and found one more to his liking. While he masticated I carefully proceeded. "Last time, under hypnosis, you told me about a friend of yours, an Earth being, and his father's death, and his butterfly collection, and some other things. Do you remember any of that now?"

"No."

"Well, did you have such a friend?"

"Yes."

"Is he still a friend of yours?"

"Of course."

"Why didn't you tell me about him before?"

"You never asked."

"I see. Where is he now, do you know?"

"He is waiting. I am going to take him back to K-PAX with me. That is, if he still wants to go. He vacillates a lot."

"And where is your friend waiting?"

"He is in a safe place."

"Do you know where that is?"

"Certainly."

"Can you tell me?"

"Nay, nay."

"Why not?"

"Because he asked me not to tell anyone."

"Can you at least tell me his name?"

"Sorry."

Given the circumstances, I decided to take a chance. "Prot, I'm going to tell you something you may find hard to believe."

"Nothing you humans come up with surprises me anymore."

"You and your friend are the same person. That is, you and he are separate and distinct identities of the same person."

He seemed genuinely shocked. "That is patently absurd."

"It's true."

Annoyed now, but under control: "Is that another of those 'beliefs' that passes for truth with your species?"

It had been a long shot, and it had missed. There was no way to prove the contention and no point in wasting any more time. When he had finished his snack I asked if he was ready to be hypnotized again. He nodded suspiciously, but by the time I had counted to three he was already "gone."

I began: "Last time you told me about your Earth friend, beginning with his father's death. Do you remember?"

"Yes." Prot was trance anamnestic—he could remember previous hypnotic sessions, but only while in the hypnotic state.

"Good. Now I want you to think back once again, but not so far back as last time. You and your friend are high school seniors. Twelfth-graders. What do you see?"

At this point prot slouched down in his chair, fiddled with his nails, and began to chew on an imaginary piece of gum. "I was never a high school senior," he said. "I never went to school."

"Why not?"

"We don't have schools on K-PAX."

"What about your friend? Does he go to school?"

"Yes, he does, the dope. I couldn't talk him out of it."

142

"Why would you want to talk him out of it?"

"Are you kidding? Schools are a total waste of time. They try to teach you a bunch of crap."

"Like what?"

"Like how great america is, better than any other country, how you have to have wars to protect your 'freedoms,' all kinds of junk like that."

"Does your friend feel the same way you do about that?"

"Nah. He believes all that garbage. They all do."

"Is your friend there with you now?"

"Yes."

"Can he hear us?"

"Of course. He's right here."

"May I speak with him?"

Again the momentary hesitation. "He doesn't want to."

"If he changes his mind, will you let me know?"

"I guess."

"Will he tell me his name, at least?"

"No way."

"Well, we have to call him something. How about Pete?"

"That's not his name, but okay."

"All right. Is he a senior now?"

"Yep."

"What year is it?"

"Nineteen seventy-four."

"How old are you?"

"A hunnert and seventy-seven."

"And how old is Pete?"

"Seventeen."

"Does he know you come from K-PAX?"

"Yes."

143

"How does he know that?"

"I told him."

"What was his reaction to that?"

"He thinks it's cool."

"Incidentally, how did you learn to speak English so well? Did he teach you?"

"Nah. It's not very difficult. You should try speaking *w:xljqzs/k..mns pt.*"

"Where did you land when you came to Earth?"

"You mean this trip?"

"Yes."

"China."

"Not Zaire?"

"Why should I land in zaire when china was pointing toward K-PAX?"

"Do you have any other Earth friends? Is there anyone else there with you?"

"Nobody here but us chickens."

"How many chickens are you?"

"Just me and him."

"Tell me more about Pete. What's he like?"

"What's he like? He's all right. Kinda quiet. Keeps to himself. He's not as smart as I am, but that doesn't matter on EARTH."

"No? And what does matter?"

"All that matters is that you're a 'nice guy,' and not too bad looking."

"And is he?"

"I suppose."

"Can you describe him?"

"Yes."

"Please do."

"He's beginning to wear his hair long. He has brown

eyes, medium complexion, and twenty-eight pimples, which he puts clearasil on all the time."

"Are his eyes sensitive to bright light?"

"Not particularly. Why should they be?"

"What makes him a nice guy?"

"He smiles a lot, he helps the dumber kids with their assignments, he volunteers to set up the bleachers for the home games, stuff like that. He's vice-president of the class. Everybody likes him."

"You sound as though you're not so sure they should."

"I know him better than anybody else."

"And you think he's not as nice as everybody thinks."

"He's not as nice as he makes out."

"In what way?"

"He has a temper. It gets out of hand sometimes."

"What happens when it gets out of hand?"

"He gets mad. Throws things around, kicks inanimate objects."

"What makes him mad?"

"Things that seem unfair, that he can't do anything about. You know."

I was pretty sure I did know. It had something to do with the helplessness and anger he felt at the time of his father's death. "Can you give me an example?"

"One time he found a kid beating up on a smaller kid. The older guy was a big redheaded bully and everybody hated him. He had broken the other kid's glasses, and his nose, too, I think. My friend beat the shit out of him. I tried to stop him but he wouldn't listen."

"What happened then? Was the bully badly hurt? Did he try to get even later on?"

"He lost a couple teeth is all. He was mostly afraid my friend would tell everybody what happened. When he didn't, and asked the little kid not to either, they became the best of buddies. All three of them."

"What do these other guys think about you?"

"They don't know about me."

"Does anyone besides your friend know about you?"

"Nary a soul."

"All right. Back to your friend. Does this anger of his show itself often?"

"Not very. Hardly ever at school."

"Does he ever get mad at his mother and sisters?"

"Never. He doesn't see his sisters much. They're already married and gone. One of them moved away."

"Tell me about his mother."

"She's nice. She works at the school. At the cafeteria. She doesn't make much money, but she does a lot of gardening and canning. They have enough to eat, but not much else. She's still trying to pay back all of his dad's doctor bills."

"Where do they live? I mean is it a house? What kind of neighborhood is it in?"

"It's a small three-bedroom house. It looks like all the others on the street."

"What sorts of things does your friend do for entertainment? Movies? Books? Television?"

"There's only one movie theater in town. They have an old tv set that doesn't work half the time. My friend reads a lot, and he also likes to walk around in the woods."

"Why?"

"He wants to be a biologist."

"What about his grades?"

"What about them?"

"Does he get good grades?"

"A's and b's. He should do better. He sleeps too much."

"What are his best subjects?"

"He's pretty good in latin and science. Not so hot in english and math."

"Is he a good athlete?"

"He's on the wrestling team."

"Is he planning to go to college?"

"He was until a few days ago."

"What happened? Is there a problem?"

"Yes."

"Is that why he called you?"

"Yes."

"Does he call you often now?"

"Once in a while."

"And what is the problem? Money? There are scholarships available, or—"

"It's more complicated than that."

"How so?"

"He has a girlfriend."

"And she doesn't want him to go?"

"It's more complicated than that."

"Can you tell me about it?"

After a brief pause, possibly for consultation with his "friend": "She's pregnant."

"Oh, I see."

"Happens all the time."

"And he feels he has to marry her?"

"Unfortunately." He shrugged.

" 'Unfortunately' because he won't be able to go to college?"

"That and the religion problem."

"What's the religion problem?"

"She's a catholic."

"You don't like Catholics?"

"It's not that I dislike catholics, or any other group de-

147

fined by its superstitious beliefs. It's that I know what's going to happen."

"What's going to happen?"

"He's going to settle down in this company town that killed his father and he's going to have a bunch of kids that nobody will associate with because their mother is a catholic."

"Where is this town?"

"I told you—he doesn't want me to tell you that."

"I thought he might have changed his mind."

"When he makes up his mind about something, nobody can change it."

"He sounds pretty strong-willed."

"About some things."

"What, for example?"

"About her."

"Who—his girlfriend?"

"Yep."

"I may be dense, but I still don't see why her being a Catholic is such a serious problem."

"That's because you don't live here. Her family lives on the wrong side of the tracks. Literally."

"Maybe they will be able to overcome the problem."

"How?"

"She could change her faith. They could move away."

"Not a chance. She's too attached to her family."

"Do you hate her?"

"Me? I don't hate anyone. I hate the chains people shackle themselves with."

"Like religion."

"Religion, family responsibilities, having to make a living, all that stuff. It's so *stifling,* don't you think?"

"Sometimes. But they're things we have to learn to live with, aren't they?"

"Not me!"

"Why not?"

"We don't have all that crap on K-PAX."

"Will you be going back there soon?"

"Any time now."

"How long do you usually stay on Earth?"

"Depends. A few days, usually. Just long enough to help him over the rough spots."

"All right. Now listen carefully. I'm going to ask you to come forward in time several days. Let's say two weeks. Where are you now?"

"On K-PAX."

"Good. What do you see?"

"A forest with lots of soft places to lie down on, and fruit trees, and all kinds of other beings wandering around. . . ."

"Much like the kind of forest your friend enjoys hiking in?"

"Something like that, but nobody is bulldozing it down to build a shopping center."

"Tell me about some of the plants and animals in the woods there on K-PAX." I was curious to find out whether the young prot had a fully developed concept of his home planet, or whether that came later. While he was describing the flora and fauna I retrieved his file and pulled out the information that prot had divulged to me in sessions five through eight. I quizzed him on the names of grains, fruits and vegetables, the various animal "beings," even about light travel and the K-PAXian calendar. I won't repeat the questions and answers here, but they confirmed my suspicion that the creation of his alien world was developed over many years. For example, he could tell me the names of only six grains at this stage.

Our time ran out just as prot decided to make a trip to one of the K-PAXian libraries. He asked me whether I would like to join him. I said I was sorry, I had some appointments.

"It's your loss," he said.

After I had awakened him, and before he left my examining room, I asked prot whether he could, in fact, talk to animals, as Giselle and I suspected.

"Of course," he replied.

"Can you communicate with all our beings?"

"I have a little difficulty with homo sapiens."

"Can you talk to dolphins and whales?"

"They're beings, aren't they?"

"How do you do that?"

He wagged his head in abject frustration. "You humans consider yourselves the smartest of the EARTH beings. Am I right?"

"Yes."

"Then obviously the other beings speak much simpler languages than yours, right?"

"Well—"

Out came the notebook, pencil poised. "So if you're so smart, and their languages are so simple, how come you can't communicate with them?" He waited for an answer. Unfortunately, I didn't have one.

JUST before I left for the day Giselle gave me another discouraging report from the police. Her contact had come up with a list of all disappearances, during the last ten years, of white males born between 1950 and 1965 in the entire United States and Canada. There had been thousands during this period, of course, but not a single one even came close to matching prot's profile. Some were too tall, some were bald, some were blue-eyed, some were dead, some had been found and were accounted for. Unless prot were a female in disguise, was much older or younger than he seemed, or someone whose disappearance had not been noticed, our patient, for all practical purposes, did not exist.

She was also waiting for the names and locations of all the slaughterhouses operating anywhere in North America between 1974 and 1985.

"You can eliminate the ones in or near large cities," I told her. "There's only one movie theater."

She nodded her acknowledgment. She looked tired. "I'm going to go home and sleep for about two days," she said, yawning. How I wished I could have done the same!

I was lying awake that night trying to make some sense of the day's events—why, I wondered hazily, was there no record of Pete's disappearance? And what good, I tried to reason, was a list of slaughterhouses without further information as to where our abattoir might be located?—when I got a call from Dr. Chakraborty. Ernie was in the clinic. Someone had tried to kill him!

"What? Who?" I barked.

"Howie!" came the chilling reply.

All I could think of as I sped down the expressway was: Jesus Christ! What have I done? Whatever happened to Ernie was my fault, my responsibility, just as I was responsible for everything else that happened at the hospital. It was one of the worst moments of my life. But even at that blackest of hours I was heartened by the glow of the city, her throbbing lights bright against the steel-gray background of the dawning sky, as full of defiant life as the night, some forty years earlier, that we futilely rushed my father to the hospital. Same glowing sky, same darkening guilt.

Ernie was still in the emergency room when I got to MPI. Dr. Chakraborty met me in the corridor with: "You are not to worry. He is very fine." And indeed he was sitting up in bed, sans mask, smiling, his hands behind his head.

"How are you feeling, Ernie?"

"Wonderful. Absolutely wonderful." I had never seen a smile quite like his. It was positively beatific.

"What happened, for God's sake?"

"My good friend Howie just about strangled me to death." When he threw his head back to laugh, I could see a red abrasion where something had been wrapped around his neck. "That old son-of-a-bitch. I love him."

"Love him? He tried to kill you!"

"No he didn't. He made me *think* he tried to kill me. Oh, it was fantastic. I was asleep. You know, with my hands tied and everything? He wrapped something around my neck—a handkerchief or something—and tightened it up, and there wasn't a damn thing I could do about it."

"Go on."

"When I stopped breathing and became unconscious he somehow lifted me onto a gurney and ran me up here to the infirmary. They got me going again in a hurry, and when I woke up I realized immediately what he had done."

"What do you think he did?" I remember saying to myself as I asked him this: I must be a psychiatrist! It was all I could do not to laugh.

"He taught me a lesson I'll never forget."

"Which was?"

"That dying is nothing to fear. In fact, it's quite pleasant."

152

"How so?"

"Well, you've heard that old adage—when you die your life passes before your eyes? Well, it does! But only the good parts! In my case, I was a child again. It was wonderful! My mother was there, and my dog, and I had all my old toys and games and my catcher's mitt. . . . It was just like living my whole childhood over again! But it was no dream. It was really happening! All those memories—I never realized what a wonderful thing childhood is until I got the chance to relive it like that. And then, when I was nine, it started all over again! And again! Over and over again! It was the best thing that ever happened to me!" There he was, his skin pale as a scallop, laughing about the event whose prospect had terrified him all his life. "I can hardly wait for the real thing!"

They had taken Howie to Ward Four. I let him stew there the rest of that day and most of the next before I found time to talk to him. I was angry with him and let him know it, but he just sat there beaming at me, his grin a perfect copy of prot's know-it-all smirk. As he was heading back to his room on Ward Two he turned and proclaimed, "Prot says one more task and I'll be cured, too."

"*I'll* decide that, goddamn it!" I shouted after him.

O N E of the night nurses told me later that the Duchess had begun to take some of her meals in the dining room with the other patients. She was shocked and offended by all the belching and farting (courtesy, primarily, of Chuck), but, to her great credit, she usually stuck it out.

At her first appearance Bess tried to get up and serve her. One glance from prot and she returned to her place. As usual, however, she wouldn't eat anything until everyone else had finished.

"How did he get her to come to the table?" I asked the nurse.

"She wants to be the one who gets to go with him," came the obvious reply. She sounded envious.

154

Session Twelve

WHILE prot was munching peaches and plums I brought up the subject of Howie and his tasks. I explained that the first one he had assigned to him (to find the "bluebird of happiness") had produced a positive effect not only on Howie, but on the rest of the ward as well. Though it had turned out successfully also, the second (to "cure" Ernie) was more problematical. I asked him if he had anything else in mind for my patient.

"Only one final task."

"Do you mind telling me what it is?"

"That would spoil the surprise."

"I think we've had enough surprises around here for a while. Can you guarantee this task will cause no harm to anyone?"

"If he does it well, it will be a very happy day for everyone, including yourself." I was not so certain about that, but my doubts were swallowed up by his self-confidence.

My father once lay down on the living room floor and asked me to make a run at him. He wanted me to push off on his knees, flip over him, and land on my feet above his head. It sounded like suicide. "Trust me," he said. So I put my life in his hands, made a run at him, and, with his help, miraculously landed on my feet. I never did it again. Prot had the same "trust me" look in his eyes when he told me about Howie's last task. And on that note we began our twelfth session.

The minute I started to count, prot fell into a deep trance. I asked whether he could hear me.

"Of course."

"Good. Now I want you to think back to the year 1979; that is, 1979 on Earth. It's Christmas Day, 1979. Where are you and what do you see?"

"I am on the PLANET TERSIPION in what you would call the CONSTELLATION TAURUS. I see orange and green everywhere. It's quite remarkable. The flora on this WORLD are not chlorophyll-based as they are on EARTH and K-PAX. Instead, light is gathered by a pigment similar to that of your red algae. The sky is green because of the chlorine in the atmosphere. There are all kinds of interesting beings, most of whom you would characterize as insects. Some are bigger than your dinosaurs. All of them are quite slow-moving, fortunately, but you have to—"

"Excuse me, prot. I would love to hear about this planet, and all the other places you have visited, but right now I would prefer to concentrate on your passages to Earth."

"Anything you say. But you asked me where I was and what I was doing on christmas of 1979."

"Yes I did, but only as a point of reference. What I'd like to ask you to do now is to come forward in time to your next visit to Earth. Can you do that?"

156

"Of course. Um, let's see. January? No, I was still on TERSIPION. February? No. I was back on K-PAX then, learning to play the patuse, though I'll never be any good at it. It must have been in march. Yes, it *was* march, that delightful time in your northern hemisphere when the ice on the streams is melting and the mayapples and crocuses are coming up."

"This is March 1980?"

"Precisely."

"And he called you?"

"Well, not for anything in particular. He just wants someone to talk things over with now and then."

"Tell me about him. What's he like? Is he married?"

"Yes, he's married to a girl he knew in—oh, I told you about that already, didn't I?"

"The Catholic girl who was pregnant when they were seniors in high school?"

"What a memory! She's still a catholic, but no longer pregnant. That was five and a half years ago."

"I've forgotten her name."

"I never told you her name."

"Can you tell me now?"

After a lengthy hesitation, during which he seemed to study my haircut (or the need thereof), he said, quietly, "sarah."

Barely concealing my elation: "Did they have a son or a daughter?"

"Yes."

"I mean which?"

"You should do something about that sense of humor, doctor brewer. A daughter."

"So she's about five?"

"Her birthday is next week."

"Any other children?"

"No. Sarah developed endometriosis and they gave her a hysterectomy. Stupid."

"Because she was so young?"

"No. Because there is a simple treatment for it that your medical people should have figured out long ago."

"Can you tell me the daughter's name? Or is that a secret?"

After only a moment's hesitation: "rebecca." When this was divulged so readily I wondered whether Pete had relented and had decided to allow prot to tell me his real name. Perhaps he was beginning to trust me! But prot must have anticipated my question: "Forget it," he said.

"Forget what?"

"He's not going to tell you that."

"Why not? Will he at least tell why not?"

"No."

"Why not?"

"You'll just use the answer to chip away at him."

"All right. Then tell me this: Do they live in the same town he was born in?"

"Yes and no."

"Can you be more specific?"

"They live in a trailer outside of town."

"How far outside of town is it?"

"Not far. It's in a trailer park. But they want to get a house farther out in the country."

A shot in the dark: "Do they have a sprinkler?"

"A what?"

"A lawn sprinkler."

"In a trailer park?"

"All right. Do they both work?"

His mouth puckered slightly, as if the fruit hadn't agreed with him. "He has a full-time job, as you would call it. She earns some money making children's clothing."

"Where does your friend work?"

"The same place his father and his grandfather did. Just about the only place in town there is to work, unless you're a grocer or a banker."

"The slaughterhouse?"

"Yessir, the old butchery."

"What does he do there?"

"He's a knocker."

"What's a 'knocker'?"

"The knocker is the guy who knocks the cows in the head so they don't struggle so much when you cut their throats."

"Does he like his job?"

"Are you kidding?"

"What else does he do? At home, for example?"

"Not much. He reads the newspaper in the evening, after his daughter has gone to bed. On weekends he tinkers with his car and watches tv like everybody else in town."

"Does he still hike in the woods?"

"Sarah would like him to do that, but he doesn't."

"Why not?"

"It depresses him."

"Does he still collect butterflies?"

"He threw out his collection a long time ago. There was no room for it in the trailer."

"Does he regret his decision to get married and raise a family?"

"Oh, no. He is truly devoted to his wife and daughter, whatever that means."

"Tell me about his wife."

"Cheerful. Energetic. Dull. Like most of the housewives you see at the a&p."

"And the daughter?"

"A carbon copy of her mother."

"Do they all get along well?"

"They idolize one another."

"Do they have a lot of friends?"

"None."

"None?"

"Sarah's a catholic. I told you—it's a small town. . . ."

"They never see anyone else?"

"Only her family. And his mother."

"What about his sisters?"

"One lives in alaska. The other is just like everyone else in town."

"Would you say he hates her?"

"He doesn't hate anyone."

"What about male friends?"

"There ain't none."

"What about the bully and the kid he beat up on?"

"One is in prison, the other was killed in lebanon."

"And he never stops off at a tavern after work for a beer with his fellow knockers?"

"Not anymore."

"He did earlier?"

"He used to joke around with the others, have a beer or two. But whenever he invited someone for supper, they always found some excuse not to come. And no one ever invited him and his family for a barbecue or anything else. After a while he began to get the idea. Now they stick to their trailer most of the time. I tried to tell him this would happen."

160

"Sounds like a pretty lonely existence."

"Not really. Sarah has a million brothers and sisters."

"And now they're going to buy a house?"

"Maybe. Or build one. They've got their eye on a few acres of land. It's a beautiful spot, a part of a farm that someone split up. It has a stream and a couple of acres of trees. A lovely place. Reminds me of home. Except for the stream."

"Tell him I hope he gets it."

"I'll do that, but he still won't tell you his name."

At that point Mrs. Trexler barged in, out of breath, whispering frantically about a disturbance in the psychopathic ward: Someone had kidnapped Giselle! I quickly hushed her up and reluctantly brought prot back from his hypnotic state, left him with Mrs. T, and took off for the fourth floor.

Giselle! It is hard to express the feelings I had in the few seconds it took me to make it downstairs. I couldn't have been more distressed if it had been Abby or Jenny in the hands of whichever lunatic had grabbed her. I saw her slouched down in my office chair, heard her childish voice, smelled her sweet, piney scent. Giselle! All my fault. All my fault. Allowing a helpless girl to "cruise the corridors" of the psych ward. I tried not to imagine a pair of hairy arms wrapped around her neck, or worse. . . .

I banged into Four. Everyone was milling around or chatting amiably, some even beginning to return to their regular routines. I couldn't believe how unconcerned they seemed to be. All I could think of was: What kind of people are these?

The kidnapper's name was Ed. He was a handsome, white, fifty-year-old man who had gone berserk six years earlier and gunned down eight people with a semiautomatic rifle in a shopping mall parking lot. Until that time he had been a successful stockbroker, a model husband and father, sports

161

fan, church elder, six-handicap golfer, and all the rest. Afterward, even with regular medication, he suffered periods of episodic dyscontrol accompanied by significant electrical activity in his brain, which usually ended with utter exhaustion and fists bloodied by pounding them against the walls of his room.

But it wasn't Giselle he had kidnapped. It was La Belle.

I never did find out whether Mrs. Trexler's tongue had slipped or whether I misheard her—I had been worried about Giselle's safety all along. In any case the kitten had gotten into the psychopathic ward, and when the orderlies opened Ed's door to take away his dirty laundry, she slipped inside. It wasn't long before he was banging on the bars of his window and threatening to wring La Belle's little neck unless he could talk to "the guy from outer space."

Villers was there to remind me that he had opposed the idea of having animals in the wards, and perhaps he was right—this would never have happened without the kitten and, furthermore, if anything happened to it, the effect on Bess and the others could be quite demoralizing. I thought Ed was bluffing; he was not in one of his violent phases. But I could see no compelling reason not to let him talk briefly with prot, and I asked Betty to send for him. Prot, however, was already there. Apparently he had followed me down the stairs.

There was no need to explain the situation, only to tell him to assure Ed there would be no reprisal if he let the kitten go. Prot, requesting that no one accompany him, headed for Ed's room. I assumed they would talk through the barred window, but suddenly the door opened and prot darted inside, slamming it behind him.

After a few minutes I cautiously approached the window and peered into the room. They were standing over by the far wall, talking quietly. I couldn't hear what they were saying. Ed was holding La Belle, stroking her gently. When he glanced toward me I backed off.

Prot finally came out, but without the kitten. After making sure the security guard had locked Ed's door, I turned to him, puzzled. Anticipating my question, he said, "He won't harm her."

"How do you know that?"

"He told me."

"Uh huh. What else did he tell you?"

"He wants to go to K-PAX."

"What did you tell him?"

"I said I couldn't take him with me."

"What did he say to that?"

"He was disappointed until I told him I would come back for him later."

"And that satisfied him?"

"He said he would wait if he could keep the kitten."

"But—"

"Don't worry. He won't hurt her. And he won't cause you any more trouble, either."

"How can you be so sure of that?"

"Because he thinks that if he does, I won't come back for him. I would anyway, but he doesn't know that."

"You would? Why?"

"Because I told him I would. By the way," he said as we were walking out together, "you'll need to find a few more furry beings for the other wards."

HERE was Howie's final task: to be ready for anything. To respond at a moment's notice to whatever prot, without warning, might challenge him with.

For a day or two he raced at tachyon speed from the

163

library to his room and back to the library—same old Howie. He didn't sleep for forty-eight hours. He was reading Cervantes, Schopenhauer, the Bible. But suddenly, as he was darting past the lounge window where he had spotted the bluebird, he stopped and took his old seat on the ledge. He began to chuckle, then to roar. Pretty soon the whole ward, except perhaps for Bess, was giggling, then the whole hospital, staff and all. The absurdity of prot's charge, that he be ready for anything that might possibly happen, had sunk in.

"It is stupid to try to prepare for life," Howie told me later, on the lawn. "It happens, and there isn't a damn thing you can do about it." Prot was over by the side wall examining a sunflower. I wondered what he saw in it that we didn't.

"What about your task?" I asked him.

"Qué será, será," he whistled, leaning back to soak up the warm sunshine. "I think I'll take a nap."

I suggested he think about the possibility of moving to Ward One. "I'll wait until Ernie's ready," he said.

The problem was that Ernie didn't want to leave. I had already proposed, at the last staff meeting, that Ernie be transferred to One as well. He had shown no sign of the debilitating phobia since his "cure"—no mask, no complaints about the food, no hog-tying himself at night or sleeping on the floor. He was, in fact, spending most of his time with the other patients, particularly Bess and Maria. He had already become quite adept at recognizing the latter's various alters, learning all their names and characteristics, waiting patiently for the "real" Maria to make an appearance, then going out of his way to keep her around, gently encouraging her interests in needlepoint and macramé. It was obvious that Ernie had a talent for helping others, and I encouraged him to consider going into one of the health or social professions. His reply was, "But there's so much that needs to be done *here*."

It was about this time that Chuck organized an essay contest to decide who would be the one to go with prot on August seventeenth. The plan called for submission of all entries by August tenth, a week before his "departure," a date that was rapidly approaching. Prot had apparently agreed to read all the essays by the seventeenth.

Several staff members noted that Ward Two was unusually quiet during that two-week period with everyone sitting off by him/herself, thinking hard, bending over periodically to write something down. The only patients who didn't seem to want to go to K-PAX were Ernie and Bess—Ernie because there was work to be done here, and Bess because she felt she didn't deserve a free trip. And, of course, Russell, who called the contest "the work of the devil."

Session Thirteen

EVER since she ran off to Texas with a guitar player at the age of fifteen, my daughter Abby has been a vegetarian. She won't wear fur, either, and has long opposed the use of animals in medical research. I have tried many times to explain to her the benefits to mankind of the latter endeavor, but her mind is closed on the subject. "Explain that to all the dead dogs," is her standard reply. We haven't discussed the subject in years.

Abby once gave me a tape recording of whale songs. At the beginning of session thirteen, while prot was digging into a watermelon, I played it for him. He stopped chewing and tilted his head to one side, much as Shasta had done when she had heard the same tape. By the time it was over he was grinning even more broadly than usual. A piece of the rind was stuck in his teeth. I said, "Can you make anything out of that?"

"Of course."

"What is it? Is it some kind of communication?"

"What did you think it was—stomach gas?"

"Can you tell me what they're saying?"

"Sure."

"Well?"

"They're passing on all kinds of very complex navigational data, temperature and solute and food type and distribution charts, and lots of other things, including some poetry and art. It is rich in imagery and emotion, which you would probably dismiss as 'sentimental.' "

"Can you give me a literal translation of all that?"

"I could, but I won't."

"Why not?"

"Because you would use it against them."

I felt a certain amount of resentment at being held personally responsible for the decimation of many of the world's cetaceans, but could think of no good reply.

"There was also a message for all the other beings on the PLANET." He paused here, peering at me out of the corner of an eye, and took another bite of fruit.

"Well? Are you going to tell me what it was? Or are you going to keep that a secret, too?"

"They're saying, 'Let's be friends.' " He finished the melon, counted, "One-two-three-four-five," and was out like a light.

"Comfortable?" I said, when I realized he had already hypnotized himself.

"Perfectly, my dear sir."

"Good." I took a very deep breath. "Now I'm going to give you a specific date, and I want you to remember where you were and what you were doing on that day. Do you understand?"

"Jawohl."

167

"Excellent." I braced myself. "The date is August seventeenth, 1985."

There was no hint of shock or other emotion. "Yes," was all he said.

"Where are you?"

"I'm on K-PAX. Harvesting some kropins for a meal."

"Kropins?"

"Kropins are fungi. Something like your truffles. Big truffles. Delicious. Do you like truffles?"

I was a bit annoyed by his attention to trivia at a time like this, though it was I who had pursued the topic. "I've never had truffles. But let's get on with this, shall we? Is anything else happening? Any calls from Earth?"

"There it is now, as a matter of fact, and I'm on my way."

"What did it feel like when the call came?"

"He needed me. I felt that he needed me."

"And how long will it take you to get to Earth?"

"No time at all. You see, at tachyon speed, time goes backward, so that—"

"Thank you. You've already explained to me all about light travel."

"Funny, I don't remember doing that. But then you must know it takes no time at all."

"Yes. I had forgotten. So now you are on Earth?"

"Yes. In zaire."

"Zaire?"

"It is pointing toward K-PAX at this moment."

"And now you'll be heading for—"

"And now I am with him."

"Your friend?"

"Yes."

"Where are you? What is happening?"

"By a river in back of his house. It is dark. He is taking off his clothes."

"He called you to Earth to go for a nighttime swim with him?"

"No. He is trying to kill himself."

"Kill himself? Why?"

"Because something terrible has happened."

"What happened?"

"He doesn't want to talk about it."

"Damn it, I'm trying to help him."

"He knows that."

"Then why won't he tell me?"

"He feels terribly hurt and ashamed. He doesn't want you to know."

"But I can't help him unless he tells me what happened."

"He knows that, too."

"Then why—"

"Because then you'd know what even *he* doesn't want to know."

"Do *you* know what happened?"

"No."

"No? Doesn't he tell you everything that happens to him?"

"Not anymore."

"Then will you help him? If you can get him to tell me what happened you would be taking the first step toward helping him deal with it."

"No."

"Why not?"

"He doesn't want to talk about it—remember?"

"But time's running out for him!"

"Time is running out for everyone."

169

"All right. What is happening now?"

"He is floating down the river. He is drowning. He wants to die." Prot stated this matter-of-factly, as if he were a disinterested observer.

"Can't you stop him?"

"What can I do?"

"You could talk to him. Help him."

"If he wants to die, that's his right, don't you think?"

"But he is your friend. If he dies you will never see him again."

"I *am* his friend. That is why I won't interfere."

"All right. Is he still conscious?"

"Barely."

"But still in the water?"

"Yes."

"There is still time. Help him, for God's sake."

"There is no need. The stream has washed him onto the bank. He will survive."

"How far downstream did it carry him?"

"Just a few jarts—a mile or so."

"What is he doing now?"

"He's coughing. He's full of water, but he's coming around."

"And you are with him?"

"As close as I am to you right now."

"Can you talk to him?"

"I can talk to him, but he won't talk to me."

"What is he doing now?"

"He's just lying there." At this point prot took off his shirt and lay it on the floor in front of him.

"You covered him?"

"He is shivering." Prot lay down on the carpet beside his shirt.

"You are lying down beside him?"

"Yes. We are going to sleep now."

"Yes, you do that. And now I'm going to ask you to come forward in time to the next morning. The sun is up. Where are you now?"

"Still lying here."

"He is sleeping?"

"No. He just doesn't want to get up."

"Did he say anything during the night?"

"No."

"Did you say anything to him?"

"No."

"All right. Now it's late afternoon. Where are you now?"

Prot got up and returned to his chair. "In zaire."

"Zaire? How did you get to Zaire?"

"It's difficult to explain. You see, light has certain—"

"What I meant was, why did you go back there? Is your friend with you?"

"It looked like a beautiful country. I thought some sightseeing might cheer him up."

"Did you talk to him about it?"

"Yes. I said, 'Let's get out of here.' "

"What did he say?"

"Nothing."

"So now you're in Zaire."

"Yes."

"Both of you."

"Yes."

"What will you do next?"

"Get to know the beings here."

"And then what?"

"We'll move on to another place."

"All right. It's six months later. February seventeenth, 1986. Where are you?"

"Egypt."

"Still in Africa?"

"It's a big continent. By EARTH standards, anyway."

"Is your friend still with you?"

"Of course."

"What did you use for money on these travels?"

"Nothing. We just took what we needed."

"And nobody objected?"

"Not after I explained who we were."

"All right. It's one year after you left the river. August seventeenth, 1986. Where are you now?"

"Sweden."

"Do you like it there?"

"Very much. They are more like K-PAXians here than anywhere else we've been."

"In what way?"

"They are less warlike, and more tolerant toward their fellow beings than the other countries we have visited."

"August seventeenth, 1987."

"Saudi arabia."

"August seventeenth, 1988."

"Queensland, australia."

"August seventeenth, 1989."

"Bolivia."

"October seventeenth, same year."

"The united states. Indiana."

"December seventeenth."

"New york."

"February seventeenth, 1990."

"The long island psychiatric hospital."

"May seventeenth."

"The manhattan psychiatric institute."

"The present."

"Same old place."

"And your friend hasn't spoken to you in all this time?"

"Not a word."

"Have you tried to talk to *him*?"

"Occasionally."

"May I try?"

"Be my guest."

"I need a name. It would be so much easier if you would give me a name to call him."

"I can't do that. But I'll give you a hint. He can fly."

"Fly? Is his name Fred?"

"C'mon, you can do better than that. Can't you think of anything that flies besides airplanes?"

"He's a bird? He has the name of a bird?"

"Bingo!"

"Uh, uh, Donald? Woody? Jonathan Livingston?"

"Those aren't real birds, are they, gene?"

"Martin? Jay!"

"You're getting waaaaaarmerrrrrr!"

"Robin? Robert?"

"Well done, doctor brewer. The rest is up to you."

"Thank you. I'd like to speak to him now. Do you mind?"

"Why should I?" Suddenly prot/Robert slouched down in his chair. His hands fell limply to his sides.

"Robert?"

No response.

"Robert, this is Doctor Brewer. I think I can help you."

No response.

"Robert, listen to me. You've had a terrible shock. I understand your pain and suffering. Can you hear me?"

No response.

At this point I took a chance. Knowing prot and, through him, something about Robert, I could not shake the feeling that if he had in fact hurt, or killed, someone, it must have been an accident or, more likely perhaps, self-defense. It was mostly speculation, but it was all I had. "Robert, listen to me. What happened to you could have happened to anyone. It is not something to be ashamed of. It is a normal response that human beings are programmed to carry out. It's in our genes. Do you understand? Anyone might have done the same thing you did. Anyone would condone what you did and why you did it. I want you to understand that. If you will just acknowledge that you hear me we can talk about it. We don't have to talk about what happened just yet. Only about how we can get you to overcome your grief and self-hatred. Won't you talk to me? Won't you let me help you?"

We sat silently for several minutes while I waited for Robert to make a move, a small gesture to indicate he had heard my plea. But he never twitched a muscle.

"I'm going to ask you to think about it for a while. We'll talk about this again a week from today, all right? Please trust me."

No response.

"I'm going to ask to speak with your friend now."

In a twinkling prot was back, wide-eyed and smiling broadly. "Hiya, gene. Long time no see. How ya been?" We talked a bit about our first few meetings back in May, the tiniest details of which he described perfectly, as if he had a tape recorder inside his head.

I woke him and sent him back to Ward Two. Cheerful as ever, he didn't remember a thing about what had just transpired.

★ ★ ★

174

THERE was a seminar that afternoon in our lecture room, but I didn't hear a word of it. I was considering the possibility of increasing the number of sessions with prot/Robert. Unfortunately, I had a meeting in Los Angeles at the end of that week and the beginning of the next, something that had been arranged months before and would have been impossible to get out of. But I suspected that even a dozen more sessions wouldn't be enough. Maybe a hundred wouldn't be enough to sort everything out. True, I now knew his first name, but I wasn't sure this would be of much help in tracing his background. It was encouraging in another sense, however: It indicated a possible crack in the armor, a hint of willingness on Robert's part to begin to cooperate, to help with his own recovery, to get well. But there were only two weeks left before prot's "departure." If I couldn't get through to him by then, I was afraid it would be too late.

"HIS name is Robert Something," I told Giselle after the seminar.

"Great! Let me check it against my list." She bent over a long computer printout. Her profile was perfect, like one of those "Can you draw me?" advertisements. "Here's one! But this guy disappeared in April of 1985, and he was sixty-eight years old. Wait! Here's another one! And he disappeared in August! No, no, he was only seven then. That would make him twelve now." She looked at me sadly. "Those were the only two Roberts."

"I was afraid of that."

"He's *got* to exist," she wailed. "There has to be a record of his existence. We must have missed something. An important clue . . ." She jumped up and began pacing around my office. Eventually she spotted the picture of my family on my desk. She asked me about my wife, where we had met, and so

175

on. I told her how long I had known Karen, a little about the kids. Then she sat down and told me some things about herself she hadn't mentioned before. I shall not record the details here, but she was on intimate terms with more than one prominent figure from the worlds of sports and journalism. The point, however, is that although she had countless male friends, she had never married. I wasn't about to ask her why, but she answered as if I had: "I'm an idealist and a perfectionist and all the wrong things," and turned her gaze to a faraway place in the distant past. "And because I have never met a man I could give myself to, utterly and completely." Then she turned to me. In a moment of helpless ego—Brown's syndrome is a very powerful force—I was sure she was going to say, "Until now." My tie suddenly needed my attention. "And now I'm going to lose him," she whimpered, "and there's nothing I can do about it!" She was in love with prot!

Caught between disappointment and relief I said something stupid: "I've got a son you might like." I was thinking of Fred, who had just landed a part in a comedy playing at a dinner theater in Newark. She smiled warmly.

"The pilot who decided to become an actor? How old was he when that picture was taken?"

"Nineteen."

"He's cute, isn't he?"

"I suppose so." I gazed fondly at the photograph on my desk.

"That picture reminds me of my own family," she said. "My dad was so proud of us. We all became professionals of one sort or another. Ronnie is a surgeon, Audrey's a dentist, Gary a vet. I'm the only dud in the bunch."

"I wouldn't say that. Not at all. You are one of the best reporters in the country. Why settle for second best in something else?"

She smiled at that and nodded. "And that picture of you reminds me of my father."

"How so?"

"I don't know. He was nice. Kind. You'd have liked him."

"I probably would have. May I ask what happened to him?"

"He committed suicide."

"Oh, Giselle, I'm very sorry."

"Thank you." Dreamily: "He had cancer. He didn't want to be a burden."

We sat in my office thinking our own private thoughts until I happened to glance at the clock on my desk. "Good grief—I've got to run. We're going to go see Freddy perform tonight. He's playing a reporter. You want to come with us?"

"No, no thanks. I've got some writing to do. And some thinking."

As we got into the elevator I reminded her that I was going out of town for a few days and wouldn't be back until the middle of the following week.

"Maybe I'll have the case solved by then! I'm supposed to get the locations of all the slaughterhouses tomorrow!"

She got off on Two and I stood there in the empty elevator feeling the tug of gravity and a profound sense of sadness and not knowing which I understood less.

Session Fourteen

I didn't get back to my office until the following Wednesday morning. As soon as I walked in I detected the fragrance of pine trees, and I knew that Giselle had been there. Perched on top of the great mound of work piled on my desk was a note neatly handwritten in green ink:

> There was only one disappearance in 1985 that occurred in a town where a slaughterhouse is located. It was in South Carolina, and the missing person was a woman. Am spending this week in the library going over newspaper files for that year.
> See you later.
>
> Love,
> G.

While I was reading it I got a call from Charlie Flynn, the astronomer, my son-in-law's colleague at Princeton.

After he had returned from his vacation in Canada, Steve had told him about the discrepancy between his and prot's account of the orbit of K-PAX around its double suns. He was very excited. The calculation, he said, had been done by one of his graduate students. Upon hearing of prot's version he had recalculated the orbital pattern himself, and it turned out to be exactly as prot had described it: a pendulum-like back-and-forth motion, not a figure eight. All the star charts prot had drawn up were quite accurate as well. I thought nothing would faze me anymore where prot was concerned, but what this trained scientist said next shocked me as much as it fascinated him. He said, "Savants are basically people with prodigious memories, aren't they? This is different. There is no way anyone could guess that orbital pattern or intuit it. I know this sounds crazy, but I can't see how he could have come up with this information unless he had actually been there!" This from a man who is as sane as you or I. "Could I talk to your patient?" he went on. "There are several thousand questions I'd like to ask him!"

I rejected this idea, of course, for a number of reasons. I suggested, however, that he send me a list of fifty of the key questions he wanted to ask prot, and assured him that I would be happy to present them to him. "But make it fast," I said. "He claims he's leaving on August seventeenth."

"Can you get him to stay longer?"

"I doubt it."

"Can you try?"

"I'm trying my damnedest," I assured him.

THE rest of the morning was taken up with meetings and an interview with the third candidate for the directorship. I'm afraid I didn't give him the attention he deserved. He seemed capable enough, and had published some excellent work. His specialty was Tourette's syndrome, and he suffered from a mild form of the affliction himself—nervous tics, primarily, though he occasionally called me "a piece of shit." But I was too preoccupied with trying to formulate a way to get through to Robert to listen. At last an idea came to mind, and unforgivably I sat up and blurted, "Ah!" Thinking I was referring to his discourse, our guest was quite pleased by my outburst and went on and on with an even greater display of facial twitching and name calling than before. I paid no attention to him—I was absorbed by the question: *Could the host personality be hypnotized while the secondary alter is already under hypnosis?*

"OKAY, ready for anything," prot said after finishing a huge mixed fruit salad and blowing his nose on his napkin. He tossed it into the bowl and looked for the spot on the wall behind me. Knowing he would jump the gun, however, I had covered it up before he could throw himself into a trance.

"I'm not going to hypnotize you for a while."

"I told you it wouldn't work," he said, breaking into the all-too-familiar grin.

"I want to talk to you about Robert first."

The smile vanished. "How did you find out his name?"

"You told me."

"Under hypnosis?"

"Yes."

"Well, flatten my feet and call me daffy."

"What happened to his wife and child?"

Prot seemed confused, edgy. "I don't know."

"Oh, come on. He must have told you *that*."

"Wrong. He's never mentioned them since I found him by the river."

"Where are they now?"

"I have no idea."

Either prot was lying, which I strongly doubted, or he was genuinely unaware of Robert's activities when he wasn't around. If that were the case the latter could try almost anything—possibly even suicide—without prot's knowledge. I was more certain than ever that I had to get through to Robert as soon as possible. In fact, there wasn't a moment to lose. I stood up and removed the tape from the spot on the wall behind me. Prot fell into his usual deep trance immediately.

"We are now in the present. Prot? Do you understand?"

"Yes. It is not a difficult concept."

"Good. Is Robert there with you?"

"Yes."

"May I speak to him, please?"

"You may, but he probably won't speak to *you*."

"Please let him come forward."

Silence. Robert slouched down in the chair, his chin on his chest.

"Robert?"

No response.

"Robert, this is Doctor Brewer. Please open your eyes."

There was a barely detectable shift in his position.

"Robert, listen to me. I am not just *trying* to help you. I *know* I can help you. Please trust me. Open your eyes!"

His eyes flickered open for a moment, then closed again. After a few seconds he blinked several times, as if vacillating, and finally they stayed open. It was little more than a vacant stare, but it was something.

"Robert! Can you hear me?" After what seemed like an eternity I detected a hint of a nod. "Good. Now I want you to focus your attention on the spot on the wall behind me."

The lifeless eyes, gazing emptily at the edge of my desk, shifted upward slightly.

"A little higher. Raise your eyes a little higher!"

Slowly his focus lifted, an inch at a time, slowly, slowly. Ignoring my presence completely, he lifted his gaze to the wall behind my shoulder. His mouth had fallen open.

"Good. Now, listen carefully. I'm going to count forward from six to ten. As I count, your eyelids will become heavy and you will grow increasingly sleepy. By the time I get to ten, you will be in a deep trance. But you will be able to hear and understand everything I say. Now this is very important: When I clap my hands, you will wake up. Do you understand?"

A tiny, but definite, nod.

"Good. We'll begin now. Six . . ." I watched carefully as his eyelids began to droop. ". . . and ten. Robert, can you hear me?"

No response.

"Robert?"

Unintelligible.

"Please speak louder."

A feeble "Yes," more like a gurgle. But someone was there! At that moment I was very, very glad I had chosen to become a psychiatrist.

"Good. Now listen to me. We are going to travel back in time. Imagine the pages of a calendar turning rapidly backward. It is now August eighth, 1989, exactly one year ago. Now it is 1988; now 1987, now 1986. Now, Robert, it is August eighth, 1985, at noon. Where are you?"

He remained motionless for several minutes before murmuring, "I am at work." He sounded tired, but his voice was clear, though slightly higher-pitched than prot's.

"What are you doing there?"

"I am eating my lunch."

"What are you eating?"

182

"I have a Dutch loaf sandwich with Miracle Whip and pickles, a peanut butter sandwich with Concord grape jelly, potato chips, a banana, two sugar cookies, and a thermos of coffee."

"Where did you get your lunch?"

"From my lunch bucket."

"Your wife made it for you?"

"Yes."

"All right. We are going to move forward eight days and two hours. It is 2:00 P.M. on August sixteenth, 1985. Where are you now?"

"At work."

"And what are you doing at this moment?"

"Knocking steers."

"All right. What do you see?"

"It is jerking around making noises. I bang it again. Now it is still." He wiped some imaginary perspiration from his forehead with the back of his hand.

"And it moves down the line where someone else cuts the throat, is that right?"

"Yes, after it is shackled."

"Then what?"

"Then another one comes along. Then another, then another, then another—"

"All right. Now it is just after quitting time. You are on your way home from work. You are home now, getting out of your car. You are going up the walk—"

His eyes widened. "Someone is there!"

"Who? Who is there?"

Agitated: "I don't know. He is coming out of my house. I have never seen him before. He is going back into the house! Something is wrong! I am running after him, chasing him into the house. Oh, God, No! NOOOO-

183

OOOOOOOOOO!" He began to wail, his head wagging back and forth, his eyes as big as the moon. Then he looked toward me and his demeanor changed radically—an utter transmogrification. He looked as though he wanted to kill me.

"Robert!" I yelled, clapping my hands together as loudly as I could. "Wake up! Wake up!" His eyes closed immediately, thank God, and an exhausted Robert sat slumped in the chair in front of me.

"Robert?"

No response.

"Robert?"

Still nothing.

"Robert, it's all right. It's over now. Everything is all right. Can you hear me?"

No response.

"Robert, I'd like to talk to prot now."

No response.

"Please let me speak to prot. Prot? Are you there?" I was beginning to feel a mounting trepidation. Had I been too aggressive? What if—?

Finally his head lifted and his eyes blinked open. "Now you've done it."

"Prot? Is that you?"

"You had to do it, didn't you? Just when he started to trust you, you went for the jugular."

"Prot, I would like to have taken it more slowly, but you are planning to leave us on the seventeenth. Our time is almost up!"

"I told you—I have no choice in the matter. If we don't leave then we'll never be able to get back."

"You and Robert?"

184

"Yes. Except . . ."

"Except what?"

"Except he's gone now."

"Gone? Gone where?"

"I don't know."

"Look hard, prot. He must be there with you somewhere."

"Not anymore. He's not here anymore. You have driven him away."

"Okay, I'm going to count back from five to one now. As the numbers decrease you will begin to wake up. On the count of one you will be fully alert and feeling fine. Ready? Five . . . one."

"Hello."

"How do you feel?"

"I think I had too much fruit. Have you got any antacid?"

"Betty will get some for you later. Right now we need to talk."

"What else have we been doing for the past three months?"

"Where is your friend Robert right now?"

"No idea, coach."

"But you told me earlier he was in 'a safe place.' "

"He was then, but he's gone now."

"But you could contact him if you wanted to."

"Maybe. Maybe not."

"All right. Let's review a few things. When you came to Earth five years ago, Robert was trying to drown himself. Remember?"

"How could I forget?"

"But you don't know why?"

"I think it's because he didn't want to live anymore."

"I mean, you have no idea what caused him to be so upset? So desperate?"

"Haven't we been over this?"

"I think he may have killed someone."

"Robert? Nah. He loses his temper sometimes, but—"

"I don't think he meant to kill anyone. I think he caught someone in his house. Someone who may have harmed his wife and daughter in some way. He is only human, prot. He reacted without thinking."

"I'm not surprised."

"Prot, listen to me. You helped Howie to cure Ernie of his phobia. I'm going to ask you to do something for me. I'm going to ask you to cure Robert. Let's call it a 'task.' I'm assigning you the task of curing Robert. Do you accept the assignment?"

"Sorry, I can't."

"Why the hell not?"

"Ernie wanted to get well. Robert doesn't. He just wants to be left alone. He doesn't even want to talk to *me* anymore."

"You've helped a lot of the patients in Ward Two. I have confidence that if you really put your mind to it you could help Robert, too. Will you please try?"

"Anything you sigh, mite. But don't hold your breath."

"Good. I think that's enough work for today. We both need a little time to reflect on this. But I'd like to schedule an extra session with you on Sunday. It's the only day I have. Would you be willing to come back for a Sunday session?"

"What about your promise to your wife?"

"What promise?"

"That you would take sundays off, no matter what. Except that you cheat and bring work home."

"How did you know about that?"

"Everyone knows about that."

"She's going to the Adirondacks with Chip for a couple of weeks, if it's any of your business."

"In that case, I would be delighted to accept your kind invitation."

"Thank you."

"Don't mention it. Is that all?"

"For now."

"Toodle-oo."

I switched off the tape recorder and slumped down in my chair, as drained of emotion as Robert must have been. I felt very bad about this particular session. I had rushed things, taken a big chance and failed, perhaps irreversibly. One thing you learn in psychiatry: Treating a psychotic patient is like singing opera—it seems easy enough to the spectator, but it takes a tremendous amount of work and there are no short-cuts.

On the other hand, perhaps I had not been bold *enough*. Perhaps I should have forced him to tell me exactly what he saw that August afternoon when he got home from work. I knew now that he had stumbled onto something terrible, and I suspected what it might have been. But this hadn't helped my patient one iota and, indeed, may have made things worse. Moreover, I had missed a golden opportunity to ask him his last name! The position of director, free of patient responsibility, suddenly seemed a very attractive idea.

J U S T before she left for the weekend Betty told me she had given up on the idea of motherhood. I said I was sorry it hadn't worked out for her. She replied that I needn't be, and pointed out that there were already more than five billion human beings on Earth, and maybe that was enough. She had obviously been talking with prot.

As we were walking down the corridor she suggested that I stop in and see Maria. She wouldn't tell me why. I glanced at my watch. I had about five minutes before I had to leave for a fund-raising dinner at the Plaza. Sensing my impatience, she patted my arm. "It'll be worth it."

I found Maria in the quiet room talking with Ernie and Russell. She seemed uncharacteristically happy, so I thought it was a new alter I had encountered. But it was Maria herself! Although the answer was obvious, I asked her how she was feeling.

"Oh, Doctor Brewer, I have never felt so good. All the others are with me on this. I know it."

"With you on what? What happened?"

"I've decided to become a nun! Isn't it wonderful?" I found myself smiling broadly. The idea was so simple I wondered why I hadn't thought of it myself. Perhaps because it was *too* simple. Perhaps we psychiatrists have a tendency to make things more complicated than they really are. In any case, there she was, nearly beside herself with joy.

I was beginning to feel better myself. "What made you decide to do that?"

"Ernie showed me how important it was to forgive my father and my brothers for what they did. After that, everything was different."

I congratulated Ernie on his help. "It wasn't my idea," he said. "It was prot's."

Russell seemed unsure about what to make of all this. "It is only by Beelzebub, the prince of demons, that this man casteth out demons," he mumbled uncertainly, and shuffled away.

188

Maria watched him leave. "Of course it's only for a little while."

"Why only for a while?" I asked her.

"When prot comes back he's going to take me with him!"

Session Fifteen

KAREN and Shasta left for the Adirondacks late Sunday morning. Shaz was as joyous as Maria had been two days earlier—she knew exactly where she was going. I promised to join them in a week or so.

Chip, busy with his lifeguard duties, had decided not to spend his time with his fuddy-duddy parents after all, but moved in with a friend whose father and mother were also on vacation. With no one in the house but me, I decided to check into the guest room at the hospital for the duration.

I made it to my office that afternoon just in time for my session with prot. I was already sweating profusely. It was a very hot day and the air conditioning system wasn't working. It didn't seem to bother prot, who had stripped down to his polka-dot boxer shorts. "Just like home," he chirped. I turned on the little electric fan I keep for such emergencies, and we got on with it.

Unfortunately, I cannot relate the contents of that interview verbatim because of a malfunction in my tape recorder, which I did not discover until the session was over. What follows is a summary based on the sweaty notes I took at the time.

While he devoured a prodigious number of cherries and nectarines, I handed him the list of questions Charlie Flynn had faxed to me for prot's attention. I had perused the fifty undoubtedly well-chosen queries myself, but they were quite technical and I wasn't much interested at that point what his responses, if any, would be. (I could have answered the one about light travel—it's done with mirrors.) Prot merely smiled and stuffed them under the elastic band of his shorts alongside the ever-present notebook.

At the merest suggestion he found the spot on the wall behind me and immediately fell into his usual deep trance. I wasted no time in dismissing prot and asked to speak with Robert. His countenance dropped at once, he slouched down to the point where it almost seemed he would fall out of his chair, and that's where he stayed for the remainder of the hour. Nothing I brought up—his father's death, his relationship with his friends (the bully and his victim), his employment at the slaughterhouse, the whereabouts of his wife and daughter—elicited the slightest hint of a reaction. I carefully introduced the subject of the lawn sprinkler, but even that evoked no response whatsoever. It was as if Robert had prepared himself for this confrontation, and nothing I could say was going to shock him out of his virtually catatonic state. I tried every professional maneuver and amateurish trick I could think of, including lying to him about what prot had told me about his life, and ending up by calling him a shameless coward. All to no avail.

But something had occurred to me when I brought up the subject of his family and friends. I recalled prot, and was greatly relieved when he finally showed up. I asked him whether there was anyone, if not me, Robert would be willing to speak to. After a minute or two he said, "He might be willing to talk to his mother."

I implored him to help me find her. To give me a name or an address. He said, again after a few moments of silence, "Her name is beatrice. That's all I can tell you."

Before I woke him up I tried one more blind shot. "What is the connection between a lawn sprinkler and what happened to Robert on August seventeenth, 1985?" But he seemed genuinely befuddled by this reference (as had the un-hypnotized prot), and there was no sign of the panic elicited by my wife's turning on ours at the Fourth of July picnic in our back yard. Utterly frustrated, I brought him back to reality, called in our trusty orderlies, and reluctantly sent him back to Ward Two.

THE next day Giselle reported that she had spent most of the previous week, along with her friend, at the Research Library tracking down and reading articles from small-town (those with slaughterhouses) newspapers for the summer of 1985, so far without success, though there were still two large trays of microfilm to go. I passed on the meager information I had managed to obtain. She doubted that Robert's mother's name would be of much help, but it led her to another idea. "What if we also search the files for 1963, when his father died? If there's an obituary for a man whose wife's name was Beatrice and who had a six-year-old son named Robert . . . Damn! Why didn't I think of that before?"

"At this point," I agreed, "anything's worth a try."

CHUCK had collected all the "Why I Want to Go to K-PAX" essays over the weekend. Most of the patients had submitted one, and a fair number of the support staff as well, including Jensen and Kowalski. As it happened, this was the time for Bess's semiannual interview. During that encounter I asked her why she hadn't entered the contest.

"You know why, Doctor," she replied.

"I would rather you tell me."

"They wouldn't want somebody like me."

"Why not?"

"I don't deserve to go."

"What makes you think that?"

"I eat too much."

"Now, Bess, everyone here eats more than you do."

"I don't deserve to eat."

"Everyone has to eat."

"I don't like to eat when there are so many that don't have anything. Every time I try to eat I see a lot of hungry faces pressed up against the window, just watching me eat, waiting for something to fall on the floor, and when it does they can't get in to pick it up. All they can do is wait for somebody to take out the garbage. I can't eat when I see all those hungry faces."

"There's nobody at the window, Bess."

"Oh, they're there all right. You just don't see them."

"You can't help them if you're starving, too."

"I don't deserve to eat."

We had been around this circle many times before. Bess's battle with reality had not responded well to treatment. Her periods of depression had been barely managed with ECT and Clozaril and, more recently, by the presence of La Belle Chatte. She perked up a little when I told her that Betty was planning to bring in another half dozen cats from the animal shelter. Until further progress was made in the treatment of paranoid schizophrenia and psychotic depression there wasn't much more we could do for her. I almost wished she had been among those who had submitted an application for passage to K-PAX.

The kitten, incidentally, was doing fine with Ed. The only problem was that everyone in the psychopathic ward now wanted an animal. One patient demanded we get him a horse!

O N Tuesday, August fourteenth, prot called everyone to the lounge. It was generally assumed he was going to make some kind of farewell speech and announce the results of the essay contest Chuck had organized. When all of Wards One and Two and some of Three and Four, including Whacky and Ed and La Belle, had gathered around, along with most of the professional and support staff, prot disappeared for a minute and came back with—a violin! He handed it to Howie and said, "Play something."

Howie froze. "I can't remember how," he said. "I've forgotten everything."

"It will come back," prot assured him.

Howie looked at the violin for a long time. Finally he placed it under his chin, ran the bow across the strings, reached for the rosin that prot had thoughtfully provided, and immediately broke into a Fritz Kreisler étude. He stopped a few times, but *didn't* start over and try to get it perfect. Grinning like a monkey he went right into a Mozart sonata. He played it pretty badly, but, after the last note had faded into perfect silence, the room broke into thunderous applause. It had been the greatest performance of his career.

With one or two exceptions the patients were in a fine mood all that day. I suppose everyone was on his best behavior so as not to jeopardize his chances for an all-expense-paid trip to paradise. But prot made no speech, no decision on a space companion. Apparently he was still hoping to talk Robert into going with him.

Oddly, no one seemed particularly disappointed. Everyone knew it was only a matter of days—hours—until "departure" time, and his selection would have to be made by then.

Session Sixteen

D ESPITE facing what should have been a very long and presumably exhausting journey prot seemed his usual relaxed self. He marched right into my examining room, looked around for his basket of fruit. I switched on my backup tape recorder and checked to see that it was working properly. "We'll have the fruit at the end of today's session, if you don't object."

"Oh. Very well. And the top o' the afternoon to ye."

"Sit down, sit down."

"Thankee kindly, sir."

"How's your report coming?"

"I'll have it finished by the time I leave."

"May I see it before you go?"

"When it's finished. But I doubt you'd be interested."

"Believe me, I would like to see it as soon as possible. And the questions for Dr. Flynn?"

"There are only so many hours in a day, gino, even for a K-PAXian."

"Are you still planning to return to your home planet on the seventeenth?"

"I must."

"That's only thirty-eight hours from now."

"You're very quick today, doctor."

"And Robert is going with you?"

"I don't know."

"Why not?"

"He's still not talking to me."

"And if he decides not to accompany you?"

"Then there would be room for someone else. You want to go?"

"I think I'd like that some day. Right now I've got a lot of things to do here."

"I thought you'd say that."

"Tell me—how did you know that Robert might want to go back with you when you arrived on Earth five years ago?"

"Just a hunch. I had a feeling he wished to depart this world."

"What would happen exactly if neither of you went back on that date?"

"Nothing. Except that if we didn't go back then, we never could."

"Would that be so terrible?"

"Would you want to stay here if you could go home to K-PAX?"

"Couldn't you just send a message that you're going to be delayed for a while?"

"It doesn't work that way. Owing to the nature of light . . . Well, it's a long story."

"There are plenty of reasons for you to stay."

"You're wasting your time," he said, yawning. I had been told that he hadn't slept for the last three days, preferring instead to work on his report.

The moment had come for my last desperate shot. I wondered whether Freud had ever tried this. "In that case, I wonder if you'd care to join me in a drink?"

"If that's your custom," he said with an enigmatic smile.

"Something fruity, I suppose?"

"Are you insinuating that I'm a fruit?"

"Not at all."

"Just kidding, doc. I'll have whatever you're having."

"Stay right there. Don't move." I retreated to my inner office, where Mrs. Trexler was waiting sardonically with a laboratory cart stocked with ice and liquor—Scotch, gin, vodka, rye—plus the usual accompaniments.

"I'll be right here if you need anything," she growled.

I thanked her and wheeled the cart into my examining room. "I think I'll have a little Scotch," I said, trying to appear calm. "I like a martini before dinner, but on special occasions like this one I prefer something else. Not that there are that many special occasions," I added quickly, as if I were applying for the directorship of the hospital. "And what about you?"

"Scotch is fine."

I poured two stiff ones on the rocks, and handed one to prot. "Bon voyage," I said, raising my glass. "To a safe trip home."

"Thank you," he said, lifting his own. "I'm looking forward to it." I had no idea how long it had been since his last drink, or if he had ever taken one at all, but he appeared to enjoy the first sip.

"To tell you the truth," I confessed, "K-PAX does sound like a beautiful place."

"I think you would like it there."

"You know, I've only been out of this *country* two or three times."

"You should see more of your own WORLD, too. It's an interesting PLANET." He took a deep slug, bared his teeth and swallowed, but his timing wasn't right and he choked and coughed for several seconds. While watching him try to get his breath I remembered the day my father taught me to drink wine. I hated the stuff, but I knew it signified the beginning of adulthood, so I held my nose and gulped it down. My timing wasn't right either, and I spewed some burgundy all over the living room carpet, which retains a ghostly stain to this day. I'm not sure he ever forgave me for that. . . .

"You don't hate your father," prot said.

"What?"

"You've always blamed your father for the inadequacies you perceive in yourself. In order to do that you had to hate him. But you never really hated him. You loved your father."

"I don't know who told you all of this, but you don't know what you're talking about."

He shrugged and was silent. After a few more swallows (he wasn't choking anymore) he persisted: "That's how you rationalized ignoring your children so you could have more time for your work. You told yourself you didn't want to make the same mistake as your father."

"I didn't ignore my children!"

"Then why do you not know that your son is a cocaine addict?"

"What? Which son?"

199

"The younger one. 'Chip,' you call him."

There *had* been certain signs—a distinct personality change, a constant shortage of funds—signs I chose to disregard until I found time to deal with them. Like most parents I didn't want to know that my son was a drug addict, and I was just putting off finding out the truth. But I certainly didn't want to learn about the problem from one of my patients. "Anything else you want to get off your chest?"

"Yes. Give your wife a break and stop singing in the shower."

"Why?"

"Because you can't carry a tune in a basket."

"I'll think about it. What else?"

"Russell has a malignancy in his colon."

"What? How do you know that?"

"I can smell it on his breath."

"Anything else?"

"That's all. For now."

We had a few more drinks in total silence, if you don't count the thoughts roaring through my head. This was interrupted, finally, by a tap on the door. I yelled, "Come in!" It was Giselle, back from the library.

Prot nodded to her and smiled warmly. She took his hand and kissed him on the cheek before slipping over and whispering in my ear, "It's Robert Porter. That's about all we know so far." Then she plopped down in the corner chair. I brought her a drink, which she gratefully accepted.

We chatted about inconsequential things for a while. Prot was having a fine time. After his fourth Scotch, when he was giggling at everything anyone said, I shouted, "Robert Porter! Can you hear me? We know who you are!"

Prot seemed taken aback, but he finally realized what I

was doing. "I tol' you an' tol' you," he snorted unhappily. "He ain' comin' out!"

"Ask him again!"

"I've tried. I've rilly rilly rilly tried. What else c'n I do?"

"You can stay!" Giselle cried.

He turned slowly to face her. "I can't," he said sadly. "It's now or never."

"Why?"

"As I a'ready 'splained to doctor bew—bew—doctor brewer, I am shed—shed—I am 'xpected. The window is op'n. I c'n *only* go back on august seventeenth. At 3:31 inna norming."

I let her go on. She couldn't do any worse than I had. "It's not so bad here, is it?" she pleaded.

Prot said nothing for a moment. I recognized the look on his face, that combination of amazement and disgust which meant he was trying to find words she could comprehend. Finally he said, "Yes, it is."

Giselle bowed her head.

I poured him another drink. It was time to play my last trump. "Prot, I want you to stay too."

"Why?"

"Because we need you here."

"Wha' for?"

"You think the Earth is a pretty bad place. You can help us make it better."

"How, f'r cryin' out loud?"

"Well, for example, there are a lot of people right here at the hospital you have helped tremendously. And there are many more beings you can help if you will stay. We on Earth have a lot of problems. All of us need you."

"You c'n help y'rself if you want to. You just hafta *want* to, thass all there is to it."

"Robert needs you. Your friend needs you."

"He doesn't need me. He doesn't even pay 'tention to me anymore."

"That's because he's an independent being with a mind of his own. But he would want you to stay, I know he would."

"How d'you know that?"

"Ask him!"

Prot looked puzzled. And tired. He closed his eyes. His glass tipped, allowing some of his drink to spill onto the carpet. After a long minute or two his eyes opened again. He appeared to be completely sober.

"What did he say?"

"He told me I've wasted enough time here. He wants me to go away and leave him alone."

"What will happen to him when you go? Have you thought about that?"

The Cheshire-cat grin: "That's up to you."

Giselle said, "Please, prot. *I* want you to stay, too." There were tears in her eyes.

"I can always come back."

"When?"

"Not long. About five of your years. It will seem like no time at all."

"Five *years*?" I blurted out in surprise. "Why so long? I thought you'd be back much sooner than that."

Prot gave me a look of profound sadness. "Owing to the nature of time . . ." he began, then: "There is a tradeoff for round trips. I would try to explain it to you, but I'm just too damn tired."

"Take me with you," Giselle pleaded.

He gave her a look of indescribable compassion. "I'm sorry. But next time . . ." She got up and hugged him.

"Prot," I said, emptying the bottle into his and Giselle's glasses. "What if I tell you there's no such place as K-PAX?"

"*Now* who's crazy?" he replied.

AFTER Jensen and Kowalski had taken prot back to his room, where he slept for a record five hours, Giselle told me what she had learned about Robert Porter. It wasn't much, but it explained why we hadn't been able to track him down earlier. After hundreds of hours of searching through old newspaper files, she and her friend at the library had found the obituary for Robert's father, Gerald Porter. From that she learned the name of their hometown, Guelph, Montana. Then she remembered something she had found much earlier about a murder/suicide that had taken place there in August of 1985, and she called the sheriff's office for the county in western Montana where the incident occurred. It turned out that the body of the suicide victim had never been found, but, owing to a clerical error, it had gone into the record as a drowning, rather than a missing person.

The man Robert killed had murdered his wife and daughter. Robert's mother had left town a few weeks after the tragedy to live with his sister in Alaska. The police didn't have the address. Giselle wanted to fly out to Montana to try to find out where she had gone, as well as to obtain pictures of the wife and daughter, records and documents, etc., in case I could use them to get through to Robert. I quickly approved a travel advance and guaranteed payment of all her expenses.

"I'd like to see him before I go," she said.

"He's probably sleeping."

"I just want to watch him for a few minutes."

I understood perfectly. I love to watch Karen sleep, too, her mouth open, her throat making little clicking noises.

"Don't let him leave until I find her," she pleaded as she went out.

I don't remember much about the rest of the afternoon and evening, although reports have it that I fell asleep during a committee meeting. I do know that I tossed and turned all night thinking about prot and about Chip and about my father. I felt trapped somewhere in the middle of time, waiting helplessly to repeat the mistakes of the past over and over again.

GISELLE called me from Guelph the next morning. One of Robert's sisters, she reported, was indeed living in Alaska, the other in Hawaii. Sarah's family didn't have either address, but she (Giselle) was working with a friend at Northwest Airlines to try to determine Robert's mother's destination when she left Montana. In addition, she had gathered photographs and other artifacts from his school years and those of his wife-to-be, thanks to Sarah's mother and the high school principal, who had spent most of the previous night going through the files with her. "Find his mother," I told her. "If you can, get her back here. But fax all the pictures and the other stuff now."

"They should already be on your desk."

I cancelled my interview with the Search Committee. Villers was not pleased—I was the last candidate for the directorship.

There were photos of Robert as a first-grader on up to his graduation picture, with the yearbook caption, "All great men are dead and I'm not feeling well," along with pictures of the wrestling teams and informal snapshots of soda fountains and pizza parlors. There were copies of his birth certificate, his immunization records, his grade transcripts (A's and B's), his citation for top marks in the county Latin contest, his diploma. There were also pictures of his sisters, who had graduated a few years before he had, and some information on them. And one of Sarah, a vivacious-looking blonde, leading a cheer at a basketball game. Finally, there was a photograph of the family standing in front of their new house in the country, all smiles. Judging by the age of the daughter, it must have been taken not long before the tragedy occurred. Mrs. Trexler brought me some coffee as I was gazing at it, and I showed it to her. "His wife and daughter," I said. "Somebody killed them." Without warning she burst into tears and ran from the room. I remember thinking that she must be more sympathetic toward the plights of the patients than I had thought. It wasn't until much later, while paging through her personnel file at the time of her retirement, that I learned her own daughter had been raped and murdered nearly forty years earlier.

I had lunch in Ward Two and laid down the law: no cats on the table. I sat across from Mrs. Archer, who was now taking all her meals in the dining room. She was flanked by prot and Chuck. Both were talking animatedly with her. She looked uncertainly from one to the other, then slowly lifted a spoonful of soup to her mouth. Suddenly, with a sound that could have been heard clear up in Ward Four, she slurped it in. Then she grabbed a handful of crackers and crumbled them vigorously into her bowl. She finished her meal with half the soup smeared all over her leathery face. "God," she said happily, "I've always wanted to do that."

"Next time," said Chuck, "belch!"

I thought I saw Bess smile a little, though it might have been wishful thinking on my part.

After the meal I returned to my office and asked Mrs. Trexler, who had regained her composure, to cancel all my appointments for the rest of the day. She mumbled something unintelligible about doctors, but agreed to do so. Then I went to find prot.

He was in the lounge, surrounded by all the patients and staff from Wards One and Two. Even Russell, who had experienced some sort of revelation after he understood that it was prot who had been responsible for Maria's deciding to become a nun, was there. When I came into the room he exclaimed, "The Teacher saith, My time is at hand." The corners of his mouth were caked with dried spittle.

"Not just yet, Russ," I said. "I need to talk to him first. Will everyone excuse us, please?" I calmed a chorus of protest by assuring them he would be back shortly.

On the way to his room I remarked, "Every one of them would do anything you asked them to. Why do you suppose that is?"

"Because I speak to them as equals. That's something you doctors seem to have a hard time with. I listen to them being to being."

"I listen to them!"

"You listen to them in a different way. You are not as concerned with them or their problems as you are with the papers and books you get out of it. Not to mention your salary, which is far too high."

He was wrong about that, but this wasn't the time to argue the matter. "You have a point," I said, "but my professional manner is necessary in order to help them."

"Let's see—if you believe that, then it must be true. Right?"

"That's exactly what I wanted to talk to you about."

We came to his room, the first time I had been there since his earlier disappearance. It was virtually bare except for his notebooks lying on the desk. "I've got some pictures and documents to show you," I said, spreading the file out on its surface, gently shoving aside his report. A few of the photographs I held back.

He looked over the pictures of himself, the birth and graduation certificates. "Where did you get these?"

"Giselle sent them to me. She found them in Guelph, Montana. Do you recognize the boy?"

"Yes. It is robert."

"No. It is you."

"Haven't we been over this before?"

"Yes, but at that time I didn't have anything to prove that you and Robert were the same person."

"And we aren't."

"How do you explain the fact that he looks so much like you?"

"Why is a soap bubble round?"

"No, I mean why does he look *exactly* like you?"

"He doesn't. He is thinner and fairer than I am. My eyes are light-sensitive and his aren't. We are different in a thousand ways, as you are different from your friend bill siegel."

"No. Robert is you. You are Robert. You are each part of the same being."

"You are wrong. I'm not even human. We are just close friends. Without me he'd be dead by now."

"And so would you. Whatever happens to him also happens to you. Do you understand what I am saying?"

"It is an interesting hypothesis." He wrote something in one of the notebooks.

"Look. Do you remember telling me that the universe

was going to expand and contract over and over again, forever?"

"Naturally."

"And you said later that if we were in the contraction phase time would run backward but we'd never know the difference because all we would have would be our memories of the past and a lack of knowledge of the future. Remember?"

"Of course."

"All right. It's the same here. From your perspective Robert is a separate individual. From my perspective the truth is perfectly logical and obvious. You and Robert are one and the same person."

"You misunderstand the reversal of time. Whether it is moving forward or backward, the *perception* is the same."

"So?"

"So it makes no difference whether you are correct or not."

"But you admit the possibility that I'm right?"

His smile widened markedly. "I'll admit that, if you'll admit it's possible that I came from K-PAX."

From his point of view there wasn't the slightest doubt about his background. Given several more months or years I might have been able to convince him otherwise. But there was no more time. I pulled the pictures of Sarah and Rebecca from my pocket. "Do you recognize them?"

He seemed shocked, but only for a moment. "It is his wife and daughter."

"And this one?"

"This is his mother and father."

"Giselle is trying to locate your mother and sister in Alaska. She is going to try to bring your mother here. Please, prot, don't leave until you talk to her."

He threw up his hands. "How many times must I tell you—I have to leave at 3:31 in the morning. *Nothing* can change that!"

"We are going to get her here as soon as we can."

Without looking at a clock he said, "Well, you have exactly twelve hours and eight minutes to do it in."

THAT evening Howie and Ernie threw prot a bon voyage party in the recreation room. There were many gifts for their "alien" friend, souvenirs of his visit to Earth: records, flowers, all kinds of fruits and vegetables. Mrs. Archer hammered out popular tunes on the piano accompanied by Howie on the violin. Cats were everywhere.

Chuck gave him a copy of *Gulliver's Travels*, which he had lifted from the bookshelves in the quiet room. I recalled prot's telling me that the (Earth) story he liked best was "The Emperor's New Clothes." His favorite movies, incidentally, were *The Day the Earth Stood Still*, *2001*, *ET*, *Starman*, and, of course, *Bambi*.

There was a great deal of hugging and kissing, but I detected a certain amount of tension as well. Everyone seemed nervous, excited. Finally, Chuck demanded to know which of them was going to get to go with him. With those crossed eyes I wasn't sure whether he was looking at me or prot. But prot answered, "It will be the one who goes to sleep first."

They all lined up immediately for a last tearful embrace, then dashed to their beds, leaving him alone to finish his report and prepare for his, and hopefully their, journey, each trying desperately to fall asleep with visions of yorts dancing in their heads.

I told him I had some things to do, but would come to say good-bye before he left. Then I retired to my office.

At about eleven o'clock Giselle called. She had found

Robert's sister's address in Alaska. Unfortunately, the woman had died the previous September, and his mother had gone on to live with the other sister in Hawaii. Giselle had tried to reach her, but without success. "It's too late to get her to New York in time," she said, "but if we find her, she might be able to call him."

"Make it fast," I told her.

For the next three hours I tried to work to the accompaniment of *Manon Lescaut* on my cassette player. In Act Three of that opera Manon and Des Grieux depart for the New World, and I understood at last why I love opera so much: Everything that human beings are capable of, all of life's joy and tragedy, all its emotion and experience, can be found there.

My father must have felt this, too. I can still see him lying on the living room sofa on a Saturday afternoon with his eyes closed, listening to the Metropolitan Opera broadcasts. Oh, how I wish he had lived and we had had a chance to talk about music and his grandchildren and all the other things that make life fun and interesting and good! I tried to envision a parallel universe in which he had not died and I had become an opera star, and I imagined singing some of his favorite arias for him while Mother brought out a big Sunday dinner for us to eat.

I suppose I must have dozed off. I dreamed I was in an unfamiliar place where the cloudless purple sky was full of moons and sailing birds, and the land a panoply of trees and tiny green flowers. At my feet stood a pair of huge beetles with humanoid eyes; a small brown snake—or was it a large worm?—slithered along behind them. In the distance I could see fields of red and yellow grains, could make out several small elephants and other roaming animals. A few chimpanzee-like creatures chased one another into and out of a nearby forest. I found myself crying, it was so lovely. But the most beautiful feature of all was the utter silence. There wasn't a hint of wind and it was so quiet I could hear the soft ringing of faraway bells. They seemed for all the world to be tolling, "gene, gene, gene. . . ."

I woke with a start. The clock was chiming 3:00. I hurried down to prot's room, where I found him at his desk writing furiously in his notebook, trying, presumably, to complete his report about Earth and its inhabitants before departing for K-PAX, letting it go until the last minute, it appeared, just as a human being might do. Beside him were his fruits, a stalk or two of broccoli, a jar of peanut butter, the essays and other souvenirs, all neatly packed in a small cardboard box. On the desk, next to his notebooks, were a pocket flashlight, a hand mirror, and the list of questions from Dr. Flynn. All six of the lower-ward cats were lying asleep on the bed.

I asked him whether he minded my looking over the answers he had formulated to those fifty queries. Without interrupting his writing he shook his head and waved me into the other chair.

Some of the questions, e.g., the one about nuclear energy, he had left unanswered, for reasons he had made clear in several of our sessions together. The last item was a request for a list of all the planets prot had visited around the universe, to which he had replied, "See Appendix," which tallied the complete list of sixty-four. This inventory included a brief description of those bodies and their inhabitants, as well as a series of star charts. It was not everything Professor Flynn and his colleagues, including Steve, had hoped for, but enough to keep them busy for some time, no doubt.

At around 3:10 he threw down his pencil, yawned, and stretched noisily as if he had just finished a routine piece of work.

"May I see it?"

"Why not? But if you want to *read* it you'd better make a copy right away—it's the only one I've got." I called one of the night nurses to take it upstairs, admonishing him to get some help and to use all the copiers that were operational. He hurried off, clutching the little notebooks as though they were so many eggs. The possibility of stalling the process occurred to me at that point, but it might well have made matters even worse and I quickly rejected the idea.

I had a feeling the report would be a rather uncomplimentary account of prot's "visit" to Earth, and I asked him, "Is there anything about our planet that you liked? Besides our fruits, I mean."

"Sure," he said, with an all-too-familiar grin. "Everything but the people. With one or two exceptions, of course."

There didn't seem to be much left to say. I thanked my amazing friend for the many interesting discussions and for his success with some of the other patients. In return, he thanked me for "all the wonderful produce," and presented me with the gossamer thread.

I pretended to take it. "I'm sorry to see you go," I said, shaking his brawny hand, though I wanted to hug him. "I owe you a lot, too."

"Thank you. I will miss this place. It has great potential." At the time I thought he was referring to the hospital, but of course he meant the Earth.

The nurse came running back with the copy a few minutes before it was time for prot to leave. I returned the original notebooks, a little jumbled but intact, to prot.

212

"Just in the nick of time," he said. "But now you'll have to leave the room. Any being within a few feet will be swept along with me. Better take them with you, too," he said, indicating the cats.

I decided to humor him. Well, why not? There wasn't a damn thing I could do about it anyway. I rousted the cats from his bed. One by one they brushed against his leg and streaked for various other warm places. "Good-bye, Sojourner Porter," I said. "Don't get knocked over by any aps."

"Not good-bye. Just *auf wiedersehen*. I'll be back before you know it." He pointed toward the sky. "After all, K-PAX isn't so far away, really."

I stepped out of the room, but left the door open. I had already notified the infirmary staff to stand by, to be prepared for anything. I could see Dr. Chakraborty down the corridor with an emergency cart containing a respirator and all the rest. There were only a couple of minutes to go.

The last I saw of prot he was sitting at his desk tapping his report into a neater stack, checking his flashlight. He placed his box of fruit and other souvenirs on his lap, picked up the little mirror and gazed into it. Then he transferred the flashlight to his shoulder. At that moment one of the security guards came puffing up to tell me that I had an urgent long-distance call. It was Robert's mother! At exactly the same instant, Chuck came running down the hall with his worn little suitcase, demanding to be "taken aboard." Even with all this commotion I couldn't have taken my eyes off prot for more than a couple of seconds. But when I turned to tell him about the phone call, he was already gone!

We all raced into the room. The only trace of him left behind were his dark glasses lying on a scribbled message. "I won't be needing these for a while," the note said. "Please keep them for me."

Acting on my earlier hunch that prot had hidden out in the storage tunnel during the few days he had allegedly gone to Canada, Greenland, and Iceland, we rushed to that area. The door was locked, and the security guard had some difficulty finding the right key. We waited patiently—I was confident we would find prot there—until he finally got the heavy door open and found the light switch. There was enough dusty old equipment to start our own museum, but there was no sign of prot. Nor was he hiding in the surgical theater or the seminar room, or anywhere else we thought he might have tried to conceal himself. It didn't occur to any of us to check the rooms of the other patients.

O N E of the nurses found him a few hours later, lying unconscious and in the fetal position on the floor of Bess's room. He was little more than alive. His eyes were barely dilatable, his muscles like steel rods. I recognized the symptoms immediately—there were two other patients exactly like him in Ward 3B: he was in a deep catatonic state. Prot was gone; Robert had stayed behind. I had rather expected something like this. What I failed to foresee, however, was that later the same morning Bess would also be reported missing.

G I S E L L E had the report translated by a cryptographer she knew, who used as a basis for this the pax-o version of *Hamlet* that prot had done for me earlier. Titled "Preliminary observations on B-TIK (RX 4987165.233)," it was primarily a detailed natural history of the Earth, especially of the recent changes thereon, which he attributed to man's "cancerous" population growth, his "mindless" consumption of its natural resources, and his "catastrophic" elevation of himself to superiority over all the other species who cohabit our planet. All of this is consistent with his use of capitals for the Earth and other planets, and lower case for individual beings.

There were also some suggestions as to how we might "treat" our social "illnesses": the elimination of religion, capital, nationalism, the family as the basic social and educational unit—all the things he imagined were fundamentally wrong with us and, paradoxically, the things most of us hold dear. Without these "adjustments," he wrote, the "prognosis" was not good. Indeed, he gave us only another decade to make the "necessary" changes. Otherwise, he concluded, "human life on the PLANET EARTH will not survive another century." His last four words were somewhat more encouraging, however. They were: *Oho minny blup kelsur*—"They are yet children."

Epilogue

ROBERT'S mother arrived with Giselle the day after prot's departure and stayed through the weekend, but there was no indication whatever of cognizance on Robert's part. She was a lovely woman, a bit confused, of course, about what had happened to her son—from the beginning she had been completely unaware of prot's existence—as were we all. I told her there was no need for her to stay longer, and promised to let her know of any change in his condition. I dropped her at Newark Airport before heading for the Adirondacks with Chip, who tearfully admitted his cocaine problem when I confronted him with it, to join Karen and Bill and his wife and daughter.

THAT was nearly five years ago. How I wish I could tell you that Robert sat up one fine day during that time and said, "I'm hungry—got any fruit?" But, despite our best efforts and constant attention, he remains to this day in a deep catatonic state. Like most catatonics he probably hears every word we say, but refuses, or is unable, to respond. Perhaps with patience and kindness on our part he will recover, in time, from this tragic condition. Stranger things have happened. I have known patients who have returned to us after twenty years of "sleep." In the meantime, we can do little more than wait.

Giselle visits him almost every week, and we usually have lunch and talk about our lives. She is currently researching a book about the deplorable infant mortality rate in America. Her article on mental illness featuring prot and some of the other patients appeared in a special health-oriented issue of *Conundrum*. As a result of that piece we have received thousands of letters from people asking for more information about K-PAX, many of them wanting to know how they can get there. And a Hollywood producer has requested authorization to do the story of Robert's life. I don't know whether anything will come of that, but, thanks to Giselle's tireless efforts, the information we received from Robert's mother, the hours of conversations I had with prot, and the cooperation of the authorities in Montana, we now have a reasonably clear picture of what happened on that terrible afternoon of August sixteenth through the early morning hours of August seventeenth, 1985. First, some biographical details.

Robert Porter was born in Guelph, Montana in 1957, the son of a slaughterhouse worker. Shortly after Robert's birth his father became disabled when a convulsing steer became unshackled and fell on top of him. In terrible pain for the rest of his life, unable even to tolerate bright light, he spent many of his waking hours with his young son, an energetic, happy boy who liked books and puzzles and animals. He never recovered from his injuries and succumbed when Robert was six years old.

His father had often speculated about the possibility of

remarkable life forms living among the stars in the sky and Robert called into being a new friend from a faraway planet where people didn't die so readily. For the next several years Robert suffered brief bouts of depression, at which times he usually called on "prot" for comfort and support, but he was never hospitalized or otherwise treated for it.

His mother took a job in the school cafeteria, which paid poorly, and the family, which also included two daughters, was barely able to make ends meet. Luxuries, like fresh fruit, were rare. Recreation took the form of hikes in the nearby woods and along the riverbank, and from these Robert gained a love and appreciation of the flora and fauna in forest and field and, indeed, of the forests and fields themselves.

He was a good student, always willing to pitch in and help others. In the fall of 1974, when he was a high school senior, Robert was presented a community service medal by the Guelph Rotary Club and, later that year, was elected captain of the varsity wrestling team. In the spring of 1975 he was awarded a scholarship to the state university to study field biology. But his girlfriend, Sarah Barnstable, became pregnant and Robert felt obligated to marry her and find work to support his new family. Ironically, the only job he could find was the one that had killed his father some twelve years earlier.

To add to their difficulties his wife was Catholic, and the resulting mixed marriage stigmatized the pair in the eyes of the residents of their small town, and they had few, if any, friends. This may have been a factor in their eventual decision to move to an isolated valley some miles outside of town.

One August afternoon in 1985, while Robert was stunning steers at the slaughterhouse, an intruder appeared at the Porter home. Mother and daughter were in the backyard cooling themselves under the lawn sprinkler. The man, a stranger who had been arrested and released numerous times

218

for a variety of crimes, including burglary, automobile theft, and child molestation, entered the house through the unlocked front door and watched Sarah and little Rebecca from the kitchen window until the girl came inside, probably to use the bathroom. It was then that the intruder accosted her. Hearing her daughter's screams the mother ran into the house, where both she and Rebecca were raped and murdered, though not before Sarah had severely scratched the intruder's face and nearly bitten off one of his ears.

Robert arrived home just as the man was coming out of the house. On seeing the husband and father of his victims the murderer ran back inside and out the rear door. Robert, undoubtedly realizing that something was terribly wrong, pursued him into the house, past the bloody bodies of his wife and daughter lying on the kitchen floor, and into the yard, where he caught up with their killer and, with the strength of a knocker and the skills of a trained wrestler, broke the man's neck. The sprinkler was still on, and remained so until the police shut it off the next day.

He then returned to the house, carried his wife and daughter to their bedrooms, covered them with blankets, washed and dried their swimsuits and put them away, mopped the bloody floor, and, after saying his final farewells, made his way to the nearby river, where he took off his clothes and jumped in, an apparent suicide attempt. Although his body was never found, the police concluded that he had died by drowning, the case was officially closed, and that is how the report went into the files.

He must have come ashore somewhere downstream, and from that point on he was no longer Robert, but "prot" (derived, presumably, from "Porter"), who wandered around the country for four and a half years before being picked up at the bus terminal in New York City. How he lived during that

219

period is a complete mystery, but I suspect he spent a lot of time in public libraries studying the geography and languages of the countries of the world, in lieu of actually visiting them. He probably slept there as well, though how he found food and clothing is anybody's guess.

But who was prot? And where did his bizarre idea of a world without government, without money, sex, or love come from? I submit that somehow this secondary personality was able to utilize areas or functions of the brain that the rest of us, except, perhaps, those afflicted with savant syndrome and certain other disorders, cannot. Given that ability, he must have spent much of his time developing his concept of an idyllic world where all the events that had accumulated to ruin his "friend" Robert's life on Earth could not happen. His vision of this utopian existence was so intense and so complete that, over the years, he imagined it down to the most minute detail, and in a language of his own creation. He even divined, somehow, the nature of its parent suns and the pattern of stars in the immediate vicinity, as well as those of several other planets he claimed to have visited (all the data he provided to Dr. Flynn and his associates have proven to be completely accurate).

His ideal world had to be one in which fathers don't die while their children are growing up. Prot solved this problem in two ways: A K-PAXian child rarely, if ever, sees his parents, or even knows who they are; at the same time, he is comforted by the knowledge that they will probably live to be a thousand.

It had to be a world without sex, or even love, those very human needs which can destroy promising young lives and rewarding careers. More importantly: Without love there can be no loss; without sex, no sex crimes. A world without even water, which might be used for sprinkling lawns!

220

There would be no currency of any kind in this idealized place, the need for which kept Robert out of college and forced him to spend his life destroying the creatures he loved, the same kind of work that had killed his father. As a corollary, no animals would be slaughtered or otherwise exploited on his idyllic planet.

His world would be one without God or any form of religion. Such beliefs had prevented Sarah from using birth-control devices, and then had stigmatized the "mixed marriage" in the eyes of the community. Without religion such difficulties could never arise. He may also have reasoned that what happened to Robert's wife and child, and his father as well, argued against the existence of God.

Finally, it had to be a world without schools, without countries, without governments or laws, all of which prot saw as doing little, if anything, to solve Robert's personal and social problems. None of the beings on his idealized planet were driven by the forces of ignorance and greed that, in his eyes, motivate human beings here on Earth.

I was puzzled at first by the question: Given his intolerable situation, why didn't Robert move with his pregnant wife to another part of the state or country, both for work and to escape the local bigotry? It was Giselle, a small-town girl herself, who reminded me that young people all over America, trapped by family ties and economic need, accept jobs they abhor and stay put for the rest of their lives, benumbing themselves on their off hours with beer and sports and soap operas.

But, despite this dreary prospect, it is possible that without the terrible events of August sixteenth through seventeenth, 1985, Robert and his wife and daughter might have enjoyed a reasonably happy life together. They certainly maintained strong family ties, both with one another and with their respective kin. But something did happen that day, something so devastating as to deal the final blow to Robert's psyche. He called on his alter ego one last time to help him deal with that unspeakable horror.

But this time prot was unable to heal the wounds, at least not anywhere on Earth, where rape and murder are of no more consequence than last night's television shows. In prot's mind the only place where one could deny such horrible crimes was the imaginary world he had created, where violence and death are not a way of life. A beautiful planet called K-PAX, where life is virtually free of pain and sorrow.

He spent the next five years trying to convince Robert to go there with him. Instead, devastated by grief and guilt, he retreated farther and farther into his own inner world, where even prot could not follow.

Why prot chose to "return" after exactly that period of time is unclear, particularly in view of the fact that his earlier visits were of much shorter duration. He may have realized that it would take considerable time to convince Robert to accompany him on his return, discovering finally that even the allotted five years wouldn't be enough. In any case prot did, indeed, depart this Earth (for all practical purposes) at the appointed time, and Robert is still with us in Ward 3B.

The staff and patients bring him fruit every day, and recently I brought in a Dalmatian puppy, who never leaves his side except to go outside, all of which he ignores. Hoping to stimulate his curiosity I tell him about all the new patients who have arrived over the past few years, including a brand-new Jesus Christ, whom Russell welcomed to Ward Two with, "I was you, once." Upon arrival all of them are told "the legend of K-PAX," which, along with the gossamer thread, brings smiles and hope and makes our job a little easier.

222

I also keep Robert up to date on the activities of Ernie and Howie, both of whom have been released and are leading highly productive lives, Ernie as a city-employed counselor for the homeless and Howie as a violinist with a New York–based chamber ensemble. The former, who until recently had never even kissed a woman for fear of contamination, is now engaged to be married. Both stop by MPI frequently to say hello to me and to Robert and the other patients, and Howie has performed for all of us on a number of occasions.

I've told him also about the wedding of Chuck and Mrs. Archer, who are happily sharing a room in Ward Two, not because they have to remain on that floor but because they choose to wait there for prot's return. Mrs. A, who is no longer called "the Duchess," looks much younger now, but I'm not sure whether it's because of the marriage or her giving up smoking. And about their "adopting" Maria, who has moved into a convent in Queens and is the happiest novice out there. She is totally free of headaches and insomnia, and none of her secondary identities has put in an appearance since she left the hospital.

Russell comes to pray with Robert daily. He has recovered completely from the surgical removal of a golf ball-size tumor in his colon, and so far there has been no sign of a recurrence.

Ed is doing well, too. There have been few violent episodes since prot's departure, all minor, and he has been transferred to Ward Two. He spends most of his time working in the flower gardens with La Belle Chatte.

All of them are waiting patiently for prot's return and the journey to K-PAX. Except for Whacky, who was recently reunited with his former fiancée when her husband was returned to prison for a lengthy stay. To my knowledge no one has told Robert about this, but perhaps, as prot undoubtedly would have, he just knows.

Perhaps he knows also that Mrs. Trexler is retired now. On my recommendation she has been seeing a psychoanalyst, and she tells me she is more at peace with herself than she has been in decades.

And that Betty McAllister became pregnant shortly before prot's departure, and is now the mother of triplets. Whether he had anything to do with this I can't say.

Of course I've also told him about my daughter Abby's new job, now that her kids are both in school, as editor of the Princeton-based *Animal Rights Forum*—prot would have liked that. And about Jenny, now a resident in internal medicine at Stanford, who plans to stay in California to work with AIDS patients in the San Francisco area. Her sexual preference and disinclination to produce grandchildren for us seems of microscopic importance compared to her dedication to helping others, and I am *very* proud of her. As I am of Freddy, who is appearing at the time of this writing in a Broadway musical. He lives in Greenwich Village with a beautiful young ballerina, and we've seen more of him in the last year than in all those he was an airline pilot combined.

But I'm proudest of all of Will (he doesn't want to be called "Chip" anymore), who has taken an interest in Bill and Eileen Siegel's daughter and calls her every day, much to the delight of the phone company. I have brought him to the hospital once or twice to show him what his old man does for a living, but when he met Giselle he decided he wanted to become a journalist. We are very close now, much more so than I was with Fred and the girls. For that, as with so many other things, I have prot to thank.

And of course I brag about my two grandsons, whom I get to see quite often—they are Shasta's favorite visitors—and who are the smartest and nicest kids I've ever known, with the possible exception of my own children. I'm proud of all of them.

I gave up the chairmanship to Klaus Villers. Despite his decree limiting the number of cats and dogs in the hospital to six per floor he is doing a far better job than I ever could have done. Now, unencumbered by all administrative duties and the talk show and as much of the other extraneous baggage as possible, I spend my working hours with my patients, and most of my free time with my family. I no longer sing at the hospital Christmas party, but my wife insists I continue to do so in the shower—she says she can't sleep otherwise. We both know I'm no Pavarotti, but I still think I sound a lot like him, and perhaps that's all that matters.

I wish I could tell Robert that Bess is all right, but she has never turned up, nor have the flashlight, mirror, box of souvenirs, etc., and we have no idea as to her whereabouts. If you see a young black woman with a pretty face, perhaps sitting on a park bench hugging herself and rocking, please help her if you can and let us know where she is.

And of course I dearly wish I could tell him where his friend prot has gone. I have played for him all the tapes of our sessions together, but there is no sign of comprehension on his part. I tell him to wait a little longer, that prot has promised to return. He hears all this, curled up on his cot like some chrysalis, without batting an eye. But perhaps he understands.

Will prot ever show up again? And how did he get from his room to Bess's under our very noses? Did this involve a kind of hypnosis on his part, or a similar ability we don't comprehend? We may never know. I fervently wish I could talk with him again, just for a little while, to ask him all the questions I never got the chance to ask before. I still think we could have learned a great deal more from prot and, perhaps, from all our patients. As the cures to many of our physical ailments may be waiting for us in the rain forests, so may the remedies for our social ills lie in the deepest recesses of our minds. Who knows what any of us could do if we were able to concentrate our thoughts with prot's degree of intensity, or if we simply had sufficient willpower? Could we, like him, see ultraviolet light if we wanted to badly enough? Or fly? Or outgrow our "childhood" and create a better world for all the inhabitants of the EARTH?

Perhaps he *will* return some day. By his own calculations he is due again soon. Giselle, who has been waiting patiently for him, has no doubts whatsoever, nor do any of the patients, nor most of the staff, who keep his dark glasses on the little dresser beside Robert's bed. And sometimes at night I go out and look up at the sky, toward the constellation Lyra, and I wonder. . . .

Acknowledgments

I am indebted to many individuals for their generous assistance, especially John Davis, M.D. for helpful discussions, and Rea Wilmshurst, C. A. Silber, Burton H. Brody, and Robert Brewer for critical readings of the manuscript. I also thank my editors Robert Wyatt and Iris Bass for their enormous skill and excellent advice, Ida Giragossian for suggesting I give them a try, Annette Johnson and Susan Abramowitz for their selfless efforts on my behalf, and my agent Maia Gregory for her wit and timely encouragement. And, as always, my wife Karen for her unflagging support of everything I have ever done.

Glossary

Å—angstrom (one ten-millionth of a millimeter)

ABREACTION—release of emotional tension brought about by recalling a repressed traumatic experience

ADRO—a K-PAXian grain

AFFECT—the emotional state or demeanor of a psychiatric patient

AGAPE—a star in the constellation Lyra

AIKIDO—a Japanese form of self-defense involving the throwing of one's opponent

ANAMNESIS—the recollection of past events

AP—a small, elephant-like being

APHASIA—inability to speak or understand spoken or written language

BALNOK—a large-leafed K-PAXian tree

BROT—an orf (a progenitor of the dremers)

c—the speed of light (186,000 miles per second)

CHOREA—a disease of the nervous system characterized by jerky, involuntary movements

CONFABULATION—the replacement of a gap in one's memory by something he or she believes to be true

COPROPHILIA—an obsession with feces

DELUSION—a false belief that is resistant to reason or confrontation with actual fact

DRAK—a red grain having a nutty flavor

DREMER—a K-PAXian of prot's species

ELECTROCONVULSIVE THERAPY (ECT)—electric shock treatment used in cases of acute depression

ELECTROENCEPHALOGRAM (EEG)—a graphical representation of the electrical activity of the brain

EM—a large, frog-like being who lives in trees

FLED—an undescribed K-PAXian being

FLOR—an inhabited planet in the constellation Leo

HOM—a K-PAXian insect

HYPNOSIS—an induced trance-like state producing vivid recollection along with an enhanced susceptibility to outside suggestion

JART—a measurement of distance (equivalent to 0.214 miles)

K-MON—one of the two suns of K-PAX (also called Agape)

KORM—a bird-like being

K-PAX—a planet in the constellation Lyra

KREE—a K-PAXian vegetable, much like a leek

K-RIL—one of the suns of K-PAX (also called Satori)

KROPIN—a truffle-like fungus

LIKA—a K-PAXian vegetable

MANO—a dremer

MOT—a skunk-like animal

MULTIPLE PERSONALITY DISORDER (MPD)—a psychological dysfunction characterized by the existence of two or more distinct personalities, any of which may be in command of the body at a given time

NARR—a doubter

NEUROLEPTIC DRUG—a compound having antipsychotic properties

NOLL—a planet in the constellation Leo

ORF—one of the progenitors of the dremers

PARANOIA—a mental disorder characterized by feelings of persecution

PATUSE—a K-PAXian musical instrument, similar to the bass viol

PROT—traveler

RELDO—a village on the planet K-PAX

RULI—a cow-like being

SATORI—a star in the constellation Lyra

SAVANT SYNDROME—a condition characterized by remarkable mental capabilities, usually associated with a low level of general intelligence

SWON—an em

TERSIPION—a planet in the constellation Taurus

THON—a K-PAXian grain

TOURETTE'S SYNDROME—a neurological disorder characterized by recurrent involuntary movements, and sometimes by grunts, barks, or epithets

TROD—a chimpanzee-like being

YORT—a sugar plum

K-PAX II
on a beam of light

For my wife's retirement fund

Sometimes one wonders whether the
dragons of primeval ages are really extinct.

—SIGMUND FREUD

Prologue

IN March 1995, I published an account of sixteen sessions with a psychiatric patient who believed he came (on a beam of light) from a planet called K-PAX. The patient, a thirty-three-year-old male Caucasian who called himself "prot" (rhymes with "goat"), was, in fact, a double personality whose alter ego, Robert Porter, had been devastated by a severe emotional trauma. The latter survived only by hiding behind his formidable "alien" friend. When prot "returned" to his home planet at precisely 3:31 A.M. on August 17, 1990, promising to reappear "in about five of your years," Robert was left behind in a state of intractable catatonia, kept alive by constant monitoring and attentive care.

Many of the patients in residence at the Manhattan Psychiatric Institute at the time of prot's tenure have since departed. These include Chuck and Mrs. Archer (all names have been changed to protect individual privacy), who only recently moved out to a retirement complex on Long Island, thanks to an annuity established by her late husband; and Ed, a psychopath who gunned down six people in a shopping mall in 1986, but who has evinced little tendency toward violent behavior since a chance encounter with prot in 1990. He now lives in a community care home with La Belle Chatte, a former feline resident of MPI. The only patient mentioned in *K-PAX* who was still with us in 1995 was Russell, our resident "chaplain," who had nowhere else to go.

Nevertheless, all our inmates, even the most recent arrivals, were well aware of prot's promised return, and as the miserably hot, rainless summer days oozed by, the tension began to mount among patients and staff alike. (Only Klaus Villers, our director, remained unperturbed. In his opinion, "He vill neffer be back. Robert Porter vill be here foreffer.")

No one anticipated prot's return more than I, however, not only because of a paternal fondness I had developed for him during the course of our sessions together, but also because I still hoped to get Robert out of the catatonic ward and, with prot's help, on the long road to recovery. But "about five years" from the time of prot's departure could have been anytime in 1995 or even later, so my wife and I went ahead with our usual plans to spend the middle two weeks of August at our Adirondack retreat.

That was a mistake. I was so preoccupied with the possibility of his imminent reappearance that I was very poor company for Karen and our friends, the Siegels, who tried every possible means to get my mind off my work. In hindsight I probably realized unconsciously that "five years" meant, to a mind as precise as prot's, sometime within minutes or hours of that exact interval. In fact, it was on Thursday, August 17, at 9:08 A.M., that I received a tearful call from Betty McAllister, our head nurse. "He's back!" was all she could say, and all she needed to.

"I'll be there this afternoon," I assured her. "Don't let him go anywhere!"

Karen (a psychiatric nurse herself) merely smiled, shook her head, and began to pack a lunch for my return trip to the city while I grabbed up unread reports and unfinished manuscripts and stuffed them into my briefcase.

The drive gave me a chance to reflect once more on the events of 1990, which I had reviewed only a few weeks earlier in preparation for his possible return. For the benefit of those who are not familiar with the history of the case, a brief summary follows:

Robert Porter was born and raised in Guelph, Montana. In 1975, when he was a high-school senior, he married a classmate, Sarah (Sally) Barnstable, who had become pregnant. The only job he could find to support his new wife and budding family was "knocking" steers in the local slaughterhouse, the same job that had killed his father some twelve years earlier.

One Saturday in August 1985, Robert arrived home from work to find a stranger coming out the front door. He chased the man through the house, past the bloody bodies of his wife and daughter, and into the backyard, where he broke the intruder's neck. Numb with grief, he attempted suicide by drowning in the nearby river. However, he washed ashore downstream, and from that moment forward was no longer Robert Porter, but "prot," a visitor from the idyllic planet K-PAX, where all the terrible things that had befallen his alter ego could never happen.

Indeed, his was a truly utopian world, where everyone lived happily for a thousand years without the tiresome need to work for a living, where there was little or no sickness, poverty, or injustice, nor, for that matter, schools, governments, or religions of any kind. The only drawback to life on K-PAX seemed to be that sexual activity was so unpleasant that it was resorted to only to maintain the (low) population levels.

After prot, a true savant who knew a great deal about astronomical matters, was brought to MPI (how he got to New York is still a mystery), it took me several weeks to understand that he was a secondary personality behind whom his primary psyche was hiding and, with the help of Giselle Griffin, a freelance reporter, to identify that tragic soul as Robert Porter. But this revelation came too late. When prot "departed" the Earth on August 17, 1990, Robert, no longer able to hide behind his alter ego, retreated deep into the recesses of his own shattered mind.

Nothing, including a series of electroconvulsive treatments and the most powerful antidepressant drugs, had been of any use in arousing Robert from his rigor. I even tried hypnosis, which had proven so effective in revealing what had happened to him in 1985. He ignored me, as he did everyone else. Thus, it was with mounting excitement that I arrived at the hospital that hot August afternoon and hurried to his room, where I somehow expected prot to be ready and eager to get on with whatever he had "come back" to do. Instead, he was weak and unsteady, though a bit impatient to be up and going, as anyone who had spent five years in the fetal position would be. He was asking (more of a croak) for his favorite fruits, of course, and blamed his feeble state on his recent "voyage." Betty had already seen that he had some liquid nourishment, including a little apple juice, and Dr. Chakraborty, our chief internist, had ordered a sedative to help him sleep, which he did almost immediately after I arrived.

It may seem odd to the reader that prot needed rest after five years of inactivity, but the fact is that the catatonic patient, unlike the comatose, is neither asleep nor unconscious but rigidly awake, like a living statue, afraid to move for fear of committing further "reprehensible" acts. It is this muscle rigidity (sometimes alternating with frenetic activity) that results in the utter exhaustion the patient feels when he is finally aroused.

I decided to let him recuperate for a few days before bombarding him with the list of questions I had been compiling for half a decade and getting on with his (Robert's) treatment and, I fervently hoped, successful recovery.

Session Seventeen

I SCHEDULED the first session (the seventeenth overall) with prot for 3:00 P.M., Monday, August 21, remembering to dim the lights for his sensitive eyes. Indeed, he
removed his dark glasses as soon as he was escorted into
my examining room by his old friend Roman Kowalski
(Gunnar Jensen had retired), and I was delighted to find
that he appeared to be fully recovered from five years of
rigid immobility, though technically it was Robert, not prot,
who had been catatonic throughout that period. He was,
in fact, much as I remembered him: smiling, energetic, alert.
The only notable changes were some weight loss and a hint
of premature graying at the temples—he was now thirty-
eight years old, though he claimed to be closer to four
hundred.

Betty had reported that he was already able to eat soft,
easily digestible foods, so I had a few overripe bananas on
hand, which he dug into with his usual relish, skins and all.

"The riper the better," he reminded me. "I like them pitchblack." He seemed utterly at home, as if our last session had been only yesterday.

I turned on the tape recorder. "How are you feeling, prot?" I asked him.

"A little tired, gene." Note to reader: prot capitalized the names of planets, stars, etc. Everything else, including human beings, was, to him, of little universal importance and therefore lowercase. "How about yourself?"

"Much better, now that you're back," I told him.

"Oh? Have you been ill?"

"Not exactly. Frustrated, mostly."

"Maybe you should see a psychiatrist."

"Actually, I've conferred with the best minds in the world about the source of my frustration."

"Does it have anything to do with your relationships with other humans?"

"In a way."

"I thought so."

"To be frank, it concerns you and Robert."

"Really? Have we done something wrong?"

"That's what I'd like to know. Maybe we could begin with your telling me where you've been for the past five years."

"Don't you remember, doc? I had to return to K-PAX for a while."

"And you took Bess with you?" Note: Bess was a psychotically depressed patient who "disappeared" in 1990 along with prot.

"I thought a change of scene would do her good."

"And where is she now?"

"Still on K-PAX."

"She didn't come back with you?"

"Nope."

"Why not?"

"Are you kidding? Would you want to come back to this place after you've seen pa-ree?" NB: the "place" he referred to was the Earth, not the hospital.

"Can you prove to me that Bess is on K-PAX?"

"Can you prove she is not?"

A familiar sinking feeling began to set in. "And how is she doing?"

"Like a fish in water. She laughs all the time now."

"And she didn't come back with you."

"Haven't we been over this?"

"What about all the other K-PAXians?"

"What about them?"

"Did anyone else come with you?"

"No. I wouldn't be surprised if no one ever did."

"Why not?"

"They read my report." He yawned. "Still, you never know. . . ."

"Tell me something: Why did you come to Earth in the first place, knowing from our radio and TV broadcasts that it was such an inhospitable planet?"

"I told you before: Robert needed me."

"That was in 1963?"

"By your calendar."

"Just in time for his father's funeral."

"In the nick."

"And you've made the trip several times since."

"Nine, to be exact."

"All right. Just for the record, then, you've been back on K-PAX for the past five years."

"Well, it's not that simple. There's the round trip, which—oh, I explained all that last time, didn't I? Let's

246

just say I stayed around for a little r and r after turning in my report to the libraries. Then I hurried on back here."

"Why were you in such a hurry?"

"Ah, I get it. You're asking me questions you already know the answers to." There it was: the familiar Cheshire-cat grin. "Just for the record—right?"

"In your case, I don't know many of the answers yet, believe me."

"Oh, I can believe that, all right. But to answer your question: I promised certain beings I would come back in five of your years, remember?"

"To take them to K-PAX with you."

"Yep."

"So what's the rush?"

"They all seemed to want to leave as soon as possible."

"And how many of them do you plan to take back with you when you go?"

Up to this point prot had been gazing about the room as if searching for familiar objects, pausing occasionally to study the watercolors on the various walls. Now he looked directly into my eyes and his smile vanished. "I came prepared this time, doctor b. I can take as many as a hundred beings with me when I return."

"What? A *hundred*?"

"Sorry. Not enough room for more."

The transcript indicates a long pause before I could think of a response. "Who do you think you'll be taking, for example?"

"Oh, I won't know that until the time comes."

I could feel my heart pounding as I asked, as casually as I could, "And when will that be?"

"Ah. That would be telling."

Now it was my turn to stare at him. "You mean you're not even going to tell me how long you'll be here?"

"I'm happy to see that your hearing is still unimpaired, narr" (pax-o for "gene," or "one who doubts").

"I'd really like to know that, prot. Can you give me some idea at least? Another five years? A month?"

"Sorry."

"Why the hell can't you tell me?"

"Because if you knew when I was leaving you'd watch me like a cat watches a bird in this carnivorous WORLD."

I had learned a long time ago that there was no use arguing with my "alien" friend. All I could do was make the best of whatever situation he sprang on me. "In that case, I'd like to schedule you for three weekly sessions. Every Monday, Wednesday, and Friday at three o'clock. Would that be all right with you?"

"Whatever you say, dahktah. For the time being I'm at your service."

"Good. There are a few more questions I'd like to ask you before you go back to your room."

He nodded sleepily.

"First, where did you land on this trip?"

"The pacific ocean."

"It was pointing toward K-PAX at the time?"

"Gino! You're finally getting it!"

"Tell me something. How do you breathe in outer space?"

He wagged his head. "I guess I spoke too soon. You still don't understand. The usual physical rules don't apply to light-travel."

"Well, what's it like? Are you awake? Do you feel anything?"

His fingertips came together and he frowned in concentration. "It's difficult to describe. Time seems to stand still. It's rather like a dream. . . ."

"And when you 'land'?"

"It's like waking up. Only you're somewhere else."

"It must be quite an awakening, finding yourself in the middle of an ocean. Can you swim?"

"Not a stroke. As soon as I bobbed up I got right out of there."

"How?"

He sighed. "I told you on my last visit, remember? It's done with mirrors. . . ."

"Oh. Right. And where else did you go before you came here?"

"Nowhere. Came straight home to mpi."

"Well, are you planning any excursions away from the hospital while you're here?"

"Not at the moment."

"If you do decide to take any side trips will you be sure to let me know?"

"Don't I always?"

"That reminds me—did Robert go with you on your trip to Labrador and Newfoundland the last time you were here?"

"Nope."

"Why not?"

"He didn't want to."

"We never saw him during the few days you were gone. Where was he?"

"No idea, coach. You'll have to ask *him*."

"Second: You're not planning any 'tasks' for the other patients (as he did for Howie, the violinist, five years ago), are you?"

"Gene, gene, gene. I just got here. I haven't even any of the patients yet."

"But you'll tell me if you come up with any such-plans?"

"Why not?"

"Good. And finally, are there any more little surprises you're not telling me about?"

"If I told you, they wouldn't be surprises, would they?"

I glared at him. "Prot—where is Robert?"

"Not far away."

"Have you spoken with him?"

"Of course."

"How is he feeling?"

"Like a sack of mot excrement." Note: A "mot" is a skunklike animal found on K-PAX.

"Did he say anything you'd like to tell me about?"

"He wanted to know what happened to the dog." He meant the dalmatian I had brought in, hoping to induce the catatonic Robert to respond to it.

"Tell him I took Oxeye home until he felt well enough to take care of him."

"Ah. Your famous carrot-and-stick routine."

"You could call it that. All right. This is my last question for today, but I want you to think about it before you answer."

He broke into another gigantic yawn.

"While you're here, will you help me make Robert feel better? Will you help him deal with his feelings of worthlessness and despair?"

"I'll do what I can. But you know how he is."

"Good. That's all anyone can do. Now—any objection to my trying hypnosis again during our next session?"

"You never give up, do you, doc?"

"We try not to." I stood up. "Thank you for coming in, prot. It's good to see you again." I went over and shook his hand. If he was still weak it didn't show in his handshake. "Shall I call Mr. Kowalski, or can you find your way back to your room?"

"It's not that difficult, gino."

"We'll move you back to Ward Two tomorrow."

"Good old ward two."

"See you Wednesday."

He threw me a backward wave as he shuffled out.

AFTER prot had gone I listened, with mixed feelings of excitement and trepidation, to the tape of this brief session. Given enough time I was sure I could help Robert overcome the barriers blocking his recovery. But how much time would we have? In 1990 we were faced with a deadline that forced me to take chances, to hurry things too much. Now I was confronted with an even worse dilemma: I hadn't the slightest idea how long prot would be around. The only clue I had was his passive response to my suggestion of thriceweekly sessions. If he were planning to leave within a few days he would undoubtedly have responded with, "They'd better be productive!" or some such remark. But I could be wrong about that, as I have been about so many things where prot was concerned.

In any case three weekly sessions were all I could manage. Though I wouldn't be teaching during the fall term, there were other unavoidable responsibilities, not the least of which were my other patients, all difficult and puzzling cases, each deserving of my best efforts. One of these was a young woman I call Frankie (after the old song "Frankie and Johnny Were Lovers"), who is not only unable to love another human being but doesn't even understand

251

the concept. Another was Bert, a loan officer at a bank, who spends all his waking hours searching for something he has lost, though he hasn't a clue as to what it is.

But back to prot. During the previous five years there had been ample opportunity to discuss his case with colleagues, both at MPI and around the world. There were no end of suggestions about how to deal with my problem patient. For example, one doctor from a former Soviet state assured me that Robert would be quickly cured by immersing him in ice water for several hours a day, a useless and inhumane practice that became obsolete decades ago. The consensus, however, was that hypnosis was still probably the best approach for Robert/prot, and I planned to begin essentially where I had left off in 1990. That is, to try to coax Robert out of his protective shell so I could help him deal with his devastating feelings about the tragic events of 1985.

In this effort I badly needed prot's help. Without it, I felt the chances for recovery were slim. Thus, I was faced with another quandary: If Robert were to get well, prot would have to "dissolve" into, and become part of, his personality. How willing would he be to play a role in Robert's treatment and recovery if it came about at the expense of his own existence?

ON Friday, the day after prot's return, I had called Giselle Griffin, the reporter who had been so instrumental in tracking down Robert's origins, to tell her he was back. She had come in regularly since prot's departure five years ago, ostensibly to check on Robert's progress, but secretly, I think, hoping to find that prot had returned, for she had fallen in love with him during the months she had spent at the hospital researching his story for *Conundrum* magazine. Of course she was often traveling far and wide, her most recent project (possibly anticipating prot's return) being an article on UFO's, which have been sighted almost everywhere. Nevertheless, she always left a beeper number and made it clear that she wanted to be informed of any change in Robert's condition.

She was very excited to hear about prot's reappearance and said she would be there "ASAP." I requested, however, that she not come to see him until he had recovered from his "journey" (i.e., the catatonia) and I had had a chance to speak with him, assuring her, perhaps erroneously, that there would be plenty of time to get reacquainted when he was stronger.

After the session with prot I phoned her again or, more accurately, left a message that she could call and set up an appointment to see him. After that I dictated a letter to Robert's mother in Hawaii, advising her that her son was no longer catatonic, but suggesting she also not visit until things were more certain. Then I toured the lower wards, intending to inform all the residents who were interested that prot was back, to pave the way for his return to Ward Two the following day.

The institute is structured so that the most seriously ill or dangerous patients occupy the top floors, while the least afflicted roam the first and second (Wards One and Two). Ward One, in fact, is primarily a temporary home for certain transient patients who come in periodically for a "tune-up," usually an adjustment in their medication, and for those who have made substantial progress toward recovery and are nearly ready for discharge. Prot was about to rejoin the inhabitants of Two, patients suffering serious psychoses ranging from manic depression to acute obsessive-compulsive disorder, but who are not a menace to the staff or each other.

I needn't have bothered. It was obvious from the moment I entered the ward that everyone already knew about prot's return. A psychiatric hospital is similar to a small town in some ways—news travels fast, and moods seem almost communicable. On this, the day before prot was to take up residence among them, the atmosphere was virtually electric with anticipation. Even some of the severe depressives greeted me relatively cheerfully, and a chronic schizophrenic, who hadn't uttered an intelligible sentence in months, inquired, I believe, after my health. And most of these patients, except for Russell and a few others, had never even met him.

GISELLE showed up at my office on Tuesday morning, sans appointment, as I expected. I had not seen her for several weeks, but I had not forgotten her piney fragrance, the doelike eyes.

She was dressed, as always, in an old shirt, faded jeans, and running shoes with no socks. Though pushing forty, she still looked like a kid—a sixteen-year-old girl with crow's-feet. Yet, there was something different about her. She was not so ebullient as she was five years ago. Gone was the coy smile I had once mistaken for coquettishness but which I had learned was a part of her truly ingenuous nature. Instead, she seemed uncharacteristically nervous. It occurred to me that she might be apprehensive about meeting prot again, distressed, I supposed, that he might have changed, or perhaps had even forgotten her.

"Don't worry," I reassured her. "He's exactly the same."

She nodded, but the distant look in those big brown eyes suggested she hadn't heard me.

"Tell me what you've been up to the last couple of months."

254

Her eyes suddenly came into focus. "Oh. I'm almost finished with the piece on UFO's. That's why I haven't been around for a while."

"Good. Are they real or—"

"Depends on who you talk to."

"What if you talked to yourself?"

"I'd say no. But there are plenty of sane, normal people who would disagree."

"Yet you believe that prot came from K-PAX."

"Yes, but he didn't come in a UFO."

"Ah." I waited, which seemed to make her nervous again.

"Dr. Brewer?"

I was pretty sure I knew what was coming. "Yes, Giselle?"

"I'd like to come back to the hospital for a while. I want to find out what he really knows."

"About UFO's?"

"About everything. I want to write a book about it."

"Giselle, you know a psychiatric hospital isn't grist for the public mill. The only reason I let you work here the last time is that you performed a valuable service for us."

"But I would be performing another valuable service this time, one that might benefit *everyone*." She curled up in the black vinyl chair across from my desk. "You're probably going to write another book about him as a patient, right? Mine will be different. I want to find out everything he knows, catalog it, check it all out, and see what the world can learn from his knowledge. Which you'll have to admit is pretty remarkable, whether you believe he comes from K-PAX or not." She bowed her head for a moment, then looked up at me with those pleading doe eyes. "I won't be in the way, I promise."

I wasn't convinced of that. But I wasn't so sure her proposal was such a bad idea, either. I knew she could be of considerable help in my dealings with prot (and later, perhaps, with Robert). "I'll tell you what. You can do it under two conditions."

She abruptly uncoiled and sat facing me like a puppy waiting for a treat.

"First, you can only interview him for an hour a day. Despite your feelings about prot, he's not here to help you write a book."

She nodded.

"And second, you'll have to have his consent. If he isn't interested in cooperating with you, that's the end of it."

"I agree. But if he doesn't like the idea, I can still visit him, can't I?"

"During regular visiting hours and under the usual conditions."

She knew, of course, that our rules were liberal, and she could talk with him most evenings and on weekends (inasmuch as reporters and curiosity seekers were screened out, it was unlikely that he would have many other visitors). "Done!" She jumped up and extended a tiny hand, which I took. "Now can I see him?"

"One more thing," I added as we headed (Giselle skipped) for Ward Two. "See if you can find out when he's leaving."

Her face fell. "He's leaving?"

"Don't worry—it won't be for a while. And when he does, he's going to take a few people back with him."

"He is? Who?"

"That's what I'd like you to find out."

When we got to Two, we found prot in the lounge

surrounded by several of the other patients, all of whom seemed to be talking at once. The ward's half–dozen cats were competing for space to rub against his legs. Rudolph, the self–proclaimed "greatest dancer in the universe," was pirouetting around the room. Russell was running back and forth crying, "Praise the Lord! The Teacher is at hand!" Milton, our peripatetic jokester, shouted, "Chairs for the standing army!" Others were mumbling incomprehensibly, and I made a mental note to ask prot later whether he could understand any of their parlance. There were presents, too: peanut butter and fruit (known from his previous visit to be favorites of his), and the gossamer thread, an invisible talisman left on the lawn one drizzly day five years earlier by "the bluebird of happiness."

When he saw Giselle he broke away from the group and approached her with arms outstretched. He hugged her warmly and then stepped back and gazed silently into her eyes. Prot obviously remembered her, and fondly.

Having other duties to perform, I left them alone and hurried to meet with my first patient of the day.

WHEN I got to my examining room I found that Messrs. Rodrigo and Kowalski were waiting outside with Michael, a twenty–two–year–old male Caucasian who had tried to kill himself on at least three occasions before coming to MPI.

He's not the only one. Suicide rates in the United States, and many other countries, have increased dramatically over the past several years, particularly among the young, and nobody seems to have a good explanation for this tragic phenomenon. There are many reasons why a person might try to take his own life—grief, stress, general depression, fail-ure of one's expectations, feelings of hopelessness—but none

257

of these in itself is the root cause of a suicidal tendency (most grieving and depressed people do not attempt to end their lives). As with all medical problems, each case has to be treated individually. The therapist must try to determine the reason for the patient's self-destructive feelings and help him deal with them by proposing more reasonable solutions to the problems causing his suffering.

Michael, for example, holds himself responsible for the death of his identical twin brother, and desperately wants to "even the score." Although it's true that he was instrumental in initiating the events that led to his twin's demise, it was an accident that could have befallen anyone. I have not been able to convince him of this, however, nor to absolve him of his deep feelings of responsibility and guilt ("Why him, not me?").

But Mike takes this logic one step farther than most. He feels himself responsible for the fate of everybody whose path he has ever crossed, afraid he might have started a chain reaction of catastrophic events. Ordinarily he keeps his distance from me and everyone else, avoiding eye contact, saying little.

Not this time. Though unkempt and sloppily dressed, as usual, he came into the room in good spirits (for him). He even tried to smile. I remarked upon this, hoping there had been a genuine change in his attitude toward life. And there was. He had heard about prot, and was eagerly waiting to meet him. "Don't worry," he added, looking me right in the eye, "I'm not going to make another attempt until I talk to the guy from K-PAX." When I looked dubious he actually grinned and raised a scarred arm in salute. "Scout's honor."

There's an old axiom in psychiatry: "Beware of the cheerful suicidal." I knew he was serious and probably would wait to hear what prot's solution to his problems might be. But I certainly wouldn't decrease his surveillance, nor move him down from Three.

As I mused about what prot could possibly do for Michael, and perhaps some of the others, I suddenly realized that his return presented us with another dilemma. All the inmates had heard about prot's earlier visit and hopes were running high, perhaps much too high, that he would be able to chase away all the dragons breathing fire down their necks, as he had done with many of our former patients. I couldn't help wondering: What would happen to a patient like Michael, whose last hopes would be dashed if prot failed to meet those rosy expectations?

THAT afternoon I cleaned off my desk, or tried to—when I was finished it looked as crowded as before—and found a paper awaiting my review, which had been due two weeks earlier. I started to read it but all I could think of was my next session with prot. Although he had only just returned, I already felt exhausted. It's at times like this that I contemplate with great seriousness an early retirement, a bug my wife keeps flicking into my ear.

Many people have the following idea about psychiatrists, and perhaps about physicians in general: We work whenever we wish, take long weekends, spend a lot of time on vacation. And even when we do come to the office we don't do any real work and for this we command enormous fees. It isn't like that, believe me. It's a twenty-four-hour-a-day job. Even when we aren't attending to our patients or on call we're running case histories through our minds, trying to think of something we might have forgotten that would help a suffering individual. And the stress of making a mistake takes its toll as well. We often sleep poorly, eat too much, don't get enough exercise—all the things we preach against.

I ended up reviewing prot's entire file again, unfortunately without any new ideas coming to mind. And I knew I wouldn't get much sleep that night or any other until Robert came forth and, together, we exorcised the demons roaring thunderously in the recesses of his tormented mind.

Session Eighteen

ON the morning of prot's next session I got a call from Charlie Flynn, the astronomer from Princeton and my son-in-law Steve's colleague, who was studying the planetary system prot claimed to have come from. His voice reminded me of a squeaky wheel. "Why didn't you tell me he was back?" he demanded, without even a "Hello." "I—"

"Whoa. You have to understand that prot is a patient of mine. He's not here for your benefit, nor anyone else's."

"I disagree."

"That's not for you to decide!" I snapped. I hadn't slept well the night before.

"Who does decide such matters? There is a great deal he can tell us. The things we've learned from him already have changed our way of thinking about certain astronomical problems, and I'm sure we've only scratched the surface. We need him."

"My first responsibility is to my patient, not the world of astronomy."

There was a brief pause while he reconsidered his approach. "Of course. Of course. Look. I'm not asking you to sacrifice him on the altar of science. All I'm asking is that you let us talk with him when he's not undergoing therapy or whatever."

I could understand his position and, indeed, the refrain was beginning to sound familiar. "I'll offer you a compromise," I told him.

"Oh, no. Submitting a list of questions like last time just won't do it."

"If I let you talk to him directly, then every astronomer in the country is going to be banging on the door."

"But I banged first."

"No you didn't. Someone got here before you did."

"What? Who?"

"The reporter who helped us fill in his background five years ago. Giselle Griffin."

"Oh. Her. But what has she got to do with this? She's not a scientist, is she?"

"Nevertheless, here's my proposal. You and everyone else can talk to him through her. Is that acceptable?"

Another pause. "I'll make you a counteroffer. I'll agree to your proposition if I can speak directly with him just once. We were in on this thing five years ago, too, and we helped identify him as a true savant, remember?"

"Okay, but you'll have to work it out with her. She has him for an hour a day."

"How do I reach her?"

"I'll ask her to contact you."

After grumbling something about reporters, he hung up. I immediately called the head of our secretarial pool to

262

request that she direct all requests for information about prot to Giselle.

"Does that include the stack of mail we've gotten over the past few years?"

"Everything," I told her, eager to get this can of worms out of my hair.

WHEN Giselle's article featuring prot came out in 1992, it precipitated a flurry of calls and letters to the hospital. Most were requests for information about prot's home planet and directions on how to get there. When K-PAX appeared three years later, several thousand more queries came in from all over the world. A lot of people, it seemed, wanted to find some way, short of suicide, to get off the planet. Since we had no answers to these questions, most of the correspondence was filed away without response.

On the other hand, all the requests for copies of his "report," an assessment of life on Earth and his dim prognosis for the future of Homo sapiens, have been honored. This treatise, "Preliminary Observations on B-TIK (RX 4987165.233)," has generated a certain amount of controversy among scientists, many of whom believe that his prediction of our imminent demise is greatly exaggerated, that only a crazy person would call for an end to established social customs, which, in prot's eyes, fuel the fire of our self-immolation.

As for myself, I take prot's report, and all his other observations and pronouncements, for what they are—the utterances of a remarkable man who may be able to utilize part(s) of his brain unavailable to the rest of us, except, perhaps, for those suffering from other forms of savant syndrome. In prot's case, however, a substantial portion of his brain belonged to someone else: his alter ego, Robert

Porter. It was Robert, a desperately ill patient, whom I so badly needed and wanted to help, even if it came at prot's expense.

"PEACHES!" prot exclaimed as he strode into my examining room. He was wearing his favorite attire: sky-blue denim shirt and matching corduroy pants. "I haven't had one of these in years! *Your* years, that is." He offered me a taste and then opened wide to bite into a ripe one himself. A jet of saliva squirted halfway across the room.

This was one of the few fruits whose seeds he did not consume. I asked him why.

"Hard on the teeth," he explained, clanking one of the pits back into the bowl. "Dentist fodder."

"You have dentists on K-PAX?"

"Heaven forbid."

"Lucky you."

"Luck has nothing to do with it."

"While you're eating, let me just ask you: Are you planning to write another report on us?"

"Nope," he replied with a great slurp. "Not unless there have been some major changes since my last visit." He paused and gave me his sincere, innocent look. "There haven't been, have there?"

"You mean on Earth."

"That's where we are, ain't it?"

"Not that you would call major, I suppose."

"I was afraid of that."

"No world wars, though," I said brightly.

"Just the usual dozens of regional ones."

"But that's progress, don't you think?"

He grinned at this, though it looked more like an animal baring its teeth. "That's one of the funniest things about this place. You kill millions and millions of beings every day, and if you murder a few less on the next one, you nearly break your arms patting yourselves on the back. On K-PAX you humans are a riot."

"C'mon, prot, we don't kill 'millions and millions' of people every day."

"I didn't say 'people.' " Another pit rang into the bowl like the peal of a cheerful bell.

I had forgotten that he considered all animals equally important, even insects. I decided to change the subject. "Have you spoken with any of the other patients since I last saw you?"

"They have spoken to me, mostly."

"I suppose they all want to go back with you."

"Not all of them."

"Tell me: Are you able to communicate with everyone in Ward Two?"

"Of course. So could you if you tried."

"Even the ones who don't speak?"

"They all speak. You just have to learn how to listen."

I have long believed that if we could understand what certain unintelligible patients were saying, i.e., how their thoughts differed from normal, we could learn a lot about the nature of their afflictions. "What about the schizophrenics? I mean the ones whose words seem garbled—can you understand what they're saying?"

"Certainly."

"How do you do that?"

Prot threw up his hands. "You remember the tape you played for me five years ago? The one of the whale songs?"

"Yes."

"What a memory! Well, there you are."

"I don't—"

"You've got to stop treating your patients as if they were carbon copies of yourself. If you were to treat them as beings from whom you might learn something, you would."

"Can you help me do that?"

"I could, but I won't."

"Why not?"

"You have to learn it for yourself. You'd be surprised how easy it is if you forget everything you've been taught and start over."

"Are you talking about my patients, or the Earth again?"

"It's the same thing, wouldn't you say?" He pushed the bowl of pits away and sat gazing contentedly toward the ceiling, as if he hadn't a care in the world.

"What about Robert?" I asked.

"What about him?"

"Have you spoken to him in the last day or so?"

"He's still not saying much. But . . ."

"But—what?"

"I have the feeling he's ready to cooperate with you."

I sat up straighter. "He is? How do you know? What did he say?"

"He didn't say anything. It's just a feeling I have. He seems—I don't know—a little tired of hiding. Of everything."

"Everything? He's not planning to—"

"Nah. He's just tired of being tired, I think."

"I'm very glad to hear that."

"I suppose that's what you would call 'progress.'"

I stared at him for a moment, wondering whether Robert might be willing to come out even without hypnosis.

266

"He's not *that* tired, gene," prot remarked.

I could feel my shoulders slumping. "In that case, we'll begin now. If you're ready."

"Whenever you are."

"Good. Do you remember the little spot on the wall behind me?"

"Of course. One-two-three-four-five." And he was out like a light.

"Prot?"

"Yes, dr. b?"

"How do you feel?"

"A little spacey."

"Very funny. Now—do you remember what happened the last time I spoke with you in this setting?"

"Certainly. It was a hot day and you were sweating a lot."

"That's right. And Robert wouldn't speak to me—remember?"

"Of course."

"Will he speak to me now?"

There was a pause before prot abruptly slouched down in his chair.

"Robert?"

No response.

"Robert, the last time I spoke with you was under very different circumstances. I didn't know much about you then. Since that time I have learned why you are suffering so much, and I want to try to help you cope with that. I'm not going to make any promises this time. It won't be easy, and you'll have to help me. For now, I only want to chat with you, get to know you better. Do you understand? Let's just talk about the happy times in your life or anything else you'd like to discuss. Will you speak to me now?"

He made no response.

"I want you to consider this room a safe haven. This is a place where you can say anything that's on your mind without fear or guilt or shame, and nothing will happen to you or to anyone else. Please remember that."

No response.

"I'll tell you what. I've got some information here on your background. I'm going to read it to you, and you stop me if I say anything that's incorrect. Will you do that?"

Again there was no response, but I thought I detected a slight tilt of Robert's head, as if he wanted to hear what I had to say.

"All right. You were a star wrestler in high school with an overall record of 26-8. You were captain of the team and finished second in the state tournament your senior year."

Robert said nothing.

"You were a good student and won a scholarship to the state university. You were also awarded a community-service medal by the Guelph Rotary Club in 1974. You were vice president of your class for three years running. All right so far?"

Still no response.

"You and your wife Sarah and your daughter Rebecca lived in a trailer for the first seven years of your marriage, and then you built a house in the country near a forest with a stream. It sounds like a beautiful place. The kind of place I'd like to retire to someday. . . ."

I glanced at Robert and, to my surprise, found him staring at me. I didn't ask him how he felt. He looked terrible. "I'm sorry," he croaked.

I wasn't clear what he was sorry about—it could have

268

been any number of things. But I said, immediately, "Thank you, Robert. I'm sorry, too."

His eyes slammed shut and his head dropped down again. Apparently the only reason he had come out was to offer this pathetic apology to me, or perhaps to the world. I gazed at him sadly for a moment before he sat up and stretched.

"Thank you, prot."

"For what?"

"For—never mind. All right, I'm going to wake you up now. I'm going to count back from five to one. You will awaken slowly, and when I get to—"

"Five-four-three-two-one," he sang out. "Hiya, doc. Did Rob say anything to you yet?" Note: When awake, prot could not remember anything that transpired while he was under hypnosis.

"Yes, he did."

"No kidding? Well, it was only a matter of time."

"The question is, how much time do we have?"

"All the time in the WORLD."

"Prot, do you know anything about Rob that I don't know?"

"Such as?"

"Why he feels so worthless?"

"No idea, coach. Probably has something to do with his life on EARTH."

"But you talk to him, don't you?"

"Not about that."

"Why not?"

"He doesn't want to."

"Maybe he does now."

"Don't hold your breath."

"Okay, I'll let you off the hook for today. See if you

can find out anything more from Robert, and I'll see you again on Friday."

"Put plenty of fruit on that hook," he advised as he ambled out.

I was on the "back forty" watching a badminton game played without shuttlecocks when Giselle came running toward me. I hadn't seen her since her encounter with prot two days earlier. "It's like you said," she panted. "He's just the same!"

I asked her whether he had told her when he was leaving.

"Not yet," she confessed. "But he doesn't seem to be in any hurry!" She looked absolutely moonstruck.

I reminded her to try to find out when it would be and to let me know "ASAP." "But be subtle about it," I added inanely.

It didn't surprise me to learn that she had already gone through all the correspondence the hospital had received about prot and K-PAX. What did, however, was the information that more letters were beginning to come in.

"But nobody knows he's back."

"Somebody does! Or maybe they just anticipated his return. But the amazing thing is that a lot of them were addressed specifically to prot, care of MPI, or to prot, K-PAX. Or to the hospital with the notation to 'please forward.' In fact, some were just addressed to 'prot,' no address given."

"So I heard."

"But don't you see what that means?"

"What?"

"It means that a lot of people wanted their letters or calls to go directly to prot, not to anyone else."

"Isn't that what you would expect?"

"Not really. Furthermore, a lot of it was marked PERSONAL AND CONFIDENTIAL."

"So?"

"So I think most people don't trust us with the letters. I wouldn't, would you?"

Perhaps she was right. I had read some of those addressed to me, many of which began: "You idiot!"

While I was mulling over this unwanted development, she added, "Besides, you may have a legal problem if you don't turn them over to him."

"What legal problem?"

"Tampering with the U.S. mails."

"Don't be ridiculous. Prot is a patient here, and we have a right—"

"Maybe you should ask your lawyer."

"Maybe I will."

"No need. I already spoke to him. There was a case in 1989 in which evidence obtained from the correspondence of a patient at one of the state institutions was thrown out of court as illegal search and seizure. On top of that the hospital was fined for tampering with the mails. Anyway," she argued further, "if he's just a part of Robert's personality as you seem to think, what harm can it possibly do?"

"I don't know," I answered truthfully, thinking more about Robert than about a stack of Santa Claus mail or what prot might do with it. "All right. But just give him the ones specifically addressed to him." I suddenly felt like a Watergate criminal trying to minimize the damage, though I didn't know what the fallout might be.

"Next item. I got a call from Dr. Flynn last night."

"Oh, yes. I was going to ask you to call him."

"I guess he couldn't wait. Anyway, I arranged for him to meet with prot."

"Just don't let him take too much of prot's time. He won't be the last caller you'll have."

"I know. I've already heard from a cetologist and an anthropologist."

"Maybe that's enough for now. . . ."

"We'll see." She skipped away, leaving me alone with Jackie, a thirty-two-year-old "child," who was sitting on the damp ground (the lawn had been watered during the lunch hour) near the outer wall, digging a hole and ecstatically smelling each spoonful of the soft earth before squeezing it into a ball and carefully stacking it on top of the others. She had a mustache of soil, but I wasn't about to stop her and suggest she wash her dirty face.

Like many of our patients, Jackie has a tragic history. She was raised on a sheep farm in Vermont and spent most of her time out-of-doors. Home-schooled and isolated from close contact with other children, she developed an early interest in nature in all its color and variety. Unfortunately, Jackie's parents were killed in an automobile accident when she was nine, and she was compelled to live with an aunt in Brooklyn. Almost immediately after that, on the playground of her new school, she was accidentally shot in the stomach by a ten-year-old boy trying to avenge the murder of an older brother. When she came out of the hospital she was mute, and she hasn't spoken a word, nor mentally aged a day, since that time. In fact, one of the nurses still puts her hair up in pigtails, as her mother used to do when she was a girl.

Though she suffered no brain damage, nothing we have tried has proven successful in bringing her out of her dream world, the childhood she loved so much. She appears

272

to live in a hypnotic state of her own making, from which we cannot arouse her.

But how she enjoys that world! When she plays with a toy or one of the cats she throws her entire being into it, focusing her concentration to the point of ignoring all outside stimuli, much like our autists. She takes in a sunset, or the sparrows flocking in the ginkgo trees, with rapture and serenity. It is a pleasure to watch her eat, her eyes closed and her mouth making little smacking noises.

It was patients like Jackie, and Michael, and others at the hospital that I vaguely hoped prot, before he disappeared again, might be able to help. God knows we weren't doing much for them. Already he was instrumental in getting Robert to come out for a moment, if only to say he was sorry. But about what? Perhaps that he wasn't going to be able to go through with it, to cooperate in his treatment. Or maybe it was, in fact, what it appeared tobe: a hopeful sign, an attempt to communicate, a small beginning.

THAT afternoon, as I was hurrying to get to a committee meeting, I spotted prot in the rec room talking with two of our most pathetic patients. One of these is a twenty-seven-year-old Mexican-American male who is obsessed with the notion that he can fly if he simply puts his mind to it. His favorite author, of course, is Gabriel García Márquez. No amount of medication or psychotherapy can convince him that only birds, bats, and insects can take to the air, and he spends most of his waking hours flapping back and forth across the lawn, never rising more than a foot or two above the ground.

How did this sorry condition come about? Manuel was the fourteenth of fourteen children. As such, he was the last into the bathtub, never got his share of the limited food, never had any new clothes, not even underwear or socks. On top of that, he was the "runt" of the bunch, barely making five feet in height. As a result he grew up with almost no self-esteem, and considered himself a failure before his life had even begun.

For reasons known only to himself he set an impossible goal: to fly. If he could accomplish this, he decided, he would be fit to join the ranks of his fellow human beings despite all his other "failures." He has been at it since he was sixteen.

The other is an African-American homosexual—I'll call him Lou—who firmly believes he is pregnant. What makes him think so? If he places his hand on his abdomen he can feel the baby's pulse. Arthur Beamish (who is gay himself), his staff physician and our newest psychiatrist, has not been able to convince him that *everyone's* abdomen pulses with the beat of the abdominal aorta and other arteries, or to persuade him that fertilization in a man is impossible due to the absence of a major component of the reproductive system, namely an egg cell.

What has led to this bizarre conception? Lou has the mind of a woman trapped in a man's body, a not uncommon gender-identity problem known as transsexualism. When he was a child he enjoyed dressing in his big sister's clothing. His unmarried mother, who had problems of her own, encouraged this practice and insisted he urinate sitting down, and it wasn't until he was twelve years old that the truth was discovered during a routine school physical. By that time Lou's sexuality was firmly established in his mind. Indeed, he refers to himself as "she," something the staff does not encourage as it would only make things worse. Oddly, a benign cyst in his bladder caused some occasional

274

minor bleeding, a fact he used to "prove," at least to himself, that he was menstruating.

Although a subject of intense verbal abuse throughout high school, he stubbornly maintained his female characteristics, wearing skirts and bras, using makeup, etc. He padded his breasts, of course, but so did some of the girls. After graduation, he and his mother moved to a different state where no one knew them, and Lou's identity was secure. He got a job as a secretary for a large corporation, and it wasn't long afterward that he fell in love with a man who happened to notice his five o'clock shadow in the elevator late one afternoon. A passionate relationship followed, and it was only a few months later that the urinary bleeding mysteriously stopped and Lou took this to mean he was pregnant. He was ecstatic. He badly wanted to have a child in order to validate his existence. Almost immediately thereafter he was afflicted with morning sickness, abdominal pains, fatigue, and all the rest. He has been wearing maternity clothes ever since.

The "father" of his child, frightened by something he did not understand, convinced Lou to seek psychiatric help, and he ended up with us at MPI. That was six months ago, and the baby is "due" in a few weeks. What will happen when it comes to term is a matter of conjecture and concern among staff members and patients alike. Lou, however, awaits that fateful day with sublime anticipation, as do some of the other inmates, who are already suggesting possible names for the new arrival.

Session Nineteen

"ITHINK I found the focus for my book," Giselle announced as I was coming out of my office.

"I'm on my way to a meeting. Want to walk?"

"Sure." She fell in beside me with quick little steps. "Isn't it space travel? UFO's? Little green men?"

"Not really. The first chapter will be about the likelihood of extraterrestrial life. The second will be a rehash of my article about UFO's. It's the other chapters I'm talking about."

"Have you asked him about UFO's?"

"Uh-huh."

"Well, what does he think?"

"He says 'There ain't any.' "

"How does he know that?"

"He says it would be like riding a pogo stick a trillion times around the Earth."

"So how does he account for all the sightings that people claim?"

"Wishful thinking."

"Huh?"

"He says that even though there are no alien ships, there are a lot of humans who would like to believe otherwise."

Klaus Villers joined us. "Hi, Klaus. What's the focus of the other chapters, Giselle?"

"Whether or not he has any special powers. If he has *one*, maybe there are others."

"You mean can he travel at superlight speed? That sort of thing?"

"Exactly. But there are other things, too."

"Such as?"

"Well, we both know he can talk to animals, right?"

"Hold on. *He* says he can talk to animals, but how do we know that?"

"Has he ever lied to you?"

"That's not the point. He may *believe* he can talk to them but that's not the same as fact. Nor is anything else he says that we can't verify."

"*I* believe him."

"That's your prerogative."

"Anyway, I'm going to try to find out whether he can or not. If he can, maybe he's telling the truth about everything else."

"Maybe and maybe not. But how do you propose to find out?"

"I'm going to ask him to speak with some animals whose history we know something about, and to tell me what they said to him."

"Well, all we have are the cats."

"That's a start. But they all came from a pound, and we know very little about them. And cats never say much anyway. I've got a better idea."

We stopped at the amphitheater. "This is where we get off." I thought Klaus would go on in, but he stopped, too. I glanced at my watch. "So what's your idea?"

"I want to take him to the zoo."

"Giselle! You know we can't let you take prot to the zoo. Or anywhere else."

"No, I mean make it an outing for all the patients in Wards One and Two. Or any others you think might want to go along." I heard Villers grunt. Whether it was a positive or a negative response, I couldn't tell.

"Look, we've got to get to this meeting. Let me think about it."

"Okay, boss. But you *know* it's a good idea." And off she went, half walking, half running, presumably to find prot. Villers stared after her.

I didn't pay much attention at the executive committee meeting, which had to do with ways to trim the budget in the wake of government cutbacks for treatment and research. I was thinking about prot's alleged "superhuman" abilities. What had he really done that was so amazing? True, he knew a lot about astronomy, but so did Dr. Flynn and many others. He somehow managed to get from his room to Bess's under our very noses five years ago. But that could have been some kind of hypnotic trick or simple inattention on our part. The only really inexplicable talent he possessed was his ability to "see" UV light, but even that had not been rigorously tested. None of these "powers" required an extraterrestrial origin. In any case, my chief concern was with Robert, and not prot.

When the budget meeting was over Klaus stopped me

in the hall. "Ve should get a cut of her book," he whispered.

OWING to prot's influence, perhaps, I decided to have lunch in Ward Two. Betty and a couple of the other nurses joined us.

Everyone waited until I sat down. Prot took his place at the end of the table and all eyes were on him as he dug into his vegetables. He refused to eat any of the hot dogs, of course, as did some of his closest followers. He also declined the lime gelatin, saying he could "smell the flesh" in it. Frankie, who was already considerably overweight, eagerly relieved them of the leftovers, gobbling them down to the accompaniment of various bodily noises.

I glanced around the table at these unfortunate souls, some of whom had been here most of their lives, and tried to imagine what their worlds must be like. Russell, for example, though much improved from his Christ-like delusions of five years ago, was still unable to engage in normal conversation, preferring instead to quote endless passages from the Bible. I couldn't begin to get inside his head and imagine a life so limited, so joyless.

And Bert. What a frustrating existence, an eternity of worry and sorrow. What was it about his brain that precluded his dealing with his undeterminable loss and moving on? Whatever it was, his easy solution to all his problems, like that of almost everyone else present, was a trip to K-PAX, where difficulties like his didn't exist. In fact, Betty told me before lunch that the patients couldn't hear enough about the place. "It's like Lenny and the rabbits," she said. (Betty has read all of Steinbeck's novels more than once.)

When we had finished eating, Milton stood up and

rapped on the table. "Went to the doctor the other day," he quipped. Some of the others were already tittering. "Told him I wanted somebody who knew what he was doing.He puffed out his chest and said, 'I've been practicing medicine for more than thirty years.' I said, 'I'll come back when you've got it right!' " Everyone was looking at me, giggling, waiting for my reaction. What else could I do but laugh, too?

I was still thinking about possible strategies to get Robert to stay around for a while when prot marched in for our nineteenth session. "Why didn't you tell me about the letters?" he inquired impishly as he reached for the fruit bowl.

"I was going to," I replied. "As soon as I thought you were ready to deal with them."

"Very interesting," he replied, biting into a persimmon.

"What—the letters?"

The fruit made his mouth pucker up. "Don't you find it amazing that so many beings want to get off this PLANET? Doesn't that tell you something?"

"It tells me we have our problems. But after all, the Earth has a population of six billion people, and only a few thousand called or wrote to you." I remember feeling quite smug about this rejoinder.

"Very likely because those are the only beings who read your book or Giselle's article. Hardly anyone on your WORLD reads much, if at all." He finished the persimmon and reached for another. "We don't have anything like this on K-PAX. You should see what they look like in UV light!" He smacked his lips loudly and gazed thoughtfully at the fruit.

280

"Do you plan to answer them?"

"The persimmons?"

"No, dammit. The letters."

"I'll try. Most will be condolences, of course. I can only take a hundred beings with me when I go back, remember?"

"How many have you lined up so far?"

"Now, gene, if I gave you an obon, you'd take a jart."

"So you won't tell me. Nor will you tell me when you'll be leaving. I must confess, prot, I'm very disappointed that you still don't trust me."

"As long as we're being so honest and direct, doctor b, perhaps you could explain to me why human beings take everything so personally."

"I'll tell you what: I'll answer that if you'll tell me how long you're going to stay around."

"No way. But don't worry—I won't be leaving for a while yet. I've got the letters to consider and a few other things to take care of. . . ." He swallowed the last of the fruit and sat back, still smacking his lips. "Ready, doc?"

Sometimes I felt as though I were the patient and prot the doctor. "Just about. I'd like to speak to Robert first."

Without a word his eyes closed and his head slumped to his chest.

"Robert?"

No response.

"Robert, can you hear me?"

If he could, he didn't let on. There was no need to waste any more time. Obviously he still wasn't ready to cooperate, at least not without hypnosis. "All right, prot, you can come back out now."

"My tongue feels like cotton," he declared.

"That's the persimmons. Okay, I think we're ready now."

He gazed at the little white dot on the wall behind me. "Weird fruit. One-two-three-four—"

I waited until I was sure he was in a trance. "You may leave your eyes closed for a while, prot."

"Whatever you say, gino."

"Good. Now I'd like Robert to come forward, please. Rob? Can you hear me?"

His head dropped again.

"Robert, if you can hear me, please nod."

He nodded almost imperceptibly.

"Thank you. How are you feeling?"

"Not very good," he mumbled.

"I'm sorry. I hope I can help you feel better soon. Please listen to me and trust me. Remember, this is your safe haven."

No response.

"I thought we might talk a little about your childhood today. Your family. About growing up in Montana. Would that be all right?"

A feeble shrug.

"Good. Will you open your eyes, please?"

They blinked open, but he avoided my gaze.

"Why don't you tell me something about your mother."

Softly but clearly: "What do you want to know?"

"Anything you'd like to tell me. Is she a good cook?"

He seemed to consider the question carefully, or maybe he was simply trying to decide whether to respond. "Pretty good," he said.

I couldn't help feeling excited about this simple answer. It came in a lifeless monotone, but it represented a tremendous breakthrough, something I was afraid might take weeks of persistent cajoling. Robert was talking!

The remainder of the session proceeded rather haltingly, but he seemed to become more at ease as we chatted about some of the basic elements of his childhood: his sisters, his friends, his early school years and favorite activities—books and puzzles and watching the animals in the fields behind the house. His pre-adolescent boyhood seemed to be a perfectly normal one, unusual only in that he lost his father when he was six (at which time prot made his first appearance), though I didn't bring that up in this session. I merely wanted to gain Robert's confidence, make him feel comfortable talking with me. The real work would come later.

The discussion ended with Robert's telling me about a memorable day he had spent, when he was nine, roaming the fields with Apple, his big, shaggy dog, and I hoped that finishing on this happy note might encourage him to come forward less reluctantly the next time. But before I recalled prot I tried something I was pretty sure wouldn't work. I reached over, picked up a tiny whistle I had brought in for the occasion, and blew it loudly. "Do you hear that?"

"Yes."

"Good. Whenever you hear that sound I want you to come forward, no matter where you are or what you are doing. Do you understand?"

"Yes."

"Good. Now I'd like to speak with prot, if you don't mind. Thanks for coming, Robert, and I'll see you later. Please close your eyes."

They drooped shut.

I waited a moment. "Prot? Please open your eyes."

"Hiya, gene. What's up?"

"The opposite of down?"

"Dr. brewer! You *do* have a sense of humor!"

"Thanks a lot. Now just relax. I'm going to count back from fi—"

"Five-four-three-two—Hey! Are we finished already?"

"Yes, we are. How did you know?"

"Just a feeling I get sometimes. Like I've missed something."

"I know how it is."

He got up to leave. "Thanks for the interesting fruit. Maybe I could take a few seeds back with me when I go."

"Take a whole basketful if you like. By the way—I saw you talking with Lou yesterday. Do you have any suggestions on what we might do with him?"

"I think it had better be a cesarean."

OUR son Will spent his last vacation weekend at home with us—he would soon be moving into a dormitory at Columbia for the fall semester. A pre-med student, he was employed for the summer as an orderly at MPI.

When he paid his first visit to the hospital five years ago and met Giselle, Will immediately announced that he wanted to be a reporter. That enthusiasm gradually faded over the years, as youthful interests tend to do, and after several return visits he declared his intention to follow his old man's footsteps right into psychiatry. I am very proud and happy that he made this choice, not just because he would be carrying on a family tradition, but also because he has a natural ability to get along with patients and they with him.

In fact, it was Will who solved a bewildering problem for us earlier in the summer, an elderly man who was pretending to swallow his medication, devising various clever methods and schemes to fool the nurses. Will caught him at it, but, with an understanding beyond his years, did not try to force the man to take his pills or report him for not doing so. Instead, he spoke to him at length about the matter, discovering, finally, that the old boy was afraid to swallow anything red. When we had the medication repackaged in white capsules the patient was home with his family within two weeks.

Will's current self-imposed project, in addition to his regular duties, is to try to decipher the ramblings of a young schizophrenic patient who (Will thinks) is trying to communicate with us through some sort of code that no one can decipher. Most of his utterings seem to be pure gibberish. But occasionally, after one of his meaningless statements, he chomps a few times on an imaginary cigar and repeats the whole thing two or three times. Here is one of Dustin's orations (a kind of poetry?), delivered with four chomps and four repeats, and carefully recorded by Will:

> Your life sure is fun when you like cabbage but be careful when you find a yellow box full of crabs or ostrich poop because then the world will stop and you can never really know if this is where someone says that you must comply because you're not going there to learn how to be grateful or to make mistakes when you're stepping out. . . .

Did Dustin have some sort of cabbage fetish, or had he had an unfortunate run-in with a crab or an ostrich? And was the cigar a phallic symbol? We stared at this nonsense for an hour after dinner until Karen sent us outside to shoot a few baskets and chase after the dogs and forget about work for a while. But Will wanted to know more about some of the other schizophrenics and the nature of the affliction in general, which he referred to as "split personality."

"The first thing you should know about schizophrenia is that although it literally means 'split brain,' it is *not* the same thing as multiple personality disorder. It's more of a malfunction of sense and logic, not a 'split' personality. The patient might hear voices, for example, or believe things that are patently false. Others suffer from delusions of grandiosity. In the paranoid type, feelings of persecution predominate. Many speak 'word salad,' but this can happen with certain other maladies, too."

"You're lecturing again, Dad."

"Sorry. I guess I still find it hard to believe you're following in the old man's footsteps."

"It's a dirty job, but somebody's got to do it."

"Anyway, with schizophrenia, you've got to be careful with your diagnosis. Nice shot."

"What's the etiology?"

"Schizophrenia usually develops early in life. Recent evidence suggests a genetic origin, or possibly fetal damage by a virus. It often responds almost miraculously to antipsychotic drugs, but sometimes doesn't, and there's no way to predict which cases—Oxie, come back here with that!"

"What about Dustin?"

"In Dustin's case, none of the neuroleptics has alleviated his symptoms in the slightest, not even a gram of Clozapine a day. But he's an unusual case anyway. I'm sure you've noticed that he plays chess and other games without any problem. He never says much, but he seems perfectly focused and logical during these encounters. In fact, he almost always wins."

"Do you think his problem has anything to do with the games he plays?"

"Who knows?"

"Maybe his parents. They visit him almost every evening. Would it be all right if I talk with them sometime?"

"Now, Will, I admire your enthusiasm, but that's something you shouldn't get involved with at this point."

"Well, I'm not giving up on him. The key to the whole thing is in that cigar routine, I think."

I was very proud of him for his perseverance, which is one of the most important attributes a psychiatrist can have. He spends part of his lunch hours and every spare minute of his time with Dustin. Of course he is quite taken with prot, too, as is everyone, but he gets little chance to talk with him because the line is so long. It's only when everyone else goes off to bed that our alien friend gets any time to himself. I only wished I knew what he was thinking about during those long, dark hours of the night.

Session Twenty

Contrary to popular belief, physicians do not hesitate to criticize each other's work, at least in private. Thus, at the regular Monday-morning staff meeting, considerable doubt was expressed about whether a simple post-hypnotic suggestion (the whistle) would summon Robert from the depths of hell. One of my colleagues, Carl Thorstein, went so far as to call it a "nutty" idea (Carl has often been a thorn in my side, but he's a good psychiatrist). On the other hand, it was generally agreed that little could be lost by doing the experiment, which had not been tried before.

Nor was there much enthusiasm for Giselle's plan to get prot to talk to animals, though the broader suggestion of a zoo outing for the inmates was well received, and I was nominated a committee of one to look into the matter. Villers admonished me "to keep ze costs as low as possible."

Some of the staff members were on vacation, so there

was little further discussion of patients and their progress, if any. However, Virginia Goldfarb mentioned a remarkable improvement in one of her charges, the histrionic narcissistic dancer we call "Rudolph Nureyev."

Rudolph was an only child who was reminded constantly that he was perfect in every way, and getting better. When he decided to take up ballet his parents responded with high praise and strong financial support. With that kind of encouragement (and considerable talent), he went on to become one of America's finest dancers.

His only problem was one of attitude. He expected every-one, even music directors and choreographers, to defer to his impeccable taste and judgment. Eventually he became so important (in his own mind) that he began to voice other demands, and finally became so impossible to work with that he was fired by the management of his dance company. When this news spread, no one else in the world would take him in. He ended up a voluntary patient at MPI when his last and only friend encouraged him to seek professional help.

His sudden improvement came about following a single lengthy conversation with prot, who described to Rudolph the breathtaking beauty and grace of the performers in a balletlike dance he had seen on the planet J-MUT. He encouraged Rudolph to try some of the steps, but it required such fantastic speed, exquisite timing, and contortion of limb that Rudolph found the work impossible to execute. He suddenly realized that he was not the greatest dancer in the universe. Goldfarb reported that his supreme arrogance had vanished immediately, and she was thinking of moving him to Ward One. There was no objection.

Beamish, peering at me over his tiny glasses, joked that we should give prot an office and send all the patients to him. Ron Menninger (no relation to the famous clinic) remarked, a little less facetiously, that perhaps I ought to delay Robert's treatment until prot had done whatever he could for the other inmates, a notion I had grappled with myself.

Villers reminded us that we were expecting three distinguished visitors over the next month or so, including the chair of our board of directors, one of the wealthiest men in America. Klaus wasted no words in emphasizing the importance of this visit, suggesting that we put our very best feet forward that day, funding efforts for the new wing having fallen below expectations.

After some other matters were disposed of, he announced that a major TV network had offered the hospital a healthy sum for an exclusive appearance by prot on one of its talk shows. Astonished by this ridiculous prospect, I asked how they even knew he had returned. Someone pointed out that it had already been picked up by the media, including one of the national news programs. I wondered whether Klaus himself had anything to do with that.

The discussion ended without resolution. Some, like me, thought it preposterous to let one of our patients be interviewed on television. Others, noting that prot was unique in all the world and that he would undoubtedly be able to hold his own with any interviewer, weren't so sure. Though we could certainly use the money, I thought we were opening another can of worms. I pointed out that we had a lot of bizarre and interesting cases at the hospital, so why not a whole TV series based on their individual stories? Villers, missing the irony of my remark, seemed quite enthusiastic. I could almost see dollar signs in his eyes, which lit up like shooting stars as he contemplated the potential windfall.

Virginia caught me after the meeting. She wanted to know whether prot might be willing to schedule a look at a couple of her other patients. She wasn't joking—Goldfarb never jokes. I assured her I would speak to him about the matter

IF I have more than cottage cheese and crackers for lunch I have a hard time staying awake the rest of the afternoon. I watched in envy as Villers put away a huge plate of roast beef, various kinds of vegetables, buttered rolls, and pie. He said very little as he gobbled down his food, and left as soon as he was finished, dots of gravy and piecrust flecking his goatee. As I watched him go, I thought: I don't know much about this man, who keeps his personal life to himself, but I'd know those drooping shoulders anywhere.

Klaus Villers is a paradox of the highest order. He exemplifies, I suppose, the public image of the typical psychiatrist—cold, decisive, analytical. Nothing appears to faze him. I have never seen the slightest hint of shock or amusement on his weather-beaten countenance, rarely sensed even the slightest emotion. Yet, for all his gruffness of character and outspoken opinions he can be soft as an oyster inside.

Perhaps the best example of this is the case of a former patient whom Klaus was powerless to help (a not infrequent situation at MPI). The man, a hopeless manic depressive from a poor family, was so fond of his doctor, for reasons of his own, that he carved several beautiful little birds for Klaus and his wife. When the man died, our "heartless" director, who barely found time or inclination to thank the man for his gifts, paid for his interment out of his own pocket, erecting a huge marker for "The Birdman of MPI." No one knows why he did this, but I choose to believe

291

that he simply felt sorry for a long-suffering patient he could do nothing for.

Klaus emigrated with his family to America from Austria more than fifty years ago. Born in 1930, he grew up during the years preceding World War II. His awareness of the atrocities going on around him may have been a factor in his decision to become a doctor, but this is pure speculation on my part. I don't even know how he met his wife Emma.

For all his intelligence he still maintains a thick German accent and, unbelievably, his wife speaks almost no English at all. Extremely introverted, she virtually never leaves their secluded home on Long Island, tending to her garden and homemaking for herself and her husband. They rarely attend extramural functions or, even after he became director in 1990, invite anyone to their lovely home (I was there only once, years ago). Apparently they see no need for social contacts, finding everything they need in each other. As far as I know they have no children.

Their only hobby is hiking. They have walked the Appalachian Trail many times, once or twice with the late Supreme Court Justice William O. Douglas, who apparently didn't have many friends either. As a result, Klaus knows every species of bird in eastern North America by sight or sound and, in fact, usually spends a part of his lunch hour each day on the lawn watching and listening. He remarked once that his wife does the same thing at exactly the same time so that, in a sense, they enjoy the experience together even though they are miles apart.

The reason I mention this now is that I had not seen him on the lawn with his field glasses for some time, or heard him whistle a bird call as he strode the corridors. In fact, he seemed to be acting a bit strangely in a number of ways, not the least of which was his plan to raise funds for the new wing (his legacy?) by getting prot to go on television. I suspected he was suffering from a mild case of depression, perhaps due to his having reached the standard retirement age of sixty-five. Or maybe he was just overworked—my own tenure as acting director was the most difficult period of my life.

I wanted to come right out and ask him if there was anything I could do to lighten his load, but I knew that would get nowhere. Besides, I had enough problems without adding him to my already overcrowded schedule.

When I returned to my office I found Giselle sitting in my chair, her feet resting on the stack of papers covering my desk, oblivious to her surroundings. "Giselle, you can't have my desk. You're only here because—"

"I think I know when he's leaving."

"You do? When?"

"About the middle of September."

"How do you know that?"

"When I told him there may be a trip to the zoo in the next couple of weeks, he said, 'I can just make it. Count me in.' "

"Okay. Good. Keep it up. Do you have any idea yet who he's taking with him when he leaves?"

"He won't say a word about that. Says he has to work out some details. But it could be anyone."

"That's what I was afraid of. Anything else?"

"I need a place to spread out."

"C'mon. Let's see if we can find you a desk somewhere."

"ALL right," I said, after watching prot devour a half-dozen oranges. "Let's get to work."

"You call this work? Sitting around chatting and eating fruit? It's a picnic!"

"Yes, I know your thoughts about work. Now—is Robert there with you?"

"Yep, he's right nearby."

"Good. I'd like him to come out for a while."

"What—without your hypnosis trick?"

"Robert? May I speak with you please?"

Prot sighed, set aside the ragged remains of an orange, and gazed dully at the ceiling.

"Robert? This is very important. Please come out for a moment. Everything will be all right. No harm will come to you or to anyone. . . ."

But prot just sat there with his know-it-all smirk. "You're wasting your time, gino. One, two—hey—where's the dot?"

"I'm not going to hypnotize you just yet."

"Why not?"

"I've got another idea."

"Will wonders never cease!"

I reached into my shirt pocket and pulled out the whistle. Prot watched me with amusement as I put it to my lips and blew. At that moment the smirk vanished and a different person appeared, only I wasn't sure who it was. He wasn't slouched in the chair as Robert usually is. "Robert?"

"I'm here, Dr. Brewer. I've been waiting for you to call." Though he seemed quite unhappy about it, he was nonetheless there, apparently ready to talk.

I stared at him, savoring the moment. It was the first time I had ever seen Robert when he wasn't catatonic or under hypnosis (with rare exceptions—see K-PAX). But the triumph was undercut by a hint of suspicion. Something wasn't right—it seemed too easy. On the other hand, he

294

had been pondering his dilemma for years, and perhaps, as sometimes happens, he was simply getting bored with living in a figurative straitjacket. "How are you feeling?"

"Not so hot." He looked much like prot, of course, but there were dissimilarities. For example, he was far more serious, not the least bit cocky. His voice was a little different. And he seemed exhausted.

"I can understand that. I hope we can help you feel better soon."

"That would be nice."

"Let me ask you first: Should I call you Robert or Rob?"

"My family calls me Robin. My friends call me Rob."

"May I call you Rob?"

"If you like."

"Thank you. Care for some fruit?"

"No, thanks. I'm not hungry."

There were so many questions I wanted to ask him that I didn't know where to begin. "Do you know where you are?"

"Yes."

"How do you know that?"

"Prot told me."

"Where is prot right now?"

"He's waiting."

"Can you speak with him?"

"Yes."

"Good. Now—do you know where you've been for the past five years?"

"In my room."

"But you couldn't move and you couldn't speak to us—do you remember?"

"Yes."

"Were you able to hear us?"

"Yes. I heard everything."

"Can you tell me why you couldn't speak or respond in some way?"

"I *wanted* to. But I just couldn't."

"Do you know why?"

"I was afraid to."

"Why were you afraid?"

"I was afraid . . ." He gazed off into some inner space. "I was afraid of what might happen."

"All right. We'll get back to that later. Let me just ask you this: You seem to be less fearful now than you were then—can you tell me why?"

He started to answer, then hesitated.

"Take your time."

"There are a couple of reasons."

"I would like very much to hear them, Rob, if you feel like telling me."

"Well, all of you have been so kind to me since I came here that I guess I felt like I owed you something."

"Thank you. I'm glad you feel that way. And the other reason?"

"He said I can trust you."

"Prot? Why now, and not before?"

"Because he's leaving soon, and I think he's becoming impatient with me."

"How soon? Do you know?"

"No."

"All right. But you were in the same situation five years ago. How is it different this time?"

"Last time I knew he would be coming back. This time he's not."

"He's not coming back? How do you know that?"

"He doesn't like it here."

"I know, but—"

"He told me you would take his place. That you would help me when he's gone."

He was appealing to me with such intensity that I went over and placed my hand on his shoulder. "I will, Rob. Believe me, I'll help you in every way I can."

With that he slowly puckered his face and began to cry. "I'm so tired of feeling bad. You don't know how bad it is." His head dropped.

"No one who's not in your shoes can understand what you've been through, Rob. But we've helped a lot of people in similar situations and I think you're going to feel better very soon."

His head lifted and he looked at me. He was no longer crying. "Thanks, dr. b. I feel better already."

"Prot? Where's Robert?"

"He's kind of tired. But if you play a nice tune on your whistle he might be back later."

"Uh—prot?"

"Hmmmmmmmm?"

"Thank you."

"For what?"

"For giving him the confidence to come out."

"Did he tell you that?"

"Yes. And he also told me this might be your last visit to Earth. Is that true?"

"It is if you get Robert back on his feet. Then there wouldn't be any need for me to come, would there?"

"No, there wouldn't. In fact, it might be better if you didn't."

"Don't worry—I know when I'm not wanted. Besides, there are a lot of other interesting places to go."

297

"Other planets?"

"Yep. Billions and billions of them in this GALAXY alone. You'd be surprised."

"Can you give us a little time before you go back? Can you give us six more weeks?"

"I can only give you what I've got."

"Will you at least tell me how much you've got?"

"Nope."

"But prot—Robert's life is at stake. Which is why you're here, isn't it?"

"I told you before: I'll give you some warning. It won't come as a complete surprise."

"I'm happy to hear that," I said glumly. "All right. Well, as long as you're here, I'd like to ask you one more thing about Rob."

"Is that a promise?"

"Not exactly. Now—is there some other reason he's suddenly speaking to me? Anything I don't know?"

"There doesn't seem to be any limit to what you don't know, my human friend. But I will tell you this: Don't be fooled by his cheery disposition. It was all he could do to come forward today. He still has a long way to go and he could retreat at a moment's notice. Be gentle with him."

"I'll do my very best, prot."

"In spite of your primitive methods? Lotsa luck." He picked up the fragment of orange and stuffed it into his mouth.

"How are you doing with the letters, by the way?"

Through orange teeth: "I've read most of them."

"Any decisions yet?"

"Too soon for that."

"Will you tell me when you've decided who's going back with you?"

"I might. Or maybe I'll save it for the tv show."

"What? Who told you about that?"

"Everyone knows about that."

"I see. And I suppose everyone knows about the trip to the zoo? And about all the people who want to talk to you?"

"Of course."

"Prot?"

"Yeah, coach?"

"You're driving me crazy."

"Tell me about it," he sighed.

Thinking he was joking, I chuckled a little. But he seemed to be quite serious. I glanced at the clock on the wall behind him—we still had a few minutes left. I stood up. "All right. You take my place and I'll take yours."

Without a moment's hesitation he jumped up and ran over to my chair. He plopped into it, squeezed the vinyl arms several times, and whirled around in a complete circle. Obviously enjoying himself, he grabbed a yellow pad and began to scribble furiously as he stroked an imaginary beard.

I took his chair. "You're supposed to ask me some questions," I prodded.

"That won't be necessary," he mumbled.

"Why not?"

"Because I already know what's bugging you."

"I'd love to hear what it is."

"Alimentary, my dear canal. You were born on a mean, cruel PLANET from which you see no way to escape. You're trapped here at the mercy of your fellow humans. That would drive any being crazy." Suddenly he banged his fist on the arm of my chair. "Time's up!" He scooted over, grabbed another orange, and bit into it. Then he whirled again and flung his feet onto my desk. "And I've got work to do," he concluded with a dismissive wave. "Pay the cashier on your way out."

I gave him a poor imitation of a Cheshire-cat grin. He screeched and bolted for the door.

It wasn't until later that I happened to glance at the yellow pad he had scribbled on. In a messy but legible scrawl he had written, over and over again, 17:18/9/20. It took me a moment to figure it out, but finally I realized: He's leaving on the twentieth at 5:18 P.M.!

NOT having been in Ward Three since before my "vacation," I decided to take a brief tour. I found Michael in 3B perusing a book called *The Right to Die*, a work he has read dozens of times, as Russell reads and rereads the New Testament.

A naked woman streaked by. Michael ignored her. He wanted to know when he was going to get to talk with prot. Unforgivably, his request had slipped my mind, but I told him I would see to it immediately. He said, jokingly, I hoped, "I could be dead by the time he gets here." I slapped him on the shoulder and continued my rounds, stopping to chat with various social and sexual deviates, tortured souls preoccupied with specific bodily functions. I watched in never-ending amazement as one of them, a Japanese-American male, undressed himself, smelled the crotch of his underwear, then dressed again, and undressed, over and over again. Another man kept trying to kiss my hand. Others performed their own endless rituals and compulsions. Yet none of these miserable creatures were more tragic than the inhabitants of 3A, the severely autistic ward.

Autism was once blamed principally on unfeeling and uncaring parents, especially the mother. It is now known

300

that autists suffer some sort of brain defect, whether genetic or induced by organic disease, and no amount of nurturing will alter the progress of this debilitating affliction.

Stated simply, autists are missing the part of brain function that makes a person a soulful human being, someone who can relate to other people. Although often able to perform extraordinary feats, they appear to do so entirely mechanically without any "feel" for what they have accomplished. The ability of the autist to concentrate on whatever it is that occupies his or her thoughts is astonishing, and typically to the exclusion of everything else. There are exceptions, of course, and some are able to hold jobs and learn to function to some extent in society. Most, however, live in worlds of their own.

I found our twenty-one-year-old engineering wizard, whom I'll call Jerry, working on a matchstick recreation of the Golden Gate Bridge. It was almost finished. On display nearby were replicas of the Capitol Building, the Eiffel Tower, the Taj Mahal. I watched him for a while. He worked deftly and rapidly, yet seemed to pay little attention to his project. His eyes darted all over the room, his mind apparently somewhere else. He used no notes or models, but worked from memory of photographs he had glanced at only briefly.

To Jerry, who may not even have noticed me, I said, "That's beautiful. How long before it's finished?"

"Before it's finished," he replied, without changing his pace.

"What's next on the agenda?"

"Agenda. Agenda. Agenda. Agenda. Agenda. Agenda—"

"Well, I've got to go now."

"Go now. Go now. Go now."

"Bye, Jer."

"Bye, Jer."

And so it was with the others, most of whom were wandering around or staring intently at their fingertips or studying the blemishes on the walls. Sometimes someone would let out a bark or start clapping his hands, but not one of them paid the slightest attention to me or glanced in my direction. It is as if autists actively practice a kind of desperate avoidance. Nevertheless, we continue to try to find some way to relate to them, to enter their worlds, to bring them into ours.

One feels sorry for such individuals, to pity their lack of contact with other human beings. Yet, for all we know, they may be quite happy within the confines of their private realms, which might, in fact, encompass gigantic universes filled with an incredible variety of shapes and relationships, with interesting and satisfying visions, and tastes and sounds and smells that the rest of us cannot even imagine. It would be fascinating to enter such a world for one glorious moment. Whether we would choose to stay there, however, is another matter.

Session Twenty-one

Still trying to come to grips with what I suspected was prot's upcoming "departure" date, I took a stroll on the grounds, where a spirited game of croquet was in progress, though what rules were in force was impossible to determine. Behind this circus I spotted Klaus over by the sunflowers talking animatedly with Cassandra, a woman in her mid-forties who has the ability to forecast certain events with uncanny accuracy. How she does this is anybody's guess, including her own. The problem with Cassandra is that she has no interest in anything else. By the time she was brought to us she had nearly starved to death. Her first words, after she had seen the lawn with its plethora of chairs and benches from which she could contemplate the heavens, were, "I think I'm going to like it here."

One of the areas in which she excels is that of weather. Perhaps this is because she's outdoors so much, winter and summer. If you've ever heard the five-day forecasts of the shameless TV weather people, you know that their predictions are very often wrong. Cassie, on the other hand, is usually right for periods of up to two weeks from the date of her prognostication. I had heard, in fact, that Villers, her staff physician, had consulted her about conditions for the proposed outing to the zoo before he would allow a date to be set. (When Milton heard that fair weather was expected for the trip, he remarked, "Only fair? Surely we should wait until it gets better.")

Animals also seem to know when changes in the weather are coming, possibly because of some unknown sensitivity to subtle variations in air pressure or humidity, though not so far in advance, probably. But how can we explain her uncanny ability to predict, with more than ninety-percent accuracy, who will become the next president or the winner of the Super Bowl, weeks or even months beforehand, something no animal can do. (It is rumored that Villers has reaped a small fortune from her desultory pronouncements, which he usually keeps to himself, claiming doctor-patient privilege.) What does she see in the sun and stars that the rest of us are missing?

I also saw Frankie waddling around the lawn under her usual black cloud. Her inability to form human relationships seems to be related in some way to autism—perhaps a similar part of the brain is involved. Unlike the true autists, however, she has no problem communicating with the staff and her fellow patients, though what she conveys is likely to be a caustic comment or jarring insult. Whether these jabs are intentional I can't say, but she was one patient I hoped prot might be able to help, despite his own misgivings about human love.

At the far corner I noticed several of the other inmates grouped under the big oak tree, shading themselves like a bunch of sheep from the heat of the August sun, except that they were all facing inward. I wondered whether something had happened. But when I started in their direction I saw prot in their midst. He was holding forth on some subject or other, commanding their complete attention. Even Russell was silent. As I approached them my beeper squealed.

I hurried to a phone and punched the number of the departmental office. "It's Robert Porter's mother," the operator said. "Can you take the call?" I asked him to transfer it.

Mrs. Porter had received my letter and understandably wanted to know how Robert was doing. Unfortunately, I could only tell her that I was pleased with his progress so far, but that much more work remained to be done. She asked when she could come to see him. I told her I would let her know the moment her son was well enough for that. She seemed disappointed, of course, but agreed to wait for further progress. (I didn't mention the possibility that she might instead find him in the same state he was in when she was here five years ago.)

I returned to the lawn. Villers had departed, leaving Cassandra to gaze once more at the heavens. Prot was gone, too, and the others were milling around under the oak tree, directionless without their magnetic leader. Frankie was still off by herself, cursing the wind.

"DR. Flynn was here yesterday with another astronomer and a physicist," Giselle told me over lunch in the staff dining room. "I gave him an hour with prot. I've never seen anybody so eager to meet someone. He actually ran down the corridor to prot's room."

"Well, did he learn anything he didn't know before?"

"He didn't get everything he wanted, but he seemed to think it was worth the trip."

"Why didn't he get everything he wanted?"

"Prot's afraid he'll use the information to his own selfish ends."

"I figured as much. Of course it's also possible that prot doesn't know all the answers."

"I wouldn't count on it."

"What sorts of things did Flynn ask him about?"

She took an enormous bite of a sandwich and continued, her jaw the size of an apple, "For one thing, he wanted to know how old the universe is."

"How old is it?"

"Infinitely."

"What?"

"You remember—it keeps expanding and contracting, forever and ever."

"Oh. Right."

"Flynn wasn't satisfied with that. He asked him how long the present expansion has been going on."

"What did prot tell him?"

"He said, 'How do you know it's expanding?' Flynn started to explain the Doppler effect but prot cut himshort with: 'When the UNIVERSE is in the contraction phase you'll still have the same Doppler shift.' Flynn said, 'That's ridiculous.' Prot said, 'Spoken like a true homo sapiens.'"

"Anything else?"

"Yes. He wanted to know how many planets there are in our galaxy, and how many of them are inhabited."

"What did prot say?"

She swallowed some of the food bulging in her cheek. "He said there are a trillion planets in our galaxy alone, and a proportionate number in all the others. And guess what percentage of these are inhabited."

"Half of them?"

"Not *that* many. Point two percent."

"Is that all?"

"All? That means there are several billion planets and moons in the Milky Way teeming with life."

"How many of these creatures are like us?"

"That's the interesting thing. According to prot, a lot of the beings around the universe resemble us. 'Us' being mammals, birds, fish, and so on."

"What about humans?"

"He says that humanoid beings have arisen or are evolving on some of these, but that they usually don't last very long. About a hundred thousand of our years, on the average."

"Not a very pleasant prospect."

"Not for us."

"What else?"

"Dr. Flynn wanted to know how we can accomplish hydrogen fusion as an energy source."

"And prot wouldn't tell him, right?"

"Oh, he told him, all right."

"Really? What's the secret?"

"You won't believe it."

"Probably not."

"It only works with a certain substance as catalyst."

"What substance?"

"Something found on Earth only in spider excrement."

"You're kidding."

"But it's not just any old spider poop."

"It's not?"

"Nope. Only that from a particular species indigenous to Libya. The stuff comes in little gold pellets the size of poppy seeds!" She started to giggle.

"Is this prot's idea of a joke?"

"Flynn didn't think so. He's already trying to figure out how to get into Libya." Then she became more serious. "Guess what else?"

"I can't imagine."

"He wanted prot to give him a demonstration of light-travel."

I finished the last tiny curd of cottage cheese. "Did he comply?"

"Yes."

"What? He disappeared again?"

"Not exactly. He got out his little flashlight and his mirror, but just then a cat ran by. It meowed, and everybody turned to look at it for a second. When we looked back, he was on the other side of the room. Dr. Flynn was flabbergasted. So was I. I had never seen him do that before." Her eyes were bright as a squirrel's.

I couldn't hide my skepticism. "Sounds like a pretty neat trick."

"Dr. B, do you know anyone else who can do that trick?"

"Well, did prot tell him how it's done?"

"No. He said we're not 'ready' for light-travel."

"I figured as much."

Another bite and the cheek swelled up again. "Then the physicist jumped in. That got pretty hairy. She asked prot about all kinds of alpha and omega stuff. I'll have to do some studying to figure it all out. But one thing I understood."

"What's that?"

"You ever hear of quarks?"

"They're supposed to be the fundamental particles of atomic nuclei, aren't they?"

"Mm-hm. But inside of them are smaller particles and inside of them still smaller ones."

308

"Good God. Where does it all end?"

"It doesn't."

"What did the physicist think of all this?"

"She wanted the details."

"Did prot give her any?"

"Nope. He said that would spoil the fun of discovering them for herself."

"Maybe he doesn't know any of the details. Maybe he's just speculating."

"He knows enough to travel at superlight speed!"

"Maybe. Anything else?"

"That's about it. They left a thick notebook of additional questions for prot to consider."

I told her about my suspicion that he only had until September 20 to answer them. She nodded unhappily. "And what about the letters? Has prot said anything about the letters?"

"He's finished with them. He gave them back to me."

"He doesn't want them?"

"Whatever he wanted from them is in his head somewhere. Of course more keep coming in. He gets some every day."

"And where are the old ones?"

"They're on the little table you gave me to use as a desk." She drew out and emphasized the word "little." "You want to read them?"

"Isn't it illegal for me to read them?"

"Not if he gives you permission."

"Would he do that, do you think?"

"He already has. I'll put them on the *big* desk in your office."

"Not all of them. Just leave me a representative sample. By the way—the faculty thinks the idea of a trip to the zoo is a pretty good one. Can you contact the officials over there and set it up?"

"I know someone who works there. All I need from you is a definite date."

"GINO! Long time no see!"

"It's only been two days, prot."

"That's a long time. You can get halfway across some GALAXIES in two of your days."

"Maybe *you* could."

"So could you if you wanted to badly enough. But you're more concerned with other things. The stock market, for example."

"But you won't tell us how to do it."

"I just did."

"Uh-huh. Anything else you feel like telling me before we begin?"

"I think some of my correspondents would enjoy a long voyage."

"Who wants to go, for example?" I casually asked him.

"Your humor still needs work, gene."

"I mean in general."

"Those who are unhappy here on EARTH."

"That's not much help."

He shrugged.

"All right. Are you finished with your grape juice?"

"Yep. Amazing stuff. Nothing in the UNIVERSE purpler than grape juice."

"Okay. Remember the whistle?"

"Of course. But that won't be necessary, Dr. Brewer."

The transition had been so subtle that I barely noticed the slight change in voice and manner, especially with the purple mustache across his upper lip. "Robert?"

"Yes."

"How are you feeling?"

"I don't know. Strange. Shaky. Not too bad, I guess."

"I'm glad to hear that. Tell me—can you come out whenever you want to now?"

"I always could. I just—couldn't."

"I understand. Will you be able to stay here for a while?"

"If you like."

"Good. As I told you under hypnosis, this is your safe haven. Please try to remember that. Now—is there anything you especially want to talk about today? Anything bothering you right this minute?"

"I miss my wife and my little girl."

I was astonished by this simple sentence. Coming from anyone else it would have been routine and long overdue. But I thought it might take weeks to get him to talk about his family. This was a profound change. How much courage it must have taken for Robert to say it! "I'd like to hear more about them if you're ready to tell me."

His eyes drifted away and became moist and dreamy. It was as if he wanted to dwell lovingly on a delightful subject for a moment before beginning. At last he said, "We had a wonderful place in the country, with a garden and a small orchard. None of the trees had produced any fruit yet, but they would have in another year or two. We had five whole acres with a hedgerow and a small pond and a stream and lots of maples and birches. Prot told me it reminded him of K-PAX, except there's hardly any water there. The whole thing was full of life. Birds and rabbits and groundhogs and some goldfish in the pond. We had daffodils and tulips and forsythia. It was beautiful in the spring and fall. And the winter, too, when the snow came.

Sally loved winter. We used to do some cross-country skiing and Becky liked to skate around on the little pond. She loved all the birds and the other animals, too. She fed the deer. The house wasn't very big, but it was just about right for us. Sally couldn't have any more children. . . ." He paused for a few moments, remembering.

"We had a big fireplace and Becky had her own room with flowered wallpaper and enough space for all her things. She had some pictures taped to the walls. Rockstars, I guess. I never got much into rock and roll. The kitchen—" He broke off suddenly and his jaw seemed to clamp shut. "The kitchen—"

"That's all right, Rob. We can come back to the kitchen later."

"Why should we do that? Are you still hungry?"

"Prot! Where's Robert?"

"He's right here, collecting himself. Didn't I tell you to be more gentle with him?"

"Listen, my alien friend. I know what I'm doing. Robert has made remarkable progress since you've been back. Give him a chance."

He shrugged. "Just don't push too hard, doc. He's dancing as fast as he can."

"Are you going to let him come back, or not?"

"Just give him a minute or two. He's been trying to forget everything for a long time. It's hard for him to cough it up on demand."

"I haven't demanded anything."

"Could we talk about something else for a while?"

It took me a moment to realize that Robert had returned. "Whatever you want to talk about is fine with me, Rob."

"I don't know what to say."

"Let's go back a little. Would you like to tell me more about your boyhood? Last time we stopped when you were twelve, I believe."

"Twelve. I was in the seventh grade."

"Did you like school?"

"I hate to admit it, but I loved it."

"Why do you hate to admit it?"

"Everybody's supposed to hate school. But I liked it. I remember the seventh grade because that was the first year we went to different rooms for different classes."

"What classes did you like best?"

"General science. Biology. We had a field and woods behind our house, and I used to walk around there and try to identify all the different trees and things. That was great."

"Did you do that with a friend? Or one of your sisters?"

"No, I usually went by myself."

"Did you like to be by yourself?"

"I didn't mind. But I had friends, too. We played basketball and messed around together. Smoked cigarettes up in the tree house. But none of them cared about my field or the woods. So I usually went there by myself. I can still remember the way the trees smelled on a hot summer day, or the ground after a rain. The crickets at night. I saw deer sometimes early in the mornings and around sunset. I watched them and found out where they slept. They didn't know I was watching them. I used to go there in the evenings sometimes and wait for them to wake up, and then I'd see where they would go."

"What about Sally? Did you know her then?"

"Yes. Ever since first grade."

"What did you think of her?"

"I thought she was the prettiest girl in school. She had hair like the sun."

"Did you talk to her much?"

"No. I wanted to, but I was too shy. Anyway, she didn't pay much attention to me. She was a cheerleader and everything."

"When did she first begin to pay some attention to you?"

"When we were juniors. I was on the wrestling team. She started coming to the matches. I couldn't figure out why she did that, but I tried very hard to impress her."

"Did you succeed?"

"I guess so. One day she told me she thought I had some good moves. That was when I asked her to go to the movies with me. It was our first date."

"What did you see?"

"*The Sting.*"

"That's a terrific film."

Rob nodded. "I'll never forget it."

"When was your next date?"

"Not for quite a while."

"Why not?"

"Like I said, I was shy. Sally had other friends. I wasn't sure she liked me that much. I couldn't understand why she would."

"How did you find out she did?"

"If you've ever lived in a small town you know how word gets around. She told someone, and *she* told someone, and so on until it got back to me that she liked me a lot and wanted to go out with me again."

"So you finally asked her for another date?"

"Not exactly. She finally gave up and asked me."

"What did you think about that?"

"I liked it. I liked *her*. She was so friendly and outgoing.

When she was with you she made you feel like you were the only other person in the world."

"And eventually you fell in love with her."

"I think I was always in love with her. I used to dream about her all the time."

"You got the girl of your dreams!"

Thoughtfully: "Yes, I guess I did." He produced a sickly smile. "I'm lucky, aren't I?"

"Do you remember any of the dreams?"

"I—I don't think so. . . ."

"All right. We'll talk about that some other time. When did you ask Sally to marry you?"

"On graduation day."

"From high school."

"Yes."

"Weren't there some problems associated with that? Didn't you want to go to college?"

"She was pregnant."

"She was carrying your child?"

"No."

"She wasn't?"

"No."

I was puzzled by this for a moment before I realized what he was saying. I asked, as gently and casually as I could, "Do you happen to know whose child it was?"

"No."

"All right. We'll come back to that later."

"If you say so, coach."

"Prot! You've got to stop popping up like this!"

"It's more like Rob popped down."

"Why didn't you tell me Rebecca wasn't Robert's child?"

"She wasn't?"

315

"No."

"I didn't know. Anyway, what's the diff?"

"On Earth people like to know who their fathers are."

"Why?"

"Blood is thicker than water."

"So is mucus."

"Just answer me this: Do you have any idea at all who Rebecca's father might be? Did Robert ever mention another boyfriend of Sarah's? Anything like that?"

"No. He didn't call me just to gossip. Anyway, why don't you ask him? He's right here."

"Thanks for the suggestion, but I think we'll call it quits for today. I don't want to push him too hard at this point."

"My dear sir, there may be hope for you yet."

I glanced at the clock. It was exactly three-fifty and there was a seminar at four. The speaker was Dr. Beamish, whose topic, one of his favorites, was "Freud and Homosexuality." "Before you go, just tell me one more thing: Is Robert all right now?"

"He's okay. He'll probably be ready to talk to you again by Friday."

"Good. Thanks again for all your help."

"No problemo."

He was still wearing the purple mustache as he turned and strode briskly out of my examining room. I had been so caught up in these unexpected developments that I forgot again to ask him whether he would be willing to speak with Mike and some of the other patients.

I didn't go to the seminar. There were several uncomfortable questions sticking like cockleburs to the edges of my mind.

316

For one thing, Robert had been literally hiding behind prot, barely saying a word for a decade, half of that in a state of catatonia. Now, abruptly, he was out and talking with only minimal encouragement. He *wanted* to talk! Though he retreated when the subject became too painful, he actually seemed fairly comfortable at times, and I wondered whether he had begun to come out in the wards as well (I made a note to check with Betty McAllister on this). It had been a dramatic, remarkable change, one that rarely happens in psychiatry.

For another, Rob attributed his sudden courage to prot's upcoming departure. But multiple personality disorder doesn't operate that way. It is Robert who calls prot into "existence" when he is needed. It would be a peculiar aberration indeed if prot refused to show up, although such a *rara avis* is not unknown in the literature. For example, there is the occasional case of a primary and secondary personality who can't stand each other, and sometimes the latter refuses to show up out of spite or the former declines to ask him to.

But prot and Robert seemed to get along quite well. Still, it occurred to me that the net effect of his leaving would be the same as that resulting from such a "family" spat. Perhaps I could get Robert angry enough with prot that he would be glad to see him depart. But would this help him to face the world on his own, or simply make matters worse?

There were other unanswered questions as well, chief of which was: Who was the father of Sally's child? And what effect did this twist of fate have on Robert's already damaged (by his father's untimely injury and eventual death twelve years earlier) psyche? It was beginning to look like the inside of an atom. Whenever we seemed to be getting somewhere more particles appeared. How deeply would we have to dig before we got to the heart of Robert's problem? And could we get there before the twentieth of September?

I discussed these concerns over dinner with my wife. Her comment was: "Maybe Robert isn't the father, and maybe he is."

I said, "What do you mean?"

"Maybe he can't admit it, even to himself. If you ask me, the key event happened much earlier than that."

"What makes you think so?"

"Well, prot made his first appearance when Robert was six, didn't he? Sometime before that. Maybe you should concentrate on his early childhood."

"I'm dancing as fast as I can, 'Doctor' Brewer!"

WHEN I arrived on Thursday morning I found a stack of "prot" letters on my desk. Some were written by people who might as well have been residents of MPI or another hospital. ("Help! Someone's trying to poison our water with fluoride!") Others had plans to "develop" K-PAX; for example, to turn it into a gigantic theme park called "Utopia." Still others wanted to spread their various religions to the far corners of the universe. But most were pathetically similar. The following is an example of one such letter:

Glen Burnie, Maryland

Dear Mr. Prot:

My son Troy is ten years old. After he saw on TV a story about how you don't kill any animals or eat meat, he won't eat it either. I don't know what to give him. He seems healthy, but I'm afraid he's not getting enough of the vitamines [sic] that you get in meat. He has thrown out all his toy soldiers, too. Now he says he wants to go to K-PAX with you. In fact, he's all packed.

I don't know what to do. Please write to him and explain that you didn't mean that earth people are supposed to be like you.

Thank you.

Yours truly,
Mrs. Floyd B—

Many of the letters were from children themselves, scrawled in large print. The two I saw were typical, I suppose. One pleaded with prot to "please stop all the wars." The other, from an older girl, apologized that she couldn't go to K-PAX now because she had to help out at home, but could she come later? If these were a representative sampling of those that prot had received, there must have been thousands and thousands of children all over the world who were ready and willing to take their chances on an alien planet rather than accept what they had inherited from their forebears. I felt both sadness and elation at the prospects for the future of our own world if these heartfelt letters were any indication of the thoughts and hopes of today's youth.

At the bottom of the stack was a piney note neatly hand-written in green ink: *I want to go, too!*

A peculiar sight: prot and Giselle hurrying through the lounge on their way to the front door, Russell following close behind and, trailing along after him, a bunch of the other patients. And, behind *them*, a string of cats. Milton danced along at the front of the pack, wearing his funny hat and playing an imaginary tin whistle. No one was saying a word. It was almost like a strange, silent dream, an image from a Bergman or Kurosawa film. I noticed that prot was carrying something in his upturned palm.

Not wanting to disturb them, I ran to the front windows and watched as he dropped his cargo onto the lawn, to shouts and applause from his coterie. I couldn't see what it was. It was only later that I learned that prot had found a spider frantically trying to claw its way up the side of one of the bathroom sinks. He and the others had taken it outside. When it disappeared in the grass Russell said a prayer and the whole thing was over.

Russ had been praying a lot lately, even more so than when he believed himself to be Jesus Christ. I'd been told he had decided that the end of the world wasn't far off. Whether this had anything to do with prot's return I couldn't say. In any case, his newfound preoccupation with death and the next world was little different from that of millions of other people walking around loose.

As I watched the group come back through the big door at the end of the lounge, prot and Giselle hand in hand, something occurred to me that I hadn't thought of before, or perhaps chose to ignore. The rebudding romance between them (despite prot's abhorrence of sex) seemed to be getting stronger by the day. How would she take it if prot disappeared and Robert took his place in the world? More to the point, might she try to obstruct Robert's treatment in some way? And would prot's evident fondness for her likewise cause him second thoughts about helping Robert to get well?

320

Session Twenty-two

On the first day of September we were honored by a visit from the chairman of our board of directors. Villers had thoroughly impressed upon everyone the importance of his arrival—the hospital was looking for a donor for whom we would name the badly needed (and still unfunded) new wing. I was awarded the privilege of hosting this distinguished businessman, whose stock portfolio gave him control of several major corporations, a bank, a television network (the one producing prot's talkshow interview, I realized), and other enterprises. Menninger joked that he was so rich he was considering making a run for the presidency. Klaus was determined to get a share of this treasure trove.

My first impression when I met him at the gate was that he must have had a very difficult childhood. Despite his great wealth and commensurate power he was noneffusive almost to the point of disappearing. He reluctantly offered me a hand that was so cold and limp that I instinctively dropped it, as if it were a dead fish. That probably cost us a few thousand, I thought with some dismay. But perhaps he was used to it.

During the entire visit he never looked my way. As we toured the grounds prior to having coffee with Villers and the rest of the executive committee, I noticed that he kept a respectable distance from me, as if to avoid contamination. Indeed, one of his bodyguards stationed himself between us at all times. Furthermore, he seemed to suffer from a mild form of obsessive-compulsive disorder. Whenever we approached anything with a corner on it he would stop and feel the sharp vortex with his thumb before moving on (I had heard that there were no corners anywhere in his office).

Oddly, he seemed discomfited by the sight of the patients milling around, particularly Jackie sitting on the grass, a mound of dirt piling up between her bare legs. Bert, checking for lost valuables behind every tree, and Frankie, who was shuffling around topless to beat the heat, did nothing to ease his consternation. Apparently he had never seen mentally disturbed people before. Or perhaps it was a case of what might easily have been himself.

Nevertheless, everything was going more or less smoothly and according to plan until Manuel loped toward us, squawking and flapping his arms. When I turned to explain to our visitor the problem with this particular patient, I saw him sprinting for the gate. The bodyguards were barely able to keep up with him. I certainly wasn't.

Villers couldn't bring himself to speak to me the entire morning. I didn't get any of the free coffee or little cakes, either. To tell the truth, I holed up in my office for the rest of the forenoon, reorganizing my files and ignoring the phone. But when I saw him at lunch he was positively apoplectic with joy. Our board chairman had sent over a check for one million dollars. More than enough to get our fundraising program off the ground, and giving him a leg up on a name above the door of the new facility.

Klaus was so delighted, in fact, that he paid for my meal (cottage cheese and crackers), a first for him.

PROT ignored the bowl of fruit when he came into my examining room and I knew that Robert had already come forward without even being asked. "Rob?"

"Hello, Dr. Brewer."

"Is prot with you?"

"He says to go ahead without him."

"That's all right. Maybe we won't need him this time." He shrugged.

"How are you feeling today?"

"Okay."

"Good. I'm happy to hear that. Shall we take up where we left off last time?"

"I guess so." He seemed nervous.

I waited for him to begin. When he didn't, I prodded: "Last time we were talking about your wife and daughter—remember?"

"Yes."

"Is there anything more you'd like to tell me about them?"

"Could we talk about something else?"

"What do you want to talk about?"

"I don't know."

"Would you like to tell me about your father?"

There was a long pause before he replied, "He was a wonderful man. He was more like a friend than a father."

Oddly, he seemed to be reciting this, as if he had prepared and rehearsed it.

"You spent a lot of time with him?"

"The year he died we were together all the time."

"Tell me about that."

Almost woodenly: "He was sick. A steer had fallen on him in the slaughterhouse and crushed him. I don't know what all was wrong with him, but it was a lot of things. He was in pain all the time. All the time. He didn't sleep much."

"What sorts of things did you do together?"

"Games, mostly. Hearts, Crazy Eights, Monopoly. He taught me to play chess. He didn't know how to play, but he learned and then he taught me."

"Could you beat him?"

"He let me beat him a few times."

"How old were you then?"

"Six."

"Did you play any chess later on?"

"A little in high school."

"Were you any good?"

"Not too bad."

This gave me an idea (I had checked with Betty, and also Giselle: Robert had not yet made an appearance in the wards). "Some of the other patients play chess. Would you like a game sometime?"

He hesitated. "I don't know. Maybe. . . ."

"We'll wait until you're ready. Okay—what else can you tell me about your father?"

Again as if by rote: "Mom got him a book on astronomy from the library. We learned a lot of the constellations. He had a pair of binoculars and we looked at the moon and planets. We even saw four of Jupiter's moons with them."

324

"That must've been something."

"It was. It made the planets and stars seem not so far away. Like it would be easy to get there."

"Tell me something about that. What did you think it would be like on another planet?"

"I thought it would be fantastic. Daddy told me that all kinds of different creatures might live there, but that most of them would be nicer than people were. That there wouldn't be any crime, or any wars, and everyone would get along fine. There wouldn't be any sickness either, or poverty or injustice. I felt sorry that we were stuck here, and that he was always hurting so much and nobody could do anything about it. But when we were outside at night looking up at the stars he seemed to feel better. Those were the best times. . . ." Rob gazed dreamily at the ceiling.

"What else did you do?"

Shakily (he was almost in tears) he replied, "We watched TV sometimes. And we talked. He got me a dog. A big, shaggy dog. He was red. I called him 'Apple.'"

"What sorts of things did you talk about?"

"Nothing special. You know—what it was like when he was growing up, stuff like that. He taught me to do things, like how to pound a nail and saw a board. He showed me how the car's engine worked. He was my friend and my protector. But then—" I waited for him to come to grips with his thoughts. At last he said, as though he still couldn't believe it, "But then he died."

"Were you there when that happened?"

Robert's head jerked to the side. "No."

"Where were you?"

He turned back toward me, but his eyes avoided my gaze. "I—I don't remember. . . ."

"What's the next thing you remember?"

"The day of the funeral. Prot was there." He was start-ing to fidget in his chair.

"All right. Let's talk about something else for a moment."

He sighed deeply and the squirming stopped.

"What was it like when you were younger, before your father was injured? Did you spend a lot of time with him then?"

"I don't know. Not as much, I guess."

"Well, how old were you when the accident happened?"

"Five."

"Can you remember anything that happened when you were younger?"

"It's all kind of fuzzy."

"What's the earliest thing you remember?"

"Burning my hand on the stove."

"How old were you then?"

"Three."

"What's the next thing you remember?"

"I remember being chased by a cow."

"How old were you then?"

"It was my fourth birthday. We had a picnic in a field."

"What else happened when you were four?"

"I fell out of the willow tree and broke my arm."

Robert went on to relate a variety of other things that had happened to him when he was four. For example, they moved to a different house. He could recall that day in some detail. By the time he turned five, however, everything became a blank. When he tried to remember, he became distressed, unconsciously wagging his head from side to side.

"All right, Rob. I think that's enough for today. How do you feel?"

"Not too good," he sighed.

"All right. You can relax now. Just close your eyes and breathe slowly. Is prot there with you?"

"Yes, but he doesn't want to be bothered. He says he's thinking."

"Okay, Rob, that's all for now. Oh—one more thing: I'd like to put you under hypnosis next time. Would that be all right with you?"

His pupils seemed to visibly shrink. "Do we have to do that?"

"I think it would help you to get well. You want to get well, don't you?"

"Yes," he said, somewhat mechanically.

"Okay. We'll do an easy test on Tuesday to determine how good a subject you are for the procedure."

"We won't be meeting on Monday?"

"Monday is Labor Day. We'll meet again next Wednesday."

"Oh. Okay." He seemed relieved.

"Thank you for coming in. It was a good session."

"Terrif. So long, doc." On his way out he grabbed a couple of pears and bit into one of them, and I knew that Rob had "retired" for the day.

"Prot?"

"Yeah?"

"Want to go to a picnic on Monday?"

"Will there be fruit?"

"Of course."

"I'm goin'!"

"Good. And I wonder if you'd do me another favor."

He mumbled something in paxo.

"I've got a patient I'd like you to talk to." I told him about Michael. He seemed quite interested in the case. "If

I let you into Ward Three will you try to help him?"

"Help him commit suicide?"

"No, goddamn it. Help talk him out of it."

"I wouldn't dream of it."

"Why not?"

"It's his life. But I'll tell you what I'll do. I'll find out why he wants to do it and see if we can work something out."

"Thank you. That's all I'm asking. I'll set something up as soon—"

"Time!" prot shrieked. "And someone's waiting!"

I thought he meant Rodrigo, who had brought him up, but when I opened the door Betty was there with Kowalski. "Problem in the wards?" I asked them.

"It's Bert."

"Where's everyone else?"

"Most of the doctors have gone home early for the weekend."

"Listen—will you and Roman take prot down to 3B? I want him to talk to Michael. I'll be there shortly."

"Sure."

Prot said, "I know the way."

"I want Betty to see this, too."

He smiled tolerantly. "Okay, coach."

I ran to the stairs and down to the second floor, wondering what could have gone wrong with Bert, who can get along for days or weeks without a fuss before becoming desperately anxious about finding whatever it is he has lost. In this respect he is like the patients suffering from manic depression (bipolar disorder), traveling the mountainous road between indifference and near panic.

Bert has been with us for only a few months, arriving not long after he spent his own surprise birthday party destroying the shrubbery and beating in the neighbor's garage door frantically searching for something. A fine athlete who looks much younger than his forty-eight years, he would seem to be a man who has everything: friends, a job he loves, excellent physical health.

All the likely things were checked out early on, of course—a safety deposit key, a briefcase, his wallet—nothing of any importance seemed to be missing. Nor did it seem to be anything so obvious as a loss of youth (his hair was still thick and flaming red), of money or religious faith, or of a family member, or even the respect of his co workers, factors that sometimes play a role in one's state of well-being. The only clue we had was a closet full of dolls his mother had discovered when she paid him an earlier visit. But even that led nowhere.

On this particular occasion Bert was accosting everyone he encountered, loudly demanding that they empty their pockets and subject themselves to a "body search." I tried unsuccessfully to calm him down, but, as usual, ended up ordering a shot of Thorazine.

While I was helping get him back to his room, one of the nurses came running up, out of breath. "Dr. Brewer! Dr. Brewer! Betty needs you upstairs right away!"

"Where—Ward Four?"

"No! Ward Three! It's prot!" My first thought was: Damn! What's he done to Michael?

I signaled for someone to take over. "What happened?" I asked the nurse as we ran for the stairs. Suddenly I remembered prot's comment about Robert's attempt to drown himself in 1985: *He has that right, doesn't he?* I had made a stupid, amateurish, tactical mistake. Prot might well have agreed with Michael's desire to end his life and tried to help him.

"It's the autistic patients," she puffed. "Something's happened to them!"

"What? What's happened to them?" But we were already banging into 3B and there was no need for further explanation. In my thirty-two years of practice I have seen some terrible and some wonderful things. Nothing could match what we found there that afternoon.

Prot was sitting on a stool facing one of the autists. It was Jerry, the matchstick engineer, who had not said six words of his own since he arrived at the hospital some three years earlier. Prot was squeezing and stroking one of his hands in a warm and tender way, as if caressing a bird. Jerry, who had not looked anyone in the eye since he was an infant, was gazing into prot's. And he was speaking! Not loudly or frenetically, but quietly, almost in a whisper.

Betty was off to one side, smiling in her teary way. We edged toward her. Jerry was telling prot about his childhood, about certain things he liked to do, about his favorite foods, his love for architectural structures. Prot listened intently, nodding occasionally. After a while he squeezed Jerry's hand one last time and let it go. At that instant, poor Jerry's eyes wandered to the walls, to the furniture, anywhere but to the people in the room. Finally he got up and went back to working on his latest model, a space shuttle on its launch pad. In short, he reverted immediately to his usual state of being, the only existence he had known for the twenty-one years of his pathetic life. The whole episode had lasted only a few minutes.

Betty, still teary-eyed, said, "He did it for three of the others, too."

Prot turned to me. "Gene, gene, gene, where the mischief 'ave you been?"

"How did you do that?"

330

"I've told you before, doc. You just have to give them your undivided attention. The rest is easy." With that, he headed for the stairs, Kowalski trotting along behind.

"And that's only half of it," Betty said, blowing her nose.

"What's the other half?"

"I think Michael is cured!"

"Cured? C'mon, Betty, you know it doesn't work that way."

"I know it doesn't. But I think this time it did."

"What did prot say to him?"

"Well, you know Michael has always held himself responsible for the death of anyone he has ever had any direct contact with?"

"Yes."

"Prot found a way out for him."

"A way out? What way out?"

"He suggested that Michael become an EMS technician."

"Huh? How would that solve his problem?"

"Don't you see? He can make up for any deaths he has caused by saving other people's lives. He neutralizes his mistakes, so to speak, one at a time. It's perfectly logical. At least it is to Michael. And prot."

"Is Mike in his room now? I'd like to see him for a minute."

"I sent him to the library with Ozzie in Security. He couldn't wait to get hold of a manual on emergency medical procedures. You'll see. He's a totally different person!"

A great many thoughts raced around my head as I stared out the window of the train to Connecticut. I was thrilled that prot had apparently been able to do something for

Michael that I, in several months of therapy, had not. And his interaction with the autists was something I would never forget. (Before leaving my office I called Villers, Jerry's staff physician, and told him as calmly as I could manage what had happened. His only comment was an unemotional "Zat is so?")

As I gazed at the houses and lawns flying by I wondered whether psychoanalysis had somehow gotten on the wrong track. Why couldn't we see things as clearly as prot seemed to be able to? Was there some simple shortcut to a person's psyche if we only knew how to find it? A way to peel back the layers of the soul and put our hands on its core, to massage it like a stopped heart and get it going again?

I recalled Rob's telling me about his nights in the back-yard with his binoculars, his father's arm around his shoulder, both of them gazing into the heavens, the dog sniffing around the fence. If I tried hard enough could I become a part of that scene, feel what he must have felt?

I blamed my father for my loneliness as a child. As our town's only doctor, he commanded a great deal of respect, and this aura seemed to transfer to me as well. The other boys treated me as if I were somehow different, and I had a hard time making friends even though I desperately wanted to be one of them. As a result I became somewhat intro-verted, a characteristic I retain to this day, unfortunately. If it hadn't been for Karen living right next door I might have ended up a basket case.

I frankly envied Rob his relationship with his father and with his dog. I, too, wanted a dog. My father would-n't hear of it. He didn't like dogs. I think he may have been afraid of them.

On the other hand, if he or I had been different, or if he had lived longer, perhaps I wouldn't have become a psychiatrist. As Goldfarb is fond of saying, "If my grand-mother had wheels, she'd be a wagon." As I stared into the hazy sunlight trying to make some sense of Robert/prot's life, I suddenly thought of Cassandra, our resident seer. Could *she* tell me what would happen if prot left or, for that matter, whether he was, in fact, departing on the twentieth?

I didn't feel much like going in on Saturday, but Dustin's parents had requested a meeting with me and it was the only time I could manage. I found them waiting in the lounge. We chatted for a few minutes about the weather, the hospital food, the worn spots in the carpet. I had met them before, of course. They seemed a genial couple will-ing to try to help their son in any way possible, visiting him often and assuring me we had their complete confidence and full support.

They had requested the meeting to discuss Dustin's progress. I told them frankly that there hadn't been much as yet, but we were thinking about trying some of the newer experimental drugs. As I talked with these gentle people, I found myself contemplating the possibility that despite their almost obsequious behavior, they might have abused Dustin in some way. A similar case came to mind involving a beloved minister and his wife who had, together, beaten their small boy to death. No one in the congregation seemed to have noticed the bruises and contusions, or they chose to ignore them. Could Dustin's be a similar case? Was he harboring injuries we hadn't yet been able to detect, present-ing us with cryptic hints to the underlying cause of his problem?

Child molestation takes many forms. It can be sexual, or involve other types of physical or mental abuse. Because of the child's fear and reluctance to tell anyone else, it is one of the most difficult aberrations to track down. A visit to a doctor will sometimes turn up evidence for such maltreatment (though physicians, too, are sometimes reticent about acting in such instances). But Dustin's medical records indicated no such problem, and it wasn't until he was in high school that he suddenly "snapped." Why it happened then is a mystery, as is the case, unfortunately, for many of our patients.

Session Twenty-three

I was gripped, as usual, by a strong sense of déjà vu as Karen and I waited for everyone to show up on a sunny, though relatively cool, Labor Day. It was here, five years ago, that I first became aware of the turmoil roiling deep inside prot's (Robert's) mind, and that I caught a glimpse of his ability to influence people's lives, not only those of the patients but members of my own family as well.

Shasta and Oxeye, the dalmatians, sniffed about the yard, keeping an eye on the front gate as well as the picnic table. They were well aware that visitors were on their way.

Only half the family would be coming to this, the last cookout of the summer. Our oldest son Fred was on location shooting a film musical (he had a part in the chorus), and Jennifer, the internist, was unable to get away from the clinic in San Francisco. In fact, we hadn't seen either of them for several months. One by one, it appears, your children separate the ties and slip away. At moments like this

I begin to feel older and older, less and less relevant, as the drumbeat of time grows ever louder and harder to ignore. Though still (barely) in my fifties, I find myself wondering whether retirement might not be preferable to running down like an old grandfather clock.

Karen keeps asking me when I'm going to put away my yellow pad, and sometimes I think it would be quite wonderful to spend my days wandering leisurely around the wards, chatting with the patients, getting to know them intimately as prot does, a knack that Will, and a few of the nurses, seem to have been born with. A busman's retirement, to be sure, but I know one or two drivers who love to spend their holidays riding around the country seeing things they had missed before. And no more cottage cheese!

Abigail and her husband Steve and the kids were the first to arrive. Abby greeted me warmly. As both of us have grown older she has begun to understand that I did my best as a father, as I, in turn, have come to grips with my own father's shortcomings. We all make mistakes, we never get it right, as she is learning for herself, which (as prot pointed out) is probably the only way any of us ever really learn anything.

Abby, perhaps sensing an ally in our alien visitor, took the opportunity, which she hadn't done in years, to ask me whether I realized yet that animal experimentation was "the most costly mistake in the history of medical science. Not that some good hasn't come of it," she went on before I could respond, "as there would be for almost any pissass approach to scientific problems. But we have to ask how much farther we might have progressed if better methodologies had been developed decades ago."

I reminded my daughter, the radical, that she might get farther with her case if she cleaned up her language a little, and if the animal-rights people would stop breaking into laboratories and terrorizing researchers.

"Oh, Dad, you're so fucking *establishment*. As if property and what you call 'bad language' were more important than the animals you kill every day. They called the war (she meant Vietnam) protesters terrorists, too, remember? Now we know that was just bullshit. They were *right* and everybody knows it. It's exactly the same now with the animal-rights movement. Fortunately," she added, only half jokingly, "all you old farts will peter out someday and things will change. The younger guys are beginning to see the folly of animal research." Then she smiled and kissed me on the cheek. Happily, all our arguments end this way.

My astronomer son-in-law Steve knew all about Charlie Flynn's interview with prot, and he reported that his colleague was busy searching the skies with renewed vigor for evidence of inhabited planets. Over the past few years Flynn has received a number of prestigious awards for his "discoveries" of several previously unknown worlds, including Noll and Flor and Tersipion, all of which were brought to his attention by prot in 1990. He and some of his colleagues were also working with officials at the State Department in hopes of visiting Libya or, at a minimum, of arranging to import as much excrement as possible from a certain spider indigenous to that country. And he had put all his graduate students to work shining lights into mirrors, hoping they would skip across the laboratory at superlight speeds, so far without success. "Ah love it," Steve drawled. "It's just like bein' in a sci-fi novel."

My grandsons Rain and Star, ages eleven and nine respectively, had a good time that day, primarily because of the dogs, I suppose, with whom they are great friends. As soon as they arrived the great Frisbee chase began, the boys' shoulder-length hair flying out behind them like little flags. Shasta Daisy, now thirteen, hard of hearing and somewhat arthritic, became a puppy again in the excitement of the chase.

Betty and her husband Walt and the triplets arrived a little later with Giselle and prot, whom Shasta recognized at once from the similar visit five years earlier. Oxeye approached him as well, though somewhat more cautiously. Perhaps he instinctively realized this was not Robert, the silent companion of his puppyhood (I had brought Oxie to the catatonic ward in a feeble attempt to get Rob to relate to him). In any case, the dogs rarely left his side all afternoon.

Finally came Will, who brought his girlfriend Dawn. Will had just finished his summer stint at MPI, disappointed that he had not been able to decipher Dustin's secret code. He was sure it had something to do with the "cigar" pantomime, but he couldn't figure out what. He came to relax on this Labor Day, his final free day before classes began, but he was also hoping to speak with prot about how he might be able to communicate with Dustin.

Nothing extraordinary happened for most of the afternoon, and we all enjoyed a terrific backyard picnic. When that was over, and everyone was sitting around talking, I took prot aside and asked him how Robert was feeling.

"He seems to be doing okay, gino. It must be your chairside manner."

"Thank you. Which reminds me—there's something I need to ask you while you're here."

"Ask away."

"In our last session, Robert called his father his 'friend and protector.' Do you know what he meant by that?"

"I never met his father. I didn't know Rob when his father was alive."

338

"I know. I just thought he might have mentioned something about him to you." I reached into my pocket and pulled out the whistle I had used to bring Robert forward during session twenty. "Remember this?"

"Not the briar patch! Oh, dear! Oh, dear! Anything but the briar patch!" Prot wrung his hands in mock dismay, though I could tell he had been expecting this. Everyone else had been warned, and all the adults present, particularly Giselle, were glancing somewhat nervously in our direction. I winked at her reassuringly. The boys, even little Huey, Louie, and Dewey, were also sitting still, the dogs at their feet. It was suddenly very quiet.

I had no idea whether it would work here, whether Robert was ready to make an appearance outside the relative security of my examining room. As soon as I touched the whistle to my lips, his head dropped for a moment, then raised again. I didn't even have to blow it.

"Hello, Dr. Brewer," he said. His eyes jerked around like a pair of frightened butterflies. "Where am I?" He removed prot's dark glasses so he could see better.

"You are at my home in Connecticut. Your second safe haven. Come on. I'll introduce you to everyone."

But before I could do that, Oxeye came running toward us, his tail flapping. He jumped up and began licking Robert's face (we were sitting in lawn chairs at the back of the yard). Obviously he recognized his former companion and was very glad to see him. Shasta, on the other hand, was less demonstrative. She had met Robert only once, when he freaked out at the sight of our lawn sprinkler.

For his part, Rob was overjoyed to see Oxie again, and he hugged him for several minutes. "I've missed you!" he exclaimed. The dog wagged his tail from ear to ear before running joyfully all over the yard, making several

339

close passes at Rob, as happy dalmatians will do. Later, Rob asked me whether we would keep his dog for him "a little longer." I assured him that we would be happy to do so, pleased that his outlook had become so positive.

Out of the confines of the hospital and prot's influence, Robert showed a side of himself I had not seen before. He was a courteous, kind, soft-spoken man who loved children, and he demonstrated for the boys a number of wrestling holds before joining in on a rip-roaring Frisbee chase with all five, and the dogs as well. If he had not been a mental patient, one would never have suspected there were demons gnawing and scratching just beneath his placid exterior.

Steve tried to engage him in a conversation about the heavens at one point, but gave up when it became apparent that Robert had only a cursory knowledge of the skies— the names of the planets and a few constellations. On the other hand, they both enjoyed comparing notes on their favorite college and professional football teams, though Robert was virtually unaware of developments in that sport since the mid-eighties.

But it was Giselle who occupied most of his time. Though she seemed to resent his presence at first, she was soon chatting quietly with him about her background and his (both came from small towns), and I certainly didn't discourage this. The more comfortable Rob became with these new and unfamiliar surroundings, the more he was likely to trust us and the better the prognosis. As I watched them I wondered whether it would be Robert or prot who would be returning to the hospital with Betty and her family.

But Rob didn't last out the afternoon. When he went into the house to use the bathroom it was prot who came out, dark glasses and all. Whether the interior had reminded him of that fateful day in 1985 I wasn't sure, but I made no attempt to recall his alter ego. I was delighted he had made an appearance at all.

When Will discovered that prot had returned he immediately pressed him about Dustin's "secret code."

"You mean you haven't worked that out yet? About the carrot and all? Ehhhh"—*chomp, chomp, chomp*—"what's up, doc?"

"Carrot?" Will stammered. "I thought it was a cigar."

"Why would he be munching a cigar?"

"Well—okay—what does the carrot mean?"

"You're smarter than your father. You figure it out."

Some of the others wanted to talk to prot as well. Steve pumped him about his own specialty, the formation of stars, and Giselle tried to get him to "speak" with Shasta, to find out whether he could learn anything about her background. Abby wanted to know how to get more people to sympathize with the plight of animals the world over. "Don't stifle your children's natural feelings toward them," he advised her. And even *they* were grilling him, wanting to know more about what life was like on K-PAX. Star, for example, wondered whether K-PAX was as pretty as the Earth.

Prot's eyes seemed to glaze over. "You can't imagine how beautiful it is," he murmured. "The sky changes from deep red to bright blue and back again, depending on which sun the illuminated side is facing. Rocks, fields of grains, faces—everything—glow in the radiant energy of the suns. And it's so quiet you can hear korms flying and other beings breathing far off in the distance. . . ."

I never did get a chance to ask him any of the host of questions I had been saving for him myself. That, like so many other matters, would have to wait for another time.

★　★　★

Although I had already brought Robert forth after hypno-tizing prot, for certain technical reasons I wanted to bypass the latter and deal directly with Rob. I had scheduled Robert's hypnosis-susceptibility (Stanford) test for early Tuesday morning, but was not surprised that it was prot who showed up. I took the opportunity to ask him, with no little trepidation, about my family and how they were doing (it was prot who put me on to Will's drug problem five years earlier).

"Your wife makes a great fruit salad," he said, stuffing his mouth to the brim with raspberries.

As patiently as I could manage, "Anything else?"

He squished the berries around in his mouth; a little stream of bloodred juice ran down his chin. "Abby seems to be one of the few human beings who understand what it will take to save the EARTH from yourselves. Of course she has some rough edges. . . ." He grinned wryly and a masticated berry tumbled from his mouth. "I like that."

"Dammit, prot, what about Will?"

"What about him?"

"Is he taking any drugs?"

"Only sex and caffeine. You humans never cease trying to find something to fulfill your boring lives, do you?"

"It may surprise you to learn, my friend, that there's no one on Earth more human than yourself."

"No need for insults, gino."

I laughed at that, perhaps out of relief. "So you think Will is doing all right, then?"

"He'll be a great doctor, *mon ami*."

"Thank you. I'm very happy to hear that."

"Anytime."

I could see from the lopsided grin that he still wasn't going to tell me when he would be leaving or who he planned to take with him. However, something else had occurred to me as I was driving in that morning. "Prot?"

"Yeth thir?" in his Daffy Duck voice. I thought: He's been hanging around Milton too long.

"Betty told me she saw you in the quiet room reading *K-PAX*."

"I was curious."

"Did you find any inaccuracies in it?"

"Only your absurd speculation that I am merely a figment of robert's imagination."

"That brings up an interesting question I've been meaning to ask you. How come I've never seen you and Robert at the same time?"

He slapped his forehead. "Gene, gene, gene. Have you ever seen me and the world trade center at the same time?"

"No."

"Then I presume you think the world trade center doesn't exist?"

"You know, there's a better way to conclusively prove or disprove that you and Robert are the same person. Will you give us a blood sample?"

"You already sampled it when I was here the first time, remember?"

"Unfortunately, it was accidentally discarded. May we have a little more?"

"There are no accidents, my friend. But why not? I've got plenty."

"I'll set it up with Dr. Chakraborty for later this week, okay?"

"Hokay, joe."

"Now—I need to speak to Robert for a while. Will you tell him, please?"

"Tell him what, Dr. Brewer?"

343

"Oh, hello, Robert. How are you feeling?"

"All right, I guess."

"Good. I brought you here to see how good a candidate you would be for hypnosis, remember?"

"I remember."

"All right. Just relax for a moment." I explained the procedure to him. He listened carefully, nodded at the appropriate times, and we began.

The procedure took almost an hour. Robert was tested for a number of simple responses to hypnotic suggestion, such as arm immobilization, verbal inhibition, etc. Whereas prot had obtained a perfect score of twelve on the same test, I was surprised to find that Robert did very poorly with a four, considerably below average. I wondered whether this represented a genuine lack of aptitude or he was fighting it. Having no good alternative, I decided to go ahead with the next session as planned, though with less confidence than I would have liked.

IF Robert was going to get well there would have to be better reasons for him to stay out of his protective shell than to retreat into it. Thus, I wanted and needed Giselle's help in his treatment, despite her stronger feelings for prot. She was strategically placed to act as a sort of liaison between Rob and the world. I asked her, over lunch, what she thought of him.

"He's okay. A nice enough guy. In fact, I like him."

"I'm glad to hear that. Giselle, I have to ask you a favor. Robert is struggling to maintain his identity, even in my examining room. He made a brief appearance yesterday at my home, but that's about it. As far as I know he's never shown up in the wards. Have you ever seen him in Two?"

"No, I haven't."

"Here's the thing. Somehow fate has placed you in a unique position to help him. Will you try to do that? As a favor to me as well as him? I'll give you free access to him—no more time limits."

"Why not just whistle him out like you did before?"

"That was a special occasion. I don't want to shock him by bringing him out in the wards before he's ready."

"What can I do?"

"What I *don't* want you to do is to try to entice Rob to come forward. What I'd like you to do is to make him feel comfortable so he'll *stay* out when he does show up."

Her eyebrows lifted. "How do I do that?"

"Just be nice to him. As nice as possible. Talk to him. Find out what he's interested in. Play games with him. Read to him. Anything you can think of to keep him around. I want him to like you. I want him to depend on you. I want you to be there for him." I almost said, "Try to love him"—but that was asking a bit too much. "Are you up to such a challenge?"

She smiled, I think, though it was hard to tell with her mouth stuffed with food. "It's the least I can do," she mumbled, "for letting me be with prot so much of the time."

"Good." I scraped my plate, wishing as usual that there were more cottage cheese. "Now—what else is happening?"

"Well, there's an anthropologist and a chemist coming later this week. To talk to prot, I mean."

"What do they want?"

"I think the anthropologist wants to know about the progenitors of the 'dremer' species on K-PAX, maybe get some idea of what our own forefathers might have been like. The chemist wants to ask him about the flora of the Amazonian rain forest, which he's been studying for twenty years or so. He wants to know where to look for drugs to treat AIDS and various forms of cancer and so on."

"Let me know what he tells them, if anything. Anybody else lined up?"

"A cetologist is coming next week. He wants prot to talk to a dolphin he knows."

"He's bringing a dolphin?"

"He's got a big tank that he pulls around to fairs and shopping malls. He's going to bring it and the dolphin to the front of the hospital so that prot can talk to him."

"Good grief—what next?"

"As prot might say, 'Anything's possible.'"

THAT afternoon I met with several of the faculty in Ward Four, where the psychopathic patients are housed. The reason for this gathering was that a new inmate had been brought in, someone who had planned and carried out a series of murders in all five boroughs of the city. Such patients are usually assigned to Ron Menninger, who specializes in psychopathy, with Carl Thorstein taking the overload.

The entire faculty, except for those unable to make it owing to other commitments, usually shows up for the first "session" with a new resident of Four—not only to help his psychiatrist evaluate his condition and possible course of treatment, but also to assess the potential danger to the rest of the staff and patients.

The new inmate, wearing bright orange-plastic shackles, was brought in by two of the security guards and asked to sit at the end of the long table. Ordinarily I'm not surprised by the general appearance of a psychopathic patient because there is no mold into which such a person fits. A "path" can be young or old, hardened or timid. He can look like a derelict or the boy next door. But I winced when this cold-blooded killer was brought in. I had been informed, of course, that she was a female Caucasian, but it was hard to imagine, even with decades of experience, that such a beautiful woman could be guilty of committing the crimes alleged to her. Yet she had been tried, found not responsible by reason of insanity, and sent to MPI for killing seven young men in various parts of the city.

Serial killings, indeed most murders, are usually committed by men. Whether this has anything to do with the male (or female) psyche, or is merely a matter of opportunity, is not at all clear. Psychopathy itself is a difficult affliction to understand. As with many mental illnesses, there seems to be a genetic defect often leading to an under-arousal of the autonomic nervous system. Persons harboring this defect, for example, exhibit little anxiety when confronted with a potentially dangerous situation. In fact, they seem to enjoy it.

In addition, psychopaths are often quite impulsive, acting mainly on feelings of the moment, seeking shortlived thrills without regard to the long-term consequences. They are usually sociopathic as well, caring little for the feelings of others and evincing little regard for what other people may think of them.

On the other hand, they are often superficially charming, making it very difficult for potential victims to spot danger in ordinary interactions with them. How does one recognize that "the nice boy (or girl) next door" can be as deadly as an anaconda?

But back to our patient. The woman, only twenty-three, was thought to have murdered seven young men, perhaps as many as nine, all from outlying towns, who had come to the big city for a good time on a Saturday night. All seven were found in deserted areas, unclad from the waist down, and penectomized. She was apprehended only when she picked up a police decoy, who barely escaped with his life, not to mention his genitalia.

But charming she was, and lovely as well. She smiled as she gazed into the eyes of every doctor in the room. Her answers to routine questions were frank, sometimes humorous, not the slightest bit antisocial. And I thought: Can we ever really know a person, even one who is perfectly sane? I knew that Ron was in for a very interesting experience. Nevertheless, I didn't envy him in the slightest, even when she wet her lips and winked at me as if to say, "Let's have some fun."

When I got back to my office I perused the "poop sheet" on our newest patient, whom I will call Charlotte. One by one her victims had disappeared and were never heard from again. The reason it took the police so long to find her was that young men come to town every weekend to pick up girls, and even under the best of circumstances it is virtually impossible to find an unknown killer in a city full of people. Probably no one would even take notice of a young couple leaving the bar or restaurant where they met, perhaps arm in arm, smiling warmly, Mr. Fly eagerly accompanying Ms. Spider to her web.

Perhaps that's why I have trouble sympathizing with spiders, even when they get trapped in a sink.

BEFORE leaving for the day I sought out Cassandra. I found her sitting on the weathered bench under "Adonis in the Garden of Eden," her raven-black hair shining in the sun, gazing at the cloudless sky from which she gets her inspiration, or so she claims. Knowing she ignores any attempt to interrupt her, I waited.

When she finally turned her attention away from the heavens I cautiously approached her. She seemed in a pleasant enough mood, and we chatted for a while about the hot weather. She predicted more of the same. I said, "That's not what I wanted to ask you about."

"Why not? Everyone else does."

"Cassandra, I wonder if you could help me with something."

"It won't be the Mets."

"No, not that. I need to know how long prot is going to be around. Can you tell me anything about when he'll be leaving us?"

"If you're planning a trip to K-PAX, don't pack your bags yet."

"You mean it will be a while before he goes?"

"When he's finished what he came to do, he'll leave. That will take some time."

"May I ask you—did you get this information from prot himself?"

She looked annoyed, but admitted she had talked with him.

"Anything else you can tell me about your conversation with prot?"

With a hint of amusement now: "I asked if he would take me with him."

"What did he say?"

"He told me I was one of those being considered."

"Really? Do you know who else is on the list?"

She tapped her head with a forefinger. "He said you would ask me that."

"Do you know the answer?"

"Yes."

"Who are they?"

"Anyone who wants to go."

But not everyone on the list will be selected, I thought dismally. A lot of them are going to be very disappointed. "All right. Thank you, Cassie."

"Don't you want to know who's going to win the World Series?"

"Who?"

"The Braves."

I almost blurted out, "You're crazy!"

Session Twenty-four

Whenever I experience a difficult patient making a first appearance in Ward Four, I always pay a visit to Ward One to try to recapture my optimism, and I did so the morning after meeting Charlotte. I encountered Rudolph in the exercise room practicing what appeared to be very novel ballet stances and moves. It reminded me of the contortionists who used to appear on *The Ed Sullivan Show*. I asked him how he was doing. To my surprise he confessed that he had a long way to go. I wasn't sure whether he meant his treatment program or his perfection of ballet technique, but I could see that he wouldn't be with us much longer.

I found Michael in the quiet room behind a book of poetry. I asked him what he was reading.

"Oh, just some Keats and Shelley and Wordsworth and those guys. An anthology. I've missed out on so much of my life. When I was in high school I wanted to be an English teacher."

"Still can be."

"Maybe. Right now I just want to balance the ledger."

"Have you looked into any EMS training programs?"

"I've already signed up for one. Starts October third." He glanced at me hopefully.

"I think you'll make it. I'll take a look at my schedule and see if we can work in a wrap-up session sometime soon."

On the way back to my office I stopped briefly in Ward Two, where my balloon of optimism began to deflate with a pronounced hiss. Bert was crashing through the lounge lifting cushions, stomping on the carpet, peering behind drapes and chairs. How sad he seemed, focused on his impossible quest like some latter-day Don Quixote.

But was Bert's case any more tragic than that of Jackie, who would always be a child? Or Russell, so focused on the Bible that he never learned how to live? Or Lou or Manuel or Dustin? Or, for that matter, some of our faculty and staff? Or millions of others who stumble about the world looking for what may not be there? Who set impossible goals for themselves and never attain them?

Milton, perhaps noticing my sudden melancholy, held forth with: "Man went to the doctor. Said he had chest pains and wanted an electrocardiogram. Doctor gave him one and told him there was nothing wrong with his heart. Came in every few months. Same result. Outlived three doctors. Finally, when he was ninety-two, there was a change in his EKG pattern. He looked the guy straight in the eye and said, 'Ha! I told you so!' "

Now in his fifties, Milton fully understands the sadness of life and tries vainly to cheer up everyone he sees. Unfortunately, he has never been able to alleviate his own suffering. He lost his entire family—father, mother, brothers, a sister, grandmother, several aunts and uncles and cousins, in the Holocaust. Only he escaped, protected from harm by a total stranger, a gentile who took the baby at the pleadings of his mother and pretended it was her own.

But is his story any sadder than that of Frankie, a woman unable to form human relationships of any kind? Not a sociopath like Charlotte, nor an autist like Jerry and the others, but someone who is indifferent toward affection, a patient who is pathologically unable to love or be loved—what could be sadder than that?

VILLERS was leaving the dining room as I was coming in. I waved at him as he passed by but he didn't see me. He seemed distracted, deep in thought, conjuring up some new money-making scheme, I assumed.

Menninger joined me instead, and I asked him about his new patient. "She's as cold as they come," he told me, "a female Hannibal Lecter. You should read her detailed history."

"I think I'll pass on that."

But Ron was enjoying himself. He loves to play with fire. "When she was five, she killed a puppy. You know how she did it?"

"No."

"She baked it in the oven."

"Did she get any treatment?"

"Nope. Claimed she didn't know the pup was in there."

"And it went downhill from there."

"Way down."

I slowly chewed up the last of the crackers. "I'm not sure I want to hear the rest."

"I'll give you the low point. After several more practice

353

runs with neighborhood pets, including a horse she stabbed to death, she killed the boy next door when she was sixteen."

"How did she get by with it?"

"She didn't. She spent some time in a reform school and then was transferred to a mental institution when she attacked one of the guards. You don't want to know what she did to him. She managed to escape from that place and was never heard from again."

"How old was she then?"

"Twenty. She was arrested a year later."

"You mean she killed those seven or eight guys in one year?"

"And that's not the worst of it. When she killed the neighbor kid?"

"Yes?"

"She left him lying in the backyard and went to a movie. After that, she slept like a baby, according to her parents."

"I'd keep an eye on her if I were you."

His eyes lit up. "Don't worry. But she's an amazing case, don't you think? I've never met anyone like her." He seemed beside himself, eager for his first session with Charlotte.

"Just be careful. She's no Sunday-school teacher."

"Wouldn't matter if she were."

"Why not?"

"Some of the most violent people in the world are Sunday-school teachers."

WHILE waiting for Robert/prot to come in for his twenty-fourth session I jotted down on a yellow pad some of the missing pieces of the puzzle I hoped to obtain from Rob, paramount of which was the question of who had fathered

Sarah's child, and what, if anything, did this have to do with Rob's mental problems? Why did he call his father his "protector"? What happened when he was five years old that he couldn't, or wouldn't, remember? None of this was going to be easy for Rob to deal with, but I was pretty sure the seeds of his trauma had begun to germinate during that early period in his troubled life, as my perceptive wife had suggested.

There was another, quite unforeseen, difficulty as well. Based on the results of the Stanford test, it appeared that Robert was trying hard to resist being hypnotized. Was he beginning to have second thoughts about cooperating with me and getting to the bottom of the quagmire he had been treading most of his life? I decided to approach his childhood only indirectly for the time being.

From his history I knew approximately when Sarah must've become pregnant, so I had some idea of when she told him about it. I tried to imagine what he must have felt upon hearing this news, and I was still staring into empty space when someone tapped on the door.

"Hi, Dr. Brewer."

"Hello, Rob. How are you feeling?"

He shrugged.

"Do you remember coming here from Ward Two?"

"No."

"What's the last thing you remember?"

"I was being tested to see whether I could be hypnotized."

"Well, you passed."

His shoulders slumped.

"And you know that in this setting there's no danger, nothing to worry about, right? Are you ready to try it?"

"I guess."

"Okay, sit down and relax. Good. Now focus your attention on that little spot on the wall behind me."

He pretended not to see it. After a moment, however, he complied.

"That's it. Just relax. Good. Good. Now I'm going to count from one to five. You will begin to feel drowsy on one, your eyelids will become heavier and heavier as the numbers increase, and by the time I get to five you will be asleep, but you will be able to hear everything I say. Do you understand?"

"Yes."

"Good. Now—let your arms drop. . . ." Rob's arms fell heavily to his sides and his eyes closed tightly. He began to snore softly. Obviously he was faking it. "Okay, Rob, open your eyes."

His eyes popped open. "Is it over already?"

"Rob, you'll have to do better than that. Are you afraid of the procedure?"

"No, not exactly."

"Good. Now let's try again. Are you comfortable?"

"Yes."

"All right. Now let yourself relax completely. Let all your muscles go limp and just relax. That's it. Good. Now find the spot on the wall. Good. Just relax. One. . .you're beginning to feel drowsy. Two. . .your eyelids are getting heavy. . . ." Robert stared at the white dot. He was still resisting, apparently caught between fear and suspicion. On three his eyelids began to flutter, and he fought to keep them open. By the count of five they were closed and his chin had dropped onto his chest. "Rob? Can you hear me?"

"Yes."

"Good. Now lift your head and open your eyes."

He complied. I checked his pulse and coughed loudly.

There was no reaction.

"How do you feel?"

"Okay."

"Good. All right, Rob, we're going to go back in time now. Imagine the pages of a calendar turning backward, backward, backward. You are slowly becoming younger. Younger and younger. You are thirty, twenty-five, twenty. Now you're a senior in high school. It's March 1975. Almost spring. You have a date with your girlfriend Sally. You're picking her up now. Where are you going?"

"We're going to a movie."

"What movie are you going to?"

"*Jaws.*"

"Okay. What is Sally wearing?"

"She's wearing her yellow coat and scarf."

"It's cold outside?"

"Not too cold. Her coat is open. She has on a white blouse and a blue skirt."

"Are you driving or walking?"

"Walking. I don't have a car."

"All right. You're at the theater. You're going in. What happens next?"

"I'm buying some popcorn. Sally loves popcorn."

"You don't like it?"

"I'll have a little of hers. I don't have any more money."

"Okay. There's Robert Shaw being eaten by the shark. Now the movie is over and you're leaving the theater. Where are you going now?"

"We're going back to Sally's house. She wants to talk."

"Do you know what she wants to talk about?"

"No. She won't tell me till we get to the house."

"All right, you're back at Sally's house. What do you see?"

Robert seemed to become edgy. "It—it's a big white house with dormers in the roof. We're going to sit on the porch and talk for a while. In one of the swings."

"What is Sally saying to you?"

"Her head is on my shoulder. Her hair is soft. I can smell her shampoo. She tells me she is pregnant."

"How does she know that?"

"She has missed two periods."

"Are you the father?"

"No. We've never done anything."

"You've never had a sexual relationship with Sally?"

His fists clenched. "No."

"Do you know who the father is?"

"No."

"Sally won't tell you?"

"I never asked her."

"Why not?"

"If she wanted me to know, she'd tell me."

"All right. What are you going to do about it?"

"That's what she wants to talk about."

"What does *she* think you ought to do?"

"She wants to get married. Only—"

"Only what?"

"Only she knows I want to go to college."

"How do *you* feel about it?"

"I want to get married, too."

"And give up your career?"

"I don't have much choice."

"But you're not the father."

"It doesn't matter. I love her."

"So you told her you would marry her?"

"Yes."

"What's happening now?"

"She's kissing me."

"Do you like it when she kisses you?"

"Yes." His reply sounded strangely matter-of-fact.

"Has she ever kissed you before?"

"Yes."

"But it never led to anything further?"

"No."

"Why not?"

"I don't know."

"All right. What's happening now?"

"We're going inside."

"It's too cold to stay on the porch?"

"No. She wants to go up to her room."

"Is she ill?"

"No. She wants me to go, too."

"Tell me what you see."

"We're going up the stairs. Trying to be real quiet because they squeak. It's dark except for a hall light. Everyone else has gone to bed."

"Go on."

"We're tiptoeing down the hallway. It's still squeaking. We're going into Sally's room. She's closing the door. I hear it lock. We're taking off our coats."

"Go on."

"We're hugging and kissing some more. She is pressing herself against me. I'm sorry. I can't help it. I put my hands under her skirt and lift it up."

"Go on, Rob. What's happening now?"

"We move toward the bed. Sally falls down on it. I'm on top of her. No! Please! I don't want to do this!"

"Why not? Why don't you want to have sex with Sally?"

"It's a terrible thing to do! I have to go to sleep now."

"It's all right, Rob. It's over. It's all over. What's happening now?"

"I'm getting dressed."

"How do you feel?"

"I don't know. Better, I guess."

"What is Sally doing?"

"She is just lying there watching me button my shirt. It's dark but I can see her smiling."

"Go on."

"I put my coat on. I have to go."

"Why do you have to go?"

"I told my mother I would be home by eleven-thirty."

"What time is it now?"

He checked his wrist. "Twenty after eleven."

"What's happening?"

"Sally's getting up and putting her arms around me. She doesn't want me to go. She isn't wearing anything. I try not to look but I can't help it."

"What do you see?"

"She's naked. I can't look. I'm unlocking the door. 'Bye, Sally. I'll see you tomorrow.' I'm tiptoeing along the corridor. Down the stairs. Out the door. I'm running. I run all the way home."

"Is your mother waiting up for you?"

"No. But she hears me come in. She asks if it's me. 'Yes, Mom, it's me.' She wants to know if we had a nice time. 'Yes, Mom, we had a very nice time.' She says good night. I go to my room."

"You're going to bed now?"

"Yes. But I can't sleep."

"Why not?"

"I keep thinking about Sally."

"What do you think about her?"

"How she smells and how she feels and how she tastes."

"Do you like those things?"

"Yes."

"But you can't go all the way?"

"No."

"Rob, can you tell me about anything that happened when you were younger that would make you dislike sex? Something that hurt you, or frightened you?"

No response.

"All right. Now listen carefully. Imagine the calendar again. The pages are turning rapidly, but this time we're coming forward. You're getting older. Twenty, twenty-five, thirty, and still you are getting older. You are thirty-eight years old. It's September 6, 1995, the present time. Do you understand?"

"Yes."

"Good. Now I'm going to count backward from five to one. As I count, you will begin to wake up. When I get to one, you will be fully awake, alert, and feeling fine. Five. . .four. . .three. . .two. . .one—"

"Hello, Dr. Brewer."

"Hello, Rob. How do you feel?"

"You asked me that a minute ago."

"You've been under hypnosis. Do you remember?"

"No."

"All right. May I ask you a few more questions now?"

"Sure." He seemed relieved it was over.

"Good. Rob, you were only five when your father was injured at work, weren't you?"

"Yes."

"Did you visit him in the hospital?"

"They said I was too young. But my mother went to see him every day."

"Who took care of you while your mother was at the hospital?"

"Uncle Dave and Aunt Catherine."

"They came to stay with you?"

He began to fidget. "No. I stayed with them for a while."

"How long?"

He answered slowly, almost in a whisper, "A long time."

"During that time, did anything happen that you want to tell me about?"

"I don't know, gino. I wasn't there."

"Doggone it, prot. Couldn't you have given us a few more minutes? Where's Robert? Is he okay?"

"Bearing up remarkably well, I'd say, under the circumstances."

"What circumstances?"

"Your relentless—how you say eet?— browbeating."

"Is he coming back?"

"Not for a while."

"Prot, what can you tell me about Robert's Uncle Dave and Aunt Catherine?"

"I just told you—I wasn't there."

"He's never told you anything about them?"

"Never heard of any Uncle Dave or Aunt Catherine."

"All right. Have some fruit."

"Thought you'd never ask." He grabbed a cantaloupe and bit into it.

I watched him devour rind, seeds, everything. I was still annoyed with him, but there was no time to waste. "As long as you've barged in—Dr. Villers asked me to sound you out on your TV appearance."

"Sound away."

"Well, are you willing to do it?"

"Who gets the money?"

I thought: Spoken like a true Homo sapiens! "Why, the hospital, I suppose. You don't need money, do you?"

"No being needs money."

"What do you suggest we do with it?"

"I suggest we let the network keep it."

"Otherwise you don't show up?"

"You got it."

"I don't think Klaus is going to like that idea. The main reason you were going on was to raise money for the new wing."

"He'll get used to it."

"Do you want to be on TV?"

"Depends. Why do they want to know what a crazy person has to say?"

"You'd be surprised who goes on talk shows. Actually, they might try to make a fool of you."

"Sounds like fun. I'll be there!"

"All right. I'll tell Villers about your decision."

"Anything else, doc?"

"The trip to the zoo has been scheduled for the fourteenth. That okay with you?"

"Yep. What a place!" He took another huge bite of melon.

I declined to pursue this comment, which could have meant anything. Instead, I seized the opportunity, while I could, to discuss the patients with him. "I saw you talking with Bert this morning."

"How very observant."

"Do you know what he's looking for, by any chance?"

"Sure."

"You do?? What, for God's sake?"

"Ah, gene. Do I have to do *all* your thinking for you?"

"Please, prot. All I'm asking for is a tiny little hint."

"Oh, all right. He's looking for his daughter."

"But he doesn't have a daughter!"

"That's why he can't find her!" He went for the door.

"Wait a minute—where are you going?"

"I don't get paid for overtime."

I called out: "Anything you can do for Frankie?" But he was already gone.

FIRST thing next morning I called Chakraborty and then went looking for prot. On the way to the lounge I ran into Betty and told her what he had said about Bert. Her response was typical: "Prot is really something, isn't he? Maybe you should give him an office and bring all the patients in to see him."

"We've already considered that," I told her resignedly. "But he doesn't want the job."

I found him in the lounge surrounded by his usual entourage, including Russell, who was now insisting that the end of the world was imminent. I asked them to let me speak to our alien friend for a moment. There was a lot of grumbling, but they finally backed away.

"Prot, Dr. Chakraborty is ready to take a little blood from you."

"I shall returrrn," he promised his followers. "Count Drrracula awaits in the crrrypt." Without another word he headed for the door. I started to call out, but I realized he knew exactly where he was going. Suddenly I had the uncomfortable sensation of being surrounded. Someone said, "You're trying to get rid of him, aren't you?"

"Prot? Of course not."

"You're trying to drive him away. Everybody knows that."

"No—I'm trying to get him to stay! For a while, at least. . . ."

"Only as long as it takes to make Robert better. Then you want him to die."

"I don't want anyone to die."

Russell shouted, "If you do not wake up I will come upon you like a thief, and you will not know the moment of my coming!" While everyone was pondering that pronouncement I made a hasty exit.

GISELLE came in late that afternoon to report on prot's meeting with the anthropologist and the rainforest chemist.

"First," I said, "any sign of Robert?"

"Haven't seen him since Labor Day."

"Okay. Go on."

"They turned out to be brother and sister. Hadn't spoken in years. I don't think they like each other much."

"What did he tell them?"

"The chemist seemed suspicious of prot's knowledge and abilities. He demanded to know the names of all the plants that produce natural products that could be used in the fight against AIDS."

"And?"

"Prot just shook his head and said, 'Why must you humans label everything a "fight"? The viruses mean you no malice. They're programmed to survive, like everyone else.' "

"That sounds like him. What happened then?"

"He rephrased the question."

"And did prot give him the information he wanted?"

"No, but he told him where to look for one."

"Where?"

"Somewhere in southwestern Brazil. He even described the plant. It's got big leaves and little yellow flowers. He said the natives call it 'otolo,' which means 'bitter.' The chemist took this all down, but he still seemed skeptical until prot told him there was a substance good for certain kinds of heart arrhythmias in another plant found in the same region of Brazil. The guy knew all about that drug. In fact, he was one of its co-discoverers. He actually kissed prot's hand. By then his time was up. He took off like a bat."

"What about the anthropologist?"

"Prot told her there were probably several 'missing links' on Earth. She wanted to know where to find them."

"Don't they already know that?"

"Nope. They're not in Africa."

"Where, then?"

"He suggested she go to Mongolia."

"Mongolia? How did they get from there to Africa?"

She gave me a look of protlike exasperation. "They didn't have cars, Dr. B. They probably walked."

"So I suppose she's off to Mongolia?"

"She leaves next week."

"You realize, of course, that it will be a long time before we know whether prot was right about any of these things."

"No, it won't. We know now."

"How do we know that?"

"What does he have to do to prove to you that he knows what he's talking about? Everything he's told Dr. Flynn so far was right, wasn't it?"

"Maybe. But savants like him only know what is already known. He can't deduce something that nobody knows yet."

"He's not a savant. He's from K-PAX."

We had been through this before. I thanked her for the report and told her I had another favor to ask of her.

"Whatever you say, Dr. B."

"We need to find out whether Bert had a daughter some time in the past. There's no record of it, but maybe it got lost somehow, like Robert's disappearance in '85 went into the books as a suicide."

"I'll get right on it. But first you'll have to give me some information about him."

I handed her a sheet from my yellow pad with all the pertinent data on it. Leaving a piney ghost behind, she was literally off and running. I only hoped she would be half as successful at this task as she had been in tracking down prot's true identity five years earlier.

Right after she left, Klaus Villers came in. I thought he wanted to discuss one of his patients, or perhaps offer some pointed suggestions about one of mine, something he truly loves to do. Instead, he spent fifteen minutes stroking his goatee and telling me the story of Robin Hood. He wanted to know what I thought about the moral implications of that myth for present-day society. I told him I thought that people shouldn't take the law into their own hands, but if they did they should be prepared to pay the consequences. Judging by the inflection of his grunts, I don't think he liked that answer.

Session Twenty-five

T HE morning before Rob's next session I sat in my office thinking about him and Sally. What could possibly have happened to preclude his having an intimate relationship with his wife-to-be, whom he dearly loved? Did the fact that she was carrying someone else's child have anything to do with it?

Even under the best of circumstances, sex one of the most difficult things human beings have to deal with. Most of us learn about it piecemeal, on school playgrounds, in the streets, from movies or TV. Some get an introductory course from their father or mother, often in the form of a how-to manual obtained from the local library. Many parents are almost as ignorant about the subject as their children.

The best place to learn about sex, just as it is for every other subject, is the schools. But that idea has come under fire in recent years. The net result of this vacuum is, of course, that teenage pregnancy and venereal diseases are rampant in our society. The kids learn plenty about sex, but they learn it from each other.

My own introduction to this mysterious subject was somewhat less than informed. One hot August afternoon my mother went shopping, leaving Karen and me home alone. We were fourteen or fifteen at the time. We turned on the sprinkler and ran through the spray, back and forth until our shorts and T-shirts were sopping wet, and nearly transparent. Then we "accidentally" bumped into each other, one thing led to another, and—well, it's the old story. Afterward, Karen was sure she was pregnant and I thought I was a rapist. We didn't touch each other again for two years.

Yet, despite all the taboos and other obstacles, most of us manage, through trial and error at least, to find a satisfactory partner and, eventually, to enjoy a more or less successful sex life. Why not Rob?

LATER that morning, Will, now back in school but still coming to MPI in his spare time to speak with Dustin and some of the other patients, stopped by my office to see if I wanted to go somewhere for lunch. Though I rarely do so, he and I went out to a nearby restaurant.

Knowing I should eat lightly or fall asleep later on, I decided on a cup of soup and a salad. Will, always a good eater, ordered substantially more.

We chatted for a while. Usually full of restless energy, he seemed withdrawn, nervous. He only picked at his food, claiming he wasn't as hungry as he thought. I may not be the world's greatest father, but even I could tell that something was bothering him, and I suspected what it might be: His girlfriend Dawn was pregnant. My own father, who

369

lived through (and never forgot) the Depression, wouldn't let me leave food on my plate; it's a habit I've never been able to break. I scraped Will's uneaten portions into my empty salad dish.

But his girlfriend wasn't pregnant (as far as I knew). It was worse than that. He was having second thoughts about medical school! Not an unfamiliar topic to me, as I had dealt with similar misgivings thirty-five years earlier. And I had known other students who couldn't take the pressure and finally dropped out. One had committed suicide. A few turned to drugs. This was what was worrying me—Will already had a drug problem.

As I gobbled his lunch, I told him about my own doubts when I was his age, that it was not unusual for a student, or even a doctor, to question his abilities, to feel overwhelmed at times by his awesome responsibility for the lives of his patients. But I also reminded him that it comes with the territory. That he, like all of us, will make mistakes. That no one is perfect and we can only do our best. And in his case, the best was quite good enough. Even prot had said so.

"Prot said that, Pop?"

"He says you're going to be a fine doctor."

"Well, if prot thinks so, maybe I can handle it after all."

Though a bit envious that it had been prot's remark, and none of my own, that had swayed his thoughts and lifted his spirits, I felt relieved that the problem seemed to have been resolved. Now he was hungry. Since I had eaten all of his food, he ordered something more. To keep him company, I had a rich dessert while we discussed Dustin and some of the other patients. Finally he pushed his plate away and took a sip of coffee.

I asked him whether he was finished. He nodded. Since he hadn't eaten everything, I scraped the leftovers onto my dessert plate.

It was a wonderful lunch, the kind I never had a chance to have with my own father. But now I had to go back and try to be a good doctor, despite my own chronic misgivings, on a Friday afternoon and a very full stomach.

"AH, cherries! No being can eat just one!"

"Prot! Where's Robert?"

Slurp! Munch, munch, munch. "He's taking the day off."

"What do you mean, 'He's taking the day off'?"

"He doesn't want to talk to you today. Give him the weekend. He'll come around." *Crunch, crunch.* "Cherry?"

"No, thanks. Why would he be more willing to talk on Monday than today?"

"He needs to psych himself up for it."

"We're running out of time, prot."

"Haven't we been over this before? Trust me, doc. You can't rush these things. Or would you rather blow your little whistle and put him back the way he was a month ago?"

"It's that bad?"

"You're getting into something he's been trying to run away from for most of his life."

"What is it? Do you know what happened to him?"

"Nope. He never told me."

"Then how do you know—"

"I've been coming here since 1963, remember?"

"So what do we do now?"

"He's almost ready to deal with it. Just give him a little more time."

The only sound on the tape at this point was that of someone's foot tapping, probably my own. "Prot?"

"What you want, *kemo sabe*?"

"Do you think he would feel more comfortable talking to *you* about it first?"

"I don't know. Want me to ask him?"

"Please do."

Prot gazed at the ceiling for a long moment. Unforgivably, I yawned. Ignoring this breach of etiquette, he exclaimed, "Well done, dr. b! He *does* want to tell me first. But he doesn't want *me* to tell *you*. *He* wants to do it."

"Will he tell you now?"

Prot threw up his hands in a now-familiar gesture of frustration. "Gene, gene, gene! How many times do I have to say this? He wants to do it on Monday. He'll tell me that morning and you in the afternoon. I think it's a pretty good deal, don't you? My advice is to take it."

"I'll take it."

"Good person."

I gazed at him through heavy-lidded eyes as he energetically devoured a couple of pounds of cherries. "Well, we've got some time left," I pointed out. "Maybe *you* would be willing to answer a few questions."

"Anything. Except how to build better bombs or contaminate another PLANET."

I didn't ask him what he figured we'd contaminate it with. Instead, I pulled out my old list of questions, the ones I had brought to the Labor Day picnic but never got a chance to ask him. Of course I had certain ulterior motives for wanting to query him. Maybe he would say something that would give me a better insight into the workings of his (and Robert's) unpredictable mind. "There are a few things you told me during your visit five years ago that I never followed up on. May I do so now?"

"I don't think anything could stop you from asking your relentless questions, gino."

"Thank you. I'll take that as a compliment. By the way, some of these were sent to me by people who read *K-PAX*."

"Hooray for them."

"Ready?"

"Aim. Fire!"

"No need for sarcasm, prot. First, what does 'K-PAX' mean?"

He adopted a stiff, pompous demeanor before proceeding. " 'K' is the highest class of PLANET, the last step in the evolutionary process, the point of perfect peace and stability. 'PAX' means 'a place of purple plains and mountains.' "

"Because of your red and blue suns."

He relaxed again. "Bingo!"

"So 'B-TIK,' what we call Earth, is the second lowest type?"

"Kee-reck. You don't want to know about the 'A' category."

"Why not?"

"Those are WORLDS already destroyed by their own inhabitants. Before that they were 'B's."

"I see. And 'TIK' means——?"

"Beautiful blue water dotted with white clouds."

"Ah, I get it."

"I was beginning to wonder."

"All right. What about Tersipion?"

"Oh, that's what *they* call it. We call it F-SOG."

"Okay. Tell me about some of the other beings you

373

have come across. Like the giant insects on—ah—F–SOG, for example."

"Use your imagination, doc. Anything you can think of, and a lot you can't, exists somewhere. Remember that there are several billion inhabited planets and moons in our GALAXY alone, not to mention a comet or two. Your species can't seem to imagine anything that doesn't work pretty much the same as you do. Your 'experts' are always saying life is impossible somewhere or other because there isn't any water or oxygen or whatever. Wake up and smell the hoobah!"

Paxo, I assumed, for coffee. I wished I had some. I thought of a former patient of mine, whom I called "Rip van Winkle." Rip would fall asleep even during intercourse. "Let's go on to some more general questions."

"Uh—Eisenhower?"

"No, not him. You told me once that K–PAXians like to contemplate the possibility of traveling forward in time. Remember?"

"Of course."

"Does that mean you can already go backward in time?"

"Not in the sense you mean it. Think—if beings could come back here from, say, EARTH year 2050, why haven't they?"

"Maybe they have."

"I don't see any of them around, do you?"

"So traveling backward in time is impossible?"

"Not at all. But maybe your future beings don't *want* to come back here. Or," he added pointedly, "maybe EARTH's future is limited."

"What about K–PAX? Is it crawling with beings back from the future?"

374

"Not as far as I know."

"Does that mean—"

"Who knows?"

"All right. You once mentioned a 'spatial fourth dimension.' Have you ever seen it?"

"Once or twice."

"So it exists?"

"Evidently. In fact, while I was back on K-PAX, I managed to stumble into it. It was wonderful—I've always wanted to do that." He paused a moment to ponder the experience. "But I fell out again right away. It must have something to do with gravity."

"Obviously. Okay, let's come down to Earth for a minute."

"Nice place to visit, but . . ."

"Cute. Now—you told me a long time ago that we humans were going 'hell-bent after solar, wind, geothermal, and tidal energy without any thought whatsoever about the consequences.' What did you mean by that?"

"Look. What happens when you dam up a river and steal its energy for your own devices? You flood everything in sight and the river becomes a trickle. So what do you think would happen if you had windmills all over your PLANET?"

"I don't know. What?"

"Use your noggin! For one thing, your climate would be changed to the point where you would think you were on another WORLD. In fact, it's already happening, haven't you noticed? The floods, the droughts, the endless strings of tornadoes and hurricanes—you name it."

"But we don't have all that many windmills on Earth."

"Exactly! And what's going to happen when you have more and more? Not to mention screwing around with your tides and internal temperatures. In the meantime, you insist on burning up the last of your fossil fuels and wreaking havoc as if there were no tomorrow."

"But prot—everything causes *some* pollution or effect on the environment. Until we figure out nuclear fusion, what are we going to use to heat our homes? Run our machines?"

"What, indeed?"

"So there's no way to win?"

"You might try reducing your numbers by five or six billion."

By now I was barely able to keep my eyes open. "But don't you think we're making a beginning? There's a lot of concern these days about the environment, for example."

"*The* environment? You mean *your* environment."

"Well, yes."

"And to make *your* environment more tolerable for *you*, you recycle beer cans, plant trees—is that what you mean?"

"It's a start, isn't it?"

"Recycling is like putting a Band-Aid on a tumor, doc. And where are you going to plant a tree when there's no place left to plant it?"

"Is that what you meant when you said in your report that we are yet children?"

Prot's gaze shifted to the ceiling, as it often does when he's trying to find words that I might be capable of understanding. I tried unsuccessfully to stifle another yawn.

"Let me put it this way: When you stop making killing seem admirable, when motherhood becomes less important than survival—not just *your* survival, but that of all the other creatures on your PLANET—you'll be on your way to adulthood."

"Lions kill! So do eagles and bears and—"

"They have no choice. You do."

"You kill plants, don't you?"

"Plants have no brain or nervous system. They feel no pain or anguish."

"Is that your main criterion?"

"That is the only criterion."

"What about insects?"

"They have nervous systems, don't they?"

"And you think they feel pain?"

"Have you ever been stepped on?"

"Not literally."

"Try to imagine it."

"Bacteria? Molds?"

"Dig right in."

"Does this mean you're opposed to abortion?"

"I assume you're talking about the *human* fetus."

"Yes."

"If it can feel anxiety or pain, don't do it."

"And does it feel anxiety or pain?"

"It certainly can the day before birth. The day after conception it is no more sensate than a grain of sand."

"Then where do you draw the line?"

"Now, gene, that's a nobrainer, wouldn't you say?"

I had to end this before I fell asleep. "Prot—when are you leaving?"

His eyes rolled up for a moment—his version of a smirk. "I still don't know, daddyo. But I can tell you this: I filed for three windows this time—just in case."

Suddenly I was wide awake. "Windows?"

"In case things get complicated again."

"With Robert?"

"With everything."

"Can you at least tell me now whether you'll be taking any of our patients with you when you go?"

"*Ad hos forgal!* Not this again!"

"Cassandra?"

He shrugged.

"Jackie?"

"Nah."

"Why not?"

"She's the happiest being in the place!"

"What about—"

"Maybe. She's obviously not happy here. But you have so much to learn from her!"

"From Frankie? A woman who's incapable of love?"

He stared at me disgustedly, almost angrily. "Sometimes I think these visits with you are a complete waste of time. What you call 'love' is a big part of your problem. You tend to limit the concept to yourself and your immediate family. Talk to frankie, doc. You might learn something. And that goes for all your other patients, too."

I thought: Did Robert's problem have more to do with love than with sex? Was he somehow betrayed by his wife and daughter? Or someone else he loved? "I've got a lot more questions left, my alien friend, but—well, I'll save them for later."

"Fine with me. I've got plenty of other things to do."

"That reminds me. In case I don't get another chance— thanks for what you've done so far. Not only with Robert but for Rudolph and Michael and for getting through to some of the autists. You've accomplished more in the few weeks you've been here than the rest of us have in the past five years."

"I told you before: You can do it, too. All you have to do is eliminate the crap from your thoughts."

"Easy for you to say."

★　★　★

After dinner that evening my wife wouldn't let me work, not even to browse through a journal. Instead, she put on a videotape of *Spellbound*, one of my favorite movies, and suggested I contemplate the possibility of finding a home upstate for our eventual retirement. Within minutes, even before Gregory Peck's first fainting spell, I had fallen asleep.

I dreamed that prot had become fully integrated into Robert, who was no longer shy and depressed, but confident and outgoing. Although he demonstrated no overt traits of prot (he couldn't see ultraviolet light, for example), other signs of him were evident in Robert's personality. His aptitude for math and science increased dramatically and he was making plans to attend college. On the other hand, he had lost none of his (and prot's) sex hangup.

Then the dream took a sudden turn. Prot came flying by accompanied by Manuel. Both of them had sprouted wings. Robert, too, had grown wings and all three of them flew around and around, motioning for me to join in. Then Russell, who looked like an angel out of Revelations, halo and all, lifted off. The other patients appeared, flying in perfect formation, and everyone rose higher and higher, prot in the lead, until they were only a dot against the sun. Desperately I flapped and flapped, but I wasn't able to get off the ground. I tried to call out, but couldn't even do that. In fact, I could hardly breathe. . . .

When I woke up I found Karen watching me with a smile, the one that says, "How sweet." I could tell I had been snoring. The movie was over.

"Decided on a retirement place?"

"No, but it's something I'd definitely like to think about."

★ ★ ★

379

I drove in to work the next day, Saturday, but couldn't seem to get much done. I felt listless, out of sorts, not myself. On my desk I uncovered the paper I hadn't yet reviewed, and a couple of tickets I had forgotten about. They were for Carnegie Hall that afternoon. Howie, a fine musician and former patient, had sent them to me. I called Karen, but she had a bowling tournament she wasn't about to miss.

For some reason I thought of prot. He wasn't in the building, so I tried the lawn. I found him examining the sunflowers, which must have looked like a row of burning stars to him. "Love to hear Howie play!" he exclaimed.

"Hurry up and get ready. We have to leave right away."

"I'm ready," he replied, heading for the gate.

Prot immediately struck up a conversation with the taxi driver, who had seen a picture of him on television. "Glad you're back," he told my alien companion. "I was hopin' you could do somethin' wid dis friggin' heat."

"Sorry, pal," prot replied. "That's up to you." The cabbie didn't say another word.

Later on, we passed a couple of kids banging away at each other with toy rifles. "I see you're still teaching your children to kill," he observed. I thought: I can't take him anywhere!

The multitude in the streets seemed to put him into a foul mood. When I asked him what CD he would take with him if he were marooned on a desert island, he snapped, "Where would I get a cd player on a desert island?"

The concert, however, was a great success. Prot seemed to be able to pick out Howie's playing from the other violinists in the chamber group. "Nice vibrato," he reported. "But he's a hair flat, just like always."

As the musicians started on their final work, the

Mendelssohn "Octet," someone in the balcony screamed, "Shut up the goddamn coughing!" The hacking stopped immediately, as did the music. All the players and half the audience gave the man a standing ovation. Prot laughed out loud. Then it became absolutely still. I had never heard the piece played so beautifully.

We visited with Howie after the concert. Looking much younger than he did half a decade earlier, he was very happy to see prot, and wondered how long he'd be around. Prot dodged the question. Howie inquired as to Bess's health, and asked about the patients still with us. "I miss them," he lamented. "In fact, I miss the whole hospital."

"You want to come back?" I joked.

"I'm thinking about it," he replied in all seriousness. "Unless there's room for me on the bus to K-PAX."

Prot didn't say yes, but he didn't say no, either.

Session Twenty-six

Villers was late for the Monday-morning staff meeting, explaining that his wife was sick and he had to take her to the doctor. Then there was a delay on the Long Island Rail Road—some "dummkopf" had pulled the emergency cord for no apparent reason.

He was further chagrined by prot's insistence that we turn down the television-appearance fee, but he soon came up with an alternative plan: an appeal for viewer contributions to the hospital, complete with 800 number. The date had been finalized for Wednesday, the twentieth of September. September 20! The day of prot's departure! Unless, of course, he had changed his mind and was waiting for the next "window," whenever that might be. . . .

Goldfarb brought up a new problem, one that hadn't occurred to me. Since my efforts at coaxing Robert out of his protective shell were meeting with some success, was it possible that it might be he, and not prot, who showed up for the taped interview? I said I didn't think that very likely given Robert's reluctance to make an appearance outside my examining room. Beamish pointed out that with prot, no one could be sure of anything. I had no good response to that.

Instead, I discussed the new information that I, or rather prot, had obtained from Bert, but this seemed almost inconsequential compared with Menninger's cheerful report on Charlotte, who had somehow managed to seduce one of the security guards into her cell and nearly bit off his nose and one of his testicles. Our security chief had been apprised of this unfortunate development, of course, and was urged to instruct the guards accordingly.

Villers, still in a bad mood, brought up the scheduled visits by the cetologist and other scientists. He wanted to know how much we were getting for these "consultations" with prot, and was further annoyed with the answer. Thorstein, looking more and more like Klaus's second in command, suggested we charge big bucks for subsequent interviews with Robert's alter ego, particularly if any patents or other useful information were to come of it.

The only other business was a reminder that one of the world's foremost psychotherapists was arriving the next morning for an all-day visit (a brief biography was passed around), and that a popular television personality and author of *Folk Psychology* was coming later in the month.

The conversation then degenerated, as it often does, to discussions of baseball scores, restaurants, weekend retreats, fabulous golf shots, etc. I mused silently about how long prot might be staying. At least until the TV appearance, I assumed, and perhaps longer. And I thought: If the appeal for funds was successful, and he managed to help us raise enough money to finance the new wing, what on Earth would we call it?

AFTER lunch, prot set up an unannounced treasure hunt without saying what the prize might be. That was all the encouragement the patients needed, and they spent the rest of the hour happily combing the lounge, the exercise room, the dining hall, and the quiet room for "buried" treasure. Even though no one knew what he or she was looking for, the joy and excitement were immense.

I was a little annoyed. Prot had not warned me he was going to do this, though technically it wasn't really a "task" for the patients, which he had agreed to tell me about in advance. I watched in both amusement and melancholy as our inmates got into the game with considerable frenzy— everyone searching high and low for something to make their lives more rewarding or, at least, tolerable.

Even some of the staff were caught up in the excitement, turning over chairs and peering under rugs. To tell the truth, I became a participant myself, hoping to find something, I suppose, that would cheer me up, make my day. Perhaps I was searching for the parallel life I had lost, the one in which my father had not died and I had become an opera singer, the one I dream about from time to time.

While all this was going on, however, prot was reported missing. No one had seen him leave. The hunt then became one of finding *him*.

Though further frustrated by this turn of events, I wasn't really worried— it had happened once before. I was sure he would be back in time for our next session. Indeed, it wasn't long after his disappearance that Giselle came running in, shouting that he had shown up again, to loud cheers from his followers. Whatever he had done while he was away, it had taken him no time at all, apparently.

My dream didn't come true that day, and I doubt that

anyone else's did either. But each of the patients turned up his very own gossamer thread, invisible to everyone else. Something to give them hope for a better world perhaps, a tenuous new lease on life.

I wondered whether my frustration showed when prot came in, followed by a cat. He sat down and started on a plum, which he shared with his "friend." I didn't even know cats liked fruit.

"Where's Robert?"

"He'll be along shortly. He's still pumping himself up. Besides," he added wistfully, "I hardly ever get any fruit anymore."

"You want to tell me where you went this afternoon?"

"Not really."

"You promised to let me know if you were planning any trips, remember?"

"I didn't plan it. It was a spur-of-the-moment thing."

"Where did you go?"

"I had some invitations to deliver."

"Personally?"

"I'm not a 'person,' remember? I'm a being."

"Why didn't you just drop them in the mailbox?"

"I wanted to be sure they got there."

"To people who are going to K-PAX with you?"

"Some are people, some aren't."

"So how many invitations were there?"

I didn't expect an answer to that one either, but he replied, cheerfully, "Only a dozen so far. Still plenty of room."

I glared at him. "Next time you plan any 'spur-of-the-moment things,' will you let me know, please?"

"It's your party."

"Thank you. Now—what about Robert?"

"What about hi—"

"Dammit, prot, did he tell you what happened to him when he was five?"

"Yes, and may I say: You human beings are sick!"

"Not everyone, prot. Just some of us."

"From what I've seen, you're all capable of just about anything."

We sat staring at each other for a while. Five or six plums later, he spat the last pit into the bowl and placed his hands behind his head, apparently sated. The cat lounged contentedly in his lap. Prot's eyes drooped shut. Suddenly he leaned forward and wrapped his arms around himself. Robert's eyes fought to reopen. He seemed weak, shaken, his confidence gone. In short, he looked much as he had in earlier sessions. Instinctively, he began stroking the cat, which purred noisily.

"Hello, Rob, it's good to see you again. How are you feeling today?"

"I'm afraid."

"Please trust me. No harm will come to you in this room. This is your safe haven, remember? We're just going to chat about whatever you'd like to tell me. Whatever comes into your mind. We'll proceed at your own pace."

"All right. But I'm still scared."

"I understand."

He sat looking at me, but said nothing for several precious minutes.

I took a chance. "Is there anything you want to tell me about the time your father was in the hospital?"

His gaze dropped to the floor. "Yes."

I was elated. Thanks to prot, Robert had made such excellent progress that hypnosis might not be necessary.

"You went to live with your Uncle Dave and Aunt Catherine, is that right?"

"Yes," he murmured.

"Are they on your father's or mother's side of the family?"

Rob slowly looked up. "Uncle Dave was Mom's brother."

"And Aunt Catherine was his wife?"

"No. His sister. Mom's sister."

"And they lived together?"

"Neither of them ever married."

"All right. Can you tell me a little about them?"

"They were both big. Heavyset. My mother's a little plump, too."

"What else? What were they like?"

"They were not very nice people."

"In what way?"

"They were mean. Cruel. But nobody knew that when I went to live with them."

"What sorts of mean things did they do?"

"Uncle Dave killed my kitten." He unconsciously picked up the cat and hugged it.

"He did? Why?"

"He wanted to teach me a lesson."

"What lesson?"

Robert turned noticeably paler. His face became contorted by uncontrollable tics. "I . . . I don't remember."

"Try, Rob. I think you're ready to talk about this now. What did your uncle do to you? Will you tell me?"

There was a long pause. I had just about decided to hypnotize him when he said, so weakly that I could barely hear him, "I had to sleep on the livingroom sofa. The first night I was there he came downstairs and woke me up."

"Why did he wake you up?"

"He wanted to lie down with me."

"And did he do that?"

"Yes. I didn't want him to. There wasn't room on the sofa for him and me both. But he got in with me anyway."

"What happened then?"

"He put his hand in my pajamas. I kept saying, 'No!' But he wouldn't listen. I was crushed against the back of the sofa and couldn't move."

"What did he do?"

"He licked my face with his big tongue. Then he felt me for a long time until—"

"Until what, Rob?"

"Until it started to get bigger."

"What did you think about that?"

"I was afraid. I didn't understand what was happening. I didn't know what to do."

"What happened then?"

"He finally got up and left."

"Just like that?"

"He said if I told anyone he would kill my kitten."

"What else?"

"The outside of my pajamas was sticky and cold. I didn't know why."

"Where did he go?"

"He went back upstairs."

"Did this ever happen again?"

"Almost every night. I used to lie there and pray that Uncle Dave wouldn't come down."

"Was it always the same?"

"No. Sometimes he put his mouth down there. Then—Then he—"

"I know this is difficult, Rob. But you must try to tell me the rest."

388

"He wanted me to put my mouth on him! Oh, Daddy, help!"

"And did you do it?"

"No! I said, 'No—I won't do it!' "

"And he left you alone after that?"

"No. The next day he killed my kitten. He picked her up and wrung her neck."

"While you watched?"

"Yes."

"What else?"

"He said he was going to do that to me unless I did what he wanted."

"Did he come back that night?"

"Yes."

"And did you do it?"

"No. I don't know. I . . . I . . . I don't remember anymore."

"What's the next thing you remember?"

"He came back about every night but I don't think he bothered me. I was always asleep."

"You were able to fall asleep knowing your uncle was coming to molest you?"

"Not exactly. I never fell asleep until he came down and got into the sofa. So I don't think he did much after that."

"Where was your Aunt Catherine all those nights?"

"She stayed upstairs, mostly. She had a bad heart. But sometimes I thought I saw her sitting on the stairs. And I heard her once or twice."

"What did she say?"

"Nothing. She just made funny noises. Like she couldn't breathe."

"And this went on until your father came home from the hospital?"

"Yes. They killed a dog, too."

"What dog?"

"I don't know. I think it was a stray. They killed it with a knife."

"Why?"

"They said that would happen to me if I told. Uncle Dave would strangle me and Aunt Catherine would stab me with the knife."

"Did you ever tell anyone?"

"Never."

"All right, Rob. We'll stop for a while."

Obviously relieved, he sighed loudly.

"Thank you for telling me all this. Are you okay?"

"I don't know. I think so." He began stroking the cat again.

I let him rest for a minute. I should have sent him back to the wards at this point, but I knew prot could depart at any time despite everything. "Rob, I'd like to put you under hypnosis now. Would that be all right?"

His shoulders slumped even lower. "I thought we were finished for today."

"Almost."

He looked left and then right, as if trying to find a way out. "All right. If you think it will help. . . ."

As before, he didn't go into the trance immediately, as prot always did, but more cautiously, fighting all the way. When I was sure he was "asleep" I induced him to return to the past, but this time all the way back to his fifth birthday. He described the cake, remembered blowing out all the candles. But he wouldn't tell me his wish or (he solemnly informed me) it wouldn't come true. It was only a short time later that his father was injured in the slaughterhouse and ended up in the hospital, and little Robin (his boyhood name) had to go live with his Uncle Dave and Aunt Catherine for a few weeks. The prospect was not an unpleasant one for him. He seemed to like his mother's older siblings, who had given him a kitten for his birthday. His sisters were taken to live with another aunt in Billings.

"All right, Robin, you're at your aunt and uncle's house and it's time for bed. Where are you going to sleep?"

"Aunt Catherine made the sofa into a bed for me. I like it. It smells funny, but it's soft and warm."

"Good. Are you going to sleep now?"

"Yes."

"Where is the kitten?"

"Uncle Dave put her in the kitchen."

"All right. What's happening now?"

"I'm just laying here, listening to the crickets. The kitten is meowing. Oh—someone's here. It's Uncle Dave. He's trying to get in bed with me. He is pushing me over."

"He's coming to sleep with you?"

"I guess so. But it's too crowded. He's pushing me against the back of the sofa. He has his arm around me. He's touching me! 'No, Uncle Dave! I don't want you to!' He's putting his hand in my pajamas. He's feeling my thing. 'Uncle Dave! Please don't. I'll tell!' "

"What did he say to that?"

Five-year-old Robert started to cry. "He says if I do he'll kill my kitten."

"It's all right, Robin. He's finished now. He's gone back upstairs. Just rest for a little while."

He continued to sob until it tapered off to a whimper.

"All right, Robin, now it's one week later, and you're getting into the sofa. How are you feeling?"

"I'm very afraid. He's going to come down. I know he's going to come down. I can't sleep. I'm so scared."

"Where is your kitten?"

"Oh, he killed her. He killed her. I think he's going to kill me, too." He was shaking. "Oh, here he comes. 'Please, Uncle Dave, please. Please God, don't do it tonight!' "

"He's getting into the sofa?"

"No. He's pulling my blanket off. I'm holding on to it but he's too strong. Now he's taking off his pajamas. I don't want to look. I'm going to sleep now." He closed his eyes tightly.

"Robin? Are you asleep? Robin?"

His eyes came open again. But the look of fear was gone, replaced by one of hatred. Bitter, intense hatred. All his muscles were tense. He said nothing.

"Rob?"

"No," he replied, through clenched teeth.

"Who are you?"

His feet began to shuffle. "Harry."

I was stunned. Not because another alter had made an appearance, but because I understood immediately what a fool I'd been, that there might be still others I didn't yet know about, perhaps watching and listening to everything that transpired. "Harry, please—tell me what's happening."

The feet stopped shuffling. "He's kneeling beside the sofa. His thing is in my face. He wants me to put it in my mouth."

"Are you doing that?"

"I have to or he will kill Robin. But I will kill *him*, too. If he does anything to Robin I will kill him. I hate him! I hate his guts! I hate his rotten thing! I am going to bite it off if he hurts Robin. Then I will kill him. I will! I will! And her, too, that fat pig." He looked as though he meant every word.

"All right, Harry. It's all over now. Uncle Dave and Aunt Catherine have gone upstairs. You are all alone. You and Robin."

Harry sat in his chair spitting violently, glowering, his eyes rising as the pair made their way slowly up the stairs.

"Harry? Listen carefully. You're going to sleep now." I waited until he calmed down, closed his eyes. A moment later I whispered, "All right, Robin. It's morning now. Robin, wake up."

"Huh?"

"Is that you, Robin?"

"Yes."

"It's time to get up."

Dismally: "I don't want to get up." But at least the horrible twitching had subsided.

"I understand. It's okay. Just rest there for a while. We're going to go forward in time now. You're getting older. You're six, now you're seven, now ten. Now you're fifteen, twenty, twenty-five, thirty, thirty-five, thirty-eight. Rob?"

"Yes?"

"How are you doing?"

"Not so hot."

"All right, I'm going to wake you up now. I'm going to count backward from five. By the time I get to one you will be wide awake and feeling fine. Five . . . four . . . three . . . two . . . one." I snapped my fingers. "Hello, Rob—how do you feel?"

I needn't have asked. He may have felt fine, but he looked sick and exhausted. "Can I go to my room now?"

"Of course. And Rob?"

"Yes?"

I got up, placed my hand on his shoulder, and escorted

him to the door. He was still holding the cat. "I think the worst is over. Everything is going to be all right now."

"Do you really think so?"

"Yes, I do. In one or two more sessions I think we'll have everything sorted out. Then you can begin to get well."

"That sounds too wonderful to be true."

"It's true. And when you get better, it will be perfectly all right for prot to leave. You won't need him anymore."

"I hope not. I don't think he's going to be around much longer anyway, no matter what happens."

"Do you have any idea—"

"You're browbeating again, coach. He doesn't know, and neither do I."

"Prot! Rob was just on his way back to Ward Two."

He shrugged and reached for the door.

"Before you go, tell me: Are there any child molesters on K-PAX?"

"No, and no adult molesters, either."

ON Tuesday morning one of the world's foremost psychiatrists arrived to spend the day at MPI meeting with faculty and staff, and to present a seminar on current research in his field. I had never met the man before, though I had read most of his books, including the immensely popular *The Lighter Side of Mental Illness*, heard him lecture at national and international conferences, and was looking forward to this rare opportunity.

He strode into the hospital wearing top hat and tails, his trademark dress. Now in his eighties, he looks twenty years younger, and keeps himself in shape by running seven miles every morning before breakfast, doing fifty push-ups at midday, and swimming an hour every afternoon before dinner. In between he gulps vitamins and minerals by the handful. He asked everyone he met where the swimming pool was. Unfortunately, the Manhattan Psychiatric Institute does not have such a facility.

I didn't see him until later, in part because I skipped the morning coffee conference (our guest had grapefruit juice) in order to visit Russell, who was in the infirmary, apparently suffering from exhaustion. He seemed okay otherwise, and was still preaching the imminent demise of the world.

I spoke to Chak about Russ's condition, but he was mystified about what was ailing him. "You are not to worry," he assured me. "He is not in immediate danger." He was thinking of transferring him to Columbia Presbyterian for further examination and testing.

"Do what you need to do," I said. "I would hate to lose him."

I poked my head into Russell's room before leaving the clinic to wave a cheerful goodbye and found him weeping. I stepped in and asked him what the matter was. He said, "When I get to heaven I hope they have hamburgers on Saturday nights. . . ." I think it was the first time I had ever heard him say anything that wasn't a quote from the Bible.

My turn to speak privately with the great clinician, whose books occupy a prominent place on my office shelves, came at two o'clock. He bounded into my office fresh as a kid (thanks to the push-ups, perhaps), swallowed several vitamin pills, and immediately fell asleep sitting up in his chair. For a moment I thought he had died there, but on careful observation I could see his chest moving under his cravat. Not wanting to disturb him, I slipped out and let him have his forty winks. It was only later that I learned he had passed out in everyone's office. Apparently he was saving his strength for the four-o'clock seminar.

When I returned to awaken and escort him to Beamish's office he finished the sentence he had started when he dozed off and leaped out of the chair like a twenty-year-old. I had a difficult time keeping up with him as he winged his way down the corridor.

Having an hour or so free before the seminar, I decided to spend them on the grounds, where I found Lou huffing and puffing around the back forty. Not having seen him for a couple of weeks I was aghast at the amount of weight he had put on. His maternity slacks were stretched to their limit. His bright-yellow blouse was unbuttoned and it fell over his swollen belly like the petals of a giant sunflower. It appeared he was literally feeding his delusion.

He blew some hair from his eyes. "Had I known it was going to be like this I never would have become a mother," he groaned. He seemed to be fingering something—a gossamer thread, I presumed.

I noticed Dustin plodding along the far wall. He always seemed to be most agitated late in the afternoon. I heard Lou say, "Why don't you give Dustin a break and keep his parents away from him tonight?"

"They're nice people, Lou. And they're his only visitors."

"They're driving him nuts!"

Just then Milton wiggled along on his beat-up unicycle, juggling a few raisins and mumbling to himself, "And I told the maestro, 'No, thank you! I want to hear the entire *ramide* or no *ramide* at all!' "

Virginia Goldfarb came by from the other direction and reminded me of the upcoming seminar by our distinguished visitor. I accompanied her to the amphitheater.

When everyone was seated and Villers had introduced our guest in a very complimentary fashion, he bounded from his chair and took the podium. It looked to be a rewarding hour. Unfortunately, when the lights were dimmed for his slides, the great man fell asleep again, and he stood snoring softly at the front of the room like an old horse wearing a top hat. The projectionist, one of our bright young residents, gravely continued with the slide show, which was pretty much self-explanatory anyway. When it was over and the lights came up, our speaker awakened, concluded his talk, and asked for questions.

No one had any. Perhaps everyone else was thinking, as I was, about the functional capacities of the elderly gentlemen who populate the halls of Congress and the United States Supreme Court, sleeping at the switch, so to speak, while the trains roll by.

Refreshed by his nap, our distinguished colleague got in his hour of swimming at a local gym before taking another snooze, this time over dinner at one of Manhattan's finest restaurants. (Villers, whose wife was still sick, had begged off and I was left to deal with the problem myself.) Somehow he managed to catch his menu on fire from the candle and, later, his head fell into his plate and mashed his "very young, tender sweet peas in unsalted butter sauce with a hush of marjoram and dill." After helping him eat, I finally got our slumbering guest into a cab and off to the airport, his forehead still flecked with food. He strode briskly into the terminal, but whether he made it home or not is anybody's guess.

As we pulled away I marveled at the accomplishments of our illustrious friend, much of which must have taken place while he was sound asleep. And I wondered whether he might not have a good deal more energy if he didn't keep himself in such great shape.

Session Twenty-seven

EARLY Wednesday afternoon, before my next session with Robert, I had a quick lunch with Giselle just to touch base. She mentioned that an ophthalmologist she knew was extremely interested in proving or disproving prot's ability to see UV light. I asked that she put him off for the moment. "Prot may be leaving soon, and there's still a lot of work to do."

"That's exactly why he should see prot ASAP!"

I told her I would let her know when a good opportunity came up.

Unfortunately, she was unable to tell me anything about prot I didn't already know. In fact, she complained that he was spending less time with her than he had earlier, and she requested copies of the taped recordings of our last few sessions. I felt sorry for her—she had become like a daughter to me—but I refused to let her listen to the tapes.

"Why not?" she demanded. "It's going into your book,

isn't it? Then the whole world will know everything he said in those sessions."

"Not everything. Besides—what makes you so sure I'm going to write another book?"

"Because you want to retire. At least your wife wants you to."

"A book isn't going to do it."

"It'll help."

"Maybe, but I still can't tell you. You know about doctor-patient privilege. If I do the book I won't identify any of the patients by their real names."

Her cheek ballooned with half a sandwich. "So don't tell me who's on the tapes!"

"Why not ask prot to tell you about the sessions? He seems to have a pretty good memory."

"I tried that."

"What did he say?"

"He doesn't want to violate your privacy."

"What does *that* mean?"

"I think he knows all there is to know about you."

"There isn't that much to know," I said, uncomfortably.

"He says we all have a lot of secrets we don't want any other being to find out about."

"Well, he's probably right about that."

"Yes, and everything else, too. In fact, it was prot's idea that I listen to the tapes. He says I can help Robert more if I know what's going on."

The retirement bug buzzed in my ear. "I'll think about it," I told her.

ROBERT strode in for his twenty-seventh session with an uncharacteristic smile on his face. Not a prot-like smirk, but certainly a grin. For the first time he actually appeared eager to talk. He hadn't even brought a cat with him.

"Rob, are you ready to tell me about Sally and Rebecca?"

The smile shrank but he said, "Yes, I think I am."

"Good. We'll stop if you begin to feel uncomfortable."

He nodded.

"Rob, how can you be sure you're not Rebecca's father?"

"Sally and I never had sex—uh—sexual intercourse."

"What did you have?"

"We just kissed and petted. That was all we did."

"Even after you were married?"

"Yes."

"Did you ever find yourself with your clothes off?"

"Sometimes."

"How did you think that happened?"

"They came off while we were kissing and petting."

"But nothing else happened?"

"No." Robert suddenly seemed less confident. He stared at his feet.

"How are you doing?"

"I'm okay."

"Do you know what sex is? How it operates?"

Uncomfortably: "I have a vague idea."

"But you've never done it."

"No."

"Sally wasn't interested?"

"Oh, yes. She was."

"Didn't you want to make love with her?"

"Yes. No. I don't know. We never—"

"All right. Let's not waste any more time. If you're ready, I'd like to hypnotize you again."

400

He looked away.

"Rob, this will probably be the last time. We're very close to the heart of your difficulty. Do you trust me?"

He took a deep breath and exhaled it harshly. "Yes."

"Good. Are you ready now?"

He took another breath and nodded. Slowly, kicking and scratching all the way, he fell into a trance. I took him back to June 9, 1975. "Rob, you and Sally have just been married. Do you remember that moment?"

"Of course. Our families were all there and it was a beautiful service."

"And after that?"

"There was a reception in the church basement. Cake and punch and some cashews and blue candy in little silver dishes."

"Okay. The reception is over. What's happening now?"

"People are snapping our pictures."

"And after that?"

"We're leaving the church. Everyone is throwing rice at us as we run down the steps and out to the car."

"You bought a car?"

"Yes. A '57 Ford Fairlane."

"Where did you get the money?"

"We used our wedding money for the down payment."

"Go on."

"We're driving away."

"Where are you going?"

"We don't have enough money for a honeymoon, so we're just going for a drive out in the country. It's a beautiful spring day. It's wonderful having Sally next to me with her head on my shoulder."

"I'm sure it is. All right, it's early evening. Where are you now?"

"The Hilltop House."

"What's the Hilltop House?"

"It's a nice restaurant in Maroney. About fifty miles from Guelph."

"How is the dinner?"

"Terrific. The best one we've ever had."

"What are you eating?"

"Lobster. We've never had it before."

"Okay. Dinner is over. Where are you going now?"

"We're driving home."

"Where is home?"

"Back in Guelph. A trailer park called Restful Haven."

"You have a trailer?"

"Sally prefers to call it a mobile home."

"Do you own it or rent it?"

"It was a present from Sally's family. It's a used one."

"All right. You're home now. What's happening?"

"We're going inside. I forgot to carry Sally over the threshold, so we're going back out and I'm picking her up and carrying her in. She's kissing me."

"What do you see, now that you're inside?"

"Somebody has put a box of diapers on the kitchen table. For a joke, I guess."

"Is Sally pregnant?"

"Yes."

"Who knows about this?"

"Probably everyone."

"You mean word gets around."

"Yes."

"Does the father know?"

"I don't know who the father is. Maybe Sally told him. We never talked about it."

"What's happening now?"

"It's starting to get dark. I'm not tired, but Sally wants to go to bed."

"Is she doing that?"

"Yes. She's in our little bathroom. . .now she's coming out. She's wearing a silk nightie. While she was in there I took off my clothes and got into bed."

"And is Sally getting in with you?"

"Yes. Actually she's jumping up and down on the bed and laughing."

"How do you feel about that?"

"I'm afraid."

"What are you afraid of?"

"We have never had sex. I've never done it with anyone. Except—"

"Yes, I know about Uncle Dave."

No response.

"All right. What is happening now?"

"Sally is snuggling up to me, rubbing her hand on my bare chest. She's kissing my face and my neck. All of a sudden I'm very sleepy. I'm falling asleep."

"Rob? Are you asleep?"

"Are you kidding? At a time like this?" His demeanor suddenly changed. He was alert, almost bugeyed. He seemed quite agitated. But it wasn't prot. Or Harry.

"Who are you?"

"Never fear, Paul is here."

"Paul? You're Paul? What are you doing here?"

"Helping out."

"How are you helping out?"

"Sally is horny as hell. She needs me. So does Rob."

"Rob? How does Rob need you?"

"I'm showing Rob how to make love to his wife."

"But he's asleep."

403

"Yeah, he always does that. But that's not my problem." He turned over and began to make kissing sounds.

"All right, Paul. It's an hour later. It's all over. Sally's asleep. What are you doing now?"

"Just lying here. Sally's head is on my shoulder. She is sound asleep. I can hear her breathing. I can smell her breath. Is that what lobster smells like?"

"Aren't you sleepy?"

"A little. I'm just going to lie here and enjoy this until I doze off." He was smiling.

"How many times has this happened before?"

"Not too many. Until now. It's been hard to find any privacy anywhere."

"Paul, are you the father of Sally's child?"

He started snapping his fingers. "How'd you guess?"

"It wasn't too difficult. Tell me: Can you hear everything that goes on with Rob?"

"Sure."

"Does he know about you?"

Snap, snap, snap. "Nope."

"How often do you come out?"

"Only when Sally needs me."

"Why not any other time?"

"Why should I? I've got a pretty good deal, don't you think?"

"From your point of view, I suppose it is. Okay, just one or two more questions."

"Shoot." *Snappity snap snap.*

"When did you first make an appearance?"

"Oh, I guess Rob was eleven or twelve."

"And he needed to masturbate?"

"He'd freak out every time he got a hard-on."

"All right. One last thing: Do you know about Harry?"

"Sure. Nasty little kid."

"All right. You lie there a while. It's getting late. You are falling asleep." Still smiling, he closed his eyes and the finger-snapping stopped. "Now it's morning. Time to get up."

His eyes opened, but he was no longer smiling.

"Rob? Is that you?"

He yawned. "Yes. What time is it?"

"It's still early. Is Sally there with you?"

"Shh. She's sleeping. God, she's beautiful."

I lowered my voice. "I'm sure she is. Now we're going to come forward in time. Imagine a calendar whose pages are turning rapidly forward. It's 1975, 1980, 1985, 1990, 1995. We're back in the present—September 13, 1995. Do you understand?"

"I understand."

I woke him up. He looked tired, but not nearly so exhausted as he had been after the previous session. "Rob, do you remember anything that just happened?"

"You were going to hypnotize me."

"Yes."

"Did you?"

"Uh-huh. And I think we've got most of the puzzle put together now."

"I'm glad to hear that." He seemed greatly relieved, though he didn't yet know what the picture looked like.

"I'm going to tell you something that you might find very disturbing. Please remember at all times that I'm trying to help you deal with your very understandable grief and confusion."

"I know."

"And remember that you can do or say anything that comes to mind. You are in your safe haven here."

"I remember."

"Good. Most of what we've learned about your past has come about through hypnosis. That's because when a person is hypnotized he is able to recall many things that his conscious mind has repressed. Do you understand?"

"I think so."

"Okay. I've hypnotized you several times now, and each time you told me some things about your past that you have consciously forgotten. Primarily because they are too painful to remember."

Robert seemed to freeze for a moment and, just as suddenly, thawed. It became clear to me then, if it wasn't before, how much he wanted to get well. I felt enormously gratified. "At some point I'm going to let you hear the tapes of all the sessions we've had so far. For now I'm just going to summarize everything we've learned to this point. If it gets too rough, just stop me and we'll pick it up some other time."

"I trust you. Please tell me what happened, for God's sake."

I told him the whole story, beginning with his burning his hand on the stove, the lumbering cow, about his father's accident and hospitalization, and about Uncle Dave and Aunt Catherine. He listened with the most rapt attention until Uncle Dave came down the stairs. At that point he shouted "No!" and buried his face in his hands. A moment later he lifted his head. I was sure it would be prot, or maybe someone else. But it was still Rob. As they used to say in the movies, he had "passed the crisis."

He asked me to go on. I told him about Harry. He shook his head as if he didn't believe it, but then he nodded for me to continue. I brought up the subject of his father's death and the first few appearances of prot, on up to his

406

junior year of high school and his first date with Sally, her pregnancy, their wedding, and Paul. Again he wagged his head, but this time he merely stared off into space as if testing the logic behind it all. "Paul, you rotten son of a bitch!" he blurted out, before breaking into a single, loud sob. That was what I had been waiting to hear.

"Paul is the father of your child."

"I figured as much."

"Do you understand what I'm telling you?"

"What do you mean?"

"The fact is that *you* were Rebecca's father. Paul is you. So is Harry. And so, believe it or not, is prot."

"That's pretty hard to swallow."

"I think you're ready to try. I'm going to make a copy of all the tapes and I want you to listen to them. Will you do that?"

"Yes."

"Good. It would be best if you did it here and left prot outside. I don't have any patient interviews Friday morning. I can ask Betty to bring you up then. Will you come and listen to the first three or four? If that works out you can hear the rest later on."

"I'll try."

"I'm also going to give you some reading material. A few case histories of multiple personality disorder."

"I'll read them, I promise. I'll do anything you say."

"Good."

"Only—"

"Only what?"

"Only—what happens next?"

"There are still a couple of loose ends to tie up. We'll try to do that next session. Then the real work begins."

"What kind of work?"

"It's called integration. We need to bring you and prot and Paul and Harry into one single personality. That won't be easy. It will depend a great deal on how badly you want to get well."

"I'll do my best, Dr. Brewer. But . . ."

"Yes?"

"What will happen to them? Will they just disappear?"

"No. They'll always be with you. They'll always be a part of you."

"I don't think prot's going to like that."

"Why don't you ask him?"

"I will. Right now he's hibernating again."

"All right. I want you to go back to your room and think about everything we've talked about."

He turned to go. Then he stopped and said, "Dr. Brewer?"

"Yes?"

"I have never been so happy in my life. And I don't even know why."

"We'll try to find out together, Rob. One last thing. Except for my home in Connecticut you have been able to talk to me only in this room. From now on I want you to consider all of Ward Two your safe haven. Will you do that?"

"I'll sure as hell try."

Our time had run over. I was late for an executive committee meeting and I couldn't have cared less.

IT wasn't quite that easy, of course—it was prot who returned to the wards. But I got a call from Betty that evening. She, in turn, had been phoned by one of the night nurses. Robert had made his first appearance in Ward Two. It happened in the lounge while he was watching a chess

408

match. He kibitzed! It definitely wasn't prot, who took no part in such "trivia." He didn't stay out long—he was just testing the waters—but it was a glorious beginning.

JUST before the scheduled trip to the zoo I made it a point to seek out prot, for two reasons. First, I wanted to make certain that it was he, and not Robert, who was going. And second, I wanted to ask him about Russell, who seemed to be languishing in the hospital, though the doctors couldn't find much wrong with him.

I found him on the lawn surrounded by his usual coterie of patients and cats. As always, there was a certain amount of grumbling when I asked them all to excuse us, though everyone was eagerly awaiting the visit to the zoo and seemed to be in good spirits. He winked at them, promising he would rejoin them in a few minutes. "What's wrong with Russell?" I asked him when we were alone.

"Nothing."

"Nothing? He won't eat. He won't even get out of bed."

"That often happens when a being is preparing to die."

"Die? You just said nothing is wrong with him."

"That's right. Every being dies. Perfectly normal procedure."

"You mean he *wants* to die?"

"He's ready to leave EARTH. He wants to go home."

"Uh—you mean heaven?"

"Yep."

I spotted Jackie somersaulting on the lawn. She, too, was happily anticipating an adventure. "But you don't believe in heaven, do you, prot?"

"No, but *he* does. And with human beings, believing is the same as truth, isn't it?"

409

"Can you help him?"

"Help him die?"

"No, dammit, help him live!"

"If he wants to die, that's his right, don't you think? Besides, he'll be back."

I thought for a moment he was talking about the second coming. Then I remembered his theory about the collapse of the universe and the reversal of time. I threw up my hands and walked off. How do you reason with a crazy person?

As I was trudging back into the building I met Giselle and some of the nurses and security guards coming out. They all grinned and waved, delighted, like the patients, to be having a rare outing, away from all this. I wouldn't have minded the trip myself, despite the heat and humidity, but I had to attend some meetings for Villers, whose wife was having surgery in the same hospital where Russell was calmly awaiting the end.

Rudolph and Michael were both discharged that morning, and I was more than elated to sign the release papers and escort them to the gate. Not as happy as they were, though. Particularly Mike, who was to take an EMS orientation class the following week. Rudolph, a totally different person from his former self, shook hands and wished me good luck with the rest of the patients. "But don't let prot get away," he admonished. "He's the best doctor you have."

That same evening, after everyone had returned fromthe zoo, Rob asked Dustin (who was perfectly normal at the chessboard) for a game. Rob lost that battle, and thenext several as well, but he appeared, at last, to be winning the war.

I got another report that Villers had spent a rare night

at MPI, sitting up until dawn talking with Cassandra. He was unshaven and not wearing a tie, something I myself had never seen. I couldn't believe he was only looking for racing tips, and I wondered whether his wife's illness might not be more serious than he let on. I made a mental note to ask him about it as soon as I found time.

Session Twenty-eight

THE Bronx Zoo is one of the premier animal-holding facilities in the United States. Occupying more than 250 acres in the heart of a major metropolitan area, it is the biggest urban sanctuary in the world. Noted for its attempts to preserve many of the planet's endangered species, it houses such diverse specimens as Père David's deer and the European bison, not to mention a variety of rare rodents, snakes, and insects.

The original idea had been to take only those patients from One and Two who were deemed capable of handling the trip. Prot vetoed this, pointing out that permanent harm could come to those who wanted to come but were not permitted. Thus, about thirty-five of our inmates boarded the bus that morning, all those (except for the residents of Ward Four) who had expressed a desire to go. They were divided into groups of six, each accompanied by three staff members—a clinical trainee, a nurse, an orderly or security guard—and a zoo volunteer.

Giselle reported to me the following morning that the outing was a tremendous success for everyone concerned, greatly boosting morale for the staff as well as the patients, and plans were soon in the works for a series of four trips a year: the zoo, the Museum of Natural History, Central Park, and the Metropolitan Museum of Art.

Prot's reaction varied from ecstasy at seeing so many different animals, to depression in finding all of them "incarcerated without benefit of trial." He proceeded from cage to cage, compound to compound, stopping at each to visit the inhabitants, and wherever he went, the elephants or zebras or swans ran trumpeting and honking to congregate as close to him as possible. He, in turn, seemed to "reassure" them, uttering various peculiar sounds and making subtle gestures. According to Giselle, the animals seemed, for all the world, to be listening to what he had to say, and he to them.

But the loudest supplicants were the chimpanzees and gorillas, who whined and screeched like so many pleading children. Prot, in turn, caused further commotion among the security people and zoo volunteers by leaping over the retaining wall and poking his fingers through the wire screens for a touch, which immediately quieted the apes, if not his hosts.

Whether any information was conveyed by this means is not certain, but we have had reports from zoo officials that many of their charges have changed their behavior patterns significantly following prot's visit. For example, the bears and tigers have ceased their endless pacing, and the incidence of bizarre conduct and self-mutilation among the primates has decreased substantially. When Giselle asked him what the animals were "telling" him, he replied, "They're

413

saying: 'Help! Let us out!' " And how did he respond to that? "I encouraged them all to hang in there—the way things are going, the humans won't be around much longer."

Of course none of this proves that anything was communicated between prot and the zoo's inhabitants. In order to test this possibility, Giselle asked him to write down any information he had obtained from them (e.g., their personal histories, which neither she nor prot would have had in their possession). When she gets his account, she plans to meet with zoo officials to determine whether there is anything of value in all this.

The only negative aspect of the outing was that some of the other patients managed to reach a conclusion similar to that of prot's, demanding to know why the zoo's inhabitants had been locked up, what crimes they had committed. Perhaps this concern had less to do with the animals themselves than with their own virtual imprisonment, which, in many cases, they see as unwarranted. Prot, for his part, has often reminded me that it's the people outside the mental institutions who should be in here, and vice versa.

I still don't know whether prot can talk to animals, but all that pales in comparison to what happened later that morning. As usual, I missed the whole thing, but those who saw it made sure I was filled in.

I was looking for Lou to see if he was still gaining weight when a contingent of manics, delusionals, and compulsives came running toward me, raving and shouting. I was beginning to feel some trepidation—were they upset that prot was disappearing on occasion and leaving Robert behind?—when one of them yelled that it was time to send Manuel home.

"Why?" I asked.

414

"Because he just flew across the lawn!"

"Where is he?"

"He's still out there!"

A cadre of patients trailing behind me, I headed down the stairs and out the front door, where I found Manuel sitting on the steps, his head in his hands. He was unashamedly crying.

"I've wanted to do that for so long . . ." he sobbed. "Now I can die."

"Do you want to die, Manny?"

"No, no, no, it's not that. It's just that I was so afraid I would die before I flew, and my life would be for nothing. Now that I can die, it's all right to live. I'm not afraid anymore."

That made some sense, I suppose, at least to Manuel. "How did you do it, Manny? How did you get off the ground?"

"I don't know," he confessed, with just a hint of Hispanic accent. "Prot said I needed to imagine exactly what it would be like to fly, down to the last tiny detail. I tried so much. I concentrated so hard. . . ." He closed his dark, shining eyes and his head tilted left, then right, as if he were reliving his imagined flight. "All of a sudden I knew how to do it!"

"I'm going to ask Dr. Thorstein to meet with you as soon as he can, all right? I think you'll be moving down to Ward One before long."

Sniffling quietly, he said, matter-of-factly, "Everything is okay now."

By this time some of the staff were also gathered around him. I asked one of the nurses whether any of them had seen Manuel lift off. No one had. Only the patients had witnessed this incredible feat.

Did they all lie? Not likely. Did Manuel fly? Also unlikely, though they claim he soared like an eagle. The important thing is that *he* believes it. From that day on he never flapped his arms again. His lifelong dream accomplished, he was happy, self-confident, at peace with the world.

I forgot all about Lou.

AS soon as he came into my examining room I asked Rob whether he had read all the material I had given him, and listened to the tapes.

"Oh, yes," he said. "It's hard to believe, but I think everything you told me is true." I gazed into his eyes for signs of uncertainty or even duplicity, and found none. Nor did he look away.

"I do, too. And I think we have nearly the whole story. There's just one missing piece of the puzzle. Will you help me fit it in?"

"I'll try."

"It has to do with your wife and daughter."

He sighed loudly. "I wondered when you were going to get to that."

"It's time, Rob. And I think you can handle it now."

"I'm not so sure of that, but I want to try."

"Good. I think we can do this without hypnosis. I just want you to tell me whatever you can about the day you came home from the slaughterhouse and found a man coming out your front door."

Rob stared straight ahead and said nothing.

"You chased him back into the house," I prodded, "through the kitchen and out the rear door. The sprinkler was still going. Do you remember any of that?"

Tears welled up in his eyes.

416

"Do you remember what happened next, Rob? This is very important."

"I caught up with the man and wrestled him to the ground."

"What happened then?"

The tears were rolling down his face. But I could tell he was thinking hard, trying to remember what he had done to the intruder who had killed his wife and daughter. His eyes darted back and forth along the wall, to my chair, to the ceiling. Finally, he said, "I don't really know. The next thing I remember is coming into the house and carrying Sally and Becky to their beds."

"And then you mopped the kitchen, said your good-byes, and headed for the river."

"I wanted to die, too."

"All right, Rob. That's enough. I'm proud of you. That must have been very difficult."

He wiped his eyes on a shirtsleeve but said nothing.

"Now I want you to relax for a minute. Close your eyes and just relax. Let your body unwind, all your fingers and toes. Good. I'd like to speak with Harry for a minute. Harry?"

No response.

"Harry, it's no use hiding. I could put Robin under hypnosis and find you that way." I wasn't so sure of this, but I hoped Harry would believe me. "Come on out. I just want to talk to you for a minute. I won't hurt you, I promise."

"You won't punish me?"

"Harry?"

His face was that of a bitter, scowling five-year-old. "I wouldn't care if you did punish me. I'd do it all over again."

"What would you do, Harry?"

"I'd kill Uncle Dave again if I got the chance." He looked mean enough to do it.

"You killed Uncle Dave?"

"Yes. Isn't that what you wanted to ask me about?"

"Well—yes. How did you kill him?"

"I broke his big fat neck."

"Where did this happen?"

"In the backyard. It was wet."

"Uncle Dave had done something to Sally and Rebecca?"

"Yes," he snarled. "The same thing he did to Robin."

"So you killed him."

"I told you I would and I did."

"Now this is very important, Harry. Did you ever kill anyone else?"

"No. Just the big fat pig."

"All right. Thank you for coming out, Harry. You can go back now. If we need you again I'll let you know."

The scowl slowly disappeared.

I waited a moment. "Rob?"

"Yes."

"Did you hear any of that?"

"Any of what?"

"Harry was just here. He told me what happened. He told me who killed the man that murdered your wife and daughter."

"*I* killed him."

"No, Rob, you never killed anyone. It was Harry who killed the intruder."

"Harry?"

"Yes."

"But Harry is only five years old, isn't he?"

418

"That's true, but he occupies a very strong body. Yours."

I could almost see a pair of lights come on in Robert's eyes. "You mean after all those years, I've been running from something that never happened?"

"It happened, Rob, and Sally and Rebecca are gone. But you didn't kill the man. Harry did."

"But Harry is me!"

"Yes, he's a part of you. But you are not responsible for his actions, not until he is integrated into your own personality. Do you understand?"

"I—I guess so." He looked puzzled.

"And there's another problem. You blamed yourself for their deaths because you had gone to work that Saturday instead of staying home with them."

"It was a nice day. They wanted me to take the day off."

"Yes."

"But I didn't because we needed the overtime pay."

"Yes, Rob. You went in that Saturday like all the rest of your fellow workers. Do you understand? Nothing that happened that day was your fault. None of it."

"But Sally and Becky died because I wasn't there."

"That's true, Rob, and we can't bring them back. But I think you're ready to face that now, don't you?"

His chest rose and fell, rose and fell. "I guess it's time to go on with things."

"It's time to begin the final phase of your treatment."

"The integration."

"Yes."

He thought about this, collected himself. "How do we do that?" He absentmindedly grabbed a banana and began peeling it.

"The first thing we do is get you to stay around as much as possible. I want you to be Robert from now on unless I specifically ask one of the others to come out."

"I don't know if I can keep prot in."

"We'll take it a day at a time. Just do your best."

"I'll try."

"From now on the entire hospital is your safe haven. Understand?"

"I understand," he said.

"C'mon—I'll go back to Ward Two with you."

IT was with a profound sense of sadness that I learned that Emma Villers had been diagnosed with an untreatable and rapidly progressing form of pancreatic cancer.

I knew something must have gone terribly wrong when Klaus appeared in my office after the session with Robert, staring and ashen. I thought it was he who was ill, and I asked him to sit down. He shook his head and blurted out the whole story. "She vas afraid of doctors," he said. "She neffer vent and I neffer made her." Pulling himself together, he added, "I am taking a leaf of absence. Vile I am gone you vill be acting director."

I started to protest—I had thought all that minutiae was behind me—but how could I? He looked so forlorn that I pounded him on the shoulder (a first for both of us) and told him not to worry about the hospital. He gave me the keys to his office, I expressed some feeble condolences and encouragement about his wife's condition, and he went away, his rounded shoulders drooping more than ever. Suddenly I remembered Russell's preaching the rapidly approaching apocalypse, and I realized, finally, what he meant: For him, for anyone, dying meant the end of the world.

I sat down and tried to get a fix on these unwelcome developments. But all I could think of was gratitude and relief that it wasn't my own wife or one of my children, and I vowed to spend more time with Karen and to call my sons and daughters more often. Then I remembered that as acting director I would have even less time than before, and I reluctantly headed for Villers's office hoping to find his desk cleaned off as, indeed, it usually is. Instead, it was much like my own, covered with unanswered letters, unreviewed papers, unattended messages and memos. His calendar was filled from eight-thirty to four-thirty or later every day for weeks ahead. And I thought, with mixed emotions: Retirement will have to wait.

ON the train home that evening I pondered Rob's rapid progress and where to go from here. It had all happened so fast, so unexpectedly, that I hadn't thought much about his treatment once he was out of his protective shell. On top of that, I had to do Klaus's job as well as my own. I knew I was in for another sleepless night.

I struck up a conversation with a fellow traveler, who had spent the afternoon with his father, a recent heart-attack victim. I told him that a coworker of mine had taken some time off to be with his dying wife. He sympathized completely, relating all the good things about his marriage of six years, how much he would miss his wife if anything happened to her. Turned out he had been married three times already and was on his way to spend the weekend with his mistress, whom, he claimed, he also loved dearly.

I thought: Not for me. In thirty-six years of marriage I have never been unfaithful to Karen. Not even *before* we were married (we were childhood sweethearts). It's not that I possess an unusual degree of loyalty, nor am I any kind of saint. The fact is, I'd be a damn fool to do anything to lose her. At that moment I fervently hoped she would get her wish and we could retire soon to some wonderful place in the country.

Then I remembered Frankie, who would never know the bliss of love and marriage. I felt as sorry for her as I did for Klaus and Emma Villers. Frankie had been Klaus's patient, and now she was my responsibility. I vowed right then to do whatever I could to get to the bottom of her problem, to put a little joy into her sad, loveless life.

OVER the weekend Will broke the code. To be certain he was right, he had run through several of Dustin's recorded "statements," and they all checked out. Will was now the only person in the world (except for prot, presumably) who could figure out what Dustin was saying.

He called me from the hospital on Sunday afternoon, as excited as I had ever heard him. "Prot was right—it was the carrot!"

"What do carrots have to do with Dustin's gibberish?"

"It's not gibberish. It's like a game with him. He sees everything in terms of roots—square roots, cube roots, and so on. There's no limit. He's a kind of savant!"

Looking back on it, I suppose I should have been more thrilled about Will's discovery. When I didn't reply, he exclaimed, "Remember that thing we worked on a few weeks ago—'Your life sure is fun . . .' and so on? The carrot is a root, see, and the four chomps on it make it a quadruple root thing: the second, fourth, eighth, and sixteenth word of the sentence, and the cycle repeats itself four times. All of his other statements are variations on that theme, depending on how many repeats and how many bites of the carrot. Get it?"

"I'm very proud of you, son. That was quite an accomplishment."

"Thanks, Pop. I'll come in some time soon and we'll talk about whether anything can be done for Dustin. I have some ideas on that."

"Really? I'd like to hear them."

"It's his parents."

"How so?"

"I think they're the problem. His father, anyway. I came in several evenings and watched them when they were together. Did you ever notice how he tries to compete with Dustin all the time? It's the only way they can communicate. At home all they did was play games. All his life Dustin has been smothered by trying to compete with his father, a game he couldn't possibly win. Don't you see? He had to devise something his old man couldn't beat him at. I've got to run, Pop. I'll come to see you in a couple of days and we'll talk about it—okay?"

"Okay, but we're not going out for lunch!"

"Whatever you say."

"Will—did you see prot today?"

"Nope. I ran into Robert once. He remembered me. But I haven't seen prot at all. Is he gone, Dad?"

"Not yet. But soon, I think."

Twenty-nine

I almost called you at home yesterday," Giselle blustered as she paced around my office.

I was trying to find the paper I still hadn't reviewed, to send it back with apologies. "What's the matter now?" I asked irritably, wondering what had stopped her.

"Where's prot? What have you done with him?"

"What—he's disappeared again?"

"Nobody has seen him since Friday."

"Robert, too?"

"No, *he's* around, but prot's gone."

"Oh. I don't think he's gone back to K-PAX, if that's what you're worried about."

"He might as well have."

"Giselle, you knew he wouldn't be here forever. He must have told you that."

"But he told me he wouldn't go without letting me know."

"Me, too. That's why I don't think he's gone."

"But it's more than that. When I saw him on Friday he seemed—I don't know—*different*. Preoccupied or something. He just wasn't his old self."

"It doesn't always happen that way, but I'm not surprised to hear it."

She plopped down in the vinyl chair. "He's dying, isn't he?"

Her disconsolation softened my irritability. "It isn't like that, Giselle. What's happening, I think, is that he's slowly becoming integrated into Robert's personality. In other words, you still have him. You'll have both of them."

"You mean Robert will become more like him?"

"A bit more like him, perhaps."

"I understand what you're saying. But it's still hard to believe."

"It's hard for Rob to believe, too."

"Either way, you're going to have a difficult time explaining it to the patients. They combed the hospital yesterday looking for him."

"What do they think when they see Robert?"

"They see a fellow patient. But they don't see prot."

"Maybe they will eventually."

"I doubt it."

"That reminds me of the favor I requested of you—remember?"

"You mean to make friends with Robert, and all of that?"

"That's right. It's very important."

She looked at her hands for a long time. "We're already friends. In fact, I like him a lot. It's just that he's not prot."

"Part of him is. Will you continue to cultivate that friendship?"

425

She turned away for a long moment. Finally she said, "I'll do what I can."

"Thank you, Giselle. I need all the help I can get. I'm counting on you."

She nodded and got up to leave. At the door she whirled around. "What about the cetologist? I promised him that prot—"

"Trust me. It'll be all right."

"Okay, Doctor B. I'm counting on you, too."

BY a show of hands I was confirmed as acting director. No one else wanted the job, not even Thorstein, at least not on a temporary basis and with the worms crawling out of the can. The remainder of the meeting was spent dividing up Villers's few patients for the duration of his absence. I took Jerry and Frankie. And Cassandra, not because I saw a fortune in milking her for predictions, but because I didn't want anyone else to be tempted. There were some objections to this, but as acting director I was able to over-rule them.

This was followed by a brief discussion of upcoming events: visits by the cetologist and the famous TV "folk psychiatrist," as well as prot's own television appearance. Goldfarb remarked that he seemed to be disappearing like a Cheshire cat, and questioned (again) whether he could be counted on to show up for the interview. I tried to calm those fears by disclosing that I was planning to try to get us out of that commitment, and that seemed to end the matter, at least for the time being.

As the conversation turned to matters of great golf games and mellow Merlots, I gazed at former patient "Catherine Deneuve"'s perfect copy of Van Gogh's *Sunflowers* and pretended I was a bee buzzing around the

426

back forty, able to see the flowers and grass and trees in astonishing vividness, much as prot seemed to be able to do. I wondered what bees thought about. The only thing that came to mind was what Hamlet said to Horatio: "There are more things in heaven and earth than are dreamt of in your philosophy. . . ."

I decided to treat Rob as if he were a boy who was more or less ignorant about sexual matters, as indeed he was. I would explain the process to him in general terms and, if I thought he could handle it, show him some videotapes that would fill in the details. In short, I was going to have to be his surrogate father, the father he never really had.

This was not an entirely unfamiliar situation. Many times a psychiatrist must play the role of parent to a patient whose experiences with his own father or mother have been disastrous. Indeed, it would not be an exaggeration to say that many analysts are the foster heads of some very large families.

Rob came in for his twenty-ninth session a couple of hours earlier than usual, as I had requested. He seemed relatively cheerful and relaxed. We chatted for a few minutes about the weekend, which he was happy to discuss in great detail. Being in the wards on his own was a new and pleasant experience for him.

"But some of the patients don't seem to like me very much," he lamented.

"Give them time," I assured him. "They'll come around."

"I hope so."

"We're going to do something a little different today, Rob."

His demeanor changed instantly. "I thought we were through with all that."

"No hypnosis today, Rob."

A sigh of relief.

"Today the subject is sex."

His reaction was perfectly normal: "Oh. Okay."

"I'm going to give you the fundamentals, then I've got some videotapes for you to watch."

He reached for an apple, his only sign of nervousness.

I explained the basic features to him. Of course he knew what I was talking about, having been exposed to the subject throughout his school years and beyond. I merely wanted to make sure there was no misunderstanding, and to observe him as we discussed the matter. He dealt with it quite well. Although he rarely looked me in the eye, neither did he seem apprehensive.

When I had finished my exposition, I pointed to the television set I had conscripted for the occasion. "I've brought in some of the tapes we have on the subject. This will give you a far better idea of what we're talking about than anything I can tell you. I think you're ready to fill in the rest of the gaps. What do you think?"

"I guess I could give it a try."

"I warn you: These are quite explicit. X-rated. Do you understand?"

"Yes."

I studied him for any change in demeanor. There was none. "If you feel any discomfort at all, just turn it off and come and get me. I'll be right next door in my office. Okay?"

"Okay."

"Good. Do you know how to run a VCR?"

"Yes. Dustin showed me."

"Dustin? No kidding. All right. You're on your own. I've got some phone calls to make. No one will bother you." I waited for that to sink in. "See the clock behind you? I'll be back at five." I left him alone to study them in whatever way he found most informative.

I was on the phone for the next several hours canceling as many of Villers's meetings and appointments and speeches as I could get away with, and trying to fit some of the others into my own crowded schedule. I also called the hospital's chief attorney, hoping to get prot out of the TV appearance. It was too late. The papers had been signed, and there was nothing left but to go ahead with it or face a lawsuit for breach of contract. After that I spent some time shuffling things around on my desk, moving piles from here to there and back again. When five o'clock finally came I tapped on the door of my examining room.

Someone yelled, "Come in!"

I found Robert slouched down in his chair, exactly as I had left him. "How are you doing?"

He was watching a film on foreplay. "Fine," he answered, without looking up. I was pleased to see it was still Rob.

"Good. That's enough for today, I think. Would you like to see some of these again sometime?"

"It doesn't seem very complicated," he replied ingenuously. "I think I'm ready to try it on my own."

I said, quietly, "I think we can manage to find someone to help you." To myself I shouted, "Right on!"

ABBY phoned us at home that evening. Karen took the call. After catching up on our various activities, Rain and Star came on. They wanted to talk to me. A new word had cropped up into their vocabulary. For example, I opined that "the Giants are going all the way this year."

"That's bullshit, Grandpa." In fact, everything I said was "bullshit."

I asked to speak with their mother.

"Sure they say 'bullshit' once in a while," she sighed. "So what?"

"They're too young for that. It gives a bad impression."

"Dad, lots of yuppie kids keep their hair neatly trimmed and wear ties and watch what they say, and they couldn't give a good goddamn about their planet or the animals they share it with. Which would you rather have for a grandson?"

"I've met some very nice yuppies."

"Oh, Dad, you're impossible. But I love you anyway. Here's Steve. He wants to tell you something."

"Hello, Steve. What's up?"

"Ah just thought you'd like to know"—his chortle sounded a bit like that of a chimpanzee—"that Charlie Flynn broke his big toe this afternoon."

"What's so funny about that?"

"He had hauled some high-intensity spotlights up into the big telescope and was trying to shine them down onto the mirror. Danged if he didn't fall off."

"Why was he doing that?"

"Light-travel," he said, giggling. "He was tryin' to get to K-PAX!"

Before hanging up we chatted a while about how absentminded scientists can be. "For example," he related, "a plumber came into the department the other day to fix a clogged sink. He took off the trap underneath, caught the dirty water in a bucket, and handed it out to one of the graduate students standin' there. He said, 'Here—get rid of this.' The kid promptly dumped the water right back into the sink!" It sounded like a whole barrel of monkeys on the other end of the phone.

As soon as we finished our conversation and I dropped the receiver down, the phone rang again. It was the head night nurse. Her voice was shaking. "Dr. Brewer?"

"Yes?"

"Dr. Brewer, you're not going to believe this."

"Believe what?"

"I don't know how to begin."

"Jane! What is it?"

"Lou just had a baby!"

"You're kidding!"

"I told you you wouldn't believe it."

"Where is he now?"

"In the infirmary. Dr. Chakraborty says he and the baby are doing fine. It's a girl. Six pounds eight ounces. Seventeen inches." I could almost see the woman grinning. When she does that, her eyes almost disappear.

"But—but—when did it happen? *How* did it happen?"

"No one knows. Except prot."

"Prot? What did he have to do with it?"

"He delivered the baby."

My head was swimming. Did prot somehow find an abandoned child somewhere and bring it in without being seen? "All right, Jane. Thank you. I'll speak to prot and Dr. Chak in the morning."

"She's a beautiful baby," was all she had to add.

STILL reeling from the news, I came in early the next morning to see Lou's impossible child for myself. I still felt it had to be some trick of prot's. But when I got to the

431

hospital I found a big truck parked on Amsterdam Avenue. I had forgotten that Giselle's cetologist friend was coming.

In the trailer was a dolphin he wanted prot to speak to. I wasn't sure, however, that prot would be available, despite his sudden reappearance last evening. In fact, it was Robert who came out of the building and greeted me and the other patients milling around the grounds. Giselle was with him.

She introduced me to the marine biologist, a tanned young man in jeans and a T-shirt bearing a great blue whale and the phrase "Cetaceans Unlimited." He couldn't wait to get started.

"Are you going to speak to the dolphin, Rob?"

"You know I can't go outside, Dr. Brewer."

"Just wondered whether you were planning to try."

"Not quite yet." In fact, as soon as we got to the big wrought-iron gate, prot flipped on his dark glasses and chirped, "Hi, Giselle. Got something for you." He gave her a handwritten version of his conversation with the zoo animals. "Hiya, gino. How are things?"

I said, "Prot, where did you get that baby?"

"She came from Lou. Pretty shitty delivery, doc. I told you it should've been a cesarean. Now, if you'll excuse me. . . ."

I was flabbergasted by this glib remark, but I followed him into the trailer without a word. For once I didn't want to miss anything. I left Betty to try to explain to the patients why everybody couldn't climb aboard.

The tank was big enough for the dolphin to swim around in a tight oval, but not much else. As soon as I was inside I heard prot whooping some kind of call. The dolphin swam faster and began to make sounds of his own. There were lesions on his skin, perhaps from some kind of infection.

432

Suddenly it stopped and faced prot directly. Giselle leaned over the top of the tank and watched with a huge smile; I stood a little farther away. The cetologist scrambled to get his recording equipment going. I wished I had thought to invite Abby to see this.

The conversation, or whatever it was, continued for several minutes. The pattern of sound was not regular, but varied in pitch and duration as does the dialogue between two human beings. At the end of the whole thing the dolphin, whose name, according to the hand-painted sign stuck to the side of the tank, was "Moby," uttered a pathetic wail, as if his heart were breaking.

Suddenly it was silent, except for the sounds still echoing around and around the trailer. Prot leaned over and offered his face to the dolphin, who licked it. The cetologist said, "I've tried to get him to do that for months." Prot, in turn, licked the dolphin's snout. He then wailed something of his own before jumping down and heading for the door.

"Wait!" shouted the scientist. "Aren't you going to tell me what he said?"

Prot stopped and turned around. "Nope."

"Why not?"

"You have the tapes. You figure it out."

"But I don't have anything to go on. Giselle, you told me he'd cooperate. Talk to him!"

She shrugged.

Prot turned and said, "I'll tell you what. If you quit 'studying' him and put him back in the ocean, and get all the others to do the same, I'll tell you everything he said to me."

"Please! Give me something—anything!"

"*Sacré bleu!* All right—I'll give you a hint. What he's

expressing is almost pure emotion. Unabashed joy, high excitement, terrible sorrow—things you humans have forgotten about, even your children. Are you blind and deaf? He's in pain. He wants to go home. Is that such an alien concept?" He marched out of the trailer, presumably to tell the patients what he and the dolphin had been talking about.

The youthful scientist, looking like a would-be prince who had been given three impossible tasks to complete, glumly watched him leave. He whimpered, "I wanted to ask him why so many of them are beaching themselves lately." All I could do was shrug, too. The dolphin, I noticed, was staring at us.

But it was Robert, not prot, who joined the patients waiting outside. Yet, when he headed off toward Adonis, some of them trailed after him! Was it Robert or prot they were following? Or someone in-between?

As I was going up the walk I heard a familiar patter behind me. Giselle caught up. "I've been thinking about what you said."

"And?"

"And I think you're right. Rob is a lot like prot."

"I'm glad you feel that way."

"And even if you're wrong," she added, "I think he needs me."

"We both do," I assured her as I hurried off to the clinic to see Lou.

I found Chakraborty poring over some sonograms and X-rays. "What do you make of it?" I asked him.

"According to the pictures, he has a uterus and one small ovary. They are connected with the rectum." There were stars in his eyes. "I have not seen anything ever like it."

"Prot has always told me we should listen more to what our patients are saying to us. After this, I'm inclined to agree. How soon can he leave here?"

"He is okay to go away in one day. Should I send him back to Ward Number Two?"

"That's up to Beamish. I'll speak to him. Let's go see Lou."

"One final thing. I am very sorry to tell you, but I took a call from the big hospital one moment ago. Russell has died. Do you want them to bring him back here? After the autopsy, of course."

I had been expecting this news, but I was nonetheless stunned. I had known Russell for many years. He was a nuisance, a pain in the neck sometimes, but I had gotten used to having him around, and so had the rest of the staff and patients. In a peculiar way, he was a sincere and good friend to all of us. Yet, only Maria, a former MPI patient who had become a nun, was with him when he died. "Yes, have them send him back here. We'll bury him on the back forty."

"I think he would be liking that very much."

Lou was sitting up drinking some apple juice. One of the nurses was nearby feeding the baby from a bottle. I shook my head in wonder. "She's a pretty little girl, Lou. Have you decided on a name for her yet?"

"When I first got here, the other patients and I decided to call her 'Protista.' "

Session Thirty

GISELLE, with the help of a city employee she knew, learned that Bert had impregnated his girlfriend while they were in high school. Without his knowledge, the girl had sought an abortion from a neighborhood quack and, unfortunately, had died in the makeshift "clinic." When Bert found out about this, he was devastated to the extent that he never went out with a woman again.

But it wasn't until thirty years later that his mother paid an unexpected visit and found his closet full of dolls and children's clothing, a futile attempt to resurrect his lost daughter. Her discovery precipitated a chain of events that led to his violent eruption and hospitalization, where vigorous treatment with a variety of antidepressant drugs failed to relieve Bert of his all-pervasive sense of loss, and he finally ended up at MPI.

Armed with these facts, I went to see him. I found him in the lounge helping Jackie build a Lego house.

Frankie was there, too, her great bulk perched precariously on the window ledge. She was staring morosely out the big window, ignoring all of us.

I found a chair and pulled it up to watch the construction project. Jackie was as involved, carefree, and happy as any nine-year-old, while Bert played the role of father, praising the laying of every new brick, not interfering unless something went awry.

"I know about your daughter," I told him.

He continued to help Jackie with her new house.

"You must miss her very much."

He pretended not to hear me.

"I have an idea you might like."

He glanced briefly in my direction, then helped Jackie figure out how to position a double window.

"Jackie needs a father. You need a daughter. How would you like to 'adopt' her? Not legally, of course—there are certain problems with that. Unofficially."

He looked at me with a pathetic appeal. But he didn't, or was unable to, say anything. Jackie added another brick to the little house. Bert's chin began to flutter.

I patted him on the shoulder and left him to contemplate the possibilities while I ambled over to talk with Frankie. She, too, was preoccupied with other matters and seemed not even to notice that I had taken a seat beside her on the sill, where Howie had once planted himself to search for the "bluebird of happiness."

"I've been talking to prot," I told her.

"Where is he?" she demanded, without looking at me. "What have you bastards done with him?"

"He isn't far away. He explained everything to me."

Frankie fixed a steely gaze on me. "Have you ever thought about doing something about your obnoxious voice?"

437

"You're unable to love anyone for the same reason he is. You find it irrelevant. It seems stupid to focus your feelings on one single person and forget about everyone else. Am I getting warm?"

She stared at me for another long moment. "I may puke,"she said.

"Go ahead and puke, but hear me out first. No one you have ever met has any concept of how you feel, and even when you explain it they still don't get it. In fact, they think you're crazy. And worse, heartless. Am I right?"

"Did you know your nose would choke a horse?"

"I'll be perfectly honest with you. I find it hard to understand how you can be indifferent toward other people. It seems unnatural to me. But I'm beginning to see how *you* can feel that way, thanks to prot. Can we work together? Maybe we can learn something from each other."

She threw back her head and brayed like a donkey.

I was extremely pleased to see how confident Rob had become. He was at ease with Giselle, the patients, the staff. Indeed, when he came into my examining room he grabbed my hand and shook it.

At the same time, I wondered whether he had made such good progress that he might suddenly find himself facing the TV cameras during prot's talk-show appearance. I didn't want to think about the consequences that might result from such a situation.

Thus, I spent a good part of the morning trying to reverse what I had worked so hard to accomplish over the past few weeks and years, i.e., explain to Robert why he should stay in the background while prot was doing the television interview. He reminded me that he was quite content to remain in the hospital, his safe haven, and leave

438

the rest of the world to prot, at least for the time being.

The other problem was getting prot, who was showing up less and less often, to come out and do the show. But he had said he would do the "gig" (as he called it), and with prot, a promise is a promise.

"You want to see some more tapes, Rob? Or are you bored with them?"

"Not exactly, but—"

"I've asked Giselle if she would like to see them, too. Would you be interested in having some company while you watch?"

His smile was faintly reminiscent of prot's, though the latter wouldn't have had the slightest interest in the films. "I'm willing if she is," he replied.

I called her out of my office, where she had been waiting. (I should mention here that Giselle and I had discussed the desirability of using condoms, should the need arise. In response she had pulled a couple from her pocket and waved them at me.) Now, I was surprised to find, she was actually blushing. Rob took her hand and led her to the sofa I had brought in.

I went back to my office and locked the door with a loud click, leaving them to their own devices, nature to take its course.

PROT seemed rather pensive during the limo ride to the television studio. He didn't even remark on all the noise and trash along the way or the state-of-the-art gizmos he found in the back of the car—the bar, the quad stereo system, the refrigerator stocked with food. Perhaps he was thinking about what he might say to the cameras. Or maybe he was uncomfortable with the new suit we had bought for him. Giselle and the security guards were quiet, too, all three of them staring blankly out the one-way windows at the passersby trying to peer in.

"Prot?"

"Hmmmmm?"

"I just wanted you to know that I had nothing to do with this."

"Sure, coach. I understand perfectly."

"But now that you're going through with it, I'd like to give you some advice."

"Give away."

"If I were you I wouldn't tell the audience they're a bunch of fools and a cancer on the Earth."

"Yes—you humans do have a difficult time with the truth."

"You could put it that way."

"You worry too much, dr. b."

"The other thing is: Please don't let Robert appear before the cameras. It could be devastating for him."

"I won't encourage him to do that, but he has a mind of his own, you know."

We were taken through a side door into the studio, where we were met by the show's producer. I'd never seen such a huge grin or more perfectly capped teeth. After some small talk, Giselle and I were shown to a little green room furnished with a couple of chairs, a table with a pot of coffee, and a great big monitor, where we were left with a very young production assistant. Prot was led away to makeup. "Good luck!" I bellowed after him. I was as nervous as the Ward Two patient we call "Don Knotts."

While we waited I asked Giselle about Rob's reaction to the sex tapes. Her smile was about as wide as that of the producer's. "We didn't watch any tapes."

"You're sure it wasn't Paul you were dealing with?"

"Positive. I could tell by his voice, for one thing. Not at all like the Paul on the tape you let me hear. It was Rob, all right. He was like a kid in a candy store."

Prot was brought on last, after the movie starlet, who appeared to have an IQ of about ten, and the male model/stripper. He was warmly welcomed when he finally came out to face the audience and the cameras, and the show's hostess, a possible manic, if not amphetamine-dependent, seemed genuinely taken with him, as are most of us who know him.

She began innocuously enough, if perhaps a bit tongue-in-cheek, by asking him about life on K-PAX, why he had come to Earth, what space travel was like, and so on. (At one point the director flashed on the screen a computer-ized juxtaposition of one of prot's star charts, which he had drawn for me much earlier when I was trying to determine the extent of his astronomical knowledge, with a picture of the real thing.) Most of it I had heard before. But she also asked him one or two things I should have thought of and hadn't. For example, how does one stop after travel-ing through interplanetary space at superlight speed? (As near as I could figure out, it's sort of programmed in.) Prot answered all the questions politely, if matter-of-factly, from behind his dark glasses. I waited for the interviewer to get to something more controversial and try to put him on the spot. At that point the band struck up a jazzy rendition of "Two Different Worlds" and there was a pause for some commercials.

I asked the production assistant whether the hoobah was decaffeinated. She gave me a strange look.

When the program returned, the hostess, winking at the camera, asked prot whether he would mind giving us a little demonstration of light-travel.

"Why not?" he replied. Giselle and I and the assistant leaned forward in our chairs as, I assume, did most of the audience. Someone brought out a flashlight and mirror. Prot grinned. Apparently he had been expecting something like this.

In any case, he placed the light on his right shoulder and pointed it toward the mirror, which he held in his outstretched left hand. The room we were in was so quiet I could hear everyone breathing. Suddenly there was a very brief flash of light and prot disappeared from the screen! The audience gasped. The camera jostled around until it found prot on the other side of the stage standing behind the microphone reserved for singers and stand-up comics. He was wearing a funny little hat. I recognized it at once: It was Milton's. He tweaked an imaginary mustache and chirped, "Bear walks into a bar, see? Takes out a pistol and plugs everyone in the place. The cops come and take him away. 'What's wrong?' the bear protests. 'Humans ain't on the endangered species list!' "

No one laughed.

"Am I going too slow for you guys? All right—how about this one: Who are the first to line up for wars, to pull the executioner's switch, to murder all their fellow beings because they taste good? Give up? The prolifers!"

No one laughed.

"You're not trying, folks—who is your leader? One more time: Two Christians get married. What religion will their children adopt? I'll give you a hint. It works for Muslims and Jews and Hindus alike.. . .Nothing? Okay. See, it has to do with where people get their so-called ideas. . . ."

The audience, shaken by what they had seen, still didn't laugh. The hostess, her tongue no longer in her cheek, asked prot to return to his seat. "How—how did you do that?" she demanded.

"I learned the routine from one of my fellow inmates."

"No—I mean how did you get to the other side of the room?"

"I told you earlier—remember?"

She requested an instant replay of what she called prot's "light-and-mirrors trick" in super slow motion. But no matter how slow the motion, prot always disappeared from the screen. In our little room Giselle laughed and clapped her hands. The production assistant gaped at the monitor and said nothing. The band started up, the 800 number flashed onto the screen, and there was another pause for commercial messages.

When the show began again, the hostess, much more serious now, brought out a prepared list of questions for prot. What follows is a verbatim transcription:

> **HOSTESS:** You have written [she was referring to prot's "report"] that there are certain things we humans must give up in order to survive as a species. One of these is religion. Can you elaborate on that?
>
> **PROT:** Certainly. Have you ever noticed that a great many of your present difficulties are based on the intolerance of one set of believers for the beliefs of others?
>
> **H:** Too many, probably, and we all see your point. What I'd like you to tell us is how we give up something that's such an intrinsic part of our human nature?
>
> **P:** That's entirely up to you. The evidence I've seen so far suggests you don't have the guts.

H: What do you mean by "guts"?

P: Religion is based primarily on fear. It started that way and it continues to this day.

H: Fear of what?

P: You name it.

H: You mean death.

P: That's one thing.

H: What about money?

P: What about it?

H: How can we give up money? What would we use instead?

P: For what?

H: To buy a washing machine, for example.

P: Why do you need washing machines?

H: Because they save time and energy.

P: In other words, you've flooded your planet with washing machines and cars and plastic soda bottles and tv sets so you'll have more time and energy?

H: Yes.

P: And in order to keep the economy going you need more and more human beings in order to buy more and more of your products. Am I right so far?

H: Well, growth is good for everyone.

P: Not for the several million other species on your PLANET. And what happens when your WORLD is full of people and cars and washing machines and there isn't room for any more?

[The music started up.]

Giselle and I looked at each other and shrugged. I went

to the little adjoining rest room. In a moment or two I heard her yell: "Dr. B! He's back!" I hurried in to find the program's hostess holding up a small dog. It was yapping frantically.

"What's he saying?" she demanded of prot.

"He wants to take a [bleep]," prot responded. The audience, now on more familiar ground, roared. They howled even more when the dog defecated, as if on cue, on top of the big desk. The merriment went on for several minutes as the hostess mugged for the cameras, got rid of the dog, and someone came out to clean up the mess. They were still laughing when it was time for the next series of commercials.

The show returned to a smattering of titters, but this ended abruptly when the dialogue resumed.

> *H:* You seem to find a lot wrong with us humans. But you have to admit we have our good points, too. If you were to use one word to charac- terize our species, what would it be?

> [Prot's eyes rolled up for a moment—he was thinking. Like everyone else who was watch- ing, probably, a number of things came to *my* mind: "generosity," "perseverance," "a sense of humor. . . ."]

> *P:* I haven't decided whether it's ignorance or just plain stupidity.
> *H:* And that's why you think that mankind won't make what you call the necessary decisions to survive as a species.
> *P:* Or womankind either.

H: Yet there are many who think we can over-come these difficulties and win this war. Why do you think that's not possible?

P: It's not impossible. Beings on other WORLDS have done it. But it's pretty much too late for that here. You've already begun to destroy your home. That's the beginning of the end.

H: So what's going to happen to us, in your view?

P: You don't want to hear it.

H: I'd really like to know. How about it, audi-ence?

[A smattering of applause.]

P: It's your funeral. All right—it will be a grad-ual decline at first, like cancer or aids. You won't notice much except for the disappear-ance of a few more nonhuman beings and the usual little wars everywhere. Fuel and mineral resources will begin to run out. Emergency meetings of nations will be held, but self-interests will prevail, as they always have, and the more desperate or greedy among you will make demands and ultimatums. These will not be met, and larger wars will break out. In the meantime your entire environmental support system will begin to collapse. There will be enormous suffering among all the inhabitants of the EARTH, even those who still possess relative wealth and power. After that, it's only a question of time. Death could come in any number of ways, but it is as certain as taxes.

[The hostess stared at him and said nothing for a moment.]

P: I told you you wouldn't want to hear it.
H: Life will just end on Earth?
P: There will still be life, but human beings will never return to this PLANET. Similar species might evolve, but the likelihood that one of them will be homo sapiens is very small. You are a rare breed in the UNIVERSE, you know. A freak of nature, so to speak.
H: And there's no way to stop this?
P: Sure. All you have to do is start over with a different set of assumptions.
H: You mean the business of eliminating money, families, religion, countries—things like that?
P: It's not really so difficult. You just have to decide whether these things are more important to you than your survival. For example— you gave up smoking, right?

[Yet another soft musical hint: "Two different worlds. . . ."]

H: Uh—yes, I did. But—
P: Was it easy?
H: It was hell.
P: But now you never miss it, do you?

[The music came up, more persistently than before.]

P: Look—why not try living without wars, religions, specieside, and all the rest for a decade or two? If you don't like it you can always go back to the hatred and killing and endless growth. . . .

H: Back after these messages.

[When the show returned, the starlet decided to get into the act. The facade of dumbness had fallen off.]

S: You forgot to factor the human spirit into your equations.

P: That's a meaningless term concocted, no doubt, by some homo sapiens or other.

S: What about Shakespeare? Mozart? Picasso? The human race has accomplished some great things, even by your standards. In fact, we humans have made this a pretty wonderful world!

[A smattering of applause.]

P: [gazing at the camera with his familiar look of exasperation mixed with mild contempt]: What kind of world is it where violence and war are not only accepted, but your youth are encouraged to practice them? Where your leaders must be constantly guarded against assassination, and airline travelers frisked for weapons? Where every vial of aspirin must be protected against poisoning? Where some of your beings make fortunes to play games while others are starving?

Where no one believes a single word your governments or your corporations say? Where your stockbrokers and film stars are more valued than your teachers? Where the numbers of human beings increase and increase while other species are driven to extinction? Where—

["Two different worlds. . . ."]

H: Don't go 'way. We'll be right back!

No one in the little room said anything. We all watched the commercials, thought our divergent thoughts. In a little while our hostess returned with: "We've been talking with prot, a visitor from the planet K-PAX, where things are a lot simpler than they are here on Earth. Prot, our time is up. Will you come back and visit us again?"

"Why—weren't you listening?" He was still wearing the funny hat and the suit and I didn't know which looked sillier on him.

"Good night, folks, good night! Good night!"

There was no applause. The audience, apparently, was still confused by what they had seen and heard. Or perhaps they merely figured his were the words of a crazy man.* Just before the show went off the air there was another extreme slow-motion shot of prot disappearing abruptly from view, and the 800 number flashed one final time on the screen.

When they brought him back to our little room he was grinning broadly. I stuck out my hand, as proud of him

---

*Some of prot's other comments, which space did not permit including here, are listed in "The Wisdom (or Craziness) of prot," at the end of this book.

as if he were my own son. Not for what he had said, but because he had kept his word and done the show without allowing Robert to make an appearance.

"See you later, doc," he said. He turned to Giselle and whispered, "Bye, kid." She hugged him. When he stepped back it was Rob, still wearing prot's sunglasses and Milton's hat, who faced us.

I was puzzled. I hadn't expected this. Had prot decided to throw Rob into the water, to force him to sink or swim? I quickly explained the situation to him—where he was, what had happened. He looked at me with a hint of amusement, just as prot might have done. When we left the little waiting room he was happy and relaxed, which was more than could be said for me.

On the way back to the hospital he played with the gizmos, waved at the staring passersby, seemed to soak up the excitement of the city, which he had never seen. "From now on, the whole world is your safe haven," I told him, though it was obviously unnecessary. By the time we got "home" he was sound asleep, his head resting on Giselle's shoulder.

THE morning after the televised interview a pair of CIA agents were in my (Villers's) office waiting for me. They demanded to speak with prot.

"I don't know where he is," I responded truthfully.

"You mean he's gone?"

"Looks that way."

They seemed dubious, but one of them suddenly came up with a notebook and scribbled something into it. He ripped out a page and handed it to me. It was a beeper number. "If he shows up again, let us know right away." I almost expected them to insist that I eat the message, but they whirled around simultaneously and rushed out the door, as if all hell were breaking loose somewhere.

After they had gone I went to look for Rob. I found him in his room with Giselle. Both were reading or, perhaps, studying. They looked exactly like a couple of college students preparing for exams in a coed dorm.

I took a look at the stack of dusty books resting on Rob's little table like old treasure chests about to be opened: *Birds of the Northeast, Moby Dick,* and several others. In his hands rested a recent tome by Oliver Sacks. As normal as apple pie, I thought, with no little satisfaction.

Giselle was taking notes from a book called *Unexplained Mysteries.* On the floor next to her chair was a typed manuscript, the first draft of her article about UFO's.

"How are you feeling, Rob?"

"Never felt better, doc," he assured me.

"I just stopped in to give you this," I said, handing him the tape Karen had made of the talk show. "And to ask you whether you would be willing to submit to a few simple tests during your regular session tomorrow."

"Anything you say," he replied, without even asking what kind of tests they were.

I hurried out, late for a meeting, which dragged on and on. Though it was supposed to be a discussion about plans for the new wing, no one wanted to talk about anything other than prot's TV appearance the previous evening. Having been through all of it before, I finally excused myself and returned to my office, where I called Robert's mother. Confident that Rob would be around for a while, I told her of my guarded optimism about his prognosis and invited her to visit him and see for herself. She was somewhat hesitant about traveling alone, but said she would come if "that nice young girl" (Giselle, whom she

451

had met on her previous visit to the hospital) would go with her.

I told her I didn't think that would be a problem.

With that pleasant chore taken care of, I took a call from Betty. "Dr. Villers phoned yesterday while you were gone. He wanted to speak with prot. He said it was urgent. He called again later, but I couldn't find prot—only Robert. I suggested he talk to Cassandra. He said it was too late for that."

"It may be too late for prot, too."

"That's too bad. He sounded desperate."

ALL the rest of that week we were inundated with calls to the 800 number. A few of the callers pledged money to the hospital. Some had a relative or friend they wanted admitted. Several producers from other talk shows wanted prot to come on their programs "and do that trick." Most of those who telephoned, however, did not apply for admission of a loved one or contribute funds toward the new wing or make prot a job offer. Instead, they wanted to know where to call or write to him, when they would see him again, how to get to K-PAX.

A few reporters called as well, asking for prot's life story and all the rest. Unable to convince them that prot *had* no "life story," and perhaps no longer existed, I finally referred them to Giselle.

Then the letters started to pour in, thousands of them, most addressed to "prot, c/o Manhattan Psychiatric Institute, New York, NY." I didn't open any of these, but I did take a look at some of the ones addressed to "prot's keepers," or the like. Some of these called him "the devil" (as Russell had at one time), and some even threatened him with bodily harm. Others thought he was a kind of Christ-like figure, "a messiah for our time," who had come to "save us from ourselves." Oddly, not one person saw him for what he really was—part of a mentally ill person who seemed to be on the road to recovery.

But prot made no appearance that week (much to Villers's great dismay). I felt somehow betrayed. If he had, in fact, "departed" this world for good, he had done so without giving us any notice, something he had assured me he would not do. Still, I couldn't help think of the last time he had "returned" to K-PAX, and the Robert he had left behind. Rob was a very different person this time, smiling and confident. Maybe that was all anyone could expect.

ONE of the things I would never forget about prot was his ability to communicate with the autistic patients. Perhaps that explains the dream I had the night after the talk show.

I was in what appeared to be a space capsule. I could see out some tiny windows into a shimmering blue sky. The cabin was further lit by some sort of instrument panel. It was dazzling. There were dozens of dials and computer screens, all aglow with green and amber lights.

Suddenly there was a tremendous noise and everything began to vibrate. I felt the force of gravity pulling me down and down and then, after a few minutes, the noise and vibration ceased and I was floating free, miles above the Earth, looking down at the most beautiful planet in the universe.

I was jolted by something, thrown far off course, blinded by a shadow blocking my view. The next thing I knew I was back on the launch pad, and the darkness was gone from the window. A giant head appeared. It was Jerry. He had given me a ride in his perfect model. A huge eye peered in at me, and his mouth opened in a toothy grin. It was wonderful—for a moment I understood him, understood everything!

But then I woke up and, as always, I understood nothing.

Session Thirty-one

THE visit from the nation's most popular psychologist was scheduled for Friday. His books, *Folk Psychiatry* and *Clean Up Your Mess*, have been on the best-seller lists for years. I was on the lawn waiting for Cassandra to notice me when word came that, unfortunately, some "urgent business" had come up and our guest was forced to cancel at the last minute.

For some reason this annoyed me a great deal. I blurted out to the nurse, "What an ass—well, the medical term is 'anal orifice.' "

On the positive side, this gave me some unexpected free time to catch up on a lot of paperwork. But as soon as I sat down there was a call from a Dr. Sternik, the ophthalmologist Giselle had mentioned earlier, who badly wanted to examine prot's eyes.

"Sure," I said, "go ahead. If you can find him."

★　★　★

The first thing I asked Rob after he sat down was what he thought of the tape of the television show starring his alter ego, prot.

He took a peach from the fruit bowl. "Weird. Very weird."

"How so?"

"It was like watching myself, only it wasn't me at all."

"As I've told you before, prot is a part of you."

"I understand that, but it's still hard to believe it."

"Have you seen him in the last couple of days?"

"Not since we left the TV studio."

"Do you know where he is?"

"Nope. Does that mean I'm ready to go home?"

"We'll see."

Someone tapped lightly on the door. "Come in, Betty! All right, Rob, I'm going to ask Betty to give you a few simple tests. For your information, these are the same ones we gave prot five years ago. I want to compare the results, see if there are any differences, okay?"

"Sure."

"Good. And after you're through here, Betty will take you to the clinic so you can give us a blood sample. That will only take a minute. And Dr. Chakraborty wants to get an EEG, which is a simple, painless recording of your brain waves."

"Fine."

Both were smiling broadly when I left them alone. Betty loves to administer tests of any kind; Rob was happy just to be in control of himself. She and Rob would miss Russell's funeral, but Betty said she didn't like funerals— she would rather remember the decedent as he was—and Rob barely knew him, if at all.

It was raining and the service was held in the lounge.

A bunch of folding chairs had been brought in and everyone was facing the open casket, which was lying on the magazine table. It was a simple pine box, which is not only the usual choice for indigent patients, but had long been Russ's own wish as well, after we declined to find him a cave with a big rock for a door.

Chaplain Green made a beautiful speech about Russell and his eternal life in heaven, filled with golden streets and singing angels, and yes, hamburgers on Saturday nights. It almost made me wish I were joining him. Then it was the turn of those who knew him best.

Some of the long-term staff stood up to say how much they would miss him, and a few of the patients paid their final respects. Even former residents Chuck and Mrs. Archer had come to add a story or two, as did Howie and Ernie, who had spent years in this institution and knew him well. For my part, what I remembered best about Russ was his in-your-face style of preaching, spouting prodigious amounts of spittle along with the Scriptures. I reminded the gathering about his early days at MPI, the days of fire and brimstone. He was something to see then, with his sandy hair blowing in the wind and his gray eyes all ablaze, and you could always depend on Russell to be around to give us God's opinion of the tiniest event. In later years he had mellowed somewhat, but he never rested in his quest for lost souls. And now, for the first time in his life, he was at peace. I stopped there, stunned for a moment by a sudden understanding of the attractiveness of suicide for some people. I only hoped that none of the patients followed the same line of thought.

After the service I mingled for a while with some of our former patients, all of whom were doing well. We discussed, with considerable nostalgia, their days at the hospital (it's strange how even a stay in a mental institution can seem like a happy time in retrospect). Chuck, especially, seemed a changed man, chatting away without the slightest comment on the odor of anyone present. But it wasn't until everyone was leaving that he said, "It was good to see prot again." Confused by his crossed eyes, perhaps, I thought for a moment he meant to say "Russell," but Mrs. A and Ernie and Maria all nodded enthusiastically.

"Hasn't changed a bit," Ernie declared.

"Was prot here?" I asked as calmly as possible.

"Didn't you see him? He was standing at the back of the crowd."

I said my goodbyes and returned to my examining room. Rob and Betty were still there, busily engaged in the testing process. Thinking that maybe our former patients had generated visions of prot from the rich loam of their imaginations, I went back to my office, where I placed a call to Virginia Goldfarb.

"No," she said, "I didn't see him. Why? Was he supposed to be there?" Same for Beamish and Menninger.

I ran to the lawn and checked with several of the other patients still milling about the gravesite. All of them had seen prot.

I wanted to get away from my desk, from the hospital, from everything. But I didn't know where to go. I wandered around for a while, ending up in Villers's office, where I occupied myself with correspondence and budget matters until I got a call from our new administrator, Joe Goodrich, a nice young man and quite competent, despite his limited experience. I could tell he had something he wanted to say to me, but was having a hard time doing it. Finally he blurted, "I just got a call from the *New York Times*. Klaus Villers killed his wife and then himself.

Apparently it happened last night. They want you to fax them his obituary. In fact, Dr. Villers left a note requesting that you take care of it."

I mumbled something and hung up. Though I hardly knew Klaus and Emma, I was profoundly saddened by this tragic news, and I wasn't sure why. Perhaps because it came so close after Russell's death and prot's apparent departure. Too much, too soon. I felt as if I were a spider at the bottom of a sink—no matter how much I struggled, I couldn't get out. And prot wasn't there to help me.

ON Saturday I drove in and forced myself to spend the day processing those parts of Rob's tests that Betty hadn't finished. Chak had also stayed late on Friday to get the blood samples off to the lab for DNA analysis and typing, though we wouldn't get the results for several weeks. I listened to a tape of *La Bohème* while I worked up the data. But I didn't sing along or even hear much of it.

At first I didn't believe the results, but I soon remembered that nothing about the case of Robert/prot could ever be routine. Here are the comparisons of some of Rob's tests with those of prot, examined five years earlier:

TEST	ROB	PROT
IQ	130	154
Short-term memory	good	excellent
Reading skill	average	very good
Artistic ability	above average	variable
Musical ability	fair	below average

General knowledge	limited	broad and impressive
Hearing, taste, smell, tactil eacuities	normal	highly sensitive
"Special" senses	none	questionable
EEG	normal (though somewhat different from prot's)	normal
Vision		
1. Light sensitivity	normal	marked
2. Range	normal	can detect light well into UV range
Aptitude	some affinity for natural sciences	could do almost anything

In addition to the above, there were also slight differences in skin tone (fairness) and voice timbre. Robert and prot were two completely different people occupying the same body like a pair of Siamese twins.

As I looked over the data something kept flitting around my mind like a trapped butterfly trying to escape. Was it guilt about Klaus's death? Finally, out flew an old adage with dull brown wings: Be suspicious of the patient who discharges himself, as Robert had begun hinting we should consider for him.

★   ★   ★

Will came into my office just as I was packing up to leave for what was left of the weekend. He wanted to talk about Dustin's parents. I reminded him to finish his studies before he began his practice. But suddenly I felt a compelling need to confess my feelings of guilt about Klaus and Emma Villers. If I had tried to cultivate a friendship with him, I told Will, get to know him as well as some of his patients seemed to, maybe I could have done something. He listened intently to the whole thing, and when I was finished he said, "Sometimes you can't do anything about a problem no matter how hard you try."

"Son, I think you've got the makings of a fine shrink."

"Thanks, Pop. Now, what about Dustin's parents?"

I sighed, "Don't worry—I'll take care of it."

"I wonder if parents aren't the cause of half the mental problems in the world," he mused.

"Damn near," I sighed. "Prot would probably say we ought to do away with parenthood altogether."

Session Thirty-two

T HE Monday-morning staff meeting began with a moment of silence for our departed colleague. After that I discussed my misgivings about Rob. By now everyone was aware that he was making excellent progress, and that there had been no appearances by prot (except, perhaps, to the patients at Russell's funeral) for several days. Someone asked whether Robert, who showed no signs of psychosis whatever, wouldn't do just as well in Ward One. I demurred: "Let's wait to hear from Virginia and Carl" (Gold-farb and Thorstein were absent for Rosh Hoshanah).

Perhaps I was being overly cautious. I suppose everyone becomes more conservative as he gets older. I had, after all, been wary about Michael, who was doing very well as an EMS trainee, despite the fact that he had attempted suicide as recently as a few months earlier. And, thanks mainly to prot, Rudolph was also gone, Manuel was on the verge of departure, Lou had gotten through a very difficult delivery, and now Bert was making excellent progress as well. Maybe he had worked similar wonders with Rob.

After the brief meeting I went to see Bert, who unburdened himself of the whole story. After his girlfriend's death, their unborn child kept growing and growing in his head like a kind of mental fetus. The headaches were excruciating. He kept everything bottled up inside for years, until he was well past forty, when his mother's serendipitous discovery eventually triggered the cascade of events that sent him to us.

This is not unusual. Many nervous or other mental breakdowns result from a sudden eruption, like a geyser, of feelings long repressed. Most of us have something locked up inside, trying to break out. One of my former teachers once remarked that if science could find some way for the brain to let off this steam, a little at a time, there would be far less mental trauma in the world, and certainly in the hospitals. Unfortunately, so little attention is paid to mental health, even as part of a regular medical checkup, that such a goal has yet to be attained.

Bert told me how he had bought dolls and clothes and spent nearly every night of his adult life bathing his "daughter" (he had arbitrarily chosen the sex of the baby), and putting her to bed, taking care of her when she was "sick," and all the rest. When he was finished, and the tears were over, I asked him again about adopting Jackie. By this time, the other patients had stopped whatever they were doing and drifted over to listen, and we all waited for the answer.

"It would be the happiest day of my life," Bert blubbered, and I had no trouble believing him.

At that moment I heard something I had never heard in over thirty years of practice. The small group of patients that had gathered nearby broke into spontaneous applause. For a second I thought they were thanking me. But of course it was Bert (and prot) they were lauding, and I happily joined them.

INFLATED with borrowed success, I headed for 3B. On the way there I thought hard about what prot had said and done to get Jerry to respond to him. It seemed simple enough—he just held his hand and gently stroked it, almost as if it were a bird or some small animal he was trying to calm.

I closed the door and eased over to where Jerry was finishing his replica of the space shuttle, complete with launch pad. Not wishing to disturb him, I crept closer.

I watched for a while, marveling at the detail, the obvious understanding of structure and function, a Michelangelo of the matchstick. At the same time, I remembered prot's comment to me about the model: "The space shuttle program is like Columbus sailing up and down the coast of Portugal."

I said, "Hello, Jerry."

"Hello, Jerry."

"Jerry, would you come with me for a moment, please?"

He froze, a sculpture in flesh and bone. Even his cowlicks seemed to become more rigid. I couldn't see his eyes, but I imagined their suspicion and fear.

"I'm not going to hurt you. I just want to talk to you for a minute."

I tugged him patiently to a chair. After a little encouragement he sat down, though now he could barely keep still. I pulled up another. Taking his hand in mine I began stroking it and speaking to him gently, as prot had done, or seemed to. I'm not sure precisely what I expected. I *hoped* he would leap up and shout, "Hiya, doc, how's it going?" or some such thing. But he never looked in my direction, never made a sound, but continued to fidget and fitfully scan the walls and ceiling.

I wouldn't give up. Like a paramedic who works over a dying patient for an hour or more, I continued to stroke Jerry's hand and arm and speak softly to him. I varied the pressure, the cadence, switched from one hand to the other—nothing worked. After that hour I was exhausted, sweating as though we had been arm wrestling the whole time. "Okay, Jerry, you can go back to work."

Without so much as a glance he jumped up and returned to his model. I could hear him muttering, "Back to work, back to work, back to work. . . ."

I decided, before lunch, to find and inform all of Klaus's patients of his death and to tell them who their new therapist would be. There was no need. All of them had heard about the tragedy and knew about the changes. What surprised me was the depth of feeling they expressed for their former counselor. In fact, they loved my longtime colleague, obviously much more than had I or the rest of the staff.

But, of course, I never had a session with Klaus. The bonds between a patient and his psychiatrist are strong, often resembling, as I have said, that of a parent and child. In Villers's case it appeared to be even stronger than that. From what I gathered he spent as much time telling them about his problems as vice versa. In so doing, he broke the first rule of psychiatry. But what he lost in effectiveness, if anything, he made up for in the affection his patients held for him, and their willingness to try to please him. I wished

465

I had made a greater effort to get to know him better myself.

As long as I was in Ward Two I decided to have lunch there. The patients, even those who had little contact with Villers, seemed strangely quiet during the meal. I noticed that they kept staring at Rob, who looked like prot but wasn't exactly him. They still came to him for help on occasion and he was perfectly willing to give it. Whether he was as effective as prot in some of his advice remained to be determined.

All of this might have been moot, however. I had nearly decided to transfer him to Ward One to see how he would deal with the change. But, assuming he did well, what would the other patients think about both of them leaving the hospital for good? One of the favorite terms now being bandied about the hospital was "anal orifice." Would they think I was a first-class orifice for letting Robert/prot go?

While I was in Two, my temporary administrative secretary had taken a message, which she later passed on to me, from Klaus's lawyer. There was to be no formal burial service for him and his wife, only a simple cremation. They had requested that I scatter the ashes around Emma's flower garden. I was touched by this entreaty and, of course, agreed to it.

IT was with a certain amount of wistfulness that I welcomed Rob to his last regularly scheduled session with me. I knew I would miss him, and I most certainly would miss prot, with whom I had spent even more time, and from whom I had learned a great deal. But of course I was nonetheless happy with the way things had turned out.

"Well, Rob, how are you feeling today?" I began.

"Fine, Doctor B. How about yourself?"

466

"A little dragged out, I'm afraid."

"You've been working too hard lately. You should slow down."

"Easy for you to say."

"I suppose so." He looked around. "Got any fruit? I seem to have developed a taste for it."

"Sorry. I forgot."

"That's okay. Maybe next time."

"Rob, at this moment you seem perfectly okay to me. Do you think you are well?"

"I've been asking myself the same question. I'm a lot better, that's for sure."

"Hear anything from prot?"

"No. I really think he's gone."

"Does that bother you?"

"Not really. I don't think we need him anymore."

"Rob?"

"Yes?"

"I'd like to hypnotize you one last time. Do you mind?"

He seemed studiously unperturbed. "I suppose not. But why?"

"I'd just like to see whether I can call up prot. It won't take long."

"Okay. Sure. Let's get it over with."

"Fine. Just focus your attention on the little dot. . . ."

He did so without the usual struggle. When he was in a deep trance I said, abruptly, "Hello, prot. I haven't seen you in a while."

There was no response except, perhaps, for a barely perceptible grin. I tried again. And again. I knew he had to be in there somewhere. But, if so, he wasn't about to come out.

After I had awakened Rob I said, "I think you're right. For all practical purposes, he's gone."

"I think so, too."

I studied him carefully. "How do you feel about my transferring you to Ward One?"

"I'd like that very much."

"I might be able to get the assignment committee's approval by tomorrow morning. Are you sure you can handle it?"

"The sooner the better."

"I'm glad you feel that way. Tell me—what do you plan to do with your life once you escape our clutches?"

He pondered the question, but not like prot would have contemplated it, his eyes focused on the ceiling or rolled up into his head. Rob simply frowned. "Well, I thought I would start by taking a trip to Guelph. See some old friends, visit Sally's and Becky's graves, the school I went to, the house I lived in. After that, I'd like to try to get into a college. It's probably too late for this year. Maybe next. Giselle is all in favor of that."

"Do you want to talk a little about your relationship with Giselle?"

"I like Giselle very much. She's not as pretty as Sally was, but she's smarter, I think. She's the most interesting person I've ever met, except for prot. That's one of the reasons I want to go back home. To say goodbye to Sally and kind of get her permission to be with Giselle. I think she would have understood."

"I'm sure she would have. Bear in mind, though, that it might be a while before you can make the trip. I may want to keep you in Ward One for a few weeks. Just to make sure there aren't any problems we've missed."

"If I'm good, do I get time off for good behavior?"

"Maybe."

"Then I'll be very good."

"You really want to get out of here, don't you?"

"Wouldn't you?"

"Yes, of course. I just wanted to hear you say it."

"I've been here more than five years. That's enough, don't you think?"

"Plenty." I glanced at my pad. "Rob, there's one more thing that has bothered me all this time, but I didn't want to ask you until you were well enough."

"What is it?"

"Prot claimed he left for a few days in 1990 to visit Iceland, Greenland, Newfoundland, and Labrador. You remember that from the tapes?"

"Yes."

"Did you go with him?"

"No, I didn't."

"Nobody saw you during that time. Where were you?"

"I hid in the storage tunnel."

"Why?"

"I wasn't ready to face anyone alone."

"Prot told you to go there?"

"No, he just gave me the key. He said, 'The rest is up to you.' "

"All right, Rob. Anything else you want to tell me before you go back to the wards?"

He thought some more. "Just one thing."

"What's that?"

"I want to thank you for all you've done for me."

"Psychiatric treatment is like a marriage, Rob—it takes a tremendous effort from both parties. You should give yourself most of the credit."

"All the same, thank you."

This time I offered him my hand. When he took it he looked me straight in the eye. He seemed as sane as any human being could ever be.The following morning Lou and her daughter were discharged. I've never seen a happier mother or a more beautiful child. When she left she promised to stop by again soon. "But first," she said, "I'm going to have a sex-change operation."

"I think that would be a very good idea."

She waved as she carried Protista out the gate. Although technically she was Beamish's patient, I somehow felt the loss of another daughter separating the ties.

ON Thursday, September 28, three of Klaus's patients and I spread the Villerses' combined ashes around Emma's beautiful flower garden at their Long Island home. At last the tears came, for all of us.

That afternoon, exactly six weeks after prot's "return" from K-PAX, Robert Porter was transferred to Ward One.

Epilogue

ROBERT did fine in One. He got along well with the staff and his fellow patients, expressed normal feelings and desires, was optimistic about his future. In the six weeks he remained there he developed his skills in chess (he even beat Dustin once or twice), studied college catalogs, pursued his interest in biology. His romance with Giselle continued to blossom to the extent that, after three weeks in what he called "Purgatory," I allowed him a weekend furlough in her custody. That worked out quite nicely, and as soon as he was released he moved in with her permanently (along with Oxeye Daisy, their dalmatian).

While Rob was waiting to be discharged, Giselle flew out to Hawaii at her own expense and brought Rob's mother back for a short visit. It was a tearful reunion—his mother hadn't talked with him in more than a decade (she had seen him only in a comatose state). While she was here I spoke with her about Rob's childhood, her husband's fatal accident, etc., as I had five years earlier. Now I learned that Rob's Uncle Dave and Aunt Catherine had died in a fire in 1966, three years after his father's death. Mrs. Porter, of course, had no knowledge of Rob's molestation by them.

She remained in New York only a few days and, buoyed by her happiness at seeing her son nearly ready for discharge, flew back to Honolulu on her own. "It's a shame his father couldn't be here for this," she told me at the airport. "He loved his son very much." I assured her that Robin loved his father, too, though perhaps for more complex reasons than she might have realized.

I think it is safe to say, at last, that all the missing pieces of the puzzle are firmly in place. The root cause of Robert's difficulties lay not, as I had thought, with the terrible tragedy that befell his wife and daughter, but came much earlier, at the hands of a pedophilic uncle. It was this severe trauma that precipitated Rob's abhorrence of sex, and the appearance of an alter (Harry) to help five-year-old Robert deal with the torment.

But why did prot appear on the scene when Robert was six? I believe that Robin felt safe only in the presence of his father, who unwittingly shielded him from the abuse he had experienced at the hands of his Uncle Dave. How devastating it must have been when his "friend and protector" died, leaving him once more at the mercy of that sick creature! Rob called into being a new guardian, one who came from an ideal place where such people as his mother's brother and sister could never exist. Fortunately, Robin wasn't compelled to stay with his aunt and uncle after all, and prot was no longer needed. In fact, it was only after his dog Apple (progenitor of the "aps," the small elephant-like creatures that roam the fields of K-PAX?) was killed that prot made his second appearance on Earth to help Robert, now nine, deal with this new tragedy.

As a result of his traumatic childhood experiences Rob struggled with sex for the rest of his youth and young adulthood, and on into his married life. In sexual matters, prot was virtually useless, and a new identity arose to deal with this problem. Thanks to Paul, Sally was never the wiser, apparently, and they enjoyed a relatively happy life together for several years.

It's not difficult to imagine what Robert must have felt when he came home one fine summer afternoon and found his wife and daughter lying dead on the kitchen floor at the hands of a deranged killer, whose terrible acts brought back his own repressed suffering. Is it any wonder that Harry came to the rescue, that all the pent-up rage he felt for his Uncle Dave exploded like a volcano and he seized the opportunity to prevent this man from performing further atrocities? Or that prot came back to try to help Robert cope with these events, something that perhaps no human being could have done? Indeed, Robert appears to have made an almost miraculous recovery, given the grim circumstances of his tragic background.

Following a trip to Montana (Oxie stayed with us, much to Shasta's delight), Rob enrolled at NYU with a major in field biology. He called me a few weeks later to tell me he was having the time of his life. That's the last I heard of him until the summer of '96, when he and Giselle visited the hospital to renew their acquaintanceship with me and the rest of the staff and patients.

Because so many people had seen prot on television and recognized him wherever Rob went, he had grown a beard. "You'd be surprised," he told me, "how well a beard disguises who you really are." Except for that I found him

473

just as he was when he left, smiling and confident, quite in control. There's a lot of prot in him, I think. But perhaps there's a little of prot in everyone. In any case, he appears to be a fully integrated human being, part of him capable of great things, another part capable of murder.

Giselle's book about prot, *An Alien Among Us?*, came out in December 1996. She reports that it is still selling "spectacularly," and she has been on the talk-show circuit all winter. But the big news, as I write this, is that she is now pregnant, and the baby is due in July. If it is a boy, they tell me they will call him "Gene."

The hospital seems strangely empty without Robert/prot. The patients keep asking when he is coming back, hoping for a ride to the stars. I don't dare tell them that prot gave his life for Robert, and that he is gone for good, because that might make matters worse. And so they wait, and hope, but perhaps this isn't such a bad thing.

Most of our former inmates, however, no longer need prot, and would probably decline a trip to K-PAX even if one was offered. Soon after Bert was discharged he met and married a lovely widow and they legally adopted Jackie, who remained, of course, with us. They visit her regularly, and her new mother is as charming a person as you'd ever want to meet. As a consequence of all this, apparently, Jackie has begun to grow up! It is as if her life was put on hold with the death of her parents, and now that she has a new set, the clock has started ticking again. No one here has ever seen anything quite like it. She even cut off her pigtails!

Lou paid us a visit after her operation. She, too, has found a partner, one who loves her as a woman, and Protista is growing fast. Her first word was (no, not "prot") "cat."

Michael and Manuel and Rudolph are also doing well, all gainfully employed and enjoying their new lives. We hear from them occasionally; they never fail to ask whether prot has returned yet.

Dustin, too, has made spectacular improvement. As a result of my laying down the law to his parents, who now visit him only once a month, he has gradually grown away from coded speeches and game-playing, and has taken an interest in other things. His communications skills have improved accordingly, and I am thinking seriously of moving him to Ward One to see how he gets along there. Incidentally, the purpose of their meeting with me in September was a feeble attempt to learn whether I was on to them, as Will and most of the patients seemed to be.

Others have not done so well. Jerry and his fellow autists remain in their own private worlds, earnestly engineering famous structures and the like. In February, Charlotte, despite being under heavy sedation as an experiment in therapy, nearly castrated and strangled Ron Menninger to death. He is now taking a more cautious approach and there have been no further incidents along that line.

Milton is still trying to cheer us (himself) up with his endless jokes, and Cassandra still sits on the lawn gazing at the stars. She predicted the results of the congressional elections months before voting day, though no one believed her at the time. (I asked her why she hadn't foretold Russell's death and Klaus Villers's suicide. "No one asked me," she replied.) And Frankie, unfortunately, is still Frankie—nasty, foulmouthed, unloved.

The Villerses left their entire estate, valued at several million dollars, to MPI (how they obtained all their wealth remains to be determined). The new wing will be called the Klaus M. and Emma R. Villers Laboratory for Experimental Therapy and Rehabilitation, though the funds won't be released for quite some time, the lawyers tell me. In the meantime, construction costs will be met from other donations and the contributions that came in following prot's television appearance.

Klaus's death left an immense void, of course, which I have tried unsuccessfully to fill. I have had to cut back on the time spent with my patients and take on a lot of onerous duties I could live without. We are currently accepting applications for permanent director, and I, for one, can't wait until the position is filled (Goldfarb and Thorstein are among the candidates).

On a more personal note, my wife will be retiring soon (thanks to the sale of the film rights to *K-PAX*), as will our old friends Bill and Eileen Siegel, who have bought a place in upstate New York and are waiting for Karen and me to join them in an Adirondack retreat of our own. Our son Will graduates from Columbia this spring. He visits the hospital once in a while to keep tabs on the patients and to advise me not to work so hard. I always say, "Tell me that when you're in my shoes!" He is still engaged to Dawn Siegel; they plan to be married "sometime" after they graduate.

Will is as puzzled as I and the rest of the staff by the results of the DNA analyses that came back shortly after Robert was discharged. The laboratory, an extremely reliable one whose clients include some of the country's finest criminologists, reported that Rob's and prot's blood DNA came from two entirely different individuals. Most of us think this must be due to human error, but of course there is no way to prove it.

And then there's the sticky question of how he was able to move, if not at superlight speed, at least fast enough to outrun a TV camera. One physicist estimated that in order to do that he would have to have traveled *at least* twenty-five miles a second, and perhaps much faster.

If that isn't enough, Giselle tells me that prot's trip to the Bronx Zoo provided certain information that no one but zoo officials (and the animals themselves) knew, such things as what their former habitats were like, some foods they missed, and so on. Based on this information, their keepers have tried to replace some of the losses, but I imagine that if prot were still here he would say this misses the point. Happily, the cetologist who visited us has transferred his dolphin, Moby, to a marine biology facility for rehabilitation pending a return to the ocean depths. The young man himself is now selling life insurance.

Regardless of what talents prot may have possessed, however, I still believe that he was nothing more (nor less) than a secondary personality of Robert Porter, and is now an integral part of him. Though many people seem to think he came from K-PAX (including Charlie Flynn, the spider coprophiliac, now mining for gold in the sands of Libya), it seems patently ridiculous to me to imagine that anyone can zip through space on a beam of light without air or heat or protection from various forms of radiation, no matter how fast he travels.

I felt betrayed at first that he "left" us without any warning whatever, especially since he had promised to give me some notice before he departed. But I keep remembering his last words to me in the television studio: "See you later, doc." And that when Robert and Giselle left the hospital to take up their lives elsewhere, Rob gave me a very uncharacteristic wink and Cheshire-cat grin. Moreover, none of the hundred "beings" he planned to take with him has yet disappeared, as far as we know. Is he hiding in Robert's brain somewhere, waiting to come forth again when the time is right?

Or is it possible that he is traveling the Earth at this very moment, searching for unhappy beings to take back to K-PAX with him? For that matter, is there any limit to what is possible? What little we know about life and the universe itself is merely a drop in the ocean of space and time. I still go out at night sometimes and look up at the sky, toward the constellation Lyra. And I still wonder. . . .

The Wisdom (or Craziness) of prot
(from his television appearance of Sept. 20, 1995)

Don't blame the politicians for your problems. They are merely a reflection of yourselves.

Many humans feel sorry for the dolphins who are trapped in tuna nets. Who weeps for the tuna?

Your recorded "history" and your "literature" and "art" are merely those of your own species; they ignore all the other beings who share your planet. For a long time we thought that Homo sapiens was the only species living on EARTH.

Religions are difficult for a K-PAXian to understand. Either all of them are right or none of them is.

Human society will always have a drug problem unless life without drugs becomes a more attractive prospect for those concerned.

Hunting is no sport, it is cold-blooded murder. If you can outwrestle a bear or chase down a rabbit, then you can consider yourself a true sportsman.

Killing someone because he killed someone else is an oxymoron.

The root of all evil isn't the lust for money, but money

itself. Try to think of a problem that doesn't involve money in some way.

Schools are not for teaching anything. They exist solely to pass on society's beliefs and values to its children.

The purpose of governments is to make your WORLD safe for commerce.

Humans love to fool themselves with euphemisms in order to pretend they aren't eating other animals—"beef" for cow, "pork" for pig, etc. This never fails to elicit gales of laughter from our beings.

All wars are holy wars.

Some humans are concerned with the destruction of their environment and the concomitant extinction of other species. If these well-meaning people were more concerned with the individual beings involved, there would be no need to worry about loss of species.

There will come a time when the human beings of EARTH will be devastated by diseases that will make aids look like a runny nose.

This above all: To thine own WORLD be true.

K-PAX III

the worlds of prot

For Karen

It often happens that the universal belief of one age—a belief from which no one was free or could be free without an extraordinary effort of genius or courage—becomes to a subsequent age so palpable an absurdity that the only difficulty is to imagine how such an idea could ever have appeared credible.

—JOHN STUART MILL

Prologue

IN April, 1990, I began the psychoanalysis of a 33-year-old mental patient who called himself "prot" (rhymes with "goat") and claimed to be from the planet "K-PAX."

I met with this young man on a regular basis for several months, during which time I was unable to shake his bizarre story and convince him of his earthly origins (he insisted he came here on a beam of light). The only useful information that emerged from these sessions was that he suffered from a severe sexual dysfunction, hated one or both of his parents, and took a dim view of human society in general.

However, after several weeks of analysis, it became clear that the patient was, in fact, suffering from a rare form of multiple personality disorder in which "prot" was a dominant secondary ego. The primary personality belonged to a man named Robert Porter, who had killed the murderer of his wife and nine-year-old daughter, and whose frustration, guilt, and grief had driven him to withdraw from the real world into an impenetrable shell guarded by his "alien" friend.

But prot, whatever his origin and nature, was a remarkable individual filled with arcane astronomical knowledge, a kind of genius savant. Indeed, he provided astronomers with valuable information on the planet K-PAX and others he claimed to have visited, as well as the double stars between which his world swung in a retrograde motion much like that of a pendulum.

Paradoxically, he seemed to possess a profound understanding of human suffering. Indeed, he was able, during his brief tenure at the Manhattan Psychiatric Institute, to hasten the recovery of a number of his fellow patients, some of whom had been with us for years. He even helped solve certain problems plaguing my own family!

Finally I managed, mainly through hypnosis, to break through Robert's carapace and make direct contact with his primary personality. For the first time, it seemed possible that I might be able to help him learn to deal with the death of his wife and daughter, and bring prot down to Earth.

The treatment, unfortunately, was interrupted by prot's announcement of his intention to return to his home planet on August 17, 1990, at precisely 3:31 a.m., a "journey" I was unable to persuade him to postpone. Faced with an impossible deadline, I tried to achieve an early resolution of Robert's crisis, which succeeded only in driving him deeper inside his protective shell. Moreover, the hospital was thrown into turmoil as many of the patients competed for a chance to go with him. Even some of the staff were lining up for the trip!

Robert declined to join him, however, and, when prot "departed" at the scheduled time, was left behind in a state

488

of intransigent catatonia. One of the other patients, a woman suffering from severe psychotic depression, did "disappear" along with prot, but what became of her and how she managed to leave the hospital is still a matter of conjecture.

The only bright spot in the episode was prot's promise to return to Earth in "approximately five of your years." And, true to his word, he returned precisely on August 17, 1995, to take over Robert's injured psyche once again and protect it from further harm.

This time prot refused to divulge the date of his next and, according to him, final departure and I had no idea how long I would have to work with Robert. But this may have been something of a blessing in disguise: I could only assume there would be enough time to complete the protocol and, hopefully, to help Rob accept, at long last, what had happened to him and his family, and get on with his life.

Ironically, thanks in part to prot's cajoling, Robert now appeared ready and even willing to cooperate in his treatment program. As a result, it soon became evident that he had experienced a number of devastating incidents early in his life, including his sexual abuse at age five by a maternal uncle, and the death of his father when he was six. The loss of his only "friend and protector" (his father) was the last straw. It was then that he brought forth a new guardian (prot), who came from a faraway planet, one that was free from violence, cruelty, and loss, where all the events that had traumatized Robert's young life could never have happened.

Once these knots had been unraveled, and the existence of two additional alter egos revealed, it became possible, at last, for him to deal with his terrible past, including the death of his wife and daughter. Indeed, he made such rapid progress that he was discharged from MPI at the end of September, 1995, and moved in with his friend Giselle Griffin, a reporter who had been instrumental in discovering his true identity five years earlier (and subsequently became a kind of liaison between Robert and the outside world). It appeared that prot and the other two personalities, Harry and Paul, had become fully integrated into the psyche of Robert Porter, who seemed to have resumed a relatively normal life, i.e., there was no sign of a multiple personality disorder or any of the secondary symptoms (headaches, mental lapses, etc.) usually associated with this condition. For all practical purposes, Rob had been released from his psychological prison after more than thirty years of incarceration.

All of these events, including excerpts of my thirty-two sessions with Robert/prot, are described more fully in *K-PAX* and *K-PAX II*, which ended with the birth of his and Giselle's son Gene in the summer of 1997. At that time it appeared the family (including their Dalmatian, Oxeye Daisy) might, at last, live happily ever after.

Unfortunately, this turned out not to be the case.

Session Thirty-three

THE call came on Thursday, November 6, during my regular afternoon "Principles of Psychiatry" lecture at Columbia University, with which the Manhattan Psychiatric Institute is affiliated. Betty McAllister, our head nurse, contacted the chair of the psychiatry department there and insisted he interrupt my lecture to give me the bad news. Giselle had reported to Betty that prot had returned suddenly and without warning as Robert was bathing his son in their Greenwich Village apartment. Though somewhat dismayed, I wasn't entirely surprised by this unwelcome development. For one thing, multiple personality regression is not an uncommon occurrence and, for another, there were certain elements of Rob's rapid recovery in 1995 that had seemed almost too easy from the beginning—his seemingly well-rehearsed responses to certain questions put to him, for example.

It wasn't an emergency, however, and I decided to finish

the lecture before returning to MPI. That was a mistake, and not the first of the long ordeal I was already dreading revisiting. I was so preoccupied with Robert's relapse that I became confused about some trivial point, much to the delight and even snickers of some of the medical students. Annoyed, I announced an immediate pop quiz; the derision turned to groans, and I left them with a question about Hessler's paradox, knowing full well there was no correct answer, requesting that a serious and (I assumed) trustworthy student collect the papers and forward them to me.

Prot and Giselle and their (Robert's) son were already waiting, with Betty, for me in my office when I returned to MPI. We greeted one another warmly. In the seven years I had known them, Giselle had become almost like a daughter to me, and prot, strange as it may seem, something of a trusted friend and advisor. He (like Rob, of course) was graying at the temples and sported a salt-and-pepper beard. I, on the other hand, had shaved mine off since our last meeting, retaining a trim mustache so as not to feel totally exposed.

He had lost none of his confidence and good cheer. Peering at me from behind his familiar dark glasses, he spouted, "Hiya, doc. Still beating your wife?" (This referred to an early session in which we were struggling to find a way to communicate with each other.)

Though I couldn't wait to interrogate prot, to find out where he had been while Robert lived his apparently normal life as a graduate student in biology at New York University, as well as devoted partner and father, I asked Betty to escort him to Ward Two while I spoke with Giselle. The prospect seemed to delight him, and he was off at once for the stairway to his former home, Betty hurrying along behind.

MPI is an experimental hospital which accepts only

492

those cases who have failed to make significant progress elsewhere. The different wards correspond to the floors on which they are located. Ward Two, for example, houses patients with various psychoses and severe neuroses. Those who make significant progress are eventually transferred down to Ward One, where they remain until they are ready to be discharged. The third floor is occupied by various sexual deviates, coprophiles, and others, as well as the autists and catatonics, and Ward Four by a number of psychopaths, those individuals who are a danger to both the staff and their fellow patients. The faculty and staff maintain offices and examining rooms on the fifth floor.

When prot and Betty had gone I closed the door, invited Giselle to sit down, and tweaked my namesake's little nose. He gurgled happily with an expression somewhere between prot's lopsided grin and Robert's shy smile. "Now," I said. "Tell me what happened."

Giselle looked worried, or perhaps merely frustrated, as people often are when they thought they had escaped from some skillet or other, only to find themselves dancing around an enormous frying pan. She gazed at me with her moist, doe-like eyes, which triggered in my mind vivid memories of our first encounter all those years ago when, curled up in that very chair, she had come to request permission to "roam the corridors" of MPI to research an article on mental illness for a national magazine.

"I don't know," she sighed. "One minute he was Robert, and the next he was prot." She snapped her fingers. "Just like that." The baby reached for her hand, apparently trying to understand where the "snap" had come from.

"What were you doing when it happened?"

"I had a headache and was trying to take a nap. When it was time for the baby's bath, I asked Rob if he would do it just this once. Rob is wonderful with Gene, gets up at night, feeds him and plays with him and all the rest, but he hates to bathe or change him. I told him about the headache, though, and he agreed to do it. But when he came back it wasn't Rob. It was prot."

"How could you tell?"

"You already know the answer to that, Doctor B. Prot is different from Rob in a thousand ways."

"What did he say?"

"He said, 'Hiya, Giselle. So you're a mommy now.'"

"And you said—"

"I was too distressed to say much."

"So who gave the little guy his bath?"

"I think Rob probably started it, but never finished."

"And that's when prot appeared."

"I guess so. He never did get the diaper on right."

"I'm not surprised. He doesn't have much experience with babies, human or otherwise. What else can you tell me?"

"Nothing. Absolutely nothing. There he was, just as if he had never left."

"Did you ask him where Robert had gone?"

"Of course!" she wailed. Then, wistfully, "He didn't have a clue."

"He doesn't know where Robert is?"

That's when the tears came. I suppose Giselle hadn't thought about the full implication of this until that moment. It meant that Robert had retreated so deeply that not even his "guardian" (prot) knew where he was hiding. The baby started crying, too. She held him to her breast while I tried to reassure her. "We'll get to the bottom of it," I promised, without a lot of conviction. I thought we had already scraped out that barrel.

She nodded and found a handkerchief. I took little Gene, who smelled wonderfully piney, like his mother. He tweaked my nose. I feigned a roar of pain, which got him crying again, and only made things worse. "C'mon," I said to Giselle, after she had calmed herself and the boy. "Let's show Ward Two your new baby."

WE found prot talking with the patients, some of whom obviously remembered him fondly. Frankie was there, fatter than ever and almost smiling, a rare occurrence for her. And Milton, whose entire family was wiped out in the holocaust, was quietly listening to whatever was being discussed, not joking or clowning around at all. Some of the others had never met prot, except by reputation, but were eagerly telling him their stories in a blatant, if pathetic, attempt to win a free trip to K-PAX, or at least to gain some sympathy for their plights. Half a dozen cats swarmed around him, too, purring and rubbing against his legs.

Of course most of the staff knew Giselle as well, and remembered her with equal affection. They were delighted to meet little Gene, and she seemed to break out of her funk for the moment. The baby, apparently unafraid of all the strange faces peering down at him, grinned up at everyone.

I took this opportunity to wade through the cats and ask prot whether he had any objection to checking back into the hospital "for a little R and R." Though he assured me he wasn't a bit tired, he nonetheless seemed overjoyed by the prospect. I suggested we meet at nine o'clock the next morning. He said he looked forward to another of our "fruitful" sessions together (the hint was not lost on me).

I bid him adieu and sought out Betty McAllister to request that she find a room for him, a private one where

495

Giselle and the boy could comfortably visit. The most I could get from her was a nod indicating she understood my instruction; she was obviously more interested in the goings-on between the patients and the Porter family. By now Milton was standing on a table telling baby jokes, such as: "Woman gets on a bus with the ugliest baby in the world. Kid's so homely that all the other passengers are laughing at it. The woman starts to sob. Man gets on at the next stop, sees the woman crying and says to her, 'It can't be that bad. Have a peanut. And take one for your monkey.'"

With that I left them all and returned to my office to pull out prot/Robert's thick file once more and ponder all the frustrations and possibilities.

THE next morning, while waiting for prot to arrive, I tried to imagine what might have occurred to trigger Robert's abrupt relapse to his sorry condition in 1990, i.e., an essentially catatonic state in which he hid from the world behind an alter ego who claimed to be from a distant planet.

It had happened, apparently, while he was bathing his four-and-a-half-month-old son. Could the baby's naked body have brought back all the suffering and terror imposed upon him by an abusive uncle when he, Robert, was a boy of five, something his own manifestly successful sex life had not precipitated? I cautioned myself not to jump to any such conclusion, though I hoped this was indeed the case. The alternative—that there was something in his early history even more devastating than these traumatic events, and the subsequent death of his beloved father—seemed far worse. Was there something we had not yet uncovered lurking in the depths of his psyche? Was the mind something like an onion, as some have suggested, revealing a new layer whenever one is peeled back, no matter how deeply we go?

The first thing prot did when he was escorted into my examining room was to remove his dark glasses (owing to the sensitivity of his eyes to visible light I kept the lamps dimmed when he was around) and go for the fruits I had provided for him. He was not disappointed. As a sort of "welcome home" gift I had filled the bowl with a cornucopia of all those available in the hospital kitchens, already cut up into bite-size pieces, as well as a napkin and fork, both of which he ignored. It was quite something, believe me, to watch him dig in, caution thrown to the winds, sucking everything up with noisy grunts and smacking sounds. When he was finished, and obviously satisfied, I suggested that it must have been a long time since he had tasted any fruit.

"Not really," he replied, licking the bristly beard surrounding his lips. "But I'll be leaving for home soon, and there won't be many more opportunities like this."

"You mean to K-PAX."

He nodded happily.

I remember feeling my throat tighten as I asked him when that might be.

Without the slightest hesitation he informed me that he would be departing Earth on December the thirty-first. At 11:48 in the morning, Eastern Standard Time, to be precise. "We won't be needing any lunch," he added wryly. Obviously cheerful and relaxed, he sat back in his chair, crossed his ankles, and placed his hands behind his head.

"Why the change of heart?"

"There's one of those peculiarly nonsensical expressions you humans are so fond of. A carryover from your muddled past, I assume." (He meant the history of our species, not my own.)

"Let me rephrase that. The last time you were here you refused to give me a date for your departure. Why is it no longer a secret?"

"My task here is almost finished. Everything is 'go,' and there is nothing you can do to screw things up, even if you wanted to."

This smug comment annoyed me. "What 'task'? Does it involve putting Robert back into a permanent catatonic state?"

"Really, gene, you humans shouldn't take things so seriously. Your lives are too short for that." On K-PAX, of course, there was no such problem: everyone lived to be a thousand.

I stared at him for a moment. "What have you done with Robert?"

"Not a thing. He's taking a break from his miserable life."

"Why? What happened?"

"No idea, coach."

"Then how do you know he's 'taking a break'?"

"He told me before he left."

"What else did he tell you?"

"That's about it."

"And you have no idea where he went?"

"Nope. He didn't say."

"If he shows up again, will you let me know?"

"*Mais oui, mon ami.*"

I was already beginning to get the feeling that I was not in control, that all I could do was make the best of things for the time being. "All right, let's talk about you for a minute."

498

"Fifty-nine, fifty-eight, fifty—"

"Very funny. Now—where have you been keeping yourself the past couple of years?"

"Oh, here and there."

"Prot, let me explain something. To you this whole thing might be a joke. The whole *world* may be a joke. But to Robert it's not funny. I would appreciate it if you would at least be more cooperative in answering my questions. Is that asking too much?"

He shrugged. "If you must know, I've been all around your WORLD (prot capitalized planets, stars, etc.; entities as trivial as people were, to him, lower case). Sort of a farewell tour, you might say."

"What was the purpose of this 'tour'? Were you entertaining the troops?"

"A few of them. But mainly I was speaking with various beings who want to go to K-PAX with me. I've only got room for a hundred of you. Oh—I told you that last time, didn't I?"

"You mean you've been—ah—selecting your 'travel companions'?"

"You could put it that way."

I casually reached for a ballpoint and some paper. "Do you mind telling me the names of some of the people on your list?"

Prot tilted the fruit bowl toward him, but it was as empty as my yellow pad, except for a little juice, which he drank up. "A: Not all of them are people. And B: Yes, I do."

"Why?"

"You know the answer to that one, my human friend."

"You mean you're afraid we'll try to stop you from

taking them with you, or talk them out of the trip—something like that."

"Well, *wouldn't* you?"

"Maybe," I admitted. "But mostly I wanted to contact one or two of them to see whether they could confirm your story. About being 'here and there' in the world, I mean."

"Would I lie to you, mr. district attorney? And anyway, you don't speak giraffe, do you? Or deer? I *know* you don't understand the languages of any of your sea beings—we've already determined that, remember?"

I could feel my frustration rising, along with my gorge, as it always did during our sessions together. "Well, how many of them are people?"

"Oh, a couple of dozen. Yours is the most unhappy species of all."

"Do any of them speak English?" I ventured.

"A few."

"But you won't let me talk to them."

"Feel free. But you'll have to figure out who they are for yourself."

"Any of them live here at the hospital?"

He grinned and said, "One or two, perhaps."

"I'll tell you what: You give me the name of just one of your passengers and I'll have the kitchen send up another bowl of fruit."

Apparently to signify that the subject was closed, he turned to study a watercolor of Vermont in the fall. "I remember that place," he murmured.

I jotted down a note to ask each of my patients whether they had been invited along for the ride to K-PAX, and to advise the rest of the staff to do the same. Not to help them get ready for the journey, but to prepare them for the disappointment of being left behind, jilted brides at an earth-bound altar.

But there was still the matter at hand: where was Robert and why had he retreated so precipitously? Apparently we were to be given less than two months to get to the bottom of it all. I didn't much like the idea of being put under the gun again. "You say you're leaving us at the end of December—any way you can extend that?"

"Sorry."

"But you said last time you were here that there were three windows open for your return to K-PAX. Isn't this the second one?"

"Uh-uh. The second one already slipped by."

"So this is your last chance?"

"Yep."

"And if you didn't—"

"You got it. We'd be stuck here forever."

"How did you miss the second window?"

"Robert changed his mind again. He vacillates a lot."

I interrupted my doodling. "Robert is going with you this time?"

"If he still wants to. You know how it is. He's of three minds on the subject."

"So you've spoken to him since you disappeared two and a half years ago?"

"On occasion."

"Was that his idea or yours?"

"Mine, for the most part."

"Was it your idea to come back to New York this last time?"

"Nope. That was his."

"Why did he call you?"

"I guess he needed me."

"Why?"

"Didn't say." He stretched languorously, like a dog waking from a nap.

"Where were you when the call came, exactly? Can you tell me that?"

"Would you believe I was back in zaire? Of course it's called 'the democratic republic of congo' now." He shook his head. "People!"

"What were you doing in Congo?"

"Didn't we just discuss that? You've really got to do something with that memory of yours, gino!"

"Bear with me, prot. What was Robert doing when you showed up?"

"Giving his kid a bath."

"Did he finish it?"

"Nope. He handed me the washcloth and off he went."

"So you finished the bath?"

"I dried him off and stuck a diaper on him, if that's what you call those things. Then I put him back in his cage."

I stared at my pad, which produced only a date and time. "Prot, can you assure me that you'll stick around here until the thirty-first of December at—ah—11:48 a.m.?"

"Nope."

"Why the hell not?"

"Even at the speed of light it will take awhile to gather everyone up and get going."

"You mean you have to pick up all of your passengers one at a time? Like a bus driver? That's pretty primitive, isn't it?"

"The only alternative, herr doktor, would be to gather them up ahead of time. Which would create a number of other problems."

I crossed out 12/31. "All right, when will you be leaving exactly?"

"Probably right after breakfast."

I wrote down 12/31 again. "And you promise you won't leave the hospital until then?"

"Nope."

"Goddamn it, prot—why not?"

"I still have a few places to go."

"What places?"

"I've got to hand it to you, gene. You don't give up easily."

"Thank you—I'll take that as a compliment. So you won't share that information either?"

"Sorry."

"All right. Just sit back and relax. I'd like to speak to Robert now."

"Lotsa luck," he mumbled as his head dropped to his chest.

"Rob?" I waited. "Robert?"

Prot/Robert seemed to slouch down even further. There was no other detectable response.

"Robert, please come forward. I only want to speak to you for a second. Just to find out how you're feeling, what's bothering you so much. I helped you before, remember?"

Nothing.

"This room is your safe haven, just like it always was."

No response.

"You must be feeling pretty bad. But whatever it is, you can trust me. Will you just say 'Hello,' so I'll know you're here?"

Not a hint of movement.

"All right. Don't go anywhere. Just relax." I carefully opened the drawer of my desk and pulled out the whistle

I had called him with under similar circumstances two years earlier. I blew it.

There was no response whatsoever.

"All right, Rob, we'll talk later. And if there's anything you want to discuss with me, just tell one of the nurses and I'll come running—okay? Now I'd like to speak with prot again. Prot? Are you here?"

At once his eyes opened and came to a focus on me. "Find him?"

"Not yet."

"That's the spirit," he said with his maddening grin, something between genuine warmth and cynical smirk.

"How long have you had that beard?" I asked him.

"A couple of your years. I may keep it. What do you think?"

"Did you know that Rob has a beard exactly like yours?"

"Will wonders never cease!"

"You don't see any connection between his and yours?"

"Why should I?"

I stared at him glumly. "Prot, I'm going to ask you a favor."

"Very human of you, doc."

"I'm going to ask you to help me get through to Robert. Like you did a couple of years ago, remember?"

"That was different. He *wanted* to come out then. I couldn't have stopped him even if I'd tried."

"All I'm asking is that you talk to him, do whatever you can to help him *want* to get whatever's bothering him off his chest. Will you do that?"

"Sure, boss. If I see him. But I can't guarantee anything."

"Just do your best. That's all I ask."

504

He shrugged. "Don't I always?"

We sat staring at each other. Finally I asked whether he had had a chance to talk to any of the other patients about their problems.

"Some of them."

"Any thoughts so far?"

"Yes."

"Want to give me a summary?"

"No."

Annoyed, I tossed my pad onto the desk. "All right. That's all for today." I consulted my calendar, but for purposes of form only. I had already decided to give prot/Robert as much time as I could manage. I only wished there were more. "We'll meet every Tuesday and Friday at nine. All right with you?"

"What's the matter with Monday, Wednesday and Thursday?"

"Prot, you're not the only resident of MPI, unfortunately."

"I'll bet you say that to all your patients."

"Not really. Okay then, I'll see you again on Tuesday. In the meantime, I'll set up an appointment for your entrance, or re-entrance, physical with Dr. Chakraborty. Okay?"

"Why? My health is good. Don't feel a day over two hundred and fifty."

"Just routine," I assured him.

"Ah, yes. I remember your penchant for routine."

"Fine. Then I'll see you next week." I got up to escort him to the door.

"*Auf wiedersehen!*" he cried as he hurried out, apparently eager to get back to Ward Two. The room he was going to, incidentally, had been vacated not long before by another patient with a tragic history. Six months earlier the man, who was affectionately dubbed "Mr. Magoo," had suddenly stopped recognizing faces, including his own. Unfortunately, the problem had a physical etiology (he had been beaned by a falling brick), and there wasn't much we could do for him except to encourage his family, friends, and co-workers to wear name tags at all times. His wife, however, rebelled against this idea and, perhaps understandably, was gone by the time he returned to their apartment.

I plopped back down in my chair and looked over my meager notes for this session. "12/31, right after breakfast," and "Check with patients about their plans re: K-PAX," I read, along with a half-page of undecipherable doodles, tangled blue strings in a dull-yellow matrix. I only hoped the threads winding through Robert's mind could be unraveled and put into some kind of order before it was too late. The last time prot "departed" under similar circumstances Rob was left in a catatonic state from which he didn't emerge for five years, when his alter ego paid a return visit. But this time he wouldn't be coming back.

The only good news arising from our encounter was Robert's telling prot he was only "taking a break from his miserable life," suggesting that, when the time was right, he might again be ready to cooperate in a treatment program. But when would that be? And why was he suddenly so miserable? I only hoped we could do more for him than for the patient who had just vacated his room, though we had precious little time to do it in.

I returned to my inner office, where Giselle was waiting. I had almost forgotten she was there.

"Well?" she demanded, though it was more like a bleat.

506

"I'm sorry, Giselle, it looks as though we're back to square one."

"But why? I don't understand."

"Sometimes a mental illness comes like a bolt of lightning. Literally. Some little spark seems to set off a whole cascade of electrical events. Until we know a lot more about the chemistry and physics of the brain, all we can do is try to get the patient back on track by whatever means is available."

She frowned. Having traveled down this road before, she knew the risks and probabilities as well as I. "Can I have access to him like you've given me in the past?"

"Of course." I had no intention of arguing with that request, as I had before. In view of her unique position as a sort of buffer between prot (Robert) and the outside world, we both knew she could be extremely helpful to all of us. Perhaps he would utter something significant when she was around, something that none of the nurses would recognize as important. "By the way, where's your son?"

"I called my mom last night. She's staying with us until we figure out what's going on."

"What about Rob's mother?"

"I called her, too. She's remarried, and living in Arizona now. She wanted to come, but I talked her out of it. There wouldn't be much point in her visiting him if we don't know where he is."

I gazed at her eager, still-youthful face. "You probably know as much about Rob's problem as I do, Giselle. What do *you* think went wrong?"

"I suppose giving Gene his bath somehow brought everything back. But why he left so abruptly and prot came back at exactly the same time . . ." She shrugged.

I had forgotten that she considered them to be two

separate individuals. "Any idea where he might have gone?"

"None at all. Unless he went back to Guelph."

"His home town?"

"Yes."

"Why Guelph?"

"I don't know. When I'm overwhelmed with something, it helps to go back to the place I grew up in. It's like returning to a simpler time, I suppose."

I nodded understandingly though I, myself, still lived in the house I grew up in, and had nowhere else to go. But neither my own childhood nor Giselle's were fraught with the misery that had befallen Robert's.

"Can I go see him now?"

"All right, Giselle. Go see what you can find out from prot that I can't."

"Thanks, Doctor B." She jumped up and pecked me on the cheek before skipping out. In another second she skipped back in. "By the way," she added. "Would you be willing to take care of Oxie until Rob comes back?"

As it happened, our own Dalmatian, Shasta Daisy, had died in August. Though she was nearly fifteen and had had a wonderfully happy life, we still missed her sleeping with us, watching everything from the back seat of the car, playing with the grandkids. Giselle had me again and she knew it.

"All right. Bring him in tomorrow and I'll take him home with me."

"Just one thing."

"What's that?"

"He's a vegetarian now."

"The dog? Is that possible?"

"Sure. It's just a matter of feeding him the right nutrients in the right proportions. I'll give you a list."

"Thanks," I mumbled.

She smiled brightly. "I knew I could count on you."

I only wished I could share her confidence.

AFTER Giselle had gone I found myself trying vainly to reorganize the piles of paper strewn all over my desk, a ritual I go through every time some unexpected and unwanted new burden is tossed onto it. There were unrefereed manuscripts, unattended meeting invitations, an unfinished paper of my own, books, reprints, catalogs, notebooks, yellow pads, Post-its and memos of all kinds. At the back of it all stood a picture of my entire family.

I gazed lovingly at the photo, remembering the event at which it was taken, a backyard picnic more than seven years ago, the time I first invited prot to the house to determine the effect of a normal home environment on his condition (I didn't know about Rob at the time). My wife Karen and I are seated in the foreground, Shasta at our feet, backed by our sons Fred on the left and Will on the right, with daughters Abby and Jennifer standing between them. It's Will's fingers that form the antenna sticking up from the back of my head.

How much things change in seven years! Will, who was in high school at the time and suffering through a nearly catastrophic cocaine addiction, is now in his third year of medical school and doing exceedingly well. He is still planning a career in psychiatry, and he and his fiancée Dawn Siegel plan to be married as soon as he graduates (they've already been living together for two years).

Jennifer, a medical student herself at the time the picture was taken, is now specializing in the treatment and prevention of HIV infections in the San Francisco area. In fact, she has become something of a celebrity in Northern

California, the subject of several newspaper and magazine articles, and is as happy in her dismal work as was Mother Teresa in hers. Though her responsibilities preclude her visiting us more than once or twice a year, we are, of course, extremely proud of her great success and dedication.

That was a year of transition for Fred, who continues to amaze us with his career as a singer and actor. He has appeared in a couple of films and soap operas, but spends most of his time on stage, and, in fact, made his first Broadway appearance last year in the smash hit *Rent* and is now in the road company of *Les Misérables* (we didn't even know he could sing until we saw him perform at a dinner theater in Newark not long after the picture was taken). Freddy lives in the East Village with a beautiful ballerina, but refuses to discuss the possibility of marriage, at least not with us. His mother continues to hope, however.

I turned my gaze on Abby, the eldest of the four, and the most outspoken. Now approaching forty, she remains active in a number of causes, particularly that of animal rights, which she claims is the coming thing. "People are beginning to realize that animals have their own feelings and sensitivities, sometimes not very different from our own," she insists. She is prot's favorite, I suspect.

Our astronomer son-in-law Steve (who took the picture) and his colleague Charles Flynn were, of course, instrumental in uncovering prot's vast knowledge of astronomical matters, including his identifying several planets associated with solar systems elsewhere in the galaxy. Indeed, Dr. Flynn has long been convinced that prot is, in fact, from the planet K-PAX.

But back to the family: Steve and Abby's children Rain and Star, now thirteen and eleven and glued to their computer monitors several hours a day, have turned into surprisingly normal adolescents, bright yet thoughtful and considerate. Rain, in fact, is planning on becoming an Eagle Scout, and has already earned several merit badges along the way. Though we see Abby's family more often than the others, we still don't see them often enough. We don't see any of them often enough.

Perhaps that will change with the new year. Karen, thanks primarily to the option payments on the film version of *K-PAX*, decided to retire at the end of the year. She already has our travel plans worked out for the next three decades and persistently reminds me that the longer I work the less time we will have left. "What about my patients?" I ask her.

"You can't stay at the hospital forever," she always tells me. "You've got to leave them to someone else sooner or later."

It's not that easy, of course, though I see her point. Sometimes I almost think it would be nice to have a multiple personality, to be able to lead two lives (or more) at the same time. Most of us, however, are stuck with just the one. I could only hope mine could be of some benefit to Robert Porter, to help him get to the bottom of his difficulty and start him again on the long road to a permanent recovery.

511

Session Thirty-four

I brought Oxeye home with me on Saturday. Karen was delighted to see him and, for that matter, so was everyone else (the Dalmatian, which I had given to Rob in a fruitless attempt to lure him out of his catatonic state, had lived with us from 1991–5). In fact, Abby and her family came up from Princeton for the occasion.

My daughter seemed to have mellowed in the last couple of years, hardly bugging me at all about her hopelessly liberal causes. Maybe she was just glad to be back home for a while. Or perhaps it had something to do with her fortieth birthday looming on the horizon. Oxie, for his part, was also happy to be with us, though he sniffed hard for Shasta and whined for a time when he couldn't find her (we buried her in her favorite spot at our summer place in the Adirondacks).

Rain and Star ran all over the yard with him that afternoon while the old folks chatted inside. Despite the negative aspects of prot's return, everyone was overjoyed that he was back as well, and hoped I would bring him home for a cookout, the setting for their earlier encounters with him.

"In the winter?" I protested.

Karen pointed out that Thanksgiving and Christmas were coming up. "Maybe you could bring him home for those."

I didn't even want to think about that. It seemed as though we had only put away the decorations a short time before.

I cornered my son-in-law Steve and asked him about his colleague, Charlie Flynn, who had recently returned from Libya (by special dispensation from Colonel Qaddafi in return for a percentage of any profits) with a tiny supply of spider excrement indigenous to that country. According to prot, this was a key component in a cold fusion reaction. Though the results of a single small experiment (in collaboration with the physics department) looked promising, the amount, unfortunately, was insufficient to catalyze a larger-scale production. Undeterred, Flynn was busy gathering feces from various native American arachnid species in hopes of isolating the key element in this material, which could well solve the world's energy problems, not to mention his own financial ones.

"Ah think he's in Mexico now, trackin' down tarantulas," Steve chuckled.

I asked him whether there had been any developments in the study of planet K-PAX and its double star system.

"Well, another of our faculty has found what looks to be a second planet in that solar system. Ah wonder why prot never mentioned it to you."

"Maybe he doesn't know about it."

"Ah wouldn't be too sure. Anyway, you might ask him. It's even bigger than K-PAX. The main difference is that it orbits far outside the double star system, not inside it like K-PAX does."

"I'll do that."

At that point Rain showed up. Now a teenager, his voice had already changed and he sported a feeble mustache, which he's decided to keep. He seemed to have shot up another several inches since we had last seen him, and was almost as tall as I was. I felt a little like "Albert Einstein," one of my patients at MPI, who was desperately trying to slow down time and could only watch helplessly as it rolled on and on, carrying him, and the rest of us, along with it like some invisible avalanche. Of course this only reminded me that the time for prot's departure was lurking, like a giant boulder, at the bottom of the mountain.

AFTER the death of our former director, Klaus Villers, I was voted acting director of the hospital in the fall of 1997. Following interviews with a number of candidates for the permanent directorship, some of whom were crazier than the patients, it was clear that the best person for the job was our own Virginia Goldfarb. Though she has a few figurative warts, as do we all, she is even-handed and fair, and makes decisions only after careful deliberation and weighing of all the options. Moreover, she keeps herself informed of developments in many areas of psychiatry, including her own specialties, bipolar disorder and mega-lomania. Finally, she practically squeaks of confidence and self-assurance, which doesn't hurt in the fund-raising department, and I think she was a fine choice to lead the Manhattan Psychiatric Institute into the twenty-first century (though I wasn't too pleased that she put me in charge of the committee supervising the construction of the new wing, which takes a whopping amount of time).

At the regular Monday morning staff meeting, chaired by Dr. Goldfarb, there was a great deal of interest in prot's return and what it might tell us not only about Robert Porter's condition, but about others suffering from the bizarre affliction known as multiple personality disorder (MPD) as well. Although regression to the various individual personalities is not an uncommon occurrence, the patient can usually be reintegrated more easily the second time around. In the case of Robert/prot, however, the problem was complicated by the disappearance of the principal alter.

That led to a discussion of what it means to be an alter ego, i.e., how does a secondary or other personalities differ from the primary one, and from the fully integrated human being? Are they completely different individuals? Or are certain things missing in the thoughts and feelings of the various alters, who are merely "parts" of a whole? Are we all simply a mix of different personalities which dominate our minds at different times? If so, which of these is responsible for our actions? All very interesting, I remarked, but what specific recommendations were there in the case of my relapsed patient, Robert Porter?

Ron Menninger pointed out that MPD differs from all the other syndromes in that aggressive drug treatment of the individual at hand, while perhaps beneficial to him, can be devastating to one or more of the other egos (at this point I wasn't even certain how many others there were in Robert's case), and perhaps to the integrated personality as a whole.

A consensus was reached that I should continue psychoanalysis, at least for a while, in hopes that probing into prot's

515

psyche might provide further information about what had happened to Robert, his primary alter, much as it had seven years earlier. For example, prot's abhorrence of money in particular, and capitalism in general, seemed to be related to the severe financial obligations incurred by Rob's family following the fatal injury of his father.

While all this was debatable, unanimous agreement was reached on one thing: no TV appearances for prot this time! Letters and calls from people who wanted to meet him or make use of his talents or follow him to a distant planet were still dribbling in more than two years after he was interviewed on a television talk show. More disturbingly, there were several communications from people in various countries who claimed they had seen him, and even a few who insisted that he had taken them aboard his space ship and examined them. A woman in France claimed she was pregnant with his child! Obviously she hadn't heard about prot's tremendous aversion to the procreation process, which was intimately related, of course, to Robert's sexual abuse as a child.

This was followed by a preliminary discussion of a possible replacement for Carl Thorstein, who was interviewing for a position elsewhere. And we had only just found someone (Laura Chang) to take the place of Klaus Villers, who had died at about the time of prot's "disappearance" in 1995.

The subject turned, finally, to a couple of the other problem patients. One of these, the aforementioned "Albert Einstein," is a Chinese–American physicist who believes that time not only flies, but is accelerating! Quite successful in his career until several months ago, he broke down while presenting a paper on the nature of time at an international scientific meeting.

We all harbor the illusion that time moves faster as we grow older. At that conference Albert hypothesized that this is indeed a physical fact having something to do with the expansion of the universe. He tearfully reported to the shocked scientists that time was literally speeding up, that life was rapidly passing him by, along with his audience and all the rest of us. After seeing his own psychiatrist he was taken to "the Big Institute" at Columbia, where he was treated vigorously, though without success, with electroshock and other therapies, and finally ended up with us. He now spends most of his time in his room, along with dozens of pencils and reams of paper, in feverish pursuit of the impossible—of finding a way to slow down time mathematically, or even stop it altogether. Ironically, when he becomes too tired to think, he sits quietly and does nothing at all, in an attempt to make the minutes crawl by as slowly as possible. Like many of our residents, he sleeps very little. Obviously in great anguish, he moans and fidgets during every analytic session and finally jumps up and runs to the door, hoping somehow to make up for lost time.

Another patient under review was a woman suffering from an unusual form of schizophrenia, or perhaps a previously unreported type of bipolar disorder (formerly called manic depression). The patient, a woman we call Alice, sometimes sees herself as no bigger than an insect in a world of giants. At such times she is terrified of being stepped on, drowning in a cup of tea, being eaten by one of the cats, and so on. At others she thinks she has become gigantic, all-powerful, utterly in control of everything around her, including the staff and the other patients. At still other times she seems perfectly normal in every way, continually pestering her doctor (Goldfarb) to "let me out of this madhouse."

517

We don't have a clue as to the cause of this curious affliction, nor that of various other phobias, compulsions, and social deviations, whose victims haven't been helped in the slightest by even the newest and most powerful neuroleptic drugs.

Carl Beamish joined Goldfarb in suggesting that prot might have a talk with some of these problem patients. In fact, I suspect this was the reason for their being included on the meeting's agenda. There were no objections, except by me. I protested, as I had earlier, that although he had shown an amazing ability to help such unfortunates in the past, our primary responsibility was to Robert and *his* treatment. Indeed, we seemed to be back where we had started in 1990, with no clear idea of what underlay Robert's difficulty in dealing with the world around him, or how to get to the bottom of it. However, I did agree to question prot about his prognoses for the other patients, while, at the same time, requesting that everyone present query their charges about their future travel plans.

My main concern, however, was in reintegrating prot's powerful personality into that of Robert Porter's so that his family could once again be reunited, Giselle could have her husband back, and baby Gene his missing father.

PROT seemed cheerful and relaxed when he came into my examining room the following morning. "Happy Veterans Day!" he cried as he went for a pear. I watched him eat the whole thing, seeds and all, smacking his lips as usual in what was at once a delightful and disgusting spectacle.

"You know about Veterans Day?"

"Only that it used to be called Armistice Day. But you changed it because it sent the wrong message."

"What message?"

Munch, munch, munch. "That peace is a good thing. You prefer to honor your warriors. Makes it easier to recruit the next batch, don'tcha know." A speck of the Bartlett flew across the room.

"You think we're a violent, warlike species, don't you?"

He stared at me in some amusement. "Well, if you ain't, why do you teach your children the 'glories' of destroying your 'enemies'?"

"I didn't teach my children—"

"You sent them to school, didn't you? They watched TV, didn't they? You even took them to Gettysburg! What were they to think about all those heroic battles in all those wars?"

I gazed at him sitting in the dim light, one of his legs drawn up under him disarmingly. "Tell me—did Robert have a set of toy soldiers?"

"I saw some of them on my first visit."

"That's the only time?"

"Yep."

"Later on—did he have any problem with the military?"

His eyebrows came up. "How on EARTH should I know?"

"He never mentioned anything about wanting to go into the military or, maybe, ways to keep out of it?"

"Nope. Never did."

I made a note to find out whether a friend or relative of Rob's had died in Vietnam. Or perhaps the killer of his wife and daughter had been wearing part of a military uniform when Robert encountered him.

As prot sank his teeth into another pear I asked him how he felt about being back at MPI. "You've added some new patients since I was here—interesting beings in every ward!"

I reminded myself to follow up on this appraisal as soon as time permitted. "Dr. Chakraborty tells me you're still in excellent shape for a man your age."

He smiled. "I told you that—remember?"

I didn't argue the matter. Mainly I had wanted to get a blood sample to compare with an earlier one, which suggested, unless someone had gotten the tubes mixed up (this happens more often than you might imagine), that his DNA was quite different from Robert's. In any case, we would have the results in a few weeks.

"You remember Steve, my son-in-law?" I asked him.

"Sure Ah do. The astronomer."

"He tells me there's another planet orbiting K-MON and K-RIL. Is that right?"

"No. That's *not* right."

"It's not??"

"That's what I said. In fact, there are *eight* others. Most are too small to detect from EARTH with the primitive methods you insist on using."

"Why didn't you tell me about these planets before?"

"My dear sir, you never *asked*."

"Well, are any of them inhabited?"

"I assume you mean by people?"

"By life of any kind."

"Nope. Except for the occasional visitor, of course."

"In other words, your solar system is very similar to ours."

"Naturally."

"Don't you find that interesting?"

He ignored the implication of this astute observation. "Not particularly. For your information, doc, and that of your astronomer relatives, most solar systems around the GALAXY conform to this pattern. But only about one PLANET in five hundred supports the kind of life you're talking about."

I smiled at him, perhaps a bit too knowingly. "Just for the record, though, do all of those solar systems have nine planets?"

He ignored the condescending grin, too. "No, and neither does yours. Many STARS have no PLANETARY COMPANIONS at all. Others have a hundred or more. The average is about a dozen. Not counting all the little rocks you call 'asteroids,' of course."

"Did you say the Earth doesn't have nine planets?"

"There are a few out beyond PLUTO you haven't found yet."

There was no way to argue this point, so I let it drop. "Hear anything from Rob?"

"Not a peep."

"And you still have no idea where he might be?"

"Nary a clue."

"Could you find him if you wanted to?"

"Maybe. But he obviously doesn't want to be found, does he?"

"Prot, I'm going to ask you another favor."

"Here we go again."

"I'm going to ask you to look hard for him. And when you find him, to give him this message: Tell him I won't bother him right now; Giselle and I just want to get some information from him. Whether he wants to stay in graduate school, for example. After that he can go back to wherever he's been keeping himself. Will you do that?"

"Pretty devious trick if you ask me, doc." He crunched up and swallowed the last of a core. "All right. I'll see what I can do."

"Thank you, prot. I appreciate that."

"No problemo." With a straight face he added, "Where do you suggest I look?"

I studied him, not knowing whether he was joking or not. Sometime during the middle of a sleepless night, I had gotten a feeble idea. I told him I would like to speak to Paul now.

"Should I think pleasant thoughts or something?"

"Sure, if you like. Think about sailing over K-PAX in a balloon or pitching to Babe Ruth or something." He closed his eyes and smiled happily, for all the world as if he were in the middle of some high adventure.

I waited for a moment. "Paul? Will you come forward please?" (Paul was the alter ego who first appeared when Robert reached puberty and, because of his earlier abuses, was unable to handle the sexual impulses of normal adolescence, for which prot was of no help whatsoever. He went on to volunteer his services with Rob's late wife, Sarah.)

Prot shifted slightly in his chair, but Paul made no appearance.

"You might as well come on out, Paul," I told him. "I can bring you forward with hypnosis any time I want."

I wasn't certain of that, but Paul was convinced, apparently. His eyes slowly opened and he stretched lazily. "Oh, hello, doc. How are things?"

I gazed into his eyes. Like prot's they were playful, mischievous. "You remember the last time we chatted? It was a couple of years ago."

"Like it was yesterday."

"What have you been up to since that time?"

"Not much."

"You haven't made an appearance since Rob left the hospital?"

"Only a couple of times a week."

I was somewhat taken aback by this matter-of-fact reply. "Really? What do you do when you come out?"

"Oh, this and that. Try to satisfy Giselle's needs, for the most part. Don't let that innocent look fool you—she's a tiger in bed. Or tigress . . . ?"

I was crestfallen. If Paul was, in fact, assuming Rob's conjugal duties at this late date, he had probably been doing so in 1995. In that case, was Robert in on the deception? Why would he want to pretend that he was making such terrific progress when he was, in fact, still as miserable as ever? Had he been using his apparent "recovery" to distract us from something even worse than his profound sexual dysfunction?

There was nothing to do but take things as they came. "Are you aware of everything Rob has been up to during the last two years?"

"More or less. He studies a lot. Dull stuff. I usually sleep when he does that. Love to sleep."

"Bully for you," I said enviously. "But you're aware of what's going on with him most of the time—is that right?"

"Okay. Okay. I have eavesdropped on Rob's private life. I need to be ready if he fails to live up to his obligations. You understand."

"Yes, I think I do, finally." In fact, I felt like a damn fool, and almost said so. "Anything else to report? Anything you've seen or heard that his doctor ought to know about?"

He scratched his chin and contemplated the ceiling. "Can't think of a thing, doc. All of his equipment seems to work okay."

"What about last Thursday? Were you aware that Rob called on prot to return?"

"Sure—I couldn't miss something as obvious as that."

"What was he doing at the time?"

"Giving the kid—my kid—a bath. He's a slippery little bastard."

"Anything happen while he was doing that? Did Rob suddenly become ill, or did he cry out, or faint—anything like that?"

"Not a thing. All at once prot was there and Rob wasn't."

"Who finished the bath?"

"Prot, I s'pose. What's the difference?"

"I don't know. Do you have any thoughts on that?" He pondered this. "Not really."

"Well, do you know where Rob went?"

"Nope. When this happens he can stay away for ages, damn him."

"Why 'damn him'?"

"Are you kidding? No Rob, no pussy wussy."

"Paul, when did Rob first call you?"

"He was—I don't know—twelve or thirteen, I guess. Something like that."

"And you've been around ever since?"

"From time to time."

"Exactly how often did he call you, and under what circumstances?"

"I told you—he needed someone to take over whenever he got an erection and had to do something about it."

"With girls?"

"With himself, mostly."

"And later on, with girls."

"Nope. Only one girl. What was her name again? Oh, yeah. Sarah. Only he called her Sally. A little dippy, but a good lay." His smile was not like prot's—there was an element of sarcasm in it. "Different from Giselle. I imagine all women are different. I've only had two." He sat up straighter, looked directly at me (until then his eyes had shifted from place to place, never focusing on anything for more than a few seconds) and winked. "You'd probably know more about that than I would. . . ."

He was quite wrong about that, but I wasn't about to go into it. "So you just—what—lie around and wait for the right moment?"

"That's about it."

"What about Harry? What has he been up to?"

"That little shit? Haven't heard from him in a long time."

"And as I recall, there's no one else there with you besides Rob, prot, and Harry—is that right?"

"I already told you that a couple of years ago. You hounded Rob like this, too, and look what happened."

"All right, Paul, that's all for today. You can go back to sleep now."

He yawned. "So long, doc. By the way, you got any other patients that need some help? I'm horny as hell."

"I'll let you know."

He shrugged, nodded, and his eyes slowly closed.

I was not unhappy to see this somewhat disgusting young man, who seemed to be interested in little besides sex, withdraw. Perhaps this said more about my own hangups than his promiscuity, but I had no time to dwell on the matter. Before prot could make a reappearance, I asked Harry to come forward. (It was Harry who took over whenever Rob was being abused by his uncle. Indeed, there is reason to believe that it was he, not Robert, who killed the murderer of his wife and daughter, perhaps confusing him for Uncle Dave.) It took a while, but he finally opened his eyes and looked around the room, blinking, presumably trying to figure out where he was.

"Hi, Harry. How are you doing?" The picture of a five-year-old boy with a beard had a somewhat comical effect.

"Okay, I guess." He frowned. "You're that doctor, aren't you?"

"You remember me?"

"What happened to your beard?" Oblivious to his own, he rubbed his nose and wiped his finger on his pants.

"Oh, I've got it in a jar at home."

His eyes widened, but he said nothing.

"What have you been up to the last couple of years?"

"Just waitin', keepin' an eye out."

"For Uncle Dave?"

"Yeah."

"Do you mind if I ask you some questions?"

He shuffled his feet. "I guess not."

"Were you around when prot came back this time?"

He felt the vinyl arms of his chair. "Who's 'prot'?"

"Never mind. Were you there when Rob left last week?"

"Uh-huh."

"What happened?"

Another frown. "I dunno." His nose seemed plugged, as if he had a cold. "He was givin' somebody a bath."

"And he left without any warning?"

"I guess so."

"Any idea where he went?"

He looked around the room. "No," he said, though it sounded more like "dough."

"All right. Did I ask you before whether you know about anyone else who lives with you and Rob?"

526

He shrugged. "I don't remember."

"Well, *do* you?"

"No."

"What about Paul?"

"Huh?"

"You've never met Paul?"

He fidgeted with his shirt buttons. "Uh-uh."

"Or anyone else besides Robin?" (Robert's childhood name.)

"Uh-uh."

"Anything else you want to tell me about Rob while you're here?"

He wagged his head.

"All right, Harry. You can go."

He looked around one last time before closing his eyes.

Again I waited for prot to reappear, but he just sat there, apparently asleep.

"Prot?"

His eyes popped open. "Present and accounted for."

"Did you hear any of my conversations with Paul and Harry?"

"Not a word. Did I miss anything?"

"Apparently you've missed quite a lot. Both of us have. All right. Our time's about up. You might as well go back to Ward Two."

"So early?" He grabbed the last pear on his way to the door. "See you Friday," he called out.

"Wait a second. I almost forgot." I retrieved a weighty bundle, held together by two enormous rubber bands, that the mail room had sent over. "This is all the stuff that came for you while you were gone. We didn't know where to forward it," I added pointedly.

Ignoring the comment he took the package. "Thanks,

doc." He riffled through some of the letters. "I hope none of these beings want to go to K-PAX. The passenger list is just about filled up."

As he left, I marveled at the confidence he exuded, his conviction that he was, in fact, a K-PAXian. There wasn't a shred of doubt in his mind. But neither is there any (in the patients' minds) that our current "Christ" is the son of God, that our resident "Croesus" is a rich and powerful woman, or that any of our other delusionals are not who they think they are. For that matter, all of us probably harbor a number of delusions, thinking ourselves more or less attractive, smarter or dumber than we really are. On the other hand, perhaps we are all exactly who we think we are. Prot is right about one thing: truth is whatever we believe it to be.

The idea I had come up with the previous night wasn't just feeble, it was decrepit. Except for the revelation that Rob had been faking his all-too-rapid recovery in 1995, neither Paul nor Harry were going to be of much help in finding out what happened the week before. Paul appeared to be little interested in Rob, much less prot, unless there was some sexual gratification in it; and Harry, who was only five, was apparently unaware of the existence of the other personalities, except, of course, for Robert. Unless there were someone in there I didn't yet know about, all I had left was prot.

But even he didn't seem particularly eager to work with Rob this time around, perhaps because of the latter's (from prot's point of view) intransigence. He had already spent several years trying to convince Robert to leave the world he was unable to deal with and return with him to the idyllic planet K-PAX, to no avail.

The questions still remained: What had happened to

Robert, and why *then*? What did it have to do with bathing the baby, if anything? On top of that dilemma, how was I going to tell Giselle that she had been sleeping with two different men, and that Paul, not Rob, was the father of little Gene? The old retirement bug began buzzing around my ears, and I didn't try very hard to swat it away. I almost felt sorry for Will, now well into his third year of medical school. But I remembered my own student days, and those difficult, exciting years of residency. If I had the chance all over again, I'd probably do exactly the same thing, make the same damn mistakes, take the bad with the good.

AFTER letting prot go a few minutes early I seized the opportunity to take a stroll on the grounds. For one thing I wanted to get a look at progress on the construction of the new wing, the Klaus M. and Emma R. Villers Laboratory for Experimental Therapy and Rehabilitation. More importantly, I have come to realize over the years that a great deal can be learned from informal encounters with the patients. The more contact we have with them the better we are able to spot subtle changes in their behavior, something that might be missed in the more formal setting of the examining room. Besides, it was a sunny November day, and there weren't going to be many as pleasant for some time.

On this particular occasion I found Ophelia sitting with Alex on a bench not far from the side entrance, and I ambled over to speak with them. Ophelia is a young woman who will do anything anyone tells her to. An orphan who was passed from one foster home to another, she became obsessed early in life with trying to please her various parents so they wouldn't dump her off on someone else. Like an anorexic, who can never be thin enough, she blamed herself

529

for each perceived failure, and tried harder and harder to please everyone. Ironically, this blatantly sycophantic behavior drove away many prospective parents. At the same time, she suffered abuse from teachers and students, employers and co-workers in whatever situation she found herself. Eventually she learned to trust no one, while helplessly complying with every wish or command. She ended up with us when she was found wandering in Central Park after having been raped by a shoe salesman.

With her was another patient whom we call "Alex Trebek," after the host of the popular television quiz show, *Jeopardy*. Perhaps because the real Mr. Trebek makes his job look so easy, our "Alex" firmly believes that he (or perhaps anyone) can do it as well as the original, and, indeed, has offered to substitute for Mr. Trebek, without notice, at any time. As with the route to Carnegie Hall, he thinks he can get there with practice, and he roams the wards and grounds shouting "Yes!" and "That's right!" and "Correct!" This in itself would not place him with us. The problem with "Alex" is that these are the only words he utters.

As with most mental patients, there is a lighter side to all this. With his mustache and sporty jacket and tie he even looks a little like the real game-show host, and many of our visitors become convinced that Alex Trebek himself is a resident of MPI, no matter what denials we might make.

I paused at their bench and asked if either had spoken with prot as yet. Ophelia inquired immediately (so I wouldn't think she was being recalcitrant, I suppose) whether I thought that would be a good idea. "Doesn't make any difference to me," I assured her. "I was just curious."

She admitted she had talked with prot for a few minutes over the weekend.

"Correct!" confirmed Alex.

530

"And did he ask you whether you wanted to go to K-PAX?"

"Would you be unhappy if I told you he did?"

"No."

"We all want to go," she confessed matter-of-factly. "But he can only take a hundred of us with him."

"You are right!"

At this point one of our "exhibitionists" darted from behind a tree and exposed a bare foot to us. When no one responded, he grabbed his shoe and slunk off.

"Well, did he give you any encouragement?"

"Would that be wrong?"

"No."

"He said the trip is still open to anyone. The passenger list hasn't been finalized yet."

"Do you want to be on it?"

"Would it annoy you if I said 'yes'?"

"Either answer would be fine."

"I told him that I would be happy to do whatever he wanted me to do."

"That's it!" Alex shouted.

Seeing Cassandra leave her favorite spot not far away, I excused myself and hurried to catch up. As always, Ophelia seemed distressed that I was leaving her, feeling, I suppose, that she had displeased me in some way.

But I needed to speak with our resident prophet, whose ability to predict future events could be of help in determining what prot had in mind for the other patients. "Hello, Cassandra!" I called out.

She stopped and tried to focus on the reality of my appearance.

I couldn't help but notice that she seemed a little down. "Anything wrong, Cassie?"

She stared at me for a few minutes before turning and wandering slowly away. I didn't like the look of that. It usually meant she had seen signs in the sky suggesting that something bad was going to happen. If so, there was no way I could get her to tell me what it was until she was ready to do so.

At this point Milton appeared. "Man comes home to find his house burned to the ground. 'Damn!' he says. 'I miss everything!'"

When I didn't laugh, he brought out three huge seeds, taken from one of the dried-out sunflowers lining the back wall, and began to juggle them. I watched Cassandra dissolve in a group of other patients, all huddled around the fountain (which had been turned off for the winter months) like a flock of sheep. Among those present were "Joan of Arc," who doesn't understand the meaning of the word "fear," and "Don Knotts," who is afraid of everything. It suddenly occurred to me that their illnesses might be related to MPD, that their "incomplete" psyches might be akin to part of a multiple personality, the other alter(s) being absent or repressed. I stood there wishing we could somehow integrate these two patients, and some of the others milling around the "back forty," to create new, and perhaps whole, individuals out of those whose psyches had become dominated by one emotion or another. But that, along with our understanding of how prot managed to "disappear" on certain occasions, would have to wait until some future time.

Milton was still juggling sunflower seeds when I left, sometimes off his foot and around his back. He was amazingly good, actually.

GISELLE was waiting for me when I returned to my office (we had agreed to meet after each Tuesday session to compare notes). I told her about K-PAX's supposed companion planets, and about the letters I had passed on to prot.

She wasn't much interested in these revelations. "He told me yesterday that he hasn't found Rob yet. Did he have any luck today?"

"Unfortunately, no. But he promised me he would make a serious effort to do so."

She seemed disappointed with our lack of progress, as, of course, was I.

"Giselle, you knew this wasn't going to be easy. In my opinion something is bothering Robert that may be even more devastating to him than the sexual abuse by his uncle and the murder of his wife and daughter, if you can believe there could be anything worse than that. It may have something to do with bathing your son."

She thought about this. "My God—you mean he was abused when he was a *baby*?"

"No, no, no, I didn't say that. But if something did happen at that early age, it's not going to be easy to get to. Even if Robert were here and willing to cooperate it would be almost impossible."

"You mean we may *never* know what happened to him?"

"I didn't say that, either. I said it's going to be very difficult. Besides, it may have nothing to do with his bathing your son."

"So what can we do?"

"All we can do is keep prot talking, encourage him to get through to Robert, and go from there. But," I cautioned her, "don't press him too hard on this. Just talk with him about whatever he wants to chat about and try to steer the conversation toward Robert once in a while."

She nodded dismally.

"By the way, did anything else happen recently in your life or Rob's? Any deaths in the family? Is he having difficulties in school? Problems at home? Anything like that?"

"Nothing. As you know, he's finishing three years of college in two, and was thinking about his senior thesis."

"Does he have a dissertation topic yet?"

"He's interested in island biogeography."

"What's 'island biogeography'?"

"It's about the fragmentation of the Earth, through development and habitat destruction, into little pieces that are too small for indigenous species to survive."

"Sounds like an interesting topic."

"It is. I might write an article about it myself some time."

"What are you working on now?"

"A piece about some of the new drugs coming out of the rainforests."

"That might fit in well with Rob's studies."

"Yeah," she muttered. "We make a great team."

I took a deep breath and jumped in. "Any problems of a—um—more personal nature?"

"You mean between Rob and me? No, not really. He seems quite happy most of the time."

There was no other way to say this. "Has he been a satisfactory sex partner?"

She blushed slightly and looked away, but I detected a mischievous smile on her face. "More than satisfactory," she assured me. "Why? Did something happen—"

"Just trying to rule out some of the possibilities," I said.

"Well, that's not one of them."

"Giselle . . ." I began. The mischievous smile evaporated. "There's something I have to tell you. Please—sit down."

She complied immediately and waited for me to go on.

I sat down too, and began to drum my pen on the stack of paper covering my desk, a compulsive habit I resort to whenever I need to break unpleasant news and don't know quite where to begin. Finally I told her that I'd spoken with Paul.

She shifted slightly in her chair. "Paul?"

"You remember—the personality who took over whenever Rob found himself in a situation involving—"

"I remember."

"It's possible he's lying, of course, but Paul tells me that it was he and not Rob who is Gene's father."

Her eyes widened, then slowly narrowed. "I know that," she murmured.

"You *know*?"

"At first he had me fooled. I became suspicious when he would start to fall asleep whenever we began to make love, and then he would suddenly be wide awake and very passionate."

"Giselle, why didn't you ever tell me about this?"

"I thought about it. But it was sort of a gradual thing. I wasn't sure until maybe a year ago. And—well, it's hard to explain. I guess I was afraid of what would happen if I did."

"What did you think would happen?"

"I was afraid you'd take him away from me." When I didn't respond, she added, "I knew that Paul was a part of Rob. So at first I thought: What's the difference? Maybe we're all different personalities at different times. You've said the same thing yourself. Rob always came back afterward, and was the same Rob as he was before."

I shook my head a bit and waited.

"Besides, I thought maybe I could help him. Encourage

Rob not to be afraid of sex. You know, take it slowly, one step at a time, until he became—well, acclimated to his phobia. Like you do with someone who's afraid of flying or spiders."

"Giselle, you know psychiatry isn't that simple."

She sighed. "You're right. I know that. But I didn't want to lose him. . . ." She was hoping, I suppose, that I would tell her she had done no harm, or at least that I understood.

I did understand. Her motives were partly selfish, partly sympathetic. I felt very sorry for her. But I also felt sorry for Rob, whose problems were infinitely more terrible. "Giselle, is there anything else you want to tell me?"

She pondered this for a moment. "He still misses his father terribly, even thirty-five years after his death. He has a picture of him on the desk in his little study. Once or twice I've heard him talking to it."

"Were you able to hear what he was saying?"

"No, not really. But once I found him crying. It was almost as if he were apologizing to his dad for something."

I knew how he felt. I have often wished that I could apologize to my father for the near-hatred I felt for him when I was a boy and he exerted such a powerful influence on my life, even seeming to have decided what I was going to do with it. It was only later, long after he died, that I realized that whatever happened to me was mostly my own doing. But I'm sure he felt some negative vibes at the time, just as I could tell when my own children resented something I had said or done wrong, however inadvertently.

"One more thing, Giselle. You understand that Paul is a part of Rob. Why not prot, too?"

"Because he told me he isn't!"

No arguing with that. "All right, Giselle, we'll meet again next Tuesday. In the meantime—"

"You'll be the first to know."

After she left I got to thinking about Paul again: how many of the discussions I'd had with Rob two years before were actually with someone else?

Session Thirty-five

I usually spend an hour or two on Thursday morning preparing for my afternoon lecture at Columbia. On this one, however, I found myself thinking about prot's first visit to MPI and how I struggled for weeks trying to determine the underlying basis for his delusion. One of the ideas I wrestled with was that of finding some way to convince him of his earthbound origins. With his impeccable logic, I surmised, this revelation might jolt him to his senses, much as a computer might "crash" after being dealt an impossible problem to solve. At that time, of course, I didn't know about Robert. Once I found him hiding behind prot it became quite a different matter, and I abandoned that strategy in favor of a more direct approach. Now, I realized, the situation had reverted to its original state. If I could prove to prot that he was, in fact, only human, and a mere part of one at that, his whole support structure might collapse and allow me to find Robert's hiding place once more. The danger here was that Rob could be left in the same condition as when prot "departed" in 1990, i.e., an intractable catatonia. On the other hand, if I weren't able to get to Robert before December 31, he would be left exposed and vulnerable anyway. As things stood, there was nothing to lose by taking some calculated risks.

I was encouraged in this endeavor by a paper I had run across a few weeks earlier. In England, in 1950, a man had come to London from an outlying village which, he claimed, was characterized by a matriarchal society. In fact, he had fled his hometown to get away from the "oppressive bitches" who "ruled" there. His therapist discovered that he lived at home with a domineering mother who dictated his every move. When he was confronted by the facts, and established in his own apartment far away from her influence, the delusion quickly dissipated and the man went on to find a wife and, presumably, live happily ever after. It was this sort of logical approach I hoped to use with prot. The only problem was to convince him that the basis for his delusion lay not with a domineering mother, but with the terrible hand fate had dealt his alter ego long before he arrived on the scene.

THE lecture did not go well. In fact, it never happened. One of the students had discovered why I had been interrupted by the department chairman the week before and, as soon as I came into the classroom, began to question me about prot. I protested client–patient relationship, but he persisted and was joined by others who wanted to know, in general terms at least, what the current situation was, pointing out that I had written two books about him and that he had appeared on a national television program, so his case was hardly "privileged." I'm a firm believer that teaching is a two-way process, that a professor is usually wise to follow the interests of his students. Thus, the rest of the hour was taken up by my summarizing what had transpired so far, the dilemmas I faced, and what my plans were for dealing with prot/Robert. I had never seen them so animated, so eager to participate. They even forgave me for the pop quiz I had sprung on them earlier.

The aforementioned student, a young man with an enormous black beard (his hero was Oliver Sacks), came up with a quick answer to the whole complex problem: get prot to perform a controlled light-travel demonstration during his next session. "If we can verify this ability," he submitted, "he must be who he says he is."

We? I thought. "He's already done that with a television camera," I retorted. "But you have to remember that he has found a way to use parts of his mind that only autists and savants are able to access. If he 'disappears,' it may mean only that he can trick us into believing it, by a kind of hypnosis or some other means we haven't been able to figure out yet."

"No, no, no," he retorted back. "I mean, get him to go to some specific place—in another part of the country, say—where you've got a colleague waiting to take his photograph. All you have to do is wait for your partner to fax prot's picture to you. You could even have him wear a funny hat or something so there wouldn't be any chance for a mistaken identity."

My expression probably said, Why is there always someone like this in every class? But I responded with, "What if he won't go?"

"Then he can't do it," the student shouted, "and you've got him!" There was a chorus of "Yes!" and "That's right!"

"Might be worth a try," I admitted, wishing I had

thought of the idea myself. In a transparent face-saving attempt I added, "But don't bet on it."

When I was finally able to take my leave, "Oliver" and two of his friends followed me out. They all wanted to sit in on my next session with prot. While I was impressed with their obvious interest in the case, I explained the impossibility of complying with their request. The hirsute young man snapped, "All right, keep him to yourself, but we expect a full report next time!"

Great, I thought. Now I could look forward to being grilled before every lecture about prot's progress. As the adage goes, give a medical student enough rope and he'll hang you with it. I was definitely getting too old for this. My wife's unflagging determination that I retire by the summer of '98 was sounding more and more attractive all the time.

WHEN I got back to MPI there was a group of five or six noisy people waiting at the front gate. The security guard had his hands full convincing them that they couldn't go in, that this was a mental hospital, that only the families or friends of the patients could enter, and even then only during visiting hours. When he saw me trying to sneak by his little shed, the guard shouted, "Dr. Brewer, will you talk to these people?"

I swallowed my annoyance; this had not been a good day. "What seems to be the problem?"

One of the group, a woman with fiery red hair and wonderful teeth, responded, "We want to see prot. We know you've got him in there. You have no right to keep him locked up."

I didn't waste any time denying that he was back. "Prot is a patient here. At the moment he's not allowed to have visitors."

541

A middle-aged man wearing a fatigue jacket and crew cut jumped in front of me. "Why are you keeping him here? He hasn't done anything wrong."

I backed up a step. "We're not 'keeping' him. He volunteered to be here."

He stepped forward. "We don't believe you. That's exactly what you'd say if you were holding him against his will."

I held my ground. "Look, I don't make the rules. What if you had a brother in a hospital and a bunch of people demanded to see him?"

"I'd ask *him* about it!"

"It's not his decision to make."

"Whose decision is it?" another man demanded, his stubbled chin jutting out towards mine.

I backed up again. "Okay, I'll tell you what I'll do. I'll ask prot if he wants to come out and talk to you. If he doesn't, that's the end of it. Fair enough?"

"How do we know you'll ask him?"

"I guess you'll have to trust me on that."

They looked at each other. One or two of them shrugged. "Okay, doc, but we're not leaving until he comes out."

"I probably won't see him until tomorrow."

"What time?"

"Nine o'clock."

"We'll be here at nine."

"THIS is from California, isn't it?" prot opined. "Not as good as the Caribbean mangoes."

"Sorry. Best I could do."

"I'll take it," he slurped. "Clean as a whistle, too," he reported. "Not a trace of any of your so-called pesticides."

542

I wondered what it looked like to him—vision tests had shown that prot could see well into the ultraviolet range, much like certain insects. "Glad you're enjoying it—it's organic. While you're eating, I'm going to go ahead and ask you a few questions, okay?"

"And if I refuse?"

"No more fruit."

"Ask away."

"How is Robert doing?"

"How should I know?"

"You mean you haven't found him yet?"

"Nope. I looked all over Ward Two and he's nowhere to be found. Besides, I've been pretty busy. . . ."

"Busy? Doing what?"

"Oh, reading my mail, chatting with the other residents, thinking. You remember thinking? You used to do it when you were a boy."

"And Rob hasn't made an appearance since you've been in Ward Two?"

"Nossirree. Maybe he's in one of the other wards."

"It's very important that I speak with him, prot."

"Why? Are you writing another book?"

I pretended not to hear that. "Just let me know right away if you find him, will you? Or tell Giselle."

"W'tever," he grunted, sucking the pulp off the big pit. His beard dripped with mango sludge.

"Good." Unable to stand it any longer, I retrieved a box of facial tissues and handed him one. He wiped off his face, as a courtesy to me, I suppose. Then, annoyingly, he flung the tissue to the floor and settled back in his chair. Frustrated, I exclaimed, "Prot, you're no more from 'K-PAX' than I am. How did you come up with a ridiculous story like that?"

He shook his head. "What does it take to get you humans to see the truth?"

"For one thing, it has to be believable."

"Ah. I remember. If you believe something, it's true, correct?"

"You could put it that way."

"My knowledge of the GALAXY doesn't convince you."

"We have computers that know everything you do."

"Not everything." Suddenly he leaned forward and popped, "What would convince you that I come from K-PAX?" He was obviously eager to play his little game, like a kid with a new chess set.

I thought about the light-travel experiment, but decided to hold it in reserve for the time being. For one thing, I hadn't had a chance to set it up with a partner yet. Instead, I tried another tack. "Do you have any photographs of your home planet?"

"Do you have any photographs of George Washington?"

"No, but we have paintings of him, letters, eyewitness testimony. Do you have any such evidence?"

He looked at me sideways. "I've seen paintings of dragons and unicorns, haven't you? Letters can be forged. And we all know how reliable 'eyewitness testimony' is, don't we, gene?"

"We also have his uniforms, his wigs, even his teeth. What tangible evidence do you have that K-PAX exists, or ever did exist?" I sat back with a smug, prot-like grin.

"What evidence do you have that your gods exist, or ever did exist?"

Exasperated, I shouted, "That's entirely different!"

"Really, gene?"

"Well, there's the Bible, but you probably wouldn't accept that as evidence."

"Who would? Your bibles weren't written by gods, gino. They were written by human beings. You live by rules that were proposed thousands of years ago. At the very least you should revise them every century or so. And what if they got it wrong in the first place?"

"All right. I'm willing to stipulate that *maybe* God didn't write the Bible, and even that *maybe* there are no gods at all, if you'll agree that *maybe* K-PAX never existed either."

"One problem."

"What's that?"

"I've been there!"

"So you're asking me to take K-PAX on faith?"

He didn't miss a beat. "Not at all. You can come with me if you want. See for yourself. I've still got room for one or two more."

There was no good response to this preposterous suggestion. But, I wondered, could religion be a more important part of Rob's dilemma than I had thought? I decided to pursue this. "Most of our religions tell us that if we have enough faith, we'll end up in heaven."

"Religions aren't a question of 'faith.' They're a matter of indoctrination."

"That doesn't prove they're wrong. Anyway, right or wrong, if religions do us good, make us feel better—"

"They do seem rather benign, don't they, my illogical friend? The fact is, they are one of your most dangerous aberrations."

"Aberrations?"

"Religions are a cop-out. They free you from taking the responsibility for your own actions."

"But surely we need to have an ethical foundation of

some kind. Without moral laws, what motive would we have to behave?"

He chuckled a little, obviously enjoying himself. "You don't behave anyway, despite your thousands of religions!"

"How easy for you 'K-PAXians' not to need any help with your lives. There's no cruelty, no injustice, no evil of any kind on your planet, is there?"

"'Evil' is a purely human concept. It exists only on EARTH. And a few other class B PLANETS."

This session, like yesterday's lecture, wasn't going quite as planned. Instead of me putting him on the spot, it was prot who had taken charge, as usual. Furthermore, I was distracted by the soiled tissue he had thrown on the floor. "Let me think about that."

"You won't regret it, believe me. And as for your gods," he added cheerfully, "maybe you're right. Maybe there's a heaven and maybe there's a hell. Anything's possible in this crazy UNIVERSE."

I had an odd feeling I had been checkmated again. I tried the more direct approach. "You know Robert pretty well. Tell me: do you think religion might have had some kind of deleterious effect on his mind?"

"I wouldn't be at all surprised. It has that effect on most of you. Wracked by doubt if you believe there's a god, torn by fear if you don't." He shook his head. "Horrible! But you'll have to ask him that for yourself. We never talked about it. Except for his wife's being a catholic."

"Did that bother him a lot?"

"No, but it bothered a lot of his so-called friends, most of whom he'd known since childhood. Go figure."

Ordinarily I would have pursued the matter of Robert's childhood friends. But this was no ordinary case, and there wasn't enough time to peer into every dark corner. "Tell me something about your own childhood on K-PAX."

He quickly produced his trademark grin and asked me what I'd like to know.

I went for the jugular. "Why don't we start at the beginning? What's the earliest thing you can remember?"

"I can remember the womb," he mused.

"What?" I sat up a little straighter. "What was it like?"

"It was nice and warm."

"About like K-PAX on a nice, sunny day?"

"It's always sunny on K-PAX."

"Of course. I had forgotten. What else do you remember about the womb?"

"There wasn't much room to move around."

"So I've heard. But it was comfortable, otherwise?"

"I suppose so. Noisy, though. A lot of pounding and gurgling."

"Your mother's heart. Stomach. Intestines."

"I could hear her lungs, too. Wheeze, wheeze, wheeze."

"You realized even before you were born what was causing all that racket?"

"Not really. Not in words, anyway."

"Okay, you remember the womb. Does this mean you remember being born?"

"Yep. What a hassle."

"In what way?"

"It's a pretty tight squeeze, coach."

"Did it hurt?"

"I had a headache for days. *Your* days, I mean."

"Of course. So you didn't much like being in the womb, and being born wasn't too agreeable an experience, either. What about when you found yourself out in the world—was that as unpleasant as all the rest?"

"Some of the smells weren't too savory."

"Like what?"

"Now, gene, are you telling me you haven't noticed that poo-poo happens?"

"Now that you mention it, I have on occasion. Do babies wear diapers on K-PAX, or what?"

"It's not cold there. They don't wear anything."

"Babies run around naked on your planet?"

"Naturally. They do on this PLANET, too. In the summer, anyway."

"So you were exposed to the elements, and to your relatives and anyone else who happened to be around. Is that right?"

"None of my relatives were there, as far as I know."

"Not even your mother?"

"Only for a little while."

"How about one of your uncles?"

"Huh?"

"Did you have any uncles hanging around?"

"I already answered that."

"Meaning you don't know for sure."

"Nope."

"Okay—you say your father abandoned your mother after you were born?"

"No, he left *before* I was born. Where I come from, no father hovers around waiting for a child to show up. It's no big deal."

"If I remember correctly, you said you've never even met your father, is that right?"

"No, I said that if we have met, our biological connection wasn't pointed out to me."

"K-PAXian fathers leave their children to fend for themselves, is that it?"

"Of course. Mothers do, too. We don't have parents to brainwash us, like you do on EARTH."

"Who does brainwash you?"

"No one does. Children are free to learn what they want, pursue whatever interests them."

"Without any kind of supervision whatever?"

"Only enough to make sure they don't harm themselves in some way."

"Who does the supervising?"

"Gene, gene, gene. We went over this years ago!"

"Refresh my memory. Who makes sure your children don't get themselves into trouble?"

"Whoever happens to be around."

"What if no one is around?"

"There is always someone around to do what needs to be done."

"An uncle, for example?"

Prot was becoming a trifle annoyed. "I wouldn't know my uncle from a lorgon" (a goatlike creature found on K-PAX).

"Well, did *anyone* bother you in any way after you were born?"

"Not that I recall."

"Would you remember if someone did?"

"Of course."

"Are you sure?"

"You should get your hearing aid checked, gino."

Another feeble attempt at K-PAXian humor, I suppose. But it also meant that prot was becoming testier, which was exactly what I wanted. "All right. Who bathed you when you were a baby?"

He slapped his forehead. "In the first place, babies don't take baths on K-PAX—there's no water, remember? In the second place, we're not obsessed with every speck of dust on our skins, as you humans seem to be. And in the third place, if I needed to be cleaned, someone would do it."

"How were you cleaned when you were a baby?"

"I was wiped off with fallid leaves. They're soft and moist."

"Who did that for you?"

"Whoever was around."

"Your mother?"

"If she was around."

"In other words, a baby is at the mercy of 'whoever is around'?"

"Spoken like a true homo sapiens."

"That's because no one would ever harm another being on K-PAX, right?"

"Now you're getting it."

"Did one of your uncles hang around the house a lot?"

He whacked his forehead again. "We don't have houses on K-PAX."

"Well, did one of them hang around your neighborhood, or wherever it was you lived?"

"What is this obsession you have with uncles?" he screeched. "We don't have uncles! We don't know anything about uncles! Do you understand?"

"Do you resent the question?"

"I resent stupidity!"

"All right. I think that's enough for one session, don't you?"

"Plenty!" he said, jumping up and heading for the door. He still had an orange ring around his mouth.

"See you Tuesday!" I called out.

The only reply was the door being slammed.

After disposing of the soiled facial tissue I listened to the tape of our conversation. It was curiously satisfying to hear him become agitated at the mention of nudity, of bathing, of putative uncles. Was baby Robin harmed in some way by someone "who happened to be around"? There was a definite sore spot being touched here, and I was pretty sure we were on the right track. The only question was, did it lead to a brick wall?

Then there was prot's abhorrence of religions, or perhaps the concept of 'faith' in general. Was Robert betrayed by someone he had faith in? Perhaps even a clergyman? I made a note to ask Giselle what she knew about his religious background.

In my office I found a message from the head of security—the people gathered on the sidewalk outside the front gate were demanding to speak with prot. I had forgotten all about them. Perhaps I subconsciously hoped they would just go away. I got the guy on the phone. "Find Giselle," I told him, "and get her to take care of it."

EARLY that afternoon I received a call from a colleague now living in Germany, though he is an American and went to medical school in the United States. In fact, we interned together at Bellevue. Though an incorrigible practical joker, he is a brilliant psychoanalyst and extremely personable as well. After chatting for a bit about our respective families he told me he had a patient in his hospital claiming to be from the planet K-PAX. "You've opened a can of worms," he cheerfully informed me. "Now there are going to be 'prots' popping up all over the place. As a matter of fact, there's another one I've heard about in China, and one in Congo, of all places."

"This isn't like your horse joke, is it?"

"Gene! Would I do that to you?"

"Yes! You did, in fact!"

"Well, maybe I did. But this involves a patient."

"All right, what's your guy like?" I asked him.

"Much like the man you've described in your books. But he calls himself 'char,' pronounced 'care.'"

"Does he like fruit?"

"Can't get enough of it."

"Can he draw star maps from various places around the galaxy?"

"No, he has another talent."

"What's that?"

"He claims he has a direct pipeline to God."

"Did you test him on that?"

"I asked him if there's really a heaven."

"And is there?"

"Yes. But there's a catch."

"What's that?"

"There aren't any people there."

"Sounds like a genuine K-PAXian to me."

"Who knows?"

"That reminds me, George. I wonder if you'd do me a favor."

"Sure."

"Do you have a camera?"

"Is the Pope Catholic? Is grass green? Do skunks—"

"Okay, okay. Here's what I'm going to do. I'm going to send *our* K-PAXian to see you. I mean, don't hold your breath, but just in case he shows up, would you get a picture of him and fax it to me right away?"

"When's he coming?"

"How about next Tuesday? At 9:15 a.m., say, which would be—what—3:15 there?"

"I'll be out front waiting for him. Does he have the address?"

"No, but I'll give it to him. Got to run. Thanks for calling, Herr Doktor. And take care of *your* K-PAXian."

"Any suggestions as to how?"

"I was hoping you'd tell *me*!"

AS soon as I hung up, I realized I was already a few minutes late for my next patient, an obsessive-compulsive who must go through one or another endless ritual before he can perform the simplest act. For example, he can't eat until he has washed his hands and face exactly thirty-two times. If he loses count he has to start over. And if he touches anything on the way to the dining room he must find a washroom and go through the whole procedure again.

But Linus's difficulties go well beyond this. A biochemist with two doctoral degrees, he was part of a team trying to map the human genome, the complete chemical sequence of the DNA strands comprising each of our forty-six chromosomes, a formidable task requiring hundreds of scientists and all the latest technology.

His problems began to surface almost as soon as he was assigned to work on the project. In his first paper (with about fifteen co-authors), one of the referees noticed some peculiarities in the sequencing of the gene which governs how we taste sourness. On careful examination, it seemed that the section of DNA Linus had worked on was identical to part of another gene, except the forty or so components had been reversed. Someone was asked to check his data, but his notebooks had somehow been misplaced or stolen, and the experiments could not be repeated by other members of the laboratory.

At this point his thesis work came under closer scrutiny

and it was discovered that none of that was verifiable either, and those original notes and data had disappeared also. To make a long and gruesome story short, our Linus knew nothing about biochemistry whatever, or much of anything else. How had he obtained his Ph.D.'s? No one knows, but it must have been a remarkable con job. (It was reported that his graduate-school seminars were so complex that no one could understand them, which presumably only enhanced his reputation as a brilliant researcher.)

A mild form of compulsive behavior was noted during his student days, but it was during the genome studies that he began to suffer from obsessive compulsions of a very serious nature. He sharpened dozens of pencils every morning before he could start to work. From this he rapidly progressed to a daily cleaning of the office he shared with a fellow biochemist. But it was when he began tidying up his *partner's* desk, and, finally, shining every piece of glassware in the laboratory before he could get going, that he was put on temporary leave and encouraged to find help.

Why would someone so patently brilliant as Linus (his IQ approaches 180) falsify his research and try to make a career out of gibberish when it would have been easier just to do the experiments honestly and report the actual results?

Obsessive-compulsive disorder is an age-old affliction closely related to certain other anxiety disorders, and often grounded in anal fixation. Monoamine oxidase inhibitors and certain tricyclics have proven beneficial in a limited number of cases, as has cingulatomy, a surgical procedure. Psychoanalysis has not been very effective, however, perhaps because free association merely increases the level of fixation on a particular obsession. The best and most common approach is to expose the patient to whatever triggers the compulsive behavior, prevent his engaging in

554

the usual rituals, and confront the underlying anxiety.

Sometimes OCD covers up a severe inferiority complex. Linus's father is a well-known chemist, and his mother a highly regarded mycologist and one of the world's foremost experts on poisonous mushrooms. Had he tried to live up to their expectations, an elusive goal shared by many highly successful people in all sorts of endeavors? Or had some specific event precipitated his abnormal behavior?

I welcomed him into my examining room for our bi-monthly session. Naturally he declined my offer of prot's leftover fruit. "Didn't wash your hands before you came up?"

Linus, who is not especially handsome in any case, screwed up his face. "No. I just don't like fruit."

"Otherwise it doesn't bother you to eat it?"

"Not particularly."

"You're a scientist," I reminded him. "Let's do an experiment."

He looked horrified. "I—I can't."

"What do you think would happen if you ate it?"

He squeaked, "I have to go wash my hands!"

"Try a bite of mango first. I assure you it's clean. Prot said so."

He stopped wringing his hands. "He said that?" I thought for a moment I was going to witness one of prot's wondrous cures. Obviously struggling to make a decision, Linus stared intensely at the fruit. But suddenly he backed away from it as if it were a gun. "Please!" he begged. "Let me go wash my hands first!" He hurried away to scrub off any contamination he may have encountered by being in the same room with me and an overripe mango. I didn't try to stop him. In fact, it occurred to me, as it has to every other member of the staff, to turn him over to prot and see what *he* could do with him.

OVER my wife's protestations I drove to the hospital early on Saturday morning. She thought we should go looking for a retirement home.

"I'm not retired yet!" I pointed out.

"It's just a matter of time!" she parried.

"We'll talk about that after prot leaves. Until then, I don't want to think about it."

She accepted that, I guess. After all, December 31 wasn't very far off.

On weekdays I usually take the train and come in the back way, but, since I had driven down, I parked in the garage around the corner and entered through the front gate. To my surprise, and no little annoyance, I found that the half-dozen or so people gathered around it had become a crowd of forty or fifty. I tried to slip through, but someone recognized me and demanded that I "let prot go."

"He can go any time he wants," I calmly reminded him.

"Then why are there guards at the gate?"

"We have some dangerous individuals here. I don't think you'd want to see them on the streets."

A few of the patients were milling about the grounds. "They don't look very dangerous," someone else observed.

"Not them. But there are others . . ."

"Is prot dangerous?"

"Not a bit."

"Then why don't you let him go?"

"I told you—he can go any time he wants! In fact, he's leaving on New Year's Eve!" While the crowd digested this news I sidled past the guard and hurried up the walk

556

to the front door of the hospital wondering why Giselle hadn't taken care of this nagging problem, and noting as I did so that time had stopped again for the crew working on the new wing. It occurred to me that Albert's problem might be solved by putting him in charge of the building committee.

As soon as I got inside I called Giselle's apartment. Her mother told me she wasn't home, adding, "I hope you can find Rob soon. We all miss him."

I called the nurses' station on Ward Two and she wasn't there, either. Still annoyed, I rounded up all the original notes in prot's file and began to go over them, looking hard for clues and inconsistencies. There *had* to be something I had overlooked before and was overlooking now. The only things I came up with were some questions about Rob's dog, Apple, who was run over and killed when Robin was nine, and the recollection that his Uncle Dave and Aunt Catherine died in a fire soon afterward. Were these two events related in some way?

Frustrated and disappointed, I decided to have lunch in Ward Three, the home of the sexual and social deviates and certain other unfortunates. As always, I was amazed how eating seems to counteract the symptoms of most mental illnesses, if only temporarily. In fact, during that brief period it was difficult to tell the autists from the coprophilics, and I wondered whether some use could be made of this observation: i.e., whether pleasurable sensations of one sort might be useful in the treatment of problems of a different sort. Would stimulating certain areas of the brain, for example, be a way of alleviating the intensity of other, less desirable, sensations? Would marijuana or cocaine overcome the unpleasantness of OCD or bipolar disorder? This reminded me of the early attempts to cure syphilis by infecting patients with malaria. The comparison seemed apt. Psychiatry is at about the same stage now as internal medicine was a century ago.

I sat across from Jerry and Lenny, two of our autistic patients, remembering the day more than two years earlier when prot had awakened Jerry from his "dream" world long enough for the latter to communicate certain thoughts and feelings he had long bottled up inside. How had prot done that? Unfortunately, this was another conundrum that would probably have to wait for future generations to solve.

As for the present, I could almost feel a certain amount of tension around the table, which was considerably quieter than usual, hardly any spitting or wailing at all. But it wasn't until everyone had finished eating (except for those who sculpt their food into birds or squish it into a homogeneous mess before starting) that one of the incurable voyeurs, sitting at the other end of the table, politely asked if prot could come to lunch next time. Total silence descended immediately, like a black curtain. Jerry and Lenny weren't exactly looking at me, but they weren't ogling the walls and ceilings, either. What could I say? I told my luncheon companions I would extend the invitation right away. The room broke into spontaneous happy laughter that went on and on. It was quite infectious. Everyone looked at everyone else and laughed even harder. I don't remember when I'd had such a good time, though I'm still not sure what we were laughing about.

THAT afternoon I listened to tapes of some of my early conversations with prot (and, less frequently, with Robert), marveling yet again at his ultraconfidence in the truth of his bizarre confabulation. A world of his own creation that was unbelievably perfect, so carefully thought out as to be seamless and, yes, almost convincing. If we could all focus our attention to such a degree on any worthwhile project, he had often reminded me, who knows what we might accomplish.

I think I dozed off for a minute and was awakened by the phone. It was Giselle "reporting in." "You looking for me, Dr. B?"

"Huh? Oh yes. Those people hanging around the front gate—have you spoken to them yet?"

"Yes, I have. They won't leave until they see prot."

"Can't you get rid of them?"

"Not until he makes an appearance."

"This is turning into a circus."

"Maybe Milton could put on his clown suit and warm them up with his juggling act."

"Get serious, Giselle. If word gets out, the media will have a field day with this."

"You worry too much, boss. Let me take care of it for you. That's why I'm here, remember?"

"Make it soon."

After some shuffling and filing I listened to a few more tapes, and it wasn't until late afternoon that I grabbed up all the ones I hadn't yet heard and headed for the parking lot. The crowd was still out front and was, if anything, larger. This problem, like all those connected with prot's "visit," just wasn't going to go away. I turned around and left by the back door.

Karen and I had tickets to the Met's lavish presentation of *Turandot* for that Saturday evening, and I looked forward to a night of relaxation and enjoyment. But this particular opera is about riddles and answers, and my thoughts came right back to prot and the unanswered questions: Why had Robert withdrawn so abruptly, how could we get him back, and what would happen to him when prot made his year-end "departure," this time for good? With the New Year looming like a guillotine, there was more urgency than ever to get to the bottom of things. But a personal note had also crept into my thinking. If I could solve this puzzle, the case of Robert/prot would be an accomplishment worthy of ending a career. If not, I would be quitting a loser.

I was encouraged, though, by a tremendous round of cheers and applause, and I took a bow, not quite knowing why. The next thing I knew Karen was elbowing me, whispering that the opera was over. "If you were going to doze through the whole thing," she added, "we could have stayed home and watched a movie on TV. You could have slept better there."

Session Thirty-six

MONDAY was one of those days when, for some reason, I felt discombobulated, as if I were on the outside looking in. I wasn't pleased with what I saw.

There was something about prot, something all-consuming, that made everything else seem unimportant by comparison. All of my "free" time seemed to go into his (Robert's) case. When I wasn't studying my notes or listening to the tapes, I was thinking about them.

Some of the other staff members were beginning to slide down this slippery slope as well. During the regular Monday meeting most of them were astonished by the revelation that prot seemed able to remember being born, and even lying in the womb. Some, especially Thorstein, saw this as a golden opportunity, suggesting I spend several more sessions pinning down the earliest moment prot could recall.

Our newest young psychiatrist, Laura Chang, agreed. She herself wanted to "pick his brain," after hours if necessary, pointing out that perhaps the root of many mental difficulties lay in the very earliest moments of our experience. It is her view, in fact, that certain formative patterns might be initiated in the late-stage embryo, who must be quite mystified indeed by all the harsh sounds he hears, the strange smells and tastes he may be aware of, assuming, of course, that he is conscious (her hypothesis) at times. I could understand their motives, having stated in the past that much could be learned from prot's apparent depth of knowledge about many esoteric subjects, whatever its nature. I reminded everyone yet again that our responsibility was to Robert, not to prot, and that this should be the basis for any protocol.

The meeting ended with a discussion of the upcoming outing, for those patients who wanted, and were able, to visit the Metropolitan Museum of Art, and notice of a long-overdue visit by the popular psychologist known to the public as "America's TV shrink," who had abruptly cancelled a similar trip two years earlier for personal reasons.

Afterward, I invited Goldfarb for coffee in the doctors' dining room, intending to speak with her about the crowd of people hanging around the gate. But she had her own agenda, high on the list of which was an attempt to schedule formal interviews between prot and some of her patients. I peered into those thick glasses, behind which her eyes looked like pinpoints, and tried to change the subject back to the circus going on out front. But she had no interest in dealing with it unless there were some disturbance or other. I pointed out that they were her responsibility. She accepted this and went over to refill her cup. I have never known anyone who could drink hot coffee as fast as Goldfarb.

The other reason I had wanted to speak with her was

to talk her into allowing me temporary leave from some of my duties, particularly those of an optional or peripheral nature, such as the various hospital and university committees I served on and, especially, chairing the one overseeing the completion, if ever, of the new wing. I even tried to foist off a few of my most difficult patients (Frankie and Linus) on her or another colleague, and blatantly inquired about the possibility of someone taking over my lecture course. Hoping this would be the coup d'état, I added, "I'm thinking of retiring next summer."

Goldfarb broke into a nasal giggle. She drained her steaming cup, got up and strode out, still chuckling. As she left I heard her whinny, "You'll never retire!"

O N my way out to give my afternoon lecture at Columbia, I ran into Giselle. "Isn't it great?" she chirped.

"Huh? What do you mean?"

"Like they said, all they wanted was to talk to prot."

"Who? Oh, you mean the people—Well, is he going to—"

"He already did."

"What? He talked to them?"

"Yesterday."

"I see. And what did he tell them?"

"He said he didn't have room for them all on this trip."

"You mean they all want to go with him?"

"Not all. But some of them did."

"What was their reaction to being left behind?"

"They asked him to come back for them!"

"And is he going to do that?"

"Nope."

"Why not?"

"He's already said he's never coming back, remember?"

"What did they think about that?"

"Not much until he told them someone else might do it." She waited, her brown eyes twinkling like a cat that had just finished a canary.

"Well, when is the next K-PAXian due to come for them?"

"He couldn't say. In fact, he couldn't guarantee that anyone from K-PAX would ever visit the Earth again."

"Didn't this make things worse?"

"Not when he told them we already have K-PAX here. He says the Earth could be just like K-PAX if we wanted it badly enough. Nobody said anything for a while, until a twelve- or thirteen-year-old boy asked him, 'How do we do that?'" She paused again in her mischievous way.

Milton slouched by, grumbling, "Hemorrhoids are a pain in the ass. . . ."

I asked her impatiently, "Okay, I'm curious. What was the answer?"

"He said, 'That's up to you.'"

"That's what I figured he'd say."

"And then he went back in."

"So why are they still here?"

"They're not. But it doesn't make any difference."

"Why not?"

"Because they were soon replaced by another group. *They* wanted to speak with prot, too."

"God, is there no end to this?"

"These people aren't crazy, Dr. B. You should go out and talk to them some time. There are plumbers, house-wives, accountants, factory workers and—well, you name it. I'd write an article about them if there were time."

"Why isn't there time?"

"If prot takes Rob with him, I expect to go, too."

"To K-PAX."

"That's right."

"Don't you know for sure?"

She looked as if she'd been shot. "Not exactly. I guess I'd better ask him about that."

"What if prot doesn't find Rob? Then you'll stay behind with *him*, correct?"

"He'll find him!"

"One more thing: Don't let him talk to anybody from the media. We've got enough trouble without that."

"Easier said than done!"

THE afternoon lecture went surprisingly well. When I told the students that a colleague in Germany was prepared to receive prot at 9:15 in the morning, "Oliver Sacks" volunteered to organize a "surveillance committee" to man every entrance to the hospital and monitor prot's possible comings and goings.

Another can of worms. Inasmuch as there was nothing to lose, however, I agreed. "But be discreet. I don't want anyone hanging around before nine or after ten o'clock. And you have to stay outside the wards. Fair enough?"

This seemed to satisfy everyone concerned, and I went on with the lecture, which, as I suspected, was one of the most muddled I ever presented. Nonetheless, the students gave me their rapt attention and, except for the scratching of pens on paper, were supremely attentive. Or perhaps they were merely mulling over prot's possible origins, as was I.

In fact, it was sometime during the presentation that a chilling thought popped into my head: *How did prot's boyhood on K-PAX compare with his alter ego's tragic life here on Earth?*

★   ★   ★

I came prepared for my next session with prot, having listened by then to all of the tapes of our earlier meetings, re-read his "report," and watched the video of his television appearance. There was no way I was going to allow him to sidetrack the interview with his superior memory and quibbling about small details. In fact, I decided to emphasize the seriousness of the hour by forgoing the fruit.

"That's the main reason I'm here!" he wailed. He sat facing me glumly, his Cheshire-cat grin only a memory. It occurred to me that maybe he was putting me on.

I started the tape recorder. "Did you find Rob?"

"Checked every closet and behind every tree. He's nowhere to be found. Maybe he went back to Guelph."

"How would he get out without anyone noticing him?"

"Maybe he never came in."

I nodded pleasantly. "Prot, I have a colleague in Germany who wants to see you for a moment." I handed him a slip of paper. "Here's the address."

Prot studied the information. "I'll try to squeeze it in."

"No—you don't understand. He wants to see you *now*. At 9:15 this morning."

"Your sense of humour still needs work gino. I've already performed this stunt for you. Even if I did it again you'd never believe it. You'd think it was some kind of trick."

"No I wouldn't! This would be the proof we need that you're really who you say you are!"

"How many times do I have to prove it?"

"Just this once."

"Sorry. No can do."

"Why the hell not?"

566

"I told you already. Besides, what if Robert shows up while I'm gone?"

"But Dr. Ehrhart is waiting!"

"Has he nothing else to do?"

"He has plenty to do!"

"So do I!"

"So you refuse to cooperate."

"I'm here, ain't I?"

Even though I knew he couldn't zip off to Germany or anywhere else, I had rarely been angrier in a session with a patient of mine. "Prot," I screeched, "why don't you just admit it? You can't do it, can you?"

"Of course I can."

"You're not from K-PAX, are you? You're a fake and a phony! Everyone knows it!"

"Surely not everyone."

"It's because of the fruit, isn't it?"

"Nope. We're not a petty, vindictive species like some others I could name."

"A lot of people are going to be disappointed."

"Won't be the last time."

I stared at him for a while to emphasize my displeasure. "Dr. Ehrhart claims that other 'K-PAXians' are popping up around the world."

"Could be. Or maybe they're lunatics."

Grabbing a yellow pad, I said, rather petulantly, I'm sure, "All right, damn it, tell me more about your phony boyhood."

"You never get enough, do you, doc?"

"I may make an exception in your case."

"No you won't. You're bound and determined to pry every little secret from everyone here."

"That's what psychiatrists are for."

"That so? I thought they were for making piles of money to 'feed their families,' like every other sapiens in this godforsaken place" (he meant the Earth).

Recalling that Robert's family had been exceptionally poor, I asked him, "You don't like the capitalist system very much, do you, prot?"

"Frankly, my dear, it sucks."

"What's wrong with it? It's worked pretty well throughout our history."

"Then why do you have so many problems?"

"Look. If there were no trading or bartering, no legal tender, everyone would have to grow his own food, make his own clothes, produce his own transportation, and all the rest. A terrible waste of time and energy, wouldn't you say?"

"At last I understand what's wrong with you—you're all nuts!"

"No need for insults, prot, or whoever you are."

"Merely an observation, my thin-skinned friend. None of you seems to have the ability to see a bigger picture, to figure out the consequences of your actions, or even to look at a problem rationally. You're a bunch of wild-eyed schizophrenics!"

"What problem?" I calmly asked him.

"And on top of that, you can't follow a conversation. Look. You've given me the pros of the money system. Have you given any thought to the cons?"

"I suppose you're talking about the way some people abuse it."

"That's a start."

"Well, I suppose it must seem unfair to the disadvantaged."

"Keep going. . . ."

"I don't know what you're getting at."

"Do you ever listen to the evening news? Read a newspaper?"

"Sometimes."

"What's the result of all that brainwashing?"

"Brainwashing?"

He tapped his fingers together and looked up at the ceiling.

"What's the result of all the focus on the 'economy,' on 'jobs,' on 'growth,' on—"

"But everyone benefits when—"

"Really, gene? Do *all* your beings benefit? Do the elephants and tigers benefit? Does your PLANET benefit?"

"You're repeating yourself. That's exactly what you said on TV two years ago."

"And you didn't hear it then, either!"

"But everyone is already aware of the environment. We all know about global warming. Scientists in every country are studying the problem—"

Prot guffawed. "When are you humans going to stop 'studying' your problems and start *doing* something about them?"

"We *are* doing something about this one! We're trying to reduce greenhouse gases to 1990 levels, for example."

"Har har har—you people kill me! It's 1990 levels that are causing the problem!"

"You don't understand. We have to balance one benefit against another. We have to compro—"

"Compromising on your environment is like removing half a tumor."

"It's not that simple, prot. Jobs are at stake. Lives are at stake."

"Exactly."

"What's that supposed to mean?"

"You're trapped in a quagmire of money and you can't seem to find a way out of it. In the meantime, your PLANET is dying. And the really nutty thing about it is that you hardly even notice. Catastrophe is right around the corner, and when you get there you'll all wring your hands and pretend you didn't see it coming."

"And how much time do you figure we have left, exactly?"

"Twenty-three years," he said matter-of-factly.

"You mean our species has only twenty-three years left on Earth?"

"Did I say that, doc? I mean that if the necessary changes aren't made by that time, certain events will be set in motion and then there will be no stopping the slide."

"And how did you arrive at that figure?"

"I didn't. It was worked out by another K-PAXian."

"Based on what?"

"She used the data from my report. It's simple. You can do it yourself. All you need is a primitive computer . . . ."

"If it's so simple, why didn't *you* work it out?"

"Same reason you didn't—I don't give a damn what happens to your murderous, self-centered species. What saddens me is that you're taking all the other beings with you."

"I give a damn!"

"Then why haven't you worked it out?"

"Look, prot, maybe you're right," I said to mollify him. "But it's time to get on with our session, okay?"

"Sure," he shrugged. "Why not? It's not my problem, anyway."

"Because you'll be leaving us soon."

"Righto."

570

"Back to K-PAX, where there *are* no problems."

"Exactly."

"Tell me more about your boyhood there. Were you poor?"

"No one is 'poor' on K-PAX! Or rich, either. It's a meaningless concept."

"Tell me what your early childhood was like."

He stared at the empty fruit bowl. Finally he said, "Okay—how early is early?"

"Oh, up to the age of six, say."

"*Your* years, of course."

"Or the K-PAXian equivalent."

"To tell you everything would take me about six years, wouldn't it? You got that much time, gino?"

"Dammit, prot, just give me the highlights."

"The whole thing was a highlight. Wasn't yours?"

I sighed. "All right. Let's say you're five. In Earth terms, of course. It's your fifth birthday today. Is there a party for you? A birthday cake?"

"None of the above."

"Why not?"

"We don't have cakes on K-PAX. Or parties. Or birthdays."

"No birthdays?"

"Our annual cycles vary a bit depending on—well, I don't suppose you want to go into the ASTRONOMICAL details."

"Not just now."

"I didn't think so. In any case, nobody cares when someone was born or how old he is. It's completely irrelevant."

"What about friends? Are they irrelevant, too?"

"You need to re-read your own books. Everyone on

571

K-PAX is a 'friend.' We don't have 'enemies.' We just don't need them, as you seem to."

"Naturally. Pets?"

"Certainly not."

"Toys? Games?"

"Not the kind you mean."

"What kind is that?"

"We don't have 'monopoly' to teach us the value of making money. Or toy soldiers to teach us the importance of the military. Or dolls to teach us the joys of parenthood. None of that crap." He thought a moment. "Besides, all of life is a game. On K-PAX life is fun. Right from the start."

"Nary a problem, is that right?"

"Only little ones, but even those are fun."

"What sorts of little fun problems did you have to deal with?"

"Oh, you know—scrapes and bruises, an occasional stomach ache, that sort of thing."

"Those don't sound like much fun to me."

"It's a part of life, don'tcha know."

"Ever get into a fight with one of your 'friends'?"

"No one fights on K-PAX."

"So how do you get the scrapes and bruises? Does someone punish you for behaving badly?"

"No one behaves badly. What's the point? And if we did, there would be no punishment."

"But someone gave you the bruises, didn't they?"

"Didn't you ever fall out of a tree, my human friend?"

"Once or twice. You never had an abusive uncle, anything like that?"

"Where do you get this 'uncle' shit? I told you—I don't know from 'uncle'!"

572

"All right. Anyone else bother you when you were a small boy? A passerby, perhaps?"

"Of course not!"

"Okay—what sorts of things did you do when you were little?"

"I watched the korms [birds], ran with the aps [small, elephant-like creatures]. I learned the names of the fruits and grains, studied the stars, traveled around, spent some time in the libraries, ate, slept—you know: I did whatever needed to be done and, after that, whatever I felt like doing."

"Did you have a bicycle? Roller skates?"

"Nah. Who needs those things?"

"You just walked wherever you wanted to go?"

"It's a good way to get around, and you see more than you do going by light."

"What about that? I mean, when did you first experience light travel?"

"Right away. Of course I rode along with someone else until I figured out how to do it."

"When you were five?"

"Long before that."

"Who did you ride with?"

"Whoever was around."

"Of course. And who were you staying with when you were five years old?"

He slapped his forehead. "No one 'stays' with anyone on K-PAX. We like to move around."

"Why is that?"

"K-PAX is a big place. There's a lot to see." (Unlike tiny Guelph, Montana.)

"Did anyone you knew die when you were six?"

That shot flew over his head, apparently. "Probably an

573

ancient fart or two. Hardly anyone ever dies on K-PAX."

"So you've told me. All right, prot. Our time is up for today. You can go now. I'll see you on Friday."

He jumped up and jogged to the door. "Don't take any wooden nickels!" he shouted on his way out.

I assumed he was putting me on again.

GEORGE must have thought the "light-travel" experiment had been a great joke. When I returned to my inner office I found a fax from him with a picture of a very old horse, ribs showing, head hanging down. An arrow identified the bony critter as "prot." I thought about calling him to explain the situation, but just then Giselle showed up. She seemed in much better spirits than she had for some time. When I mentioned this obvious change, she exclaimed that if prot found Rob and took him to K-PAX, she would definitely get to go along, too!

"He told you that?"

"Yep!"

"My godson going, too?"

"Yep!"

"Then I guess you'd better help him find Rob, right?"

The smile vanished. "How can I do that?"

I asked her to start by filling in any missing details she might have about Rob's background, things she might have learned in her two years of sitting at the breakfast table with him, watching movies, making plans over a glass of wine, and all the other occasions which contribute to a happy and intimate relationship. Unfortunately, she didn't know much more about him than I did. They rarely discussed his childhood—it was painful for him (and for her as well)—or his previous marriage (for the same reasons). However, she did tell me a couple of surprising things about his likes and dislikes. For example, although he was interested in most scientific subjects, including field biology, the focus of his academic studies, he actually disliked astronomy. He wouldn't even watch reruns of the old *Star Trek* series or the myriad spin-offs. Another peculiar characteristic was his abhorrence of bathtubs. He took showers exclusively, and wouldn't even enter the bathroom when she was in the tub.

I thought: Did something happen while little Robin was taking a bath? "Anything else you can think of?"

"Nothing out of the ordinary."

"Any religious beliefs?"

"Rob isn't an atheist, but he's not very religious, either. More of an agnostic, I suppose."

"Did he ever tell you about his toy soldiers, discuss the war in Vietnam, anything like that?"

"He has toy soldiers?"

"When he was a boy he did."

"So did my brothers and everybody else I know."

"Did he ever rail about being poor when he was growing up, or profess any negative feelings about the free-enterprise system? Or what it might be doing to the environment?"

"He's a biologist, Dr. B. Of course he talks about the degradation of the environment. But he has never showed any communist leanings, anything like that, if that's what you mean."

"Does he think the Earth is going to hell in a hand-bag?"

"No more than anyone else. Why? Did prot tell you Rob had radical ideas on all these things?"

"Not exactly. I'm still trying to get a handle on Rob's problems. Do me a favor, Giselle. Will you think about this some more, and when we meet again could you give me a report on anything unusual that might come to mind about Rob's behavior the past couple of years? And make me a complete list of his likes and dislikes, particularly any strong ones. Will you do that?"

She blinked those big, doelike eyes. "Sure, if you think it will help."

I chose not to divulge my misgivings about that.

AS I was passing through the lounge I encountered Frankie sitting in her customary place on the wide windowsill staring at the lawn. I asked her why she didn't get her coat on and go outside for a walk. She replied, characteristically, "It's shitty out there."

"Frankie, it's a beautiful day!"

"Beauty is in the eye of the beholder," she scowled. "Or so they say. I wouldn't know—I've never encountered it."

"Don't you think the sunshine is beautiful? The green grass, especially in late November? The leaves blowing in the wind?"

"What's so beautiful about death and decay?" She stared at my left cheek. "That's the ugliest mole I've ever seen."

"Isn't there *anything* you think is beautiful?"

"K-PAX sounds pretty damn good."

"Nothing good about the Earth? How about the mountains? The seashore? Music? You like opera?"

"Can't stand it."

"Why?"

"They're all just fucking glorified soaps. Make me want to puke," she added before waddling off and nearly running into Alice, who was in her "giant" phase, clomping through the lounge with enormous, loud steps. She shrugged Frankie off as if she were a mosquito.

It was times like these that I wished I had gone into some other line of work. Frankie always left me depressed. She holds all of us responsible for the death of her mother, who was given the wrong medication when she was in a hospital for some minor ailment. It was a famous case back then, and I remember reading about it myself. But accidents happen, even to the best of us, and Frankie might have come to realize that, had her father not killed himself a year later, followed by an older sister. (Ironically, the nurse responsible for the mix-up married Frankie's lawyer and became a wealthy and well-respected woman.) Though Frankie herself shows no tendency toward suicide, she remains hopelessly embittered toward everyone and everything. Of all the patients here she seemed the least likely to get any help from prot—he had a difficult time with human relations himself.

I heard a commotion behind me. "Dr. Brewer! Dr. Brewer!"

Wondering what crisis was breaking this time, I turned to find Milton running toward me. "Uncle Miltie" wasn't wearing his usual funny hat, nor was his shirttail sticking out through his fly. In fact he looked like a different person altogether. It suddenly occurred to me that maybe this was the "real" Milton.

"Dr. Brewer!" he panted as he slid to a stop in front of me. "Let me out! Prot says I'm cured!"

"Well, Milton, I'd prefer you let the rest of us be the judge of that."

"No—you don't understand. I *am* cured."

"I know you believe that, and maybe it's true. Would you like to schedule an appointment so we can talk about it?"

"No need!"

577

"Really? Convince me. What makes you think you're well enough to leave us?"

"Prot says so."

I studied him for a minute. Gone were any obvious signs of psychosis. He was steady, clear-eyed, not going for laughs. This was a man who had lost his entire family in the holocaust. Not through some stupid mistake, as in Frankie's case, but as a result of one of the blackest periods in human history. Yet all the profound sadness underlying his jokes and clowning was no longer clouding his eyes. "Tell me—what happened to you today?"

"I spoke with prot. He had the answer to all my problems."

"What is that?"

"Forget our history."

"Forget the holocaust??"

"Forget everything! We don't have to live in the past, regretting everything we've done or that anyone else has done. We don't have to look for retribution, to continue the cycle over and over. We don't even have to forgive anyone. We can start all over, as if the events of the past never happened. This can be day one! It is for me!"

"Does this make sense to you, Milton?"

"Perfect sense, Dr. Brewer."

"And you think your memories won't come back?"

"Of course they won't. There *is* no past! This is the beginning of time!"

"I'd like to talk to you about this some more, but I want to speak with prot first. That okay with you?"

"Whatever you say. Should I plan to move down to Ward One?"

"That's up to Dr. Goldfarb and the assignment committee, but I think there's a good chance of that if you continue to improve."

"I guarantee it. You'd be surprised what a burden the past can be!"

"*That* I won't argue with!"

WHEN I got back to my office our esteemed director was there, pacing back and forth, smoking a cigarette. Goldfarb stopped smoking ten years ago.

"What's wrong?" I asked her.

"You remember the visit we had from the CIA after prot's TV appearance two years ago?"

"How could I forget? They reminded me of Laurel and Hardy."

"Well, they're back."

"What did they want?"

"They wanted to know why we hadn't told them prot had returned. They wanted to talk to him."

"What did you tell them?"

"I asked them if they had a search warrant." Like my daughter Abby, Goldfarb is among the last of the liberals.

"Did they have one?"

"No. But they did have a request signed by the President."

"You mean *the* President?"

"The."

"How did they know prot was here?"

"Everyone seems to know that."

"So did you give them the go-ahead?"

"No. I said I had to speak to his doctor first."

"What do they want to talk to him about?"

"They want to know how he's able to travel at light speed. For security reasons, they tell me."

579

"I'm tempted to deny their request."

"Are you prepared to deny one from the President of the United States?"

"Maybe."

"Good! To tell you the truth, I didn't think you had it in you."

"But I think the decision should be up to prot."

She tamped out the cigarette on her watch crystal (an old habit) and dropped the butt into a jacket pocket. "That's only the beginning."

"What do you mean?"

"They want to be here when he leaves."

"What for?"

"Same thing. They want to set up cameras and all sorts of other equipment to record the event."

"How they going to get all that into his little room?"

"They've already thought of that. They want him to use the lounge."

"Of course you said no to that."

She examined her shoetops, which were suede and matched her green wool skirt. "Not exactly."

"What do you mean?"

"I offered them a compromise. I said only if we let the press in to cover it, too."

"What? You want to—"

"There's a difference between meddling in a patient's affairs and simply observing him. If they keep out of the way and don't try to interfere with whatever happens . . ."

"That's a pretty fine distinction."

"Look. The new wing is running a million and a half over estimates. We're going to need all the publicity we can get to generate the funds necessary to complete the goddamn thing."

580

I started to laugh.

"Something's funny?"

"I was just thinking: prot's going to love ending his visit with another fundraising appearance."

After she left I realized I had forgotten to tell her about Milton.

Session Thirty-seven

W HEN I entered prot's room on Wednesday morning, escorted by a couple of felines, he exclaimed: "Look what the cats drug in!" Several other inmates were in attendance.

I wasn't amused. "Prot, I need to talk to you."

"Anything you say, doc." A tiny nod and all the other patients trailed out, but not without a little muttering and nasty stares, even from the cats.

I sat down in his chair. "What did you tell Milton?"

"You mean about treating his life as a bad joke?"

"Yes."

"I told him to forget your history. It's nothing but a bloody mess, a catalog of false starts and wrong turns, doomed from the beginning."

"He should forget *all* of our history?"

"*Every* human being should forget it."

I wondered whether he was joking again. "Look, prot.

I appreciate your attempts to help the patients. We all do. But I don't think you should try to treat them without discussing it with their doctors first."

"Why?"

"Because mental illness is a very complex matter—"

"Not really."

"Prot, I know you've helped others in the past. But a wild suggestion like that could backfire if—"

"It worked, didn't it?"

"And in the second place, how can we forget our history? Someone has said that if we forget history, we are doomed to repeat it."

"You repeat it anyway! You have a war, then another war, then another and another. You never learn a thing from them, except how to kill more beings more efficiently. Your history serves mainly to remind you who to hate. But your petty wars and other peccadilloes are a small matter compared to your determination to destroy your own WORLD. Basically you got off on the wrong feet in the beginning. Everything you've tried—feudalism, communism, capitalism, nationalism, sexism, racism, speciesism—has failed. The only way to get out of a vortex like that is to start all over again."

I reminded myself never to argue with a crazy person. "Thanks. I'll pass that on. The other thing I wanted to talk to you about involves a couple of visitors we had - yesterday."

"You mean the g-men."

"You know about them?"

"Everybody knows about them."

"So you know they want to speak to you."

"They want me to go to germany, too?"

"No, I think the TV demonstration convinced them

you can travel on a beam of light. But they want to know exactly how you do it."

"It's done with—"

"Mirrors. Yes, I know. Would it be all right with you if Giselle schedules a meeting between you and them?"

"If she wants."

I stood up. "When will she be coming in?"

"Any time now."

"She tells me she's going to K-PAX with you. Is that true?"

"If rob goes, she wants to go, too."

"And if he doesn't want to go? Or you can't find him?"

"I imagine she'll want to stay here with him. Odd, isn't it?"

"What's odd about it?"

"Your beings would rather live on a doomed PLANET than go to paradise and leave someone you love behind. It's a most interesting phenomenon."

"In any case, do you think you should get her hopes up like that?"

"I merely answered her questions. The hope is her own idea."

"But you *might* include her on your list."

"Many of the sapiens I've talked to would go if they had the chance. And almost *all* the other beings. You've made life on EARTH miserable for them, you know. It's turning out to be more difficult than I thought to narrow the list down to a hundred."

"Before you make a final decision, the residents of Ward Three want to speak with you as well. Will you come for lunch today?"

"Will there be fruit?"

584

"I guess that can be arranged."

"I'll be there!"

I needed coffee. In the doctors' dining room I found Laura Chang reading a journal and sipping a cup of tea. She had been with us only a couple of months and, as yet, I didn't know her very well, except that she came with a fine academic record and excellent recommendations. About all I knew for sure was that she had been a championship ice skater in her youth but had sustained an unfortunate injury that shortened her career and precluded a trip to the 1988 winter Olympics. As a result of this and the subsequent depression she became interested in medicine and then psychiatry.

I asked her how she was getting along with her patients, whether she had any unanswered questions about the hospital, or any problems with the staff or facilities.

"That pounding and drilling in the new wing is driving me crazy!" she replied without looking up from her article (on the relationship between autism and oxygen deprivation in the fetus).

"Well, it'll all be finished in another twenty or thirty years."

Chang was not amused. "It's like going to the dentist every day!"

I went for a cup of "rainforest blend." On the other side of the room I could hear Thorstein and Menninger discussing Cassandra. Or Thorstein, anyway. He has the kind of voice that would carry across Grand Central Station. It appeared that Cassie had withdrawn even more into her thoughts and dreams than ever. This was not unusual—all the patients have their ups and downs. What was puzzling, however, was that she seemed to be the one resident on whom prot was having a negative effect. Even prot can't win them all, I mused.

When I got back to Chang's table she was still buried in the journal. I gazed at her shiny black hair, the bright, youthful face, and for a moment I caught a glimpse of the future. Despite the astronomical expense of medical and psychiatric training, the cost-cutting outlook of the health-care providers, and all the other difficulties associated with the practice, I realized with no small degree of pleasure that the current crop of clinicians was among the best ever to come out of the various residencies. Maybe because the greater challenges aren't for the faint-hearted.

"Any other complaints?" I asked her. "Anything you want to talk about?" What I really wanted to know, of course, was whether she was having trouble with any of her patients.

She looked up from her article. "I *would* like to know more about prot."

"You mean about Robert. Prot is really only a second-ary personality."

"But if I understood you correctly at the last staff meeting, you're having a problem getting through to Robert. What have you tried?"

Good God, I thought. She wants to help *me*. I didn't know whether to be flattered or insulted. But what the hell—maybe she could spot something I'd missed. I gave her a short summary of prot's first and second "visits," and a brief review of what had been accomplished, if anything, during our four sessions since his reappearance two weeks earlier.

"The whistle didn't bring him out this time?"

"Not as far as I could tell. He's withdrawn even deeper into his shell than he was when I first saw him seven years ago."

"But it worked before?"

"Yes."

"With hypnosis or without?"

"Without. It was a post-hypnotic suggestion."

"Ever try it when the patient was under hypnosis?"

My chin dropped. Then I burned the roof of my mouth. What a fool I was! It had been so easy to bring Rob forward in 1995 that I assumed hypnosis wouldn't be necessary this time around.

Without another word she returned to her journal. But her eyes were even brighter than before, and I'm almost sure there was a hint of a smile on her face.

THE Thursday lecture was another disaster. When I reported that prot wouldn't cooperate in the light-travel experiment, there was a collective roar. A discussion broke out (as if I weren't even there) about whether this proved prot was only human after all. When I finally gained control and began to talk about eating disorders, there was a constant shifting in seats, shuffling of papers, coughing and hacking, and the inevitable, "Are we going to be responsible for this on the final exam?"

I was tired and went through the material as fast as possible. And, as before, I was preoccupied by thoughts of prot and all the unwanted complications his presence at the hospital always brought, though I had been informed that his joining the residents of Three for lunch the day before had had a considerable salutary effect. And there was definitely a change in Milton. Not only was he no longer telling endless jokes and juggling vegetables and riding around the lounge on his unicycle, he couldn't seem to do those things anymore, couldn't even *remember* any jokes. In the not inexpert opinion of Betty McAllister and some of the other nurses, he was as sane as they were, and should be transferred to Ward One, if not discharged immediately.

But what about Cassandra? Why had she become more withdrawn than she was on her arrival, and what did this have to do with prot? Of course my thoughts were focused primarily on Robert. I *had* to find him again, perhaps while his "alien" friend was under hypnosis. Failing that, I planned to go at him with what might have happened to him as a baby, jolt him into consciousness one way or another. I only hoped the shock wouldn't be just another short circuit.

ONCE again I withheld the bowl of fruit. I wanted prot to feel edgy, uncertain. He came into my examining room, glanced around, shrugged, and took his seat. "How are you today?" I asked him perfunctorily.

"Peachy keen," he replied, rather pointedly I thought.

"Have you seen the CIA yet?"

"S?^/, sen^·or, I see the cia by the seaside."

"What did you tell them?"

"I told them it was done with mirrors."

"What else?"

"They wanted to know if I'd explained the procedure to any foreign powers."

"Well?"

"I said, 'What you mean, "foreign," white man'?"

I concealed a weak grin. "And?"

"They wanted me to sign something promising I wouldn't do that."

"Did you?"

"No."

"What'd they say?"

"They offered me some stocks and bonds."

I couldn't hold back a snort. "Anything else?"

"They asked me not to try to leave this place."

"Did you agree to that?"

"I said I would stay until December the thirty-first. Except for a few brief excursions, perhaps."

"What did they think of your making 'excursions'?"

"They said they would be watching me."

"Since you brought that up, I wonder if you would tell me something I've been wondering about: How do you get out of the hospital without anyone seeing you?"

"Can you see a photon?" he asked with an all-too-familiar grin.

"But that's what light is composed of, isn't it?"

"More or less."

"Well, can you go through doors?"

"Now, gene, you know light doesn't go through doors."

"Does that mean if we put you in a room without windows you wouldn't be able to get out?"

"Of course not. I'd just open the door and leave."

"What if the door were locked?"

He wagged his head. To him I must have appeared to be the stupidest person on Earth. "Gino, there isn't a lock on EARTH I couldn't open. But if you want to play another of your little games . . ."

"What if there were no door?"

"If there's no door, how would you get me in there?"

"Well, we could build the room around you."

"And what would keep me from leaving while the walls are going up?"

"Well, we could—" But time was passing rapidly, and there wasn't anymore to waste. "Ah, skip it. See that little dot on the wall behind me?"

He warbled, "That oooooooold black magic has me

[pause] innnnnn its spellllll. . . . Onetwothreefour—" and dropped into his customarily deep hypnotic state.

I waited a moment before saying gently, though confidently, "Rob, would you please step forward for a moment? I have something very important to discuss with you."

There was no indication he had heard me.

"Rob, I think I might know what's bothering you. What's causing you so much anguish. May I tell you about it?"

I waited for another long minute. It was like speaking to the dead. Well, I thought, what can we lose? I pulled out the whistle and blew it as loudly as I could.

There wasn't a twitch, not a flutter. But of course he might have been faking a response in 1995. As a former mentor was fond of saying, "When all else fails, try a sledgehammer."

"Rob, I think you may have been abused in some way very early in your life, maybe when you were a baby. Something that you yourself may not even be aware of, and it ties in with your later encounters with Uncle Dave and Aunt Catherine. It was something terrible and it irreversibly changed your life, but whatever happened wasn't your fault, and we can repair the damage if you'll let us. Do you understand?"

No response.

"Rob? Can we talk about this for a minute?" I waited. "All right. If you'll just indicate in some way that you hear me, you can go for now. I won't bring this up again until you're ready to talk about it—okay?"

Not a nod, not a whisper.

"All right, Rob. Please think it over until we meet again in a few days. I'll see you then."

I waited for another little while. "Prot? Are you there?"

His eyes popped open. "Hiya, doc, how you been?"

"Peachy keen," I replied glumly. "I'm going to wake you up now. Five, four, three—"

"Are we done?"

"Apparently we're back to square one. Again."

"The best place to be!"

"In that case, let's start where we left off last time. You were six, in Earth terms, and so far you've had a perfect childhood on K-PAX, with no problems whatever, except for the odd scrape or bruise, of course." Missing or ignoring the hint of sarcasm, he waited for me to proceed. "What happened after that?" I prodded him.

"After what?"

"After you were six."

"I was seven."

"Har har har. Tell me about your life as a boy of seven. For example, did you have any friends your own age?"

"Everyone on K-PAX—"

"Let me rephrase that. Did you have anyone your age to play—I mean, to interact with? Of your own species, that is."

"Not really. As you know, there aren't many children around. Not like on EARTH, where almost everyone seems to think it's his and her duty to breed and breed and choke your WORLD to death as quickly as possible."

I jotted down: Environment rantings really about procreation/sex? "Let's talk about *you* today, shall we? I remind you that if your parents hadn't conceived you, you wouldn't be here."

"If Giselle had wheels, she'd be a wagon."

"Do you think you shouldn't have been born?"

"Irrelevant, incompetent, and immaterial. I didn't get a vote in the matter."

"If you had gotten a vote, how would you have voted?"

"If Giselle had wheels, she'd be—"

"All right. Who did you associate with when you were a boy?"

"Whoever happened—"

"—to be around. Yes, of course. But could you be more specific?"

He named a few names, none of which I had heard before.

"Okay," I interrupted. "What sorts of things did you do with these—uh—beings?"

"The same as anyone does. We ate and slept and watched the stars and talked about all sorts of things."

"What sorts of things did you talk about?"

"Whatever came to mind."

At that point something came to mine. "Tell me: Who told you about the Earth?"

"No one told me. I heard your radio waves when I was in the library. Along with those of other PLANETS."

"How old were you then?"

"Oh, thirty-five or so. Three and a half in your terms."

"Are all K-PAXian kids interested in astronomy?"

"Oh, sure. K-PAXians love to talk about other PLANETS, other GALAXIES, other UNIVERSES, that sort of thing."

"When did you first come to Earth?"

"You remember. In 1963, your calendar."

"How old were you then?"

"Sixty-eight."

"Was it your first trip to another planet?"

"No. But it was my first solo flight."

"I see. Do you remember the details?"

"Every one of them."

"Would you mind filling me in on them, please?"

"Not at all." But he just sat there.

I rephrased the question.

"I got a call from someone named 'robin.' He said he needed me. So I hopped on over."

"He called you on the telephone?"

"Of course not—we don't have telephones on K-PAX."

"So how did you know he needed you?"

"I suppose I happened to be tuned to his wavelength."

"His wavelength?"

"Have you forgotten *all* your high-school physics, gino? A wavelength is the length of a wave."

"And you just went."

"Yep."

"What were you doing when the call came?"

"Eating some likas. Watching a yellow hom dig a hole."

"And where did you land when you got here?"

"In china."

"How did you get to Montana?"

"Same way I got to china."

"Light travel."

"Kee-reck."

"So you found Rob—"

"In no time at all."

"What was he doing when you got there?"

"Attending a funeral."

"What did he say when you showed up?"

"Not much. His father had just died."

"So he was pretty unhappy?"

Prot paused here. "It was the first time I had encountered sadness. It took me a little while to understand what was wrong with him."

"What did you decide it was?"

"I figured it probably had something to do with his father's demise."

"Wouldn't that make you sad?"

"I don't know who my father is."

"Of course. So you couldn't possibly be sad when he dies."

"I probably wouldn't even know about it."

"How convenient."

"Is that another of your famous non sequiturs?"

"What did Robert want from you?"

"He didn't say. I think he just wanted someone to commiserate with."

"I can understand that. But why you?"

"You'll have to ask *him*."

"He doesn't seem to want to talk to me. Will *you* ask him?"

"Sure. If I see him."

"Thank you. Now—how long were you on Earth?"

"A few days."

"Just long enough to help him over the worst of it, is that right?"

"I suppose you could put it that way. After a while, he didn't need me anymore."

"So you went back to K-PAX."

"Righto."

"Back to your wanderings and stargazing and all the rest."

"Yes, indeedy."

"And that's how you spent your childhood."

"Pretty much. An orange or a banana would taste good right now, don't you think?"

"I'll see that you get some at the end of the session."

"Thankee kindly."

"No problemo. Now—how old were you when you got to puberty?"

"A hundred and twenty-eight."

"What's that like on K-PAX?"

"About like it is here. Hair sprouts up everywhere. Stuff like that."

"Any change in your feeling about girls?"

"Why should there be?"

"When did you become interested in girls?"

"I'm interested in everything."

"I mean sexually interested."

"You're playing dumb again, aren't you, gene? No one on K-PAX is sexually interested in anyone else."

"Because the sex act is so unpleasant."

"Very."

"Tell me—if it's so unpleasant, why do any of your beings want to produce children at all?"

"Not many of them do."

"Just enough to keep your species alive?"

"'Species' don't live. Only individuals do."

"I'll rephrase that. Your species propagates only enough to maintain itself?"

"No. As a matter of fact, our species will probably disappear in a few thousand years."

"Doesn't that bother you?"

"Why should it?"

"Why *should* it? Because there wouldn't be any more dremers (K-PAXians of prot's species)!"

He shrugged. "Here today, gone mañana. A drop in the ocean of time."

"All right. Tell me this: Is sexual activity unpleasant right from the start?"

"From the very beginning."

"Did you ever get an erection when you were a boy?"

"Once in a while."

"What was it like?"

"It usually meant I had to urinate."

"You never touched your penis except to urinate?"

"No."

"Did you ever have any sexual feelings when you had an erection, good or bad?"

"Pretty bad. I got up and peed right away."

"So, in your entire—ah—four hundred years or so, you've *never* been with a woman? Or a man, for that matter? Or masturbated, not even once?"

"Nothing could be farther from my mind."

"And no one ever made an attempt to seduce you at any time in your life?"

"Only on EARTH. Unsuccessfully, of course."

"Have you ever seen anyone else do it? Of your own species, I mean."

"Do what?"

"Engage in sexual activity of any kind."

"No. It hardly ever happens on K-PAX, you know."

"You've never seen anyone kiss or touch someone of the opposite sex?"

"Of course we touch. But only in what you would call a 'platonic' way."

Something, no doubt extraneous, occurred to me. "If I remember correctly, you told me once that there is no such thing as marriage on K-PAX—is that right?"

"Yes, and may I say it's a pretty stupid idea on EARTH, too."

"Well, without love or marriage, how do you know who to produce a child *with*?"

596

"It's no big mystery. You bump into someone who, for some reason or other, feels a compulsion to add to the population of the species and—"

"How would you know if someone wants to do that?"

"He or she will tell you, of course. We don't have all these silly games you play on EARTH."

"Where do you 'bump into' members of the opposite sex? Are there bars? Things like that?"

"No bars. No restaurants. No exercise parlors. No grocery stores. No churches. No—"

"While you're traveling, then?"

"Usually. Or in the libraries. You'd be surprised how many interesting beings you can find in a library."

"And you just *do* it, without thinking much about it?"

"Oh we think about it very carefully before going ahead with it."

"You have to weigh the pros and cons."

"Exactly."

"And everyone on K-PAX knows how unpleasant sex is."

"Certainly."

"Who teaches you about that?"

"Whoever is—"

"Whoever is around. I know, I know. All right. What if someone wants to conceive a child with you and you don't want to do it?"

"Nothing."

"What about animals?"

Another little prot-like snicker. "We're all animals, gino."

"Did you ever see any other species on your planet copulate?"

"Once in a while."

"Do they seem to be in pain?"

"Absolutely. There's considerable resistance, a lot of noise and commotion."

"Do all your beings have this problem?"

"I don't consider it a problem."

"Prot, which do you hate most—money or sex?"

He wagged his head again. "You still don't get it, do you, doc? Money is a dumb idea. Sex is horrible."

I nodded, surprised to discover that our time was up.

But prot wasn't finished. "Your beings seem to be endlessly fascinated by the subject of reproduction. That's all your popular songs are about, and your movies and sitcoms, etc., etc., ad nauseum. Love, sex, love, sex, love, sex. You humans aren't easily bored, are you?"

"It's an important subject for most of us."

"Pity. Think what you could accomplish if you spent all that time and energy on something else."

"We'll take this up next session, all right?"

"Whatever you say. Don't forget to have some fruit sent over. I'll be in my room."

"Just curious—what are you going to do after you've had the fruit?"

"Thought I'd take a nap."

"Sounds exciting."

"It can be." He flipped on his dark glasses. "Cheers."

I wondered what he meant by that. As he was going out the door, I shouted, "Prot!"

He whirled and peered over the dark glasses. "Yeeeesssss?"

"Do you ever dream when you sleep?"

"Sure."

"Try to remember one for next time, will you?"

"That won't be too hard. They're always the same."

598

"Really? What are they about?"

He rolled his eyes. "*Ka raba du rasht pan domit, sord karum—*"

"In English, please."

"Okay. I see a field of grains, with trees and beautiful flowers mixed in here and there. Nearby a couple of aps are chasing each other, and in the distance a bunch of—well, something like your giraffes are munching rummud leaves. A whole flock of mountain korms are flying by, barking their exuberant calls. . . ." He opened his eyes and gazed at the ceiling. "And the sky! The sky is like one of your sunsets—pink and purple all the time. You might say it's a picture-postcard scene, except we don't have pictures. Or postcards. The air is so clear you can see some of the rills on our closest moons. But the best parts of it you don't see. You feel and smell and taste them. It's so utterly calm that you can hear for miles. The air is sweeter than honeysuckle, only not as cloying. The ground is soft and warm. You can lie down anywhere. There is food wherever you look. And you are free to go anywhere without the slightest fear. Each moment is limited only by your imagination. And it's wonderfully peaceful. There's no pressure to work or do anything you don't want to do. Every single moment is a happy time, a time without—"

"All right, prot. It sounds great. I'll send you down a basket of fruit right away. What would you like?"

"Bananas!" he replied instantly. "I haven't had any of those for a while. The riper the better!" he reminded me.

"I remember."

He smiled in anticipation as he made his way to the stairs.

After he had gone I found myself scribbling: LOVE! SEX! LOVE! SEX! on my yellow pad. In fact I made it into a little tune. I had a feeling this had been a key session, yet I couldn't put my finger on exactly why. Was his problem a question of doing something almost unspeakable (in his mind) to someone he loved? Did this involve sex in some way? To prot, sex was the worst idea in the universe, worse even than his other bugaboos—money, religion, governments, schools, and all the rest. Despite his milk and honey protests, life was so calamitous for prot and his fellow "K-PAXians" that most of them would rather become extinct than reproduce themselves. I couldn't help feeling more than a little saddened by this terrible truth: The ultimate solution to his, and perhaps everyone's, problems was death itself. I didn't much like the ring of that.

Then there was the matter of dreams, a direct pipeline to the unconscious mind. There are whole journals devoted to the dream state, as well as to the phenomenon of sleep itself, though no one seems to know what purpose either of them really fulfills. It has been hypothesized (by Sagan, among others) that sleep evolved as a way to keep prey animals out of the clutches of predators during periods of highest risk. My own view is more or less the opposite: that sleep became a way to reduce anxiety and boredom while animals were in hiding. If so, it may serve the same function in human beings. In any case, the need for sleep has been with us for millions of years, as has, perhaps, the dream state.

The analysis of dreams can be a powerful component of psychotherapy. Dreams may be a way of bringing into the conscious mind events that are normally repressed. For example, a man who fears heights might persistently dream of falling out of windows. And a woman who is concerned about the sexual advances of a co-worker might dream of being attacked by men with clubs (phallic symbols). Though subject to more than one possible interpretation, dreams can give us important insights into what is literally "on someone's mind." Sometimes they can tell us things that don't come out even under hypnosis! Though it didn't seem likely that an analysis of prot's relentlessly idyllic one would be productive, I kicked myself for not making an effort to analyze Robert's dreams when I had had the opportunity. Now there were no dreams of Robert's to analyze. There was no Robert!

I kicked myself again.

Session Thirty-eight

O<small>N</small> Saturday, while raking the final leaves of autumn, I thought about a persistent dream of my own, one so familiar that I recognize it as a dream even as it happens. It always takes place in the same surroundings, my own house, though all the rooms are empty. After searching for a very long time (I don't know what I'm searching for), I step into a room and find a man there. He is carving something with a knife. I creep closer, trying to determine what he is whittling out. Closer and closer, until I can almost see the familiar figure in his strong hands. At this point I always wake up. Whether it's because I recognize it as the end of the dream or I don't really want to find out what he's carving, I can't say.

Of course it's my father, and it's my life he's forging for me.

I have other, more pleasant dreams as well: winning the Nobel prize for medicine (in my acceptance speech I can't think of a thing to say); passionate love with my wife, which sometimes turns into the real thing; playing basketball with my children, none of whom has ever grown up.

But prot had only one beautiful dream, as befit his singularly happy life in his perfect world. Where no one had to work, food was plentiful, and life was always fun, harmonious, and interesting. Had he always had this idyllic dream, even from the beginning? While stuffing the crunchy, redolent leaves into a large plastic bag, I thought about his previous "trip" to Earth and my serendipitous discovery of Robert, without which we might never have learned anything about his actual background. Suddenly I recalled asking prot, the first time he was under hypnosis, to relate the earliest experience he could remember. He replied, without hesitation, that it was Robert's father's funeral. Now he was claiming that he could remember being born, and even before. Could this be the wedge, the key, the inconsistency in his story I had been searching for?

Karen shouted that lunch was ready. The previous evening had been her retirement dinner, and nearly everyone there got up to tell a story about her career as a psychiatric nurse in one of Connecticut's finest general hospitals. For example, a colleague reminded us of the time she had missed lunch, and he had found her eating the leftovers of some of the patients, who later complained that they hadn't finished yet.

There were gifts, too, including *What's Your Opera IQ?*, a quiz book covering everything she might possibly want to know about the subject. Of course it was a joke. Karen hates opera, and accompanies me only so I'll watch her favorite old movies with her once in a while on TV. Nevertheless, I somberly thanked everyone for the thought, and promised to test her knowledge periodically. Other, more serious, gifts included travel and cookbooks, which she browsed through in bed half the night, the new bowling ball I had given her lying between us.

Though technically she had to go back before the end of the year to pick up her last check and take care of some loose ends, this was her first day of de facto retirement, and she had spent most of the morning in the kitchen simmering a hearty soup, kneading a sourdough bread, preparing a beautiful salad, and baking an apple pie for dessert. A far cry from my usual cottage cheese and crackers.

The rest of the afternoon was spent drowsily discussing family matters, making travel plans. One question that had put a damper (in my mind) on a permanent move to the country was what to do with the house I had grown up in with Karen right next door. In my mind's eye I watched her come out to play, her teeth sparkling, her nose freckled, her hair shining in the sun. I reminded her that I didn't want to lose all those wonderful memories.

"Don't be silly," she replied. "We'll rent it to one of the kids. Why don't you speak to Fred about it?"

I mumbled something and began to doze off.

"You'd better hang up your yellow pad pretty soon," she pointed out, "before you start falling asleep at meetings!"

I didn't tell her that had already happened more than once. But at least I hadn't yet fallen asleep with a patient.

THE Monday staff meeting, usually a pretty somnolent affair itself, was rather animated this time. There was a great deal of excitement about the abrupt change in Milton, who had been with us for years and, we'd all assumed, would be here forever. Now he was waiting in Ward One for word that he would be discharged, and was eagerly anticipating

604

life beyond these walls, regardless of what it held. It was the kind of thing we hope will happen to all our patients, but which rarely does.

This success, of course, brought more pressure for me to encourage prot to talk to all the other inmates, particularly those pathetic figures who seemed like permanent fixtures, among them Linus, Albert, Alice, and Ophelia. And, of course, Frankie. Everyone in the room seemed perfectly willing to give him the credit if these patients could be given a new lease on life, as had Milton and others before him, including even a couple of former psychopaths.

And I thought: Should I encourage prot to spend more time with these unfortunate beings? Did the potential good outweigh the risks to my own patient, Robert? It was the old ethics question come to life—was it right to sacrifice one person for the benefit of two or three others? I didn't know the answer then, and I don't know it now.

But one thing I did know: He wasn't going near any of the psychopaths this time, if I could help it. I didn't want someone like Charlotte, who had killed and disfigured at least seven young men, to take advantage of his openness and generosity. Even if he had no use for his genitalia, I didn't want him to lose them at the hands of a deranged psychotic.

"ONETWOTHREE—" said prot before he fell into the familiar trance. I hadn't said a word.

"Can you hear me?"

"Of course."

"Good. Just relax. I'd like to speak to Robert for a moment." As long as prot was under hypnosis, there was nothing to lose by trying. Maybe Rob had thought about our last session, had a change of heart.

I waited for several minutes. He didn't come forward, of course, but I thought perhaps I could wear him down a little. "Rob? Did you think about what I said last time?"

No response.

"We're not going to discuss anything you don't want to talk about. I'd just like you to tell me whether you heard me at our last meeting, and whether you can hear me now. If you can hear me, please raise your left hand."

The hand didn't budge.

"Rob? We're wasting time. I know you can hear me. Now listen up. When you were here two years ago we talked about some of your problems, and we made great progress in solving them—remember?"

No response.

"When you were well enough to leave the hospital, you took a trip to your old home town, you started work on your bachelor's degree in field biology, you married Giselle and had a son. You named him Gene, after me. Okay so far?"

No response.

"I think you did that because you thought you owed me something. Well, I agree with you. You do owe me something. All I'm asking in return for everything we've accomplished together is for you to say you can hear me. That's all I'm asking. We can talk about whatever it is that's bothering you some other time. Fair enough?"

Nothing.

"Rob? I'm going to count to three. When I get to three, you're going to lift your left hand. Here we go: one . . . two . . . three!"

I looked hard at his hand, but not even a finger budged.

"All right, we're just going to sit here until you lift your hand."

We sat there, but the hand didn't move.

606

"I know you want to do it, Rob. But you're afraid of what will happen if you do. I assure you nothing will happen. This is your safe haven, remember? Nothing bad can happen to you here. Nor can you cause harm to anyone else. Do you understand? After you lift your hand you can go back and rest until next time. All right? Okay, here we go. Now—*lift your hand*!"

No response.

"Rob, I'm tired of screwing around. *LIFT YOUR GODDAMN HAND!*"

Not an iota.

"All right, Rob. I understand. You're feeling so bad that nothing matters to you. Not love, not loyalty, not your son, not anything. But consider this: I, Giselle, little Gene, your mother—did I tell you Giselle called her?—your classmates and friends, all the staff and residents at MPI, everyone you know wants to help you through this difficult period if you will only let us. Please think about that, will you? I hope you'll be feeling better the next time I see you. You may go now. Talk to you later," I added matter-of-factly. "Okay, prot. You can come back out."

He lifted his head and his eyes opened. "Hiya, doc. What's happening?"

"Not much, I'm afraid. But I hope that will change soon."

"For the better, I hope."

"So do I."

He closed his eyes. "Fivefourthree—"

"Wait!"

His eyes popped open again. "What? Am I doing it wrong?"

"No, not at all. But I'd like you to remain hypnotized for a while."

"What for?"

"Let's call it an experiment. How old are you now, by the way?"

"Three hundred—"

"In Earth terms, please."

"Thirty-nine years, ten months, seventeen days, eleven hours, thirty-two minutes, and—"

"That's close enough. Okay—now I want you to go back to when you were seventeen years old. In Earth terms, of course. You're rapidly getting younger. Robert is in high school. You visited him then. Do you remember?"

"Certainly. We talked about it earlier."

"Right. Rob's girlfriend Sarah had just become pregnant. He didn't know what to do."

The young prot shifted some imaginary gum in his mouth. "He was in deep shit, as you humans so elegantly put it."

"And you came to help him out."

He shook his head. "People—there seems to be no end to their problems!"

"All right. We've been over that before. Now I want you to go back to the time you were nine Earth years old, which is about ninety on K-PAX, right? You're becoming younger and younger. A hundred and twenty, a hundred, and now ninety. Understand?"

"Uh huh. I'm ninety."

"Right. You've just turned ninety. There aren't any birthday presents, of course. Does that bother you?"

"Why should it?"

"Okay. What are you doing right now?"

"I'm looking at the yort trees over by the adro field. I think I'll go and eat a couple of yorts."

"Okay. You do that. Who else is around?"

"Some ems are jumping about in the trees. I see a korm flying above them, and a lot of aps running around in the field. . . ." It was obviously a peaceful and beautiful prospect, like his only dream.

"Any other dremers around?"

"Only one."

"Who is he?"

Ninety-year-old prot chuckled. "He's not a he. He's a she."

"Your mother?"

"No."

"An aunt? A neighbor?"

"We don't have any of those on K-PAX."

"A stranger? Someone you don't know?"

"No."

"What's her name?"

"Gort."

"Is she a special friend of yours?"

"Every being is a friend."

"Nothing remarkable about Gort?"

"Every being is remarkable."

"Have you known her long?"

"No."

"All right, prot. You're getting younger now. Younger . . . Younger . . . We're going to go back to the time you were fifty years old."

Prot's eyes closed immediately. After that he didn't move. I waited. He still didn't move. I was beginning to worry that something might have happened to him. At the same time, I found myself unspeakably elated: Had this devastating period (age five) in Robert's life somehow affected the mind of fifty-year-old prot as well?

"Prot?"

No response.

I was definitely becoming concerned. "Prot? Listen carefully. We're going to go forward again to when you were ninety, okay? You're getting older now. You're sixty, seventy, eighty. Now you're ninety again. Please open your eyes."

They popped open. He seemed a bit confused.

"We were talking about Gort, remember?"

"Yes."

"Good. Bear in mind now that you are ninety years old. I want you to tell me something you *remember* about your eightieth birthday."

"We don't have birthdays on—"

"Yes, yes, I know. I mean, tell me what you were doing when you became eighty years old."

"I went to K-REM."

"What is that—another planet?"

"No. It's one of our purple moons."

"What's it like?"

"Like your sahara desert."

"How long did you stay?"

"Not long."

"Did you go with someone else?"

"Yes."

"A man?"

"Yes."

"How old is he?"

"Eight hundred and eighty-seven."

"Must have been one of his last trips."

He shrugged.

"All right. Now you're getting younger again. You're eighty and still getting younger. Seventy-five, seventy, sixty-five. Okay, now you're sixty. What are you doing at this moment?"

Prot's eyes closed again.

I waited, but he said nothing.

"Okay, prot," I said quickly. "You're getting older again. You're sixty-five, sixty-eight, sixty-nine, seventy. At this moment you're seventy again. What are you doing right now?"

"Seeing how far I can jump."

"Okay. Now listen carefully. I want you to tell me something that happened to you when you turned sixty years old."

He pondered the question for a moment. "I don't remember."

The hairs on the back of my neck began to tingle. "You don't remember when you were sixty?"

He fiddled with the arm of his chair. "No."

"Nothing at all?"

"No."

"What's the earliest thing you remember?"

With no hesitation he said, "I remember a casket. Before that it's a bit hazy."

I could actually feel the muscles in my chest tighten. "What can you tell me about that hazy period just before you saw the casket?"

The young prot frowned hard with concentration. "I'm down on the ground," he murmured. "Someone is bending over me."

"Who is it? Who is bending over you?"

"I don't know her. She is wiping my face with something."

"She is cleaning you?"

"I suppose so. I'm groggy. And my head hurts."

"Why does your head hurt?"

"I don't know. I think I fell out of a tree. But I don't remember. . . ."

"Now this is important, prot. How old were you when this happened?"

"Sixty-eight."

"And you don't remember anything that happened before you were sixty-eight?"

He sniffed and wiped his nose on his shirt sleeve. "No."

My God! I thought. The seminal moment didn't come with Robert's abuse when he was a baby, or even at age five with Uncle Dave, but later! It was something that happened about the time of his father's death. Something so horrible that it overshadowed all the other terrible things that had befallen him. Did he actually witness his father's demise? Or even his suicide? Was it possible that he was asked to *assist* in it? Could it have been—God Almighty—a mercy killing? I saw that our time was almost up, and perhaps just as well. I needed to think about all this.

"Okay, prot, I'm going to bring you back to the present. You're beginning to get older. You're seventy-five now, and rapidly getting older. Eighty, ninety. Now you're a hundred, two hundred, three hundred, and now we're back to the present time, and you're here on Earth. Do you understand?"

"Of course I understand, doc. What's the big deal?"

"Good. Very good. Now I'm going to wake you up. I'm going to count backward from five to one, and—"

"I know all that. Fivefour—Hiya, coach. We done for the day?"

"Almost. I just want to ask you a couple more questions."

"Will they *never* end?"

"Not until we get some answers. Tell me what you remember about your sixty-eighth—I mean, tell me about the day you became sixty-eight years old."

612

"Haven't we—"

"Yes, but I want to hear it again."

He repeated, quickly and mechanically, "I got a call from someone named 'Robin.' He said he needed me. So I hopped on over. It was the first time I had encountered sadness. It took a little while to understand what was wrong with him. . . ."

"His father had just died."

"Yes."

"What do you remember before that?"

"Everything."

"Being born, and all that."

"Yep."

"Prot, are you aware that when you were under hypnosis you couldn't remember anything that happened to you before you were sixty-eight?"

"Get out of town!"

"How do you explain that?"

"Explain what?"

"That you can't remember any of that stuff when you're under hypnosis."

"No idea, coach. Unless it has something to do with the kroladon."

"The what? What's a kroladon?"

"A memory-restoring device."

"Your memory was restored with this thing?"

"Clever deduction, gino."

"Why didn't you tell me about this before?"

"It never came up."

The tape of this session is silent for a full two minutes. Finally I sighed and asked him, "How does this 'device' work?"

"Search me. I think the kroladon doesn't actually

restore memory, but only re-imprints it on different circuits."

"All right. How did you lose your memory?"

"I'm a little unclear about that. You see, there's a little gap between the time you lose it and when the kroladon re-programs it. Otherwise—"

"Well then, damn it, *when* did you lose it?"

"When I was sixty-eight."

"Just before your first trip to Earth."

"Pre-SOISS-ly."

"At pre-SOISS-ly the time of Robin's father's death!"

Without looking at the clock, which showed that our session was over, prot suddenly exclaimed, "Fruit time!" and hurried out.

I didn't try to stop him.

This was crazy, an absurd situation. Contrary to all logic, the *unhypnotized* prot could remember, with the help of a "memory-restoring device," events in his life beginning with the womb, while the *hypnotized* prot couldn't remember a thing that happened before his "sixty-eighth" birthday. Perhaps because he didn't exist prior to that time? Did he *create* his own early childhood? Was the "kroladon" *him*? I could hear my former mentor David Friedman cajoling me to "pursue, pursue, pursue." On the other hand, he was also fond of uttering gibberish like "How now brown cow?" at the most unexpected times. Helped him to think, I suppose.

I mumbled that phrase three or four times, but didn't come up with anything at all, except for an image of a puzzled cow. I did, however, decide to pursue, pursue, pursue, no matter where it led.

GISELLE had come up with a list of Robert's likes and dislikes, and from that came a few suggestions for the things

614

he probably missed most in his current noninteractive state. Things like his son, Giselle herself, his mother, mushroom and black olive pizza, and chocolate-covered cherries. And, of course, his father. Not much we could do about that, but maybe something could be done with the rest.

I remembered the hint of a reaction when I had mentioned his mother. "But that might have been wishful thinking," I confessed.

"Should we get her to pay him a visit?"

"I doubt it would help. She was here before when he was catatonic, remember? He never even acknowledged her presence, and all it did was upset her even more."

Her eyes lit up. "I bet he'd respond pretty fast if his father came to see him!"

"Giselle, you know that's impossible."

"Is it? I have an actor friend who could play him pretty well if we get him something to base it on! Do you think it might be worth a try?"

I had to admit it might jolt something out of Rob. The other side of the coin, of course, was that it might make matters even worse. But time was running out and, at this point, maybe anything was worth trying.

"The only problem," she added, "is that he's rehearsing for Off-Broadway. But I'll see if he can squeeze it in."

"Okay, but let's not rush into anything. I've got something else in the fire." I told her about prot's inability to remember his early childhood under hypnosis, and my plans to pursue this.

Her only reaction was a stunned, "Is that possible?"

I shrugged. "Where prot is concerned, anything's possible!"

★　★　★

O N my way through the Ward Two lounge the next morning I came across Alice and Albert chatting animatedly on the big green sofa. "Alex Trebek" was hanging around, apparently serving as moderator. I marveled, as always, at how far advanced a mental institution is compared to the outside world: a young black woman, an older Chinese–American, and a middle-aged Caucasian deep in conversation with no consideration of age, race, gender or nationality. Here, everyone is equal. Maybe prot was right—all our differences are based on past mistakes and cruelties, and if we could somehow forget our respective histories and start over, who knows what might come of it.

Of course they clammed up as I approached. But I soon learned that all three had been given certain "tasks" to perform. A familiar uneasiness set in.

"May I ask who gave you these 'tasks'?"

"Why, prot, of course," Alice proudly informed me.

"That's right!" Alex verified.

I had mixed feelings about this revelation, but I had learned not to rush to judgment in matters involving our alien visitor. "And what 'tasks' did prot assign to you, Alice?"

She deferred to Albert, who replied, "Theoretically, very simple ones. You see, Alice has a problem with space, and I with time. But prot pointed out that the space–time continuum is a kind of symbiosis, whereby space can be increased at the expense of time, and vice versa. If we can learn to trade one for the other, we would both be cured!"

I resisted the temptation to remind them that their doctors would be the judge of that. They all seemed so pleased that there might be a simple answer right around the corner that I didn't have the heart to discourage them.

"What about you, Alex? Did prot give you something to do, too?"

"Yes!"

Albert explained that prot had suggested he do his own show right here in the hospital.

"Will you be setting that up, Alex?"

"Correct!"

"He's going to get to work on it right after lunch," Alice added.

"How about you, Albert? You and Alice getting right to work, too?"

"Immediately. In fact, we were just discussing it when you came along." They all stared at me impatiently.

I took the hint. "Well, I've got to run. Good luck to all three of you!"

No one offered a farewell. They were already back to whatever they had been considering earlier. Their tasks seemed harmless enough, I thought, and might take their minds off their problems, if only for a little while.

On my way out to find prot, I literally bumped into him. Or would have, had he not stepped aside at the last moment, though he didn't seem to be looking in my direction. "It was the best I could do on short notice," he volunteered, when he finally noticed me.

"What—the 'tasks' you've been giving out?"

"Isn't that what you wanted to see me about?"

"Well, that was one thing. Actually, I have no problem with any of that as long as the patients' expectations aren't raised too high."

"All I can do is point the way. The rest is up to them."

"Well, we'll see how successful your 'treatment program' is. But the other reason I was looking for you was to invite you to the house for Thanksgiving tomorrow."

"What—and watch you cut open a dead bird? No, thanks."

"Well, how about the day after? What about Friday?"

"Relax, gino. Take a weekend off. Anyway, I won't be here Friday."

"What do you mean you 'won't be here'?"

"Is that a difficult concept for you?" He repeated each word slowly and distinctly. "I—won't—be—here." As if to emphasize his point, he turned to go.

"Where are you going? You're not leaving the hospital again, are you?" I called after him.

"Not for long!" he shouted back.

Session Thirty-nine

THIS year Thanksgiving happened to fall on my birthday. Abby and her family came for the occasion, along with Will and his fiancée. They arrived early, Abby bearing the turkey (much to my surprise—she's a devout vegetarian), and Dawn helped with the preparations. I played a couple of games of chess with the boys (I could still beat them, though not by much), but it only reminded me of Ward Two and the slow-moving matches in the game room, which led to thoughts of prot and his "temporary leave" from the hospital.

I was still preoccupied with that dilemma when my son Fred, who had finished the tour with Les Mis, and daughter Jenny, all the way from California, made an unexpected appearance. It was the first time in years the whole family had been together.

Both of them hugged me, but all I could think to say was, "What are you two doing here?"

"It's Thanksgiving, Daddy, remember?"

"And Mom's retirement," Freddy added.

"And your birthday."

"It was supposed to be a surprise." They each handed me a package.

I wasn't surprised—I was dumbfounded. "I suppose your mother put you up to this."

"Well, she was in on it, but it was actually prot's idea," Fred replied.

"Prot?"

"He came to see us last month."

"Last month??"

At that point the kitchen contingent burst in, there was another round of hugs and kisses, and we were soon on our way to the dining room, happily accompanied by our other guest, Oxeye Daisy. I won't go into detail about the dinner, except to say that it was the most beautiful, and also the first, soy turkey I had ever eaten.

None of us has ever been much on public (or private) speaking, but I thought I should say something on the occasion of my sixtieth. So, after we were all completely stuffed, I rambled awhile about the delights and significance of having one's family around, how this becomes more and more meaningful with the passage of time, and so on. "For this I guess we have prot to thank," I added. "And I thank all of you wonderful people for being here."

Perhaps to shut me up, Freddy now raised his glass and said, "To prot!" and we all clinked ours against those within reach.

After the usual chitchat about the year's events, the strange weather, and the football standings (Abby's husband Steve toasted the Jets, who were still in the running), Will stood up. Across the table, Karen gave me a huge, knowing smile. We had both been waiting for them to select a wedding date. "Dawn and I are going to be parents!" he announced.

There were cries of joy and more clinking. Far too diplomatic to press them on when they were planning to tie the knot, "Grandma" asked our daughter-out-law when the baby was due.

"In June," Dawn replied cheerfully.

Jenny raised her glass. "To June!"

"To the new baby!" Abby chimed in.

"Happy birthday, Dad," Fred added.

"Have a great retirement, Mom," offered Will.

"To Oxie!" cried Star.

"*La chiam!*" Rain shouted. Clink. Clink. Clink.

I don't know why, but sad, happy tears began to roll down my cheeks. I took a sip of wine, hoping no one would notice.

Will disappeared and came back with a huge devil's food cake (my favorite) ablaze with what seemed like a dangerous number of candles. Having practiced for this moment, I proceeded to blow them all out, one at a time, around and around, except for the one in the center, which refused to be extinguished. There were groans all around.

"That one's prot's," thirteen-year-old Rain announced confidently. "Mom, can I have some wine?" Abby gave him a sip of hers. Nothing timid about that boy, I thought proudly. Maybe we have another doctor in the family!

Ever the optimist, Karen pointed out that sixty is the beginning of the second half of your life, when you get a chance to do all the things you didn't get around to in the first half. "Unless you wait until it's too late," she added, holding my gaze meaningfully.

Later, after the presents had been opened (I got a

"retirement planner" from Karen), I took Will aside and asked him how medical school was going.

"Great!" he told me.

"Still thinking about psychiatry?"

"No doubt about it."

We gabbed about what he was learning in med school and the rewards (and headaches) of residency and practice. I thought: Nothing can be better than this! I only wished my own father, the small-town doctor, could have been here with us.

"Your mother was wondering when you and Dawn are getting married."

"I don't know, Pop. Maybe never."

"Do you think that's the best thing?"

"It all seems so irrelevant."

"Maybe for you, but how about the baby?"

"Dad, you need to have a talk with prot."

The rest of the family drifted in. Freddy and I sang a few Broadway tunes. Fred is a far better singer than I ever was, but I like to think he got his talent from me. The grandchildren performed a little comedy skit. I don't know who they got that from.

I usually go in to my office on the Friday after Thanksgiving, but this time, despite the guilt feelings, I stayed home. Abby and her family, along with Will and Dawn, left on Thursday evening, but both Fred and Jenny stayed over. Freddy was going back to his own apartment in the city that afternoon because his beautiful ballerina-girlfriend was returning from a visit with her own family, and Jenny wasn't flying back to San Francisco until Sunday.

Although his mother resisted the temptation to suggest that Fred follow his younger brother's example, she nonetheless asked him some pointed questions about his "roommate," whom we had rarely seen. Poor Fred finally blurted out, "Laura doesn't want any children!"

After an embarrassing silence the conversation turned to Jenny's specialty, the treatment of patients suffering from AIDS. She was quite optimistic about the whole thing, reporting that deaths from the disease were on the decline for the first time in its history, and that a vaccine was on the way. When I made the facetious comment that she would soon have nothing to do, she reminded me that thousands of people were still dying from HIV infections every year, and the global incidence of the virus was still on the rise. I remembered an earlier comment by prot that some day human beings would be devastated by diseases "that would make aids look like a runny nose." I only hoped I wouldn't be around long enough to see that.

When I had a chance to talk to Freddy alone, I learned that after finishing his national tour he was, once again, "temporarily unemployed." This gave me an idea. I told him about the situation with Robert, that perhaps the only thing that might shake him out of his present state might be an appearance by his father.

He said, "Sure," and asked to see pictures of Mr. Porter, and a description of what his voice might have sounded like. I told him I would send him a couple of photos from the file and have Giselle contact Rob's mother about her husband's manner of speaking and anything else that might be helpful.

After his reaction to the question about his apartment mate, I deferred inquiring about what he thought about taking over the house if we decided to vacate it. Instead, I asked my son, the former airline pilot, whether he ever missed flying.

623

"Do you miss getting your teeth drilled?" he replied.

At about lunchtime there was a call from Dr. Chakraborty. I took it in the den, where I still, even at this late date, felt I was imposing on my father's private sanctuary. "Hello, Chak. What's up?"

"There is bad news and there is also bad news," he informed me gravely.

I sighed, "Tell me the bad news first."

"You are not going to believe this," he assured me.

"Believe what?"

"It is the DNA work. There is no question about it. Prot and Robert Porter's DNAs are entirely different. It is confirmed."

"How different?"

"The odds they are not coming from the same person are seven billion."

"But—"

"I told you you would not be believing it."

I gazed at my desk, which was even more cluttered than the one in my office, and promised myself I would wade through it all sometime soon. "Chak, let's write a paper on this."

"It can be done. But no one will be believing it."

"You're probably right. Okay, what's the other bad news?"

"Prot has disappeared once more."

"Did anyone see him leave?"

"No. He was here one minute and gone away the next."

"Don't worry. He'll be back."

"I am not worrying."

I wasn't worried, either. He had done this before, and had always returned. But something else occurred to me on the way to the dining room: *Would Paul and Harry's DNA also be different from Robert's?* Indeed, might this be a simple way to diagnose multiple personality disorder? A Nobel prize, I dreamily reflected, would be as good a way as any to end a career. . . .

BY the time of the Monday meeting the entire staff knew that prot had disappeared and there were the usual questions about how he had managed to slip through our fingers again. I reported that I had asked Betty McAllister to make sure someone kept an eye on him at all times, but he had managed to get the nurses to rescue a cat from a closet shelf and when they turned around he was gone. As before, the surveillance cameras in the corridors and at the gates recorded nothing of him at all, and a search of the premises also proved fruitless. Still, no one seemed overly concerned about his disappearance, and I thought: It's amazing how quickly we get used to even the most bizarre events.

On the other hand, no one was prepared for my summary of the previous session with him, in which the hypnotized prot couldn't remember anything of his early childhood, nor for the results of the DNA analysis. Both seemed preposterous, and there was no hesitation in telling me so. Before I could mention that I had already thought of it, Goldfarb recommended getting DNA samples from the other alters. Chang suggested I focus in on the precise moment that prot lost his memory and compare this to the exact time Robert called him to Earth. Menninger wondered whether the results of the last session might not mean that his so-called memory of K-PAX was contrived. Thorstein also "smelled a rat."

The meeting was interrupted by a tap on the door.

625

Betty stepped in to let us know that prot was back and that someone had seen him at the Bronx zoo over the weekend. "My God!" Goldfarb exclaimed. "He's taking the animals!"

I wasn't going to provide any fruit for prot, but after he had somehow managed to bring the whole family together for Thanksgiving, I couldn't refuse him. There was also a mushroom and olive pizza, freshly baked in the hospital kitchens, and some chocolate-covered cherries from Lilac Chocolate in the Village, supplied by Giselle.

While he was scarfing down the various fruits as if there were no tomorrow, I turned on the tape recorder. "First of all, I want to thank you for getting Fred and Jenny to come for the holiday. How did you do that?"

"I just asked them."

"If *I* had asked them, they might not have showed up."

"That's one of the most interesting things about your species. Most humans will respond to an obviously unselfish request, even when they would refuse a selfish one. A remarkable trait, don't you think?"

"Secondly, you want to tell me where you've been the past few days?"

"Oh, out speaking with some of my friends."

"You mean non-human friends?"

"Mostly."

"In the zoo, for example?"

"Among other places."

"Are you taking some of them to K-PAX?"

"One or two, maybe."

"There's something I'm curious about."

"There's hope for you yet, doctor b."

626

"Won't that—bringing back alien species to K-PAX—screw up the ecology on your planet?"

"Not unless they develop human views on the subject."

"But—oh, never mind." I knew I wouldn't get anywhere with this.

Even though it was still three hours to lunchtime, the aroma coming from the covered tray was beginning to make my mouth water. "You want some pizza?" I asked him.

"Not if that's cheese I smell in there, and I think it is."

"Oh, for God's sake, prot, what's wrong with cheese? Nobody killed any cows to get that."

He snorted, a testament to my bottomless ignorance, I suppose. "Maybe you should look into that a little deeper."

"I'll do that," I promised him. "But first I'd like to speak with Robert."

"Onetwo—" His head fell to his chest so abruptly that I wondered whether Robert might be eagerly waiting to come out.

"Rob?"

He wasn't.

"Rob, I've got some surprises for you. Smell that pizza?" I reached over and lifted out a slice. The cheese strung out more than a foot. "Here. Go ahead."

He didn't move a muscle. I took a noisy bite myself—anything for science. "It's delicious," I informed him. "Your favorite kind."

There was no response.

"Well, maybe you're right. A little early, isn't it? Okay. How about a chocolate-covered cherry? Just one won't hurt."

He wasn't the slightest bit interested. To encourage him, I tried a couple. They were wonderful.

I offered him an evening with Giselle, a visit from his

son, even one from his mother. He didn't seem to care about any of this. I played my hole card. "Your father may be coming to see you soon. Would you like that?"

I thought I saw one of his hands twitch briefly and heard a muffled sound of some kind, but it didn't show up on the tape of this session. I waited for a moment in case he changed his mind about coming out. He didn't. "All right, prot. Come on back."

He quickly raised his head. "*Finito?*"

"For the moment. Please unhypnotize yourself."

"Fivefour— Find him yet?"

"No, I didn't. Any suggestions?"

"Perhaps you're barking up the wrong tree."

"What tree would you suggest I bark up?"

"I was thinking of the tree of knowledge."

I glared at him. "Last time you told me about a 'memory-restoring device,' remember?"

"Of course."

"There's something about the—uh—'kroladon' that I don't understand."

"I'm not surprised."

Prot seemed to be getting more arrogant every day. But perhaps that was just my own frustration coming out. Or maybe it was *his*. "Does it bring forth *all* your memories? Even the bad ones?"

"We don't have bad memories on K-PAX."

"I see. So if I asked you something about your past, anything at all, you'd tell me?"

"Why not?"

"Even if it were uncomfortable for you?"

"Why would it be uncomfortable?"

"All right. Let's talk some more about your childhood on K-PAX."

"You seem to be obsessed with childhood, gino. Is that because your own was so terrible?"

"Dammit, prot, when this is over, you can ask me any questions you like. Until then, we'll concentrate on *you*. Okay?"

"It's your party."

"Some party. Now—I want you to think back again to your boyhood on K-PAX. You're fifty-nine point nine now. Understand?"

"I think I can manage that."

"Good. Great. Okay, you're sixty now, and time is passing rapidly. You're watching the stars, eating, talking and running with your friends of whatever species, the days—I mean the time—is going by, and soon you're sixty-eight point one. Some more time goes by, and you become sixty-eight point two. And so on. Point three, point five, point seven, point nine. Do you remember anything about those days?"

"Everything."

"Naturally. Now I'd like to put you under again."

"Under what?"

"Prot, please just go to sleep."

"One—"

"Prot? Can you hear me?"

"Of course."

"Good. Now I want you to think back to the time you were sixty-eight point five. What do you remember about that time in your life?"

He thought for a moment. "Nothing."

"Can you describe something that happened when you turned sixty-eight point six?"

"I remember looking up at the stars."

"Is this the first thing you remember?"

"Yes."

I sat bolt upright. "Go on."

He put his hands against his temples and frowned. "My head hurts. I remember wandering toward K-MON for a while. I came to a balnok tree and smelled its bark. Balnok bark smells terrific! I chewed on some, then I found a rock that I hadn't seen before, and I asked someone what it was. He told me it was a silver ore, and the blue and green veins were morgo and lyal salts. It was so lovely that I—"

"Excuse me. Were you wearing any clothes at the time?"

"No. Why should I?"

"What about the man?"

"No. And he wasn't a man. He was a cras [pronounced 'crass']."

"What's a 'cras'?"

"A progenitor of the dremers."

"The dremers evolved from the crasses?"

"That's another way to put it."

"Did he harm you in any way?"

"Of course not."

"What happened after he told you what the rock was?"

"He went his way and I went mine. In a little while I got a call from—"

"All right. We'll return to this later. Right now I want you to go back just a bit. Something happened to you earlier. Maybe you fell out of a tree—something like that. You might have been knocked out. When you woke up, you had a headache and you were lying on the ground. Someone was wiping your face, and you couldn't recall what had happened to you. Do you remember that moment?"

He closed his eyes. "Uh—"

"Do you remember what happened to you? How you came to be lying on the ground with a headache?"

He frowned hard and then stared at the ceiling as if trying to find some answers there.

"Try to remember, prot. It's very important."

"Why?"

"Prot—please try to cooperate! I think we may be getting somewhere."

"Where?"

The tape indicates that I took a long, deep breath at this point. "I don't know yet. For now, please try to remember how you got that headache!"

He paused again. "I—there's a—a dremer. He is lying in a hollow log. I am cleaning him with a fallid leaf. . . ."

"Tell me more about this—uh—being. What does he look like? Is he young or old?"

"Not old, but not young, either. He is broken. He is in—in great pain, and—I don't remember anything else."

"Try!"

"I remember running. I am running, running, running as fast as I can. I'm running so fast that I bang against a tree. Then someone is wiping my face. My head hurts. . . ."

"Okay, what happened after that?"

"I found some balnok bark to chew on, but the headache didn't go away. I told you about the silver ore. Later on, I heard someone calling me. It was Robert. He needed me, and I went to help him."

"Don't you think it a little strange that someone would call you for help right after you lost your memory?"

"Not really. Beings are crying out for help all over the UNIVERSE."

"I see. All right—this is your first experience with interplanetary travel, right?"

"No. I'd been doing that for quite a while."

"You had traveled to other planets?"

"I'd been skipping around our solar system since I was twenty-five or so. As a passenger, of course."

"But none of these trips came about as a result of your being 'called for help' by someone."

"Nope."

"And—even though you had never even been out of your own solar system—on your first trip to another one you travel halfway across the galaxy by yourself."

He shrugged. "That's where your PLANET *was*."

"Weren't you afraid? Didn't it bother you to be so far away from home at so young an age?"

"Home is wherever we are. The UNIVERSE is our home."

"Who told you that?"

"Everyone."

"No small-town family ties for K-PAXians, right? But didn't you feel the need to have an adult go with you? To get you out of trouble if need be?"

"Why should I get into trouble?"

"Well, you might run into some dangerous animals, for example."

"I did."

"You did?"

"Yes. Homo sapiens."

"All right. Let's go back to the time just before you got the call. You were bathing someone. Do you know who it was?"

"No."

"Concentrate, prot. You were bathing this man, and suddenly you started running. Why?"

"I— He—"

"Take your time."

"Something was wrong."

"What was wrong, prot? What was wrong?"

"I don't know. That's where it's fuzzy. The next thing I remember is running away from him." He was becoming agitated.

I hated to close this session, but, unfortunately, I had to attend a fundraising luncheon (one of the things I had tried unsuccessfully to eliminate from my cluttered schedule) on Long Island. I was tempted to skip it, but I was the featured speaker. "All right, prot, you may unhypnotize yourself."

"Five—"

"That's all for today. I'll see you on Friday."

He left, but without the usual jaunty step, or so it seemed to me. I, too, was washed out, and I finished off the pizza and chocolates. Perhaps, I thought, I can make the talk a short one.

TO my surprise, the CIA was present at the fundraiser, along with several members of the press. Both groups stared at each other suspiciously. I have no idea how they got wind of the event, but the whole thing took on an entirely different character.

I began by describing progress on the new wing, and how it would provide needed space for new facilities and instrumentation to carry out important research well into the twenty-first century. Before I got any farther, however, someone asked a question about prot. I admitted he had returned, but declined to comment on the nature of his treatment. Nonetheless she (and others) persisted: Who was he, really? Where had he been? Could he really do all the things I had reported in my books, particularly travel faster

633

than the speed of light? How long was he staying? Where was he going? Who was he taking with him? Was he really behind some of the "miraculous" cures we had achieved in recent years? Why were so many people hanging around in front of the hospital? And on and on. Unfortunately, I didn't have many of the answers. Indeed, it occurred to me that I really didn't know very much about prot, about multiple personality disorder, about anything.

And the lunch was no picnic, either. I toyed with a plate of linguine (with a sauce of wild mushrooms and black olives), and couldn't even look at the Death by Chocolate cake. My stomach was churning and the unanswerable questions kept coming. It was like a nightmare. Worst of all, there wasn't a single financial contribution, much to the chagrin of Virginia Goldfarb and our financial officer, who were becoming more and more frustrated by the cost over-runs associated with the construction of the new wing, another affair I was nominally in charge of.

THE next morning, just as the sun was coming up, it finally dawned on me why Cassandra might have been a little depressed recently—she may have seen something in the skies that indicated she wouldn't be among the passengers selected for the journey to K-PAX. But, if so, she might well have some information on who *would* be going, especially now that the time of departure was rapidly approaching. Of course I didn't expect a mass exit on New Year's Eve, a flock of patients streaming into the heavens like a gaggle of featherless geese. But if I could get the names of those on the "waiting list," it might help the staff deal with the terrible, though certain, letdowns among those who were lining up for the trip.

Prot, prot, prot. Where have you come from and where

are you going? How is it that some people, or even their alter egos, are able to convince others they know all the answers, hold the keys to the kingdom? Can anyone explain how a charismatic figure can talk three dozen people into taking a cyanide trip to Comet Hale-Bopp? And these weren't even residents of a mental institution!

In the shower I didn't have enough energy to sing the toreador song from *Carmen*, though it burrowed through my head like some relentless worm. I keep holding up a cape and prot keeps goring me. How now brown cow?

I recalled in detail the previous day's session. We were coming closer and closer to the truth, but never quite getting there. Every opened door led to another empty room. How could I overcome the imperfections of a "kroladon" and get him to tell me what went on between prot (Robert) and a broken middle-aged man (his father) just before all hell literally broke loose? Perhaps I needed to sharpen the focus. Pound at that tiny interval of time just before little-boy prot ran away. Take it minute by minute, second by second until he reveals something about what happened. "*Tor-re-a-dor, en garrr-de!*"

Later that morning, while shivering on the back forty waiting for Cassandra to complete her meditations, I got a beep from Betty McAllister—my afternoon interview with a new patient had been cancelled. I immediately asked her to try to arrange an extra session with prot for that hour.

When I returned to the lawn, Cassie was gone. I didn't have time to track her down—there was a building committee meeting at ten o'clock. I took a stroll around the back forty, peering up at the open walls rising from the ground, the helmeted workers milling around above. What were they thinking about? Lunch? A daughter's birthday? Going home after work? A weekend football game? A trip to K-PAX?

Session Forty

WHILE waiting for him to make an appearance I reviewed what I knew, exactly, about the moment before prot started running from the man he was bathing. All I really knew was that suddenly young prot was running away. What in God's name had happened at that seminal moment? Had something equally devastating happened to six-year-old Robert? And what was the connection between the two?

I had rescued a whole bowl of elderly bananas from the hospital kitchens. Prot went for them immediately, gobbling them down like a man starving. When he was finished and had sat back licking his fingers, I turned on the tape recorder and we went over the crucial events again without hypnosis. But he was unable to add a thing to fill in the brief gap in his memory. I uncovered the white dot and asked him to hypnotize himself. When he was in his usual deep trance I took him back to age sixty-eight and asked him to recall the details surrounding his bathing the broken, middle-aged dremer. He could barely remember the episode, and the only thing new I could get out of him was that the man started to rise from the hollow log (bath tub) just before prot departed the scene.

"Try to remember, prot! Was he reaching out to touch you? To grab you?"

"I— I don't— He was trying to—"

"Yes? What was he trying to do?"

"He was trying to *hit* me!"

"Why? Do you know why he was trying to hit you?"

"I— I— I—"

"Yes? Yes?"

"I can't remember. *I can't remember! I CAN'T REMEMBER! DO YOU UNDERSTAND?*"

"All right, prot, calm down. Just relax. That's right. Relax. Good. Good. . . ."

He took several deep breaths. I brought him out of hypnosis and he was immediately in complete control again, as if nothing had happened.

I decided to try a different approach. "Space travel is somewhat risky, isn't it?" I ventured.

A familiar look of exasperation mixed with condescension crept over his face. "Gene, gene, gene. Didn't you have a bicycle when you were young?"

I suddenly remembered my father running alongside my new bike, finally pushing me off, my feeling of pride when I wiggled my way down the driveway by myself. "Yes. Yes, I did."

"Space travel to us is like riding a bicycle would be to you. Did you worry about falling down every time you jumped onto it?"

"Not after the first few tries."

"Egg-zack-a-tickly."

"Tell me—what's it like flying through empty space at several times the speed of light?"

"Like nothing."

"You mean there's nothing like it."

"No, I mean there's no sensation at all."

"Is it like being unconscious? Or asleep? Something like that?"

"Something like that. It may be akin to what you call 'hypnosis'."

I didn't miss the irony here, but there was no time to dwell on it. "No feeling of hunger or thirst, of getting any older. No sensation of any kind."

"Nope."

"Why don't you burn up in the atmosphere, like a meteor?"

"Same reason light doesn't burn up in the atmosphere."

"When you 'landed,' didn't you stop with a bit of a jolt?"

"No."

"How do you stop?"

"Simple, if you have the right program."

"You mean it's done by computer?"

"Of course."

"You bring a computer along wherever you go?"

"Sure. So do you. We're all basically computers with legs, haven't you noticed?"

"Are you saying the whole thing is programmed into your brain and you have no control over it?"

"Once the matrix is in place, it's a done deal."

"It overrides your own will power, is that it?"

"There's no such thing as 'will power,' my friend."
He sounded rather wistful about this, I thought.

"We're all just a bag of chemicals, is that what you mean? No one has any control over his actions."

"Can hydrogen and oxygen stop themselves from making water?"

"You're talking about predestination."

"No, but you can call it that if it helps you to understand. I'm not saying your life is predetermined from beginning to end, only that in any given situation you will act in a predictable way, which is determined by the chemistry of your brain. You dig?"

"So if, say, a person killed his father, it's not his fault, right?"

"Of course not."

"Have you discussed this with Rob?"

"Many times."

"Then why does he feel guilty about his father's death?"

"He's a human being, ain't he?"

I stared at him for a moment. "Prot, something just occurred to me."

"Bully for you, doctor brewer."

"Did your whole body make the journey from K-PAX? Or just your 'spirit' or some sort of 'essence'?"

"Do I look like a ghost to you, doc?"

The tape indicates someone tapping furiously on a notepad with a ballpoint pen. "Then why—oh, the hell with it. Just a few more questions about your first trip to Earth, okay?"

"I'll save you some time. Though there was no sensation of growing older during the journey, I aged about seven of your months. The trip was uneventful, I didn't run into anything, I landed safely, took a look at the beings in china, attended a funeral in montana, commiserated with robert, the details of which you have ample notes and

639

recordings, and made it back to K-PAX in one piece. Anything else?"

"Yes. Do all K-PAXians have this ability to pursue someone clear across the galaxy at a moment's notice?"

"Of course."

"Quite a talent."

"Not at all. Bear in mind that our species is several billion years ahead of yours. You'd be surprised at what you can learn just by sticking around long enough. Besides that, information is coming in all the time on every wavelength. The UNIVERSE is full of interesting vibes if you know how to listen."

"And without a moment's hesitation you vibed right across the galaxy to him."

"Right into the mortuary. Ugly word, don't you think?"

"What happened after the funeral?"

"We went to his house."

"What did he do after you got there?"

"He lay down on his bed and stared at the ceiling."

"Could you talk to him?"

"I could, but he didn't feel much like talking back."

"You came all the way from K-PAX and he wouldn't talk to you?"

"Nope. But it didn't matter."

"Why not?"

"After watching him for a while, I knew exactly how he was feeling."

"How? Had the same thing happened to you?"

His eyes rolled up and his fingers came together. At last he said, "K-PAXians can sense what's bothering another being."

"You can read minds?"

640

"Not exactly. It's difficult to explain. . . ."

"Try me."

He paused for another moment. "You could call it advanced semiotics. It's a combination of things—facial expression, subtle changes of color, especially in the UV range, tone of voice, body language, eye movements, frequency of swallowing, breathing pattern, smell, and—uh—a few other things."

"What things?"

"Oh, taste, smoothness of skin, pH, the kinds of radiation being given off, stuff like that. You feel exactly what the other being is feeling."

"You're an empath?"

"That's awfully *Star Trek*, coach, but—yes, all K-PAXians are what you call 'empaths.' It's easy when you don't consider yourself the center of the UNIVERSE."

"You think 'aps' are empathic, prot?"

"Sure. Just like most other beings. Have you ever tried to put anything over on a dog?"

He was right about that. Our Dalmatians somehow sensed what we were up to even before we did.

"And that's why you seem to understand the patients' problems better than their own doctors do."

"You could too if you could get outside your prison."

"Prison?"

"You know—the confines of your assumptions and beliefs."

Once again we seemed to have detoured. But suddenly I had another inspiration, a great one this time. "With all your marvelous insight into human nature, do you know what's bothering Robert right now?"

My excitement evidently came through loud and clear, because he chuckled before replying, "No."

"Why not?"

"Because I don't know where he is!"

"Well, can't you communicate with him somehow? Send out a signal on his 'wavelength' or something? Isn't he sending out some 'vibes'?"

"Nope. He doesn't seem to want any help."

"Damn it, prot, he's right there with you somewhere!"

"If he is, I don't see him. Do you?"

Of course I did, but he would never believe it. "All right. Let's go back to when you were sixty-eight point six. Somehow you helped young Robert get over his loss. How did you do that?"

"I told him the facts of life."

"You mean—"

"Nah, not that. About how the UNIVERSE works."

"What good did that do?"

"It seemed to make him feel better."

"How?"

"I explained to him that death is nothing to fear, that time will eventually reverse itself and that his father will live again."

"I see. And did he believe that?"

"Why shouldn't he? It's as true as my sitting here."

"So if you wanted to help Robert now, you'd just remind him that his father is not really dead, that he will live again in a few billion years—something like that?"

"He already knows that. But he's probably figured out the corollary."

"What corollary?"

He shook his head. "Hel-LO-o! That everything else that's happened to him would repeat itself as well."

Another brainstorm (which turned out to be another puny sprinkle) rumbled through my head. "Then do you

642

have any suggestion as to what might help him? If we can find him, that is?"

"A trip to K-PAX would do him a WORLD of good."

"Would that help him forget—"

"No, but he would soon realize that nothing that happened to him here could ever happen there. Besides, he could actually see and talk to his father whenever he wanted to."

The hair on the back of my neck was tingling again. "What? How?"

"Now, gene, I told you about the—uh—what you call 'holograms' a long time ago."

"Oh. That." Tap, tap, tap. "So you would be willing to take Rob back with you when you go?"

"He got the first invitation—remember?"

"Why didn't he go with you the last time, do you suppose?" I asked him smugly. "Didn't he believe you?"

"There's something he wants to get off his chest first."

Unforgivably, I was becoming frustrated and annoyed. "Why doesn't he *do* it, then?" I shouted.

"Do what?"

"Get it off his chest, goddamn it!"

"Calm down, doc. Just relax. Good. Good. . . . He can't."

"Why not?"

"It's too terrible."

"Do you know what it is that's so terrible?"

"Haven't got a clue."

"I have! I've got a clue! I just need him to fill in a few details! Will you tell him that?"

"If I see him."

"I'm going to need your help on this, prot."

"If you can find him I'll speak to him."

"Thank you *so* much."

"It's the least I can do."

I tried to stay calm. "One last question: if everything is predestined, what's the point of living?"

"What's the point if it's not?"

Drained dry again, I watched him saunter out. Maybe, I thought, I should just ask him directly to tell me everything he knows about Rob that I don't. At least he couldn't come up later with some revelation and claim I never asked him about it. What the hell happened to prot's/Robert's father in that log/bathtub? Whatever it was, it was predestined, in prot's mind. The best way I know to alleviate a major guilt complex.

I ran into Carl Beamish in the restroom. Standing there side by side we heard a distant noise that sounded like a crowd at a basketball game. Memories of sweat and locker rooms and shiny gymnasium floors popped into my head. Karen never missed a game those four years I played on the high-school team. How I wished my father could have been there, even once. Might there be some sort of parallel universe, I mused, where different outcomes and missed opportunities come to be?

"Too much coffee?" Beamish opined, apparently noting that I was still standing at the urinal long after he had finished. Before I could reply another roar came from outside. I asked him what he made of it. "Maybe," he suggested, "prot has gone out to talk to the people at the front gate."

I was already late for my session with Linus, but I made a mental note to press Goldfarb on the preposterous situation in front of the hospital as soon as I found time. If I did, of course, she would probably appoint me chair of a committee of one to look into it.

"Doesn't that circus out there bother you at all?" I asked Beamish.

He looked at me as if I were crazy. "I only hope he has room to take me along, too!"

I had invited Giselle to lunch. When she finally arrived in the dining room I demanded that she tell me what was going on at the front gate.

"You should come and see for yourself, Dr. B!"

"Why won't they leave?"

"Most of them do go away after he talks to them, but more keep coming. There must be a couple thousand people out there right now. Some are bringing their dogs and cats to get a look at prot. And when he starts to speak there isn't a single bark or meow. It's absolutely quiet."

"I thought I heard cheers this morning."

"He always gets that when he tells them the Earth can be a K-PAX if we want it to be."

"That's it?"

"What more can he say?"

"I heard two cheers."

"The last one was when he was finished and went back inside."

"Go get your lunch."

By the time she got back I had already eaten my cottage cheese and crackers. Now I had to watch as she ate her mound of food. Fortunately, I had a one o'clock meeting.

"Giselle, I don't have much time. What did you learn from Rob's mother?"

She opened a manila envelope, which contained a set of snapshots, mainly of Rob's father, a few with the whole family. Most were taken when little Robin was only a baby. Gerald Porter was a big, robust man then. There was one of him in the slaughterhouse where he worked, wearing a bloody rubber apron. The later pictures were quite different. By the end of his life he had lost most of his muscle tissue. His face was drawn, there were dark circles around his eyes, his expression was that of someone trying to pretend he wasn't in pain, at least for the photos. His clothes were several sizes too big, mostly corduroy trousers and blue denim shirts. His thick black hair was parted on the right, I noted. "No home movies," she said, "but these are pretty revealing."

"I'll pass them on to Fred. What about his voice?"

"His mother said he used to be a deep baritone. Sang in the church choir. Toward the end it became rather squeaky, tired, high-pitched. He almost never slept, she told me. Couldn't eat much, either."

"The pain?"

"Terrible."

"What about Rob's relationship with his father? Did she notice anything unusual about it? Did she see any changes in him after his father came back from the hospital?"

"We didn't get into all that. Maybe you should talk to her yourself."

I stopped by my actor son's East Village apartment that evening to deliver the folder and discuss a timeframe for his visit to the hospital. The buzzer at the stoop elicited no response but the lock was broken so I went on up and tapped on the door. No answer. Disappointed, I searched my pockets for a pen. While I was writing Fred a note, a wiry man with a long gray ponytail showed up. I considered giving the package to him, but decided against it. He sidled into an apartment across the barely-lit hall, where he was greeted with a hug by another man wearing only shorts and an undershirt. The wall was cracked even worse than the one on Fred's side. I slid the folder under the door, along with a request to call me, and grabbed a taxi to Grand Central.

THE following day, Thursday, I happened to glance into the quiet room and spotted Ophelia. There was something noticeably different about her, but I couldn't put my finger on it. Alex was there too, busily consulting an encyclopedia, an atlas, and a gazetteer. Ophelia waved. Usually she pretends not to see me, fearing I might judge her too harshly about something or another, I suppose. I motioned for her to step outside so we wouldn't bother Alex.

"How are you today, Ophie?"

"I think I'm cured. How are *you*?"

"Ophelia! What happened?"

"I'm not afraid anymore."

"That's right!" I heard Alex shout.

"Why not?"

"Prot ordered me not to think of a rabbit."

I had to smile. "And you did."

She giggled. "I didn't mean to. I couldn't help it."

Alice appeared from behind a sofa, spotted us, and dashed from the room squeaking like a mouse.

"So you disobeyed his command."

"Yes."

"And now you think you're cured."

"Yes. No, I take that back. I *know* I am."

She still wasn't well, of course. She couldn't have made that much progress in several months of analysis, let alone a few minutes with prot. "That's great, Ophie. I guess we'll have to take up your case in the staff meeting next Monday."

"No need to do that. I've already been assigned to Ward One."

"Ward One? Who assigned you to Ward One?"

"Prot did."

"Correct!" Alex called out.

"Ophelia! You know prot doesn't run the hospital!"

"Of course I know that. But the order was counter-signed by Dr. Goldfarb!"

THE afternoon lecture was another bust. I had long ago given up following the syllabus I had drawn up at the beginning of the year (actually more like twenty years ago) and, as had become my habit, I began by briefing the students on my lack of progress in finding Robert, adding something about Ophelia and the other patients prot had managed to help in one way or another. "Oliver Sacks," naturally, turned the discussion back to prot. "Maybe you could get him to speak to us," he suggested. "You know—tell us what he's learned about the patients and how we can better deal with them ourselves."

I might have reminded him that he didn't have any patients yet. Instead, I barked, "He's not here to teach a bunch of medical students how to become psychiatrists. In any case, I don't think the world is ready to be treated by a clone of prot 'disciples,' do you?"

"I don't know. All I'm suggesting is that we could listen to what he has to say and see if we can learn anything from it. Draw our own conclusions."

"Sorry."

From around the room came roars and mutterings.

"All right, all right! I'll tell you what I'll do. I'll get him to jot down a few of his thoughts about the patients, and I'll bring them next time. Assuming he agrees to do so. Fair enough?"

Oliver wasn't finished. Oliver is never finished. "Ask

him also what he *doesn't* understand about them. I think that would tell us a lot about *him*."

"That is correct!" someone piped up.

Reluctantly I agreed, and abruptly changed the subject. "We're going to end the hour by talking a little bit about sexual deviation."

For once I had their full attention—even prot seemed forgotten for the moment.

Session Forty-one

PROT fell into a trance immediately. "Okay, prot, please unhypnotize yourself."

"What—" He stared bug-eyed around the room. "Where am I?"

"All right, we'll dispense with the comedy today."

"My dear sir, I don't think you'd know comedy if it rose up and bit you on the hiney." He reached for a cluster of red grapes and stuffed them into his maw, stems and all, along with a hunk of ripe peach.

"I'm willing to agree with that if you'll tell me something I don't know about Rob."

Prot laughed heartily, like a little boy who's discovered something silly. His mouth was a rainbow of color. "I was wrong, doctor b. You *do* have a sense of humor."

"You mean you're not going to divulge even one of his little secrets?"

"No, I mean there are a million things you don't know about rob. Or anyone else, including yourself."

"Then it should be easy for you. Fill me in. What are some things I don't know about Rob?"

"Well, for example, you don't even know that he tried to commit suicide on at least two occasions."

"He what? When?"

"After his wife and daughter were killed—remember?"

"Of course I do. He tried to drown himself in the river behind his house."

"Very good! But what about the first time—do you know about that?"

"What first time?"

"When he was six and a half. He tried to hang himself in his room."

"At *six*?"

"Actually, he was closer to seven. To be precise, he was six years, ten months, nine days—"

"And that's when he first called you? After the suicide attempt?"

"By george, I think you've finally got it."

"He called you because he didn't want to die."

Prot pushed another bunch of grapes into his mouth. "No, my human friend, he called me because he *failed* to die."

"You knew this and never told me? There are a few things you don't understand about human beings yourself, my alien friend."

"I already know more than I want to."

"Please," I implored (it came out more like a whine), "let's not debate that issue today. Just tell me why Rob wanted to kill himself."

"Because his father died."

"But there wasn't anything he could do about it, was there?"

"He thought it was his fault."

"Why was it his fault?"

"I don't know. You'll have to ask *him*."

"Goddammit, prot, he won't talk to me!"

"Maybe you've been asking him the wrong questions."

"I haven't asked him anything," I shot back. "He's not here, *remember*?"

"If you had asked the right things in the first place, maybe he would be!"

It was all I could do not to explode. Instead, I tapped my yellow pad rather vigorously with my pen. "Do you have any suggestions about what the right questions might be?"

Prot gazed at me as if I were a complete idiot. "Well, you might try to find out how his father died, for example."

"But—he died of natural causes, didn't he? Resulting from a work-related injury suffered months earlier, as I remember."

"Did you read the death certificate?"

"No. Did you?"

"Nope."

"Then how do you know how he died?"

"What do you get when you add two and two?"

"I suppose you're going to tell me the answer is five."

"It depends on what dimension you're in."

"Are you trying to tell me that two and two are five in Rob's case?"

"Only that you might try looking at the situation from a different angle."

"What if I don't know what angle to look at the situation from?"

"Well, I suppose you could re-examine your educational system. . . ."

"You mean my training as a psychiatrist?"

"No, dear boy, I mean your training as a perceptive being. Of course it might take you a few thousand years."

"Prot, we don't *have* a few thousand years."

"Give or take a few decades."

"Prot, I'm asking you flat out to tell me anything you know that I don't know."

"You have a rutad hanging out of your nose."

"A what?"

"A bugger."

"Oh." He watched with some amusement as I took out my handkerchief and removed the offending particle. "Is that all you have to say?"

"About your proboscis?"

"Or anything else."

"For the time being."

"All right. We're going to change the subject."

"Back to 'uncles,' I suppose."

"Maybe. There are still a few questions I want to ask you about your childhood on K-PAX."

"Will they be relevant this time, gino?"

"Let me decide that."

He shrugged. "Decide away."

"Thank you. All right. I'm going to ask you something about the time you were a baby on K-PAX. Less than twenty years old. Anything happen to you during that first twenty years that was unpleasant for you in any way?"

He scratched his head, for all the world like an ordinary human being. It's always fascinated me that trying to recall some obscure fact causes one's scalp to itch. "Not really. Pretty routine babyhood."

"All right. Let's shift to a later time. You're exactly fifty-five years old. Do you have a pet?"

"We don't have pets on K-PAX."

"Well, is there anything that follows you around? Goes where you go? Any animals that are around more than others?"

"There was a folgam that hung around sometimes."

"What's a 'folgam'?"

"Something like a cat, only smaller."

I was jolted by the recollection that five-year-old Robin's pedophilic Uncle Dave secured his silence by killing a kitten (and a stray dog), and threatening to do the same to him. "Cat?"

"See ay tee. Cat."

"But cats are carnivores, aren't they?"

"Not on K-PAX."

"A vegetarian cat."

"I just said that, *nicht wahr*?"

"You said there 'was' a folgam. What happened to it?"

"He wasn't an 'it.' He was a 'he.'"

"What happened to him?"

Prot frowned and pressed his lips together. "He went off somewhere."

"He disappeared?"

"No, he wasn't of the Cheshire variety. He just went away."

"And you don't know where."

"That's it!"

"You woke up one morning and he was gone."

"Correct! Except we don't have 'morning' in the sense you mean it. You see, with our two suns—"

"All right, all right. What happened after the folgam went away?"

"Not much. I went to a library and retrieved some information about folgams."

"Why?"

"I wondered whether they always went away like that."

"You missed your folgam, didn't you, prot?"

"He wasn't 'my' folgam. I was just curious."

"Did you ever have another folgam follow you around?"

He checked his fingernails. "No."

"Was anyone else around when your folgam ran away?"

He considered this. "Off in the distance I saw someone, but I couldn't tell who it was."

"Too far away?"

"Yes."

"Was he fat or thin?"

"He seemed to be rather heavy for a dremer."

"You hadn't seen him before?"

"I told you—I couldn't tell who he was."

"Okay. Now let's return to the time you were sixty-eight. Remember? You woke up with a headache and all the rest?"

He nodded suspiciously.

"Before this happened you were bathing someone, right?"

He nodded again.

"Was he 'a little heavy for a dremer'?"

"No."

"So it wasn't the same being you saw after your—the folgam ran off."

"Nope."

"Do you know who he was?"

"Yes, I do."

"You do?" I could feel my heart beginning to pound. "What was his name?"

"I don't know."

"Do you know your father's name?"

"As far as I know, I never met my father."

"Well, what kind of relationship did you have with the dremer in the hollow log?"

"The usual. We talked about various things, looked at the stars, admired the korms."

"What did you talk about in particular?"

"A lot of things."

"Sex?"

"That's not something that comes up very often on K-PAX. There isn't that much to say about it."

"Did he—uh—demonstrate any sexual activity toward you?"

"Of course not! Why should he?"

"But you had seen him before."

"Many times."

"Anything unusual happen on those occasions?"

"No."

"So tell me—why were you bathing him?"

"Haven't we been over this?"

"Not in any detail."

"All of a sudden you're a detail man?"

"That's right!"

"I was cleaning him because he couldn't clean himself."

"Why not?"

"He couldn't move his arms and legs very well."

"They were injured?"

"I doubt it. We have ways to repair people who are injured."

"What was his problem, then?"

656

"I don't know."

"Was he in any pain?"

"Yes."

"Didn't you give him something for that? Some balnok bark to chew on, for example?"

"It didn't do him much good."

"I see. And had you ever cleaned this man before?"

"No."

"All right. You say you had seen this dremer many times. How long had you known him?"

"For a while."

"Why is that? Don't K-PAXians move around a lot?"

"He couldn't walk very well. So he didn't move around much."

"What about yourself? Didn't you move around a lot? Leave him behind?"

"Children don't move around as much as adults. Anyway, we seemed to be going in the same direction most of the time."

"So you saw him fairly often?"

"More often than most beings, I suppose. So what?"

"But you don't know his name."

"I already told you that!" he snapped.

"After you hit your head on something and lost your memory, you never saw him again—right?"

"Never."

"Why not?"

"Who knows? I suppose he finally moved on."

"Could he have died?"

This seemed to jolt prot for a second. But he said, simply, "It's possible, of course."

"How old was he?"

"Four hundred or so, I suppose."

"Pretty young for a K-PAXian."

"Just approaching middle age."

"Does anyone ever die at that age on K-PAX?"

"Hardly ever."

"But it's possible."

"Yes, it's possible! What isn't?"

"Prot, I want you to think about this next question before you give me an answer. Could the man have been your father?"

"I doubt it," he replied without hesitation.

"Why not?"

"I told you: I've never met my father."

"You're lying, aren't you, prot?"

"Moi? I've never told a lie in my life."

"K-PAXians have a lot of different talents, don't they? I think one of them is to lie convincingly enough to fool everyone else. Is that possible?"

"Anything's— I mean, of course it's *possible*, but it doesn't happen to be true."

"You know who your father is, don't you? Or at least you suspect who he is."

"I've told you time and again that I don't!"

"And you lied about it time and again, didn't you?"

"No! I didn't!"

"The man in the hollow log is your father, isn't he?"

"No! I mean . . . I don't know who my father is, don't you understand that? It's a simp—"

"But it's *possible* that the man in the log is your father, isn't it?"

"YES, IT'S POSSIBLE, GODDAMN IT!"

I swiveled away. "Thank you, prot. That's all for today." I busied myself with my notes. A few seconds later I peeked around, but he was already gone. How now, brown prot? Maybe our educational system sucks, but it seems to be getting us somewhere, *nicht wahr*? In another few years of badgering, I assured myself, I may be able to get to the bottom of all this!

But there were only a few weeks left, not enough time to get even halfway down. With the hourglass rapidly draining, should I focus all my remaining time and attention on Rob himself, press him on what it was he wanted to "get off his chest"? Was it to confess a role in his beloved father's death, as I was beginning to suspect?

I sought out Giselle and found her in the lounge, sitting in Frankie's favorite window seat, the very spot where former patient Howie, some seven and a half years earlier, had sought out "the bluebird of happiness." I asked her what she was contemplating.

"Oh, Dr. B, I was just thinking about all the people we'll be leaving behind. Look at Alex over there, trying to be someone he's not. He's wasting his life, and it's too precious for that. And all the other patients. Most of them don't even know what they're unhappy *about*. Or who live in fear but aren't sure what they're afraid *of*. We can't take them *all* with us. It's sad, isn't it?"

I refrained from observing how sad her own dream would be when it ended. Instead, I told her about the brief conversation I had had the previous evening with Rob's mother. "Robin and his father were very close when he was six, and they spent all their time together the summer he died. His dad called him 'Robbie'—I'll mention that to Fred. Another thing I found out was that the man was incontinent. He even wore a diaper, like a baby! And one other thing might be relevant: because of all the hospital bills, the family was going to lose the house. He was pretty distraught about that."

"The house? Why?"

"Because they couldn't make the payments. On all of his medical bills, either. They were in pretty bad shape, financially. I think that's why prot's so down on the free-enterprise system!"

"But they *didn't* lose the house, did they?"

"No. He had some life insurance. Not much, but enough to keep the creditors away for a while."

Giselle thought about this for a moment. "What did Rob's mom know about—uh—"

"Not much. The girls were already in their room, asleep. She heard a commotion and went to see what had happened. She found her husband in the bathtub. He was already dead by then. She thought he died of a heart attack. Prot isn't so sure. Can you get a copy of the death certificate?"

She nodded, emitted a huge sigh, and slouched toward the door.

Before leaving the lounge I stopped alongside Alex, who was sitting in the big overstuffed chair in the corner paging through the huge encyclopedia, taking notes onto a yellow tablet identical to one of my own. A visitor might have thought he was one of the staff, hard at work researching a difficult patient's problems. "Hello, Alex, how's it going?"

"Almost ready," he replied *sotto voce*, without looking up.

"Keep up the good work," I murmured, half to myself. It wasn't until I had left the room that I realized he had responded in a most unAlex-like manner. Of course! I thought. Until he spoke to prot, no one had ever given him a chance to actually *be* who he wanted to be, a deeply felt desire haunting most people, even those outside these

660

walls. I wondered whether this would work for some of the other patients. What if we catered to their whims? Gave them a chance to actually be who they wanted to be, at least for a little while?

THE morning was taken up by a visit from the popular "TV shrink," who had cancelled a similar appearance two years earlier. He was a roly-poly, apple-cheeked little man, someone who would make the perfect Santa Claus. A farmer by trade, he smelled faintly of manure. I wondered what my former patient Chuck would have thought of him.

He had been scheduled for the whole day, but once again had to cancel the afternoon portion because of certain unspecified but pressing engagements. Though I was secretly glad because I had more than enough work to attend to, his seeming arrogance annoyed me, just as it had in 1995. But perhaps this had more to do with the fact that his books (unlike my own) have made him a wealthy man. Nevertheless, I was looking forward to meeting him because one can always learn something about communicating with one's patients from a colleague who does it so effectively on a nationwide scale.

The first thing he said, when Thorstein (who picked him up at Penn Station—he doesn't fly) escorted him into my office, was, "Life is like false teeth." I had no idea what that meant but I nodded wisely, not wanting to start off our relationship by seeming dense.

I offered the famed guru some coffee. Wagging a pudgy finger, he iterated, "You build a house one card at a time!" Assuming this to be an affirmative response, I buzzed one of the secretaries to bring us some. While we were waiting I asked him where he had studied. "A grain of sand is worth more than all the handwriting on the wall," he declared with a twinkle. (I found out later he hadn't gotten past the eighth grade.)

I tried to shift the conversation to something less personal. "How do you like New York?"

"The bigger the goose, the smaller the gander!" he shouted, pounding his fist on my desk. This went on for half an hour, and I was quite relieved when Thorstein arrived to take him away.

A makeshift seminar was set up for eleven o'clock, disrupting the schedules of staff and patients alike. Nevertheless, it was quite well attended. I won't present a verbatim transcript of that discussion; suffice it to say it was a continuous litany of aphorisms, homilies, nursery rhymes, Biblical quotations, and old wives' tales, commencing with "What is a lie, but the truth in disguise?" and ending with "You can catch more flies with honey than you can with vinegar, but vinegar is cheaper." Unfortunately there was no time for questions, but he was rewarded with a generous round of applause as he hurried out the door to his "pressing engagement."

At lunch afterward, though no one could argue about anything the great philosopher had said, neither could anyone tell me why life is like false teeth.

LOSE a few, win a few. The meeting with Linus turned out to be a breakthrough. I merely asked him why he felt it necessary to check over his room exactly thirty-seven times before he could leave it, a question I'm sure I have put to him a dozen times before. In any case the answer, same as always, was, "So that I don't make any more mistakes."

I suppressed a yawn. "Mistakes like what?"

"Like I did on that paper. You know, the one about the DNA sequence of one of the taste genes."

"You mean you made the mistake of using the wrong data when you wrote it up for publication?"

"No, I mean I should have selected a gel that wasn't so obviously a phony."

Had Linus been talking with prot? I sat up straighter. "You're *admitting* you cheated on that? You fudged the data?"

"I fudged *all* my data."

"You—but why? Everyone I've talked to and the reports I've read all say that you have a brilliant mind and could easily plan meaningful experiments and come up with significant and important results."

"That's true."

"So why screw around with the data? Wouldn't it be easier just to do the experiments?"

"I hate doing experiments."

"You hate—then why did you go into molecular biology?"

"Dr. Brewer, have you met my parents?"

"Yes, I have. They're top scientists, both of them. That alone should have given you a leg up on everyone else."

"But neither of them ever asked me what I wanted to do with my life. They both assumed I would follow in their formidable footsteps. They never even asked for my opinion, and if I tried to give one, they ignored it. One thing led inexorably to another—what could I do?"

I understood his dilemma. In fact, I identified with him. I almost *empathized* with him. My own father had assumed I wanted to follow in his footsteps. Who knows—if left to my own devices, I may have anyway. The point is I didn't seem to get a vote in the matter. I even felt obligated to follow his wishes long after he was dead!

I asked Linus what he would do with his life if he could start all over again.

"I'd like to be a cowboy," he told me with the straightest face I had ever seen. I felt as though I were being watched by a dog and it was suppertime.

"Maybe something can be done about that."

He actually crawled over to me, wrapped his arms around my ankles, and cried. The truth is, I joined him. I brushed down his hair and wept for him, for myself, for all of us.

FREDDY came to dinner on Sunday. (We had invited the ballerina, too, but she couldn't make it. A good thing, though—he ate enough for two people.) Although he had auditioned for a number of parts he was still without employment, except for a little drama coaching at one of the city's high schools. He seemed a trifle down, and acted as if there were something he wanted to tell us. The last time it was giving up flying—was he becoming disillusioned with his acting career? It certainly seemed a poorly-paid profession. Or was he worried, like most of us, about being a failure at what he did? Whatever it was, he kept it bottled up inside in typical Fred fashion.

I gave him all the information we had about Robert's father, and I could see him mulling it over, forming some sort of characterization in his mind. In the end we scheduled a "dress rehearsal" for the following Saturday. He would come to the house in some old baggy clothes and we would go over the setup and what to expect when he came to the hospital, a visit we planned for the following week. I realized, with no little regret, that he had never been to my office.

We watched a ballet on TV that afternoon. Was Fred

so attentive because he was trying to please me? Or was it simply that he had learned a lot about the art from his roommate? Perhaps he was studying the dancers in order to increase his chances of landing a role on Broadway. Who would know? Who can get inside another person's head, even that of someone close to us? Only his mother seemed completely happy, humming away in the kitchen. She disliked ballet, and wasn't going to pretend otherwise. Karen has always been exactly who she is, nothing more, nothing less. And, in her case at least, that's quite enough.

Session Forty-two

THE Monday morning staff meeting was a halcyon affair, with Linus's transfer to Ward One in process and Milton, who had been in other institutions for more than three decades before coming to MPI, about to be discharged altogether. Carried away by the general good feeling, I contemplated the perfect copy of Van Gogh's *Sunflowers*, painted by a former patient, and nibbled on a cinnamon donut, knowing I would regret it later on when I stepped on the scales. I rationalized this by professing that I would be quite willing to have a cinnamon donut every time a patient is discharged.

"You'd better start stocking up, then," Beamish roared, "because I've got someone else who's ready for Ward One, in my opinion."

I stared at the tiny glasses, which weren't much bigger than his eyes. "Who?—Ophelia?"

"That's right! How did you know?"

666

"I've noticed some changes."

Menninger agreed. "She's like a different person."

"Maybe she *is* a different person," I suggested, not knowing what the hell I was talking about.

"Whoever she is, she's no longer psychotic," Beamish assured us. "I can't even get a good neurosis out of her anymore."

Goldfarb looked around the room. "Any dissenters?" There were none.

"Let's get rid of her!" she exclaimed, flinging her pen onto the big mahogany table. A crude expression, perhaps, but it's one of Goldfarb's favorites, something of a talisman, I suppose. "Anyone else ready for Ward One?"

"I think Don and Joan are ready, as long as they go together," Chang replied. "It's wonderful—between the two of them they seem to make a whole human being."

"Same with Alice and Albert," Goldfarb chipped in, "though they're probably not ready to move down yet. But we should give prot the credit for putting them together."

That was true in the latter case, but it was I who had first thought of pairing "Don Knotts" and "Joan of Arc," though at this point who would have believed me? I did manage to point out that there were some patients who didn't seem to be affected much by prot's visit—Frankie, Cassandra, the autists, the deviates, the psychopaths.

"Give him time," said Menninger. "Give him time. Cassie, at least, has broken out of her depression. Maybe prot had something to do with that." I replied rather sheepishly that I would speak to her about it.

In view of all the upcoming vacancies in Ward Two there was room for a group of new patients waiting to make the move from "the big institute" (at Columbia) to MPI.

667

"Let's bring them over early," Chang proposed. "Let prot have a crack at them before he goes." Mine was the only dissenting vote.

The meeting wound up with a discussion of the annual outing to the Metropolitan Museum of Art. It was set for Monday, the fifteenth, when the venerable institution is normally closed. We would have the place all to ourselves (I suspect this gesture on the part of the museum staff was more for the benefit of their paying patrons than for our patients, but it was nonetheless appreciated).

"What's going on with the new wing?" Thorstein demanded. "I was on the lawn this morning and there doesn't seem to be much happening." Everyone looked at me accusingly.

"I spoke to the foreman last week. It's got something to do with the holidays and with a union vote and something else I didn't quite get. He doesn't speak much English."

"No problem," Goldfarb said with a smirk. "At this rate, we're not going to need the damn thing anymore." Goldfarb had made a joke! She lifted her pen. "Anything else?"

I mentioned the crowd at the front gate, which seemed to be getting bigger every day.

"What's the big deal?" Thorstein wanted to know. "They seem to be an orderly bunch. All they want is a word from prot. Anyway, the fault lies with you."

I found myself hoping he would be successful in finding a position elsewhere. "*Moi?*"

"If you hadn't written those books, no one would know he was here."

"What are they going to do when he leaves?" mused Beamish.

"The question is, what are *we* going to do when he leaves?" Goldfarb muttered, deadly serious again.

I found Betty waiting for me in my office. She seemed nervous, even agitated. I asked her where the disturbance was.

"Right here," she wailed.

"What do you mean?"

"I've got an appointment in an hour to have a root canal done."

"So?"

"I'm afraid of the drill."

Betty's teeth have never been very good. Now I knew why. "What is it about the drill that bothers you?"

"I'm afraid it's going to get loose and shoot through my skull."

"Betty! The odds against that are astronomical!"

Her hands were picking away at each other. "I know. But it doesn't help."

I could see she was terrified. "Well, do you want me to recommend someone to help you get through this?"

"I— Maybe. I thought you could just say something real quick that would do it."

"Nothing is that easy in this business, Betty—you know that. How did you get through the previous visits to the dentist?"

"My husband always took me. But he can't go today."

I thought immediately of sending prot with her, but quickly rejected the idea. "I don't think this is something we can solve in an hour. Do you want to change the appointment until we can look into it a little more?"

"I can't. If I wait any longer she'll have to pull it, and that's worse."

At that moment my wife walked in. "Hi! I was in town today, and for some reason I found myself heading this way. I thought we might have lunch together. Hi, Betty—want to come with us?"

"I can't," she replied dismally.

"What's the matter?"

Betty repeated the whole story.

"I understand perfectly," Karen assured her. "I have the same problem. What time's your appointment? I'll go with you. Then we'll have a nice lunch somewhere."

As if a valve had opened, all the tension drained immediately from Betty's face. On their way out, Karen gave me a wave over her shoulder and a little smile that seemed to say, "See? It's easy if you empathize with your patients."

I didn't even know she had a problem with dentists.

I went to see for myself how Cassandra was doing. While I was looking for her on the lawn (she liked to be outside where she could contemplate the heavens, regardless of how cold it was) it occurred to me that perhaps she was a kind of autistic savant, someone who devotes so much of her mental capabilities to one single activity that she actually *can* see a pattern in events that the rest of us can't, and merely reaches some perfectly logical conclusion about the long-term results.

I found her sitting on her favorite bench in her old worn coat, her arms wrapped around her as if she were confined to a straightjacket. I waited for a few minutes while she tuned in to me.

"Hi, Cassie. How are you feeling?"

"Just fine." She even smiled a little.

"Good. I'm glad you're feeling better."

"Prot told me not to give up hope."

"About what?"

"About a trip to K-PAX. He says someone else might come back for me later on."

"Can we talk about that for a minute?"

"He's leaving on the thirty-first."

"Yes, I know. What I was wondering was, have you figured out who he's taking with him this time?"

"Not for sure. Only how many of us will get to go."

"Really? How many will there be?"

"Two."

"Only two?" I sniggered. "I thought he was supposed to take a hundred of us to K-PAX."

She glared at me through the hair falling over her eyes. "That's right. But only two of *us*."

"You mean the people who live here at the hospital."

"Yes."

"But you have no idea who they will be."

"Not yet," she sighed, turning back to the sky.

"Do you have any idea *when* you might know who he'll be taking with him?"

But she was already gone, lost in the stars.

On my way back to the big front door I reflected yet again on how little we know about the human mind. As if to prove my point, I ran into Alice and Albert coming out, accompanied by a couple of cats. The A's now seemed inseparable. "How are you two doing?" I inquired.

"Great!" Albert exclaimed, whipping out a tape measure. "Alice's last 'big' phase was a full two centimeters short of the time before, which was two short of the one before that!"

Alice, brandishing a stopwatch, added, "And Albert

671

was two minutes closer to estimating the duration of an hour than he was last week! Isn't it great?"

"Wonderful!" I said, and meaning it. "Keep it up!"

"In another month or two, we'll be cured!"

I wasn't so sure about that, but I doubted they would be among the lucky winners of an all-expenses-paid trip to K-PAX.

A dense crowd was still milling quietly about the front gate. Some of them glanced in occasionally to see who was on the lawn, but it wasn't prot, and they had no interest in the rest of the patients. Not surprising, actually, since most people feel the same way toward the mentally ill and, by and large, hope they'll just disappear. Unfortunately, so do the HMO's.

AS I was leaving the hospital to give my "Principles of Psychiatry" lecture, Giselle stopped me in the corridor with an envelope addressed to "dr. eugene n. brewer, EARTH." Of course it was from prot, and it contained the list of things he did and did not understand about our patients (as well as the rest of us), which I had asked him to compile for the benefit of my students. I perused the "list," which was neatly typed on a 3x5 card:

> *what I know about homo sapiens*
> you've been brainwashed from the beginning—by your parents, your relatives, your neighbors, your schools, your religions, your employers, your governments. no wonder you're such a mess.

> *what I don't understand about homo sapiens*
> how anyone can shoot a deer.

I stuck it back in the envelope. "Tell prot I'll pass this on. By the way, did you get a copy of Rob's father's death certificate?"

"Nope. They're still looking for it. I'll try to have it for you in time for tomorrow's session."

With that I headed for Columbia to face the wrath of my students. To my surprise, however, they took prot's microtreatise with great equanimity. In fact, as I proceeded to unload as much information as I could cram into the tiny hour, I didn't hear another word about him. It was as quiet as a funeral in there, but what they were all thinking about was anybody's guess.

THREE more weeks! As I waited for prot to show up for our forty-second session together, I reflected on the death certificate, which had arrived only that morning. Rob's father had, in fact, died from "natural causes." There was no autopsy. The cause must have seemed obvious to the local doctor: a heart attack or massive stroke brought on by the unremitting stress of living inside a terribly battered body. Nothing very surprising there.

Without saying a word, prot sauntered in and grabbed up a handful of kiwis, which he noisily devoured.

"Prot, please relax now and feel free to put yourself—"

"I wish you'd make up your mind, doctor. Onetwo—"

"Thank you."

"What for?" he mumbled.

"Never mind. How do you feel?"

"Like I'm traveling on a beam of light."

"Good. Now just relax." Uncertain about whether he was under or just pretending, I checked his pulse: thirty-eight, about normal for the hypnotized prot. "Okay, prot, I'd like to speak to Robert for a minute."

Prot/Robert drooped into the usual slouch, but of course there was no sign of comprehension or movement. "Rob, it's me. Dr. Brewer. Gene. How are you feeling today?"

No response.

"Prot tells me you'd like to get something off your chest. Is that true?"

Not a sign of cognition.

"Well, I'm here. What is it you wanted to tell me?"

I waited for several minutes in case he was on the verge of responding. But there was no indication of any such attempt. "Rob, please listen to me. You don't have to say anything, but I want you to hear what I've got to tell you. If you can hear me, please nod."

There wasn't the slightest hint of movement.

"I know you can hear me, Rob. So just listen. I've got a theory about what happened when you were a boy and I'd like to run it by you, all right? If it's right, don't say anything [a sneaky trick, but sometimes one has to resort to them]. But if it's wrong, please let me know. Otherwise we'll be off on the wrong foot, heading in the wrong direction. Understand?"

No response.

"Think back for a moment to the summer of 1963 when you were six and your father began telling you about the stars. Think of all the wonderful nights you spent gazing into the heavens with him out in the back yard. Remember he told you about the sun and the planets and comets and asteroids and meteors and so on, and how exciting that was? And then he told you about all the billions of stars in the sky, and how a lot of them could have solar systems like our own, and that there were probably intelligent beings on some of the planets out there? How they might be different from us but maybe not so different? And how we might be able to communicate with them and that it might even be possible some day to visit them or that we might have visitors from one of those faraway worlds? Remember how nice it was out in the yard on those warm summer nights with his arm around your shoulder? How you helped your father back into the house when it was time to go to bed? Then your mother tucked you in and kissed you and said goodnight? Wouldn't it be wonderful to be able to go back there and live that time over again? Even for a little while?"

Rob sat like a stone.

"But one night he soiled himself while you were outside and he needed to be cleaned up. Your mother was busy or wasn't feeling well, and she asked if you would help him with his bath just this once. You said you would, and supported him while he made his painful way to the bathroom. You helped him get undressed and into the tub—remember? You kicked his dirty clothes toward the hamper and began to wash him.

"But you were dirty too, so you got out of your pants and T-shirt. Then, while you were leaning over him, his hands began to grope for you. You didn't like what was happening. You remembered the time you were living with your aunt and uncle and everything you'd been trying to forget came back."

Rob seemed to fidget a little, and I think I heard a little choke.

"Not only did your father seem to be behaving like Uncle Dave, but at that moment you knew you could no longer depend on your 'friend and protector' to keep you from harm. *There was no one in the whole world you could trust!* You threw down the washcloth and ran out of the bathroom and into the back yard. Your dad fell back into the tub. You were so distressed that you kept running on into the woods behind the house. It was dark and you stumbled and fell and hit your head against a rock or a tree. You passed out, and when you finally woke up and decided you had better go back inside, you heard your mother screaming. Despite your splitting headache you ran in and found that your father had died after you left him in the tub. He was lying under the water. You were terribly confused. You thought it was your fault because he had fallen and, if you hadn't run away, he would still be alive. Isn't that right, Rob? Isn't that what happened when you were six?"

I watched him carefully but, except for the sound of heavy breathing, he didn't twitch a muscle.

"You never forgave yourself, did you, Rob? You were never able to shake the guilt and sorrow, were you? Rob, please tell me if I'm wrong about any of this."

I waited for quite a while but his breathing quieted and there was no further response.

"Then I can assume my theory is correct and that everything happened more or less as I described it. If not, please indicate this by blinking your eyes once."

His eyelids didn't flicker. But a tear rolled down his cheek!

"All right, Rob. In a moment I'm going to let you go back to where you were a little while ago. But I want you to think about something in the time between now and your next visit. I want you to know something you didn't know before. Your father's death was brought on by the extreme stress on his body resulting from the injury he had suffered months earlier at the slaughterhouse. It was sudden, but it could have happened at any time. He wasn't reaching for you, he was reaching *out*, already feeling the

676

effects of whatever it was that killed him. Isn't that possible, Rob? You couldn't have done anything about it even if you had stayed with him. Do you understand? It wasn't your fault. It wasn't anyone's fault. On Earth people die sometimes, despite anything we might do. You didn't kill your father, Rob. If anything, you made his last few weeks some of the happiest of his life. You gave him something that he needed and wanted. You gave him your love."

Not a movement, not a whisper.

"All right, you can go now. I'll see you again in a few days. Think about what I've told you."

I waited another moment before saying, "Okay, prot, you can come on back now."

"Ehhh—what's up, doc?"

"Not a damn thing. Please unhypnotize yourself."

He complied immediately. Stifling a yawn, he said, "Hiya, gino. Did you find robert?"

"I think so, but I'm not sure."

"Wouldn't you recognize him if you saw him?"

"I'm not even sure about that."

He shook his head. "He looks a little like me. Except—"

"I know what he looks like!"

He jumped up. "Well, if we're through here, I'll just be on my way. . . ."

"Not so fast."

"You call this fast, earthling?"

"Did you hear anything I just said to Rob?"

"You think I would eavesdrop?"

"No. But it might've happened accidentally."

"Well, I never heard a word. You could have been talking to santa claus for all I know. Or any of your other mythical beings."

"Please sit down."

Prot plopped back into the vinyl chair.

"All right. I just wanted to tell you what you missed. I presented Rob with a theory about what happened to him when he was six. How his father died and how he reacted to it. Want to hear about it?"

"Why not? We've still got eleven minutes and thirty-eight seconds left."

I started to recap the highlights of my "conversation" with Robert, then had a better idea. I rewound the tape and played it for prot, who seemed fascinated by it. Afterward I forgot to turn the tape recorder back on for a few seconds, but, as I remember it, he said something like, "Your primitive methods never cease to amaze me."

"Damn it, prot, I'm not interested in your assessment of my technique or of the human race right now. What I'd like to know is whether you think my hypothesis is credible."

"Anything's—"

"Yes, I know, but is it *likely*?"

"I'd say no."

I remember rubbing my temples hard at this point, but the pain didn't go away. "Why not?"

"He didn't die of a heart attack, or any other 'natural' cause."

"He didn't? How do you know that?"

"I was there, remember?"

"But you didn't show up until the funeral, did you?"

"When I saw the body, I realized that what happened to rob's pa could only happen on EARTH. Never on K-PAX."

"What happened to him?"

"He drowned."

Suddenly I realized the full implication of what he was telling me. "Are you saying that Rob's father committed suicide?"

"Did I say that?"

"But how else—"

"Maybe it was an accident. Or maybe somebody done him in. To mention a couple of obvious possibilities." He stood up, flipped on his dark glasses, which made him look like an aging rock star, and sauntered out.

After he left I sagged down in my chair like a sack of excrement. I thought for a moment that this must be similar to what Robert felt. Then of course I realized he was feeling much worse than I could possibly even imagine. But why was he so utterly devastated by what had happened? Did he—did Harry—come forward when Rob's father was in the bathtub? My God! It was Harry who killed him, mistaking his intentions! By drowning him, probably. When Rob saw what had happened, he ran away.

But this was only speculation of the worst kind. Maybe his father simply tried to get up, fell, and hit his head on the tub. I had to find out the truth. And the only way to do that was to drag it out of Harry.

I cancelled my regular meeting with Giselle; I didn't want her to know anything she might inadvertently convey to prot, which might somehow tip off Harry. I looked over my schedule for the next three days. Booked solid. No time even for a quiet cup of coffee. There was nothing I could do but wait until Friday.

Session Forty-three

T HE *Jeopardy* game took place in the lounge late Wednesday afternoon. The contestants, as voted on by the other patients, were "Albert Einstein," "Linus Pauling," and prot. There were no electronic signaling devices, no flashing scoreboards. Instead, hands were raised and Goldfarb was called upon to judge whose was first. Betty (who had managed to survive phase one of the root-canal procedure) kept the scores, and I was elected to blow the whistle when time was up for each half. The other patients and staff served as the audience.

Everything went very well at first, though Alex nervously brushed his hands through his wavy hair several times—I had never seen the real Alex Trebek do that. He had constructed his own category board and was, of course, quite familiar with the answers and questions. At the end of round one the scores were nearly even, much to the delight of the crowd. Every single answer had been properly questioned by one of the three contestants.

Then things began to fall apart. He got mixed up on an answer involving some arcane scientific term, and forgot where Patagonia was (he had some crib sheets, but couldn't seem to find what he needed in the rush and jumble). Albert and Linus tried to help, but prot just stood there with a silly grin on his face. Finally Alex stopped altogether and, despite lots of encouragement from the audience, threw down his notes and walked away, mumbling, "I don't want to be Alex Trebek. It's a lot harder than I thought."

"Do you think he's ready for Ward One?" Goldfarb whispered.

I countered, "Maybe we should wait until we're sure he doesn't want to be Mary Hart."

THE new patients from the Big Institute arrived on Thursday, and a special orientation session was set up to acquaint them with their new home. This was done by pairing each of them with one of our long-term residents, who showed them around and introduced them to the rest of the inmates. However, the tours came to a halt in a big circle around prot, and there were the usual high expectations of what he could do for them once they were settled in, despite the limited time frame.

There were seven in all. One, a man suffering from DeClerambault's syndrome, was certain that Meg Ryan was in love with him. Another was constitutionally unable to tell the truth. (I was pretty sure what prot would do with him: suggest he run for public office.) Yet another thought himself the ugliest man in the world, a "toad," in his opinion.

The women in the group weren't much better off. There was a variant case of Cotan's syndrome (nothing

681

exists), but in her case everything existed except her. To put it another way, she thought herself invisible to all of us and, consequently, felt no compulsion to dress after a shower, stole food from others' plates, etc. Another (my new responsibility) thought that real people were speaking to her from the television set. And there was a woman who simply could not get enough love (love, not sex). First thing she told her new doctor (Beamish) was that "No one ever called me 'J'aime.'" And finally, we had a new "Jesus Christ," but with a twist—she, too, was a woman, the first female Messiah to grace the institute in our long history. She had, of course, been a carpenter.

The "Magnificent Seven," Menninger called them. But all I could see was an enormous amount of frustrating work ahead. Like one of my previous charges, a postal carrier who went berserk because he could never finish the job ("No matter how many pieces I deliver they just keep coming!"), I could see a future with endless patients waiting to get in, like the people crowding around the front gate.

I had asked Jasmine Chakraborty to stand by in my office, which is adjacent to my examining room. (How he got his first name is a long story, and one of the reasons he left India.) Chak, too, had been making retirement noises lately, though he is only forty-eight. Or hinted, at least, that it was time "to make a new change," as he put it. I hoped he wasn't thinking of a move to the planet K-PAX.

Prot banged in and grabbed a huge handful of raisins, which he crammed into his mouth.

There was no more time to waste. "All right. I'd like to speak to Harry now. Harry?"

Prot seemed surprised, but stopped chewing and his feet began to shuffle around.

"Harry, this is Doctor Brewer. I'd like to speak with you for a minute."

Like Robert, Harry appeared to be hiding. But in his case, I could see him.

"Harry, c'mon out. If you don't, I'm coming in to get you."

Harry scowled, annoyed that he'd been found so easily. Apparently he didn't like raisins—he spat them back into his hand and dumped them onto the table next to the bowl.

"Harry, I'm mad as hell at you."

His feet stopped moving and his eyes opened wide. "I didn't do nothin'."

"Harry, what happened to Robin's father?"

"I didn't do it."

"Do what, Harry? What happened to Robin's dad?"

"He died."

"I know that. But how did he die? What happened to him?"

"I don't know. We ran out of the bathroom."

"Why? Why did you run out of the bathroom?"

"Rob was afraid."

"Of what? What was Robin afraid of, Harry?"

"He was afraid of his daddy."

"What was his daddy trying to do to him?"

"He swung at Robin."

"He tried to *hit* him?"

"Yes."

"Why?"

He seemed to shrink away from me. "I don't know!" It occurred to me that perhaps he was lying about this to protect his alter ego. Or perhaps himself.

"Where did you run to?"

"We ran out into the woods. We was running as fast

as we could. I tried to get Robin to slow down. He ran right straight into a tree. I tried to tell him to stop, but it was too late."

"What happened after that?"

Harry settled down a bit and started to chew on a fingernail. "I don't—I don't remember."

"What's the next thing you remember?"

"We were in bed and there were some people around."

"Who were they?"

"I don't know. They were strangers."

"Okay, Harry. I just want to ask you one more thing. Did you push Robin's father before you ran out? Or hit him with something? Anything like that?"

"No!"

"All right, Harry, just a couple more questions. Have you seen Robin lately?"

"Not for a long time."

"Do you know where he is?"

He shook his head.

"Okay, Harry, thank you. You've been very helpful. Now I'm going to ask you a big favor."

He looked puzzled.

"We need to take a little blood sample from you. It won't hurt much. You'll hardly feel it. Dr. Chakraborty works with me. He'll come in and do it, okay?"

He shifted around nervously. "What for?"

"We need to make sure it's all right. It's like a little checkup. You've been to the doctor before, haven't you?"

"No."

"Well, it'll only take a minute." I called Chak in.

Harry's mouth puckered up. "I don't want to. . . ."

The door opened. "Hi, Harry, how are you doing? I am Doctor Chakraborty. You may call me Doctor

684

Jackrabbity if you want. I would like to take only a teensy-weensy bit of blood from your arm if you won't mind."

Harry started to squall. I thought: Here's a kid who may well have killed a grown man and he's afraid of a little needle. What a very strange thing is the human mind!

Chak tried to calm him by talking about his own five-year-old boy, who also hates to have blood taken. "Jag wants to be an astronaut, Harry. What do you want to be?"

Harry wasn't interested in discussing it. He was crying his eyes out.

"Okay, Gene, I'm finished."

"Harry? It's all over. Thank you for coming in. You may go now."

The crying ceased immediately. Harry was out of here.

Before prot could return I called out, "Paul? This is Dr. Brewer. May I speak to you for a moment?"

Paul yawned. "That was a pretty dirty trick you pulled on old Harry, there. You didn't tell him you were going to suck blood out of him." He grabbed the pile of chewed-up raisins and popped them back into his mouth. "If you had, he never would have showed up."

"Paul, this is Dr. Chakraborty. He'd like to take a little from you, too."

"Sure. Why not?" He held out his arm.

"Other arm, please," Chak said.

While "Dr. Jackrabbity" was preparing a fresh needle and syringe, I asked Paul if he knew anything about the death of Rob's father. "Not a thing," he said. "I wasn't around then."

"I know. But I thought you might have heard something. From Rob or Harry—someone."

"Nope."

"Finished."

"Thanks, Chak."

"There is no problem," he said as he hurried out with the precious blood samples.

"Seen Rob anywhere around today?" I asked Paul.

He began to tap a foot nervously. "Nope."

"Do you know where he is? How we might find him?"

"No idea."

"Well, where did he go in the past when prot up?"

He shrugged. "I never paid much attention. When prot came, my chances of gettin' laid were nil or less."

"Speaking of that, I need to ask you a very important question, and I would appreciate a truthful answer."

He looked pained, but didn't protest his honesty.

"Paul, I know you come out whenever Rob has a sexual encounter. What I want to know is whether you ever pretended to be Robert at other times. Specifically, in this room."

His face actually turned red, and he said, sheepishly, "Once in a while."

"When, for example?"

"When you talked about his sex life. He doesn't even like to *think* about it, you know."

"No other times?"

"Hardly ever."

"And Rob was really Rob in his other dealings with Giselle?"

"I really don't care about the rest of his life, doc."

"Okay, Paul. You may go."

"What—already?"

"Just wanted to take a blood sample. Thanks. Bye-bye."

"You got some damn good-looking nurses around here, you know that? I'd sure like to—"

"Good-bye, Paul. Thanks for stopping by. I'll call you again if I need you."

686

He stared at me glumly, but finally went back to wherever he hung out when he wasn't needed.

Prot reappeared and went again for the bowl of raisins. "Any luck, doctor b?"

"Another strikeout."

"Ah, those handy sports terms." Bits of the dried fruit flew from his mouth. "Y'all seem to think life is just one big ball game."

"Is that so bad?"

"Even your so-called scientists spend most of their time playing games when the answers are right there staring them in the face."

I brushed a bit of raisin off my knee. "What answers?"

"Well, for example, whether the UNIVERSE is going to collapse again or expand forever."

"According to my son-in-law, some astronomers think it's going to be an endless expansion."

"So what? You haven't got all the evidence yet. Why do you humans tend to jump to conclusions before all the facts are in?"

"I think everyone realizes this is mostly speculation," I replied weakly. "Anyway, why don't you give us some hints if you already have all the answers?"

"Okay, since you can't destroy anyone with it, though you'd probably like to, I'll give you a hint. The 'missing mass' is right there in Einstein's equations. You just haven't put two and two together yet."

"Thanks. I'll pass that on."

He tipped up the bowl and took in the last raisin. "Well, if there's nothing else . . ."

"There *is* one thing. Have you had a chance to talk with any of the new patients?"

"Sure."

"What do you think?"

"About what?"

"Dammit, prot, about the patients!"

"Sorry, doctor. I've decided to retire from psycho-analysis. They're your responsibility from now on."

"Wonderful."

"Don't underestimate yourselves. You can do it. You've just got to get rid of a lot of the false assumptions you seem to cherish. Believe me, it's as simple as that." He stood and stretched. "Well, I've got things to do. *Au revoir.*"

"But our time isn't—"

After the door slammed I thought: Another session wasted. I didn't even press him on the question of how Rob's (or his own) father died. On second thought, it wasn't a total bust. I was convinced that Rob, in the guise of Harry, at least, didn't kill his father. But if he had drowned accidentally, how did it happen? Maybe I was trying to make too much of the situation. Perhaps prot was wrong and he *did* die of natural causes. In either case, why would Rob feel so incredibly guilty about it? What the hell was it he wanted and very much needed to "get off his chest," but could not?

It was time to play the trump card. To get his "dad" in here to confront Rob, to get the truth out of him before it was too late.

THAT evening I called Steve and told him about prot's advice to the world's astronomers. To my surprise, he seemed quite excited about this. "Einstein's equations? You mean general relativity?" There was a long pause and I thought for a minute he had gone. "Only problem," he went on, "is how does that help us to find the missin' mass?" Another pause. "Unless he's sayin' it has somethin' to do with acceleration and gravity. . . ." I heard panting. "Mah God!" he shrieked. "That's it!"

"Steve? Steve?"

I called back a few seconds later but the line was busy.

ON Saturday night, while Karen and I were decorating the tree (less than two weeks to Christmas and I hadn't done any shopping yet), a middle-aged man came to the door. He was unshaven, his eyes bloodshot, but his clothes were clean, if threadbare and patched. I thought he was looking for work or a handout, though he didn't seem to be drunk or schizophrenic, as many homeless people are. "Got a match?" he squeaked in a hoarse, high-pitched voice. I didn't, but I hesitated to let him in. His face, however, was drawn, and he seemed to be in pain. His breath was raspy. I told him to wait and I would see if I could find one.

As I turned toward the living room I heard him say, "Aren't you going to let me in?" The voice had dropped an octave and had become much stronger. "Remember the Robert Frost poem you read to us when we were kids? Home is where—"

"Fred!"

He grinned. "Well, were you convinced?"

"I certainly was! That's exactly how I imagined Robert's father would be like!"

"Let's hope that's the way Robert remembers him!" He took off his coat and headed for the living room. "If I know you guys, you're decorating the Christmas tree tonight."

Session Forty-four

No staff meeting on the fifteenth; this was the day of the outing to the Met Museum, one of four seasonal "getaways" we provide for all the patients who can, and want to, go. As luck would have it, I decided not to take part, opting instead to speak to the building contractor and get some other nagging work done.

It was a sunny day, and nearly all the patients in Wards One and Two (with a smattering of Threes) gathered on the front lawn, some of them toting a cat. Prot, of course, took this opportunity to address the crowd outside the gate, reiterating his regret that he could take none of them with him to K-PAX, reminding them that there wasn't much time left to change things here (on Earth), and all the rest. None of the visitors seemed to want to leave, however, until he departed for the museum.

While waiting for the bus to arrive, prot, like some

two-legged sheepdog, herded everyone tightly together in the center of the front lawn. Without a word he produced a small flashlight, placed it on his shoulder, aimed it at a little mirror he pulled out from somewhere, and suddenly (according to both the hospital staff and eyewitnesses outside the gate) everyone disappeared.

"It was unbelievable," Betty told me later (they came back on the bus). "One minute we were standing on the lawn, the next we were on the steps of the Met. But there wasn't any sensation of movement at all, or of time passing. In fact, nobody felt a thing."

I should point out here that the integrity of Betty McAllister is beyond reproach. Moreover, Drs Beamish and Chang breathlessly confirmed everything she told me. Not having witnessed the event myself, however, I was still dubious, to put it mildly. "Are you sure you weren't the victim of some sort of hypnotic trick?" I asked her.

"I thought of that, too. But how do you explain the accounts of all the people outside the fence who saw us disappear?"

"Maybe they were fooled, too."

"What about the surveillance cameras? Did you see the tapes?"

"I saw them."

"Well? Can't you admit, finally, that he's who he says he is?"

"Maybe and maybe not," I said, thoroughly confused. "It still could be some kind of trick."

I had known Betty for twenty-five years, and we had always gotten along extremely well. But what she said next stung me to the quick. "Gene," she exclaimed, "you're blind as a bat!"

"You could be right about that. But my responsibility

is still to my patient, Robert Porter. What do you suggest I do about *him?*"

Unfortunately, she, like prot and everyone else, had no easy answer for that.

I left Fred in my office with Giselle and stepped into the examining room. Two weeks left, and I was so damn tired I didn't know whether I could keep up with prot for even that long. In fact, when he came in he caught me dozing. I awoke with a jolt and stared blankly at him, wondering who he was. "Did you really take forty people to the Met yesterday?" I demanded when I realized where we were.

He took a huge bite out of a pineapple and nodded matter-of-factly.

"Then why did you ride the bus back?"

"Thought I'd take one last look at the city."

"I see. And what did you think of it?"

"I thought: At the rate you're going, the whole EARTH will look like this some day."

"Is that such a bad thing?"

"It is if you're a giraffe."

We had already wasted enough time. "All right. Let's get down to business."

He wagged his head and blurted out a chuckle.

"Giselle got us a copy of the death certificate. You were right—it's somewhat vague on the cause of death. Would you like to elaborate on that?"

"Not particularly."

"Okay, damn it, would you please tell me what you know, even if you wouldn't like to?"

"He fell and hit his head."

"Was he pushed, or was it an accident?"

Prot shrugged. "How should I know?"

"You won't help me at all on this?"

"I *am* helping you. You just don't realize it yet."

"All right, fine. I'd like to speak to Robert now."

"No hypnotic tricks?"

"I don't think we're going to need that anymore."

He swallowed the last chunk of pineapple, murmured, "He's all yours," and his head sank to his chest.

"Rob?"

Of course there was no response.

"Rob, I have a surprise for you today. How would you like to see your father again?"

His head jerked, as if it had been tapped with a sledge-hammer. But he said nothing.

"He's waiting outside, Rob."

I heard him swallow, as though he were choking back a sob.

"Shall I ask him to come in?"

He made a few more guttural noises.

"Well, if you don't want to see him, I'll just ask him to go." I stood up and moved toward the door. There was a definite strangled whine. "Maybe he can come back in a week or two." I added, reaching for the knob.

"Noooooooooooo!" he gurgled. "Please! I want to see my daddy!"

I motioned for Fred to come in. He went straight to my patient and put a hand on his shoulder. "Hi, Robbie," he rasped. "I've missed you."

Rob fell to his knees, weeping much like Linus had earlier. He thrust his arms around Fred's legs and repeated, over and over again, "I'm sorry, Daddy. I'm so sorry. Oh, God, I'm so sorry. . . ."

I began to gurgle a little myself. It was exactly what I had been waiting to hear. What I didn't expect, however,

693

was what happened next. Robert gasped, rolled over, and passed out.

While I ran to examine him, Fred, taken aback, apologized for what had happened. "I'm sorry, Dad. I didn't mean to—"

"Not your fault, Freddy. You were perfect." Rob, however, had gone back to his familiar catatonic state. He had finally unloaded the thing he had wanted to get off his chest. Now it was simply a matter of pulling him out of the catatonia. Unfortunately, that could take years.

Only then did it occur to me that this was exactly the state Rob had been left in seven years ago. Had prot gone somewhere else? "Prot? Prot?"

He sat up. "How did I get down on the floor, coach? Howdy, Fred."

"You left us for a while."

"I didn't get very far, did I?"

"I'd say it was a giant step."

"But of course you want *two* giant steps."

"I'll settle for your delaying your trip to K-PAX for another five years."

"Sorry."

"In that case, that's all for today. And prot?"

"Narr?"

"Please don't take any more of the patients or staff from the hospital grounds without permission, okay?"

He held up three fingers, as if giving the Boy Scout oath, and said, solemnly, "I hereby promise not to take any of the patients or staff from the hospital grounds. Until the thirty-first of December, of course." He saluted and left.

After he had gone Fred confided, "I used to think you just sat around gabbing all day, Dad. I had no idea what you really did. Now I see it's a lot of work and a big responsibility. And I think you're probably very good at your job."

All I could think of in reply was, "Your work isn't nearly as easy as I thought either, son."

He hugged me. "I've always wanted to hear you say that." Neither of us wanted to let go. Of each other, of moments like this, of sweet life.

WE finally went to my inner office, where Giselle was waiting. Freddy asked her if he might be able to talk to prot that morning (I had told him she was acting as prot's "Chief of Staff"). She said she thought that could be arranged. I wondered whether something was bothering him that he wanted to discuss with our "alien" friend, but I didn't want to bring up personal or family matters in front of Giselle. She may have been like a daughter to me, but she had only seen Fred once or twice.

Inasmuch as he had been instrumental in getting through to Rob, on the other hand, it seemed perfectly reasonable to report to her, with Fred present, on the progress we had made that morning.

"Rob was there?" she exclaimed. "He spoke to you?"

"Of course he was there!" I exclaimed in return. "Don't you understand that wherever prot is, Rob is there, too?"

"Not necessarily," Fred interposed.

I was wondering whether I should have left him outside. "Why do you say that?"

"Well, his father was there a little while ago, but his father wasn't there."

"But MPD is a far different thing from playacting, Fred."

"Maybe. But how do you know it wasn't just prot

695

pretending to be Rob? Or maybe it's been Rob all along pretending to be prot. Or someone else altogether pretending to be all of them. For that matter, how do you know that multiple personality disorder isn't really just a matter of playacting?"

My son, the shrink. I didn't have time to give him a lecture on the principles of psychiatry, but I did point out that the various personalities originating from a single individual exhibit a number of differences in physical characteristics.

"Anybody ever do any tests like that with actors playing different roles?" he wondered.

Unfortunately, we didn't have an opportunity to pursue the matter. Fred had an audition coming up, and Giselle escorted him to Ward Two and his "consultation" with prot. Nor had I had the chance to tell her that her husband had slipped into a state of catatonia once again.

I sat there trying to make sense of what had happened. But I couldn't get Fred's questions out of my mind. It did, in fact, seem that Paul had been impersonating Rob at least part of the time in 1995. Did he come out that morning, pretending to be Robert, to apologize to his father for him? Was it possible he could have been playing the role of Harry as well? Or, for that matter, prot? Or was I making too much of all this? Wasn't it more likely that what had transpired in my examining room was exactly what it seemed to be: The grief and guilt underlying Rob's illness was born of something he had done to his father? Was it, in fact, a mercy killing, rather than an assisted suicide, an attempt to end his father's suffering, something that neither Harry nor Paul participated in?

Maybe it was time to admit that this case was too much for me. To admit that I might never find out what was behind Robert Porter's problems. To call in someone else. But the only person who seemed to be able to help with such a tangled case was prot himself, whoever he was.

Session Forty-five

AFTER the alleged flight to the Met, many of the staff, as well as virtually all of the patients, of course, were now firmly convinced that prot was who he said he was. Not long after that unbelievable journey I got a call from the research ophthalmologist who had wanted to examine prot's visual capabilities in 1995 (after learning that he was able to see ultraviolet light, much as certain insects and a few other earthly creatures can do).

"You'll have to talk to Giselle Griffin about that."

"I already did. She told me to call you."

"All I can do is ask him."

Since it would have been difficult to truck all of the necessary equipment up to MPI, I sent prot, who was perfectly willing to cooperate in this venture—perhaps he had finalized his list of fellow travelers—to Dr. Sternik's office and laboratory at NYU, along with a security officer.

They left on Wednesday morning and didn't return until late afternoon.

Sternik called me at six o'clock, just as I was packing my briefcase to leave. When I had talked to him earlier his voice was steady, confident. Now he spoke uncertainly in quavery tones, obviously shaken. He confirmed that prot could see light down to around 400 Å and added, "I've examined every part of his eyes and they are quite normal in all other respects. Unusually healthy eyes, in fact. Except for his retinas. Besides the usual rods and cones, there seem to be little hexagonal crystals scattered around the fovea. Whether they have anything to do with his ultraviolet vision or not, I haven't a clue. But I've never seen anything like it. . . ."

I waited for him to go on. There wasn't much I could offer, anyway.

"I was wondering," he said finally, "whether prot would be willing to donate one of his eyes to us."

"Well, I don't—"

"In the event of his death, of course. I think we might learn some very interesting things from those retinas."

I promised him I would speak to prot about it. "But he's leaving us on the thirty-first."

"Leaving? Where's he going?"

"Says he's going back to the planet he came from."

Without a moment's hesitation he cried out, "I'll give him a hundred thousand dollars for an eye!"

I promised to pass on the offer, but advised him not to hold his breath.

THE next day I was swamped with patients, meetings (one in mid-town), and my regular lecture at Columbia, the last of the semester, during which I had to cram in all the material I hadn't gotten to earlier. On top of everything else I had suffered through another restless night, with thoughts of recent events racing around in my head at tachyon speed. But all of them kept circling round and round the central question: Who was prot? Suppose he was an alien from halfway across the galaxy, or Santa Claus, or the tooth fairy, or God Himself. How would this help my patient, Robert Porter? I pondered the alternative—that he was merely an alter ego, a human being from Guelph, Montana. Whatever he was, Robert remained catatonic. When I finally got up I felt a bit more achy than usual and a little lightheaded, and I wondered whether I was coming down with something. It couldn't be the flu, I told myself; I had been vaccinated in October along with the rest of the staff.

Somehow I got through the morning (though I fell asleep during a session with one of my patients, the first time I had ever done so). I was tempted to cancel the lecture, but how could I? It was the last one, and I still had enough material for three more classes.

But the students had heard about the lightning-quick trip to the museum, and already knew about the results of prot's retinal exam. Bleary-eyed, I threw my notebook on the desk, gave them a huge reading assignment, assured them that everything I hadn't discussed in class would be on the final exam, and told them exactly where the case of Robert Porter stood. What the hell, I rationalized, maybe they could come up with something I hadn't.

The discussion was led, of course, by "Doctor Sacks," who declared: "It's as plain as the nose on your face. The father asked his son to help him commit suicide. It probably took many discussions out on the lawn at night, in the guise of watching the stars, but finally, as his dad got worse

700

and worse, the boy became convinced. Now imagine his dilemma—here he was, six years old, and his beloved father was in enormous pain. Wouldn't you want to help him end the misery? At the same time he knew it was wrong to kill his father. He was caught between a rock and a hard place. One night his father said he couldn't stand it any longer. He begged Rob to help him do it. Maybe the boy held him down in the tub, or tied him down so he couldn't get out, something like that. Of course when it was all over and he realized what he had done, he ran out of the bathroom and kept on running, trying to get away from it all. But no matter how far or how fast he ran, he couldn't get away from himself. Not in a million years. It would be enough to drive anyone crazy!"

"And how does prot fit into all this?"

"He called out for help. Prot was the only one who heard him."

"You think he came from K-PAX to help someone he didn't even know?"

"He's here, ain't he?"

I dismissed the class early and went home.

THE next day I had a low-grade fever, pain in every joint. I've always thought that people who are sick should stay home and not spread their illness to everyone they might come into contact with. But there was no choice—I *had* to keep my appointment with prot. So, feeling like a Typhoid Mary, I forced myself to get up and go to the hospital.

I shuffled in a few minutes late for our session. He was already in his usual place, gorging on tangerines. "Prot, I'd like to talk to you."

"Talk away."

"But first I'd like to speak to Rob."

He gawked around. "Where is he?"

"Never mind that for now. Please—just sit back and relax."

He sighed and rolled his UV-sensitive eyes, but his head finally drooped down.

"Rob?"

No response.

"Rob, I want to apologize to you for what I said a couple of sessions ago. I accused your father of attacking you in the bathroom. Now I think it was something else. It may have been an accident. He may have fallen and hit his head. But I don't think you'd feel all this guilt if that were the case."

I waited a minute to let this sink in. If he agreed, he didn't acknowledge it.

"Rob, did your father ask you to help him kill himself? I think he did, and you finally agreed. But you were overwhelmed with guilt about this, weren't you, Rob? Isn't that why you ran out of the bathroom when it was over?"

There was no indication that he had even heard me.

"Okay. Thank you, Rob. You may go. Prot?"

His head came up.

"All right. I'm putting the white dot back on the wall. Go ahead and hypnotize yourself whenever you're ready."

When I turned around, he was already "out."

"Good. Now I'd like to speak to Robert again. Rob? C'mon out, Rob—I know you're there." When nothing happened I repeated almost verbatim the speech I had given a few minutes earlier, ending with the suggestion that he had been talked into helping his father commit suicide.

"You had no choice, Rob. Under the circumstances, I would probably have done the same thing. Almost anybody would have."

Again there wasn't the slightest acknowledgment.

At this point I decided there was nothing to lose by playing the only card left in the deck. "But he didn't just ask you to help him die, did he, Rob? In fact, he *made* you do it, didn't he? He threatened to tell your mother about Uncle Dave, didn't he? And if he did that, your Uncle Dave would kill you, isn't that right?"

The only response was a kind of deep sigh, more like a snore.

"That wasn't a very nice thing your father did to you, was it, Rob? In fact, you realized he was no better than your uncle. You knew he would take advantage of you at every opportunity. You realized then that your father wasn't a god, as you had thought. In fact, he was just the opposite. *Your father was a piece of shit, wasn't he, Rob?*"

He made another noise, but I didn't wait for more.

"You hated him, didn't you, Rob? You hated him with all the passion in your young soul, with all the frustration and disgust you felt for Uncle Dave. You took your frustration and hopelessness out on your father, didn't you? You grabbed a baseball bat or something, and when he was in the bathtub and couldn't get away from you, you let him have it, isn't that right? You killed him, didn't you? You brought that club down on his head and watched him sink into the water, isn't that what happened? Isn't it, Rob? *ISN'T IT?*"

His head came up and his eyes, like those of some animal in the dark, flashed at me. "You fucking asshole!" he snarled. "You dirty, rotten bastard! You motherfucking son-of-a-bitch! You're the dumbest, lousiest, shittiest turd in the universe! *I loved my father. Can't you understand that? He was the most wonderful man in the world. That's why I . . ."*

"What, Rob? What did you do to your father?"

But he had broken down sobbing. At last, at last, at long last, I thought: This is what I've been waiting for. "All right, Rob, I understand. Take your time. When you're—"

"That's why I tried to do to Daddy what Uncle Dave wanted me to do with him!" He broke down completely. "Oh, God, I can't stand it!"

With all the strength I could muster I grabbed his shoulders and shook them. "Rob, stay with me for just a minute longer! Are you saying you tried to—"

Still sobbing, he stuttered, "That's when he took a swing at me. And then he tried to get up. But he slipped and fell and banged his head on the back of the tub. He was dead, I knew it. So I ran away. Oh, Daddy, I'm so sorry. Please, please forgive me! I was only trying to make you feel better. . . ." That was the last word he said before his voice trailed off into a long, diminishing wail.

I waited a few minutes, vainly hoping he would get hold of himself, but there wasn't a movement or a sound. I sank down in my chair. "Thank you, Rob," I whispered. "Thank you for trusting me, my friend. The worst of it is over. Now you can rest. You can finally rest. . . . Prot?"

"Hiya, doc. What next?"

"Please unhypnotize— Thank you."

"What for?"

"For all your help."

"You're welcome, doc." He seemed puzzled. "You said you wanted to talk to me after you spoke with Robert. Was that what you wanted to tell me?"

"Not exactly. I was going to ask you what you know about retrieving someone from the catatonic state. But now

704

I don't think that will be necessary. I think he's going to be okay."

"He told you that?"

"Not in so many words."

"Well, I'll hold his seat open a little while longer, just in case he's changed his mind. You know how these human beings are." He turned briskly and hurried out the door.

I sat for a long time after he had gone, just staring after him. How lucky I had been to get into medicine, and then psychiatry. How I wish I could thank my father for pushing me into it!

That state of euphoria lasted about ten seconds. Then I remembered we still had a very long way to go to lead Robert out of the maze. And, despite everything we had accomplished, it might never happen. Totally exhausted, I fell asleep in my chair. It was another hour before Betty found me. I had missed an assignment committee meeting in which two more of our patients were judged to be ready for Ward One.

I slept almost the whole weekend, and still felt weak on Monday. Nonetheless I made it to the hospital in time for the regular staff meeting.

The hot topic for discussion this time was Frankie. It appeared that over the last few days she had suddenly rallied, lost all her bitterness toward the human race and become almost cheerful. Everyone looked at me; she was, after all, my patient, and had been for more than two years. I shrugged feebly, murmured something about a virus.

"Sounds like prot's work," Thorstein observed. "I wonder how he did it."

Everyone looked at me again. "I'll ask him," was all

705

I could come up with. The refrain was becoming all too familiar.

But I ran into Frankie first. She was in the exercise room doing calisthenics, something I had never seen her engage in, nor any other kind of game or exercise. "How are you feeling?" I asked her inanely.

"Wonderful. Fine fucking day, isn't it?" She continued the rhythmic, mesmerizing jumping jacks, the blobs of fat slightly out of sync with the rest of her body. One of the cats, who normally would have nothing to do with her, watched her bounce up and down like a ping-pong ball.

"Yes, it is. So—have you been talking to prot?"

"Once or twice."

"Did he tell you anything that might have cheered you up at all?"

Perspiring and breathing heavily, she switched to a series of squat thrusts. "Now that you mention it, he did." She farted loudly.

The "two Al's" happened to come by. "I'd recognize one of your glaciermelters anywhere," Albert snorted. (This wasn't such a silly statement, actually. Recent studies have shown that the feces of the mentally ill contain chemicals related to the nature of their illnesses. Shit happens, and it is telling.)

"Could you tell me what it was he said to you, Frankie? Did he give you a 'task' or something?"

"That's affirmative," she puffed.

"What was it? To start exercising?"

"Egg-zack-a-tickly. He told me to get in shape for a very goddamned long journey."

I thought: Oh, shit! "Did he say what journey you needed to prepare for?"

She merely looked up toward the sky with a very -
prot-like grin.

"You want to consider a transfer to Ward One?"

"No, thanks," she grunted. "Not worth the trouble."

Session Forty-six

"How's the virus?" prot asked me when he came in. I started to say I was feeling better, but quickly realized he might be inquiring about the well-being of the bugs themselves. He downed half-a-dozen pomegranates in about three minutes. After he had finished and settled into his chair, I asked whether he was, in fact, going to take Frankie with him to K-PAX.

"She's not very happy here, wouldn't you say, gino?"

"Seemed to be doing all right when I saw her yesterday."

"That's because she knows she'll be getting out of here soon."

"To K-PAX."

"Yep. Where none of the terrible things that befell her on EARTH can happen to her."

"Because there are none of us lowly human beings there, you mean."

"You said it, I didn't."

"But Frankie is human! So is Bess!"

"No they aren't! That's why you locked them up here in your jail!"

"They aren't *Homo sapiens?*"

"Of course they are. But being 'human,' my dear sir, is a state of mind. And a nasty one at that."

"All right. Who else is on your list?"

"Only ninety-nine other beings, unfortunately."

"All right, Mr. Spock. I'd like to speak with Robert now."

"Very well, captain." His head drooped down slightly. It was a familiar sight.

"Rob? Can we talk?"

He declined the offer.

I was on thin ice again, but I remembered one of our former director Klaus Villers' maxims: Extraordinary cases require extraordinary measures. "Rob, what do you think of going to K-PAX with prot? Everything would be different there. You could forget the past, get a fresh start. Does that idea appeal to you?"

There was no sign it did.

"I'll tell you what. Just nod if you'd like to get away from all this. Do you want to go to K-PAX, Rob?"

I watched him closely for any sign of movement. It was barely possible even to tell whether he was breathing.

"Rob, there's something you may not know. On K-PAX you would be able to see your father again any time you want. Did you know that?"

I thought he jerked his head a little, though it might have been wishful thinking on my part.

"That's right, Rob, they have a wonderful device there, a computer with all-sense capability. You can roam the

709

fields of your boyhood, wrestle the Hulk, visit with your father before he was injured in the slaughterhouse, play chess or watch the stars with him, whatever you'd like to do. Sound good?"

Was it a hint of a smile I saw, or only my imagination?

"You could talk to your father, tell him how sorry you are, and life would go on as if nothing had happened. Would you like that, Rob? Think about it!"

I literally felt my heart jump as his head slowly began to rise. Slowly, slowly, slowly. Finally, he murmured, "Would Giselle and our son get to go, too? I'd like Dad to meet them."

I choked back a sob. "That's up to prot, Rob. Want to speak to him about it?"

He nodded once before his head fell back to his chest. Almost immediately he looked up again. "Was Robert here?"

"You just missed him."

"I thought I felt some pretty strong vibes."

"He was right here, prot. But only for a minute or two. See if you can find him, will you? He can't have gone far." My eyes were very tired, and I closed them for a moment. The next thing I knew I was alone; both prot and Robert were gone.

GISELLE, of course, was elated that Rob might be going to K-PAX. Before I could tell her the rationale for my promise to him, she exclaimed, "I've got so much to do!"

"Wait!"

She whirled around. "Yes?"

"What will you do if Rob changes his mind again?"

"I haven't got time for mind games, Dr. B. I've got to find prot. See you later!"

I wondered, sadly, what would happen when prot "departed" and left all three of them behind. Would I have the whole Porter family as patients? I went home to try to recover from the lingering effects of the virus and to discuss retirement plans with my wife.

IT finally turned colder on Christmas Eve, and seemed more like winter. Nonetheless, the crowd outside the front gate was still in an upbeat mood, drinking hot beverages obtained from a vendor and singing songs of the season. Someone had even put up a Christmas tree, which had been decorated with stars of all sizes and shapes. I could also see a menorah or two, candles lit. Not Rockefeller Center, but beautiful nonetheless.

Nothing much was going on inside the walls. It was a day of parties in all the wards, the first in Ward Four, and we worked our way down from there. I still didn't feel well enough to play Santa Claus, and turned that duty over to prot, who delighted in belting out "Ho, ho, ho's" at every turn. There was a gift for each of the residents, and cake and punch. The psychopaths were released from their cells one or two at a time. Perhaps it was only the spirit of the season, but they all seemed in complete control, not an evil thought among them. Even Charlotte, in her orange shackles, seemed cheerful and composed. Of course she has always gotten along well with men, right up to the time she bites off some part of their anatomy.

Ward Three was a bit more relaxed, there being little danger to the staff except for the odd pie in the face or the rare occasion when one of the sexual deviates occasionally pinched a nurse.

I found Jerry working on a perfect replica of the Statue of Liberty, right down to the patina of green oxides and the little silvery sun reflector in her torch. "Some cake or cookies, Jerry? They're your favorite—chocolate chip!"

"Chocolate chip, chocolate chip, chocolate chip," he mumbled, apparently without comprehension. But he grabbed the one I offered and whisked it into his mouth without missing a beat. I watched him work for a while, wondering, as I did so, how prot had managed to get through to him two years earlier and why the rest of us couldn't. Maybe he was right – if we could learn to really feel what they feel . . . But I was too old to start over. I only hoped my son Will and "Oliver" and the rest of their generation would have more success than I, that psychiatry would soon be making the kinds of miraculous strides being revealed almost daily in other fields of medicine. And I thought: What a wonderful time to be born!

The Ward Two party was combined with Ward One's. I'd never seen the patients in such a happy state. Especially the "Magnificent Seven," who seemed to be an optimistic bunch, despite their various problems. I wondered whether they were anticipating visits to "Dr. prot" and expecting to move down to One soon, as had Albert and Alice, who were perfectly all right as long as they stayed together. Indeed, having little choice, apparently, they were planning to be married as soon as they were discharged.

Alex had brought some work to the party. He was one of those who had been transferred to One, having announced he wanted to be a librarian. What could be more sane? He was reading a book called *Computers for Nitwits*. When I asked him about it he explained that everything was on computers these days. "Why, I wouldn't be surprised if books and magazines became obsolete altogether!" I could only hope he was wrong about that. Karen and I had planned to spend a significant part of our retirement devouring all the books we had never found time to read.

The changes in Linus and Ophelia were tremendous. Linus was the happiest guy at the party—somewhere he had found a cowboy hat and was practicing his rope twirling—and Ophelia the loudest. In fact, she wanted to order everyone around, trying to make up for lost time, I suppose. Well, I thought, not all sane people are angels.

I found prot surrounded by several of the other patients, and the usual dozen cats. I was surprised when he asked to speak with me. Everyone else pretended to be annoyed, but they knew he wouldn't be far away. Not, at least, until the thirty-first.

When we were ensconced in a corner he said, "Robert sends you his apologies."

"For what?"

"He won't be seeing you again."

"You spotted him?"

"Yep."

"But we have two more sessions!"

"He has nothing more to tell you before he goes."

All I could think of was: God Almighty, what have I done? "What about Giselle and little Gene?"

"We'll work something out."

"Still scheduled for December thirty-first?"

"Right after breakfast."

"Can't you—"

"No way, José."

"In that case," I sighed, "I wonder whether you'd like to spend Christmas with Karen and me. Abby and Steve and the kids will be there too, and maybe Fred."

"Why, shore, if there aren't any dead birds on the table (I had told him about the soy turkey on Thanksgiving).

"They all want to say good-bye."

"Where they going?"

IT rained on Christmas. Betty and her husband brought prot, but that was the last they saw of him that day. Steve, who had been appointed acting chair of the astronomy department now that Flynn was combing the world for supplies of spider excrement, cornered him most of the time. I didn't mind. After toying with the idea of trying to call forth Robert, I decided against it. Seeing all the food and gifts and decorations might have brought back childhood memories and made things even worse. This would be a non-session. Only Will, who was spending the holiday with Dawn's family in Cleveland, was missing. And, of course, Jenny out in California. But both called to wish us a Merry Christmas and it was almost as if we were all together again.

Steve wanted to know everything prot had to tell him about the moment before the Big Bang, whether there was really a theory of everything, how soon the universe would stop expanding and begin to contract, what would happen at the time of the Big Crunch, and so on. Above all, however, he wanted prot to be the first to know that his newly programmed computer confirmed his hypothesis that if the expansion of the universe were accelerating, a new cosmological constant would slow it back down again.

Prot yawned. "Yes, I know."

"One more thing: Hawking has said that even though nothing can escape from black holes, they can still leak radiation. True or false?"

"False!"

"They don't?"

"No—they can leak *everything*! Otherwise how do you

explain the BIG BANG, which started out as the BLACKEST HOLE of all time?"

"How can I thank you for putting me on to all this?"

"Tell your fellow humans to stay away from the STARS until they learn that all the other beings in the UNIVERSE aren't there for their benefit."

Later, when we had gathered around the table, he remarked, "You humans are at your best this time of year, when you begin to notice there are other people around besides yourselves. Why not share this generosity of spirit with the other beings on your PLANET, just for this one day?" He finished his glüg (Karen is of Scandinavian origin) and asked for more.

Abby, at least, had long been convinced. This time it was a yam duck. And Karen had prepared his usual enormous fruit salad. Prot gobbled it all down, then sat back and patted his bulging stomach. "I'm going to have to go on a diet when I get back," he sighed. I thought: How very human!

The subject turned to our plans for the upcoming year, beginning with the New Year's Eve party Karen was planning for all our friends. Someone brought up the subject of the big celebration two years hence.

"One of the saddest things about your beings," prot informed us, "is that you're all looking forward to a new millennium, when things will be better than they are now. But you're all going to wake up in the next century and everything will be just like it was before. Except for one thing, of course," he added, almost as an afterthought. "It will be your last."

But Rain wasn't convinced. "Prot, what's the first thing we have to do in order to survive the next century?"

"Everything."

"Everything?"

"It's all interrelated. For example, you can't reduce your numbers until you eliminate your religious beliefs. And you can't do that as long as there is an abundance of ignorance and a dearth of education. But you can't change that as long as people with the most money use it to maintain the status quo. And if you maintain the status quo, your environment will soon collapse. But you can't protect the environment from collapse until you reduce your numbers—shall I go on?"

"Let's open the presents first!" shouted Star, to everyone's relief.

There were the usual gifts—ties, shaving lotion, computer games for the kids, a squeaky toy for Oxie, dried fruit for prot. But there were also presents under the tree *from* him. He handed one of them to me. "You first."

Hoping not to find any unwanted surprises, I carefully opened the little box. Inside was a smaller one. And inside that an even smaller one. And inside that there was one so tiny I was sure I would never be able to get it open. I didn't know whether to laugh or cry. The others opened their gifts and, without a word being spoken, everyone carefully separated his or her pea-sized box from the rest.

"Let's sprinkle them on the tree," Star suggested, and we all did so.

Prot lifted his glass and wished us all a Merry Christmas. "And a happy retirement to all the fogeys present. May they live a thousand years!" Glasses clinked like so many bells.

Afterward, while Steve was having his last shot at prot, I cornered Fred to report on Robert's progress. "He's through the worst of it," I assured him. "Now I think he can accept what happened to him and go on to the next

716

stage—grief. Fortunately, given enough time, we can do something about that."

He nodded, but seemed distracted by something. It appeared that this was the moment he had chosen to tell me what had been bothering him recently. Or perhaps longer. If he didn't want to be an actor anymore (and I understood how difficult the profession was), what then? Was it possible he had decided he wanted to be a doctor, like me? Would there be another psychiatrist in the family? I prodded him a little. "Were you able to talk to prot the other day?"

"Yes. He helped me to decide."

"Decide what?"

"To tell you something I've been wanting to tell you for a long time."

I didn't like the sound of that. "I'm listening, son."

"Dad," he blurted out, "I don't want the house, and I don't want to get married."

"You mean—"

"No, I'm not gay. In fact, I've got more women than I can handle."

"I thought it was the ballerina."

"Actually, it's two ballerinas and a flight attendant and an assistant producer. At the moment."

"Sounds like you need help, Fred."

"No, thanks, Dad. I'm having way too much fun. It's the house I wanted to talk to you about, mostly. I know you were thinking of passing it on, and I know how much it means to you to keep it in the family. But it's not right for me. And neither is the suburban life."

"Why now, Freddy? Why are you telling me now?"

"I think it was what happened in your examining room. I didn't want to be sorry later on, when it might be too late, for not sharing these things with you."

That I could understand.

"Does this mean you don't want to be a psychiatrist?"

"Why in the world would I want to be a psychiatrist? I love acting. In fact, I was going to tell you that I just got promoted to the Broadway production of *Les Mis*!"

It was my turn to hug *him*. "That's great news, Freddy. Congratulations!"

"Thanks, Dad."

But the surprises weren't over yet. With prot they never are. As everyone was leaving, he took me aside and whispered, "Karen has breast cancer. It's no problem now, but someone ought to take a look at it."

That night, when we had finally gotten to bed, I casually asked her when she was due for a mammogram.

"Funny you should ask about that. I just had one a month ago. It was negative. But prot suggested I make another appointment."

"Are you going to do it?"

"Right after the first of the year."

"Happy New Year," I said dismally.

"Don't be silly. This is what happens when you get old. Things start to go wrong. That's why we need to enjoy life now, before it's too late."

At that moment I promised myself I would definitely hang up my yellow pad as soon as possible after prot's imminent "departure."

I found out later that before he had showed up for Christmas he had somehow gotten into Ward Four and offered his genitalia for the taking by Charlotte. "I have no use for them," he apparently told her.

She merely laughed at him, explaining that she only took those from men who tried to hit on her. It was then that the whole sordid story of her own abuse by her *grandfather* came out. (As prot might have said, "People!") As of this writing she's engaged in intensive psychotherapy with Carl Thorstein, and he tells me there is some hope for a future for her after all!

It's events like this that make psychiatry and, for that matter, life on Earth, so thoroughly unpredictable.

Session Forty-seven

WHEN prot came in for our final session, I had a basket of shiny apples ready for him.

"Red Delicious!" he exclaimed. "My favorite!"

"Yes," I murmured. "I know." After he had disposed of most of them, cores and all, I told him I wanted to say good- bye to Robert and the others.

He nodded and closed his eyes contentedly.

I waited for a moment. "How do you feel, Rob?"

No reply.

"Did you think about what we discussed last time?"

Probably, but he wasn't about to go through any further trauma on the eve of his departure for paradise, and who could blame him? All I could do was wish him godspeed. Maybe there was a slight response to that heartfelt senti- ment, maybe not.

I watched him a few more minutes, wondering what he was thinking as he sat there frozen in time. Was he running in the field behind the house with his big dog, Apple? Gazing at the stars with his beloved father? Watching TV with his girlfriend Sarah? Tossing a giggling Gene into the air? Farewell, Rob. Farewell for now, my friend.

"Paul?"

He wasn't too eager to show up, either.

"Anything you want to get off your chest before you go?"

Apparently there wasn't.

I couldn't help thinking: He's going to be awfully disappointed by the women on K-PAX. "Good-bye, Paul, or whoever you are. And good luck to you."

He lifted his head for just a moment, winked, and replied, "I make my own luck."

"And Harry, you little devil. Take care of yourself and Rob."

Harry didn't make a move. He wasn't about to come out and get stuck with a needle.

"And don't get into any trouble!" I added like a worried father.

Though it doesn't show up clearly on the tape, I distinctly heard a muffled, "I won't!"

"Okay, prot, you can come on back now."

"Hello, hello, hello, hello," he spouted. One for each of them, I suppose.

"I just wanted to thank you again for all you've done for our patients."

"Not at all. I was well compensated for it." (He meant the fruit, presumably.)

"Prot, I've just got a few loose ends to tie up, okay?"

"If you say so. But there will always be more, no matter how many you tie up."

721

"No doubt. But I'd just like to clear up a few small matters before you go. For example, was Rob here last month? Or did he go to Guelph? Or somewhere else?"

"No idea, coach. You'll have to ask *him*."

It was far too late to point out that I *was* asking him. "Tell me this, then. Where did *you* go when you briefly left the hospital, now and two years ago?"

"To prepare those who would be going with me. And to offer my condolences to those who wouldn't."

"How did you know who wanted to go?"

He locked his hands behind his head and smiled, for all the world like someone who has accomplished some important task a little ahead of time. "The humans sent letters, remember? The others conveyed their wishes through the—uh—what you would probably call 'the grapevine.'"

"You mean the message is passed on from one being to the next—something like that?"

"Only far more complicated. When an elephant knows something, every elephant in the WORLD knows it."

"How can we verify that?"

"Ask them!"

"All right. Here's another question for you. You claim you age about seven months every time you come to Earth, right?"

"That's right!"

"So how could you travel halfway across the galaxy when Robin needed your help, and get there in time?" I asked smugly. "For that matter, why didn't it take seven months for his cry to get to K-PAX?"

"Gene, gene, gene. Haven't you heard anything I've said in the past 7.65 years? It takes no time at all to go from one place to another on the highest overtones of light energy. But time is relative for the traveler, and *he* ages a certain amount. Get it?"

"Not really." But there was little point in pursuing the matter. And it was time to say my final good-bye. "Any last words for me before you go, my alien friend?"

"Remember what I told you. You can solve the problems of any other being, and even a whole PLANET, if you could just learn to put yourself in his or her place. In fact, that's the *only* way you can do it."

"Thanks, I'll try to remember that."

Sensing there was nothing left for me to say, perhaps, he stood up.

"Just one last question."

"That'll be the day."

"Why only a hundred passengers? Why not two hundred? Or a thousand? Or a million?"

"I had no idea when I came here that damn near everybody wants to get off this WORLD. But next time . . ."

"Does that mean you've changed your mind and you'll be coming back?"

"Not a chance. But there might be others, and they'll know the score."

"How soon?"

He shrugged. "Maybe tomorrow. Maybe never. But if any other visitors do show up here, I hope you'll treat them well."

"Red Delicious and pitch-black bananas."

"Maybe my trip hasn't been for nothing after all!" He grabbed the remaining apples, stuffed them into a pocket, and, with a backward wave, was out the door.

"See you tomorrow," I murmured to myself as I stepped into my office, where Giselle was waiting with her son. She wanted him to say good-bye to me. Instead, he went for my nose.

"Thanks for everything you've done, Doctor B. Gene. And, if we don't see you again after tomorrow, don't worry about us. We'll be fine." She hugged me hard.

The only thing left to say was, "God bless us, every one."

THAT afternoon, prot, accompanied by most of the staff and patients, strode out to the front gate to say his final farewells to the huge crowd that had accumulated there. Someone had built a small platform next to the guardhouse and, despite the cold and snow, prot hopped onto it and stepped up to the microphone. There was an enthusiastic roar from the festive multitude, many of whom were waving "K-PAX" flags, which went on for several minutes. People were throwing gifts of fruit and flowers onto the little stage. Prot grinned broadly at them. (Someone told me later that it seemed he was speaking directly to every individual there, which included several dogs and cats, a few birds, and even a fish or two, held up high in their little bowls so he could see them.) Scattered here and there also were several vans and television cameras. Police were all over Amsterdam Avenue, which had been closed to traffic. I also spotted the G-men, unmistakable in their crew cuts and trim blue suits, up near the makeshift podium.

At last everything settled down and it became very quiet. "I'll be leaving you soon," he began, "and I shall miss you all."

Cries of "No!" were quickly stilled by an uplifted hand.

"Many of you understand that a great many changes need to be made to turn your beautiful EARTH into the paradise it could be. I have said consistently that how you do this is something you have to work out for yourselves. Yet I keep getting cards and letters telling me you don't know where to begin. Nothing could be simpler. *First, do no harm, either to your PLANET or any of your fellow beings—*"

Suddenly a shot rang out. At exactly that instant prot tilted his head to the side and the bullet whizzed past him, piercing his left ear. A scuffle broke out in the crowd and several people grappled with the gunman. Someone took the weapon away, and another man grabbed the woman's arm and twisted it around her back. She screamed, and there was a lot of other noise and confusion.

Prot, the blood running down his cheek, lifted his hand again and said, without raising his voice in the slightest, "Leave her alone. She's just following orders she received years ago from her family, her friends, and almost everyone else she knows. Don't hurt her, don't throw her in jail. Teach her."

By now, Chak had climbed onto the podium and clamped a gauze onto prot's damaged ear. He went on as if nothing had happened. "And now, my friends, I must leave you. Some day, if you somehow survive the twenty-first century, other K-PAXians may visit you. And who knows—some of your grandchildren may make the trip to the other side of the GALAXY. It's not so far away, really." He waved again, jumped down from the platform, Chak trailing along behind, and trotted back inside.

Long after the commotion had died down, the crowd finally began to disperse, except for a few souvenir hunters who lingered. In an hour or two the sidewalk was clear, and cars and taxis were once again honking past the gate. It was as if prot had never been here.

★ ★ ★

THAT evening there was another huge party in the Ward Two lounge, organized by my wife and Betty McAllister. Everyone was there, including most of the former patients who had departed the hospital in the past seven and a half years: Howie, Ernie, Chuck and Mrs. Archer, Maria in her nun's habit, Ed and LaBelle Chatte, Whacky and his voluptuous girlfriend, Lou and her daughter Protista, Rudolph, Michael and his new wife, Jackie and her stepfather, Bert, and all the others who had come into contact with prot. Some of my own family were there, too, including Abby and Steve and the boys, Freddy and two of his lady friends, and Will and Dawn, who was beginning to look something like the *Mona Lisa*. Cassandra was already predicting that the unborn child, a boy, would grow up to be a psychiatrist! I told her we would see about that.

Frankie, the lucky winner of an all-expenses-paid trip to Utopia, was all smiles (though she affectionately called everyone she ran into an "anal orifice") as were Giselle and little Gene. They were all so happy, in fact, that I almost wished I were going with them. I knew, of course, that tomorrow morning the sky was going to fall and I would have to deal not only with their devastating disappointment, but with that of Robert Porter as well.

Even so, I didn't want to spoil the party, and it was well past midnight when it finally broke up and all the patients made their tearful farewells and went to their beds. I finally escorted prot, along with Giselle and her son, to his room, where they would all spend the night, or what was left of it. "Well, thanks again," I murmured, taking his hand.

"Enjoy your retirement, gino," he responded. "You've earned it."

Giselle thrust the baby into his arms and gave me

another hug and a kiss, smack on the mouth. Prot, with no experience in such matters, held him as though he were the most fragile thing in the universe.

I took my godson from him and kissed him on the forehead. "Good-bye, kid," I told him, tweaking his little nose. "Don't take any wooden yorts."

"My beings didn't raise no dummies," I distinctly heard him reply, unless prot was an expert ventriloquist along with everything else.

I was up early the next morning with Chak and the rest of the medical staff, trying to prepare for anything that might happen. I was especially concerned about a possible storm of mass hysteria, which would have been a nightmare. "Not to worry at all," he kept telling me. "Everything will be very fine."

We got to the dining room before seven, but prot and his "family" were already there, gorging themselves on cereal (with rice milk) and fruit. It was a quiet breakfast, most of the patients having decided to let them enjoy their last meal on Earth in private.

Prot, wearing his usual blue corduroys and denim shirt, seemed his normal self—unconcerned, confident. He lapped up at least a quart of orange juice, several dishes of prunes, and one last bunch of overripe bananas. I noticed that his ear was still bandaged. K-PAXians, it appeared, were as slow to heal as the rest of us.

"Well, it's time," he said, when all the fruit was gone except for the dried ones, which he was taking with him.

There was a last piney hug from Giselle, and even a quick one from Frankie. "Get that nose fixed," she admonished. Prot thanked me for "your patience" (patients?), and hoped that "all your mental problems will be little ones."

727

A few of the inmates and staff said their final farewells and wandered over to the lounge, where many of the others had already assembled, as had the CIA, with their sensors, recorders, and cameras. The press photographers waited impatiently on the other side of the room. Apparently there was little time left. Prot immediately gathered the three of them together, brought out his little mirror and flashlight, and gave one last wave (each of us was sure he was waving to him or her). Frankie, blowing kisses, shouted, "Good-bye, you bastards! Fuck you all! Fuck you . . . ! Fuck you . . . !"

I yelled at prot, "Say hello to Bess for me!" He winked, but whether this meant "I will" or he was complimenting me on my sense of humor, I'll never know. In any case he clearly mouthed, "Don't eat anyone I know!", held out his little mirror, propped the flashlight on his shoulder, switched it on, and in an instant he was gone.

I didn't know what Giselle and the others' reaction would be when it was over, but I expected Robert to collapse on the spot where prot had stood, as he had done the last time prot departed. Instead, he disappeared too, as did Frankie, Giselle, and the boy. All of them had simply vanished.

A few minutes later I got a call from my wife. "Oxie is gone," she chirped, without the slightest hint of disappointment.

Somehow I wasn't surprised.

Epilogue

SHORTLY after prot and the others had "disappeared," there was a call from the Bronx zoo. Several of the primates had somehow gotten out and hadn't been found. To this day none of them has turned up anywhere, but whether they accompanied prot on his final "journey" to K-PAX, no one knows.

But this we do know: About a dozen humans from around the world were also reported missing shortly after our group of five (counting Oxeye) departed. Many of these declared, on the morning of December 31, that they were waiting for someone to pick them up. Some even left notes giving a forwarding address: K-PAX. The only former patients who disappeared at about the same time as the others were Ed (and his cat LaBelle)—prot, apparently, had fulfilled a long-standing promise to them—and Mr. Magoo, the man who couldn't recognize faces, which would be of little consequence on K-PAX.

So far as we can determine, however, none of the children who wanted to go with prot were chosen. Indeed, there have been several reports that prot visited some of the juvenile applicants at one time or another over the past two years to explain why he wouldn't be taking them with him. In every case he told them the same thing he had told all the young people hanging around the gate for the past month: They could have K-PAX right here if they wanted it badly enough, it was up to them, etc.

As for the seventy or so remaining "seats," we can only guess that they were filled by various beings from giraffes to bugs. The only thing we can be fairly certain about is that there were probably no sea creatures included in the passenger list.

So where are prot and all the others? Maybe they're hiding out in some cave in Antarctica or under the canopy of a dense South American jungle. Or perhaps they are all on K-PAX. Wherever they went, they disappeared without a trace and haven't been seen since, except for a number of reports of his abducting a few more rural Midwest couples for sexual purposes, and flying over large cities like some latter-day Superman. Prot, of course, would have dismissed these as "background noise."

It all boils down to this: There are two possible explanations for what happened to them, equally plausible in my view. The first is that prot was no more and no less than a secondary personality of a deeply disturbed young man devastated by the terrible events of his boyhood. Like certain autists he was somehow able to reach into recesses of his brain that the rest of us, for whatever reasons, can't get to. This would account for his ability to trick us into believing he could travel faster than light, come up with complex cosmological theories, and so on.

730

Moreover, he somehow managed to change not only the spectral acuity of his eyesight but the structure of the DNA within the very cells of his body. (Only prot's DNA differed from Robert's. That of Paul and Harry did not.) He may also have been able to read minds, though there isn't much clear evidence for that. And certainly bodies, thank God. He correctly diagnosed not only former patient Russell's bowel tumor in 1990, but my wife's breast cancer seven years later. (Karen had a tiny malignancy removed early in 1998 and the prognosis is excellent.) Not to mention all the psychiatric patients he set on the road to recovery with his uncanny intuition. The little boxes he gave us all for Christmas, incidentally, turned out to be infinite regressions. No matter how powerful the microscope, there was always another box inside.

The only other possible explanation is that prot can see UV light and travel at tachyon speeds, and that he is on K-PAX right now introducing a hundred of our fellow beings to his Garden of Eden in the sky. Fantastic, yes, but little more so than the former hypothesis, I have come to believe.

Let's examine the latter explanation for a moment. Does it fit the data? How can we account for the fact that prot and Robert seemed to occupy the same body, at least at times? Is it possible that only prot's spirit or essence came to Earth, something that he himself denied? More to the point, if only the essences of the hundred space travelers left the planet, where are their bodies? Alternatively, did prot's entire being make the trip to Earth and, for reasons beyond our understanding, could somehow replace Robert at a moment's notice? But if he really was a space traveler, how do we account for the apparent similarities in the lives of prot on his ideal planet and Robert here on Earth?

I have thought about these possibilities long and hard, believe me, and the only conclusion I have been able to reach is that the truth is "all of the above." Or to put it another way, the answer is a combination of both explanations. Isn't it possible, for instance, that planet K-PAX is a kind of alternate world to our own, a parallel universe, so to speak, one of the roads not taken on Earth? Do we all have alter egos floating somewhere among the stars?

Whatever the answer, there are a great many questions still lying in the folder labeled "Robert Porter." For example, how did Rob manage to fool us in 1995 with his apparent "pseudorecovery," and who else was in on the deception? And was it Harry who did away with the intruder who murdered Rob's wife and daughter, and what would have happened if that vicious killer hadn't appeared that fateful day in August, 1985—would Robert and his family have lived a relatively normal life? What if six-year-old Rob had never bathed his father? Or little Gene? Or if his father had never been injured in the first place? Or Giselle had wheels? Will prot and the others ever return? Wherever they are, have they found, at last, a measure of the peace they all so desperately sought?

In brief, I don't know the answers to any of these questions. All I know is that I have hung up my yellow pad and moved to an old farmhouse in the Adirondacks (courtesy of the film version of K-PAX), where Karen and I, and our mixed-breed dog Flower, plan to sit and watch the sun go down till the end of our days. I leave the world in the hands of the next generations, who, I dearly hope, and choose to believe, are up to the job.

In one case, at least, I have absolute faith in the future. My son Will, now doing his residency at Bellevue, is going to be a fine psychiatrist, of that I am certain. He has an ability I never had, that of empathizing with his patients and getting things out of them that no one else can. He claims he learned this trick from prot, but I think it was something he was born with. He and Dawn are now the parents of a beautiful baby boy who resembles his grandfather in many ways (you should compare our baby pictures!), and they come up to see us whenever they get a chance, though Will claims that taking care of the old house, in addition to his professional duties, takes most of his time.

Freddy visits less often, usually for a brief "weekend" (following his Sunday matinée). Now living with a new soulmate in the West Village (the real thing this time, he tells us), he is still a regular cast member of the popular Broadway show *Les Misérables*.

With prot's help, our son-in-law Steve is now chair of the astronomy department at Princeton. Consequently, he has little time for research or anything else, including us (his predecessor, Charlie Flynn, incidentally, is now a student at a Midwestern theology school). But his and Abby's kids, now approaching adulthood (too soon!), are our most frequent visitors, especially in the summer, when they usually stay for several weeks, claiming they don't miss their computers a bit. Abby herself survived turning forty, and is more active than ever in various "rights" causes.

Jennifer, the "real doctor" in the family, doesn't visit us as much as we'd like (though we have been to see *her* once or twice), but she keeps us informed on the progress of her AIDS practice and research. She tells us, in fact, that she is participating in a program to test a new vaccine against HIV and it looks as though it is going to be a godsend.

Do I miss the grind? Not much. Retirement is every bit as good as it's supposed to be. I do keep up with some of the psychiatric literature and visit the hospital once in a while, where Jerry and I usually have a heart-to-heart, his head against my chest, or vice versa. And I have met the woman who took the pot-shot at prot, now a patient at MPI. She claims she was acting "under orders from God." Whenever I see her I remember prot's telling me that wherever there are religions there will always be fanatics.

Thorstein is still there, as are Goldfarb and all the rest; they were kind enough to rename the lecture hall between the first and second floors the "E.N. Brewer Auditorium" (the new wing is still under construction), probably hoping for a large donation from me. Although that expectation hasn't yet been realized, I am nevertheless deeply grateful for the honor.

But I'm beginning to feel like an outsider there, especially since most of the old, pre-prot patients are gone. Just as well. Let Will be the next Brewer beating his brains against the prots and Christs and the other unfortunate people who end up within those walls.

Not that we aren't keeping busy (I still haven't found time to read *Moby Dick*, or try the unicycle Milton presented to me on the eve of his departure). Karen is firmly in charge of our travel schedule and all our social and cultural engagements, including an occasional performance at the Met, and keeps us pretty busy. But now I see opera (and a number of other things) in a rather different light since prot's visits. It is, after all, limited to the joys and tragedies of people. If there's one thing I learned from him, it's that we humans seem to be concerned with only a tiny part of some larger whole. According to prot, every being has just as much right to its life as we do, a view I have finally come to share, though I still have a slice of pizza or a hot fudge sundae once in a while. But no more cottage cheese!

And I spend more time now looking at the sky. In

fact, Karen bought me a four-inch reflecting telescope for my retirement present, and most clear evenings, summer and winter, will find me outside contemplating the stars. Sometimes I look toward the constellation Lyra and wonder whether our hundred beings are up there and what they are doing (part of me will always regret not accepting prot's offer of a free trip to K-PAX when I had the chance). I sincerely hope they have found peace and contentment, and that there is another world out there where my father is still alive and I became a singer instead of a psychiatrist. Whether that is true or only a dream, there's one thing I'm absolutely sure of: There are millions of planets we don't yet know about, worlds we can hope to visit or communicate with some day, and the Earth and the beings on it aren't at the center of the universe. Rather, I see us, the galaxy, and even the universe itself as a tiny part of the wisdom, beauty, and mystery of God.

Suggested Additional Reading

Abbey, Lloyd, *The Last Whales* (Grove Weidenfeld, New York, 1989).

Amory, Cleveland, *Mankind?* (Harper and Row, New York, 1974).

Bliss, E.L., *Multiple Personality, Allied Disorders, and Hypnosis* (Oxford Press, New York and Oxford, 1986).

Buell, R., and Zimmer, N., *Aspects of Love: The Doctor/Patient Relationship* (Cityscape Press, Buffalo, NY, 1991).

Calder, Nigel, *Einstein's Universe* (Viking Press, New York, 1979).

Carson, Rachel, *Silent Spring* (Houghton Mifflin, Boston, 1962).

Cavalieri, Paola, and Singer, Peter, *The Great Ape Project* (St. Martin's Press, New York, 1993).

Confer, W.N., and Ables, B.S., *Multiple Personality* (Human Sciences Press, Inc., New York, 1983).

Croswell, Ken, *The Universe at Midnight* (The Free Prees, New York, 2001).

Davison, Gerald C., and Neale, John M., *Abnormal Psychology* (John Wiley & Sons, New York, 1994).

Dressler, Alan, *Voyage to the Great Attractor* (Alfred A. Knopf, New York, 1994).

Ehrlich, Paul, *The Population Bomb* (Ballantine Books, New York, 1968).

Eisenberg, Evan, *The Ecology of Eden* (Alfred A. Knopf, New York, 1998).

Ferris, Timothy, *The Whole Shebang* (Simon & Schuster, New York, 1997).

Friedman, C.T.H., and Gaguet, R.A. (eds.), *Extraordinary Disorders of Human Behavior* (Plenum Press, New York, 1982).

Garrett, Laura, *The Coming Plague* (Farrar, Straus and Giroux, New York, 1994).

Griffin, Giselle, *An Alien among Us?* (Scientific Publications, Inc., Montpelier, VT, 1996).

Havens, L., *A Safe Place* (Harvard University Press, Cambridge, MA, 1989).

Hawking, Stephen, *A Brief History of Time* (Bantam Books, New York, 1988).

Jamison, K.R., *Touched With Fire* (The Free Press, New York, 1992).

Lear, Jonathan, *The Fifty Minute Hour* (The Other Press, New York, 1982).

Mason, Jim, *An Unnatural Order* (Simon & Schuster, New York, 1993).

Masson, Jeffrey M., & McCarthy, S., *When Elephants Weep* (Delacorte Press, New York, 1995).

McKibben, Bill, *The End of Nature* (Random House, New York, 1989).

Melville, Herman, *Moby Dick* (Harper & Bros., New York, 1851).

Neale, J.M. *et al.*, *Case Studies of Abnormal Psychology* (J. Wiley, New York, 1982).

Payne, K., *Silent Thunder* (Simon & Schuster, New York, 1998).

Putnam, F., *Diagnosis and Treatment of Multiple Personality Disorder* (Guildford Press, New York, 1989).

Quammen, David, *The Song of the Dodo* (Simon & Schuster, New York, 1996).

Rapoport, J.L., The *Boy Who Couldn't Stop Washing* (E. P. Dutton, New York, 1989).

Rees, Martin, *Our Final Hour* (Basic Books, New York, 2003).

Restak, R.M., *The Mind* (Bantam Books, New York, 1988).

Robbins, J., *Diet for a New America* (Stillpoint Publications, Walpole, NH, 1987).

Sacks, Oliver, *The Man Who Mistook His Wife for a Hat* (HarperCollins Publishers, New York, 1985).

Sacks, Oliver, *An Anthropologist on Mars* (Alfred A. Knopf, New York, 1995).

Sagan, Carl, *The Dragons of Eden* (Random House, New York, 1977).

Sagan, Carl, *Cosmos* (Random House, New York, 1980).

Sagan, Carl, *The Demon-Haunted World* (Random House, New York, 1995).

Schell, Jonathan, *The Fate of the Earth* (Alfred A. Knopf, New York, 1982).

Scully, Matthew, *Dominion* (St. Martin's Press, New York, 2002).

Singer, P., *Animal Liberation* (Avon Books, New York, 1975).

Sizemore, C.C., A *Mind of My Own* (W. Morrow, New York, 1989).

Stone, I., *The Passions of the Mind* (Doubleday, New York, 1971).

Taylor, Gordon R., *The Biological Time Bomb* (New American Library, Cleveland, 1968).

Treen, A., and Treen, S., *The Dalmatian* (Howell Book House, New York, 1980).

Treffert, D.A., *Extraordinary People* (Harper & Row, New York, 1989).

Wise, S., *Rattling the Cage* (Perseus Books, Cambridge, MA, 2000).

Wolman, B. (ed.), *The Therapist's Handbook* (van Nostrand Reinhold, New York, 1983).

Yalom, Irvin D., *Love's Executioner* (Basic Books, New York, 1989).

Acknowledgments

I thank Lois Weinstein for climbing this mountain with me, and my editors Mike Jones and Isabella Pereira for being both efficient and co-operative.

PROT'S
REPORT

Foreword

I remember my first encounter with prot as if it were yesterday (he would probably say it *was* yesterday). His demeanor annoyed me considerably until I connected his lopsided grin with that of my late father, for whom I held a deep-seated resentment. Perhaps I was also a bit frustrated by the case itself. Prot was an apparent delusional with no obvious background. Identifying him was like trying to crack open a billiard ball with a feather, and came at a time when I, as interim director of the Manhattan Psychiatric Institute, was covered up with numerous other duties.

But it soon became apparent that prot, regardless of his background and origin, was remarkably empathetic and could sense in an instant whatever was troubling anyone he ever met, including both inmates and staff. Perhaps this is what drew all of us to him, a feeling that he *understood*, and what's more, could help. Dozens of patients who otherwise might still be residents of MPI were soon discharged when prot got to the heart of their problems and helped solve them. It was quite remarkable to witness the recovery of intractable psychotics who had been with us for years, and perhaps even more so was the recidivism rate: 0 (with the notable exception of his own alter ego, Robert Porter). I can't help but wish that every mental institution harbored a visitor or two from K-PAX, or some other wonderful place completely different from Earth, whose inhabitants, even the sanest among us, seem to be blinded in many important respects by our own mental baggage.

But prot left an even wider and deeper legacy than that. During the five years he traveled the Earth with Robert, he made incisive observations on the behavior of its inhabitants, with particular emphasis on Homo sapiens, whom he designated "a freak of nature." It was our human activities that seemed to fascinate him most, though not always in a positive way. Calling us "a cancer on the EARTH," he offered a simple (to him) solution to all our social and environmental problems: start over with a different set of assumptions. Practically everything we had ever done, all the choices we had ever made in the long history of our species, was ill-considered, inappropriate, or just plain stupid, according to prot. Among our "disastrous" notions were the institutions of government, capitalism, religions, schools, even motherhood—in short, virtually the entirety of our human belief systems and values. All this he recorded in a little red notebook he carried with him at all times.

This is not the place to rewrite the K-PAX trilogy, but for those who haven't read it, a brief summary may be in order. Prot was brought to the Institute in May, 1990. With patience, luck, and a little hard work, we eventually learned that there was a very sick man (Robert Porter) he was "fronting" for, a man who had suffered several terrible traumas in his life beginning when he was only five years old. After seven years of therapy, interrupted by a return visit to K-PAX and a two-year hiatus during which prot roamed the Earth looking for a hundred traveling companions for his final journey to the stars, I was forced to conclude that he was both Robert's alter ego and, at the same time, a visitor from space. Whether or not this is the correct interpretation, both of them left us at the end of 1997 and haven't been seen since.

There are some who would disagree with this admittedly empirical conclusion, but no one denies that prot possessed a remarkably disinterested and logical mind, one with a great deal to say about life on Earth as viewed by a true outsider. While we might dislike, or even resent, many of his observations, there is an underlying ring of truth in them that cannot easily be dismissed.

It was his custom to write a "report to K-PAX" on all the planets he had visited during his frequent travels. In August of 1990, when he was about to return to his home planet "for a little r & r," prot allowed us to make a copy of his copious notes about the Earth, written in a language he called pax-o. Fortunately, we had a Rosetta Stone to help us decipher his writings, a translation he had made of *Hamlet* into his native language. With the help of a professional linguist (Dr Carol Boettcher, Columbia University Department of Linguistics, to whom I am deeply grateful) I was able to convert most of his notes into modern English. Where there was no equivalent word or phrase in Shakespeare's great play, but the meaning seemed clear, she has filled in what she believes were prot's intentions. When the meaning was *not* clear, she or I made a stab at it, based on my familiarity with him and his way of thinking. These are enclosed in brackets. Words and phrases in parentheses, on the other hand, are prot's own clarification of meaning to his K-PAXian readers. Otherwise, the entire text is included here without modification except for certain grammatical corrections, such as the use of capital letters to begin sentences.

Prot wrote his notes in bits and pieces, whenever he had time to jot down a paragraph or two (he was surrounded by patients most of the time), interspersing the history and present condition of the Earth with his observations at the hospital and elsewhere. Consequently, his report is somewhat disjointed, though that may simply be the way K-PAXians do these things. When possible, I have connected the various sections into a continuous whole. For the sake of clarity (and to make printing easier), his occasional notes, scribbled in the margins, have not been included. However, I have retained prot's convention of capitalizing stars, planets, and other heavenly bodies, and using lower case for everything else, including the names of individuals.

Over the years there have been numerous requests for copies of prot's report, including those from the assistant secretary-general of the United Nations, and the heads of the FBI, CIA, and other governmental agencies, as well as scientists, sociologists and religious leaders, and these have been honored. But there have also come thousands of requests from the general public, which were impossible to fulfill in unpublished form. I sincerely hope this volume will satisfy that demand, and that readers everywhere will find some interest, if not comfort, in the workings of prot's remarkable mind.

750

Preliminary Observations on B-TIK (RX 4987165.233)

This is a report on the condition of a PLANET in great [turmoil]. I write it for the information and amusement of my fellow K-PAXians, though I suspect that a certain "psychiatrist" will want a copy of it before I leave the place.

During regular visits to this small WORLD, I have gotten to know many of the countless beings here, including the dominant species, homo sapiens, which means, ironically, "thinking (or 'wise' or 'logical') man." By observing the sapiens, I have seen for myself how a class B PLANET can become an A. [Note: on prot's scale, a "K" planet is the most highly evolved. The lowest, an "A," is what's left when a "B" planet self-destructs.] Their inability or refusal to think about what they are doing to their WORLD has put them at the brink of extinction. Despite this apparent genetic aberration, the humans are nevertheless an interesting, if contradictory, species.

Everything I write here should be self-explanatory

except for time units, which are used arbitrarily and without a hint of logic on B–TIK, so a few definitions are necessary:

a "day" is one rotation of the PLANET
an "hour" is 1/24 day
a "week" = 7 days
a "month" = 30 (or 28 or 29 or 31) days
a "year" = 12 months = 1 revolution of B–TIK around its parent STAR

Other terms are more difficult to define. "To commit a crime" means to violate certain human rules, which vary from place to place. Beings who do so are locked in cubes called "prisons," or medical facilities like the manhattan psychiatric institute, where I await my return to K-PAX. Although I had committed no such violations, I was taken, near the end of my journey, to this facility for treatment of "delusion" (did you know that all K-PAXians are delusional?).

I decided to stay. There was plenty of fruit and it was as good a place as any to write this report.

I'VE just been to the next upward level visiting the "sexual deviates." On most K PLANETS, and even some I's and J's, there are many beings who find the sex act so abhorrent that they actively avoid members of the opposite gender. On EARTH, no one can get enough of it.

The only thing different about the deviates is that they pursue it to the exclusion of everything else. It's like spending all your time inducing vomiting.

MOST sapiens live in loose packs, in places they call "towns" or "cities." These are grouped into "states," which in turn

752

make up the "countries." The latter fill every square jart [0.214 miles] of the PLANET except for the great bodies of water called "oceans" or "seas," and the frozen poles. In different words, human beings consider themselves the "owners" of their WORLD. A bizarre concept, wouldn't you say?

It is the division of the entire surface into countries which causes many (but not all!) of the problems faced by the sapiens. Oddly enough, to these beings their country is far more important than the PLANET, and they are perfectly willing to destroy a territory in order to control it. They are even prepared to die to keep out the humans of other territories, unless such beings have been specifically invited. In fact, they are quite willing to go to *other* countries to die if they perceive a long-term threat to the integrity of their own "homeland." This doesn't always work, and borders and countries change with amazing frequency.

Some of you will think this is a [put-on?]. I assure you that every word is true.

B-TIK, as seen from space, is one of the most beautiful WORLDS in the GALAXY. Its watery oceans, reflecting the color of its sky, combined with wispy white clouds, make it a very inviting WORLD as seen from a safe distance.

When I arrived here twenty-seven (EARTH) years ago, my first impression was that the PLANET was just as lovely as it appeared to be from space. The air was warm and fresh, the vegetation lush, and the sounds were those of bird, mammal and insect beings of every possibility. And wonderful fruits were hanging everywhere. It was what the domineering species would call a "paradise," which means, again ironically, the beauty and perfection of B-TIK before the sapiens came to be.

I walked a tiny part of the surface for a while, sometimes pulling a fruit or a vegetable and sitting in the shade of a tree to rest from my journey and absorb the exquisite surroundings. The only feature that diminished my sense of contentment was the strong light intensity resulting from the close proximity of their yellow STAR. This was painful to my eyes until I [rigged up] something from sticks and grasses to cover them.

Of course I knew about the oceans. But there was an incredible amount of water everywhere—rivers, streams, lakes, swamps, pools—sometimes it even falls from the sky! A very strange sensation, being "rained on," as they call it, and not at all unpleasant. Many of the animal beings of B-TIK seem to need a great deal of water, drinking it regularly and staying in the open when it falls from those puffy clouds, which darken as they're about to release their voluminous moisture. Some species even live in it: hairless, finned beings who never leave the lakes and rivers. Water in abundance!

As country china turned away from its SUN, the light intensity decreased, and I removed my makeshift eyeshades. At the transition point, a whole new set of beings came out and the others went somewhere to sleep. These new arrivals had bigger, more efficient eyes for seeing in the darkness. They, too, wandered around looking for something to eat. In fact, many beings spent most of their waking hours seeking food.

This is very different from the operation of the sapiens, who devote much of their lives to doing work for others of their species in order to be allowed the currency with which to purchase their sustenance. When they've "earned" the right to live, they're too old to enjoy it! [Untranslatable K-PAXian expression]

★   ★   ★

BESIDES the deviates, the third level is occupied by people who would rather eat [feces] than the meals provided for them. Imagine what this says about the food here!

AS soon as I was sufficiently acclimated I traveled to guelph, in country united states, to find the boy who had called me here, robert porter. I located him at his father's disposal, and he was quite distressed. Even so, he asked me to come to his house, where he gave me a pair of "sunglasses" and clothes to wear (the naked body is peculiarly offensive to most members of his species).

Robert, or robin, as he wanted to be addressed, was the first sapiens I had ever encountered, and he was a [mess]—well-devastated by his father's demise. I could understand how he felt: a shortened life is indeed a tragedy, even with the endless recycling of the UNIVERSE. You can never know what would have happened to that being if his life had not ended before its natural completion.

After that first visit I made several more to EARTH, but I usually went straight to guelph without any sight-seeing. His needs were great and, like those of most B-TIKians, many.

Rob's most recent blow came five years ago, and it must have been as traumatic as his father's premature ending because he wouldn't even tell me about it. I respected his decision, of course, but it was clear that B-TIK wasn't the place for him. In fact, I had allowed that period of time to try to convince him to return with me to K-PAX. I underestimated. Even after this allotment he has barely said a word. Sometimes I think he would rather die than deal with whatever is bothering him. A true homo sapiens! If he chooses that route, of course, I would be able to bring back another being in his place. Wherever we went during those five revolutions, there was no shortage of volunteers.

VIRTUALLY every nonhuman being wanted to go with us (most were exhausted by the need for constant vigilance). But some of the sapiens were even more miserable. Many of them clung to us when we tried to leave them. One person threatened to make holes in us with small projectiles if we refused to take him along. I tried to explain the error in his logic, but he laughed quite loudly and insisted he was only joking. Still snorting, he offered me the projectile-launching device. What did he think I was supposed to do with it? We didn't wait around to find out.

Others pleaded, begged, and cried. A female promised to kill herself if she was left behind. An astonishingly violent species, the sapiens, much like the zorts of B-POM (now A-POM).

B-TIK is a young PLANET, only 4.6 billion years old. It was formed in the usual way of debris left over from the coalescence of its companion STAR. When it finally cooled, rain fell and fell from the sky and the depressions filled with water. As on many other WORLDS, single-celled plants and animals organized themselves quickly and were the predominant beings for millions of years. Eventually they began to differentiate into multi-cellular organisms, and became larger and more complex. At first these creatures lived in the abundant seas. After a time, some species moved onto the land and adapted themselves to life outside the waters. From these came new life forms in astonishing variation. There are more species of all sizes, shapes, and colors living on B-TIK than on a dozen other PLANETS combined! Some evolved into primates, and one of these, unfortunately, became human beings.

OF the sixty-four PLANETS I have visited, I have never encountered the sapiens anywhere else. Fled once told me that she found a few of them on B-LOD, where they were living in caves. Since there were few other fauna there, they subsisted on grains and legumes. She thinks their WORLD might progress to a C in the next few thousand cycles [a K-PAXian revolution cycle is about twenty years], but with this species you can never be certain of anything.

DESPITE the abundance of vegetation on B-TIK, the first sapiens began to eat the dead beings they sometimes found. Soon they were killing live animals in order to satisfy their newly-acquired taste for flesh. Unlike other beings, however, they did this not only for sustenance, but also for pleasure. This peculiar aberration has been part of their nature from the beginning. And, unlike the other carnivores with whom they shared the EARTH, the humans killed far more than they needed for survival. After a hundred thousand years of this behavior, it's a wonder there are any nonhuman animals left on the PLANET. They even exterminated their own progenitors!

IN the American forests 0.62 years ago we ran into a young sapiens, a hunter. He was "taking a break" from the killing, and we had an interesting chat. He considered himself a "naturalist." Loved the great outdoors, he told me. I asked him why he wanted to kill parts of the nature he "loved." He looked [pained], and indicated that his father and grandfather had taught him the hunting procedures. It was a family tradition. He described the "great times" the three of them had before his progenitor companions had been accidentally eliminated from the hunt. One of his goals was to travel to other countries and try his hand at taking a few "trophies" from them.

I told him I was a scientist studying the power of light, gave him a mirror, showed him how to hold it, and pointed him in the right direction. When I stepped back, the beams of the setting sun encountered his reflector and off he went to C-DAK, where the dominant species are vast numbers of large, vicious, carnivorous beings. No doubt he has had many great times there.

MY visits to EARTH have provided the opportunity to learn exactly how the sapiens' genetic defect manifests itself: somehow it prevents the species from developing or maturing. Here is what I have learned from the writings of the humans themselves and what I have been told by surviving individuals of other species, those who have not yet been driven to extinction.

Like the dominant beings of certain other B PLANETS, homo sapies began to see themselves from the beginning as self-important individuals rather than as a minuscule part of something larger and more significant. When there was a choice between their survival and that of other members of their species, they invariably chose themselves. This self-centeredness pyramided downward to the family members, and further to the tribal unit, all in the name of survival. One's own family came before other families, the tribe before all other tribes. Eventually, as the human population increased and became organized into bigger and bigger units, one's state was defended against other states, and his country came before all others. At the bottom of the pyramid came the WORLD's sapiens population as a whole. And below *that*, everything else in the UNIVERSE.

Their religions (beliefs in powerful, unseen gods) confirmed that they were the center of all existence. Not only were they the only important species on EARTH, but in the entire COSMOS. If there is anything to the theory of MULTIVERSES, sapiens would undoubtedly consider themselves at the center of them all.

BESIDES the deviates and [shit]eaters, there are many other patients at mpi. Some of these are quite content with their [lot], and are as happy as a being can be. Others cry out for succor every minute of their terrible lives. I have concluded from this that a B–TIKian is judged insane when he is at either end of the happiness scale. In different words, you can't win.

I listened to the more wretched sapiens for several hours each day. In many cases, it was the first time any being had seriously considered their plights and how they came to be incarcerated at the hospital. Instead, their "doctors" chose to try one drug and then another to "normalize" them and get them back into the self-centered and violent society which, in many cases, was the cause of their problems in the first place.

Patient howie, for example, was classified as "obsessive-compulsive" because, in order to please his demanding father, he wanted to understand everything about existence. An admirable trait, perhaps, but a bit too much for a human being.

This quest for knowledge is not a problem for most people, who prefer to spend their time watching televised "sports" programs and "situation comedies" on visualized microwave broadcasts. In fact, it was the latter that first suggested to me how infatuated the sapiens are with their sexual desires. These "shows" are about almost nothing else, and certainly not anything like political or environmental concerns—viewers would tune them out, I've been told.

PATIENT ernie is here because he is pathologically afraid of dying. The fear of this inevitable process seems to be programmed into all the sapiens, though perhaps not to the consuming degree that it occurs in ernie. Most people manage to suppress the terror until faced with it directly, at which time it explodes and they "freak out," to use a colorful sapiens expression. It was this anxiety, in fact, that brought about the next step in human evolution, the invoking of comforting beliefs to allay those fears.

At first these beings presumed that powerful deities must be everywhere (though none were ever seen), a god for every dread and, eventually, for every need. When the sapiens began to barter flesh or grains, they assumed, in another moment of "inspiration," that their gods might also be amenable to such trades, and they began to offer them food and clothing in exchange for favorable weather or to cure illnesses or heal wounds. Few seemed to notice that the gods never accepted any of these offerings or that the weather patterns remained random and unchanged, that the SUN "rose" and "set" every day regardless, that rain came and went, and that rivers flooded their banks at regular intervals. But beliefs are the same as truth to these beings, an equation passed down through the millennia. (It is worth noting that the humans of the present time still refer to the "rising" and "setting" of their STAR. This is a good example of how such misperceptions become deeply and permanently ingrained once they have become a part of the sapiens' convictions.)

★   ★   ★

760

ANOTHER peculiar misconception is that the heart is the seat of all emotions. If a sapiens is cruel, he is called "heartless." They often love someone with "all their heart." They know things "by heart," they "lose heart," and buy whatever "their heart desires." One wonders what happens to these feelings, no matter how heartfelt, when a transplant occurs.

A woman in country france once told us that she had been taken aboard a [spacecraft] and sexually molested by the beings living there. I pointed out that no spacecraft has ever visited EARTH or any of the other nearby PLANETS. She took off some of her clothes and showed rob and me where she had been penetrated: under the armpits, at the backs of her knees, and on the top of her head. She was certain she was pregnant with multiple little aliens. Praying for another visitation, she left us her coverings and rode off on a make-believe bicycle.

You'd be surprised how many sapiens there are like her on B-TIK.

AS with the other animal beings, the strongest member of the sapiens tribes became their leader, the one to make decisions and barter with other groups. Females, who bore and raised the children, rarely rose to the level of chief. This tradition, as with the others, has carried over for thousands and thousands of years.

But the strongest member was not necessarily the smartest. The more clever individuals began to take charge of the most mysterious and fearsome aspects of their harsh lives, and an uneasy partnership developed between the tribal leaders and those who claimed to be able to communicate with the gods. These "priests" became experts at

761

appeasing the deities and in explaining what went wrong when the gods weren't happy. In exchange for such crucial services, the spiritual leaders gained a measure of respect, comfort and security without the tiresome need to do work of any kind. This, too, has continued unchanged to the present time.

ON this day howie found the "bluebird of happiness," a goal I knew would take his mind off his determination to learn everything there was to know about his WORLD. He was so excited that I thought he might experience a urinary accident. What surprised me was that most of the other patients were as thrilled as he was. There was genuine joy in their faces when howie ran down the corridors with the news, and I am certain they were delighted to see another sapiens so happy. And the more joy there was to share, the happier they became! A very interesting phenomenon, don't you think?

THE all-consuming delight experienced by some of the patients is much like that of the nonhuman animals. They are totally involved in the *moment*, to the exclusion of every concern about the past or future. All the beings of the EARTH (except for the humans) live this way, in the present. The birds of the spring (the time between the cold and warm months on this WORLD, when its axis begins to tilt toward the SUN) clearly demonstrate this principle. All over the PLANET they sing loudly, and every molecule of their being joins in. They don't worry about whether life has meaning, or if any gods approve of their music. Their joy is infectious, and every animal, even some of the sapiens, feels it.

The same is true for the other beings. I have seen

whales [breach] the waves for no reason other than the ecstacy of it, monkeys swing happily from tree to tree, and wolves roll contentedly in the beams of the SUN. Their joy is so intense that they find it difficult to describe.

Human children also experience such uninhibited happiness until the time they are taught the "realities" of their WORLD.

THE sapiens even bring sexual intercourse into their everyday speech patterns. Humans all over B-TIK, especially the males of the species, describe almost everything as "fucking." Fucking this, fucking that. They do their fucking jobs and go home to their fucking wives and take out the fucking garbage. Their children pick this up very quickly. Is it any wonder they are so fucking bored?

I wrote earlier about the creation of a deity for every perceived fear or need. Eventually, subspecialties arose. Those priests who developed expertise in the healing of wounds and illnesses (with the help of the gods) became physicians. The tribal units, especially if they were large, or possessed a particularly strong leader, learned that they could reap benefits from smaller tribes through force, and the more militant members of such groups became specialists in the "art" of war. Thus, smaller bands became incorporated into larger units until sizable territories were controlled by one or another tribe. From this came discrete lands bounded by rivers or mountains, and therefore easy to defend against other sapiens, and from these rose, finally, the large and powerful nations.

Few questioned the authority of the leaders, or of their priests or medical specialists or military commanders. Children were instructed in the use of fighting techniques, usually in the form of "games." Those who were adept at these contests became the next wave of generals. Those who were particularly clever at recognizing signs of disease or preparing useful remedies became physicians or scientists. Those who firmly believed, or pretended to believe, that the gods could be appeased by this or that recitation or sacrifice became clergymen. All others were expected to work for the benefit of the tribe or state. And so it went, from then until now, and promises to continue as long as human beings dominate the EARTH.

ONE of the favorite myths on B-TIK is that the sapiens would quickly forget about their respective countries and unite to fight invading beings from another WORLD.

That alone should tell you a lot about this species.

SINCE K-PAXians don't discuss nonsequiturs like religion, family matters, sports, and all the other topics that concern the sapiens almost full-time, doctor gene asked me today what we find to talk about. None of the subjects I mentioned—other UNIVERSES, for example—interested him much. If that wouldn't interest him, what would? I realized then that I wasn't leaving a moment too soon. If I stayed any longer I might end up right where I was.

This is one of the great mysteries about the human beings—their vast indifference to how the COSMOS came about, how the SUN and the EARTH were formed, how life came to be—in short, almost everything about their existence. They practically worship ignorance, and choose to live in a kind of Dark Age. Astonishing for a "thinking man," is it not (especially one who supposedly worships the creations of the gods)? What do we make of a species that has little curiosity or sense of wonder?

The rest of the GALAXY knows everything that's going on here, yet the sapiens are strangely unembarrassed by this fact. Obviously they have no sense of shame. Or of humor, either. When I told my [shrink?] an EARTH joke I had heard on I-RUD (Q: Why did the chicken cross the road? A: She was being chased by a sapiens with a hatchet.), it elicited not the faintest hint of a smile.

WE did find a few countries that are more like K-PAX than the others. One of these was sweden, where the sapiens treat each other with somewhat more respect than the people of most other places on EARTH. They are less warlike and more inclined to view other humans as equals, and they treat their nonhuman beings less like inanimate objects than do most others.

But visits to even the best of the B-TIKian countries always make me homesick for K-PAX, where life is good for everyone regardless of their color or number of legs. Where there is no fear, violence, or greed, no government or religious propaganda, and every being is happy almost every moment of his or her existence. If I were to characterize PLANET EARTH with a single word, it would probably be "sad."

Riddle: Does anyone care?

Besides the deity called "jesus christ," a denizen of many B-TIKian mental institutions for some reason, there were several peculiar mental types at the institute. One of the female patients seemed to be a different person almost every time I met her, a victim of something called "multiple personality disorder." This was apparently brought about by sexual abuse. A curious phenomenon in a WORLD where every such encounter is an act of abuse, yet almost everyone devotes much of his/her time attempting to satisfy this apparent need.

I was puzzled for a time about how the genetic defects in the homo sapiens manifested themselves in a kind of permanent lack of development lasting 100,000 years or more. But after talking with several of the humans around the PLANET, I began to see a consistent pattern of malaise, almost listlessness. Again, it seems to be related to fear.

Young humans learn to fear not only the things that might negatively affect their ordered lives, but anything that might disrupt the order itself! In short, they learn to conform, and parents who don't succeed in instilling this trait are considered failures by their peers. Children are praised when they recite the dogmas they have been indoctrinated with, and ostracized when they do not. They are programmed from the beginning to behave exactly like everyone else—flesh and blood robots. (It would be fascinating to study whether this easy programmability is yet another genetic aberration in this species. Anyone interested?)

IN a desperate attempt to prove that I was merely human, gene tried to get me to tell him how to travel on a beam of light and produce cold nuclear fusion. When I refused, he proclaimed we couldn't do those things! How did he think I got here?

I told him about the ultimate fate of the UNIVERSE, but I don't think he believed that either, perhaps because the idea of living his life over again was not a pleasant prospect for him. By now I was beginning to understand something of his own tragic history—where he was "coming

766

from," to use sapiens terminology. In short, he was raised by his parents. If I were human I probably wouldn't want to live my life over again, either.

ROBOTS teaching robots. They call them "schools" on B-TIK, places where children from five to eighteen years are forced to go and almost none of them wants to. These are some of the things they are "taught" in these boxes:

  that it's perfectly acceptable to kill and eat other
      beings, or use them for any other purpose imag-
      inable
  that their history is one of endless wars among them-
      selves and the important thing is not to avoid
      these conflicts, but to win them
  that science is a matter of learning countless facts
  that money is not only necessary, but "capitalism"
      is the only economic system that works
  that work is an ethical necessity
  that their country is the best one on EARTH
  that motherhood is not only good, but is expected
  that the most important goal of any school is to
      defeat representatives of other such facilities in
      mindless games

  This is no joke!
  Here are some of the things *not* taught in the schools:

  how to prevent the deterioration and ultimate
      destruction of the only PLANET they inhabit

767

that the lives of nonhuman beings are worthy for
their own sakes

that their wealthy, and therefore powerful, are using
the other sapiens to their own ends

what the actual requirements for human nutrition
are

how to accept differences and resolve conflicts
between countries

that ignorance is not an admirable goal

that violence to any being, whether real or "make-
believe," leads to violence to others

Surprisingly, religions are not discussed in most schools.
The myths of the sapiens are deeply ingrained into their
consciousness before they ever get to the boxes, and they
violently dislike (fear) having their comforting dogmas chal-
lenged by proponents of any of the other 10,000 varieties.

On K-PAX, this would be like eating only one grain
and pretending there aren't any others until death occurs.

NURSE betty brought in a furry, forgal-like being who,
like all non-human animals, was distrustful of the sapiens.

The baby cat ran across the lounge and jumped into
my lap. What a fascinating being she is! She actually trem-
bles with happiness at the slightest touch. Very emotional,
though she pretends otherwise, like many of the humans
here.

WE once met a sapiens who had become separated from
his son in a shopping mall (a place to buy all the unnecessary products made on B-TIK, accompanied by loud
"music"). He was frantic with worry. The boy wasn't
hard to find—he was the only child wandering around with

768

dripping eyes. When I brought them together, the father hid his fear and pretended to be very angry with the boy.

Why are these beings afraid to show their real emotions? Do they think other sapiens will take advantage of them? Or perhaps they all suffer from a form of multiple personality disorder.

The mall, incidentally, pulsed with young humans. What kind of a WORLD can it be where apprentice adults have nothing that interests them more than buying body coverings and [cosmetic trinkets?]?

DURING the past few years rob and I visited several facilities designed to hold or murder nonhuman beings—zoos, slaughterhouses, circuses, [pounds], laboratories. In all cases the feeling of the animals was remarkably uniform: why are we being held captive; I miss my family; what I wouldn't give for a mouthful of fresh grass; and so on. A pitiful situation for everyone but their "keepers."

Yet none of the jailed or mistreated beings were angry with their captors. They just wanted to go home. Many of the dogs and cats told me that they would try to do better if given another chance. The elephants sometimes pointed their trunks toward the sky and wailed piteously. The great apes often injured themselves. The tears of the whales were washed away and unnoticed. The pigs and cows couldn't believe they were about to be murdered, even when they heard the screams of those ahead of them. If the sapiens were to turn off their television sets and other noisemakers and stop talking for even a minute, they might be able to feel the suffering, hear the collective pleading of all the [incarcerated] animals around the world, together crying, "Let's let [bygones be bygones?]—please let us out!"

Perhaps part of the problem is that the sapiens don't

consider themselves to be in the animal category. Do they think they are plants?

ANOTHER amazing fruit—the pomegranate. Like a thousand tiny STARS exploding in your mouth all at once! Of all the good things about the EARTH, the wonderful variety of fruity tastes are among the very best.

Gene attempted something he called "hypnosis" on me today. When the trick didn't work, I asked him to explain what it was supposed to accomplish. He tried, but I got the clear impression that he didn't understand the process himself. Nevertheless, he wanted to try it again the next time we met!

ONE of maria's alternate "personalities" offered to give me "a good time" this night. It occurred to me that the violent treatment of nonhumans on B-TIK may be related to her condition. Perhaps the sapiens get some sort of sexual satisfaction from harming other beings?

THE means by which the rich and powerful sustain the [status quo] is quite clever (for the sapiens). The cornerstone is the economic system itself. People are encouraged to buy unnecessary products to increase their comfort levels, to impress their fellow sapiens, and to put money back into the system so that their own businesses will flourish. Great weight is put on quantities like "housing starts" and the "the gross national product," which become ends in themselves. Both, of course, are natural results of increased human population, which fuels the economic engines. Is it any wonder that their leaders don't discourage the production of more and more human babies, regardless of their effect on the PLANET?

★   ★   ★

ANOTHER batch of patients on the third level are called "autists." These are beings who can't stand to talk to other sapiens, can't even bear to look at them. These may be the sanest humans of all.

I once read a B-TIKian book called *The Travels of Gulliver*. The author got it about right.

THE role of government officials is to make certain that their constituents fear the loss of their money-making work. This is seen in every election period, when politicians of all denominations promise more jobs (regardless of kind) than their opponents can come up with. At the same time, each promises to lower government taxes on products and wages so that there will be more money to buy even more unneeded devices.

The question you are all asking yourselves is: Why don't those who do most of the work (for a tiny fraction of the profits) refuse to do it? Or at least vote to increase the taxes on the wealthy to pay for their society's needs? Answer: Their leaders dangle the hope that they, too, can become rich if they work hard enough or win a state-supported gambling game.

It's time for lunch. I hope it's not flavored cartilage again.

ONE of the most remarkable things about B-TIK is the flowers. These are found elsewhere in the GALAXY, but not in the great variety and abundance seen here. Their purpose is to attract insects to spread their [gametes] to the receptors of others of their species. On EARTH even the plants are preoccupied with sex!

The trees are just as spectacular. We have a few on K-PAX, of course, those that don't need much water, but not nearly so many as still cover large areas of this PLANET

771

despite their constant diminishment by human activity. I am particularly impressed by the those of red wood, which are extremely hardy and live for thousands of years. Even the human beings are awed by them. Other varieties, though not so tall, are beautiful as well, especially in the "autumn" (the opposite of spring). At that time of year the colors of their leaves rival those of the flowers. The [holograms?] in our libraries do not convey the full intensity of the sights, sounds, and aromas of the fields and forests. I think I'll try to re-program these when I get back.

Maybe I'll bring a sample of the aromatic soil. Wait till you smell it!

ONE [redeeming] feature of the sapiens is that even they sometimes seem to realize how utterly foolish they are. They love to make fun of each other, and even themselves. I have seen sapiens of all countries laugh at themselves until they cried.

THE rich variety of the fauna is also astonishing, beings of every imaginable size and shape. The number of [beetle?] species alone is staggering, and they come in a million different patterns and colors. I have never seen anything like it anywhere else in the GALAXY.

Insects in general, for the sapiens, are something to be despised, to be swatted, poisoned, and stepped on at every opportunity. Otherwise the humans, for the most part, take little notice of the amazing iridescence of the beetles, or the astonishing variety of the other animal species, or the rich and vibrant colors of the spring flowers or autumn trees, the EARTH itself. Sometimes I think they don't know what they have.

★ ★ ★

ERNIE, having overcome his fear of death, thanks to howie's showing him what it was like, is ready for the larger WORLD. But now there's another problem (there always is with the sapiens): despite his years locked in a hospital, he doesn't want to leave. Not because he's afraid of what's outside the walls—he wants to stay and help the other patients.

You never know what these humans are going to do next!

THOUGH they pretend otherwise, most sapiens love war. This is seen in their "national anthems," in the preservation of old battlefields and implements of destruction, and in their enjoyment of films depicting what they call "the blood and guts" of military campaigns. Statues are erected, and even peaceful holidays call for military parades. But the propaganda is far more subtle than that. War and combat are ingrained into the human way of thinking like deep roots in fertile soil. They "fight" everything from tooth decay to cancer, "declare war" on poverty and certain drugs, "battle" their opponents in all types of contests and games, where their anthems are played and their flags (painted cloths representing one or another country) guarded by armed soldiers. People even fight for the right to carry weapons!

The religions are a key part of the program, the sapiens' literature recording the driving out of this or that foe from various territories. But the funniest, or saddest, element of all this is that every religious and government leader promises his [constituents] that a particular deity is on their side in the largest and smallest encounters. Think about that—all two hundred countries of EARTH have one or another god (sometimes the same one!) protecting its soldiers from harm and ensuring ultimate "victory." And it has been this way since the beginning of time.

Here comes patient chuck ...

Chuck wanted to [unload] on me again. This seems to make him feel better, as it does with all the other patients. It must be something like lancing a boil.

A kind of economic segregation has arisen all around B-TIK. Those different from the majority are allowed to secure only the lowest-paying jobs, the ones most humans find exhausting or distasteful. Anger and frustration build, and those at the bottom of the scale try to correct the imbalance by taking what they need from the wealthier sapiens. The result is that many of the former are placed in locked cubes, out of sight of the more prosperous majorities.

The cycle returns again to the elected officials, who promise the voters they will be "tough on crime" (criminals). Rarely does one of them indicate a desire to look into the causes of the frustration and, if he does so, is usually defeated in the succeeding election. In any case, his constituents already know the causes and have little interest in providing solutions at the cost of their own jobs or increases in their tax rates. It's expensive enough just to live their own comfortable lives and to build the cubes into which criminals are locked, without spending even more money to eliminate the frustrations. Cubes are cheaper and, for some reason, more satisfying.

I may have given the impression that all humans are "a piece of shit" (yet another colorful B-TIKian term). This is not true. Some sapiens are virtually K-PAXian in their pacific nature and empathy. On our travels we came across people who shared everything they had with rob and me.

Others have devoted most of their lives to righting the injustices perpetrated on their fellow humans by the more ruthless among them. There are growing numbers of sapiens concerned about the plight of nonhuman beings and of the EARTH itself. These beings would be welcome on K-PAX, or any other PLANET. Here, unfortunately, they are still in the fractional minority.

In fact, most humans are quite friendly and likeable as individuals. It's when they band together that the trouble starts. Their worst attributes are reinforced in the larger communities, where selfish desires always seem to prevail. Again, I think this may be related to fear. The dominant tend to intimidate the weak and the caring, who are afraid to lose what little they have. It's a paradox unique to homo sapiens.

Another mystery for the next visitor to solve.

ON level four are sapiens who feel the need to harm others of their own species. Yet there are many more such beings outside these walls who produce tobacco or meat products or weapons of all kinds, which kill thousands of people every day. [Untranslatable K-PAXian expression]

SAPIENS love to justify their behavior toward the other beings by invoking their "superior" brainpower. I thought I would die laughing when I first heard that one. What could be dumber than beings who destroy their own home for the sake of cheap and easy short-time gains, especially when they have nowhere else to go?

IN fact, most people seem to have a serious and compelling need to feel superior to someone—anyone—else. For a hundred millennia the males of the species have considered themselves superior to the females, and the lighter-skinned humans decreed they were better (in what way?) than those with darker coverings. These fallacies have diminished more recently, though they are still in evidence throughout their tiny WORLD. But the superiority felt by the sapiens over their fellow inhabitants of the EARTH has been relentlessly maintained to the present time.

Human children are nurtured with the milk of other animals, sometimes from the first moments of their lives. As soon as they are able to eat solid food, it comes to them in little jars of flesh. Later, they are fed muscles and organs of all kinds, often disguised by euphemistic names (for example, "hamburger" or "hot dog" for ground-up parts). It is only after many years that the children realize what they have been eating, and by then it is difficult to change, especially when fleshy food is continually put before them and there seems to be no alternative. To ease their consciences and [assuage] their guilt, they rationalize the practice and pass it on to the next generation. And so it goes from millennium to millennium.

THIS day I watched a television program. Then another one on a different wavelength. And a third. All of them were about a wife "cheating" (having sexual relations with another person) on her legalized companion, or the opposite way. Same story, different "actors." I thought maybe the countless female viewers chose which one to stare at because of the commercial messages. But they, too, were all the same.

The sports programs, on the other side, allow a male human to live his otherwise dull life [vicariously].

The nonhuman animals of B-TIK are relegated to lower-class standing in a variety of clever ways:

776

if a person is base, callous, cruel, or gross, he is an
    "animal"—never mind that human beings are
    the only species who exhibit these traits
human animals eat, nonhumans "feed"
humans conceive children; other animals "breed"
nonhumans don't even have children; they produce
    "cubs", "kids", "foals", "lambs", "joeys", and
    the like
people don't kill nonhuman animals. They merely
    "hunt", "catch", "harvest", "manage", "cull",
    "slaughter", and "sacrifice" them
sapiens make love; all other animals "mate"
etc., etc., etc.

ANOTHER subtle method of indoctrination, but quite effective. It has even been used to justify the enslavement and extermination of various "unfeeling, animal-like" races of homo sapiens themselves! One of the most recent of these [purges] is called the "holocaust."

If you're a chicken (a non-flying bird) on B-TIK, every day is a holocaust.

IN country botswana we came across a cow farm surrounded by fences so that other animals couldn't enter. Many of the wildebeests had died of thirst. The survivors told me they could smell the water but couldn't get to it. I made a hole in the fence and let them drink. The farmer came at us with a knife. When I reappeared behind him, he dropped it and fell to his knees. I explained the situation to him and he bowed many times and promised not to close the hole.

Another time, in switzerland, I saw a woman with her face pressed against the window of a restaurant (a place to eat for money). I told the proprietor about K-PAX and he let her in.

THAT'S how it is with the sapiens. It seems that they can be re-educated, but only one at a time. And there are so many of them!

SOME humans blame technology for all their problems. Others expect it to solve them all. They remind me of the blind giants on E-FAP, who put out their eyes so they won't see the beings nibbling on their feet.

IN recent times, a few astute sapiens have begun to notice that the wholesale destruction of nonhuman beings has driven many of these species to extinction. The disregard for the individual worth of nonsapiens is only one of the reasons for this mass specieside. The other is the vast over-population of the EARTH with the humans themselves.

Again, this is closely tied to their manifold religions, none of which seem to be concerned about the choking of their PLANET by incredible numbers of homo sapiens. In fact, many of their books encourage people to "multiply and subdue the EARTH." This is a clear case of getting the message wrong. What their gods must have said, if they said anything, was, "DO NOT MULTIPLY AND SUBDUE THE EARTH—THIS CAN ONLY MEAN TROUBLE!"

And get this: to ostensibly save a few of the nonhuman species from extinction, they put them in prisons. This prac-tice is for whose benefit, one wonders.

HERE is another example of human schizophrenia: many people consider their dogs and cats to be part of their

778

families, but willingly eat any other animal that moves. What could be crazier than that?

THE sapiens' endless production of more and more copies of themselves has endangered even their own survival. The only convenient source of materials and energy, the EARTH itself, has nearly run out of both. Here is the solution the "thinking men" have come up with for the problem of more humans and less resources: produce more resources! As an example, they vigorously investigate, with their limited methods and intellect, what they call "alternate" forms of energy, all of which have as much negative impact on their PLANET as the burning of their dead fossils. I have been coming here since 1963 (the number of years since the demise of the deity called Jesus Christ, murdered, of course, by the sapiens in power at the time), and rarely have I heard anyone in a position of authority propose that humans reduce their swollen numbers as a way to minimize their energy (and other) problems. Instead, as a result of government propaganda, they plant trees and recycle garbage. Apparently this makes them feel as if they're doing something, and takes their minds off the real causes of their environmental problems. People!

CURIOUS thing: most sapiens put their dead relatives in the ground to rot. Who can understand these beings?

HERE is an example of how fear underlies all sapiens thoughts and actions: Rob and I stopped to rest one hot night in a cool, freshly-dug grave. A drunken sapiens, taking a shortcut to his home, fell in with us. Suddenly realizing where he was, he began clawing feverishly at the sides of

779

the hole, trying desperately to climb out of the darkness. I said, "You'll never make it, buddy." But he did.

ONE of the most amazing of the EARTH beings are the whales. Far more intelligent than the sapiens, they have nonetheless been persecuted and nearly annihilated since humans took to the seas in their floating vessels. They haven't the slightest interest in retaliation, preferring extinction to "fighting back".

What gentle, complex minds they have! They can think on several levels at once: singing, feeding their children, performing mathematical calculations, creating poetry, contemplating their surroundings, and a dozen other mental activities all at the same time.

I helped one to escape from a place called "sea world," where he was confined to a watery tank not much bigger than himself. In return, he described all the species of sea plants and animals within several jarts of our location in the "pacific" ocean. He even gave me a brief ride down to the depths of the sea. A unique experience, I assure you!

He said the ever-increasing noise levels were making it very difficult to communicate and to navigate the waters, or even to think. I told him it wasn't much better on the land.

THERE is nothing like these beings on K-PAX. If I could, I would bring him home for a visit. But there's not enough water in all the underground resources to provide him a place big enough to survive. Perhaps we should suggest that the beings of another of the watery PLANETS offer them sanctuary until such time as the humans further evolve or destroy themselves, whichever comes first.

★   ★   ★

ASIDE from the death and destruction perpetrated by the sapiens, the waste is astonishing. The time they spend on sports alone would be enough to completely rebuild their WORLD. Think what they could accomplish if they were to eliminate all the [crap] from their thoughts!

THERE are many things I'll miss when I leave B-TIK—the wonderful fruits, the great variety and emotional warmth of the nonhuman animals, the lush vegetation, the snow-topped mountains, the wide fields of golden grains and, of course, a few of the sapiens. But one thing I won't miss is the constant barrage of "love" and "sex" emanating from the radios, television screens, magazines (flimsy books), and almost everything else. If I stayed here a million years, I would never be able to comprehend the preoccupation these beings have with their obsessive indulgences, which can only lead to loss and disaster.

Even their religious books command them to love one another (rarely any other species), as if this can be mandated by their various gods. Love (as I understand the term) stems from a mysterious delight in certain characteristics exhibited by another being. If that is the case, how can one be commanded to love someone whose attributes are repugnant to him? Or, if so, what meaning has a similar feeling toward a being you like? Surely the gods must have meant, instead, for sapiens to *respect* one another.

Love, for the sapiens, is often (but not always) equated with sex. How, I ask, can something allegedly beautiful be linked to something so painful and disgusting? It truly [boggles] the mind! And it's everywhere—it seems to be the only reason males and females come together, regardless of how much they pretend otherwise. It is quite amusing to watch them dance around the subject, like a double

STAR, until it finally becomes mutually desirable (if that's the right word).

To lighten things a little, I offer this humorous [tidbit?].

There are six billion homo sapiens on B-TIK, and the numbers are increasing by the minute. So what gets its share of the money individual humans are taxed? Fertility research! I don't think I've heard anything funnier anywhere else in the GALAXY.

WE accidentally attended a religious meeting once, rob and I. It was in country united states, state of alabama. The day was wonderfully warm, like on K-PAX, and we heard loud music coming from inside the little god-worshiping structure. We were drawn in. Strange relationship, music and religion. The clear rhythms seemed to get the human beings set up to hear the propaganda. One wonders what other messages are conveyed to the sapiens through the vibrations of music.

There was a lot of wailing and shouting during the speaking phase of the meeting, some of them begging to be cured of various afflictions. I detected an enormous amount of fear in these beings, yet those anxieties were almost completely [alleviated] by participation in this "service." It must be something like gene's hypnosis trick.

ROB has decided to stay. With all the troubles he's seen, he prefers to live here than go to a place where none of the things that befell him could happen. Incomprehensible, wouldn't you agree? And thoroughly human.

B-TIK is one of the most beautiful small WORLDS in the GALAXY. In fact, the EARTH could truly become a paradise if the human inhabitants stopped trying their very best to "multiply and subdue" it. Their cancerous population growth, mindless consumption of its natural resources, and catastrophic elevation of themselves to superiority over all the other species who co-habit their PLANET have corrupted it for everyone, including themselves.

Given their evolutionary history, however, perhaps the PLANET was doomed from the beginning. In any case, their self-centeredness has outlived its usefulness, if it ever had any. The "idea" that they are entitled to everything they can get their hands on is reinforced daily by their governments, their laws, their parents, their schools, their entertainment media, their religions. If they are to survive the next century, their juvenile egos will have to mature and learn to rely on values other than family, country, and gods to give their lives meaning. Countless humans have said to me, "It's more complicated than that!" But to a child, everything is complicated. Apparently nothing short of genetic manipulation will fix the defect, and even that is [fraught] with difficulties—who is going to decide which genes to manipulate?

As B-TIK moves inexorably toward catastrophe, there will be more and more sapiens who will slowly awaken and wonder what went wrong. Unfortunately, it is almost too late to reverse the damage, even though a simple treatment of all their social and environmental illnesses—the elimination of capital, nations, religions and parental indoctrination—is readily available. Yet, with only a quarter of a century left to initiate the necessary changes, the majority of them continue to go on with their robotic ways as if there will be no tomorrow. Ironic, no?

Without these adjustments the prognosis is not good, and the sapiens will not survive another century. If they manage to evolve before they self-destruct, however, they could become admirable citizens of the UNIVERSE, and certainly some of the more interesting ones. But they still have a long way to go. Even after a thousand centuries of experience, they are yet children.

Afterword

I'VE probably read prot's "Report" a hundred times since 1990, and it never fails to amaze me. Not because of the occasional grain of truth imbedded in the pages, but because of what it has to say about his alter ego, Robert Porter, who is decidedly human. All of prot's "solutions" to the world's problems are connected, in one way or another, with those of his Earthly "twin."

For example, his utter abhorrence for the sex act and contempt for the family unit could just as easily be explained by Robert's abuse at the hands of a pedophilic uncle and the fateful day in 1985 when an intruder raped and murdered his wife and daughter. Similarly, Rob's family's near-poverty, the negative effects on his future of the rigid tenets of religious dogma, and the failure of society in general to address these issues might all have contributed to prot's negative assessment of our economic and social structures.

Regardless of their origins, however, prot's observations

deserve serious consideration, in my opinion. Since my retirement I have spent a good deal of time looking into the way we humans have treated the Earth and everything on it, and the picture is a grim one. The endless religious and ethnic clashes in the Middle East, in Northern Ireland, in Bosnia and Africa and India, have destroyed or ruined countless lives (both human and nonhuman). Human overpopulation has also caused enormous suffering around the world, and it is projected to become far worse. The economic disparity between rich and poor nations continues to increase by the hour. Schoolchildren remain ignorant about everything except the most basic subjects, and sometimes even those, and no one wants to spend another cent to rectify this problem. We ignore all these problems at our peril.

Am I suggesting that we forego our religious beliefs, practice strict birth control and refuse to send our children to schools? Of course not. But I have come to believe that, if we are to avoid catastrophe, we must take some steps toward those ends. We can certainly cut down on the purchase of items we don't need, for instance. This will require some adjustments for a while, but the economy will eventually come to a new equilibrium. To offset this situation we could impose higher taxes on the wealthy among us. No doubt this will provoke outcries from a number of people, but this, too, will pass.

The schools could certainly do a much better job of educating our children about the problems we face as a planet, and almost everything else. Why are we so eager to go to war? Why do so many people not know who their Senators are? Or who wrote *Middlemarch*? Or the rudiments of genetics? Or where to find Chad on a map? Or the basics of classical music and art? Or the difference between a quark and a quasar? At a minimum, the schools should teach that ignorance is not something to be proud of, and maybe that's enough.

We could certainly phase out the consumption of meat, which is one of the most environmentally destructive practices we maintain and totally unnecessary for human nutrition. And then there's the mindboggling waste associated with the production of weapons and other preparations for war. National interests should be respected, but of what use are they if the world itself is in serious jeopardy?

Religion is a bit trickier than the others. People (including me) hold onto their beliefs as if their lives depended on them, regardless of the animosity generated by intolerant beliefs all across the globe. Nevertheless, it should at least be possible to admit that there is more than one way to find truth and to understand God.

Of course all of these things will take a tremendous amount of sacrifice and effort. Might it be worth it? I sincerely believe so. Indeed, we may have no choice. Skin cancer and average global temperatures are already on the rise, our climate changes are wreaking economic havoc, and the rainforests and the unique species, including medicinal plants, they harbor are rapidly disappearing. And these are only the tips of the melting icebergs. Arable farmland is shrinking, water and energy resources are drying up, blackouts and brownouts are becoming more frequent, and on and on.

Will prot's suggestions save us from ourselves? Who knows? But even the greatest optimists among us would probably admit that they may be a lot better than doing nothing. In any case, I'm willing to give them a try if you are. . . . .

Acknowledgements

I thank my wife Karen for setting me straight on this one.
I'm also grateful to Dr Carol Boettcher, Dept. of Linguistics, Columbia University, for the initial translation of prot's report into English, and brother Bob and friend Jalel Sager for incisive comments.

It was probably Isaac Bashevis Singer who first compared the treatment of animals with the events of the holocaust.

A note on the author

Before becoming a novelist, Gene Brewer studied DNA replication and cell division at several major research institutions. He lives in New York City and Vermont with his wife and mixed-breed dog, Flower.